Praise for the Nina Borg Thrillers

"Terrific . . . What's for sure is that, stop—it's as if the poor kid's life de as fast as possible . . . Looks like an tionally lacerating Scandinavian m

"Here's something you don't often see in Nordic noir fiction—a novel written by two women about the criminal mistreatment of women and children, compassionately told from a feminine perspective and featuring female characters you can believe in . . . The first collaborative effort of Lene Kaaberbøl and Agnete Friis, and it packs an almighty punch." —*The New York Times Book Review*, Notable Crime Book of the Year

"[Nina] joins the sisterhood of run-amok heroines like *Homeland*'s Carrie Mathison and Lisbeth Salander of *The Girl with the Dragon Tattoo*. Nina doesn't just have a bee in her bonnet—she has a whole hive. And it's buzzing away in her latest adventure."
—John Powers, NPR's *Fresh Air*

"Fans of Nordic crime fiction, rejoice: Something is rotten in Denmark. But never fear, Red Cross nurse Nina Borg is on the case . . . A wild ride." —*New York Post*

"A gripping and elegant tapestry of a novel. A seamless weaving of psychological depth and rocket-paced plotting, the story hooked me in and the strong, complicated, and fascinating women at its center kept me utterly riveted cover-to-cover. Nina Borg is one of my new favorite heroines!"—Lisa Unger, *New York Times* bestselling author of *In the Blood*

"A moving story . . . [Kaaberbøl and Friis] tell a socially conscious— and, at times, critical—tale about immigration issues that apply both to Denmark and the U.S. without sacrificing the urgency of the best thrillers." —Oprah.com

"A frightening and tautly told story of the lengths to which people will go for family and money." —*USA Today*

THE BOY IN THE SUITCASE

&

INVISIBLE MURDER

BOOKS 1 AND 2 OF
THE NINA BORG SERIES

LENE KAABERBØL AND **AGNETE FRIIS**

Published by
Soho Press, Inc.
853 Broadway
New York, NY 10003

Library of Congress Cataloging-in-Publication Data is available upon request.

ISBN 978-1-61695-772-8

Printed in the United States of America

10 9 8 7 6 5 4 3 2 1

THE BOY
IN THE
SUITCASE

LENE KAABERBØL AND **AGNETE FRIIS**

TRANSLATED FROM THE DANISH BY

LENE KAABERBØL

HOLDING THE GLASS door open with her hip, she dragged the suitcase into the stairwell leading down to the underground parking lot. Sweat trickled down her chest and back beneath her T-shirt; it was only slightly cooler here than outside in the shimmering heat of the airless streets. The strong smell of decaying fast food from a jettisoned burger bag did nothing to improve the flavor of the place.

There was no elevator. Step by step she manhandled the heavy suitcase down to the level where she was parked, then realized that she didn't really want it in her car until she knew what was in it. She found a relatively private spot behind some dumpsters, sheltered from security cameras and the curious gazes of passersby. The case wasn't locked, just held closed by two clasps and a heavy-duty strap. Her hands were shaking, and one of them was numb and bloodless from carrying the ungainly weight for such a distance. But she managed to unbuckle the strap and unsnap the locks.

In the suitcase was a boy: naked, fair-haired, rather thin, about three years old. The shock rocked her back on her heels so that she fell against the rough plastic surface of the dumpster. His knees rested against his chest, as if someone had folded him up like a shirt. Otherwise he would not have fit, she supposed. His eyes were closed, and his skin shone palely in the bluish glare of the fluorescent ceiling lights. Not until she saw his lips part slightly did she realize he was alive.

AUGUST

THE HOUSE SAT on the brink of a cliff, with an unhindered view of the bay. Jan knew perfectly well what the locals called it: the Fortress. But that was not why he looked at the white walls with a vague sense of dissatisfaction. The locals could think what they liked; they weren't the ones who mattered.

The house was of course designed by a well-known architect, and modern, in a functional-classical way, a modern take on the Swedish "funkis" trend. Neo-funkis. That's what Anne called it, and she had shown him pictures and other houses until he understood, or understood some of it, at least. Straight lines, no decoration. The view was meant to speak for itself, through the huge windows that drew the light and the surrounding beauty into the room. That was how the architect had put it, and Jan could see his point, everything new and pure and right. Jan had bought the grounds and had the old summer cottage torn down; he had battled the municipal committee until they realized that they most certainly did want him as a taxpayer here and gave the necessary permissions; he had even conquered the representative of the local Nature Society with a donation that nearly made her choke on her herbal tea. But why should he not establish a wildlife preserve? He had no interest in other people's building here, or tramping all over the place in annoying picnic herds. So there it was, his house, protected by white walls, airy and bright, and with clean uncluttered neo-funkis lines. Just the way he had wanted it.

And yet, it was *not* what he wanted. This was not how it was supposed to be. He still thought of the other place with a strange, unfocused longing. A big old pile, an unappealing mix of decaying 1912 nouveau-riche and appallingly ugly sixties additions, and snobbily expensive because it was on Strandvejen, the coast-hugging residences of the Copenhagen financial elite. But that was not why he had wanted it—zip codes meant nothing to him. Its attraction was its nearness to Anne's childhood home, just on the other side of the tall unkempt whitethorn hedge. He couldn't help but imagine it all: The large family gathered for barbecues under the apple trees, he and Anne's father in a cloud of Virginia tobacco, holding chunky tumblers of a very good Scotch. Anne's siblings by the long white patio table, with their children. Anne's mother in the swing seat, a beautiful Indian shawl around her shoulders. His and Anne's children, four or five, he had imagined, with the youngest asleep in Anne's lap. Most of all, Anne happy, relaxed, and smiling. Gathered for the Midsummer festival, perhaps, with a bonfire of their own, and yet enough of them there so that the singing sounded right. Or just some ordinary Thursday, because they felt like it, and there had been fresh shrimp on the pier that day.

He drew hungrily at his cigarette, looking out across the bay. The water was a sullen dark blue, streaked with foam, and the wind tore at his hair and made his eyes water. He had even persuaded the owner to sell. The papers were there, ready for his signature. But she had said no.

He didn't get it. It was her family, damn it. Weren't

women supposed to care about such things? The near-ness, the roots, the close-knit relations? All that stuff. And with a family like Anne's, so . . . right. Healthy. Loving. Strong. Keld and Inger, still obviously in love after nearly forty years. Anne's brothers, who came to the house regu-larly, sometimes with their own wives and children, other times alone, just dropping in because they both still played tennis at the old club. To become part of that, in such an easy, everyday manner, just next door, on the other side of the hedge . . . how could she turn that down? But she did. Quietly, stubbornly, in true Anne-fashion, without argu-ments or reasons why. Just no.

So now here they were. This was where they lived, he and she and Aleksander, on the edge of a cliff. The wind howled around the white walls whenever the direction was northwesterly, and they were alone. Much too far away to just drop in, not part of things, with no share in that easy, warm family communion except by special arrangement now and then, four or five times a year.

He took a last drag and tossed the cigarette away, step-ping on the butt to make sure the dry grass didn't catch fire. He stood for a few minutes, letting the wind whip away the smell from his clothes and hair. Anne didn't know that he had started smoking again.

He took the photo from his wallet. He kept it there because he knew Anne was much too well raised to go snooping through his pockets. He probably should have gotten rid of it, but he just needed to look at it some-times, needed to feel the mixture of hope and terror it inspired.

The boy was looking straight into the camera. His bare

shoulders were drawn forward, as if he hunched himself against some unseen danger. There were no real clues to where the photo had been taken; the details were lost in the darkness behind him. At the corner of his mouth, one could see traces of something he had just eaten. It might be chocolate.

Jan touched the picture with one forefinger, very gently. Then he carefully put the photo away again. They had sent him a mobile phone, an old Nokia, which he would never himself have bought. Probably stolen, he thought. He dialed the number, and waited for the reply.

"Mr. Marquart." The voice was polite, but accented. "Hello. Have you decided?"

In spite of having made his decision, he hesitated. Finally the voice had to prod him on.

"Mr. Marquart?"

He cleared his throat.

"Yes. I accept."

"Good. Here are your instructions."

He listened to the brief, precise sentences, wrote down numbers and figures. He was polite, like the man on the phone. It was only after the conversation had ended that he could no longer contain his disgust and defiance. Furiously, he flung the phone away; it arced over the fence to bounce and disappear on the heathered slope beneath him.

He got back into his car and drove the rest of the way up to the house.

LESS THAN AN hour later, he was crawling about on the slope, looking for the damn thing. Anne came out onto the terrace in front of the house and leaned over the railing.

"What are you doing?" she shouted.

"I dropped something," he called back.

"Do you want me to come down and help?"

"No."

She stayed out there for a while. The wind tore at her peach-colored linen dress, and the updraft blew her fair shoulder-length hair up around her face, so that it looked as if she were falling. In free fall without a parachute, he thought, only to check that chain of thought before it could continue. It would be all right. Anne would never need to know.

It took him nearly an hour and a half to find the stupid phone. And then he had to call the airline. This was one trip he had no wish to let his secretary book for him.

"Where are you going?" asked Anne.

"Just a quick trip to Zürich."

"Is something wrong?"

"No," he said hastily. Fear had flooded into her eyes instantly, and trying to calm it was a knee-jerk reaction. "It's just a business thing. Some funds I need to arrange. I'll be back by Monday."

How had they ended up like this? He suddenly recalled with great intensity that Saturday in May more than ten years ago when he had watched Keld walk her up the aisle. She had been fairytale pretty, in a stunningly simple white dress, pink and white rosebuds in her hair. He knew at once that the bouquet he had chosen was much too big and garish, but it hadn't mattered. He was just a few minutes away from hearing her say "I do." For an instant, his gaze caught Keld's, and he thought he saw a welcome and an appreciation there. *Father-in-law.* I'll take care of her, he silently promised the tall, smiling man. And in his mind added two promises that weren't in the marriage vows: he would give her anything she wanted, and he would protect her against everything that was evil in the world.

That is still what I want, he thought, tossing his passport into the Zürich case. Whatever the price.

SOMETIMES, JUČAS HAD a dream about a family. There was a mother and a father and two children, a boy and a girl. Usually, they would be at the dinner table, eating a meal the mother had cooked for them. They lived in a house with a garden, and in the garden there were apple trees and raspberries. The people were smiling, so that one could tell they were happy.

He himself was outside the house, looking in. But there was always the feeling that any minute now they would catch sight of him, and the father would open the door, smiling even wider, and say: "There you are! Come in, come in."

JUČAS HAD NO idea who they were. Nor could he always remember what they looked like. But when he woke, it would be with a feeling of muddled nostalgia and expectation that would stay with him all day like a tightness in his chest.

Lately he had dreamed the dream a lot. He blamed it on Barbara. She always wanted to talk about how it was going to be—him and her, and the little house just outside Krakow, close enough that her mother would need to take only one bus, and yet far enough away for them to have a bit of privacy. And there would be children. Of course. Because that was what Barbara wanted: children.

The day before it was to happen, they had celebrated. Everything was done, everything ready. The car was packed, all preparations were in place. The only thing that could stop them now was if the bitch suddenly changed her pattern. And even if she did, all they had to do was wait another week.

"Let's go to the country," said Barbara. "Let's go find someplace where we can lie in the grass and be alone together."

At first he refused on the grounds that it was best not to alter one's own pattern. People remembered. Only as long as one did what one always did would one remain relatively invisible. But then he realized this might be his last day in Lithuania ever, if everything went according to plan. And he didn't really feel like spending that day selling security systems to middle-range businessmen in Vilnius.

He called the client he was due to see and canceled, telling them the company would be sending someone Monday or Tuesday instead. Barbara called in sick with "the flu." It would be Monday before anyone at Klimka's realized they had been playing hooky at the same time, and by then it wouldn't matter.

They drove out to Lake Didžiulis. Once, this had been a holiday camp for Pioneer children. Now it was a scout camp instead, and on an ordinary school day at the end of August, the whole place was completely deserted. Jučas parked the Mitsubishi in the shade beneath some pines, hoping the car wouldn't be an oven when they returned. Barbara got out, stretching so that her white shirt slid up to reveal a bit of tanned stomach. That was enough to make his cock twitch. He had never known a woman who could arouse him as quickly as Barbara. He had never known anyone like her, period. He still wondered why on earth she had picked someone like him.

They stayed clear of the wooden huts, which in any

case looked rather sad and dilapidated. Instead they followed the path past the flag hill and into the woods. He inhaled the smell of resin and sun-parched trees, and for a moment was back with Granny Edita on the farm near Visaginas. He had spent the first seven years of his life there. Freezing cold and lonely in the winter, but in the summer Rimantas moved in with *his* Gran on the neighboring farm, and then the thicket of pines between the two smallholdings became Tarzan's African Jungle, or the endless Mohican woods of Hawkeye.

"Looks like we can swim here." Barbara pointed at the lakeshore further ahead. An old swimming platform stuck into the waters of the lake like a slightly crooked finger.

Jučas stuffed Visaginas back into the box where it belonged, the one labeled "The Past." He didn't often open that box, and there was certainly no reason to mess with it now.

"There are probably leeches," he said, to tease her.

She grimaced. "Of course there aren't. Or they wouldn't let the children swim here."

Belatedly, he realized he didn't really want to stop her from taking her clothes off.

"You're probably right," he said, hastily.

She flashed him a quick smile, as though she knew exactly what he was thinking. And as he watched, she slowly unbuttoned her shirt and stepped out of her sand-colored skirt and string sandals, until she stood barefoot on the beach, wearing only white panties and a plain white bra.

"Do we have to swim first?" he asked.

"No," she said, stepping close. "We can do that afterwards."

He wanted her so badly it sometimes made him clumsy like a teenager. But today he forced himself to wait. Playing with her. Kissing her. Making sure she was just as aroused as he was. He fumbled for the condom he always kept in his wallet, at her insistence. But this time she stopped him.

"It's such a beautiful day," she said. "And such a beautiful place. Surely, we can make a beautiful child, don't you think?"

He was beyond speech. But he let go of the wallet and held her for several long minutes before he pushed her down onto the grass and tried to give her what she so badly wanted.

AFTERWARDS, THEY DID swim in the deep, cool waters of the lake. She was not a strong swimmer, had never really learned how, so mostly she doggy-paddled, splashing and kicking. Finally she linked her hands behind his neck and let herself be towed along as he backstroked to keep them both afloat. She looked into his eyes.

"Do you love me?" she asked.

"Yes."

"Even though I'm an old, old woman?" She was nine years older than him, and it bothered her. He didn't care.

"Insanely," he said. "And you're not old."

"Take care of me," she said, settling her head on his chest. He was surprised at the strength of the tenderness he felt.

"Always at your service," he murmured. And he thought that perhaps the family in the dream was him and Barbara, perhaps that was the point of it all—him and Barbara, in the house just outside Krakow. Soon.

Just one little thing to be done first.

SATURDAYS WERE **S**IGITA'S loneliest days.

The week went by quite quickly; there was work, and there was Mikas, and from the time she picked him up at kindergarten shortly before six, everything was done in a strict routine—cook, eat, bathe the child, tuck him in, lay out his clothes for the morning, tidy up, do the dishes, watch a little television. Sometimes she fell asleep to the drone of the news.

But Saturdays. Saturday belonged to the grandparents. From early morning the parking lot in front of their building was busy as cars were packed full of children and bags and empty wooden crates. They would return Sunday evening laden with potatoes, lettuce, and cabbage, and sometimes fresh eggs and new honey. Everyone was going "up to the country," whether the country was a simple allotment or a grandparental farm.

Sigita was going nowhere. She bought all her vegetables at the supermarket now. And when she saw little four-year-old Sofija from number 32 dash across the pavement and throw herself into the bosom of her hennaed, sun-tanned grandmother, it sometimes hurt so badly that it felt as if she had lost a limb.

This Saturday, her solution was the same as it always was—to make a thermos full of coffee and pack a small lunch, and then take Mikas to the kindergarten playground. The birch trees by the fence shimmered green and white in the sun. There had been rain during the night, and a couple of starlings were bathing themselves in the brown puddles underneath the seesaw.

"Lookmama thebirdis takingabath!" said Mikas, pointing enthusiastically. Lately, he had begun to talk rapidly and almost incessantly, but not yet very clearly. It wasn't always easy to understand what he was saying.

"Yes. I suppose he wants to be nice and clean. Do you think he knows it's Sunday tomorrow?"

She had hoped that there might be a child or two in the playground, but this Saturday they were alone, which was usually the case. She gave Mikas his truck and his little red plastic bucket and shovel. He still loved the sandbox and would play for hours, laying out ambitious projects involving moats and roads, twigs standing in for trees, or possibly fortifications. She sat on the edge of the box, closing her eyes for a minute.

She was so tired.

A shower of wet sand caught her in the face. She opened her eyes.

"Mikas!"

He had done it on purpose. She could see the suppressed laughter in his face. His eyes were alight.

"Mikas, don't do that!"

He pushed the tip of his shovel into the sand and twitched it, so that another volley of sand hit her square in the chest. She felt some of it trickle down inside her blouse.

"*Mikas!*"

He could no longer hold back his giggle. It bubbled out of him, contagious and irresistible. She leaped up.

"I'll get you for this!"

He screamed with delight and took off at his best

three-year-old speed. She slowed her steps a bit to let him get a head start, then went after him, catching him and swinging him up in the air, then into a tight embrace. At first he wriggled a little, then he threw his arms around her neck, and burrowed his head under her chin. His light, fair hair smelled of shampoo and boy. She kissed the top of his head, loudly and smackingly, making him squirm and giggle again.

"Mamadon't!"

Only later, after they had settled by the sandbox again and she had poured herself the first cup of coffee, did the tiredness return.

She held the plastic cup to her face and sniffed as though it were cocaine. But this was not a tiredness that coffee could cure.

Would it always be like this? she thought. Just me and Mikas. Alone in the world. That wasn't how it was supposed to be. Or was it?

Suddenly Mikas jumped up and ran to the fence. A woman was standing there, a tall young woman in a pale summer coat, with a flowery scarf around her head as though she were on her way to Mass. Mikas was heading for her with determination. Was it one of the kindergarten teachers? No, she didn't think so. Sigita got hesitantly to her feet.

Then she saw that the woman had something in her hand. The shiny wrapper glittered in the sunshine, and Mikas had hauled himself halfway up the fence with eagerness and desire. Chocolate.

Sigita was taken aback by the heat of her anger. In ten or twelve very long paces, she was at the fence herself. She grabbed Mikas a little too harshly, and he gave her an offended look. He already had chocolate smears on his face.

"What are you giving him!"

The unfamiliar woman looked at her in surprise.

"It's just a little chocolate . . ."

She had a slight accent, Russian, perhaps, and this did not lessen Sigita's rancor.

"My son is not allowed to take candy from strangers," she said.

"I'm sorry. It's just that . . . he's such a sweet boy."

"Was it you yesterday? And the other day, before that?" There had been traces of chocolate on Mikas's jersey, and Sigita had had a nasty argument with the staff about it. They had steadfastly denied giving the children any sweets. Once a month, that was the agreed policy, and they wouldn't dream of diverging from it, they had said. Now it appeared it was true.

"I pass by here quite often. I live over there," said the woman, indicating one of the concrete apartment blocks surrounding the playground. "I bring the children sweets all the time."

"Why?"

The woman in the pale coat looked at Mikas for a long moment. She seemed nervous now, as though she had been caught doing something she shouldn't.

"I don't have any of my own," she finally said.

A pang of sympathy caught Sigita amidst her anger.

"That'll come soon enough," she heard herself say. "You're still young."

The woman shook her head.

"Thirty-six," she said, as though the figure itself were a tragedy.

It wasn't until now that Sigita really noticed the

careful makeup designed to eradicate the slight signs of aging around her eyes and her mouth. Automatically, she clutched her son a little tighter. At least I have Mikas, she told herself. At least I have that.

"Please don't do it again," she said, less strictly than she had meant to. "It's not good for him."

The woman's eyes flickered.

"I'm sorry," she said. "It won't happen again." Then she spun suddenly and walked away with rapid steps.

Poor woman, thought Sigita. I guess I'm not the only one whose life turned out quite different from expected.

SHE WIPED AWAY the chocolate smears with a moistened handkerchief. Mikas wriggled like a worm and was unhappy.

"Morechoclate," he said. "More!"

"No," said Sigita. "There is no more."

She could see that he was considering a tantrum, and looked around quickly for a diversion.

"Hey," she said, grabbing the red bucket. "Why don't you and I build a castle?"

She played with him until he was caught up in the game again, the endless fascination of water and sand and sticks and the things one could do with them. The coffee had gone cold, but she drank it anyway. Sharp little grains of sand dug into her skin beneath the edge of her bra, and she tried discretely to dislodge them. Leafy shadows from the birches shimmered across the gray sand, and Mikas crawled about on all fours with his truck clutched in one hand, making quite realistic engine noises.

Afterwards, that was the last thing she remembered.

A SEAGULL, THOUGHT JAN. A damned seagull!

He should have been back home in Denmark more than an hour ago. Instead he sat on what should have been the 7:45 to Copenhagen Airport, frying inside an overheated aluminum tube along with 122 other unfortunates. No matter how many cooling drinks he was offered by the flight attendants, nothing could ease his desperation.

The plane had arrived on schedule from Copenhagen. But boarding had been postponed, first by fifteen minutes, then by another fifteen minutes, and finally by an additional half hour. Jan had begun to sweat. He was on a tight schedule. But the desk staff kept saying it was a temporary problem, and the passengers were asked to stay by the gate. When they suddenly postponed boarding again, this time by a full hour, without any explanation, he lost his temper and demanded to have his case unloaded so that he could find some other flight to Copenhagen. This met with polite refusal. Luggage that had been checked in was already aboard the plane, and there was apparently no willingness to find his bag among the other 122. When he said to hell with the bag, then, and wanted to leave the gate without it, there were suddenly two security officers flanking him, telling him that if his bag was flying out on that plane, so was he. Was that a problem?

No, he demurred hastily, having absolutely no desire to spend further hours in some windowless room with a lock on the door. He was no terrorist, just a frustrated businessman with very important business to attend to, he explained. Airline security was very important business, too, they said. Sir. He nodded obediently and sat himself down on one of the blue plastic chairs, silently cursing 9/11 and everything that awful day had wrought in the world.

At long last they were told to begin boarding. Now everything suddenly had to be accomplished at breakneck speed. Two extra desks were opened, and staff in pale blue uniforms raced around snapping at passenger heels if anyone strayed or loitered. Jan sank gratefully into his wide business-class seat and checked his watch. He could still make it.

The engines warmed up, flight attendants began explaining about emergency exits *here* and *here*, and the plane began to roll forward on the pavement.

And then it stopped. And stayed stopped for so long that Jan became uneasy and checked his watch again. Move your arses, he cursed silently. Get this stupid aircraft off the ground!

Instead the voice of the captain was heard over the PA system.

"I'm sorry to inform you that we have yet another hitch in our schedule. On departure from Copenhagen airport on the way down here, we were hit by a bird. The aircraft suffered no damage, but of course we have to have a mechanical overhaul of the plane before we are allowed to fly it again, which is the reason for the delay we have already suffered. The aircraft has been checked and declared fully operational."

Then why aren't we flying? thought Jan, grinding his teeth.

"The airline has a quality-control program, in compliance with which the documentation for our check-up has to be faxed to Copenhagen for signature before we are given our final permission to take off. At this time, there is only one person on duty in Copenhagen qualified to give us that permission. And for some reason, he is not to be found at his desk . . ."

The pilot's own frustration came through quite clearly, but that was nothing to the despair that Jan was feeling. His heart was pounding so hard it physically hurt his chest. If I have a heart attack, will they let me off the damn plane? he wondered, and thought about the advisability of faking one. But even if they let him out, it would still take time to get on some other flight, even if he forked out the cash it would cost to arrange a private one. He had to face the fact that he wouldn't make it.

What the hell was he going to do? He feverishly tried to think of anyone he might call on for help. Who would be loyal and competent enough to do what needed doing? And should he call Anne?

No. Not Anne. Karin would have to do what was necessary. She was already involved to some extent, and the fewer people the better. He took his private mobile phone from his briefcase and tapped her number.

The flight attendant descended on him like a hawk on a chicken.

"Please don't use your mobile, sir."

"We're stationary," he pointed out. "And unless the

airline wants to be sued for a six-figure sum, I suggest you back off and let me call my company *now*."

The flight attendant noted the no doubt exceedingly tense set of his jaw and decided that diplomacy was the better part of valor.

"A short call, then," she said. "After which I must ask you to switch it off again."

She remained by his seat while he made the call. He considered asking her to give him his privacy, but there were passengers all around him, and he wouldn't be able to speak freely in any case.

Tersely, he instructed Karin to go to his Copenhagen bank for the sum he had just had transferred from Zürich.

"There is a code you have to supply. I'll text you. And bring one of my document cases, one that has a decent lock. It's a sizeable sum."

His awareness of the listening flight attendant was acute, and he had no idea how to say the rest without sounding like something out of a pulp-fiction thriller.

"In fact, I'll text you everything else," he said quickly. "There are a number of figures involved. Text me back when you have read my message."

Though the show was over for now, the flight attendant still stayed demonstratively next to his seat while he texted his message and waited for the reply. It took a worryingly long time to arrive.

OK. But you owe me big-time.

Yes, he wrote to her. *I realize that.*

He wondered what it would cost him—particularly her compliant silence. Karin had acquired a taste for the finer things in life. But at heart she was a good and loyal person, he told himself soothingly, and she had several compelling reasons to stay on his good side. He had after all been very generous as an employer, and in certain other ways as well.

At that moment, the plane jerked forward and began to move, and he wondered whether he had after all been premature in involving her. But it turned out they were being taxied off the runway to a parking area. The captain explained that they had lost their slot in the busy departure schedule of the airport and were now put on indefinite hold while waiting first for their permission to take off to arrive from Copenhagen, and secondly for a new slot to be assigned to them. He was very sorry, but he was unfortunately forced to switch off the air conditioning while they waited.

Jan closed his eyes and cursed in three languages. *Fandens. Scheisse. Fucking hell.*

NINA LOOKED THE man right in the eyes.

"I think you had better leave," she said.

It had no effect. He stepped even closer, deliberately looming over her. She could smell his aftershave. In a different situation it might have been a pleasant scent.

"I know she is here," he said. "And I demand to see my fiancée right away."

It was a hot August day, and there were white roses from the garden in the blue vase on her desk. Outside Ellen's Place the sun was shining on dusty lawns and white benches. Some of the children from the A Block were playing soccer. One team was yelling in Urdu and the other mostly in Romanian, but they seemed to understand each other all the same. Recess, thought Nina with a small, detached part of her brain. Her colleagues Magnus and Pernille had deserted her in favor of the cafeteria ages ago, and she could see the psychologist Susanne Marcussen having lunch with the new district nurse in the outside picnic area. It was 11:55, and except for the soccer game, a heavy siesta-like tranquility had descended on Danish Red Cross Center Furesø, a.k.a. the Coal-House Camp. Or at least, things had been tranquil until the man in front of her had marched into the clinic four minutes ago. She threw a quick look at the telephone on her desk, but whom would she call? The police? So far, he had done nothing illegal.

He was in his late forties, with medium brown hair swept back from his temples, tanned and immaculate in a short-sleeved Hugo Boss shirt and matching tie. Apparently no one had thought to stop him at the gate.

"Get out of my way," he told her. "I'll find her myself."

Nina stood her ground. If he hits me, I can press charges, she thought. It would be worth it.

"This is not a public area," she said. "I'm going to have to ask you to leave."

This had even less effect than it had the first time. He looked straight through her to the corridor beyond.

"Natasha," he called. "Come on. Rina is already waiting in the car."

What? Nina tried to catch his eyes.

"She's at school," she blurted.

He looked down at her, and the smile that curled his lips was so smug that it physically sickened her.

"Not anymore," he said.

A door clicked open softly. Without turning around, Nina knew that Natasha had come into the corridor.

"Don't hurt her," she said.

"Darling, as if I would," said the man in the Boss shirt. "Shall we go home now? I bought pastries from that bakery you like."

Natasha nodded briefly.

Nina involuntarily reached out to stop her, but the small, blond Ukrainian girl walked right past her without looking at her. Nina knew the girl was twenty-four, but right now she looked like a lost and terrified teenager.

"I go now," she said.

"Natasha! You can report him!"

Natasha just shook her head. "For what?" she said.

The man put his hands around her slender neck and

drew her close for a provocatively deep kiss. Nina could *see* the girl stiffen. He let his hands move down her back and slid them inside the tight waistline of her denim jeans until he was clutching both her buttocks. His hands bulged under the fabric. With an abrupt jerk, he forced her pelvis against his own.

Nina could taste the acid of her own stomach. She felt like taking the blue vase and smashing it against the head of that *vicious* bastard, but she didn't. She knew that this was a show put on for her benefit, to sneer and parade his victory. The more reaction she gave him, the longer it would continue.

Nina still remembered the brilliant happiness of the Ukrainian girl when she showed off her engagement ring. "I stay in Denmark now," she had said with a dazzling smile. "My husband is Danish citizen."

Four months later she showed up at the center with one hastily packed bag and her six-year-old daughter, Rina. She looked as if she had dragged herself out of a war zone. There were no outer signs of violence except for a few minor bruises. Hitting her was not his thing, it seemed. Natasha wouldn't tell them exactly what he did, she just sat there with tears she could not control rolling down her cheeks in a steady, unstoppable flow. At length, severe abdominal pains had forced her to agree to being examined by Magnus.

Nina had rarely seen Magnus so angry.

"*Jävla skitstöfel*," he hissed. "*Fy fan*, I wish I knew someone with a baseball bat." When Magnus was particularly upset, his native Swedish tended to come through in his swearing.

"What did he do?" said Nina. "What's wrong with her?"

"If the bastard would only stick to using his miserable little prick," said Magnus. "But you should see the lesions she has, in her vagina and in her rectum. I've never seen anything like it."

And now the Bastard was standing right in front of her, kneading Natasha's buttocks with his greedy hands, while his eyes, gazing across Natasha's shoulder, never left Nina's. She had to look away. I could kill him, she thought to herself. Kill, castrate, and dismember. If I thought it would do any good.

But there were thousands like him. Not exactly like him, but thousands of others who circled like sharks, waiting to exploit the desperation of the refugees and take their chunk of the vulnerable flesh.

Eventually, he pulled his hands out of Natasha's jeans.

"Have a nice day," he said, and left. Natasha followed him as if he had her on a leash.

Nina jerked the receiver off the phone and dialed an internal number.

"Teacher's room, this is Ulla speaking."

"Is it true that the bastard who is to marry Natasha has picked up Rina?" asked Nina.

There was a silence at the other end. "I'll look," said the English teacher. Nina waited for six minutes. Then Ulla Svenningsen came back on the line. "I'm sorry," she said. "He turned up just as the bell went for the recess. He had brought her a popsicle, the children say, and she ran right up to him."

"Bloody hell, Ulla!"

"Sorry. But this is not a prison, is it? Openness is part of the concept."

Nina hung up without saying goodbye. She was shaking with fury. Right now she was in no mood to listen to excuses or politically correct sermons on the importance of opening up to the community.

Magnus appeared in the doorway, out of breath and glasses askew, and big beads of sweat everywhere in his large, kind dog-face.

"Natasha," he gasped out. "I just saw her getting into a car."

"Yes," said Nina. "She went back to the Bastard."

"*For helvete da!*"

"He took Rina first. And then Natasha just followed."

Magnus sank into his office chair.

"And of course she won't report him."

"No. Can't we do it?"

Magnus took off his glasses and polished them absentmindedly on the lapel of his white coat.

"All he has to say is that it's nobody's business if he and his fiancée like rough sex," he said dejectedly. "If she won't contradict him . . . there's nothing we can do. He doesn't hit her. There are no X-rays of broken arms or ribs that we can beat him over the head with."

"And he doesn't abuse the child," sighed Nina.

Magnus shook his head.

"No. We could report him for that, at least. But he is too smart for that." He looked at the clock on the wall. It was 12:05. "Aren't you going to lunch?"

"I seem to have lost my appetite," said Nina.

At that moment, her private phone vibrated in the pocket of her uniform. She took it.

"Nina."

The voice at the other end did not introduce herself, and at first she wasn't sure who it was.

"You have to help me."

"Err . . . with what?"

"You have to pick it up. You know about such things."

It was Karin, she realized. Last seen at a somewhat inebriated Old Students Christmas Lunch, which had ended in a furious shouting match.

"Karin, what's wrong? You sound weird."

"I'm in the cafeteria at Magasin," said Karin, naming the oldest department store in Copenhagen. "It was the only place I could think of to go. Will you come?"

"I'm working."

"Yes. But will you come?"

Nina hesitated. Suddenly, all kinds of things were in the air. Old favors. Unsettled accounts. And Nina knew full well she owed Karin at least this much.

"Okay. I'll be there in twenty minutes."

Magnus raised his eyebrows.

"I'm having lunch after all," said Nina. "And, err . . . I'll probably be at least an hour."

He nodded distractedly. "Oh, all right. I suppose we can hold the fort without you."

"MRS. RAMOŠKIENĖ!"

A piercing light struck one of Sigita's eyes. She tried to twist away but found she couldn't, someone was holding her, someone held her head in a firm grip.

"Mrs. Ramoškienė, can you hear me?"

She was unable to answer. She couldn't even open her eyes on her own.

"It's no use," said a different voice. "She's out of it."

"Whew. That's a bit ripe."

Yes, thought Sigita dizzily. There really was a foul odor, of raw spirits and vomit. Someone ought to clean this place up.

"MRS. RAMOŠKIENĖ. IT will be a lot easier if you can do some of it yourself."

Do what? She didn't understand. Where was she? Where was Mikas?

"We have to insert a tube in your throat. If you can swallow as we push, it will be less uncomfortable."

Tube? Why would she want to swallow a tube? Her confused brain took her back to the absurd bets of the schoolyard. Here's a litas if you eat this slug. Here's a litas that says you're too chicken to swallow the earthworm alive. Then a grain of logic asserted itself. She must be in a hospital. She was in a hospital, and they wanted her to swallow a plastic tube. But why?

She couldn't swallow, as it turned out. Couldn't help. Couldn't stop herself from struggling, which brought a new pain, sharp enough to pierce the fog of her confusion. Her arm. Oh God, her arm.

It is very hard to scream with a plastic tube in your throat, she discovered.

"MIKAS."

"What is she saying?"

"Where is Mikas?"

She opened her eyes. They felt thickened and strange, but she forced them to open all the same. The light was blinding, and white as milk. She could only just make out two women, darker shapes amidst the whiteness. Nurses, or aides, she couldn't make out the details. They were making the bed next to hers.

"Where is Mikas?" she said, as clearly as she was able.

"You must be quiet, Mrs. Ramoškienė."

An accident, she thought, I've been in an accident. A car, or perhaps the trolley bus. That's why I can't remember anything. Then came the fear. What had happened to Mikas? Was he hurt? *Was he dead?*

"Where is my son?" she screamed. "What have you done with him?"

"Please calm yourself, ma'am. Mrs. Ramoškienė, will you *please* lie down!"

One of them tried to restrain her, but she was too afraid to let herself be restrained. She got up. One arm was heavier than the other, and a bitter green wave of nausea washed over her. Acid burned her much-abused esophagus, and the pain took her legs from her, took away all control, so that she ended up on the floor next to the bed, clutching at the sheets, still struggling to get up.

"Mikas. Let me see Mikas!"

"He's not here, Mrs. Ramoškienė. He is probably with your mother, or with some other relative. Or a neighbor. He is perfectly fine, I tell you. Now will you please lie down and stop screaming so. There are other patients here, some of them seriously ill, and you really mustn't disturb them like this."

The nurse helped her back into the bed. At first she felt simple relief. Mikas was all right! But then she understood that something wasn't quite right, after all. Sigita tried to see the woman's face more clearly. There was something there, in the tone of her voice, in the set of her jaw, that was not compassion, but its opposite. Contempt.

She knows, thought Sigita in confusion. She knows what I did. But how? How could some unfamiliar nurse in a random ward in Vilnius know so much about her? It was so many years ago, after all.

"I have to go home," she said thickly, through the nausea. Mikas couldn't be with her mother, of course. Possibly with Mrs. Mažekienė next door, but she was getting on now and could become peevish and abrupt if the babysitting went on too long. "Mikas needs me."

The other nurse gave her a look from across the neighboring bed, smoothing the pillowcase with sharp, precise movements.

"You might have thought of that before," she said.

"Before . . . before what?" stammered Sigita. Was the accident her fault?

"Before you tried to drink your brains out. Since you ask."

Drink?

"But I don't drink," said Sigita. "Or . . . hardly ever."

"Oh, really. I suppose it was just a mistake, then, that we sent you to have your stomach pumped? Your blood-alcohol level was two point eight."

"But I . . . I really don't."

That couldn't be right. Couldn't be *her*.

"Rest a little," said the first nurse, pulling the blanket across her legs. "Perhaps you will be discharged later, when the doctor comes by again."

"What's wrong with me? What happened?"

"I believe you fell down some stairs. Concussion and a fracture of your lower left arm. And you were lucky it wasn't worse!"

Some stairs? She remembered nothing like that. Nothing since the coffee and the playground and Mikas in the sandbox with his truck.

GETTING AWAY FROM the center was actually a relief, thought Nina, as she drove up the ramp to Magasin's parking garage and eased her small Fiat into the none-too-generous space between a concrete pillar and somebody's wide-arsed Mercedes. Sometimes she got so sick and tired of feeling powerless. What kind of country was this, when young girls like Natasha were compelled to sell themselves to men like the Bastard for the sake of a resident's permit?

She took the elevator to the top floor of the building. As soon as she stepped out of the narrow steel box, the odor of food overwhelmed her—roasted pork, hot grease from the deep-fryer, and the pervasive aroma of coffee. She scanned the cafeteria and finally caught sight of Karin's blond head. She was seated at a table by the window, in a sleeveless white dress that struck Nina as an off-duty version of her nurse's uniform. Instead of one of the chic little handbags she normally sported, one hand rested possessively on the black briefcase on the chair next to her, while the other nervously rotated her coffee cup, back and forth, back and forth.

"Hi," said Nina. "What is it, then?"

Karin looked up. Her eyes were bright and tense with an emotion Nina couldn't quite identify.

"You have to fetch something for me," she said, slapping a small round plastic circle onto the table. A token with a number on it, Nina observed, like the ones used for public lockers.

Nina was starting to feel annoyed.

"Don't be so damned cryptic. What exactly is it I'm supposed to fetch?"

Karin hesitated.

"A suitcase," she finally said. "From a locker at the Central Station. Don't open it until you are out of the place. Don't let anyone see you when you do open it. And hurry!"

"Bloody hell, Karin, you make it sound as if it's stuffed full of cocaine, or something!"

Karin shook her head.

"No. It's not like that. It's . . ." She stopped short, and Nina could see the barely suppressed panic in her. "This wasn't the deal," she said feverishly. "I can't do this. I don't know how. But you do."

Karin got to her feet as if she meant to leave. Nina felt like grabbing her and forcing her to stay, much like she had with Natasha. But she didn't. She looked down at the token on the table between them. 37-43, read the white numbers against the black plastic.

"You're always so keen on saving people, aren't you?" said Karin with a bitter twist to her mouth. "Well, here's your chance. But you have to hurry."

"Where are you going?"

"I'm going home to quit my job," said Karin tightly. "And then I'm going away for a while."

She zigzagged her way to the exit, skirting the other tables. She clutched the briefcase under her arm rather than carry it by the handle. It looked wrong, somehow.

Nina watched her go. Then she looked at the small shiny token. A suitcase. A locker. *You're always so keen on saving people, aren't you?*

"What the hell have you gotten yourself into, Karin?" she muttered to herself. She had a strong feeling that the wisest thing to do would be to leave number 37-43 there on the sticky cafeteria table and just walk away.

"Oh hell," she hissed, and picked up the token.

"Mrs. Mažekienė? It's Sigita."

There was a moment's silence before Mrs. Mažekienė answered.

"Sigita. Thank the Lord. How are you?"

"Much better now. But they won't let me out of here until tomorrow. Is Mikas with you?"

"Oh no, dear. He is with his father."

"With *Darius*?"

"Yes, of course. He picked him up even before your accident. Don't you remember, dearie?"

"No. They say I'm concussed. There is so much I don't remember."

But . . . Darius was in Germany, working. Or was he? He didn't always tell her when he came home. Officially, they were still only separated, but the only thing they had in common now was Mikas. Might Darius take Mikas back to Germany with him? Or to his mother's house in Tauragė? He didn't have a place of his own in Vilnius, and she very much doubted that the party-crowd friends he occasionally stayed with would welcome a three-year-old boy.

Her head hurt furiously. She couldn't think things through with any clarity, and she didn't feel very reassured by the knowledge that Darius had Mikas, but at least she knew where her son was. Or with whom, at any rate.

"It looked so awful, dearie. I thought you were dead! And to think you had been lying on those stairs all night!

Now, you just have a good rest at that fine hospital, and let them look after you until you're better."

"Yes. Thank you, Mrs. Mažekienė."

Sigita snapped her mobile shut. Getting hold of it at all had been a challenge, and smuggling it into the loo with her even more difficult. The use of mobile phones was prohibited inside the hospital, except for a certain area in the lobby, which might as well have been the moon as far as she was concerned—she still couldn't walk without hanging onto the walls.

Awkwardly, she opened the phone again and pressed Darius's number with the thumb of her right hand. She was unable to hold the phone in her plaster-cased left, or at least not in such a way that she was able to operate it.

His voice was happy and warm and full of his presence even on a stupid voicemail message.

"You have called Darius Ramoška, but, but, but . . . I'm not here right now. Try again later!"

That was actually completely appropriate, she thought. The story of his life, or at any rate, the story of their relationship. I'm not here right now, try again later.

THEY HAD STARTED going out together the summer she was due to finish elementary school, and he was about to begin his second year of secondary school in Tauragė's Education Center. The summer had been unusually hot that year. In the schoolyard, only the most energetic of the little kids felt like playing on the heat-softened tarmac. The older students sat with their backs against the gray cement wall, with rolled up sleeves and jeans, chatting lazily in what they felt was a very grown-up manner.

"Are you going away for the holiday, Sigita?"

It was Milda asking. And she knew very well that the answer was no.

"Maybe," said Sigita. "We haven't really made plans yet."

"We're going to Palanga," said Daiva. "To a hotel!"

"Really?" drawled Milda. "How cool. We're just going to Miami."

All around her, there was a sudden awestruck silence. Envy and respect were almost as visible in the air as the heat shimmer over the asphalt. Miami. Outer space seemed more accessible to most of them. A holiday meant Daiva's fortnight at a Palanga resort hotel, or perhaps a trip to the Black Sea, if they got really lucky. No one in their grade had ever been further away than that.

"Are you sure?" said Daiva.

"Of course I'm sure. The tickets are already booked."

No one asked where the money came from. They all knew—Milda's father and uncle brought used cars home from Germany, fixed them up, and sold them to the Russians. That this was good business had been obvious first from the children's clothes, and Milda's new bike, then from the BMWs they drove, and finally from the big new house they built just outside town. But all the same—Miami.

"I'd rather go to New York," Sigita heard herself say. And immediately wished she could have swallowed every last syllable.

Milda threw back her head and laughed.

"Right, then, you just tell your father that you want to go to New York," she said. "He'll buy the ticket right away . . . just as soon as he sells those shirts."

Sigita felt the heat rise in her cheeks. Those damned shirts. She would never hear the last of it. They would haunt her to the end of her days, she felt sure.

They were everywhere in the flat. Thousands of them. They came from a closed-down factory in Poland, and her father had bought them for "practically nothing," as he put it. Practically nothing had still been enough that they had to sell the car. And even though her father kept talking about "top-shelf merchandise" and "classic design," he had managed to sell fewer than a dozen. For nearly two years they had been hanging there from broomsticks and wires screwed into the ceiling, crackling, plastic-shrouded, and "fresh from the factory," above the couch, above the beds, even in the loo. She never brought friends home anymore; it was simply too embarrassing. But not nearly as embarrassing as being forced to take "samples" with her to class in the hopes that some of her friends' parents would feel a sudden urge to buy one.

Her father had been severely out of his depth since the Russians went home. Back then, in the Soviet era, he had been a controller at the canning factory. It did not pay much better than working on the line, but back then it hadn't been the money that mattered, it had been the connections. No one could just buy what they wanted, it had to be arranged. As often as not, her father had been the man who could arrange it.

Now the factory had closed down. It sat behind its barbed-wire fence, a gray and black hulk with empty window frames, weeds breaking through the concrete paving. The old connections were worthless, or worse than worthless. The people who did well these days were the ones who knew how to trade, fix, and organize—in the black economy as well as in the white.

Sigita got up. The sun hit her like a hammer, and once she was on her feet, she really had no idea where to go.

"Leaving so soon?" said Milda. "Oh, I suppose you are in a hurry to go home and book that New York hotel?"

It was at that moment that he came to her rescue.

"Sigita? Don't forget we're going to Kaliningrad on Saturday, right?"

Darius. Tanned and fair-haired, with that relaxed and well-trained confidence none of the other boys had. His shirt was left casually open to reveal a crisp white T-shirt underneath, and neither garment had come from Poland.

"No," she said. "It'll be fun. Have you heard that Milda is going to Miami for the holidays?"

"Oh," he said. "You must say hello to my uncle, then. He lives there."

IT HAD TAKEN her years to see that Darius's shining armor was eggshell thin. He couldn't rescue her, had never really been able to. God only knew what he was doing with Mikas right now. Had he brought her little boy with him to some bar where Darius's party buddies would let him finish their beers? She shuddered. She *had* to get out of this damned hospital in a hurry.

THE RAILWAY STATION was crammed with irritable Monday crowds, and there was a nearly visible mist of exhaled breaths and collective sweat in the great central hall. People were tetchy in the heat, with their clothes and their tempers sticking to them, and over the PA came the announcement that the 13:11 to Elsinore was delayed by approximately twenty minutes. Nina felt a tension that made her unwilling to be so physically close to a lot of strangers. She tried to move so that they wouldn't touch her, but it just wasn't possible. Finally she reached the stairwell leading down to the left luggage cellar. The sharp smell of cleaning chemicals was weaker here and couldn't quite mask the stench of well-aged urine. The scratched metal lockers hugged the walls, long white rows with black numbers on them. 56, 55 . . . She checked the token again. 37-43. Where on earth was section 37?

She found it at last, in a quiet blind alley leading off the more heavily trafficked main corridor. Right now, there were only two travelers in here—a young couple struggling to fit a large backpack into one of the lockers.

"It won't fit," said the girl. "I told you. It's too big."

By the girl's accent, Nina took them to be American, or perhaps Canadian. Should she wait until they had left? But other tourists would come, and at least these two were intent on their Battle of the Bulging Rucksack. She pushed the token into the automated system controlling section 37, and there was a crisp metallic *click* as locker 43 came open.

Inside was a shiny dark-brown leather suitcase, a little old-fashioned, with a long tear down one side so that the green lining peeked through. Otherwise there was nothing very noticeable about it. No address labels or tags, of course. She knew it would be foolish to open it now. People who pick up their own bags don't open them to check what is inside. And Karin had said the same thing—*don't open it until you're out of there. Don't let anyone see.* Oh, Karin. What are you up to? Nina thought. It was difficult to imagine that it might be anything very sinister or serious. Karin was so . . . "unadventurous" wasn't quite the word, but still. It was just hard to picture easygoing, hedonistic Karin involved in anything dirty, illegal, or dangerous. But there had been that unwonted panic in her voice: *This wasn't the deal.* What had she meant by that?

Nina dragged the suitcase out of the locker. It was heavier than it looked, at least forty pounds, she guessed. Not easily carried for any length of distance, and the underground parking lot in Nyropsgade, where she had left the Fiat, was a couple of blocks away. But Copenhagen's Central Station did not provide complimentary trolleys like those in airports, so there was nothing else for it.

The young couple had begun taking things out of the backpack to slim it sufficiently for the narrow locker. The young man dropped a toilet bag, which hit the floor with a clang and came open. Mascara, eyeliner, hair mousse, and deodorants spilled across the tiles. One of the deodorants curved towards Nina and came to a spinning stop at her feet.

"Oh, hell," he said. "Sorry."

Nina smiled mechanically. Then she took the suitcase in the firmest grip she could manage and began to walk, trying to look halfway natural. Sweet Jesus, it was heavy. What on earth was in it?

IT WAS ONLY when she reached the car-park that she opened it. And found the boy.

He was unconscious. His skin was cool, but not alarmingly cold. Some automated professional part of her noted that his pulse was slow, but again not dangerously so, his respiration deep and also slow, his pupils slightly contracted. There was little doubt that he had been drugged, she thought. He wasn't about to die on her, but he needed treatment—fluids, and perhaps an antidote, if they could work out what had been used on him. She seized her mobile and pressed the first two emergency digits, then paused before the final one.

Her eyes fell on the suitcase. So ordinary. Normal. The tear in the leather had made it easier for the boy to breathe, but there was no way to tell whether it had been made intentionally to ensure him a certain supply of oxygen. People who put little children in suitcases do not, Nina thought, care terribly about their wellfare.

Steps somewhere, and the slamming of car doors, then the growl of an engine starting up. The sounds echoed back from the concrete walls, and she ducked instinctively behind the dumpster so as not to be seen. Why? Why didn't she get up instead and call for help? But she didn't. She caught a glimpse of silver metal and shiny hubcaps, then the car was gone.

She had to get the child to her own car, but how? She could not bear to close the suitcase and carry him like that, as if he were baggage. She ran to the Fiat instead, and got a checkered picnic blanket from the trunk, tucked it around him, and carried him against her shoulder. Mother and child, she thought. If anyone sees me, I'm just a mommy who has just picked up her exhausted toddler from kindergarten.

He seemed feather light, much less of a weight than he had been in the suitcase. She could feel his breath against the side of her neck, a small warm puffing. Dear sweet Jesus. Who would do this to a child?

She lowered him onto the back seat and checked his pulse once more. A little faster already, as if he were reacting to his surroundings. She grabbed the plastic water bottle from between the front seats and moistened his lips with a wet finger. His tongue moved. He was not deeply unconscious.

Hospital, police. Police, hospital. But if it was just a question of calling 911, why hadn't Karin done it herself? Bloody hell, Karin, Nina cursed silently. Are you mixed up in this? "I can't do anything, but you can," Karin had said. But just what the *hell* was it she was supposed to be doing?

MONDAY MORNING, SIGITA was finally released. She had called Darius at least a dozen times, but all she got was the stupid answering machine.

She still didn't understand what had happened. She really didn't drink, certainly not to the point of falling down stairs in a state of blind oblivion. And why had she let Darius take Mikas away? That had happened before the stairs, so Mrs. Mažekienė had said. Sigita felt a tiny persistent sting of fear. What if Darius would not give Mikas back to her? And how was it that she had ended up at the foot of the stairs with a broken arm and a concussion? Darius had never hit her, not once, not even during the bitterest of their fights. She couldn't believe he had done so now. But perhaps some accident . . . ? If there was one person on God's green earth who could inspire her to get drunk, it was surely Darius.

She considered taking a taxi back home to Pašilaičiai, but the habits acquired through years of enforced parsimony were not easily shaken. After all, the trolley bus stopped practically at her doorstep. For the first few stops, inside Vilnius proper, the bus was crowded to sardine-tin capacity; her plaster cast got her the offer of a seat, which she gratefully accepted, but even so, the pressure of other human bodies made nausea rise in her gullet until she was afraid she would not be able to contain it. One more stop, she told herself. If it doesn't get better after that, I'll get off and call for a cab. But the pressure did ease as they left the center of the city and the rush-hour current ran the other way. When she finally got off by Žemynos gatvė , she had to sit on the bus-stop bench and just breathe for a little while before she was able to walk on.

She rang the bell by Mrs. Mažekienė's front door before going into her own flat.

"Oh, it's you, dearie. Good to see you on your feet again. What a to-do!"

"Yes. But, Mrs. Mažekienė, exactly when did Darius pick up Mikas?"

"Saturday. How peculiar that you don't remember."

"When on Saturday?"

"A little past noon, I think. Yes. I had just had my lunch when I saw them."

"Them? Was someone with him?"

Mrs. Mažekienė bit her lip, looking as if she thought she might have said too much.

"Well, yes. There was this lady . . ."

It stung, even though Sigita had been the one to kick Darius out, and not the other way around. But of course there was a "lady." Had she really imagined there wouldn't be?

"What did she look like?" she asked, in the unlikely case that it had been Darius's mother or sister.

"Very nice. Quite young. Tall and fair-haired, with nice clothes. Not tarted up like some," said Mrs. Mažekienė.

Which meant it wasn't Darius's sister, for sure.

Then another thought came to her. A nice-looking, tall, fair-haired young woman. Quite a few of those around, of course, but still . . .

"Can you remember what she was wearing?"

THE BOY IN THE SUITCASE

"A light summer coat. One of those cotton coats, I think. And a scarf."

The woman from the playground. The one who wanted a child so badly. Sigita felt a chill go through her. What if Darius had a girlfriend now who longed for children . . . Sigita remembered the silver gleam of the chocolate wrapping, Mikas's chocolate-smeared cheeks. The sly, ingratiating bitch. Watching them, watching Mikas, worming her way into his trust with the forbidden chocolate gift. Suppose it hadn't been a Russian accent after all, but a German one. Some Irmgard he had picked up where he worked now.

"Dearie, are you all right?"

"Yes," said Sigita through her teeth, though nausea sloshed in her throat like water in a bucket. "But I think I had better go lie down all the same."

THE FLAT LOOKED the way it always did. Clean and white and modern, light-years away from the shirt-ridden hell of Tauragė. Even Mikas's toys were lined up in tidy rows on the shelves. Only one alien object disturbed the symmetry: an empty vodka bottle glared at her from the kitchen worktop, next to the sink.

She tossed it into the bin with unnecessary force. Did they get her drunk first? She didn't believe, couldn't believe, that she had just let Darius and his German slut waltz off with Mikas in tow.

Her mobile rang.

"Sigita, where the hell are you? Dobrovolskij will be here in half an hour, and we need those figures!"

It was Algirdas. Algirdas Janusevičius, one half of Janus Constructions, and her immediate boss.

"Sorry," she said. "I just got out of hospital."

"Hospital?" Irritation was clear in his voice at first, but he managed a more suitably worried tone when he spoke again. "Nothing serious, I hope?"

"No," she said. "I fell down some stairs. But I won't be in for a few days."

His silence was palpable at the other end of the line.

"Sorry," she said again.

"Yes. Well. It can't be helped. But . . . the figures?"

"There's a green folder in the cabinet behind my desk, under Dobrovolskij. The accounts are almost the first thing you'll come across."

"Sigita, for God's sake. Not *those* figures."

She knew what he meant, of course. When one worked for Dobrovolskij, there were unwritten accounts as well, numbers and sums that never made it into the official records. The reason Sigita had become indispensable to Algirdas so quickly was that she was able to hold it all in her head. Even old man Dobrovolskij himself, who was not easy to please, had come to trust in Sigita's accuracy. She knew what had been agreed, down to the last litas.

Except that right now she would have some trouble remembering her own phone number. The only thing her head held at the moment was a gray fog of nausea and confusion.

"I'm really sorry," she said. "I'm a little concussed."

This time, the silence was even heavier. She could almost hear the panic in Algirdas's breathing.

"How long . . . ?" he asked cautiously.

"They say most people get their full memory back inside a few weeks."

"A few *weeks*!"

"Algirdas, I didn't do it on purpose."

"No . . . no. Of course not. We will just have to manage somehow. But . . ."

"Yes. As soon as I can."

"Take care." He hung up. She let the hand holding the phone sink into her lap.

Her head hurt. It was as though some great fist were squeezing it in rhythmic throbs, to match the beating of her pulse. She tapped out Darius's number again.

"You have called Darius Ramoška . . ."

She sat for a long time in one of the white wooden chairs by the kitchen table, trying to think.

Then she called the police.

THE BOY LAY unconscious on the back seat, with the checkered picnic blanket covering his thin, unmoving body. And Karin wasn't answering her phone.

Nina closed her eyes, trying to concentrate. 1:35. It should be 1:35 . . . Her hands shook slightly as she turned her wrist to check her watch. 1:36, stated the stark, digital numbers. Close enough. Relief flooded through her, making it a bit easier to think.

Sorry, Karin, she silently told her friend. You ask too much, this time.

She pulled the blanket a little higher so that it was not immediately obvious a child was asleep beneath it. Rolled down the window just a notch, so air would get into the car. Locked the Fiat and left, walking with long, quick strides she knew were nearly as fast as running.

SHE CUT THROUGH the central hall of the railway station, heading for the green and white sign that proclaimed the local police presence. She entered the small office, wondering what one actually said in such a situation. Good afternoon, I've just found a child?

The officer at the reception desk looked tired. Not the easiest job in Copenhagen, probably.

"What can I do for you?" she asked.

"Err . . . I have a child in my car—"

Nina's hesitant explanation was interrupted by a crackle from the woman's radio. Nina couldn't hear what was being said at the other end, but the officer snapped

THE BOY IN THE SUITCASE

a hasty "Copy that. I'm on my way," and headed for the door at a run.

"Please wait here," she called over her shoulder, but Nina had already followed her back into the central hall. She watched the officer and one of her uniformed colleagues fairly sprint for the stairwell leading down to the left luggage lockers. Following still further, into the basement, was not actually a conscious decision.

She heard the racket as soon as she started down the stairs. Everyone in the facility had stopped their various baggage maneuvers, and some had already gathered at the entrance to the passage where locker number 37-43 was situated. Nina felt a warning flutter along her spine, like an insect moving over her skin, but she still had to look.

A man was kicking at the metal doors with frightening ferocity. She caught a brief glimpse of the back of his head, hair clipped so short it looked almost shaved, and of a set of enormous shoulders encased in a shiny brown leather jacket that was surely too hot for this weather. When the officers reached him, he shook off the first one as if she were a child he no longer wanted to play with. Then he seemed to collect himself.

"Sorry, sorry," he said, rolling his r's in a way that almost made them into d's. He stood quite still, letting the police officers calm down from violence alert to dialogue mode. "I pay. Is broken, I pay."

Then he suddenly turned his head, looking directly at her. She didn't know what made him pick her out of the crowd, but she saw his muscles bunch tensely as fury tightened his face and narrowed his eyes. He remained still, and didn't speak, but even so she sensed the violence he was holding in check.

What had she done to deserve such rage? She had never seen the man before.

But of course the locker he had been kicking to pieces was not just any locker. It was number 37-43. And she suddenly knew where the rage had come from.

She had taken something that was his.

SHE HAD TO employ every shred of self-control she possessed to stop herself from running all the way back to the car. He won't be able to follow, she told herself, the police are there. She walked as quickly as she could without turning heads.

But she remembered how he had shaken them off like a dog shakes a flea from its fur, and the only plan she was able to form was that they had to get away, she and the boy, as far away from that man as they could possibly get.

WHEN THE STOLEN Nokia beeped in his brief-case more than three hours later, Jan's plane was still sitting on the pavement, and he was still in his business class seat, sweating like a pig. This time no flight attendant swooped down on him when he pulled out his phone. Cabin personnel had long since given up on that particular score, and at least twenty other people around him were engaged in multilingual phone calls, explaining why they would be delayed.

"Mr. Marquart." In spite of the hiss and crackle of a bad connection, the man's fury came through loud and clear, not so much in his words as in his tone of voice.

"Yes . . ."

"I delivered. As agreed. The woman came and took the goods. But she left no money. You did not pay."

What?

Jan protested. He himself was stuck in a plane, he explained, but he had directed his assistant to go in his stead, and he was sure she had followed his instructions.

"Mr. Marquart. There was no money."

Jan tried to imagine what could have happened.

"There must be some misunderstanding," he said. "As soon as I get back, I'll clear it up."

"That would be a very good idea," said the man, and cut the connection. The very restraint of his phrase sent a chill through Jan even in the midst of the overheated cabin. It signaled that this was a man who did not have to resort to threats. A man best not angered.

Jan jabbed out Karin's number with some ferocity. She didn't answer, and he left no message apart from a curt "Call me!"

He stared sightlessly at the back of the seat in front of him. Sweated. Sipped the water, and the lukewarm gin and tonic he had accepted a few hours ago when he thought he had accomplished a feasible Plan B. It took him nearly half an hour to accept that he would have to call Anne.

"Have you seen Karin?" he asked. And listened, while Anne's soft voice told him that yes, Karin had returned, but had left again rather quickly. She had been in her flat above the garage for only a few minutes.

"Was she carrying anything?" he asked. "When she arrived? And when she left?"

"I really don't know," said Anne vaguely. "Were you thinking of anything in particular?"

"No," he said. "It's nothing. It'll have to wait till I get back."

As the plane finally started to taxi out onto the runway, he leaned back against the blue leather upholstery, wondering feverishly how he could have been so wrong about her.

I should have done it myself, he thought bitterly. But that is just so typical. You make immaculate plans. You are in control. And then a fucking *seagull* wrecks it all.

THE VILLA IN Vedbæk was perfectly situated, thought Nina.

It had neither ocean view nor idyllic woods in the background, but for privacy it couldn't be matched. Neatly clipped hedges screened the sprawling redbrick and the graveled parking lot from prying eyes, and the surrounding well-to-do family homes oozed respectability. Whether that had been at the front of Allan's mind when he chose to buy his way into this particular general practice in the northern suburbs was dubious, as it had never really been part of his plan to moonlight as a medical resource for illegal immigrants; but it suited Nina's purpose beautifully.

She checked the rearview mirror. The boy hadn't moved in all the time she had had him in the car, nor made a sound. The blanket was undisturbed, and only a few wisps of blond hair poked from its folds.

Tock, tock.

A measured rapping against the window glass made Nina jerk. It was Allan. His tall, gangly form cut off the sun as he bent to peer into the car. Then he rapped on the glass once more, but before she had time to react, he moved on, and was now trying to open the rear door, in vain. She must have locked it without thinking. She realized she was still gripping the steering wheel, fingers locked whitely around the rim, and it took her a second to make her hands unclench. She reached back and unlocked the rear door with stiff fingers, then got out of the car herself.

Allan had already lifted the boy gently out of the car, the blanket still wrapped around him. He held the child against his shoulder.

"What do you know?"

He was headed for the house, and Nina had to lengthen her stride to keep up.

"Nothing. Or almost nothing. Someone left him in a suitcase!"

Nina closed the door behind them and followed Allan as he strode towards his office. Jolly children's drawings decorated the walls, and behind his computer sat a small gnome-like clown doll, obviously intended for the cheering up of young patients.

The clown would not serve them now. The suitcase boy hung limply in Allan's arms, like one of Ida's cast-off Raggedy Anns, thought Nina, with a familiar taste of metal in her mouth. It was her personal taste of fear. It always came to her when adrenalin rushed through her body, into every last cell of it, reminding her of the camps at Dadaab and Zwangheli and other hellholes in which she had lived and looked after the children of others. (And it reminded her of the day he died.)

Nina pushed away the thought as soon as it entered her mind and instead locked her focus on Allan and the boy. Allan had rolled the small, soft body gently onto the couch, his middle and index finger resting against the side of his neck. His face was alight with concentration, and she saw a single bead of sweat trickle down his throat and into the open neck of his white shirt. This was not the time to talk to him.

The sphygmomanometer sat on Alan's desk, within

handy reach, but the cuff was much too big for the boy's thin arm. She found a smaller one and attached it. The child did not react to the high-pitched whine, or to the pressure from the inflating cuff. 90/52. She turned the display so that the digital numbers were visible to Allan.

Allan frowned and slid his hand across the boy's chest, setting the stethoscope against the smooth, white skin of the chest, and then, in a quick precise move, to the abdominal cavity. He then rolled the boy onto his side with a gentleness that, for a moment, caused a strange tender warmth in Nina's own chest. He listened again, and finally let the boy slip down to his original position, resting on his back with his arms spread wide.

Still this disturbing lack of life, thought Nina. As if he were caught in some limbo, neither dead nor alive, simply a thing. Allan cautiously lifted one eyelid and shone his pen-sized flashlight at the boy's pupil.

"He has been drugged," he said. "I don't know with what, but it doesn't seem to be exactly life-threatening."

"Should we give him naloxone?" asked Nina.

Allan shook his head.

"His respiration is okay. Blood pressure is a little on the low side, and he is somewhat dehydrated, but I think he will simply sleep off whatever it is and wake naturally. And in any case, we can't give an antidote when we have no idea what the original substance was."

Nina nodded slowly, dodging Allan's gaze. She knew what he had to say next.

"You will of course take him to a hospital."

"But you said he would wake on his own . . ."

Allan gestured, indicating his collection of medical reference books.

"There's a million drugs out there that someone could have given him, and I have no idea what is really wrong with him, nor do I have the facilities to do the proper tests. You simply have to take him to Hvidovre."

Nina made no reply at first.

She had had so little time to look at the child. At first she had thought him to be barely three years old, but now, examining his face, she thought he was merely small for his age. Closer to four, perhaps. She touched his cheek gently, tracing the soft lines of the mouth. His hair was short and so fair it was nearly white, the skin parchment thin and almost bluish in the light streaming through the blinds.

"I don't know where he's from," she said. "I don't think he is Danish, and I know someone is looking for him. Someone who wants to . . . use him for something."

Again, Allan frowned.

"Pedophilia?"

Nina shrugged, trying to recall as much as she could about the man who had been kicking at the locker. Huge. That was the main impression. Perhaps thirty years old, with hair so short it hardly left an impression of color. Brown, perhaps? Like the weather-inappropriate leather jacket. She tried to imagine the police issuing an APB and knew immediately that this description would match any number of large men. And she pictured the boy, alone in a hospital room, while some social worker or child care specialist sat in the staff room filling out endless forms. Would they be able to protect the boy against the rage she had seen in the man's eyes? Once he woke up, what would the Danish authorities do with him? Send him to some institution or refugee center like the Coal-House Camp? Nina suppressed a shudder. Natasha's bastard of a fiancé had sauntered straight into the camp to pick up Rina without anyone even noticing she had gone. Far too many of the so-called unaccompanied minors simply disappeared from the camps after a few days. They were collected by their owners.

"I'm not letting them take him to the camps," she snapped, glancing around the office. "Children vanish from them almost every day. He's not going to any of those places."

Finally she saw what she was looking for. Behind the matte glass doors of the cabinets by the door she made out the contours of Allan's special emergency kit, which she knew to contain a couple of bags of IV fluid.

Last year, Allan had gone with her to attend an elderly man who had fled the Sandholm asylum center and was hiding with some relatives in the city. He had been due to be sent back to some refugee camp in Lebanon, but instead he was slumped on a mattress in a loft above an old tenement flat in Nørrebro. It was at least 115 degrees Fahrenheit up there under the rafters, and in other circumstances it might have been a rather trivial case of heat stroke. But because they didn't have the range of equipment an ordinary ambulance would have had, they nearly lost him. Since then, the infusion sets had been a fixture in Allan's emergency bag. As yet, he had not had to use them, as far as she knew. He wanted out. In fact, he had wanted out for a long time, but there was not exactly a waiting list for the unofficial post of MD to the illegal immigrants that the network struggled to aid, and Nina had hung on to his phone number. Just in case, she thought with a sardonic inner smile that didn't quite reach her lips. Just in case she came across a three-year-old boy in a suitcase.

She grabbed the infusion set and the IV bag off the shelf and felt a sense of calm descend as the familiar equipment came into her hands. She had done this a thousand times. Torn the clear wrapping in a single jerk, freed the needle, uncoiled the plastic tubing. She cast around for something to place the bag on, so that it would be higher than the boy, and finally cleared a space for it on the shelf above the couch, where various toys resided. Then she took hold of the boy's inanimate arm, exposed the veins under the white skin, and let the needle slide in.

Allan, standing next to her, shook his head and sighed.

"I'll lose my license if they find out about this. If anything happens to him . . ."

"They won't. Why should they? And I'll take good care of him," said Nina. "He'll be all right."

Allan looked at her with a strange uncertainty Nina wasn't sure she cared for. Then he turned to the boy again, this time completely removing the blanket, which until now had shrouded the boy's lower body.

"Did you find him like this?" he asked.

Nina nodded.

"Would you be able to tell whether anything has been done to him?" she asked. "Whether he has been . . . abused?"

Allan gave a partial shrug and rolled the boy onto his

side again, so that his back was turned to them. Nina again felt the sour metallic taste in her mouth, and turned to look out the window. There was a slight breeze now, and she could hear the leaves of the large chestnut tree outside rustle in the hot wind. Except for that, there was barely a sound. No voices, no cars, no children. People in Vedbæk obviously weren't as noisy as those in the inner city, she thought, suddenly aware of the sweaty stickiness that made her T-shirt cling to her back.

Behind her, Allan spoke in carefully measured tones.

"I see no evidence of abuse, but one can never tell with complete certainty. People can be horribly inventive about such things."

Allan pulled off the thin white plastic gloves with a snap, covered the boy to the waist once more, and gently stroked his forehead.

"This is my professional advice to you, Nina," he said, looking at her directly for the first time. His eyes were the color of corroded steel. For God's sake, thought Nina, the man might have stepped right off the pages of a Harlequin romance, fit and tanned in an affluent kind of way that spoke of tennis courts and long sailing trips in the boat she knew he kept in Vedbæk harbor. A note of casual ease was introduced by the dark blue denim jeans, trendily scuffed at the knees to just the right degree. A handsome, humane suburban GP who did everything right and proper, even running great personal risks by doing his bit for the network. His place in the practice was on the line, she thought. This was so obviously a good man.

And yet she felt a guttering animosity. In a minute, this nice, humane man would tell her that he couldn't help her anymore. That there was nothing further he could do for the boy.

Allan sighed again, a mere exhalation of breath.

"My professional advice is that you take this boy to Hvidovre Hospital. And if anything goes wrong . . ."

Nina knew what he was about to say, but now it didn't matter, because she also knew she had won the essential victory: he wouldn't call the police.

"If anything goes wrong, and questions are asked of me and this practice, then that is the advice I have given you. And I want to hear you accept it."

She nodded quickly.

"I'll take him to Hvidovre Hospital," she obediently replied, with a quick glance at her watch.

3:09.

She had been there for more than thirty minutes.

Allan looked at her again with the skeptical expression that reminded her so much of her long, exhausted fights with Morten. Morten, who seemed to think that she could no longer be trusted to handle anything alone. Least of all the children. He didn't say it outright, but she could hear it in the way he spoke when he gave her detailed instructions on how to make Ida's lunch box, or how to dress Anton for school. He spoke slowly and clearly, enunciating each syllable, all the while trying to fix her eyes on him as though she were hard of hearing, or mentally defective, or both. More than anything, she could see it in his eyes when he packed his bags for his monthly shifts on the company's North Sea oil rigs. Leaving her alone with the children had begun to scare him.

He no longer believed her. He no longer believed in anything she said.

Nor did Allan, it would seem. But at least he was not about to stop her. The suitcase boy was not his responsibility, and never would be. Only for that reason was he letting her go.

"Keep the IV going until the unit is empty," said Allan. "After that, I want you gone. Don't let anyone see you leave. And Nina . . ."

He caught her eyes again, and she could see that his impatient irritation had returned.

"I'm through with this," he said. "Don't come back."

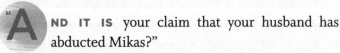**A** **ND IT IS** your claim that your husband has abducted Mikas?"

Evaldas Gužas from the Department of Missing Persons looked at Sigita with visible skepticism.

"We are separated," she said.

"But he is the father of the child?"

She could feel herself blushing. "Of course."

The office was stifling in the summer heat, and a house fly buzzed desperately in the window overlooking the street, caught between the net curtain and the glass. Gužas's desk looked to be a scarred veteran of the Soviet era, several years older than Gužas himself was. Sigita would have preferred an older policeman, not this young, black-haired, sharp-featured man of thirty at the most. He had doffed his blue-gray jacket and loosened his burgundy tie, so that he looked for all the world like a café patron on holiday. It didn't give a serious impression, she thought. She wanted experience, steadfastness, and efficiency, and she wasn't sure she was getting it.

"And this alleged abduction . . . you say it happened Saturday?"

"Saturday afternoon. Yes."

"And you waited two days to come to us because . . . ?"

He left his unfinished sentence hanging in the humid air.

She nearly lowered her eyes, but resisted the impulse. He would only see it as uncertainty and become even more skeptical than he already was.

"I was in hospital until this morning."

"I see. Can you relate to me the circumstances of the alleged abduction?" he asked.

"My neighbor saw my husband and a strange young woman take Mikas to a car and drive off with him."

"Did the child resist?"

"Not . . . not as far as Mrs. Mažekienė was able to see. But you see, the woman has been spying on us for some time, at least two or three days, and she gave Mikas chocolate. That's not normal!"

He clicked his ballpoint pen a couple of times, watching her all the while.

"And where were you when this happened?"

Now she could not keep the uncertainty from coming out in her voice.

"I . . . I don't remember clearly," she said. "I've suffered a concussion. Perhaps . . . perhaps they attacked me."

The words felt odd in her mouth because she didn't herself believe that Darius was capable of something like that. But the woman. She didn't know the woman, did she?

"And at which hospital were you treated?"

Her heart dropped like a stone. "Vilkpėdės," she said, hoping that would be the end of it. But of course it wasn't. He reached for the phone.

"Which ward?"

"M1."

She sat there on the uncomfortabe plastic chair, frustrated and powerless, as he was put through to the ward and had a brief conversation with someone at the other end. The fly kept buzzing and bumping into the glass. Gužas listened more than he talked, but she could guess what he was being told. Alcohol content in the blood, fall on the stairs.

"Mrs. Ramoškienė," he said, replacing the receiver. "Don't you think you should simply go home and wait for your husband to call?"

"I don't drink!" She blurted out the words even though she knew they would only confirm his suspicion.

"Please go home now, Mrs. Ramoškienė."

MECHANICALLY, SHE GOT on the number 17 trolley bus at T. Ševčenkos gatvė. Several stops too late, she realized that she had failed to get off at Aguonų gatvė to change lines. It was as if the city in which she had lived for more than eight years had suddenly become strange to her. The sunlight pierced her eyes like needles. Only once before in her life had she felt this helpless.

Please go home now, Mrs. Ramoškienė. But to what? Without Mikas, the whole thing made no sense—the flat, the furniture, all the clean and new things she had fought so hard for.

God's punishment, a voice whispered inside her.

"Shut up," she said under her breath, but it did no good.

She hadn't attended mass since leaving Tauragė. Not once in eight years. She didn't *want* to believe in God, but it was as if it wouldn't let her go—the hot, waxy scent of the candles, the old women who could barely kneel but insisted on doing so all the same, the flowers on the altar, the sense of solemnity that had made her sit quietly even when she had been so young her legs dangled from the pews in white stockings and shiny black shoes—that one day of the week one should make the effort, her mother said, and dress in one's best. Her first communion . . . she had felt so grown-up, so important. She was old enough to *sin*. The word unfolded inside her, releasing a scent of darkness and sulphur, of guilt and lost souls. But above all, sin was *interesting*. Interesting like Mama's sister, Aunt Jolita, who lived in Vilnius and had done things that no one would explain to Sigita. Sinners were far more interesting than ordinary people—it even said so in the Bible. Now this world of sin and confession had opened to her, too. It was peculiarly intoxicating to be a part of the chorus of response when the congregation murmured its "*Esu kaltas, esu kaltas, esu labai kaltas.*" I am guilty, I am very guilty. She went at it with a will.

"Shhhh," said her mother, twitching her scarf into place. "Not so loud!"

By and by she learned the correct volume—not self-promotingly loud and shrill, nor so low that it sounded reluctant; a sincere murmur reaching the nearest without echoing through the dome. Esu kaltas. There was a beauty, a sweetness to it.

Until the day when she actually had something relevant to confess and couldn't bring herself to say it. At first she had tried for teenage rebellion by stating flatly that she wasn't going. Had it been only her mother, she might have carried it off. But when Granny Julija looked at her and asked her if anything was wrong, her weak attempt at mutiny collapsed. No, there was nothing wrong. Nothing at all. Granny Julija had patted her arm and told her that she was a good girl. It was all right to doubt a little sometimes, she said. God could take it. Then Sigita had had to hurry up and change into her Sunday best, so that they wouldn't be late. On the outside, everything was the way it had always been. On the inside, the world had come to an end.

THE CHURCH OF St. Kazimiero was silent and nearly empty now. Two older women were busy cleaning. Volunteers, probably, like they would have been at home in Tauragė, thought Sigita. One of them asked if Sigita needed anything.

"Thank you, no," said Sigita. "I just want to sit here for a while."

They nodded kindly. The need to "sit for a while" was understood by any true believer. Sigita felt like a fraud. She was no longer a believer of any kind.

If that is so, what are you doing here? whispered the voice inside her.

She couldn't explain it. She felt as if she was standing at the edge of an abyss, but she was in no way counting on God to rescue her. On the contrary. *I don't believe in any of it. Not anymore.* But when she looked up at the image of the Holy Virgin, she could no longer hold it back. The Madonna cradled the Baby Jesus tenderly, her face aglow with love. And Sigita fell to her knees on the cold flag stones and wept helplessly, hard involuntary sobs that echoed harshly under the vaulted ceilings. *Esu kaltas. Esu labai kaltas.*

SHE HAD ONLY just left the church when her mobile phone started vibrating in her bag. She fumbled through the contents one-handedly, with the bag hanging from her plaster-encased lower arm, until wallet and makeup purse and throat lozenges tipped out onto the pavement and rolled in all directions. She had eyes for nothing except the phone. The call was from Darius, she noticed, as she snatched it from the ground.

"What's up with you?" he said in his usual happy warm voice. "You've called about a million times."

"You have to bring him back here. Now!" she snapped.

"What are you talking about?"

"Mikas! If you don't bring him back, I'll call the police." She neglected to tell him that she had in fact already done so. They just didn't want to know.

"Sigita. Sweetie. I have no idea what you're talking about. What is wrong with Mikas?"

Years of training had made her an expert. She was able to tell, by now, if he was lying or telling the truth. And the confusion in his voice sounded one hundred percent genuine.

Strength drained from her legs like water from a bath tub, and she dropped to her knees for the second time, in the middle of the sidewalk, surrounded by the debris from her bag. A distantly tinny Darius-voice was shouting at her from somewhere: "Sigita. Sigita, what is it? Where is Mikas?"

She was no longer at the edge of the abyss. It had already swallowed her. Because if Darius did not have Mikas, who did?

5 :10 P.M.

Whose turn was it to pick up Anton today? Suddenly Nina couldn't remember, and felt a long, cold tug in the pit of her stomach, as though she was about to be pulled under by some deep, chill current. The after-school child care program provided by the city would have closed at 5:00. Her son might be standing by the gate right now, accompanied by a seriously cross member of the staff.

She had seated herself on the couch with the unknown boy half in her lap, his bare white body curled against her. A few damp streaks had appeared in his hair. His skin felt warmer now, and after the fluid had begun to run into him, he seemed more alive. Not awake, but alive, at least. Once, he whimpered in his sleep, turned a wrist, moved his leg a bit. It had to be a good sign, thought Nina. She had done the right thing in staying away from the hospital, and even though she had felt her resolution firm every time she thought of the furious man at the railway station, it was still an enormous relief. The boy hadn't died. He lived, and she could tell by the tiny twitches beneath his eyelids that he was on his way back up from the deep darkness he had rested in.

Yet mixed with the relief was a new sense of panic, as thoughts beyond mere survival started to surface. What on earth had she been thinking since she fled from the railway station?

Not a damn thing, she thought sardonically, running a

finger under the strap of her wristwatch to ease it away from the overheated skin underneath. There hadn't been a single thought in her head apart from the panicked urge to get away. Bring him to safety. And now she would soon have a wide-awake naked boy in her arms, and absolutely no idea what she was going to do with him.

She needed to buy time. She leaned over and tugged her bag toward her, fumbling inside for her mobile. Thank God Morten was home this week. He would have to deal with things until . . .

Her finger hovered over the Place Call-button for a few seconds while she prepared herself as best she could. She had never been particularly good at lying to Morten, and time hadn't improved her skills, despite frequent practice. It wasn't that she wanted to be able to lie to him about important things. Just little everyday fibs that would make life run so much more smoothly. Like being able to say that her new top had cost 200 kroner rather than 450, or that it hadn't been she who had forgotten the picnic invitation from Anton's school. Other people got away with such things, why couldn't she? She was an adequate liar with everyone but Morten, she thought. But Morten saw through her feeble attempts in seconds. Somehow, she lacked her usual protective coloration when she was with him. It seemed to her that he could look directly into the bubbling mass of unfinished thoughts churning inside her. It was why she had fallen in love with him, and why he was so hard to live with now. Sometimes a lie would go by without comment, but it didn't feel like success; it was more as if he couldn't really be bothered to discuss it with her. He let her off the hook.

Nina touched the call button tentatively; the phone was already damp from the heat of her hands. Then she pressed it, and raised the phone to her ear, careful not to disturb the boy with her shift of position.

There was a tiny click as he answered, followed by a faint, surf-like noise. She could hear Morten's fumbling with the phone, and distant children's voices in the background. Thank God. He was picking up Anton, then. It might even be his turn today. Her mind felt curiously blank when she tried to remember.

"Yes." Morten's voice succeeded in being angry and resigned at the same time. "Where are you?"

It was the voice of a man who felt that she no longer deserved to be talked to as an equal. Or even as an adult.

Nina moistened her lips, looking down at the child in her arms. She had to come up with something not too far from the truth, she thought, or he would slice her explanations into ribbons before they were half finished.

"Karin called me, earlier today," she finally said. "She wasn't feeling very well. She really needed help. I've had to stay with her so that I can take her to a doctor if it becomes necessary."

Silence at the other end. Then she could hear shouting again, and Anton's thin voice asking for something.

"No," said Morten without putting down the phone, "No ice cream. It's Monday, and you know the rules." In the background Nina could hear Anton's voice rising, getting ready for the full campaign. Which might be her good luck.

"Okay," said Morten. "But I didn't think the two of you were that close anymore?"

He didn't sound angry anymore, just a little tired.

"I've known her for fifteen years. With history like that, you don't just turn your back on people."

"It's okay," he said. "But perhaps you might have called me, instead of leaving that to the staff here."

Damn. Nina shrunk a little. It *had* been her turn, had to have been, and somehow she would have felt better about it, more secure, if Morten had thrown a fit. Now there was just the unrythmic rattle of the receiver and the indistinct snatches of a new heated argument between Morten and Anton. Morten had already forgotten she was there.

"I'm sorry," she murmured, trying to press her ear more closely to the phone. "I just forgot."

"Yes, I suppose you did," he said, his voice cold and weary. "I thought things were better. I thought you were going to stop forgetting your own family. Any idea when you will be home?"

Nina swallowed. The boy had turned slightly, and one small hand opened and then closed around her arm. His eyes were still closed.

"Oh, I suppose I can leave here around eight," she said, trying to sound carefree and unworried. "It won't be very late, I promise."

Again the static hiss of wind and a connection on the point of breaking up.

"I'll see you when I see you," said Morten, the last few words nearly lost in the roar of the wind and the sound of Anton's eager pestering. "Or not. It's up to you."

Morten's voice had gone dark and distant. Then there was just silence, real silence, as the connection was finally severed.

Nina exhaled soundlessly and let the phone slip back into her bag on the floor. Then she eased herself away from the boy and stood up. Her heart beat a hard, cantering rhythm, and she needed to move, as if the disquiet she felt could be dispelled by mere motion. She stooped to snatch up the phone once more and pressed a new number while pacing up and down, imposing her own restlessness on the whole room.

He was listed merely as "Peter" in her phone book, and actually that was almost as much as she knew about him, except that he lived somewhere in Vanløse. He was the only contact in the network whose number she had. Normally it was the other way around—they called her. The people the network looked after could not saunter into the office of their local GP, or take their children to the emergency room if they were ill. Could not, in fact, approach authority in any form. So when there was need, Nina was sent for, or Allan. Or so it had been. Might she perhaps ask Magnus to step in, if Allan was serious about quitting? Unfortunately, though, Magnus did not have access to a handily secluded private practice in Vedbæk.

"Hi, this is Peter," announced a happy-sounding voice, and Nina nearly said "Hi" herself when the voice went on without pausing: "I am on holiday from the fifteenth of August to the twenty-ninth, so you'll just have to do without me!"

Bloody hell. Nina rested her forehead against the wall, closing her eyes for a minute. She had never done this bit before. Not with an unaccompanied child. The network would sometimes find some basement room or empty summerhouse for a family to stay in, or help them across to Sweden—that wasn't too complicated. Such people could, after all, look after themselves in most respects. But was there anyone out there who would take on an abandoned three-year-old? And if there was, how would she find them?

Nina opened her eyes, examining the boy in a slightly different way. He could come from anywhere, she thought. Anywhere in Northern or Eastern Europe. Denmark, Sweden, Poland, Germany. She drew a hand through her own short, dark hair, which felt sticky and damp in the humid air. She would be wiser once the boy woke up, she supposed; meanwhile, she just had to get hold of Karin. She was the one who had started all this, and Nina had no doubts that Karin knew more than she had been willing to say when she'd sat there in Magasin's cafeteria, nervously twisting her coffee cup.

This time, she let the phone ring until it stopped, but Karin still didn't answer, and Nina brushed at the faintly lit display with a restless finger, as if to clear away invisible dust.

The boy stirred, and the blanket slipped to reveal a naked shoulder.

Clothes, thought Nina, and felt relief at having a practical solution to focus on. She had to get some clothes for the boy so they wouldn't draw any more attention than they had to. She peered at the IV bag. Nearly empty, which meant she would be able to get out of here soon.

She tried Karin once more. Same depressing lack of results.

Why the hell couldn't the woman just answer her phone?

JUČAS KNEW HIS rage was both a weakness and a strength. When he was training he could sometimes use it to wring the last reserves from his body, and achieve those explosions of force that made his blood throb in a way that was almost better than sex. Following a set like that, he could *see* it: the veins lay on top of his muscles like plastic tubing, and the pump was visible, bang bang bang, just as he felt it in every fiber. God, he loved that feeling. In such moments he felt strong, and he had to supress a desire to leap onto the bench and yell out his invulnerability to the world, like some action hero from the American films he liked to watch: *You don't fuck with me, man.*

At other times, the rage helped him do things he didn't really like doing. It was always there, just under the surface, a hidden power he could call on at need. Then the men became swine, and the women bitches, and he could do what had to be done. But it was dangerous to unleash it, because it also meant a loss of control. He couldn't always stop once he had started, and he didn't think as clearly as he normally did. Once he had hit the man who was the swine at that moment so hard that the guy never really recovered, and Klimka had told him that if that happened again, Jučas would be fired. In the most permanent way. It was just about then that he realized the rage could kill him one day if he wasn't careful, and he had actually stopped taking both the andros and the durabolines immediately, because they made the rage that much harder to control. It was around that time he had met Barbara, too.

When he was with Barbara, the rage was sometimes so distant he could pretend it had gone away. It might even *be* gone one day, he thought, when he never had to work for Klimka again, when he and Barbara had their house just outside Krakow, and he could spend his days doing ordinary things like mowing the lawn, putting up shelves, eating dinners Barbara made him, and making love to the woman he wanted to spend the rest of his life with.

But there hadn't been any money. Every time he thought of the empty locker, fury sent accurate little stabs through him like a nail gun. God, he could have smashed the bitch's skull in.

He had deliberately chosen a locker in the dead-end passage; there were fewer people, and it was out of sight of the staff in the security booth. At first he had taken up position in the actual basement, so that he would be able to see when the suitcase was picked up, and by whom. But he had been there only about ten minutes when the security staff began to get nervous. He could tell they were watching him, taking turns at it, first one, then the other. They put their heads together and talked. Then one of them reached for the phone. Damn. He got out his own mobile and held it so that it shielded part of his face as he went past their window and up the stairs to the central hall.

In the end, he'd had to station Barbara there, while he himself tried to watch both the other two exits from the car. It was far from perfect. If only it had been the Dane himself, whom he knew by sight. But now it was to be some female Jučas had never laid eyes on. Oh, well. He would be able to recognize the suitcase, at least.

Twelve o'clock came and went with no suitcase-dragging woman in sight. He kept phoning Barbara, just to be sure, but he could hear that he was only making her nervous. He decided to give it an hour; after all, the Dane had had to make contingency plans, so some delay was understandable. But in the end, he had to send Barbara down to check on the locker.

A few minutes later, she came up the stairs by the street exit, and he could see it a mile off: something was wrong. She was walking with tense little reluctant steps, her shoulders hunched.

"It wasn't there," she said.

So he had to go see for himself, of course. And she was right. Somehow, the woman must have gotten past either him or Barbara. The suitcase was gone, and no money had been left in its place. When he saw that, he lost it for a moment so that the uniformed piglets got all scared, and he had to smile and pay to calm their frightened little hearts.

And in the middle of all that, he had felt it. Her eyes on him. She might have been any old tourist except for the intensity of her gaze, but he picked her out of the crowd immediately. The woman. She had been scared, too. And more than that. He had seen her note what locker it was he had been smashing. When she turned and ran, he was sure. She was the one. She had taken the suitcase. But why had she come back? Did she think she could come here to gloat, and he wouldn't know? He would show her differently. Even through the rage, he saw her clearly. Thin as a boy, with very short dark hair; for a moment he imagined sticking his cock into something like that, but who would want to, unless they were queer? Bloody boy-bitch. He would stick her, all right, but with something else.

HE CALLED THE Dane right away. Was fed a truckload of excuses about delays and honest intentions. Could he believe the man? He didn't know. Anger was still guttering in his stomach as he walked up the steps to the street, past three Russians engaged in a blatant dope deal. Morons. Couldn't they be just a little discrete? The biggest one, obviously meant to be the muscle, cast a nervous eye over Jučas. It improved his mood a fraction. Look your fill, he thought. I'm bigger than you are, pal.

Outside in the street, heat surged from the pavement and the sun-warmed bricks. The leather jacket had been a bad choice, but he'd thought Denmark would be colder, and now he didn't really feel he could take it off. He sweated a lot, people did when they were in good shape, and he didn't like Barbara to see him with huge underarm stains on his shirt.

"Andrius?" Barbara called to him through the open car window. "Is it okay?"

He forced himself to take long deep breaths. Couldn't quite produce a smile, but he did manage to ease his grip on the car keys.

"Yes." Deep breaths. Easy now. "He says it's a mistake. He is on his way home, and when he gets here, we will get our money."

"That's good." Barbara was watching him with her head cocked slightly to one side. For some reason, it made her neck look even longer. More elegant. She was the only one who ever called him by his given name. Everyone else just called him Jučas. He didn't event think of himself as Andrius, and hadn't since his Granny died and he was sent to Vilnius to live with his father because no one had any idea what else might be done with him. His father rarely called him by name at all, it had been either "boy" or "brat," according to his mood. Later, in the orphanage, everyone had gone by their last name.

He let himself drop into the front seat next to her, wincing at the contact with the sun-scorched fabric. The Mitsubishi had a certain lived-in appearance after two days on the road. Paper mugs and sandwich bags from German Raststellen littered the floor, and the food-smeared car seat the boy had been strapped into gave off a sour odor of pee. He really ought to dismantle it and sling it in the back of the van, but right now the fug was too much for him and he didn't want to spend another minute in the car.

"Are you hungry?" he said. "We might as well do something while we wait for him to call."

Suddenly, Barbara's face came alive.

"Tivoli!" she said. "Could we go there? I was looking through the fence earlier, and it all looks so beautiful."

He had not the slightest wish to endure the wait surrounded by screaming toddlers, cotton candy, and balloon vendors, but the surge of expectation in her eyes melted his resolve. They paid a day's wage to get in, and ate a pizza that only set him back about seven or eight times as much as it would have cost him in Vilnius. But Barbara was loving every minute. She smiled more than she had done at any time during the long tense drive here, and his nerves began to settle. Perhaps everything would still be all right in the end. It might be just a mis-understanding. After all, if the Dane was stuck in a plane and couldn't do much, it wasn't surprising somebody screwed up. He would pay. He had said so. And if he didn't, Jučas knew where he lived.

"There's a bit of oregano on your chin," said Barbara. "No, let me . . ." She blotted the corner of his mouth gently with the red-and-white-checkered napkin, smil-ing into his eyes so that the rage curled up inside him and went to sleep.

Later they walked around a ridiculous little lake in which someone had placed a disproportionate schooner, so large it would hardly be able to turn if anyone had the misguided idea to try to actually sail it. Barbara put two fat Danish coins into an automat and was rewarded with a small bag of fish fodder. As soon as they heard the click from the automat, the fish in the lake surged forward so that the water literally boiled with their huge writhing bodies. The sight turned his gut, he wasn't quite sure why. At that moment, the phone finally rang.

"I just got home," said the man at the other end. "There is no sign of the goods or the money. Nor of the person I sent to do the trade."

Bitch. Swine.

"I delivered," he said, with as much calm as he could muster. "Now you must pay."

The man was silent for a while. Then he said:

"When you give me what I paid for, you will get the rest of the money."

Jučas was struggling both with his temper and his English vocabulary. Only Barbara's hand on his arm made it possible to win at least one of those battles.

"You sent the woman. If she don't do what you say, is not my problem."

Again, the silence. Even longer, this time.

"She took a company car," the Dane finally said. "We have GPS tracking on all of them. If I tell you where she is, will you go and get her? She must have either the money or the goods, or both. Or she must know where they are. Bring her back to me."

"Is not what we agreed," said Jučas through clenched teeth. He wanted his money, and he wanted to get out of this stinking, stupidly expensive country where even the fish were fat.

"Ten thousand dollars extra," said the man promptly. "To get the money and the goods, and bring her back."

The screaming from the roller coaster was getting on his nerves. But ten thousand dollars was ten thousand dollars.

"Okay," he said. "You tell me where she is."

NINA WRAPPED THE blanket more tightly about the boy, picked him up, and left Allan's office with the skinny body in her arms. He felt feather light compared to Anton, but of course Anton was no longer a toddler. He went to school. He was a big boy now.

She was careful to make sure that the lock on the main door of the practice clicked behind her. The parking lot, thank God, was still empty. She levered the body carefully into the back seat and closed the door with a soft push. It was 6:44.

"What do I do now?" she muttered, then caught herself with some irritation. Talking to herself now. Not cool. She hadn't done that much since she started secondary school and had had to leave that and other childish habits behind if she wanted to survive socially. But sometimes, under pressure, it came back. It seemed to help her concentrate.

She started the car and let it roll down the graveled drive. Her hands were shaking again. She noted it with the same detached interest she would have awarded a rare bird at her bird feeder. She had to lock her fingers around the rim of the steering wheel to stop the annoying quiver that spread through her arms, then her palms to the tips of her fingers.

Karin had not returned any of her calls. Nor had Morten. Nor had there been any sign of police or other authorities. The last would of course have been unlikely, but the sense of being hunted would not leave her. It just didn't seem right that she could be driving around for hours with a three-year-old boy who wasn't hers. Somebody had to be missing him—someone other than the furious man at the railway station.

Nina turned up the volume of the car radio to be ready to catch the news. It was 6:46 according to the display on her mobile. She slowed slightly and regained enough control of her fingers to tap out Karin's number once more.

After seven long rings, there was, finally, an answer.

"Hello?"

Karin's voice sounded both hopeful and reserved.

Nina took a deep breath. It would be so easy for Karin to cut the connection if Nina came on too strongly. She had to be careful. Had to coax Karin into giving the answers she needed.

"Karin."

Nina softened her tone persuasively. Like she did when Anton was in the grip of one of his nightmares—gently, gently.

"Karin, it's Nina. I have the boy with me here in the car. He is okay."

Silence. Then a long hiccoughing breath and a heavy sigh. Karin was battling to control her voice.

"Oh, thank God. Nina, thank you so much for getting him out of there."

Another long silence. That seemed to be it. Nina cursed inwardly. Thank you for getting him out of there? How about an explanation? How about a bit of help? Something, anything, that would tell her what to do with her three-year-old burden.

"I have to know something about him," she said. "I

have no idea what to do with him. Do you want me to take him to the police? Do you know where he comes from?"

Nina heard the rising shrillness in her own voice, and for a moment she was afraid Karin had gotten spooked and hung up. Then she heard a faint, wet snuffling, as if from a cornered and wounded animal.

"I really don't know, Nina. I thought you had contacts . . . that your network would be able to help him."

Nina sighed.

"I have no one," she said, and felt the truth of it for the first time, at the very pit of her stomach. "Look, we need to talk properly. Where can I find you?"

Karin hesitated, and Nina could practically hear the doubts and fears ripping away at her.

"I'm in a summer cottage."

"Where?"

Nina waited tensely, while Karin fumbled with her phone.

"I don't want to be involved in this. I can't. It wasn't supposed to be a *child*."

The last word was nearly a wail, a high-pitched hysterical whimper, and Karin could no longer control the violent sobbing that Nina guessed had been coming even before she answered the phone.

"Where is the cottage?" she repeated, striving for a note of calm authority. "Tell me where you are, Karin, and I will come to you. It will be all right."

Karin's breath came in harsh bursts, and her silence this time was so long that Nina might have ended the call, had she not been so desperate herself.

"Tisvildeleje."

Karin's voice was so faint that Nina could barely make it out.

"I've borrowed the cottage from my cousin, and it's . . ." There was a crackling sound as Karin fumbled for something, possibly a piece of paper. "Twelve Skovbakken. It's at the very end, the last house before the woods."

There was a click, and this time, she really was gone.

Nina turned to the sleeping child with the first real smile she had been able to manage during the six hours that had passed since she opened a suitcase and found a boy.

"I've got it covered," she said, feeling her hands unclench on their own. "Now we will go find out what has happened, and then I will see to it that you get back home where you belong."

SIGITA WAS DESPERATE enough to ask him to come.

Darius's mobile phone voice became ill at ease.

"Sigita . . . You know I can't."

"Why not?"

"My job."

He worked for a construction company in Germany. Not as an engineer, as he sometimes told people, but as a plumber.

"This is *Mikas*, Darius."

"Yes. But . . ."

She ought to have known. When had she ever been able to count on him? But Mikas . . . she hadn't imagined that Mikas meant so little. Darius liked the boy and often played with him for anything up to an hour at a time. And Mikas worshiped his father, who would always appear at the oddest times, carrying armfuls of cellophane-wrapped toys.

"Are other people's toilets really more important to you than your son?" she choked.

"Sigita . . ."

She hung up. She knew it wasn't his job that was stopping him. If it had been something he really wanted to do, like a football match or something, then he called in sick without worrying about it. He was not a career chaser. His job didn't mean all *that* much to him.

It wasn't because he couldn't, it was because he wouldn't. He wanted to stay in his new life, probably with a new girlfriend, too, and had no wish to be drawn back to Vilnius and Tauragė, to Sigita and her tiresome demands.

Pling-pliiing. The mobile gave off its tinny "Message received" signal. The text message was from Darius.

Call me when Mikas comes home, it said.

As though Mikas were a runaway dog who would appear on her doorstep when it became sufficiently hungry.

"Are you all right, madam?"

She looked up. An elderly gentleman in a gray suit stood watching her from a few yards away, supported by a black cane.

"Yes," she said. "It's . . . it was just . . . it's over now."

He helped her to her feet and began to collect her scattered belongings.

"It's important to drink enough when it is this hot," he said kindly. "Or so my doctor is always telling me. I often forget."

"Yes. Yes, you are quite right."

He tipped his pale gray Fedora to her as he left.

"Good afternoon, madam."

SHE WENT BACK to the police station in Birželio 23-iosios gatvė. Sergeant Gužas's face took on a look of resignation when he saw her in his doorway.

"Mrs. Ramoškienė. I thought you were going home."

"It's not him. Darius didn't take him" she said. "Don't you understand that my son has been kidnapped?"

Resignation gave way to tiredness.

"Mrs. Ramoškienė, a few hours ago you claimed that

your husband had taken the boy. Am I to understand that this isn't so?"

"Yes! That's what I'm telling you."

"But your neighbor saw—"

"She must have made a mistake. She's old, her eyesight is not very good. And I think she has only met Darius once."

Click, click, click. The point of his ballpen appeared and disappeared, appeared and disappeared. A habit of his, it seemed, when he was trying to think. Sigita could barely stand it. She wanted to tear the pen away from him, and only the need to appear rational and sober held her back. He simply *has* to believe me, she thought. He has to.

Finally, he reached for a notepad.

"Sit down, Mrs. Ramoškienė. Give me your description of the chain of events once more."

She complied, doing the best she could to reconstruct what had happened. Described to him the tall, fair-haired woman in the cotton coat. Told him about the chocolate. But then she reached the gap. The black hole in her mind into which nearly twenty-four hours had disappeared.

"What's the name of the kindergarten?"

"Voveraitė. He is in the Chipmunk Group."

"Is there a phone number?"

She gave it to him. Soon he was talking to the director herself, Mrs. Šaraškienė. The compact ladylike form of the director popped into Sigita's mind's eye. Always immaculately dressed in jacket and matching skirt, nylons and low-heeled black pumps, as if she were on her way to a board meeting in a company of some size. She was about fifty, with short chestnut hair and a natural air of authority that instantly silenced even the wildest games whenever she entered one of the homerooms. Sigita was just a little bit afraid of her.

Gužas explained his errand; a child, Mikas Ramoška, had been reported missing. A woman involved in the matter might have made contact with the boy in the kindergarten playgrounds. Was it possible that one or more of the staff had observed this woman, or any other stranger, talking to the children or watching them, perhaps?

"The chocolate," said Sigita. "Don't forget the chocolate."

He nodded absently while listening to Mrs. Šaraskienė's reply.

Then he asked directly, apparently completely unaffected by Sigita's presence: "What is your impression of Mikas Ramoška's mother?"

Sigita felt heat rush into her face. The nerve! What would Mrs. Šaraškienė think!

"Thank you. I would like to talk to the group leader in question. Would you ask her to call this number as soon as possible? Thank you very much for your time."

He hung up.

"It seems one of the staff has in fact noticed your fair-haired woman and has told her not to give the children sweets. But Mikas wasn't the only child she contacted."

"Maybe not. But Mikas is the only one who is gone!"

"Yes."

She wasn't going to ask. She didn't *want* to ask. But she blurted it out anyway:

"What did she say about me?"

The tiniest of smiles curled his upper lip, the first sign of humanity she had observed in him.

"That you were a good mother and a responsible person. One of those who pay. She appreciates your commitment."

There was no fee as such to be paid for Mikas's basic care, but the kindergarten had an optional program funded by parents who paid a certain sum into the program's account every month. The money was used for maintenance and improvements, and for cultural activities with the children—things for which the city did not provide a budget. It had been a sacrifice, especially the first year after she had bought the flat, but to Sigita it was important to be "one of those who pay."

"Do you believe me now?"

He considered her for a while. Click, click went the damned pen.

"Your statement has been corroborated on certain points," he said, seeming almost reluctant.

"Then will you please *do* something!" She could no longer contain her despair. "You have to find him!"

Click, click, click.

"I've taken your statement now, and we will of course send out a missing persons bulletin on Mikas," he said. "We'll look for him."

At first Sigita felt a vast relief at being *believed*. She opened her purse and pushed the picture of Mikas out of its plastic pocket. The picture had been taken at the kindergarten's midsummer celebration, and Mikas was in his Sunday best, with a garland of oak leaves clutched in his hands and an uncertain smile on his face. He had objected to wearing the garland in his hair because he didn't want to look like a girl, she recalled.

"Thank you," she said. "Will this do? It's a good likeness."

She put it on the desk in front of Gužas. He took it, but there was something in the way he did it, a certain hesitation, as if he wasn't sure how much use it was going to be. It was then she realized that it was much too soon to feel any kind of relief.

"Mrs. Ramoškienė . . . is there any chance that the couple who took the boy are someone you know, or perhaps someone you are related to?"

"No, I . . . don't think so. I certainly didn't know the woman. But I didn't really ask Mrs. Mažekienė about the man because I thought it was Darius."

"We will try to get a description from your neighbor. Have the kidnappers tried to contact you in any way? Any demands, or threats? And can you think of anyone who might want to pressure you for any reason?"

She shook her head silently. The only thing she could think of was that it might be something to do with Janus Construction, with Dobrovolskij and other clients like him, and the figures she kept only in her head. But how? It didn't make sense. And in any case, no one had said a thing. No threats. No demands.

She realized that he was watching her intently, and that the clicking of the pen had finally ceased.

"What do they want with him?" she said softly, hardly daring to say it out loud, because it made it that much more real. "Why do people steal someone else's child?"

"When a child is taken, it is often personal—aimed at

a specific child, for specific reasons that might be to do with custody rights, or with something the kidnappers want from the parents. But there is a second category. One where the motives are less personal, and in those cases . . ." He hesitated, and she had to prod him on.

"What then?"

"In those cases, the perpetrators just take a child. Any child."

He didn't come right out and say it, but she knew immediately what he meant. She knew that children were sold in the same way some people sold women. A crushed and wordless whimper forced itself out of her. Esu kaltas, esu kaltas, esu labai kaltas. It's all my fault. Desperately, she tried to stop the images that flickered through her head. She wouldn't, she couldn't think of Mikas in the hands of people like that. It would destroy her.

"Please. Please, will you find him for me?" she begged, through a hot flood of tears that blurred the room and made intelligible speech almost impossible.

"We will try," he said. "But let us hope that Mikas belongs to the first category. They are often found, sooner or later."

Again he didn't say it, but she could hear the unspoken words all the same: we never find the others.

SHE DIDN'T REALLY have the time.

Nina's sense of urgency made it feel all wrong to contemplate a mundane shopping expedition, but the devil did, after all, reside in the details, and at a minimum she needed one set of T-shirt, shorts, and sandals sized for a three-year-old if she and the boy were to remain relatively secure and invisible for a while.

She scanned the storefronts on Stationsvej and cursed softly to herself at the lack of choice. There weren't all that many shops to begin with, and most of them now had closed doors and dead, unlit windows. But as she approached the end of the street, more appeared, and two of them, amazingly enough, sold children's clothes. Both clearly saw themselves as up-market; one even had a French name—La Maison Des Petites. Outside, the racks sported brightly colored rompers in a trendy retro '70s style, and when she peered through the window, she spotted a mannequin that looked to be about the right size. *And* the shop was still open. A big retail chain like Kvickly would have been better, not to mention cheaper, but so far all she had seen along the way had been a co-op with nothing much but food products. She was running out of time. The boy was lying on the back seat like a small, ticking bomb; traveling discretely with a screaming three-year-old in tow was difficult enough in itself—if the child was naked, it would be plain impossible. First rule of survival: don't draw attention to yourself.

She turned into Olgasvej and squeezed the antiquated

little Fiat into a space between two larger cars parked along the curb. She twisted in her seat to draw the blanket more thoroughly over the boy, who already seemed too close to the surface. One small arm came up to tug reflexively at the woolly material, pulling it off his face again.

Nina got out of the car, quickly scanning her surroundings. On a day as hot as this, presumably most of the inhabitants of Vedbæk would have retired to the beach, or to shady gardens and barbecued patio meals. But there were still people in the streets. On the opposite sidewalk, a suburban family sauntered past, the father thin-legged in shorts that were *too* short, the mother in a white summery top exposing her sunburnt, peeling shoulders. Their two young daughters both held giant ice cream cones, and the parents were engaged in heated conversation. A little further up the street on Nina's side, a senior citizen was walking a heavy-set basset hound, and a tight little group of long-haired teenagers had just turned the corner from Stationsvej and were headed Nina's way.

"All right," said Nina, deliberately leaning across the back seat through the open door. "I'll get you an ice cream, but that's it, okay? No more pestering." She paused artistically, covertly eying the dog walker, who was now within easy hearing, but moving at a draggingly slow pace. "Mama will be back in a jiffy."

She locked the doors quickly, then trotted resolutely back towards Stationsvej. The teenagers seemed not to have noticed her, or the little show she had provided. They moved only enough for her to edge past them and forge on. Behind her she heard their odd mix of conversation and intense texting. Good, she thought. Much too self-absorbed to be a problem.

LA MAISON DES PETITES seemed to think that what every parent really wanted was to dress their offspring like small replicas of the children they themselves had been in the '70s. The colors were bright and loud, the fabrics mostly linen and organically produced cotton, so that the little ones were not exposed to unwanted chemicals. All very well-intentioned, but Nina winced at the thought of what it would do to her bank balance.

A discretely perfumed young mother, hair tucked back by the big dark fashionable sunglasses riding on top of her head, glided past with a fat baby on her hip. Again, Nina became conscious of her sticky T-shirt and the far from fragrant odor of sweat she projected. And of fear, probably. Right now she fitted into this affluent suburban idyll about as well as a Saint Bernard in a two-room flat.

She dug out five pairs of underpants from a jumble box of Summer Sale offers in the middle of the shop. Then she rifled through the piles of jeans and T-shirts. How many days should she plan for? How long would he have to stay with her?

She had no idea, but decided to err on the side of optimism. One pair of jeans, one pair of shorts, and two light long-sleeved cotton shirts . . . That would have to do for now. Biting her lip, Nina eyed the footwear shelves. A pair of sandals were really a necessity. She piled the goods onto the counter and tried to look as little as possible at the salesperson as she ran the scanner over the brightly colored price tags.

"That'll be two thousand four hundred fifty-eight kroner," said the young woman behind the counter, smiling
with superficial courtesy. Nina forced herself to return
the smile. Overcoming her reluctance, she tapped her
credit card pin-code into the register and received the
big white carrier bag with a measured nod.

Outside, the heat was unremitting. Nina checked her
watch. 7:02. She had been gone from the car for twelve
minutes. She crossed to the corner of Stationsvej and
Olgasvej and looked toward the Fiat. No signs of unusual
activity. No collection of worried onlookers, no curious
faces. An elderly man in an oversized T-shirt shuffled
past the car without giving it a second glance. The boy
must still be alseep, thought Nina in relief. There was
a supermarket just across the street. If she hurried, she
might have time to pick up a few groceries. She wasn't
exactly hungry, but she had had nothing since breakfast,
and she knew she would have to eat something soon.

It didn't take her long to grab a loaf of white bread, a
bag of apples, and two bottles of water. That was all she
could think of, until she was approaching the exit and
her eyes fell on the ice cream freezer next to the toiletry
section. Cold, she thought. Sweet. Plenty of calories. Just
the thing. She transferred a foil-wrapped ice cream cone
from the freezer to her basket and began to load her purchases onto the conveyor belt. The pimply teenage girl
at the register was the only living, breathing human in
sight. For some reason Nina couldn't take her eyes off the
girl's unusually long, square nails as they clicked against
the display.

Nina piled her purchases into a yellow plastic bag and

hurried back into the brightness of the sunlight. She had been gone for sixteen minutes now, and she suddenly knew sixteen minutes was too long. She had the horrible sensation that time, vitally important time, had once again slipped through her fingers, and she headed for the Fiat at a near-run.

The car was where she had left it, of course, but something was wrong all the same. A woman with a thumb-sucking toddler in a stroller had taken up position a few feet from the car and was anxiously scouting up and down Olgasvej. Nina's stomach dropped, but she still managed to slow to a speed she thought more appropriate for her role as a slightly frazzled but responsible mother.

"Is that your car? Is that your boy in there?"

The woman's voice rose into an indignant descant the moment she caught sight of Nina.

Nina only nodded. The distance to the car seemed to stretch into infinity, and now that the woman had found someone to focus her outrage on, her temper was visibly rising like the tide. Close up, she was older than she had appeared at a distance, one of those thirty-something women who took such infinite care with their appeareance that only faint lines at the corner of their eyes betrayed their age when they smiled or frowned. Now indignant anger narrowed her eyes and added years to her face. It didn't become her, thought Nina, and felt her own muscles tense in response.

The stroller was parked so that it blocked the entire sidewalk, and the woman had her hands set on her hips in a confident stance.

"I've stood here waiting for you for nearly twenty minutes," she announced, pointing demonstratively at her watch. "You don't just leave a child in a car like this. And in this heat! He might die of heat stroke. It's completely irresponsible, and frankly dangerous."

Nina considered her strategy. The woman had not been there for twenty minutes, and Nina had made sure the Fiat was shaded by one of the big chestnut trees along the road, and had left all the windows ajar. The boy was in no danger of dying from the heat in such a short time, and nobody knew it better than Nina. She had seen children lie for days without proper shelter in 120° weather and still live long enough to die from malnutrition. The outraged mother was clearly one of those overzealous idiots who enjoyed showing others what a wonderful parent she herself happened to be. But knowing this was of little use. The main objective was to get away without drawing any more attention to herself or the boy. Nina lowered her eyes and forced a contrite smile.

"I had promised him an ice cream cone, and there was a line at the check-out," she said, trying to edge past the aggressively parked stroller.

"Oh? And I suppose the Maison Des Petites was terribly busy too?" countered the woman, and Nina cursed under her breath. The big white carrier bag from the fashion boutique was hard to explain away, and she decided not to try. Instead, she turned her back firmly on the indignant woman, unlocked the car—and came close to knocking down both woman and stroller as she took a startled pace backwards.

The boy was sitting up.

The blanket was still wrapped about his legs, and he was staring at her through the half-open window with huge dark blue eyes.

Nina forced herself to stand still while possiblities and half-formed plans flitted feverishly through her head. Should she simply get into the car and drive away? Should she speak to him? And if she did, what would happen if he answered?

Then she recalled the ice cream cone.

She tore her attention away from the confused, fearful gaze of the boy for as long as it took to rummage through the yellow plastic bag and fish it out. She peeled off the shiny blue wrapper and held out the cone to him through the open window, hardly daring to meet his eyes again. Apparently, she didn't have to. She saw instead how a small pale hand slowly moved toward the rim of the rolled-down window and took hold of the ice cream.

"Atju."

The boy's voice was faint, but he spoke the word slowly and clearly, as if to make sure she didn't misunderstand.

"No," she said quickly. "They were all out of those. You'll have to make do with this one instead."

Then she marched around the front end of the car as quickly as she could and got into the driver's seat. The indignant voice followed her as she backed and turned, sounding loud and clear through the open windows.

"You don't even have a proper car seat for him," shrilled the woman. "I simply don't understand how someone like you can call herself a mother. I simply don't . . ."

SIGITA WOULD HAVE liked to stay at the police station, but Gužas evicted her politely but firmly. He had her phone number, he would call. He repeated his exhortation to go home.

"But perhaps you shouldn't be alone. The boy's father?"

"He works in Germany. He's not coming."

"Well, a relative, then. Or a friend."

She just nodded, as if she were still someone who possessed such things. She did not want to admit to him just how alone she was. It felt shameful, like some embarrassing disease.

Her headache was so strong now that it hovered like a black ring at the edge of her field of vision; her nausea swelled once more. She ought to eat something, or at least drink a little, like the old man had told her to: *It's important to drink enough when it is this hot.* She bought a small square carton of orange juice at tourist price from a man selling candy and postcards and amber jewelry at a bright green cart. The juice was lukewarm and didn't taste particularly nice, and the citric acid burned her sore throat.

They'll find him, she whispered to herself. They will find him, and he will be all right.

There was no conviction in the words. Normally, she didn't see herself as a person with a very lively imagination. She was much better at recalling facts and figures than at picturing places she had never been, or people she had never seen. She didn't read a lot of novels, and saw only the films that were shown on TV.

But right now she could imagine Mikas. Mikas in a car, hidden under a rug. Mikas wriggling and crying while strangers held him down. Mikas calling for his mother, and getting no answer.

What had they done to him? And why had they taken him?

Her legs shook. She sat down on the wide stone steps leading to the river. A couple of years ago, the city had put up benches here, but they quickly became a magnet for addicts and homeless people, and now the seats had been removed, so that only the galvanized steel supports bristled from the concrete like stubble. Below, the Neris moved sluggishly in its concrete bed, brown and shrunken and tame compared to its winter wildness.

HER FIRST SUMMER with Darius, the river had been their secret place. If you followed the bank far enough away from the bridge, the paved pathway gave way to a muddy trail through the jungle of reeds. Insects buzzed and whirred, gnats and tiny black flies, but there were no people, no prying eyes or wagging tongues, and that was a rarity in Tauragė. They could even bathe. Together.

She didn't know anyone else like him. The other boys were idiots—giggling and drawing crude pictures of penises on school books. Milda's older brother had once pinched Sigita's left nipple and tried to kiss her; he was basically just as mean as Milda, only in a slightly different way.

Darius was completely different. He seemed utterly relaxed and at ease with himself, and so much more mature than any of the others. He told her he had been named after the hero pilot Steponas Darius, just like Tauragė's mainstreet, Dariaus ir Girėno gatvė. That was rather fitting, she thought. She could easily imagine Darius doing great things one day.

When he wanted to take off her blouse, she stiffened, at first. He stopped what he was doing, and slid both hands down to her waist.

"You are so tiny," he said. "My hands go almost all the way around you."

A deep shudder went through her that had nothing to do with cold. His hands moved up inside her blouse and brushed her breasts very lightly, very gently. She raised her face to the sun. Don't do that, said Granny Julija's voice in her head, you will go blind. But she let the sunlight blind her for a few more moments before she closed her eyes. Her hands spasmed into fists, clutching two handfuls of shirt from his back, and his tongue touched hers, then her lips, then the inside of her mouth. He had given up on the blouse and concentrated his efforts on her skirt and knickers. She stumbled and was thrown off balance, and he did nothing to hold her, but let himself fall with her instead, so that they hit mud and sun-warmed river water with a wet thud. His weight came down on top of her so hard that she was too winded to move or speak, which he took for acceptance.

"God, you're fine," he whispered, spreading her thighs with eager hands.

She could have stopped him. But she wanted it too. Her body wanted it. Even her head wanted it, in a way. She wanted to know what it was like—this sinning business. And it was good that she didn't really have to *do* anything except lie there and let him at her. She was prepared for pain; there had been whispers and sniggers in the girls' lavatories at school, that the first time was difficult, and that it hurt.

But it didn't. It was almost too easy, too right, to lie with him like this, pushed down into the soft warm mud by the weight of him, to feel him move between her legs and then inside her, like a welcome guest that might have stayed for so much longer than the brief moment it actually took.

He hunched over her, and then slid out. Lay there completely spent for a while, as the buzzing of the insects slowly returned, and the sound of the train on the railway bridge in the distance, and the rustle of the reeds in the wind. For an instant, a dazzling blue dragonfly hovered over his shoulder before zooming away.

Was that it? thought Sigita. Was that really all?

He rolled off her. He hadn't taken off any of his clothes; only his fly was open. She, on the other hand, was suddenly conscious of how inelegant she looked, with her knickers round one ankle and her skirt rucked up so that her entire pelvis was exposed. Somehow, he had also managed to push up both her blouse and her bra to get at her breasts, something she had barely noticed because so much else was going on. She hastily tugged her skirt into place and wanted to pull down her blouse also.

But this was when he did something that none of the other boys would have done. The thing that was just Darius. He pushed her gently back into the mud. He kissed her, a deep wet kiss that went on till she could hardly breathe. And then he touched her, outside and in, so that she gasped in surprise.

"Darius . . ."

"Shhh," he said. "Wait."

He used only his hands and his mouth. And he kept at it till the light and the sounds went away. Till she shuddered from head to foot. Till something wild and unfamiliar throbbed inside her, over and over, and she knew for certain that she was no longer any kind of virgin, and never would be again.

She felt no guilt at that moment, nor did she think of shame, or sin, or consequences. That came later.

AUGUST TWILIGHT HAD begun to gather over the bay when Nina turned off the former fishing village's main street and continued up the sparsely paved road that led through the near-deserted holiday cottage park. Tisvildeleje these days was populated mainly by commuters and tourists, and now that the school holidays had ended, most of the visitors had left. There were still a few cars with German license plates outside the biggest and most luxurious of the houses, and a couple of children whacked away at a tetherball, the pole wobbling ominously with each swing. Except for that, the lawns lay deserted and scorched from the unremitting sun of this late, hot summer. Last year had been rainy and dull, but this year the sky had seemed permanently blue since May, and by now leaves, shrubbery, and grass had long since lost any vestige of lushness and formed a dry landscape of burnt yellows and dusty greens. Nina checked her watch. Exactly 8:20.

She parked in the lane by the mailbox, behind a blue VW Golf with a streamer in the rear window. *M-Tech*, it said. *Solutions That Work*. Was it Karin's? It didn't seem like the kind of car she would choose, but Nina could see no other, more likely vehicle. She peered up the long winding drive. The cottage looked to be quite old; it was painted a deep dark red, with white frames and tiny romantic window panes from before the age of double glazing. It was set some distance from its neighbors—the last one before the woods, just as Karin had said.

Nina jammed her keys and her mobile phone into the pockets of her jeans and got out. The boy was watching her covertly, beneath half-closed eyelids. She opened the rear door and touched his wrist gently. He felt warm now, but not fevered, she noted with professional routine. There was no doubt that he was fully conscious, even though he was lying very still, the now somewhat greasy blanket wound around his legs.

He is trying to disappear, thought Nina. Like the baby hare she had once come across as a child, in the back garden, where it had been desperately trying to hide. When she had picked it up, it hadn't struggled or resisted. It just crouched in her hands, feather-light and downy. In her six-year-old ignorance, she had thought it liked her. But when she put it on her bed, it had already had the same distant look as the boy in the back seat, and later that night, she found it limp and dead in the shoe box she had provided for it.

Was the boy giving up in the same way?

Nina shivered, and not entirely because the day had finally begun to cool. She couldn't leave the boy in the car, she decided. He was awake, and even though he didn't know her from Adam, coming with her had to be better than the alternative—being left locked in a car in the gathering darkness, not knowing where or why.

He hadn't moved a muscle, but as she reached for him now, he suddenly scooted back with such abruptness that the blanket slipped off him and dropped onto the floor of the car.

Nina hesitated.

She didn't want the child to be afraid of her. She didn't like that he looked at her as if she might be a monster little different from the man in the railway station, but she had no idea how to win his trust.

"What on earth have they done to you?" she whispered, sinking down onto her haunches and trying to catch his eyes. "Where do you come from, sweetie?"

The boy made no answer, only curled himself into a tighter ball at the opposite end of the seat, as far away from her as he could get. She could see a dark stain on the seat where the blanket had slipped, and the boy smelled unpleasantly of body sweat and old urine. Nina felt a surge of tenderness, just as she did when Anton or Ida had a temperature or threw up, back home in the Østerbro flat. She would bring them crushed ice, berry juice, and damp cloths; the urge to be good to them and make them well again was so overpowering it filled her entire being. So simple to be a good mother then, she thought. It was everything else that got to be so complicated.

She pointed to the house, then put her hands togther like a statue of a praying saint and rested her cheek against them in a parody of sleep.

"First, we'll get you something to eat," she said, trying to smile. "And then we'll find a bed for you to sleep in. And after that, we'll see."

The boy made no sound, but she had to have done something right after all, because he uncurled and slid an inch or two in her direction.

"Good boy," she said. She remembered an article she had read a few years back about children's ability to survive in even the most brutal of environments. They were like little heat-seeking missiles, it had said, aiming themselves at the nearest source of warmth. If a child lost its mother, it would reach for its father. If the father disappeared, the child would head for the next grown-up in the line, and then the next, seeking any adult who would provide survival, and perhaps even love.

She showed him the clothes she had bought, and when she began to dress him, he helped. He obediently held out his arms so that she could put them into the sleeves of the new T-shirt, and ducked his head so that it was easier for her to pull it on. A clean pair of underpants followed. That would have to do for now, but even that much suddenly made him seem much more like a normal three-year-old. He came into her arms easily, as she lifted him from the car. Again she was struck by the difference between his weight and Anton's.

Now that he was awake, he didn't allow her to hold him against her shoulder. He sat warily straight on her left hip as she walked up the gravel path to the veranda.

"Hey, little one," murmured Nina, softening her voice into a maternal cooing. "No need to be afraid anymore."

His warm breath came quickly and carried a sour smell of fear and vomit.

On the veranda, someone had arranged a row of large pots containing herbs and pansies; their well-watered plumpness looked odd against the aridness of the rest of the garden. By the half-open door, a pair of bright yellow galoshes sat next to a small pet carrier. Nina remembered that Karin had spoken of a cat, at that drunken Christmas party. Mr. Kitty, she had called him. She had acquired this male presence when she'd decided once and for all that she was tired of looking for Mr. Right and the two point one children she was statistically entitled to.

At the moment, Nina could detect no sign of either kitty or Karin.

She raised her free hand to knock on the door, but it moved as she touched it, swinging open at her first knock. Unhindered, Nina stepped right into the little darkened hallway. There was a clean detergent-borne scent of citrus and vinegar, and Karin's shoes and boots were lined up neatly by the half-open kitchen door.

It was very quiet.

"Karin?"

Nina's foot came down on something soft, which gave way under her heel with a slight crunch. Startled, she backed up and steadied herself against the wall.

"Karin?" she called again, but this time with little expectation of an answer. She inched forward, running her hand over the door frame until she felt the sharp plastic contours of a switch. The light came on with a faint click, revealing a half-eaten sandwich on the floor. It was still partially wrapped, and had been acquired from the deli of the local Kvickly, she could see.

Nina felt a sharp cold jab in her stomach. It was possible that Mr. Kitty had made illegal forays into the groceries and dragged his booty into the hallway, but the house was entirely too silent considering the distraught and loudly sobbing Karin that Nina had been talking to just ninety minutes ago.

She lowered the boy to the floor of the hallway and stood undecided on the threshold.

"Stay here," she whispered, pointing at the floor. "Don't go anywhere."

The boy made no reply, only looked at her with solemn

eyes. New cracks of black fear had begun to open in his gaze; he had been frightened to begin with, and her indecision was not improving matters. She had to do something quickly.

"Karin!"

Nina walked quickly through the kitchen and into the compact living room. Karin had turned on a small, green lamp above the settee. The television was on, but with the sound turned down. TV2 News. Nina recognized the scarlet banner headlines and the usual respectable suit of the anchor.

She strode across to the window, which overlooked the garden on the other side of the house. She could see very little, only the tall pines of the plantation behind the cottage, and an unkempt lawn littered with leaves and pine cones. Nina dug into her pocket for her mobile phone, pressed the recall button and waited for the call tone. Immediately, there was an answering trill from a real phone somewhere in the house. The sound seemed to be coming from behind a closed door that probably led to the bedroom, and although the distance couldn't be great, it sounded oddly muffled, as if someone had dropped it into a bucket. A quick glance assured her that the boy's small straight form was still standing motionless by the kitchen door. She looked at the phone again. 8:28.

The numbers on the pale blue display had a calming effect on her. She slid the phone back into her pocket and pushed open the bedroom door.

Karin lay curled on the bed, with her forehead resting against her knees, as though she had been practicing some advanced form of yoga. But Nina saw it the second the image was processed against her retina.

Death.

There was a peculiar quality about dead people. Little things that seemed insignificant on their own, but added up to an umistakable impact, so that Nina was never in any doubt when she encountered it. The slight out-turned wrist. The leg that had slipped limply from its orignal position, and the head resting much too heavily against the mattress.

Nina felt the first rush from her flight instinct. She forced herself to approach the bed, while new details flooded her senses. Karin's fair hair spread around her head like a flaxen halo mixed with red and dark brown nuances. The sheet beneath her had soaked up far too much blood, and when Nina carefully turned Karin's upper body, Karin's mouth opened, and vomit mixed with blood sloshed over her lower lip and ran down her chin and into the soft folds of her throat. Two of her teeth were missing, and there was red and purple bruising on her face and neck. A lot of the blood seemed to come from a wound above the hairline, at her left temple, and when Nina probed it cautiously, the skull gave beneath her fingers, too soft and flat. Death had not been instantaneous, thought Nina. She had had time to curl up here, like a wounded animal that left the herd to die alone.

And now. So much blood.

She didn't mind blood, she reminded herself soothingly. She was okay with it, had, as a matter of fact, been one of the most steadfast at nursing school when it came to dealing with bodily fluids. (Since that day twenty-three years ago she had become very good at it. She had decided to become good at it, and it had worked.)

Nina stepped back from the bed and managed to twist to one side before she threw up, in short, painful heaves. She had eaten nothing since this morning, and all that sploshed onto the clean wooden floor was dark yellow gall and grayish water.

It was then she heard the scream. A shrill, heart-rending note of terror, like the scream you hear in the night when a hare is caught by the fox.

SIGITA WAS SITTING on the stone steps by the river, waiting for the nausea and headache to subside enough so she could walk on. Her good hand was clenched around her mobile. It had to ring. It had to ring so that she would know Mikas was all right. Or so she knew at least he wasn't what Gužas called the second category; those who were never found.

No. Don't even think it. Don't think about what strangers might do to the perfect, tiny body, don't let the thought in even for a second. It would only make it real. It would break her, it would tear her open and rip out her heart so that she wouldn't be able to breathe, let alone act. She clung to the phone like an exhausted swimmer to a buoy.

It didn't ring. In the end she pressed a number herself. Mrs. Mažekienė's.

"Mrs. Mažekienė. The man who took Mikas—what did he look like?"

The old woman's confusion was obvious, even over the phone.

"Look like? But it was his father."

"No, Mrs. Mažekienė. It wasn't. Darius is still in Germany."

There was a long silence.

"Mrs. Mažekienė?"

"Well, I did think that he must have gained some weight. He looked bigger than I remembered."

"How big?"

"I don't know . . . big and tall, now that I think about it. And hardly any hair, the way it had been cropped. But that's all the rage these days, isn't it?"

"Why did you think it was Mikas's father, then?"

"The car looked like his. And who else would be going off with the boy?"

Sigita bit down hard on her lip to avoid saying something unforgiveable. She is just an old woman, she told herself. She didn't do it on purpose. But Mrs. Mažekienė's mistake had cost them nearly 48 hours, and that was very hard to forget.

"What kind of car was it?" she asked, once she had regained some self-control.

"It was gray," Mrs. Mažekienė answered vaguely.

"What make of car?" But she knew even as she asked that it was hopeless.

"I don't know much about cars," said Mrs. Mažekienė helplessly. "It was . . . ordinary, like. Like Mikas's father's car."

The last time Sigita had seen Darius, he had been driving a dark- gray Suzuki Grand Vitara. So presumably it was a gray SUV of some kind, or perhaps a station wagon. Or a van. If Mrs. Mažekienė couldn't tell Darius's rather slender form from what sounded like that of a crew-cut doorman's, then there was no reason to think that she could distinguish between an off-roader and a Peugeot Partner. It wasn't much to go on.

"It had a baggage box on the roof," said Mrs. Mažekienė suddenly. "I remember that!"

Dobrovolskij's eldest son, Pavel, sometimes drove a silver Porsche Cayenne. It resembled the Vitara about as much as a shetland pony resembles a Shire horse, and she had never seen it with a baggage box on its expensive roof. But it was enough to make her call Algirdas.

"Hi," he said. "Are you feeling better?"

She didn't reply to that.

"How did the meeting with Dobrovolskij go?" she asked instead.

"So-so. He wasn't happy that you weren't there."

"But there wasn't any . . . trouble?"

"Sigita, what is it you want?"

She didn't know how much to say. She had never told Algirdas much about her personal life, and it seemed awkward to start now. But what if? What if Mikas's disappearance had something to do with her job?

"Mikas is gone."

He knew, she thought, that she had a son. She had brought Mikas along to the Christmas pantomime last year, when Janus Corporation had suddenly decided it needed to do something for the children of its employees.

"Mikas? Your little boy?"

"Yes. Someone has taken him."

There was an awkward pause. She could almost hear the gears click inside Algirdas's mind as he tried to work out whether this would rock *his* boat in any way. Algirdas was a pleasant enough employer most of the time, friendly, informal, not a bully or a tyrant. But she sometimes thought that he felt the same way about his staff as she did about computers: they were just supposed to work—he didn't care what was inside.

And now I don't work anymore, she thought. And he doesn't know whom to call in order to get me repaired.

"Does this have anything to do with your concussion?" he finally asked.

"Possibly. I don't remember what happened. I thought Mikas was with Darius, but he isn't."

"But why are you asking about Dobrovolskij?"

"Pavel Dobrovolskij has a silver Cayenne. And Mikas was taken away in a gray or silver SUV." She was aware that she was twisting facts to provide more substance for her suspicions than they really warranted. But if it was Dobrovolskij, then Mikas didn't belong to the second category. If it was Dobrovolskij, one could find out what he wanted, and then do whatever it took to get Mikas back.

"Sorry, Sigita, but you're off your head. Why the hell would Dobrovolskij take your boy? Besides, I think Pavel sold the Cayenne. He said it was easier to fit an elephant into a matchbox than to park that monstrosity in downtown Vilnius. Did you tell the police?"

"Yes."

"Let them deal with it, then."

"But they're not doing anything! There's just this one pathetic man clicking his bloody ballpoint pen!"

"What does his pen have to with anything?"

"And he says they will look for Mikas now, but I don't think anything is really happening. They're never found. Not the ones where it's not personal." She realized she was being incoherent. Knew, too, that this was entirely the wrong way to be with Algirdas, that it would only make him retreat. She forced herself to breathe more calmly, waiting until the words presented themselves in the proper order. "Algirdas, I have to know if you are involved in something that

Dobrovolskij wouldn't like. Or if any of the payments have been incorrect."

"Bloody hell, Sigita. It's your autistic head that's keeping track of everything. I just pony up when you tell me to."

Normally, she would be able to remember. Normally she would know if even a single litas was missing.

"Besides, you're making him sound like a gangster. He isn't."

"But he knows people who are," she said stubbornly. In the river below the steps, a black plastic garbage bag was floating past, buoyed up by the air trapped inside. For one horrible moment all Sigita could think about was that it was large enough to contain a dead child.

"Look, Sigita. I'm really sorry your boy has disappeared, but Dobrovolskij can't possibly be involved. For God's sake, don't get him mixed up in this."

She didn't say goodbye. She barely managed to turn off the mobile before her abdomen contracted, and she threw up orange juice and warm stomach acids all over her skirt and bare legs.

NINA TURNED JUST quickly enough to see the boy's shadow disappear from the doorway. She heard the rapid patter of his bare feet through the living room, then the creak of a door. Her own legs were momentarily paralyzed by a hot, melting sensation, and when she finally managed to move, her ankles and knees wobbled dangerously.

A couple of long strides took her through the door, and then into the kitchen. Out of the window above the sink she saw his flaxen head bobbing past in the darkness; he was running away. She continued her wobbly flight through the hallway and out onto the veranda. In the humid air outside, her face and throat felt flushed and pulsing with heat.

The black pines in the plantation behind the house were blurred by mist; she couldn't see the boy anywhere, but she heard the snapping of branches as he fled among the trees. Following the sound, she took off at the fastest run she could manage.

Pine boughs whipped against her face, and the tall, dry grass at the forest's edge was a rustling, prickly barrier, impeding her steps. Fortunately, she could now see the boy's white hair like a will-o'-the-wisp among the black tree trunks in the gathering darkness. She was closing in on him.

She ducked the low branches as best she could, then had to veer sharply to one side to avoid the bristling remnants of a fallen tree. Her right ankle protested, but she did manage a second burst of speed. She snatched at the boy's shoulder, but lost her grip again, and he stumbled on. Her next attempt was more succesful. She caught his arm and clung to it, forcing him to stop.

Wordlessly, she pulled him down onto the mossy grass and closed her arms around him. Under the twisted T-shirt, his heart was beating fast and hard against his bared ribs, and his breath was a hot flush against her neck.

Then she heard it.

It might have been a completely insignficant sound. A faint click, as of a door being cautiously closed, somewhere in the summer night. The sound could come from any of the other cottages skirting the forest's edge, thought Nina, as she inched backwards into deeper cover, pulling the boy with her. She could no longer see Karin's cousin's cottage, but at the end of the winding drive her own red Fiat was perfectly visible.

More sounds. Footsteps, this time, and a rustling as if someone was moving through tall, dry grass. Nina saw the man from the railway station in her mind's eye. The pale, narrowed eyes, the tense jaw, the ferocity of the kicks he aimed at the busted locker.

Had he found Karin and unleashed that fury in her?

Nina looked at her watch.

8:36.

Her watch was usually 29 seconds slower than the more accurate time given by her mobile. For some reason she hadn't corrected that imprecision. She rather liked having to figure out what time it really was.

She hugged the boy tight against her chest. His little warm body was twitching, small jerks of protest, but he made no sound. Did he understand the need for silence, or was it merely traumatized resignation?

She listened again, but the rustle of the footsteps, if that was what they were, had stopped. Should she call the police? She fumbled at the pockets of her jeans, first on the right, then on the left.

No phone.

She checked again, but knew it was futile. She had dropped it. Where and when, she had no idea.

New little bursts of adrenalin exploded in her head. The phone had been her only line of contact to the real world— to Morten, to the network and her job, and now to the police. She was alone now. Completely alone with the boy.

The crash of a door being slammed rang through the silence.

Her heart gave a wild leap and raced even faster under her sweat-soaked T-shirt. She stumbled to her feet, still with the boy locked in her arms.

And then she ran.

The boy's body was tense with resistance and difficult to manage, and she felt the extra weight now in her knees and ankles. She was getting older, she thought, too old to be fleeing with a child in her arms.

Seconds later, she reached the Fiat and yanked open the door to the driver's seat. She glanced up at the cottage through the foliage of the birches flanking the drive. She could see no signs of any human presence up there, and for a moment she began to doubt her senses. Had the footsteps really been footsteps? Or had it really just been the wind rustling the grass, or perhaps Mr. Kitty? Her phone. Should she go back and look for it? Did she dare? She felt an irrational urge to protect the still, unliving body in there, to guard it against . . .

Against what? It was too late. For Karin, everything was too late. Now Nina had to think of the boy, and of herself. Yet still she hesitated, child on her hip, as she peered through the dusty, dry leaves. Then she froze. A light had come on in the kitchen, and she saw someone move about in there. Then the dark form seemed to grow bigger as it approached the window, and for a moment, she saw the pale outline of a face.

Nina practically threw the boy into the passenger seat. She thrust the key into the ignition with frantic haste, and the second the engine caught, she backed wildly down the lane, careening from one side of the road to the other. The long grass hissed against the sides of the car, and once, a stone or a root knocked against the undercarriage. The other cottages all had black, dark windows and empty drives. No help to be had there. Gravel from the road whipped up against the windscreen when she finally managed to turn the car around and continued, still at much too furious a speed, down the partially paved road towards the sea. It was only then she realized that she had forgotten to turn on the headlights.The boy next to her had begun to scream so loudly that anyone would think she was trying to kill him.

Nina forced a deep breath into her abdomen, slowed the car a fraction, and turned on the lights with a dry little click. The boy's screaming softened into sobs, but he was now crouched on the floor of the car, his arms clutched around his head. And suddenly, amidst the soft, gurgling sobs, intelligible words began to form.

"Mama. Noriu pas Mama!"

Sweet Jesus, she thought. He has a mother somewhere.

JAN HAD DECIDED to spend the night in the company's downtown flat in Laksegade. This was mainly in order to avoid Anne. With her peculiar Anne-radar she had naturally spotted something wasn't going quite according to plan, and right now he had to keep his distance from her, or she might realize just how much of a shambles the whole thing was. Besides, it would be much easier to deal with Karin without Anne somewhere in the vicinity.

He bought a TV dinner in Magasin's delicatessen and heated it in the microwave of the small kitchen. Karin's betrayal still left a bitterness in his mouth. How he could be so wrong? But it would seem she was both less loyal and more mercenary than he would have guessed. At home, in her flat above the garage, he had found only two things worth noticing: the empty briefcase and a note announcing in bold letters, "I QUIT."

So that was gratitude for you. Normally, he was a better judge of whom to guard against, and whom to trust. And Karin had known what was at stake. Even now, he couldn't quite rid himself of the feeling that it was all a misunderstandng. That once he got to talk to her, everything would work itself out.

But the Lithuanian hadn't called, which had to mean he hadn't found her. Jan felt his stomach cramp at the thought of what this would do to him and his life. The chances that it would ever be normal again lessened with each hour that went by. He didn't exactly have all the time in the world—didn't she understand that?

He made himself a cup of coffee and tried to watch the news, but he couldn't concentrate. Perhaps he should go for a run in Kongens Have? But he hadn't brought his running clothes or shoes, and although Magasin's Men's Department was just around the corner, he didn't feel like another shopping expedition. He had already purchased a shirt and some underwear for tomorrow, the way he often did when he had been working so late that making the drive back to the house wasn't practical.

The flat was cramped as a coffin compared to the house, but there was something about it that he liked. His assistant, Marianne, had seen to the redecoration, and she had hit a note that made him feel comfortable here. Sort of a luxury version of a student's digs. Old armchairs draped with pale rugs. Retro lamps she had found in flea markets. Seven different plates, rather than a single pattern, and equally unmatching coffee mugs. Marianne liked doing that kind of thing. "It needs personality," she had said. "Or you might as well put people up in a hotel." Perhaps the place reminded him of the small flat he had shared with his student friend Kristian, back when the world was new, when they both had dreams of becoming IT millionaires. Briefly, he wondered what Kristian was doing now. As far as he knew, Jan had been the only one to make the millionaire dream come true.

What an absolutely bloody day. He stretched, and felt a twinge from the operation scar just above his hip. He scratched it reflexively. What the hell was the Lithuanian doing? And what the hell was Karin thinking?

Suddenly, the door phone buzzed aggressively. Jan set the mug on the worktop and went to press the button.

"Yes."

"It's Inger."

A fraction of a second ticked by before he realized which Inger. His mother-in-law.

"Inger," he said, trying to put a smile into his voice. "Come in!"

She was slim and fair like Anne, exactly the same figure. Right now she was wearing one of her bright African dresses, her bare, tanned arms sporting four or five carved ebony bracelets. This was the sort of thing Inger could carry off—making something like that look exactly right.

"Anne said you were here," she said. "So I thought I would seize the moment."

"What a lovely surprise," said Jan. "Would you like a cup of coffee?"

"No thank you," she said. "I just want to talk to you."

"Oh dear," he said, trying for a humorous note. "What have I done now?"

She didn't buy his attempt at levity.

"Anne is upset," she said.

"Did she say that?"

"Of course not. Anne is Anne. She would never say a thing like that. But something isn't right with her, and I am asking you now. Is it Aleksander?"

His heart pounded madly.

"No, no," he said. "That's all been taken care of."

She looked at him directly. Her eyes weren't quite as blue as Anne's were; there was more gray in them.

"What, then?" she asked. "Is there something wrong between the two of you?"

His smile felt as if it were glued to his face, and he was sure the lack of naturalness was showing. Why could he never do things right? He admired Inger. She was a wonderful woman, feminine and strong at the same time, just the sort of soulmate a man like Keld deserved. He so wanted her to *like* him.

"I would never hurt Anne," he said.

Her eyebrows shot up.

"No," she said. "I didn't think you would. But that wasn't the question I asked."

Wrong again. Sometimes he felt as if there were a little man inside his head with one of those ear-splitting buzzers they used on quiz shows whenever a contestant got it wrong.

"Then I'm not sure I know what you mean," he said. "We're fine."

She sighed. Shook her head.

"Do you know," she said. "I don't think so." She got up, hitching the strap from her stylishly fringed handbag onto one bare shoulder.

"Are you leaving already?" he said.

"There doesn't seem to be much point in staying," she said, and again, he had the feeling that he had failed some test he didn't really understand.

"Have you talked to Keld about this?" he burst out.

Again, she gave him one of those very direct, gray-blue looks. She shook her head once more, but he wasn't certain it meant no. What if she had been sitting out there in the Taarbæk villa, discussing it with Keld, in the conservatory, perhaps, over a glass of late evening wine and some really good cheese, talking about him, about him and Anne and their marriage, wondering if everything were the way it should be . . . his stomach became a small, rock-solid lump at the thought.

"Goodnight," she said. "I hope you work it out." She put a hand on his arm for a moment before she left, and he was pretty sure that there was pity in her glance.

He stood by the window, watching her walk down the street. From the rear, she could still pass for a young woman, her stride full of energy and grace, her feet turned slightly out. Once, she had laughingly told him she had been a ballet child for three whole years before they kicked her out. "And you never stop walking like a duck after that." She still took some kind of dancing class in the evenings.

He discovered he was shaking all over. Stop it, he told himself. In a little while, the Lithuanian will call. He will have found Karin. And there is still time. It will all be fine.

Just before midnight, the phone rang, but it wasn't the Nokia. It was Anne, on his personal mobile.

"The police have been here," she said, and he could hear the fragile cracks in her voice. "They say that Karin is dead."

THE DOBROVOLSKIJS WERE Russian, but not from the Soviet era. The family had lived in Vilnius for more than a hundred years, and old man Dobrovolskij himself, the present patriarch, still inhabited one of the old wooden mansions behind Znamenskaya, the Orthodox Church of the Apparition of the Holy Mother of God. Sigita had been there once before, with Algirdas, and they had been served black Russian tea on the porch, in tall glasses so gilded that they were only barely transparent.

Sigita paused by the garden gate, suddenly indecisive. Now that she was actually here, it was hard to imagine that the Dobrovolskijs could be holding Mikas somewhere in that beautiful, freshly painted house. And there was no silver Cayenne parked by the curb.

If Dobrovolskij had anything to do with this, he wouldn't do it here. Not in his childhood home, so close to the Church its huge silvery dome could be seen through the treetops. Where others tore down the old wooden houses and built modern brick monstrosities as soon as they came into money, Dobrovolskij had instead carefully renovated. The delicately carved trimmings shone with fresh yellow paint, the intricate window frames and shutters likewise; and though there might still be a well in the garden outside, it was for decorative purposes only. Sigita knew for a fact that there were three shiny new bathrooms in the house—that had been part of the agreement between Janus Construction and the old man.

She had stood there long enough to be noticed. The white lace curtain in one window twitched, and a little later a young dark-haired girl came out onto the porch.

"Mrs. Dobrovolskaja is asking whether there is anything we can do for you?" she said, her Lithuanian heavily accented. Her slim, girlish figure was dressed in a white T-shirt and a pair of black Calvin Kleins, and Sigita guessed her to be some kind of Russian relative, or perhaps an au pair. Or both.

Sigita cleared her throat.

"I'm sorry. This may sound odd. But do you know if Pavel Dobrovolskij still owns a silver Porsche Cayenne?"

"Has something happened?" The girl focused on Sigita's plaster cast. "An accident? Is he all right?"

"No, nothing has happened . . . or, not in that way. I had a fall on the stairs."

"Is it broken?"

"Yes."

"What a pity. I hope it will soon be new again." She smiled awkwardly. "Forgive me. My Lithuanian is not yet very good. I am Anna, Pavel's fiancée. How do you know Pavel?"

"It's really more my boss who knows him. Algirdas Janusevičius. They do projects together from time to time. My name is Sigita."

They shook hands.

"The Porsche?" said Sigita. "He still has it?"

Anna smiled.

"He's trying to sell it. He calls it an elephant. But no one has bought it yet. If you're interested, you can see it in Super Auto's showroom in Pusu gatvė. It's only two blocks from here."

THE PORCHE CAYENNE stood proudly in the best window at Super Auto, behind bars and armored glass, and without license plates. A price sticker announced that Sigita could become the happy owner of this vehicle if only she were willing to pay six years' wages for it. Algirdas had been right, thought Sigita miserably. There was absolutely no evidence that Dobrovolskij had taken Mikas, or had anything to do with his disappearance.

Not until she felt that straw break did she realize how hard she had been clinging to it. It had to be Dobrovolskij because Dobrovolskij was someone she knew, he had a face, she knew where he lived. If it was Dobrovolskij, Mikas would come back to her.

But it wasn't Dobrovolskij.

SIGITA WALKED TO the nearest trolley stop on legs that felt disconnected. The trolley stop did not represent a conscious decision, more a conditioned reflex. She had lived in this neighborhood herself, once, in two attic rooms in one of the wooden houses where the well was anything but decorative. For three years she had climbed the narrow stairs every day with a couple of ten-liter plastic water containers in her hands, one for Mrs. Jovaišienė, who owned the house, and one for herself. If she needed to bathe, she had to use the public facilities some blocks away, so usually she took sponge baths and relied heavily on a wonder-product called Nuvola, which came in an aerosol can; one sprayed it into one's hair, waited for a few minutes, and then brushed vigorously, after which everything would be as clean as if one had just showered. Or that was the theory. Once a week she borrowed Mrs. Jovaišienė's little hand-cranked washing machine, but most of the time she just washed her clothes in the sink, like they had done back home in Tauragė.

Mrs. Jovaišienė was probably dead by now. She had been over ninety. Sigita deliberately avoided Vykinto gatvė, where the house was, although that would have been the shorter route. She didn't want to see it. Didn't want to be reminded of that time. Mikas was all that mattered now, she told herself.

Back home in Pašilaičiai, the flat was unchanged. White. New. Empty. She closed the blinds to the afternoon sun and lay down on the bed with all her clothes on. A few seconds later, she was asleep.

THE YEAR SIGITA became pregnant, winter had come early to Tauragė. The first snows fell at the end of October. Her father had just taken over the position of caretaker in their building, after Bronislavas Tomkus had moved out. In practice, this meant that Sigita had to help her mother shovel the walks before she could go off to school and her mother could leave for her job at the post office. Her father had "the thing with his back," of course. He did insist on directing his troops, though, entertaining them with a series of humorous remarks to keep up morale.

"It's the secret weapon of the Russians, that is," he said, pointing to the packed snow. "Direct from Siberia. But they won't get us down while we have good, strong women like you!"

He jokingly praised Sigita and her mother as brave defenders of the Independence to everyone passing on the half-cleared sidewalk. It was all rather unbearable.

At least the cold weather meant that Sigita could wear heavy sweaters without arousing comment. She had begun to cut all phys-ed classes, but she knew it was only a matter of time before Miss Bendikaitė would contact the headmaster, who in his turn would contact her parents.

Sexual education was not in any way part of the curriculum at Tauragė Primary and Secondary School, but Sigita did realize what it meant when she had missed her period in August, and again in September. She just wasn't exactly sure what to do about it. Theoretically, she could have bought a pregnancy test at the pharmacy in City Square, but Mrs. Raguckienė, who sat at the register, had gone to school with her mother. And in any case, what good would a test do? She already knew what was wrong.

She hadn't told Darius. By the end of August, he had been sent to the States to stay with his uncle and attend an American high school for a year. Sigita rather thought that this unprecedented generosity owed much to the fact that his mother didn't consider Sigita a suitable girlfriend for her golden boy. Sigita had written him a letter, but without mentioning her condition. Her own mother sorted all mail outbound from Tauragė, and the airmail paper was so terribly, transparently thin.

She missed him. She missed him so much it made her breasts and her abdomen ache. She counted this longing as one more item on the list of sins she had omitted to tell Father Paulius about, but she had no plans to confess.

Eventually she realized that the tenderness in her breasts meant something other than merely thwarted passion. But to write the words: *I am pregnant*, or, *You're going to be a father* . . . No. She just couldn't do it.

One Thursday night in the beginning of December she packed as many clothes as she could fit into her gym bag. It had to be the gym bag, because the suitcases were kept in a locked storage room in the building's long, window-less attic, and besides, walking down Dariaus ir Giréno gatvé with a suitcase would definitely cause eyebrows to lift. Someone might even try to stop her. It also had to be Thursday, because that was the day when her mother went to visit Granny Julija, and her father always took that opportunity to go play cards with some of his old mates from the canning factory.

She left no letter. She would have had no idea what to say in it. Only her little brother Tomas saw her leave.

"Where are you going?" he asked.

"Out," she said, unable to even look at him.

"Mama said you had to mind me."

"You are twelve years old, Tomas. You can mind your-self by now."

She caught the last bus to Vilnius. It took nearly five hours to get there, by which time it was past midnight, and the big city of her dreams had closed for the night. There were no trolley busses, and she couldn't afford a taxi. She asked the busdriver for directions and began to walk through the silent streets, with the freezing snow crunching under the soles of her boots.

Her aunt was astonished to see her. She had to say her name twice before Jolita even recognized her.

"But Sigita. What are you doing here? Why didn't your mother call me?"

"I wanted to visit you. Mama doesn't know."

Jolita was older than her mother, but looked younger. The hair brushing her shoulders was a uniform black, and a pair of huge golden loops dangled from her earlobes. She was wearing a royal blue kimono dressing gown, but despite this, it didn't seem that she had been in bed when Sigita rang the bell. From the flat behind her came a series of soft jazz notes and the smell of cigarette smoke.

Jolita's penciled eyebrows shot up.

"You wanted to *visit* me?" she said.

"Yes," said Sigita. And then she started crying.

"Little darling . . ."

"You have to help me," sobbed Sigita. "I'm going to have a baby."

"Oh dear Lord, sweetheart," said Tante Jolita, drawing her into a silky, tobacco-scented, and very comforting embrace.

KARIN IS DEAD. Karin is dead. Karin is dead.

The thought was pounding away inside Nina's skull as she turned onto Kildevej and headed back toward Copenhagen. She was nearly certain now that no one had followed her from the cottage. The first harried miles on the narrow road through Tibirke, she had checked her mirror every other second.

Karin is dead, she thought, gripping the steering wheel still harder. She had tried to wipe her hands on a crumbled, jellybean-sticky tissue she had found in the glove compartment, but the blood had had time to dry and lay like a thin rust-colored film over her palm and fingertips.

Unbidden, the feel of Karin's skull came back to her. Like one of those big, luxurious, foil-wrapped Easter eggs Morten's parents always bought for Ida and Anton, and which always got dropped on the floor somehow. The shell under the foil would feel flattened and frail, just like Karin's head. She had been able to feel individual fragments of bone moving under the scalp as she probed.

She had been killed. Beaten to death. Someone had hit her until she was dead.

Nina hunched over the steering wheel, trying to control her nausea. Why would anyone want to kill Karin? Karin was one of the least dangerous people Nina had ever met, big-bosomed in a rather maternal way that had always made Nina think of warm milk and homemade bread. Secure. She had always been secure.

Nina wiped her eyes with one hand; she felt her gaze

drawn to the unwinding ribbon of the road's central white line and had to yank it back up with an act of will.

They had always stuck together, back at nursing school. Studied together, gone to parties and Friday drinks together, even though on the face of it they didn't have much in common. Nina was small and skinny and went in for the pale, doomed, and emaciated look. Karin, on the other hand, would have looked completely at home in a propaganda film from the Third Reich. Tall, blond, and buxom, with generous hips and smooth, golden skin. And she had been so wonderfully uncomplicated. Not stupid, not at all, just—uncomplicated, and with an overwhelming potential for happiness. Or that, at least, was how Nina had seen her, and it might have been why she stuck around, hoping for some of that happiness potential to rub off, needing to be with someone whose world was just as round and perfect as Karin herself was.

That Karin, in the end, had been the one who found it most difficult to realize her dream of a family, of husband and children, had always been a mystery to Nina. But for some reason or other, the men around Karin never stayed. Nina was the one who had acquired the whole package without ever really wanting it, and that may have been what came between them in the end.

While Nina had had her first child and gone off to save the world in foreign climes, Karin had worked as a private nurse to a Danish family stationed in Brussels, and later at some posh and probably hair-raisingly expensive clinic in Switzerland. They tried to meet during those interludes when they were both in Denmark at the same time, but it became more and more obvious that the distance between them was growing.

Like the time when she had been pregnant with Anton. Very pregnant, actually, and very nearly due. She could still recall the hurt, offended look in Karin's eyes when Nina opened the door to her in the new flat in Østerbro she and Morten had just moved into. It had been that rarest of times when everything seemed right with the world, and she had felt, perhaps for the first and only time in her life, at peace with herself. She had gained fifty-five pounds and enjoyed every ounce of it, feeling pleasantly round, firm and soft at the same time.

Karin hadn't said anything. Not even congratulations.

Since that visit, the phone calls had come at greater and greater intervals, and when she had seen Karin at that ill-fated Christmas party, already a little soused and wearing a pair of glittery reindeer antlers on a headband, it had been four years since they had last met.

Nina, too, had become rather drunk rather quickly, but she did remember Karin telling her that she was home to stay. That she had found a great job near . . . Kalundborg, wasn't it? And what else?

Nina frowned, trying to recall the scene more precisely. There had been little handcrafted schnapps glasses and chubby Santa-shaped candles on the table, vats of beer, and for some reason the kind of confetti people usually used for New Year's.

Karin was a private nurse again, she had said, and she was raking it in. Nina suddenly remembered seeing a peculiar weariness in Karin's eyes. She had had entirely too much schnapps, and she sat there twisting a plastic beer glass between her hands and telling Nina exactly how much she brought home every month, after taxes. And that she didn't even have to pay rent because there was this great flat that went with the job, with a brilliant view of the bay. The dim light deepened the furrows on her brow and made little vertical lines appear around her mouth, and for the first time ever, Nina had felt a dislike for her friend. It was as if she didn't know her anymore, and as the evening wore on, she had been full of contempt for the choices Karin had made. They were both dead drunk by then, even more so than when they used to party together when they were students. And Nina was feeling tired, and mean, and sick at heart.

Perhaps that was why she had said it. That she was still saving the world. That she was happy. That she had the perfect family, and the perfect husband, and that she spent her spare time helping all the children, women, and crippled little men no one else in all of fucking Denmark seemed to care about.

She had told Karin about the network.

The first part of it was a pack of lies, but it felt fantastic to say it. The rest was true. She did spend a lot of time on the network. Too much, thought Morten. Sometimes he complained that she was only in it for the adrenalin fix, but it was more than that; she still needed to save the world, still needed to feel that she wasn't powerless.

Nina wiped her eyes again, and eased her foot off the accelerator. This was not a motorway, although she was not the only driver who seemed to be driving like it was. The boy was quiet now. He crouched on the seat next to her, his knees drawn up to his chest, staring wide-eyed at the fields slipping past, and the dark forms of dozing horses under the trees.

She thought of the words that had tumbled out of him in that desperate wail, and tried to recall the unfamiliar sounds. The word "Mama" had been easily distinguishable, but other than that Nina could not identify a single syllable. Not one. Nor could she recognize the general tone of it. It was probably some Eastern European language, she thought, especially considering the boy's fair hair and skin. On the other hand, she didn't think it was either Russian or Polish. Not enough z-sounds. She cursed at her lack of linguistic skill and rubbed the bridge of her nose with one hand. God, she was tired. It felt as if she had been awake for days, and she had to force her eyes to focus on the digits of the car's clock.

8:58.

She wondered what Morten and the children were doing now. Ida would probably be in her room, hypnotized by one of her endless computer games. And Anton would be in bed, bedtime story over and done with. If Morten had been in a mood to read to him, of course. He might have been too angry. He had asked Nina to stay away, hadn't he? Or what was it he had said? Nina could no longer recall the exact words.

Had he asked her to come home?

Probably not. Nina felt a clean, cold calm spread from her chest to her stomach.

Morten didn't get angry very often.

In many ways, he reminded her of those big, soft dogs who let their ears get nipped and their tails get tugged day in and day out. The kind of animal you are completely certain is the nicest dog in the world, until one day it explodes in a fit of rage and sinks its teeth into the leg of the pesky seven-year-old boy next door.

Morten was actually capable of scaring Nina a little on such occasions, especially because his anger was directed at the whole world even though the spark that triggered it was usually something she had done. When they had had a bad fight, he became curt and dismissive with Ida and Anton. As if they were an extension of her and all the things about her that he couldn't stand.

On such rare days Morten found it hard to cope with Anton, and Ida was asked to turn off the television in her room for no better reason than that it annoyed him that it was on.

Nina pictured him now, sitting alone on the sofa with the laptop open on the low coffee table in front of him, restlessly surfing job ads, trekking equipment and cheap trips to Borneo or Novo Sibirsk. Anything that would give him a fleeting sense of what life could be like without her.

Her skin suddenly felt chill despite the muggy heat still trapped in the car. What was she going to do? She would learn nothing more from Karin now than she already had, and that was practically nothing.

SHE LEFT ROUTE 16 by Farum and stopped at a Q8. Stiffly, she turned in her seat to look at the boy. His eyes were closed now, and he lay huddled against the opposite door like small, limp animal. He must be completely exhausted, she thought.

She was no more than a few minutes away from the

Coal-House Camp. And what then? Tuck him into one of the baby blue cots in Ellen's House? Sit by his bedside, praying and hoping that the man from the railway station wouldn't find them?

He had already found Karin. She was almost certain about that. Found her and killed her, despite the fact that Karin had left her job and the flat with the great view of the bay and had tried to hide in a small summer cottage on the Northern coast.

The boy didn't stir as she got out of the car. She closed the door as gently as possible so as not to wake him, edged past the trailers for rent, and headed for the store. To one side of the door was a wooden pallet loaded with firewood bagged in purple sacking, on the other a huge metal basket full of sprinkler fluid promising to be especially effective against dead insects on the windshield. Right now it seemed completely absurd that there were people in the world who cared deeply about such things.

Inside, the boy behind the counter, much too young for his job, eyed her with the special wariness convenience store staff acquire after dark: Is this it? Is this where it gets unpleasant and dangerous, is this where armed strangers stick a gun in my face and tell me to open the till? The fact that she was female immediately lowered his anxiety levels, and she tried to smile disarmingly to soothe him even further, but the smile felt more like a rictus.

Oh hell, she thought. I still have blood on my hands. Maybe on the T-shirt too. She hadn't even thought to check. What the hell was she using for brains? She tucked her hands into her pockets and asked to borrow a telephone. And perhaps a bathroom?

Helpfully, he showed her into a small lounge-like area at the back of the store. She opted for the bathroom first, and used the cloyingly perfumed soap from the dispenser to rub the last rusty remnant from her nails and the wrinkles on her knuckles. Miraculously, the T-shirt had escaped smears and stains. She didn't have the patience to use the blower, but wiped her hands on her jeans instead.

Then the telephone.

She dialed the number for North-Zealand Police, helpfully provided on the message board by the phone together with details on how to reach the local cab company, Auto-Aid, hospital emergency room and other useful services. But as the line established the connection with a click, she caught sight of herself on a surveillance monitor mounted above the counter.

"Nordsjælland Police."

Nina stood motionless while clumsy thoughts waddled through her tired brain. These days, there was no such thing as a truly anonymous call.

"Hello? This is Nordsjælland Police, how can I help you?"

You can't, thought Nina, and hung up. The certain knowledge that there was nothing more she could do for Karin came back to her. She had to concentrate on the boy.

HE HADN'T MOVED. He was still curled against the door of the car, and she wondered if she should put him in the back seat instead, where he would be more comfortable. But the feeling of being hunted and observed had come back. She started the Fiat and turned onto Frederiksborgvej. At least she felt more awake now, and coherent thought no longer appeared an unsurmountable task. She hit the motorway at the Værløse exit and joined the flow of cars gliding towards the city in the dense, warm summer night. One thing, at least, was clear now. Her only key to the mystery of where the boy came from was the boy himself.

THE PHONE WOKE her. It was Darius.

"Sigita, damnit. You set the cops on me!"

"No. Or . . . I went back and told them it wasn't you. That you didn't have him."

"Then kindly explain why two not very civil gentlemen from the Polizei were here a moment ago, turning over the whole place!"

He was really mad at her, she could tell. But she was pleased. Gužas was actually doing something, she thought. Ballpoint-clicking Gužas. He had contacted the police in Düsseldorf, which was where Darius lived at the moment.

"Darius, they have to check. When the parents are divorced, that's the first thing they think of."

"We're not divorced."

"Separated, then."

"Did you really think I would take him away from you?"

She tried to tell him about the woman in the cotton coat and the mistaken conclusions drawn by Mrs. Mažekienė, but he was too angry to listen.

"Honestly, Sigita. This is too fucking much!"

Click. He was gone.

Dizzy and disoriented, she sat on the bed for a little while. She had been asleep for less than an hour. It was still afternoon. And she still had a headache. She opened the door to the balcony, hoping it would clear the air, and more importantly, her mind.

That seemed to be a signal Mrs. Mažekienė had been

waiting for for a while. She was sitting outside on her own balcony, surrounded by a jungle of tomato plants and hydrangeas.

"Oh, you're home," she said. "Any news?"

"No."

"The police were here," she said. "I had to make a statement!" She sounded proud of the fact.

"What did you tell them?"

"I told them about the young couple, and about the car. And . . . erh . . . they asked about you, too."

"I imagine they would."

"If there were other boyfriends, and so on. Now that you're on your own again."

"And what did you tell them about that?"

"God bless us, but I'm not one to gossip. In this building, we mind our own business, is what I told them."

"I think you know that I don't have a boyfriend. Why didn't you just say so?"

"And how would I know such a thing, dear? It's not as if I watch your door, or anything. I'm no Peeping Tom!"

"No," sighed Sigita. "Of course not."

Mrs. Mažekienė leaned over the railing. "I've made cepelinai," she said. "Would you like some, dearie?"

The mere thought of doughy yellow-white potato balls made nausea rise in her throat again.

"That's very kind of you, but no thanks."

"Don't forget your stomach just because your heart is heavy," said Mrs. Mažekienė. "That's what *my* dear mother always used to say, God rest her soul."

My heart isn't heavy, thought Sigita. It is black. The blackness was back inside her, and she suddenly couldn't stand another second of Mrs. Mažekienė's well-intentioned intrusions.

"I'm sorry," she said abruptly. "I have to . . ."

She fled into the flat without even pausing to close the balcony door. It wasn't nausea that seized her, but weeping. It ripped at her gut and tore long, howling sobs from her, and she had to lean over the sink, supporting herself with her good hand, as though she were in fact about to throw up.

Several minutes passed before she could breathe again. She knew that Mrs. Mažekienė was absorbed in the spectacle from the vantage of her own balcony, because she could still hear a soft litany of "There, there. There, there, now," as if the old lady were trying to comfort her by remote control.

"There is no harder thing," said Mrs. Mažekienė, when she heard the sobbing ease a little. "Than losing a child, I mean."

Sigita's head came up as if someone had taken a cattle prod to her.

"I have not lost a child!" she said angrily, and marched over to close the balcony door with a bang that made the glass quiver.

But the double lie cut at her like a knife.

AUNT JOLITA WORKED at the University of Vilnius. She was a secretary with the Department of Mathematics, but in reality her job consisted mostly of assisting a certain Professor Žiemys. The reason she and Sigita's mother were no longer on speaking terms became obvious fairly quickly. Every Monday and every Thursday, the Professor came to see Jolita. On the Thursday Sigita arrived, Jolita had just kissed him goodbye by her front door. It had been his cigarettes Sigita had smelled.

At first, Sigita couldn't understand why this should shock her so. Jolita wasn't married and could do what she wanted. This was not Tauragè. The Professor did have a wife, but surely that was his business.

In the end she came to the conclusion that the shocking thing was that it was all so *petty*. She had always known Jolita had done something awful, something Sigita's mother could not condone in the depth of her Catholic heart. Jolita had sinned, but no one had been willing to explain to Sigita precisely how and why. As a child, she had vaguely imagined something to do with dancing on a table while drunken men looked on. She had no idea where that peculiar vision had come from. Probably some film or other.

And now, the reality had proved to be so mundane and regulated. Every Monday, every Thursday. A bearded, stooping man more than fifteen years her senior, who always forgot at least one pair of glasses if Jolita did not remind him. She might as well have been married, or nearly so. It might all have been youthful and passionate once, but if so, that was a very long time ago.

Sigita had fled to Vilnius to escape Tauragè's judgment. To be free of prying and gossip, of moralizing parochial prejudice. Of everything *provincial*. Since she was nine or ten, she had been a highly secret admirer of Jolita's courage; she imagined that her aunt had done everything she herself dreamed of: that she had broken free and made a life for herself on her own terms, up there in the impossibly distant big city. This was why Sigita had sought her out. Jolita would understand. She would be able to see they had kindred souls, rebellious and free. And when Jolita had embraced her and let her move in with no questions asked, it had seemed an affirmation of everything she had dreamed.

But on Mondays and Thursdays, Jolita became anxious. She cleaned the flat. She bought wine. She awkwardly told Sigita she couldn't stay in the flat, but must keep away from five in the afternoon until midnight at the earliest. Highly embarrassing, it would seem, if the Professor were to meet Jolita's uncouth country niece, who had been so stupid as to get herself knocked up at age fifteen. If Sigita didn't leave quickly enough, Jolita's gestures became increasingly jerky and hectic. She would press money on Sigita, so she could buy herself a meal somewhere, go out on the town, see a film, that would be nice, darling, wouldn't it? Damp, crumpled notes would be pushed into Sigita's hands as Jolita damn near forced her out the door. Sigita saw a lot of films that winter.

It occurred to her that Jolita was not free or independent at all. She hadn't acquired her job by sleeping with the Professor—the job came first, and the Professor later—but that was seventeen years ago, and no one remembered that now. If the Professor were to lose his position, Jolita would be sacked as a matter of course. For the university, as for many others, the Independence hadn't been all sweetness and light and patriotic hymns. Funds were at a minimum, and everyone fought like hyenas for the pitiful scraps and jobs that there were. Jolita's whole life dangled by the thinnest of cobweb threads.

Her position, her salary, her flat, her entire way of life . . . everything depended on him. Mondays and Thursdays.

Jolita didn't think Sigita should go to school.

"You can do that next year, darling, when this is all over and done with," she said, jiggling the coffee pot to try to gauge its contents. "Another cup?"

"No, thank you," said Sigita distractedly. She was seated on one of the ramshackle wooden chairs in the kitchen; she had to sit with her legs apart to accomodate her belly. "But Jolita. There will be a baby, then."

Jolita froze for a minute, with the coffee pot raised in front of her as though it was an offensive weapon. She looked at Sigita seriously.

"Little darling," she said. "You're an intelligent girl. Surely you don't imagine that you'll be able to keep it?"

THE CLINIC HAD recently been established in a big old villa in the Žvėrynas Quarter. There was a smell of fresh paint and new linoleum, and the chairs in the waiting room were so new that some of them still sported their plastic covers. Sigita sat heavily on one of them, squatting like a constipated cow. Sweat trickled down her back, soaking into the awful, bright yellow maternity dress Jolita had acquired through a friend at the University. For the past four weeks, this had been the only garment that would fit Sigita's bloated body, and she hated it with a will.

At least it will soon be over, thought Sigita. And clung to that thought as the next spasm gripped her. A deep grunting sound escaped her, and she felt like an animal. A cow, a whale, an elephant. How the *hell* had it come to this? She gripped the edge of the table and tried to inhale and exhale, all the way, all the way, as she had been taught, but it made not the slightest bit of difference.

"Aaaaah. Aaaaaah. Aaaaaah."

I don't want to be an animal, she thought. I want to be Sigita again!

Jolita came back, accompanied by a slight, redhaired woman in a pale green uniform. Why not white? Perhaps it was meant to match the new mint green paint on the walls.

"I'm Julija," she said, holding out her hand. Sigita couldn't release her grip on the table, so the woman's gesture transformed itself into a small pat on the shoulder, presumably meant to be soothing. "We have a room ready for you. If you can walk, that will probably be the most comfortable for you."

"I. Can. Walk." Sigita hauled herself upright without letting go of the table. She began to waddle after the woman whose name was the same as Granny Julija's. Then she discovered that Jolita wasn't following. Sigita stopped.

Jolita was wringing her hands. Literally. One slim-fingered hand kept stroking the other, as though it were a glass she was polishing.

"You'll be fine, darling," she said. "And I'm coming back later."

Sigita stood utterly paralyzed. She couldn't mean . . . surely, she couldn't expect Sigita to go through this alone? Unthinkingly, she reached for her aunt with a begging gesture she regretted seconds later. Jolita backed away, staying out of reach.

"I'll bring you some chocolate," she said, smiling

with unnatural brightness. "And some cola. It's good for when you're feeling poorly." And then she left, walking so quickly she was nearly sprinting. And Sigita suddenly realized why.

It was Thursday.

NINA PARKED THE Fiat in the narrow, cobblestoned part of Reventlowsgade, squeezed in between a row of classic Vesterbro tenements on one side and the Tietgensgade embankment on the other. On top of the embankment, the traffic moved past in uneven, noisy jerks.

The boy wriggled as she pulled the shorts up around his skinny waist, but he was apparently pleased with the slightly over-sized sandals. He picked at the velcro straps with his short, soft fingers, and Nina cautiously stroked his hair. She found the water bottles, unscrewed the cap of one of them, and held it out to him.

"Atju."

The boy accepted the bottle earnestly, and drank with clumsy greed. Some of the water sloshed onto his chin and the new T-shirt, and he silently wiped his mouth with the back of his hand.

The motion was so familiar that for a split second, Nina felt as if she might be sitting in a car with an ordinary child on their way home from a long day at the kindergarten. Slowly, she repeated the word to herself. Atju. Wasn't that the same thing he had said when she gave him the ice cream earlier?

It had to mean thank you.

Nina recognized the slight nod and lowered eyes that most children learn to produce as an automatic reaction. "Thank you" was the first phrase taught by any parents with the slightest ambition to raise a polite child. It couldn't be a coincidence, thought Nina. Both times, she had been giving him something. The word was clearly designed for such situations. So, thank you. It made her task a little easier, as "Mama" was probably a too universal to be much use.

Nina opened the door and got out of the car. Heat still clung to the pavement and brick walls, and the heavy diesel fumes rising from the central railway station stung her nostrils with every breath. A faint puff of wind whirled a scrunched-up cigarette pack along the curb, until it came to rest against a tuft of yellow grass poking up between the paving stones.

The boy permitted her to lift him from the car only with reluctance, and once out, insisted on walking himself. He became tense and unmanagable in her arms, arching his spine and throwing back his head in silent protest, and when she gave in and let him slide to the sidewalk, she thought she had caught a glint of triumph in his tired eyes. He landed neatly, his new sandals meeting the pavement with a crisp and satisfied smack. Then he reached for her hand as though that was the most natural thing in the world. He was used to walking this way, thought Nina. He was used to holding someone's hand.

THEY WALKED UP Stampesgade and turned right along Colbjørnsensgade, and then on to Istedgade. The boy's hand rested in hers, lightly as a butterfly, as they slowly moved past Kakadu Bar and Saga Hotel. There were still quite a few people about in the warm, dark night; outside the cafés, the guests were sipping beers and lattes and colas, barefooted in sandals, and still dressed only in light summer dresses or shorts.

The first prostitutes Nina saw were African. Two of them, both of them rather solidly built, and dressed in high boots and brightly colored skirts stretched tightly over muscular, firm thighs. The women stood less than five yards from each other, yet they didn't talk. One had propped herself against a wall with a cigarette between pursed lips, and rummaged hectically through her bag at regular intervals. The other did nothing at all except stand there, watching every car that turned the corner.

No one took any notice of Nina and the boy, and it struck her that they must look relatively normal, walking together like this. A little late to be out and about, certainly, considering the usual bedtime of children his age, but nothing that would raise eyebrows. Vesterbro might contain Copenhagen's red light district, but it was also a neighborhood full of ordinary families, some of them with young children. Vesterbro was becoming hip, and fashionable cafés had sprung up among the topless bars and porn shops.

The boy dragged his feet a little, but she still felt no resistance in the hand resting confidently in hers. In a doorway a little further down the street, two women argued heatedly. They were both blond, with skinny legs and remarkably similar emaciated faces. The argument stopped abruptly, as suddenly as it has begun, and one of them reached into her handbag and handed a can of beer to the other.

Nina paused, and the boy stood obediently quiet at her

side while she tried to obtain eye contact with one of the women, the one now holding the beer can. She, in her turn, ignored Nina and looked at the boy instead.

"Hi there, sweetheart."

Her voice was blurred and bubbly, as though she were talking to them from the bottom of a well. When the boy didn't react and Nina kept standing there, she finally raised her eyes to Nina's, with a grimace of confusion on her face.

"Yes?"

Nina took a deep breath. "I'm looking for . . ." Nina hesitated, fumbling for the right words. The woman's gaze was already wandering again. "The Eastern European girls, where are they? Do you know?"

The woman's pale blue eyes widened in astonishment and distrust. Her pupils moved in tiny rapid jerks, and her mouth tightened. Nina realized she must look like the enemy, that the woman might consider her world to be under attack from the semi-detached, permanent-income, husband-toting kind of person who would condescend to and disapprove of people like her. She might suspect Nina of being a journalist, or an outraged wife, or even a tourist vicariously fascinated by the prospect of sleaze and degradation. In any case, the woman clearly did not relish the role of practical guide to Vesterbro's night life. Her eyes glinted aggressively.

"Why the hell are you asking?"

She moved half a step closer, and Nina felt the heaviness of her breath waver in the air between them.

Truth, she thought. I'll give her the truth, or a small part of it, at any rate.

"The boy needs his mother," she said, pulling the child onto her arm. "I have to find her."

For a few wobbly seconds, the woman maintained her stance, chest pushed forward and eyes glinting. Then the appeal to the maternal instinct had its effect. She slumped, taking another sip of her lager, and studied the boy with renewed interest.

"Poor little dear," she said, reaching out to touch his cheek with a bony finger.

He jerked his head out of reach and hid his face against Nina's shoulder, which made the beer-can woman scowl. She teetered off, pulling her friend with her. But she did answer the question as she went.

"They're everywhere at the moment," she said. "Some in Skelbæksgade, some at Halmtorvet. There are probably some in Helgolandsgade, too. They're bloody everywhere, and you have a long night ahead of you if you don't know her usual spot."

"Where do they come from, do you know?"

Nina wasn't sure the woman heard her, but just before they turned the corner, her friend twisted to look at Nina.

"Most of the white girls are from Russia," she said. "But there are others, too. Prices are way down because of them. The stupid little tarts ruin it for everyone else."

THE DOOR BUZZER let off a snarl, startling Sigita out of a strange sort of absence. Not sleep. Nothing as peaceful as sleep.

"This is Evaldas Gužas, from the Department of Missing Persons. May we come in?"

She buzzed them through. Her heart had begun to pound so hard that the material of her shirt was actually quivering with each beat. They have found him, she thought. Holy Virgin, Mother of Christ. Please let it be so. They have found him, and he is all right.

But as soon as she opened her door to Gužas and his companion, she could tell that he was not the bearer of such good news. She still couldn't help asking.

"Have you found him?"

"No," said Gužas. "I'm afraid not. But we do have a possible lead. This is my colleague, Detective Sergeant Martynas Valionis. When I told him about the case, it rang a few bells."

Valionis shook Sigita's hand.

"May we sit down for a moment?"

"Yes, of course," said Sigita politely, all the while silently screaming *get on with it*.

Valionis perched on the edge of the white couch, put his briefcase on the coffee table, aligning it with the edge with unconscious perfectionism, and brought out a plastic folder.

"I am about to show you some photographs, Mrs. Ramoškienė. Do you recognize any of these women?"

The photos were not glossy portrait shots, but printed hastily on a none-too-efficient inkjet, it seemed. He held them out to her one at a time.

"No," she said, to the first one. And the next.

The third photograph showed the woman with the chocolate.

Sigita clenched the paper so hard that she scrunched it.

"It's her," she said. "She's the one who took Mikas."

Valionis nodded in satisfaction.

"Barbara Woronska," he said. "From Poland, born in Krakow in 1972. Apparently she has lived in this country for some years, and officially she is working for a company selling alarm and security systems."

"And unofficially?"

"She came to our attention for the first time two years ago when a Belgian businessman made a complaint that she had tried to blackmail him. It would appear that the company uses her as an escort for their clients, particularly the foreign ones, when they visit Vilnius."

"She's a *prostitute*?" Sigita never would have guessed.

"That is perhaps a little too simple. Our impression is that she works as what's known as a honey trap. She certainly seems to have an uncommonly high consumption of prescription eyedrops."

Sigita didn't understand.

"Eyedrops?"

"Yes. Medicinally, they are used to relax the muscles of the eyes, which is useful in certain instances. But if they are ingested, in a drink, for instance, they have the rather peculiar side effect of causing unconsciousness and deep sleep within a short time. It's not uncommon for a hard-partying businessman to wake up in some hotel room, picked clean of his Oyster Rolex, cash, and credit cards. But Miss Woronska and her backers seem to have refined the technique a bit. They arrange so-called compromising photographs while our man is unconscious, and afterwards suggest to him that he agrees to an export deal on, shall we say, very lucrative terms for the Lithuanian companies involved. Only this time, the Belgian got stubborn, told them to publish and be damned, and came to us. Miss Woronska was one of the participants in the arranged photograph. The other was some little girl who could hardly have been more than twelve years old. One quite understands why the police have not heard from their other victims."

Hardly more than twelve . . . Sigita tried to push away the mental images. She couldn't make it square with the neat and elegant woman in the cotton coat. When people did something like that for a living, shouldn't it somehow show?

She stared at the printed page. It was not a classic identification photo of the kind made after arrests. Barbara Woronska was not looking directly at the photographer, her head was turned slightly to the left, bringing out the elegance of her long neck. The quality was grainy, as if the picture had been too much enlarged, and the expression on her face was . . . peculiar. Her mouth was half open, her eyes stared blankly. Even though only her face and neck were showing in the photo, Sigita suddenly felt convinced that Woronska was not wearing any clothes, and that this was a detail from one of the "compromising photographs."

"But why . . . what made you think that she was the one who took Mikas?"

"Two things," explained Valionis. "Item one: the Belgian had an alarming alcohol content in his blood in spite of swearing to us that he had had only one drink in the company of the delectable Miss Woronska. When our doctor examined him, he found lesions in the man's throat consistent with intubation—in other words, someone could have inserted a tube and poured alcohol directly into his stomach while he was unconscious. It's a good way of demoralizing and incapacitating someone, if you are willing to take the risk. People have been known to die from it, from acute alcohol poisoning."

Sigita's head came up.

"But . . . but that is . . ."

Evaldas Gužas nodded. "Yes. I'm sorry no one believed you. At this stage, unfortunately, we cannot prove that this was what was done to you, as it is not now possible to distinguish any orignal injury from those stemming from the intubation you had to undergo at the hospital. But everyone I have spoken to has characterized you as a sober and responsible person, so . . ." He left the conclusion hanging in the air, unsaid.

Some of Sigita's general misery eased a little. At least they believed her now. At least they would be serious about looking for Mikas.

"And . . . Mikas?"

"The other thing that rang a bell was the fact that Barbara Woronska had been identified as one of four possible suspects in another case involving the disappearance of a child," said Valionis, consulting his notebook briefly.

Sigita's hands shook.

"A child?"

Valionis nodded.

"A little over a month ago, a desperate mother reported her eight-year-old daughter missing. She had been picked up from the music school where she took piano lessons twice a week by an unknown woman who presented herself as a neighbor. The piano teacher was not suspicious, as the mother works as a nurse and has often sent others to pick up the child when she herself has a late shift. Unfortunately, the piano teacher was not able to give us a very good description and would only say that it might be one of these four women." He tapped the photographs with one forefinger.

"But where is she now?" said Sigita. "Haven't you arrested her?"

"Unfortunately not," said Gužas. "Her place of employment tells us that they haven't seen her since Thursday, and she has apparently not been living at her official address since March."

"But how come she is not in jail? With all this, how come she is still out there, stealing other people's children?"

Valionis shook his head with a disgusted grimace.

"Both cases were dropped. The Belgian went home very suddenly, and all we got from him was a letter from his lawyer to the effect that his client was dropping all charges. And the nurse just as suddenly maintained that it had all been a misunderstanding, and the child was home and quite safe."

"Isn't that a little odd?" asked Sigita.

"Yes. We are convinced that they both gave in to some form of pressure." Evaldas Gužas's gaze rested on her with an ungentle emphasis. "Which is why I have to ask you yet again, Mrs. Ramoškienė. Does anyone have any reason to subject you to that kind of pressure?"

Sigita shook her head numbly. If it hadn't been Dobrovolskij, she couldn't imagine anyone else feeling any need to pressure or threaten her.

"Surely they would say something?" she said. "I haven't heard a thing."

Helplessness gripped her once more. Again, an unbearable image flitted through her mind: Mikas in a basement somewhere, on a dirty mattress, crying, afraid. How can anyone stand this? she thought. I can't. It will kill me.

"I implore you to contact us if you hear anything at all," said Gužas. "It's impossible for us to stop people like this if no one will talk to us."

She nodded heavily. But she knew that if it became a choice between saving Mikas and telling the police, the police didn't have a prayer.

Valionis closed his briefcase with a crisp snap. The two officers got to their feet, Valionis gave her his card, and Gužas shook her hand.

"There is hope," he said. "Remember that. Julija Baronienė got her daughter back."

Sigita felt a brief spasm in her chest.

"Who, did you say?"

"Julija Baronienė. The nurse. Do you know her?"

Sigita's heart leaped and fluttered.

"No," she said. "Not at all."

SHE STOOD ON her balcony and watched the two men cross the parking lot below, get into a black car, and leave. Her right hand had come to rest just under her navel, without any directions from her. Certain things are never entirely forgotten by the body.

Contrary to everything Sigita had heard about first-time births, it had been quick, and very, very violent. In the beginning she had yelled at everyone in sight, telling them to do something. In the end she just screamed, for four hours straight. It was Julija's hand she clung to, the nurse who was somehow also Granny; and Julija stayed with her so that she felt at times that this was the only thing that held her to this world: Julija's strong, square hands, Julija's voice, and Julija's face. Her eyes were dark, the color of prunes, and she did not let go, nor did she let Sigita do so.

"You just keep at it," she said. "You just keep at it until you finish this."

But when the baby did come, Sigita could hold on no longer. She slipped, and something flowed out of her, something wet and dark and warm, so that there was only cold emptiness left.

"Sigita . . ."

But Julija's voice was already distant.

"She's hemorrhaging," said one of the other sisters. "Get the doctor, *now!*"

Sigita kept on slipping, into the chill and empty dark.

IT WAS NEARLY a day and a night before she came back. She was in a small, windowless room lit by fluorescent ceiling lights. It was the light that had woken her. Her eyelids felt like rubber mats, her throat was sore. One arm had been tied to the side of the bed, and fluids were slowly dripping into her vein from a bag on a thin metal pole. Her body felt heavy and alien to her.

"Are you awake, little darling?"

Her aunt Jolita was by the bedside. The fluorescent lights bleached her skin and dug deep shadowed pits beneath her eyes. She looked like a tired old woman, thought Sigita.

"Would you like some water?"

Sigita nodded. She wasn't certain she could talk, but in the end she tried anyway.

"Where is Julija?"

Jolita frowned, her penciled brows nearly meeting in the middle.

"Your grandmother?"

"No. The other Julija."

"I don't know who you mean, darling. Here, have a sip. Now all you have to do is rest up and get better, so that we can get you home."

That was when it happened. When Jolita said the word *home*. Something huge and black exploded in her head, her breasts, her belly. Its edges were so sharp and *evil* that it felt as if something was there, even though she knew that it happened because something was lacking. Because something had been taken out of her.

"Is it a boy or a girl?" she asked.

"Don't think about it," said Jolita. "The quicker you forget about the whole thing, the better. It will have a good life. With rich people."

Sigita felt tears slide down her nose. They felt scalding hot because the rest of her was so cold.

"Rich people," she repeated, testing to see if that might make the Blackness go away.

Jolita nodded. "From Denmark," she said brightly, as if this was something special.

The Blackness was still there.

TWO DAYS LATER, Sigita was standing next to the bed in a gray sweatshirt and a pair of jeans she hadn't been able to fit into for months. Standing was tiring, but she still couldn't sit, and getting out of bed was so painful that she didn't want to lie down again. Finally Jolita returned, accompanied by a fair-haired woman in a white lab coat. Sigita had never seen the woman before.

"Goodbye then, Sigita, and good luck," she said, holding out her hand.

It felt odd, being called by her first name by someone she didn't know at all. Sigita nodded awkwardly, but returned the handshake. The woman handed Jolita a brown envelope.

"There is a small deduction for the extra days," she said. "Normally, our girls leave us inside a day."

Jolita nodded absently. She opened the brown envelope, peeked inside, then closed it again.

"I'll need your signature here."

Jolita took the pen.

"Shouldn't I be the one to sign it?" asked Sigita.

Jolita hesitated. "If you wish," she said. "But I can do it too."

Sigita looked at the paper. It wasn't an adoption form.

It was a receipt. For payment received on delivery of "Ass. herbs for the production of natural remedies." The amount signed for was 14.426 litai.

This is no adoption, thought Sigita suddenly, with glacial clarity. This is a purchase. Strangers have bought my child and paid for it, and this is my share of the loot.

"Can't I at least see it?" she asked. "And meet the people who are taking it?" Her breasts were swollen and throbbed painfully. Julija had provided her with a tight elastic bandage that she was to keep wrapped around her torso for at least a week, she had been told, to stop the milk from coming.

The woman in the white coat shook her head. "They left the clinic yesterday. But in our experience, that's best for both parties anyway."

The Blackness stirred inside her, carving new passages in her body, flowing into her veins. She could feel the chill beneath her skin. It was already done, she thought. Now all that was left was the money. She held out a hand toward Jolita.

"Give it to me."

"Little darling . . ." Jolita looked at her in confusion. "You make it sound as if I was about to steal it!"

Sigita merely waited. In the end, Jolita passed her the envelope. It was thick and heavy with the notes inside it. Sigita clutched it in one hand and waddled for the exit. The stitches stung with every stride.

"Sigita, wait," said Jolita. "The receipt!"

"You sign it," she said, over her shoulder. "It was all your idea anyway."

Jolita scribbled a hasty signature and said goodbye

to the woman. Sigita just walked on. Into the corridor, through the waiting room, and out the door.

Jolita caught up with her on the rain-drenched pavement.

"Let's get a taxi," she said. "Let me take you home."

Sigita stopped. She turned and looked at Jolita with all the new coldness she now possessed. "You go home," she said. "I'm going to a hotel. I don't want to see you again. Ever."

THERE WERE FOUR Baronienės in the Vilnius phone book. Sigita called them all, asking for Julija. No result. Then she tried Baronas, in case the telephone was registered to the husband only. Eight of those. Two didn't answer, one had an answering machine that made no mention of any Julija, two said they didn't know anyone of that name. The sixth call was answered by a woman's voice with a cautious "Yes?"

Sigita listened intently, but she wasn't sure whether she recognized the voice.

"Is this Julija?" she asked.

"Yes. To whom am I speaking?"

"Sigita Ramoškienė. I would just like to—"

She got no further. The connection was severed with an abrupt click.

JUČAS DROVE THE car all the way down onto the beach. It was dark now, and there were no people. Behind him, the thicket of pines formed a black wall. He took off all his clothes except his underpants. The sand was still warm beneath the soles of his feet, and the water tepid and so shallow that he had to wade several hundred feet before it became deep enough for him to swim.

There was no significant surf, no suction. Just this flat, lukewarm water that could not give him the stinging shock he craved. It had to be there, he thought, further out—the cold, the undertow, the powers. He considered quite soberly the possiblity of simply continuing until he met something stronger than he was.

Barbara was waiting at the hotel. He hadn't told her much, just that he had to help the Dane with something before they could get their money.

There would be no Krakow now, he thought, digging into the water with furious strokes that did, after all, make his muscles burn a little. In his mind he could still see the smiling family, the mother, the father, the two children, but large brown rats had begun to gnaw at the house so that it was disappearing bite by bite, and now one of the rats had started on the leg of the smallest child, without causing the child or the parents to smile any less.

He stopped his progress abruptly, treading water. He knew where those rats came from. Could still remember them scuttling away as he had come into the stable with the lantern and had found Gran on the floor next to the feed bin. No one had ever thought it necessary to tell him what she had died from. But dead she was, even a seven-year-old boy could tell as much. And the rats had known it, too.

He had succeeded in finding waters too deep for him to touch bottom. But he began to swim for the coast, this time with smooth, methodical strokes. He would not let the rats win. And there was still a trail of sorts that he might follow.

He thought about his clothes. What to do with them. In the end he dipped the sleeve of his shirt into the petrol tank of the car and made a small bonfire on the beach. He had only vague notions of DNA and microscopic fibers, but surely fire would deal with most of that.

The first thing to go wrong had been the woman herself. It hadn't been the one he had seen in the railway station—the bony, crew-cut boy-bitch. This one was fair-haired like Barbara and had even bigger breasts. It would have been so much easier if it had only been the other one.

But she tried to run the minute she saw him, and surely she wouldn't have done that if she had been innocent? His reflexes took over, and he hit her a few times on the arms and legs when he caught her, just to stop her from trying to run again. She was terrified. She gabbled at him in a language that was probably Danish, then seemed to realize that he didn't understand. She began speaking English instead. Asked him who he was, and what he was doing there? But he could tell from her eyes that she knew precisely why he had come. And she was so scared that a trickle of yellow pee ran down one leg and made a damp spot in the middle of her white dress.

Why wouldn't the stupid woman just *tell* him, he thought? What was she thinking? That if she said "no" enough times, he would apologize for the inconvenience and go away?

There always came a point when they knew. Some tried to escape, or scream and beg. Others simply gave up. But the time always came when they knew. Once he had torn away all the things they used for protection—nice clothes, perhaps, or an immaculate home, courtesy and starched curtains, a name, a position, an illusion of power and security: *this can't be happening to us . . .* once he had made them understand that yes, it was happening, it could happen to anybody, and right now it's happening to you. Once the disbelief had vanished. Then there was only one raw reality left: that he would not stop until they gave him what he had come for.

Despite her terror, it took a long while for the fair-haired Danish woman to get to that point. Much longer than he was used to in Lithuania. Perhaps the layer of security was thicker here, like the layer of fat on the fish in the Tivoli lake. Peeling it off took time. But in the end she was just trying to figure out what he wanted her to say.

He asked about the money. I put it back, she said. Jan has it. She kept saying that, so it might be true.

Then he asked about the boy. Who was the bitch who had collected him? Where was he now? Who had him?

That was when he came upon a core of resistance in the middle of all that soft blondness. She wouldn't tell him. Lied to him, saying she didn't know. And that was when he became angry.

He had had to leave her for a while, afraid of losing it, afraid that he had already lost it. He'd stood outside on the porch for some minutes, just breathing, listening to the irritating whine of the mosquitoes, as if they all had little miniature engines that were tuned too high. A small gray tabby suddenly appeared from under the bushes on the opposite side of the lawn. It stopped some distance away, meowing with a curious questioning intonation. But it seemed to realize something was wrong, because it came no closer, and immediately afterwards darted back into the shrubbery and was gone.

When he went back in, she had succeeded in crawling onto the bed. Her breathing sounded wrong, too wet and bubbly, and she didn't react when he came into the room.

"Ni-na," she gurgled. "Ni-na."

He wasn't even sure whether it was in answer to the questions he had asked, or whether she was just calling for someone she imagined might help her. But he took her mobile from the bedside table to check if there was a Nina. There was. He took down both the number and her last name and tossed the phone on the bed.

"Ni-na," she said once more.

She doesn't even know I'm here, he thought. Then he saw the pool of blood spreading beneath her head.

THE FLAMES WERE dying. He kicked some sand over the embers, then decided to bury the remains of the bonfire properly. With a bit of luck they would never be found. Then he got himself a clean dry shirt from his bag in the car.

He tried to view the situation with a clear mind. One had to. At the moment, he didn't know where the money was. The blonde had said she had given it back to the Dane. The Dane said the blonde had it. Jučas believed the blonde more than he believed the Dane.

And the boy? Perhaps that gurgling "Ni-na" had actually been the answer. Maybe she was called Nina, the dark-haired boy-bitch who had ogled him back at the railway station. What if she had the brat, and this was why the Dane was suddenly so uncooperative about paying? At the price they had set, it wasn't too surprising if he wanted delivery of the goods before he handed over the cash.

Once Jučas was fully dressed again, he called Barbara. He had checked her into a hotel before leaving the city. More unnecessary expense, but he couldn't take her with him.

"Is there a phone book in the room?" he asked.

She said there was.

"I need you to find an address for me," he said. "But don't call Directory Enquiries, and don't ask the operator. Is that clear?"

"When will you be back?" she asked, and he could hear the anxiety in her voice.

"Soon. But you have to do as I say, it's important."

"Yes. Yes, okay. What is it you want me to do?"

"Look up someone in the phone book. See if there's a listing for a Nina Borg."

HELGOLANDSGADE.

The street was narrow and a bit claustrophobic. On one side was the newly refurbished Hotel Axel with its brilliant white facade and a big golden dragonfly hovering above the entrance. It had become trendy, thought Nina, to spend the night in Vesterbro, with a view of hookers and pick-pockets.

A group of teenage girls had taken up position directly opposite the hotel's entrance. They looked like ordinary school girls, thought Nina in surprise. No leather, no fishnet stockings or bleached hair. They looked like regular young people ready for a night on the town. And yet, there was somehow no doubt what they were here for.

The four girls all checked the street regularly, eyeing the passersby. Every little while, one would separate herself from the herd, walk a few steps, perhaps get out her mobile, but without ever calling someone. Then she'd return to lean on the small black motor scooter they were all gathered around. While everyone else moved on, they stayed.

Nina gripped the boy's hand a little more tightly, then approached them. A couple of phrases in accented English rose above the noisy conversation of a couple of drunks going the other way.

"Nineteen. You owe me."

One of the girls laughed loudly, and took a couple of

tottering steps backwards, on heels that were far too high for her.

They had been betting on her age, thought Nina, but she couldn't tell whether the others had guessed too high or too low. She shivered. Ida would be fourteen at her next birthday.

"Excuse me?"

Nina deliberately made her voice soft and neutral. These girls wouldn't want to talk to anyone except for necessary business, her instincts told her.

All the girls turned to regard her, and once more, Nina was struck by their youth. The heavy makeup and pale glittery lip gloss just made them look like little girls disguised as grown-ups. Nina half expected some tinny voice to announce that these were the contestants in some bizarre American Little Miss beauty pageant, so that any minute now, one of them might break into song.

One of the four took up a stance directly in front of her, legs apart and arms crossed over her chest, presumably in an effort to look menacing. She was small and very slim, her dark eyes darting nervously.

"I need some help with this boy," said Nina. "I need to know if you can understand him."

The girl cast a glance up the street, then looked at Nina again, her skepticism obvious.

"Atju," said Nina, pointing at the boy. "Do you know what it means? Do you know which language?"

Something moved in the girl's sullen face. Nina could practically see her deliberating the pros and cons, and separating them into two untidy piles. Nina quickly stuck her hand into the pockets of her jeans and came up with a crumbled hundred-kroner note. That obviously helped. The girl discreetly transferred the note to her own pocket.

"I'm not sure. I think maybe Lithuanian."

Nina nodded, smiling as softly as she knew how. She was definitively out of cash now.

"And you are not from Lithuania?"

The answer was self-evident, but Nina wanted to keep the conversation going, to hang on to the slight thread of a chance she had been offered.

"Latvia." The girl shrugged. "Marija is Lithuanian."

She stepped aside a little, indicating the tall, gangly girl who had laughed before, and who might or might not be nineteen years old. She had long dark hair, gathered in a ponytail at the back of her head. There was something coltish about her, thought Nina. Her legs seemed too long for her body, the knees wide and bony in comparison, and her movements had all the gawky awkwardness of a growing teenager.

Her face, too, was sullen, and she looked uncertainly at Nina.

"Do you know the word *atju*?" asked Nina.

An involuntary smile flashed across the girl's face, probably at Nina's attempt at pronunciation.

"It's *ačiu. Ačiū.*"

Her A was a little longer than Nina's, and it sounded exactly right in a way Nina's attempt had not. Something soft and girlish came into the young woman's face as she repeated the word, and she exposed a row of perfect white teeth still too big and too new, somehow, for the adult makeup.

"That is Lithuanian," she said, smiling again, and raising a flat hand to her chest. "I am from Lithuania."

Again, Nina pointed to the boy.

"I need to talk to this boy. I think maybe he is Lithuanian too."

If the girl would help her, she would be able to get information from the boy. He might even be able to tell her how he had ended up in a suitcase in a baggage locker at the central railway station. If only the girl would agree to go somewhere a little more quiet.

"Could you help me talk to him?"

The girl cast a quick look over her shoulder, and now there was a wary expression on her face. She was having second thoughts, and when a young man in a black T-shirt suddenly crossed Helgolandsgade and headed their way, she started visibly.

"When we talk, we don't make any money."

Her eyes were still on the black T-shirt man, who had increased his pace and was clearly homing in on Nina and the girls. The girl with the ponytail stepped back and deliberately turned away from Nina.

"Tomorrow," she said softly, not looking Nina's way at all. "After I sleep. Twelve o'clock. Do you know the church?"

Nina shook her head. There had to be thousands of churches in Copenhagen, and she didn't know any of them.

T-shirt man had almost reached them. He wasn't much older than the ponytail girl, thought Nina. He wouldn't have looked out of place, she thought, as a carpenter's or plumber's apprentice. Not so tall, but muscular, with short fair hair and a tattooed black snake winding its way up his well-defined biceps.

The girl's lips were moving silently, as though she was practicing the name before she said it out loud.

"Sacred Heart," she finally said.

T-shirt man stopped. He seized the girl's upper arm in a no-nonsense grip, and jerked her along the sidewalk, not even glancing at Nina. A few paces further on, the sound of the first slap rang across the street. The ponytail leaped and fell as the girl's head snapped back. He hit her three times, all of them hard, flat blows. Then he let go of her.

Nina snatched the boy onto her arm and stalked off in the direction of Istedgade. Anger pounded through her body in a hot red pulse, but there was nothing she could do now. Not while she had the boy with her. Hell, she probably couldn't have done much even if she had been alone. The thought did not lessen her fury.

Just before she turned the corner, she looked down Helgo-landsgade again. The man was already gone, possibly lost somewhere in the shadow of a doorway or a service entrance. The ponytail girl was heading back towards the black motor scooter. She was hunched forward as she walked, her long gangling arms wrapped around her upper body.

One of the other girls touched her shoulder briefly as she rejoined the group, and as Nina turned away, she could hear their high clear voices behind her, already laughing again in a flat, harsh, defiant way. They had another bet going, and the girl with the ponytail was laughing louder than any of them.

NINA CARRIED THE boy all the way back to the car. He was awake, but the small firm will that she had noticed when they were getting out of the car in Reventlowsgade had left him again. His legs dangled in a ragdoll fashion against her thighs and belly with every step she took. When she reached the car, he wouldn't even stand on his own while she unlocked the car. She covered the dark, sour-smelling stain on the backseat with the checkered blanket, and let the boy slide out of her grasp and onto the seat. Then she got into the back beside him and simply sat there, staring into the neon dark. She was exhausted. It was exactly 11:00, she noted. For some reason, it pleased her when she caught the hour on the hour; perhaps it was the flat precision of the double zeros.

Traffic up on Tietgensgade had become more scattered. In the old Vesterbro apartment buildings on the other side of the street, she could see into the still-lit kitchens. On the ground floor, a young man was making coffee in a bistro coffeepot, calling back his half of a conversation to someone behind him. He put the coffeepot on a tray with a collection of cups and turned away from the window with a smile on his face. Nina couldn't help wondering if the lives of other people were really as simple as they looked. As simple, and as happy.

Probably not, she thought drily. It was a distortion of a kind she was an expert at providing for herself, or so her therapist had informed her. She was always busy telling herself that she was the only one who didn't fit in, while everyone else was one big happy community. And she was also an expert at making herself believe that she was the only one who could save the world and put things right, while others were too busy buying flat-screen televisions and redecorating their kitchens and making bistro coffee and being happy. It was this distorted view that had sent her on several panicked flights from Morten and Ida, back before Anton was born, and for some years now, she had actually believed Olav when he told her that she was mistaken, and that such distortions were bad for her and the people around her.

Now, with the boy next to her, it didn't seem so easy and clear-cut.

Nina leaned her head back against the upholstery and felt her own tiredness beating against the inside of her eyelids.

She wished she could call Morten. Not to talk to him, because that would do no good. But just so that she could hear his voice, and the television news in the background, and remind herself that there was a normal world out there. She touched her pocket where the mobile ought to be, and was no longer.

She locked the doors and turned on the car radio. There might be something on the news about a missing child. Something that proved that the boy existed, that someone was looking for him. She got the bread out of its bag and offered a slice to the boy. He accepted it and took a careful bite, without looking at her. They sat like that, silently eating, the boy with his eyes lowered in quiet reserve, she with her hand cradling the back of his pale, downy neck. When he had finished, he curled up next to her, and Nina carefully folded one end of the blanket over him like a duvet. She let herself slide a little lower, drawing up her knees until they rested against the seat in front of her, and closed her eyes again. Instantly, a flickering wave of sleep threatened to sweep her away.

Sleep. God. She really had to, sometime soon. Tomorrow she could find a phone somewhere and call Morten. Perhaps his voice would not be so cold and hostile, then. His mood was always better in the mornings, and she might even be able to tell him about the boy.

She forced her eyes open once more to look at the child. He had fallen asleep with his eyes still slightly open, a soft glitter of wariness beneath the lowered lids, but his breathing was soft and regular, his lips slightly parted. Like Anton's, when he lay with his head resting limply against the Spiderman web of his pillow.

Nina's own eyes closed.

FINALLY, PEACE REIGNED in the flat. Anton had refused to go to sleep, and had sulked and peeved until nine o'clock so that Morten had missed the news, and Ida had played her music defiantly loud instead of using her headphones the way the house rules dictated. He hadn't had the energy to call her on it. Apparently, she was now done with that particular outburst of teenage rebellion, and the weird, irregular clop-clop pata-pow sounds from her computer game were muffled enough that he could ignore them.

He had opened both the kitchen and the living room windows in the vain hope of catching a breeze, but the air seemed to have congealed, and the long day still stuck to him like the damp back of his shirt. He considered taking a shower, but this was the first time since he had picked Anton up from daycare that he had been able to sit down quietly with a cup of coffee and the newspaper. He would save the shower for later; it might make it easier to fall asleep.

There were days. There were days when he just wanted to pack all this in a time capsule and come back and open it in, say, four years' time. Imagine being able to *do* something; God, how he longed to go prospecting for minerals in the tundra, or go to Greenland again, or Svalbard, and return only when he had had his fill of mosquitoes and polar bears, and quite ready to take up family life exactly as it was, with all the pieces in the same positions on the board. Or nearly the same—there were one or two moves he would like to rethink.

It wasn't that he didn't want all of this, the children and the flat and the mortgages and the securely salaried job he had. He just wished he could have the other things as well. Once he had imagined that he would be able to do both—go to Greenland for three months, perhaps, while Nina held down the fort at home. But that was before she had run away the first time. Running away was exactly what it was, he had never had any doubts about that. And it had happened just as abruptly as if she had simply left him for good. He would never forget that day. It remained under his skin like a poison capsule, and every once in a while, something would prick a hole in it so some of the poison leaked out.

It had happened five months after Ida was born. They lived in Aarhus then, in an uninspiring but cheap two-bedroom flat near Ringgaden. Nina had just graduated from nursing school, and he was doing a Ph.D. at the Department of Geology. Coming home from the department one day, he had heard Ida crying—no, *screaming*—the minute he came into the stairwell. He took the terazzo steps three at a time and practically took the door off its hinges. Ida was strapped into her baby chair on the kitchen table, her chubby face swollen and scarlet from prolonged sobbing. She had no clothes on, not even a diaper, and the pale green plastic kiddy tub on the kitchen floor was still full of bathwater. Nina was standing with her whole body pushed up against the door to the back stairs, looking as if something had her cornered. With one look at her he understood talking to her in that state would do no good;

expecting any kind of answers or assistance or action from her was futile. He had no idea how long she had been standing like that. Long enough for Ida to have wet herself and the baby chair rather thoroughly, certainly.

The day after, she had called him from a phone booth in Copen-hagen Airport. She was on her way to London, and from there to Liberia, as a volunteer nurse for an organization called MercyMedic. This was not a position she had obtained with just a day's notice, of course. But although the decision had been some time coming, and the preparations had to have been made at least some weeks in advance, she hadn't bothered to discuss it with him, or even tell him about it. Now that he thought about it, it had actually been Karin who helped her, back then. Some French surgeon she was acquainted with had been willing to overlook Nina's lack of job experience. And Morten was left alone with a five-month-old little girl.

Only much later had she succeeded in explaining herself to him, at least to some extent. He had noticed that she was finding it harder and harder to sleep, that she was constantly watching Ida, day and night, that she seemed to be afraid of disasters, real or imagined. He had tried to calm her fears, but facts and rationality didn't seem to have much effect on her conviction that something horrible could happen to the child.

"I was bathing her," she had told him, not that day, but nearly a year later. "I was bathing her, and suddenly the water turned red. I knew it wasn't, not really. But every time I looked at her, the water was red all the same." Only the severest form of self-control had made it possible for her to lift Ida from the bathtub and strap her safely into the chair. And the fact that she had not actually fled from the flat but had waited there until he came home . . . he knew now that that had been a miracle of impulse control.

He had spoken occasionally to colleagues of hers who had been stationed with her at various global hotspots. They admired her. They said she was nearly inhumanly cool and competent in the middle of the most horrible crises. When rivers washed away bridges, when a light grenade set fire to the infirmary tents, when patients arrived with arms or legs blown away by landmine explosions . . . then Nina was the one who could always be counted on. She led a remarkably efficient one-woman crusade to save the world. It was only her own family who could reduce her to abject helplessness.

Ida was standing in the doorway before he realized that the pata- pow sounds from her room had died away.

"Is she coming home?" she asked. She was wearing neon-green shorts and a black T-shirt that read *I'm only wearing black until they make something darker*. A small silver sphere in one nostril represented his latest defeat in the teenage wars.

She never says "Mom" anymore, he suddenly thought. It was either "she" or sometimes "Nina."

"Of course she is," he said. "But she may have to work through the night." He was aware that the last statement was a fairly transparent piece of arse-covering, but he wasn't quite sure whose arse. Was it out of some remnant of loyalty to Nina, or was it just that he didn't like to sound clueless?

"Oh."

Ida withdrew, showing neither relief nor disapproval.

"Bedtime," he called after her.

"Yeah, yeah," she drawled, managing to suggest that she *might* be going to bed now, but only because she felt like it.

He put down the paper and stared into space, unable to focus his mind on the words. Nina had lied to him. He had heard it clearly in the pauses, in the way she was distancing herself from what she said. That, more than the fact that she had entirely forgotten about Anton, had been what got to him. But he hadn't had the energy to confront her, just as he hadn't had the energy to fight Ida over the headphones issue. Lately, he had been in danger of running out of energy altogether.

Things *were* better. Or so he had thought. No, they really were. Olav had helped her. Helped both of them, in fact. During an otherwise fairly routine debriefing after things had become a little rough in Tbilisi, the Norwegian therapist had somehow made Nina realize that she needed help. Not so much because of Tbilisi, Dadaab, or Zambia, but because of the obsessions that drove her to *be* in Tbilisi, Dadaab, or Zambia.

Nina had come home. Her hair almost shaved to the skull, her body reminiscent of a stick insect's, but with a new . . . well, serenity was perhaps not quite the word. Balance, maybe. A cautiously maintained equilibrium that made him believe they might after all be capable of staying together, of loving each other again. They had moved to Copenhagen. A new beginning. She had begun working for the Red Cross Center at the Coal-House Camp, he had become a "mud logger," as other geologists somewhat condescendingly described his job—collecting and analyzing bore samples from the North Sea oil rigs and other none-too-exotic locations. They both agreed that family was now the priority, if the torn ligaments that bound them together were to have a chance of healing.

Well. He was still here. She was still here. Except that she had lied to him this afternoon. And he didn't know, he couldn't be sure, that he would not get a phone call tomorrow or the next day from Zimbabwe or Sierra Leone or some place equally distant and dangerous.

God damn you, Nina. He set down his mug and got up with an unfocused sense of urgency. He wanted to get away from here. Out of the flat. Just for a few hours. Or a few years. If only everything would still be here when he returned.

A LITTLE AFTER four in the morning, the door buzzer woke him. It wasn't Nina who had lost her key, as he had half expected. It was the police. One in uniform, one in a suit.

"We would like to talk to Nina Borg," said the suit, presenting his ID with a motion that had become habit many, many years ago.

Morten felt too much coffee turn into acid in his stomach.

"She's not here," he said. "She's staying with a friend. Is anything wrong?"

"May we come in for a moment? I'm afraid this is a murder inquiry."

HE BARONAS LIVED in a small wooden house which stood like an island amidst an advancing tide of project developments. The bareness of the grounds between the new apartment buildings made their modest garden seem like a veritable jungle. A small red bicycle was padlocked to the fence with heavy duty chains.

Sigita opened the gate and approached the house. A smell of frying onions greeted her; Julija Baronienė was cooking supper, it appeared. Sigita pressed the bell button on the peeling blue doorframe. Almost at once, a boy of twelve or thirteen answered. He was wearing a white shirt and a tie and looked somehow unnaturally clean and well-groomed.

"Good evening," said Sigita. "May I speak to your mother?"

"Who may I say is calling?" he said cautiously. It sounded as if he had orders not to let just anybody in.

"Tell her it is Mrs. Mažekienė from the school board," said Sigita, so that the door would not be slammed in her face with the same precipitous speed that had severed the telephone connection.

The boy stood still for a long moment, and Sigita suddenly realized that he was trying to weigh all the possibilities that this might somehow be to do with him. She smiled reassuringly.

"Er, come on in," he said. "Mama is making supper, but she'll be right with you."

"Thank you."

He showed her into the living room and disappeared, presumably to report to the kitchen. Sigita stood in the middle of the room, taking in her surroundings. The sofa was large, soft, and pale brown, clearly a recent purchase, but apart from that, everything had been here for a long time. The floor was dark from innumerable coats of shellack, and in front of the couch was an Afghan rug that glowed in strong red, white, and turquoise hues. Three of the walls had beautifully carved bookshelves from floor to ceiling, which by the style of the carpentry looked to be as old as the house itself. The shelves sagged from the weight of books and sheet music, and by the fourth wall, between the two tall windows, was an upright piano in shiny dark mahogany, with keys so old and worn they were slightly concave, the ivory yellow with age.

The door opened, and a small, compact woman entered, with a girl who must be her daughter physically hanging on to her in a manner that seemed too young for the seven or eight years she looked to be. A waft of kitchen smells entered with her, and when they shook hands, Sigita felt a cool dampness that somehow made her think that Mrs. Baronienė had been peeling potatoes.

"Julija Baronienė," she said. "And this, of course, is my Zita." Zita stared at her feet and showed no inclination to say hello to the stranger. Her hair was parted into braids, the immaculate partition showing like a straight white line against the darkness of her hair. "You'll have to excuse her," said her mother. "Zita is a little shy— and very much her mama's little girl."

She hasn't recognized me, thought Sigita. And why

should she? It's all such a long time ago. But Sigita knew at once, the moment she saw the copper hair and the warm, prune-colored eyes. This was *the* Julija.

"I suppose that is only natural," said Sigita. "Considering what's happened to her."

Julija Baronienė stiffened.

"Why do you say that?" she asked.

No point in beating about this particular bush, thought Sigita.

"I'm not from the school board," she said. "I've come to ask you how you got Zita back. You see—the same people have taken my little boy." Her voice broke on the last few syllables.

With a small mewling sound that made Sigita think of drowning kittens, Zita turned completely into her mother's embrace and hid her face against her belly.

For a moment, Julija Baronienė looked as if Sigita had jabbed a knife into her body. Then she made an obvious effort and forced a smile.

"Oh, that silly story," she said. "No, no, that was all a big misunderstanding. It turned out Zita had been picked up by the mother of one of her friends, right, Zita?" Zita did not reply, nor did she let go of her mother. Her anxiety made her seem far younger than she was.

"It was awfully embarrassing to have wasted police time like that. But . . . but of course I'm sorry for you and your little boy. Are you sure it's not a misunderstanding too? He could be with a friend. Or perhaps he may have wandered off somehow?"

"He's only three. And my neighbor saw them take him. Besides . . ." She hesitated, then ploughed on.

"There *has* to be a connection. Don't you remember me at all?"

Julija's gaze fluttered around the room before it finally came to rest on Sigita. This time, Sigita saw recognition flare in the prune-colored eyes.

"Oh," was all she said.

Sigita nodded. "Yes," she said. "I'm sorry I lied to you. But after you cut me off on the phone I was afraid you wouldn't even talk to me if you knew . . . if you knew who I was."

Julija Baronienė stood perfectly still, as if the revelation had completely robbed her of the ability to speak or move. In the background, Sigita heard the sound of a door slamming, and voices talking, but she kept her eyes squarely on Julija.

"Just tell me what you had to do," she said. "I won't tell the police, I promise. I just want my Mikas back."

Julija Baronienė still said nothing. The door to the sitting room opened.

"Hello," said the man entering. "Aleksas Baronas. Marius tells me you are with the school board?" He held out his hand politely. He was somewhat older than Julija, a kind, balding man in a grayish-brown suit that hung a little loosely on his frame. It took a moment before he realized something was wrong.

"What is it?" he asked abruptly, when he noticed how fiercely Zita clung to her mother.

Julija apparently had no idea how to answer him. It was Sigita who had to explain.

"My little son has been abducted by the same people who took Zita," she said. "I just want to know what I should do to get him back."

He recovered more quickly than his wife.

"Such stupid nonsense," he said. "Can't you see you're scaring the child? Zita has never been abducted, and she won't be, ever. Isn't that right, sweetheart? Give Papa a kiss. Julija, I'm sorry to rush you, but we need to have dinner now, or we'll be late for Marius's concert."

Zita was persuaded to release her leechlike grip on Julija. Her father caught her up and held her on his left arm, and she threw her arms around his neck.

"I don't wish to be rude," he said. "But my son is playing in a concert tonight, and it's quite important to us."

Sigita shook her head in disbelief.

"How can you . . . how can you pretend like this? How can you refuse to help me? When you know what it's like?" She pressed her hand against her lower face as if that might hold back the sobs, but it was no good.

The man's friendly manner was showing cracks.

"I must ask you to leave," he said. "Now."

Sigita shook her head once more. Tears were streaming down her face, and there was nothing she could do to hinder them. Her throat felt thick and tender. She tore a ballpoint pen from her handbag and seized a random sheet of music from the piano. Ignoring Baronas's involuntary squawk of protest, she wrote her name, address, and phone number in large jagged letters across the page.

"Here," she said. "I beg you. You have to help me."

Now it was Julija Baronienė's turn to cry. With a half-choked sob she turned and fled the room. Zita wriggled free of her father's embrace to follow, but he stopped her.

"Not now, sweetheart. Mama is busy."

Zita looked up at her father. Then she suddenly turned

and walked with swift steps to the piano seat. She sat, back completely straight, eyes closed. Then she began to play the scales, slowly, methodically, with metronomical precision. Up and down. Da-da-da-da-da-da-da-dah, di-da-di-da-di-da-di-dah. Da-da-da-da-da-da-da-dah . . .

A look of pain flashed across Baronas's face. Then he, too, went to the piano, and gently stopped the jabbing fingers by grasping the girl's wrist. He looked at Sigita.

"Otherwise she goes on for hours," he said, looking completely lost. They had smashed up his family, thought Sigita, smashed it and broken it, and he had no idea how to put it back together.

She looked down at Zita's hands, still resting on the worn ebony, as if she would go on playing the instant he released her. Sigita shuddered, and in her mind, the unbearable picture show came back, Mikas in a basement, Mikas alone in the dark, Mikas surrounded by threatening figures who wanted to harm him.

"Please," said Zita's father. "Please go. Can't you see we could not help you even if we wanted to?"

ALL THE WAY home Sigita thought about Zita's hands. Eight-year-old fingers, bent like claws against the yellowed piano keys. All except for the little finger of her left hand, which wasn't bent like the others, but stuck out from the rest. On that finger, Zita had lost the entire nail.

JAN HAD BEEN prepared for steel tables and striplit ceilings, cold, white tiles or possibly even refrigerated drawers. But the lights in the chapel of the Institute of Forensic Medicine were soft and unglaring, and the still body lay on a simple bier, covered by a white cotton sheet, with a pair of candles lending an unexpected note of grace.

"Thank you for coming," said the officer who had led him in. Jan had already forgotten her name. "Her parents live in Jutland, so it's good to have a preliminary identification before we ask them to make the journey."

"Of course," said Jan. "It's the least I can do."

He felt acid burn at the back of his throat even before they lowered the sheet to show him her face.

She was a thing. That was what caught him most off guard—the degree to which humanity had vanished along with her life. Her skin was wax-like and unliving, and it was in no way possible to imagine that she was merely sleeping.

"It's Karin," he said, though it felt like a lie. This was not Karin anymore.

The shock went far beyond anything he had imagined. He felt like one of those cartoon characters hanging in the air above the abyss, foundations shot to hell, kept up only by the lack of the proper realization: that it was time to fall.

"How well did you know Karin Kongsted?" asked the woman officer, covering Karin's face once more.

"She had become a good friend," he said. "For the past two years, just about, she had a flat above our garage, and although it is completely separate from the rest of the house, still . . . it's different from the way it would have been if she had been merely a nine-to-five employee."

"I undertstand you hired her as a private nurse. How come you need someone like that?"

"I had to undergo renal surgery a little over two years ago. That was how we met Karin. And since then . . . well, we came to appreciate both her professional and her personal qualities. It was a major operation, and there are still medical issues. Complications sometimes arise. It's been very reassuring to have her nearby. She is . . . she was a very competent person."

It felt completely absurd to stand here next to Karin's dead body and talk about her like this. But the woman wasn't letting him off the hook just yet.

"I hope you understand that I have to ask you where you were tonight? You weren't at home when we called."

"No, I was home only briefly, then I had to go to the office. The company I run is not a small one."

"So we understand."

"I was probably at the office until seven. Then I went to a flat we keep—the company, that is—and worked from there for a little while. I had intended to spend the night there."

"Where is this flat?"

"In Laksegade."

"Can we call on you there later? It will be necessary to hold a formal interview."

He thought quickly. The Nokia was still in his brief-case. And the briefcase was still in Laksegade.

"I probably should go home to my wife," he said. "She must be very distraught. If you like, I can come to the local station tomorrow. Perhaps tomorrow morning?" Show cooperation, he counseled himself. It might be important later.

"We would appreciate that," she said politely. "Although the case is now being handled by the homicide depart-ment of the North-Zealand Regional Police." From her own briefcase, she drew a small leaflet with the stirring title "Regional Police Reform: This Is Where to Find Us." She circled an address in ballpoint pen. "Can you come to this office tomorrow at 11 A.M.?"

HE WONDERED IF they were watching him. The taxi slid through the midnight traffic like a shark through a her-ring shoal, and he couldn't tell whether any specific car stayed behind them.

Don't be paranoid, he told himself. They could barely have established cause of death yet, and they surely hadn't the manpower to follow everyone con-nected to Karin. Yet he couldn't help glancing around as he alighted on the sidewalk outside the Laksegade flat. The taxi drove off, leaving the street empty and deserted. There was a certain time-bubble quality to the place—the cobbled stones, the square-lantern-shaped streetlights, even the fortress-like headquarters of the Danske Bank, which from this angle looked more like a medieval stronghold than a modern corporation domicile.

He let himself in and snatched up the briefcase. There had been no calls to the Nokia while he'd been gone.

Twenty minutes later, he had fetched the car and was on his way home. Now he felt reasonably certain that he wasn't being followed—the motorway was sparsely trafficked at this hour, and when he turned off at a picnic area between Roskilde and Holbæk, his Audi was the only car in the parking lot.

He got out the Nokia and made the call. It was a long wait before the Lithuanian answered.

"Yes?"

"Our agreement is terminated," said Jan, as calmly as he was able.

"No," said the man. Just that: the bare negative.

"You heard me!"

"The money was not there," said the Lithuanian. "She said she gave it back to you."

"Don't lie to me," said Jan. "She took it." He had seen the empty case in her bedroom. Empty, that is, except for that nasty little note: I QUIT. "She took it, and now she is dead. Did you kill her?"

"No."

Jan didn't believe him.

"Stay away from me and my family," he said. "I don't want anything more to do with you. It's over."

A brief pause.

"Not until you pay," said the Lithuanian, and then hung up.

Jan stood for a moment, trying to breathe normally. Then he banged the phone against the pavement a couple of times until he was confident it was thoroughly broken. He went into the foul-smelling bathroom, picked the SIM card from the wreckage of the phone, and flushed it down one of the toilets. He then wiped the phone itself thoroughly with wet paper towels and dumped it into the large garbage bin outside, stirring the contents with a twig until the phone had sunk from sight into the malodorous mix of apple cores, pizza cartons, ashtray contents and other road-trip debris.

What else?

He had to. He absolutely had to.

First the little plastic box. No more than two by two centimeters square, and a few millimeters thick. No larger, really, than the SIM card, but the few drops of blood trapped within contained coded information a thousand times more complex than the electronic DNA of the mobile phone. He ground it beneath his heel and dropped the remains into the garbage bin.

Then the photo. He took it from his wallet and looked at it one last time. Tried to come to terms with losing it, and everything it meant. Clicked his Ronson and let the tiny flame catch one corner and flare, before he let that, too, vanish into the bin, still smouldering.

He got back into the Audi and waited for his hands to stop shaking, at least enough so that it would be safe to drive on.

SIGITA'S MOBILE GAVE a muffled ring inside her purse the minute she opened her own front door. The sound went through her like a shockwave, and she emptied the purse onto the coffee table. Anything less drastic just wouldn't let her get to it quickly enough.

"Yes?"

But it wasn't Julija Baronienė, a change of heart. Nor was it an unfamiliar voice telling her what she should do to get Mikas back.

"LTV may be willing to broadcast a Missing Person alert on Mikas," said Evaldas Gužas. "Particularly if you will come to the studio and make a direct appeal to the kidnappers."

Sigita stood stock still. A few hours ago, she would have agreed without hesitation. But now . . . she thought of Julija Baronienė and her family, of their obvious fear. And of Zita, one nail missing.

"Wouldn't that be dangerous for Mikas?" she asked.

She sensed his deliberation and almost thought she heard the clicking of his ballpoint pen accenting his thoughts.

"Have you heard from his abductors?"

"No."

"This means that more than forty-eight hours have gone by without a single attempt at contact," said Gužas. "Is this not so?"

"Yes."

"This is most unusual. Instructions usually arrive

promptly, to prevent the parents from calling the police."

"Julija Baronienė did call."

"Yes. Within hours of the girl's disappearance. But less than twenty-four hours later, she withdrew her allegations."

"And you think this was because she had been threatened."

"Yes."

"But that means it *is* dangerous."

"It's a question of weighing the options," he said. "We have reported Mikas missing and sent out the description of his presumed kidnappers to every police station in Lithuania. We've contacted the police in Germany, where the boy's father now lives. We have even approached Interpol, although there is no indication that Mikas has left Lithuania; on the contrary, the link to Mrs. Baronienė's case gives us reason to believe that it is a local crime. All of this to no avail. We are no closer to locating your son, or his abductors. And this is why I'm considering asking the public for help."

The public. The mere word sent tremors of unease through Sigita's body.

"I'm really not sure . . ."

"LTV would broadcast your appeal in connection with their late- night news show. We know that this usually causes a great many people to call in, and some of these calls have been helpful in the past. As we are able to show a photo of one of the presumed kidnappers this time, we are very hopeful that it will be beneficial to the investigation at this point."

He always talks as if he has swallowed one of his own reports, thought Sigita. I wonder what he sounds like when he is off duty? She was temporarily distracted by a mental image of Gužas up to his waist in cold water, dressed as the complete angler and sporting a newly caught fish. "The direction of the current gave reason to suspect that trout might be active in the upper left quadrant of the search area," commented off-duty Gužas in her head.

I'm very, very tired, Sigita told herself. Or else it's the concussion. It was as if the imagination she normally kept effortlessly locked down was suddenly bubbling up from the nether reaches of her mind like marsh gas. It made her uncomfortable.

"We have asked your husband, and he has agreed that the broadcast should be made. But we would really like for you to make that direct appeal in front of the cameras. In our experience, this has an effect even on people who would not normally contact the police. Especially when children are involved."

She rubbed her whole face with her good hand. She was exhausted. Too little to eat and drink all day, she thought. Her headache had become so constant she was almost getting used to it.

"I don't know . . . Will it really help?"

"I wouldn't suggest this to you if there had been any communication from the abductors. Any opening for negotation or coercion. In those circumstances, public uproar might serve only to increase the pressure on the kidnappers and might endanger the life of the child. But there has been no such communication. Is that not so?"

He is testing me, thought Sigita. He still doesn't believe me.

"No," she said. "But if it's dangerous for Mikas, I won't do it."

"It's a question of weighing the options," he repeated. "I am not saying it is completely without risk, but in our estimation, it is our best chance of finding Mikas right now."

Sigita could hear her own pulse. How could one decide something so vital when it felt as if one's head belonged to someone else?

"We can of course make the broadcast without your consent," he finally said, when the silence had gone on for too long.

Was that a threat? Suddenly, anger roared through her.

"No," she said. "I won't do it. And if you go ahead without me, I'll . . ." But there was no way to finish. What threats could she make? He had all the weapons.

She sensed a sigh somewhere at the other end of the connection.

"Mrs. Ramoškienė, I am not the enemy," he said.

Anger left her as suddenly as it had arrived.

"No," she said. "I know that."

But once she had disconnected, she couldn't help but wonder. What was more important to an ambitious young officer like Gužas? Arresting the criminals, or saving the victims?

Her blouse was sticking to her back, and she decided to wrap a plastic bag around the cast and attempt a shower. She had to squirt the shampoo onto her scalp directly from the bottle, instead of measuring a suitable dollop into her palm, and it was equally impossible to wrap the towel around her head in the usual turban-style afterwards. When it was time for the late news, she turned on the television with a fresh attack of nerves. Despite Gužas's words there was no dramatic report on three-year-old Mikas Ramoska, missing since Saturday. And then of course all her doubts came rushing back. Should she have done it? Was there someone out there who had seen her little boy? Someone who might help?

When the phone rang, she snatched at it with such clumsy haste that it clattered to the floor. She retrieved it with another snatch and pressed "Accept Call" even though she didn't recognize the number.

"Hello?"

"It's me."

"Er . . . who?"

"Tomas."

She nearly said "Who?" once more before she realized that the caller was her little brother. She had never heard his grown-up voice, only the first hoarse cracks of puberty. He had been twelve when she fled from Tauragė and they had not spoken since.

"Tomas!"

"Yes."

A pause. Sigita had no idea what to say. What does one say to a brother one hasn't talked to in eight years?

"We heard from Darius's mother that Mikas is . . . that he has disappeared," Tomas eventually said.

"Yes." Her throat tightened, and only that one word escaped.

"I'm sorry," he said. "And . . . er . . . I was just thinking. If there's anything I can do . . . ?"

An unexpected wave of tenderness washed through her. It stole what little strength she had in her arms and legs, so that she slumped down onto the couch with the phone in her lap, while tears burned their way down the side of her nose yet again. Normally, she never cried. Today, she had long since lost count.

"Sigita?"

"Yes," she managed. "Thank you. Thank you so much. I am so glad you called."

"Er, you're welcome. I hope they find him."

She couldn't say another word, and maybe he realized. There was a soft click as he hung up. But he had called. She had only ever had sporadic news from home, and since she and Darius had separated, her most reliable source of Tauragė information had dried to a trickle. And right now there were a thousand things she wanted to know. What Tomas had been doing since leaving school. If he was still living at home. If he had a girlfriend. How he was.

If he had ever forgiven her.

But perhaps he had. He did call her, after all.

SIGITA WENT TO bed, but sleep was a hopeless enterprise. The hideous sense of imagination she had suddenly developed kept tossing images up inside her eyelids, and she didn't know how to turn it off.

If you hurt my boy, she thought, I will kill you.

It was not an outburst of anger, as when two drunks yell at each other—"I'll fucking kill you!" or the like. It was not like that.

It was a decision.

Somehow, it made her calmer. She could almost believe that the kidnappers would be able to sense her decision and realize what the price of harming Mikas would be. Just because she had determined that it should be so. This was of course hopeless nonsense, as the rational part of her well knew. Nonetheless, it helped: *If you hurt him, I will kill you.*

In the end, she went out on the balcony and sat in the white plastic chair she kept there. The heat absorbed by the concrete during the day was being released now that the air was cooler, and there was no need to put anything on over her night dress. She thought of Julija Baronienė, who had her child back. She thought of Gužas, and of Valionis. Had they gone home, or were they still at work? Was Mikas important enough? Or were there so many missing children that no one would work twenty-four-hour shifts just because another one had disappeared?

They wanted me to go on television, she thought. That must mean that he is important. She remembered the little English girl who had disappeared, but couldn't recall her name. It had been all over the news for months, and even the Pope had become involved. And still the girl had not been found.

But Mikas will come back, she told herself firmly. If I believe anything else, I won't be able to stand it.

A taxi drew up in the parking lot in front of the building. Sigita automatically looked at her watch. It was past 2 A.M.—an unusual time to arrive. A woman got out and glanced around uncertainly. Clearly a visitor, trying to get her bearings. Then she headed for Sigita's block.

It's her, thought Sigita suddenly. It's Julija!

She leapt to her feet so quickly that she stubbed her toe on the doorframe. It hurt, but that was irrelevant. She hopped to the intercom and pressed the lock button the moment the buzzer sounded. She limped out into the stairwell and followed Julija Baronienė with her eyes, all the way up.

Julija stopped when she caught sight of Sigita.

"I had to come," she said. "Aleksas wouldn't hear of it, and I had to wait until he was asleep. But I had to come."

"Come inside," said Sigita.

HOW PECULIAR THAT one still says things like "Have a seat" and "Would you like some coffee?" even when life and death and heart's blood is at stake, thought Sigita.

"May I call you Sigita?" asked Julija, twisting the coffee cup nervously in her hands. "I still think of you like that, even though you are a grown woman now."

"Yes," said Sigita. She had seated herself in the armchair, or rather, on the edge of it. Her right hand was clenched so hard that the nails bit into her palm, but she knew somehow that trying to rush the woman on the couch would be a bad idea. She suddenly remembered Grandfather's carrier pigeons. How they sometimes landed on the roof of the coop and wouldn't come all the way in, so that their recorded flight time would be minutes slower than it might have been.

"No use trying to hurry things," her grandfather would say. "Sit on the bench beside me, Sigita, they'll come when they come."

Grandfather had died in 1991, in the year of the Independence. Granny Julija didn't care about the races. She sold the best pigeons to a neighbor and left the rest to their own devices until the roof blew off the coop during a winter storm five or six years later.

Sigita looked at Julija and forced herself to sit quietly, waiting.

"You mustn't tell the police," said Julija in the end. "Do you promise?"

Sigita promised. It still didn't seem to be enough.

"He was so angry because we had called them. He said he had had to hurt Zita because we told, and that it was all our fault." The hand that held the cup was trembling.

"I won't say anything," said Sigita.

"Promise."

"Yes. I promise."

Julija stared at her unremittingly. Then she suddenly put the coffee cup down. She raised her hands to the back of her neck and bent her head so that she could take off a necklace she was wearing. No. Not just a necklace. It was a crucifix, thought Sigita. A small golden Jesus on a black wooden cross; despite the miniscule size, the pain in the tiny face was evident.

"Do you believe in God?" asked Julija.

"Yes," said Sigita, because this was not the time to mince the nuances of faith and doubt.

"Then swear on this. Touch it. And promise that you won't go to the police with anything I tell you."

Sigita carefully put her hand on the crucifix and repeated her promise. She wasn't sure that this meant more to her than the assurances she had already given, but it seemed to ease Julija's mind.

"He gave us an envelope. So that we could see what we had made him do, he said. Inside was one of her nails. An entire nail. I knew it was hers, because I had let her play with my nail polish the day before." Julija's voice shook. "He said that if we went to the police later on, he would take Zita again, and this time he would sell her to some men he knew. Men of the kind who enjoy having sex with little girls, he said."

Sigita swallowed.

"But Julija," she said. "If he is in prison, he can't take Zita."

Julija shook her head wildly.

"Do you think I can risk that? People don't stay in jail forever. And besides, I know for a fact that he is not alone."

Sigita thought it a miracle that Julija had come at all.

"I didn't know he would do that," whispered Julija, almost as if she could hear Sigita's unspoken words. "I didn't know he would take your child."

"But you got Zita back," said Sigita. "How did you do that?"

Julija was silent for so long that Sigita grew afraid she wouldn't answer.

"I gave him you," she whispered, in the end. "He wanted to know your name, and I told him."

Sigita stared at Julija in utter bafflement.

"He wanted to know my *name* . . . ?"

"Yes. You see, we never register the girls. At the clinic, I mean. Their names aren't recorded anywhere, because the parents—that is, the new parents—all get a birth certificate that makes it appear that the child is their own."

A deep pain burned somewhere in Sigita's abdomen. I was right, she thought blindly. This is God's punishment. This is all my fault because I sold my firstborn child. There was a kind of black logic to it that had nothing to do with reason and the light of day.

"But why . . . what did he want with me?"

Julija shook her head. "It's not really him. He is just the one who actually does things. It has to be the other one. The Dane."

"What do you mean?"

"He came to the clinic some months ago. He wanted to know who you were, and he was willing to pay a fortune to find out, but Mrs. Jurkiene couldn't tell him because nothing was written down. But he recognized me because I had been the one to hand over the baby, back then. Yours, that is. And he asked me if I didn't remember something, anything, about who you were and where you came from. And of course I did remember, because you nearly died, and I looked after you for so many days. But I told him I didn't."

Julija was crying as she spoke, in a strange noiseless fashion, as if her eyes were merely watering.

"He didn't want to believe me, and he kept offering me all this money if only I would tell him something. And all the while the other man stood there in the background with his arms across his chest, and it was so obvious that he was there to look after the Dane and all his money. You know, like a bodyguard. I didn't understand why he wanted to find you after so many years. And in the end, he went away, and I thought that was the end of it. But it wasn't."

"The Dane." Sigita tried to bring her wildly straying thoughts into some sort of order. "Was he the one who . . ."

"Yes. He was the one who got your child. The first one, that is." Julija looked at her with bright, dark eyes. "We thought we were doing a good thing, you understand? For the girls, and for the babies. They were always rich people, because getting a child that way is very expensive. We thought they would be good to them and treat them like they were their own. Why else was it so important that no one should think they were adopted? And the women were always so very happy. They would cry and cry, and hug the babies tight. But with the Dane, it was just the man who picked up the baby, and I never saw the wife. I've thought about that afterwards."

"You said you *thought* they would be good to them . . . Don't you think so anymore?"

"Yes. In most cases, anyway. But I've given the clinic my notice. I don't want to work there anymore. It won't be easy, because the salary was good, and Aleksas is a schoolteacher and doesn't make very much. But I don't want to work there anymore."

"But I don't understand. Was it the Dane who took Zita?"

"Not directly. It was that bodyguard. I don't know his name. And it was more than a month later, when I had almost forgotten about the Dane. But the bodyguard didn't believe I couldn't remember about you. And he had Zita. So I told him your name was Sigita, but that wasn't enough. He wanted to know your last name, too, and where you lived. I didn't know anything about that. That was too bad for Zita, he said, because she really, really wanted to come home to her mama again. So in the end, I searched the files until I found it. The receipt for your money. It wasn't your name on it, it was your auntie's. But it must have been enough, because he let Zita come home."

Ass. herbs for the production of natural remedies: 14.426 litai.

Oh yes, Sigita remembered the receipt. But she couldn't make head or tails of the rest.

"If you do as they say," said Julija, "don't you think they'll let you have your little boy back? Like Zita?"

"But I don't know what they want me to do," wailed Sigita desperately. "They've told me nothing!"

"Maybe something has gone wrong," said Julija. "Maybe the bodyguard can't get hold of the Dane, or something."

Sigita just shook her head. "It still makes no sense." Then she suddenly raised her head. "You said you don't register the girls. But what about the people who get the babies—does it say anything about them?"

"Yes, of course. Otherwise we wouldn't be able to register the births."

"Good. Then get me his name."

"The Dane?"

"Yes. Julija, you owe me that. And his address, if you can."

Julija looked terrified. "I can't."

"Yes, you can. You did it to save Zita. Now you must help me save *my* son. Otherwise . . . " Sigita swallowed, not liking it at all. But this was for Mikas. "Otherwise, I may have to go to the police after all. Then *they* can come and search your files."

"You promised! You swore on the body of Christ!"

"Yes. And I really don't want to break that promise."

Julija sat there, frozen like a trapped animal. It hurt to look at her.

"I'll try tomorrow morning," she finally said, "before the secretary gets there. But what if I can't find it?"

"You can," said Sigita. "You have to."

THE PHONE RANG a little before nine the next morning.

"His name is Jan Marquart," said Julija. "And this is his address."

NINA WOKE BECAUSE someone was beating on the car window, a series of hard rythmic blows. She opened her eyes in time to see a stooping figure reel across the street and continue in the direction of the Central Station. Above Reventlowsgade's numerous streetlights the sky was brightening to pale gray.

The back of her neck was sore, and the ache called back a vague memory of struggling with the weight of her own head during the night. It had not been a good way to sleep, but even this lack of comfort had not been enough to keep her awake. Cautiously, she released her knees from their braced position against the back of the seat. Tendons and muscles protested sharply as she opened the door and stretched her legs onto the pavement.

The boy was still asleep. He had rolled over during the night and his outflung arms rested on the seat, palms upward. He had forgotten where he was, thought Nina with a degree of envy. Even in sleep that mercy had eluded her, and she felt no less tired than the night before.

She rose slowly and walked a few steps beside the car, trying to ease the pins and needles in her legs. It was still more than six hours before she could meet the girl from Helgolandsgade, and in a little while, the sun would begin the process of turning Vesterbro into a diesel-stinking oven. She had to find some temporary refuge for herself and the boy, preferably somewhere that included the possibility of a shower. She could smell her own body—the sour odor of old sweat assaulted her nostrils every time she moved. She felt sticky and exhausted.

The boy stirred in the back seat, still half asleep, but surfacing slowly. He stretched, and then lay there for a long moment, eyes open and staring into the gray uphol-stery of the seat in front of him. Then he turned his head and looked at her. The smooth, soft look given to him by sleep vanished in an instant and was replaced by rec-ognition and disappointment. But there was a change. The sulky resignation was still there, but the hostility had gone. Perhaps there was even a hint of familiarity, a sense of belonging inspired by everything they had been through together the day before. Karin's empty gaze, the nauseating pool of congealing blood beneath her head. The chaotic escape from the cottage, the hookers in Hel-golandsgade, and the slices of untoasted white bread.

He knew whom to stick with right now. He just didn't know why.

Nina produced a faint smile. That was all she could manage. It was still only 5:43, and the thought of yet another long and lonely day with the boy on her hands seemed to leech her of all strength. Completely unsurmountable.

She might go home.

The idea felt heretical after yesterday's long flight, but the cold and stilted conversation with Morten seemed so distant now, floating only somewhere at the very back of her mind. Had he really been as angry as she thought? Maybe not. He might even be capable of understanding why she and the boy had had to disappear. If she could only find the right way to tell him. She might say that the story about Karin was only an excuse she had made up, that it had been the network that had called her, and that the boy would only be with them for a few days before being sent on to relatives in . . . in England, maybe. That might seem sufficiently safe and manageable even for Morten.

Morten didn't like that she worked with the illegal residents. In principle, he agreed that something must be done. He was unwavering in his opposition to the government's policy when it came to refugees and other immigrants, and when yet another story about grotesque deportations and broken families hit the news stream, he would be genuinely upset and outraged. The problem he had with the network and her commitment to it was purely personal. Morten didn't think it was good for her. He thought she was using it as a form of escape from herself and her own children, from what was supposed to be their family life. When he was in a good mood, he called her his little adrenalin junkie. When he was angry, he didn't say very much, but his antipathy to the network rose in direct ratio to the number of nights and evenings she spent away from their Østerbro flat.

Right now, there was nowhere else in the world she would rather be. God, how she wanted it. She wanted to sneak up the stairs with the boy in her arms, put on the kettle to make coffee. Leave the boy in front of the television, perhaps, while she herself slipped into their tiny bathroom and pulled the octopus-patterned shower curtain in front of the door. She would stand under the hot shower for a long luxurious moment with her own bottle of eco-friendly shampoo, without perfume and smelling only of simple cleanliness. Afterwards she might pad out into the kitchen on bare feet and set the table for breakfast with oatmeal, raisins, sugar, and milk. The children would have to leave for school, of course, and the boy might then sleep another few hours in Anton's bed before they had to head back to Vesterbro to find the girl from Helgolandsgade.

She would do it. Yes. She would go home. The relief was deep and physical, as if someone had quite literally lifted a weight off her shoulders. She raised her eyes to the mirror and gave the boy a genuine smile as she eased the car away from the curb and headed for Åboulevarden. Everything looked so different in the morning, even on such a morning as this. Morten would help her. Of course he would. Why had she ever doubted it?

MORTEN MADE COFFEE for the detective sergeant and for himself. The uniformed officer had declined, but accepted a cola instead.

His hands moved mechanically in a set of practiced routines that needed little guidance from his brain: fill kettle, click switch, rinse pot, open coffee can.

You don't know whether she is dead or alive, a cynical voice inside him whispered. And you're making coffee.

"Milk or sugar?"

"Milk, please."

He opened the refrigerator and looked vaguely at flat plastic packages of cured ham, mustard bottles, cucumbers, jars of pickled beets. Half past four in the morning. He could smell the bed-sweat on his own body and felt dysfunctional and unhygienic.

"She said that Karin was ill, or wasn't feeling very well, I don't quite recall her exact words. But she had to help her."

"And when was this?"

"Yesterday afternoon. A little past five. She was supposed to pick up Anton. Er, that's our youngest. She should have picked him up from daycare. But she had forgotten."

"Was that unusual?"

He shook his head vaguely, not exactly in denial; it was more a gesture of uncertainty.

"She used to be . . . a little absent sometimes. But not anymore. No. She . . . I think she was distracted, perhaps because she was worried about Karin. They were at nursing school together, and they used to be close. But it's been awhile. Since they saw each other last, I mean."

He put the bistro pot on the table. Then cups. Milk, in the little Stelton creamer that had been a present to them from his mother and father.

She could be dead. As dead as Karin.

"You haven't seen her at all?" he asked.

"No. A neighbor heard someone scream, and found the body."

"Scream? Karin?"

"We don't think so. We think she had already been dead some time by then. We don't know where the scream came from, but our witness was definite he had heard it. He didn't see anyone, but he heard a car drive off. We don't know what kind of car. We don't know whether it may have been your wife leaving the scene, or someone else. We still have searchers combing the area with dogs. That was how we found your wife's mobile."

Uncertainty was nothing new. He had suffered days and even weeks of it before, when the gaps between her calls had grown too long, and one heard disquieting things on the news. This was worse. More specific. Closer to home. He felt a strange brooding anger. This wasn't Darfur, dammit. It wasn't supposed to happen here, not now that she was home again.

The sergeant drank his coffee.

"How tall is your wife?" he asked.

"One meter sixty-nine," answered Morten automatically. And then froze with the cup halfway to his mouth because he didn't know whether this was something they needed to know in order to identify her, or her body.

Then he realized there might be a third purpose behind the question.

"You don't think that . . . that she . . . that she might have anything to do with the murder?"

"We are still waiting for the autopsy results. But it would seem that the blows were struck with overwhelming force. We tend to think that the assailant must have been male."

The reply did not provide any relief.

Suddenly, Anton was in the doorway. His hair was damp with sweat, and the too large Spiderman pajama top had slipped off one shoulder.

"Is Mummy home yet?" he asked, rubbing his face with the back of his hand.

"Not yet," said Morten.

Anton frowned, and it seemed that it was only now that he registered the presence of two strangers in the room. The uniform made his eyes pop still wider. His mouth opened, but he didn't say anything. Morten felt paralyzed, completely unable to come up with an explanation that would make sense in a seven-year-old's universe.

"Go on back to bed," he said, trying to sound casual and everyday normal. Anton gave a brief nod. The sound of his bare feet beat a rapid retreat along the corridor.

"Will you please ask your wife to contact us immediately if she comes back?" said the sergeant. "She is an important witness."

"Of course," said Morten with a growing feeling of complete helplessness.

If she comes back.

TRAFFIC ON JAGTVEJEN was warming up in the gray dawn, but the smaller streets around Fejøgade were still quiet and uncrowded. Perhaps that was why she saw the police car right away. With no blinking blue lights, it looked like a white taxi at first glance, but it was parked in an offhand, slanted manner, as if the driver could not be bothered to do a proper curbside parallel parking. Nina had time to think that this was the kind of sloppy parking Morten hated, and that he would be irritated if the car was still here when he came down to take the children to school. Then she realized that the bump on the car's roof were cop lights, not taxi lights. And that someone was up and about and had the lights on, up there in their third-floor flat.

Morten would not normally be up this early. He had flexible working hours when he wasn't out on the rigs, and even though he was alone with the kids today, as long as he had them up and ready for breakfast at 7:30, he would be fine. It was now 5:58. Much too early for normality.

Nina continued past her own front door at an even speed. It was of course possible that the cops had merely needed somewhere quiet to park while they enjoyed their morning coffee. But why, then, was Morten up? Were they looking for her? And was it because of Karin, or because of the boy?

She didn't want to believe it. The thought of having to give up her fantasy of a hot shower and a normal family breakfast caused a wave of exhaustion that dug into her already depleted reserves. She slipped the Fiat into an empty slot further up the street and sat there with her hands on the wheel and her foot on the clutch, trying to make up her mind.

There was a part of her that wanted it over and done with.

There would be no need for drama. She could hand over the boy to professional, caring adults in a quiet and orderly manner, without causing him undue anxiety. And if she really put her mind to it, she might even convince herself that she was doing the right thing. That the boy would be safe and cared for at some institution on Amager, and that the man from the railway station from now on would be a single bad memory in an otherwise happy and safe childhood. Immigraton had proper interpreters available to them, they didn't need to chase after Lithuanian hookers with ponytails and coltish legs. If the boy did have a good and loving mother somewhere, surely they would find her.

God only knew how she wanted to believe it. Every single day, she practiced her detachment skills, trying not to care about everything that was wrong with the world. Or rather . . . to care, but in a suitably civilized manner, with an admirable commitment that might still be set aside when she came home to Morten and her family, complete with well-reasoned and coherent opinions of the humanist persuasion. Right now she felt more like one of those manic women from the animal protection societies, with wild hair and even wilder eyes. Desperate. She had her good days, fortunately, but every time she dared to think that this serenity might be permanent, there would be a Natasha and a Rina, or a Zaide or a Li Hua, and her defenses would be blown to shreds, so that once more, reality grated on her naked skin like sandpaper.

Nina turned off the engine. She got out, closing the car door gently, and looked back at her own solid-seeming brown front door, and at the windows up there. She could make the choice. She could do like everyone else would do—take the boy gently by the hand, and go up there to meet the police, safe in the knowledge that she had done everything that could reasonably be expected from a responsible adult. Then she could come clean with Morten, telling him everything in one of those hot confessional rushes that would lead to a familiar, reassuring row about her priorities and his anxiety about her, and finally, finally, to tears and intimacy. Her hands on his face, sliding from his forehead to his cheekbones, then round to the back of his neck, damp under his short brown hair. Infinite relief.

All of that could be hers if only she would let herself believe what no one else seemed to have any trouble believing: that Denmark was a safe haven for the broken human lives that washed up on its shores.

Up there behind the windows, someone was moving, back and forth, jerkily, like a predator in an inadequate cage. Her conscience winced as she recognized Morten's tall, near-athletic form. Then another man appeared, shorter, rounder, gesturing slowly and soothingly.

A pro, thought Nina, feeling her antagonism increase. Morten was in the hands of one of those policemen who had attended courses in how best to talk to civilians under pressure.

He would be saying things like "We are doing everything possible, and we are very good at what we do" and

"We are highly trained professionals, and the best thing you can do for Nina now is to trust us."

He would be telling her much the same thing as he took the boy away from her. "We will do everything in our power to find out what has happened here."

Morten suddenly stepped up to the window, looking out. Inadvertently, she backed a couple of paces. Had he seen her? The last softness had gone from the dawn, and daylight exposed her fully to anyone who cared to see. But she was some distance away, and the Fiat was shielded by other cars. She stood still, conscious that movement attracted attention. But she couldn't make herself look away. Finally, he turned away from the window, and she dared move again. She leapt into the car, slammed the door, and hurriedly revved the engine. The Fiat practically leapt into the street, and then stalled. She had forgotten about the parking brake. Cursing, she got the engine started once more and engaged the clutch. Flight responses had taken over, coursing through her body, and turning back was no longer an option.

Had Morten seen her? And if he had, would he tell the police?

A sudden flashback washed through her tired mind. About a thousand years ago, when they had made love for the first time, he had raised her face to his and stared into her eyes, and there had been a startling moment of utter intimacy, utter trust. Now, she wasn't even sure he would let her drive off without setting the cops on her. She could only hope.

A glance at the mirror reassured her that at least the cop car was still unmanned, parked with its lights off by the curb. Then a clumsy gray SUV, complete with tacky roof box, pulled out behind her, blocking her view. Well, at least she was getting away for now, she thought, with the boy safely in the back seat. Then she felt a treacherous little hope that Morten had in fact seen her, but was letting her drive off on purpose. Had he perhaps even given her a discrete, acknowledging wave? Was he even now quietly rooting for her, hoping she would succeed in what she was doing? Trusting her this time, and willing to wait patiently until she returned to him and the flat, to Anton's crappy little drawings stuck to the refrigerator door, to the bathroom shelves that Ida had begun to fill with styling gels and cheap, glittery lipsticks. And when all this was over, the flat and everything it contained would be enough for her. It would. It had to be.

Nina turned onto Jagtvej just as the lights turned amber. Morning traffic was not yet closely packed in the two-lane part of the road, but behind her, she heard beeping horns and a squeal of brakes. The gray SUV behind her had followed her into the intersection much too late and was stuck untidily crosswise, fender to fender with a similar monster that was now blocking all traffic in the direction of Nørrebro.

Nina couldn't help feeling a certain unholy glee as she shifted easily into fourth gear and continued unhindered in her small and rather unremarkable vehicle. She hoped those two CO_2-offenders had a fun time exchanging insults and phone numbers and moaning about the dents in their ridiculously large fenders. A sort of cosmic justice, she thought—the bigger you get, the more you bump into things.

THE DRIVER OF the Landrover was yelling at Jučas and jabbing an aggressive forefinger at him. Jučas didn't understand a single word the idiot was saying, nor did he care. He held up both hands disarmingly, and only the acute awareness that there was a police car parked no more than two hundred meters away kept him from punching the guy's lights out instead. It wasn't even rage, just frustration. But God, it would have felt good to plant a fist in that self-righteous, arrogant face and feel the cartilage crunch.

He forced himself to smile.

"No damage," he said, pointing to the Landrover's intact front. "No damage to you. My car, not so good, but okay. Have nice day." Milky white shards from the Mitsubishi's headlights decorated the pavement, but nothing could be done about that now. What he needed was to get away, as quickly as possible, before the boy-bitch managed to disappear again. He ignored the continued protests of the Landrover-man, in English now, got back into the Mitsubishi, reversed, and managed to get free of the other vehicle.

" . . . driving like an idiot, what do you think the red lights are for, Christmas decorations?"

Jučas just waved, and drove off. Hadn't she turned right at the next intersection?

"Did you see where she went?" he asked Barbara.

It was some time before she answered.

"No," she said. Nothing else.

He threw a quick glance at her. She looked oddly distant, as if the whole thing was no longer any of her business. But perhaps the fender-bender had left her a little shocked.

"No harm done," he said. "It's just a broken headlight. I can fix it myself, if we can find a garage."

She didn't answer. Right now he had no time to coax and cajole and work out what was wrong with her. He signaled a right turn, but of course he had to wait interminably while about a hundred bicycles went past. What the hell was wrong with people in this city? Couldn't they afford cars? It seemed as if half the population insisted on teetering along on two wheels, endangering the traffic.

Next intersection. He hesitated, causing a chorus of horns behind him. He could see no Fiat. Decided on a left turn, and ended up in a one-way hell full of "enclosed areas" and fucking flower beds that apparently had to be placed in the middle of the street. Reversing aggressively, he tried to get back to the main street, but it was hopeless. Three or four one-way streets later, he had to realize that the battle was lost.

"Fucking hell!"

He hammered both hands against the steering wheel and braked abruptly. Sat there for a moment, fighting his temper.

"She had the boy with her," said Barbara suddenly.

"Did she?" Jučas glanced at her sharply. "Are you sure?"

"Yes. He was in the back seat. I could see his hair."

Right now, he would have preferred the money. But the kid was currency in his own way, and better than nothing.

"You said they were going to adopt him," said Barbara.

"What? Yes. So they are."

"Then what was he doing in that car? I thought his new parents were picking him up?"

"Yeah, so did I. But this Nina Borg person got in the way."

"And why was it that you took his clothes off?" she asked. "For the picture?"

He inhaled a mouthful of air and blew it slowly back out. Easy now.

"To make it harder for them to trace him," he said. "And stop this. You're only making it worse, asking so many questions."

He hated the way she was looking at him now. As if she didn't trust him anymore.

"Hell," he hissed. "I'm not one of those filthy perverts. And if you think that for a moment, then . . ."

"No, " she said, very quickly. "I don't think that."

"Good. 'Cause I'm not."

HE DROVE AROUND for a bit, on the off chance. But the Fiat stayed gone. Finally he went back and parked near her house again.

"Stay in the car," he told Barbara. "She'll be back. Call me when the cops leave, or if you see her and the boy."

"Where are you going?" she asked, looking at him once more, but this time in a different way. He smiled. It was okay. She still wanted him to look after her, and that was just what he planned on doing.

"I have a couple of things to do," he said. "It won't take long."

T WAS 7:07, and the public swimming pool in Helgasgade had been open for exactly seven minutes. Nina laid down the deposit for two towels at the ticket booth and continued up the wide brown stairs to the the women's changing rooms on the first floor.

They were almost alone among the many empty lockers, and the three women there were silent and introverted, folding their clothes with their backs to one another, guarding their privacy in a very public space. One was young, Nina noticed, the two others middle aged in the determinedly well-trained way. None of them looked at Nina and the boy, who stood beside her on the damp, smooth tiles, hunched and slightly shivering in the early morning chill.

Nina took the boy to the bathroom, and he peed obediently, with his pelvis thrust forward and his hands folded behind his neck. Anton had done the same thing, remembered Nina, because he could then claim that there was no need for him to wash his hands afterwards. Perhaps that was a brand of logic universal to little boys. Nina smiled at the thought.

When they returned to the changing rooms, the three women had all gone out into the echoing cavern of the swimming pool area, and Nina proceeded to undress, her movements awkward and heavy. There was a stiffness in her muscles, joints and tendons, like the aftermath of the flu, and she took her time. There was no hurry. She parked the boy on one of the wooden benches fixed to the wall with solid-looking brackets, turned on the water, and let the hot spray hit her chest and stomach.

She hadn't been eating enough lately. She could see it in the way her ribs protruded under the skin. She had always been skinny, too skinny, but since the birth of her children it seemed nothing stuck to her. Her face had become narrow and somewhat hollow-cheeked, and she had lost whatever softness she had once possessed around her collarbones, shoulders, and hips. Forgetting to eat was not a smart move. But it happened whenever she worked too much, or when Morten went off to Esbjerg and the rigs. She simply lost her appetite, and fed the children mechanically without bothering to feed herself.

"We'll get something to eat later," she promised the boy. "A big English breakfast, how about that?"

He didn't react to her voice except to sit and watch her, eyes huge and curious, legs dangling. Nina turned her back again and began to lather her body with the liquid soap from the automat on the wall. It had a sweet and perfumed smell that felt almost too extravagant for the gray shower room, and Nina was caught up in a moment's pleasure, enjoying the heat and the scent of it. Her skin felt warm, soft, and alive, and the steam rose about her and obscured mirrors and glass partitions. She worked up a new helping of frothy lather and washed her hair rather roughly. She had had it cut quite short again not so long ago. Morten didn't understand why, but he wasn't the one who had to struggle with the heavy, frizzy burden of it. It had curled nearly to her shoulders before she had it cut, and the relief had been enormous. Not least in her job, where she no longer had to wonder what would be the politically correct way of wearing it today. Many of the male inhabitants of the Coal-House Camp saw the female staff as a combination of prison wardens and service functions. They felt superior and humiliated at the same time, one of the center's psychologists had once explained. Possibly it was true. Whatever the cause, conflict always lurked just beneath the surface, and Nina had tried to appear as sexless and neutral as possible. When she had her hair cut so short, it was an oddly mutual relief. Some of her provocative femininity seemed to have disappeared along with the hair, and Nina didn't miss it. Morten did, but she had long ago stopped regulating her appearance in accordance with his opinions.

Nina slid a wet hand down across her navel and the rigidly defined muscles of her abdomen. Despite her two pregnancies, there was nothing much that was ripe and womanly about her body now. Poor Morten.

The boy moved impatiently on the bench. Collecting her drifting thoughts, she turned off the shower and began instead to fill one of the white plastic kiddy bathtubs that were scattered about the shower room. The boy did not resist as she pulled off his new clothes and sat him down in the tub. Crouching next to him, she carefully began to wash his shoulders, chest, back, and feet. Deliberately, she did not touch him elsewhere, but just let him sit in the tub as she used the shower to rinse away the soap. The boy took all this with surprising calm. His fingers trustingly followed the little currents of hot water tricklinging down his chest and belly, and when a frothy bubble almost miraculously released itself from the edge of the tub and fell with a wet pop against the tiles of the floor, he sent Nina a gleeful smile of delight and surprise—the first she had ever seen on his face since their common journey had begun yesterday afternoon.

Nina felt a new warm sense of relief spreading in her abdomen. She couldn't positively *know*, and she was no expert on responses to pedophilia and child abuse, but it seemed to her that the boy was free of such hideousness. If something like that had happened to him, surely he would have acted differently? More frightened, less trustful?

The relief was almost painful in its ferocity. The boy was still whole. Rescue, in its most complete sense, was still possible.

She turned off the water and dried him gently with one of the towels. Then, silently, they began to dress, and Nina combed his hair with her fingers.

Who was he?

She watched patiently as he insisted on pulling the T-shirt over his head himself. He might have been a child smuggled into Denmark for the purpose of some sort of prostitution or abuse, but would he then be stored like luggage in a central station locker? Nina didn't know very much about that type of crime. She certainly saw her share of human degradation and brutality in her job, but the motives there were usually unsubtle, and the methods simple enough that even the most moronic of criminals could join in. It didn't take a brain surgeon to batter the last few pennies out of an Iraqi father who had already paid almost everything he possessed to the traffickers who had arranged his journey to the border. Nor was it especially difficult to lure Eastern Euopean girls into the country and sell them by the hour in places like Skelbækgade. A few beatings, a gang rape or two, and a note bearing the address of her family in some Estonian village—that was usually enough to break even the most obstinate spirit. And the real beauty of it all for the cynical exploiters was that ordinary people didn't care. Not really. No one had asked the refugees, the prostitutes, the fortune hunters, and the orphans to come knocking on Denmark's door. No one had invited them, and no one knew how many there were. Crimes committed against them had nothing to do with ordinary people and the usual workings of law and order. It was only dimwit fools like Nina who were unable to achieve the proper sense of detachment.

She felt too much, and she knew it. Especially where the children were concerned, her skin felt tender and brittle, like the thin, pink, parchment-like new growth that spread to cover healing wounds. It had been bad after Ida's birth, but when Anton arrived, her sensitivity to the children of the Coal-House Camp had taken on monstrous proportions. It was her imagination, of course, but sometimes it felt as if their gazes clung to her, spotting her vulnerablity, tearing through her pitiful defenses and into her soul.

Unaccompanied children would usually be older than the boy from the suitcase, thought Nina, from about ten years of age and up. Often, the staff would have time to form only the most fleeting of impressions. Some of them, particularly the Eastern European ones, had been sold by their parents and trained by backers to beg and steal, and they were instructed to escape the refugee centers at the first opportunity if they were picked up on the streets. The moment their mobiles rang, they were off on the next suburban train, disappearing back into the metropolitan underworld they had come from. Other children might continue on to Sweden or England, where relatives awaited. Still others were obviously alone in the world, brought to Denmark for the sole purpose of making money for their owners. All in all, more than seventy percent would disappear from the camps without anyone ever really knowing what became of them.

But the suitcase boy was surely too young to be of use to even the most cynical gang of thieves. Might he be some kind of hostage? Or was he meant to be part of a social security scam? That had happened before, particularly in the UK, she had heard.

He was beautiful, thought Nina suddenly. She didn't know how much that meant among pedophiles, but somehow it made him seem more vulnerable. It was all too easy to imagine that some pervert bastard somewhere had ordered a small European boy for a night's pleasure. Or several nights. She looked at the boy standing in front of her with his T-shirt back to front and the new sandals carefully strapped to his small, narrow feet, and the thought of him sharing a bed with some unknown adult man was sickening and utterly unbearable.

Nina forced herself to smile at him.

Where would he end up if she delivered him to the police? Some orphanage in Lithuania? Or perhaps with a relative who would merely sell him again to the highest bidder? Perhaps with a crew-cut, bear-shouldered

stepfather, whose huge hands had beaten Karin to death?
Nina felt a shudder deep in her abdomen. She had to
know more. She had to know.

She pushed open the changing-room door and took
the boy's hand in a firm grip. She must find them some
breakfast, and then work out which church might be the
one the girl from Helgolands-gade had meant when she
talked about the Sacred Heart.

THE ADDRESS WAS in Denmark. Naturally. Sigita didn't know why she had assumed that the Dane lived in Lithuania. She stared down at the carefully penned block capitals and wondered what to do.

Gužas had called half an hour before Julija did. He wanted to know whether she had changed her mind about the TV appeal, and whether there had been any attempt at contact from the abductors. She had told him no. And she had said nothing about Julija and the Dane.

I'll have to go to Denmark, she thought. I have to find that man and ask him what I must do to get Mikas back.

But a sickening little thought kept worming its way into her mind. What if there was nothing he wanted her to do? What if he already had what he wanted, and didn't give a damn about her?

He collects my children, she thought, with a chill of horror. Now he has two.

The other child had come into her dreams during the few hours when sleep had finally claimed her. It had come out of the darkness, large as an adult, but with the face of a fetus, blind and hairless, and a naked, sexless body. It held out its arms to her and opened a toothless, unfinished mouth.

"Mama . . ." it whispered. "Mammaaaaaaaah . . ." And she drew back from it in horror. But suddenly she saw that it was holding something in its arms. Mikas. The long bluish limbs glistened wetly with embryonic fluid, and Mikas struggled in its grasp like a fish in the tentacles of a sea anemone.

"Mikas!" she screamed, but the fetus child was already distant. It retreated further and further into the dark, taking Mikas with it.

She woke up with her nightgown twisted about her, sticking damply like an extra layer of skin.

Sigita called the airport. There was a flight leaving for Copenhagen at 1:20, and a single ticket would cost her 840 litu. Sigita tried to recall the state of her bank balance. There would be enough for the ticket, just, but what about the rest? It would be difficult to manage in a foreign country with little or no money. And everything cost more abroad, or so she had heard.

Might Algirdas give her an advance on her salary?

Perhaps. But not without asking questions. Sigita bit her lip. I have to go, she thought. With or without money. Unless I call Gužas now and leave it all to him. And if I do that, they may harm Zita. She thought about the small, shattered family, of Zita's clawlike hands on the piano keys, and Julija's terror and despair. She couldn't do anything to make it worse. She mustn't. And it might not be just Zita, either. It could be Mikas too. She couldn't stop thinking about the torn-off nail Julija had received in an envelope. And that was nothing. *Nothing* compared to what people like that were really capable of.

1:20. It would be hours before she could leave for the airport.

She decided to visit her Aunt Jolita for the first time in eight years.

BANG, BANG, BANG, bang. The big yellow pile driver was pounding the foundations of the new building into the earth with resounding thumps, and a little further off, a huge crane was raising yet another prefabricated concrete element into its place. It appeared that someone had decided that there was room for a new apartment building on the green square of grass framed by the old gray and white Soviet-era blocks. Dust and diesel fumes permeated the air, and the pavement was being ground into the mud under the weight of caterpillar vehicles. Sigita felt a pang of pity for the original inhabitants. Pašilaičiai, where she lived, had barely existed ten years ago, and she often felt it was not so much a neighborhood as a constant building site. Only recently had such luxuries as streetlights and sidewalks been reestablished after the latest round of construction mayhem.

Once she was through the door, the appalling noise receded a little. She walked slowly up the stairs to the third floor and rang the bell.

A thin, gray-haired woman answered. It actually took a few moments before Sigita recognized her aunt. Jolita stared at her for several seconds, too.

"What do you want?" she asked.

"I need to ask you some questions."

"Ask away."

"Can't we do this inside?"

Jolita considered it for a moment. Then she stepped aside, letting Sigita into the narrow hallway.

"But be quiet," she said. "I have a tenant who is a bartender. He works until four or five in the morning, and he gets furious if you wake him up before noon."

The bartender lived in what used to be the sitting room, it turned out. Jolita preceded her into the small, elongated kitchen instead. At the tiny table, an elderly woman was seated, having coffee. A further two unused cups were set on the table in constant readiness, upturned on their saucers to protect them from dust and flies, just like Sigita's mother always did. The aroma of percolating coffee rose from a brand-new coffee machine, still sitting next to the box it had come in. On the table, too, were a bottle of sherry and a platter full of marzipan-covered cupcakes.

"This is Mrs. Orlovienė," said Jolita. "Greta, this is my niece, Sigita."

Mrs. Orlovienė nodded, with a certain degree of reserve.

"Mrs. Orlovienė rents the back bedroom," Jolita continued her introduction. "So you can't just move back in, if that's what you are thinking."

"No," said Sigita, somewhat taken aback. "That's not why I'm here." Whatever had happened to the Aunt Jolita she remembered? The coal-black hair, the colorful makeup, the jazz music and the professor's cigarettes? About the only remnant of that Jolita were the golden pirate-style hoops that still dangled against her wrinkled neck. They now looked absurd rather than exotic. How on earth could a person age so much in eight years? It was frightening.

"Perhaps you've come to apologize, then?" suggested Jolita.

"*What?*"

"Oh well, I was just thinking. It wasn't completely inconceivable that you should finally feel a little guilty about the way you have spat in the face of a family that only ever tried to love you and help you."

Sigita was so stunned that at first she couldn't even defend herself.

"You . . . you . . . I . . ." she sputtered. "I never spat in anyone's face!"

"Eight years without a single word—if that's not spitting, what is?"

"But . . ."

"At first I felt sorry for you. In trouble like that, at such a young age. I wanted to help you. But you did to me exactly what you did to your parents. Disappearing like that, without ever looking back, without so much as a thank-you."

Sigita stood there with her mouth open. She suddenly noticed how bright-eyed the little Mrs. Orlovienė had become, watching the drama with parted lips as if it were a soap opera.

"Your Granny Julija died, did you know that?" said Jolita.

"Yes," Sigita managed. "Mama . . . Mama sent a letter." Two weeks after the funeral. That had hurt, badly, but she had no intention of letting her aunt know that.

"Coffee?" offered Mrs. Orlovienė, holding out one of the unused cups. "Is it broken?" She nodded at the plaster cast.

"Yes," said Sigita automatically. "And no, thanks. Jolita, did someone come here asking about me?"

"Yes," said Jolita without blinking. "There was a man here, some weeks ago. He wanted to know your last name, and where you lived."

"And what did you do?"

"I told him," said Jolita calmly. "Why shouldn't I?"

"He was quite polite," nodded Mrs. Orlovienė. "Not entirely what I would call a nice young man, but quite polite."

"What did he look like?" asked Sigita, although she was fairly certain she already knew.

"Big," said Mrs. Orlovienė. "Like one of those—what are they called now?" She raised both skinny arms to mime a bodybuilder pose. "And hardly any hair. But quite polite."

At long last, Sigita's thoughts began to line up in an orderly fashion instead of tumbling over each other in random chaos. She knew that Aunt Jolita would never have taken in tenants unless she had been forced to. There was obviously no longer any Professor on Mondays and Thursdays. Probably no job, either. And yet here were sherry and cakes and a brand new percolator.

"Did he give you money?" she asked Jolita.

"Is that any of your business?"

That meant yes. Sigita spun and seized the old coffee tin Jolita usually kept noodles in. Noodles, and certain other things.

"Sigita!" Jolita tried to prevent her, but Sigita had moved too quickly. She hugged the tin against her chest with the plaster cast and wrested the lid off with her right hand. When Jolita tried to tear the tin away from her, it clattered to the floor, sending little macaroni stars shooting off in all directions across the worn linoleum. Sigita instantly put her foot down on top of the brown envelope that had also been in the tin.

"What the hell were you thinking?" she screamed, suddenly beside herself with fury.

"Shhhh!" hissed Jolita. "You'll wake him."

"A complete stranger wants to give you money to tell him where I am. He looks like a gorilla. What the hell were you thinking? Don't you realize that he has taken Mikas?"

"That's hardly my fault!"

"You made it easy." Sigita's voice was shaking. "You sold me. Without even warning me. And then they took Mikas!"

Mrs. Orlovienė sat with her mouth open, on the point of dropping her coffee cup. At that moment, the door flew back on its hinges. In the doorway stood a young man, dressed only in black boxers and a foul temper. His hair had been dyed blue and stuck out in odd directions, still coated with several layers of gummy styling gel.

"Stop that fucking racket," he snarled. The two older women were instantly silenced. Mrs. Orlovienė slid a little lower in her chair, as if being smaller would help. Jolita stood her ground, but her hands had begun the nervous rubbing movement Sigita knew so well. The young man transferred his furious glare to Sigita.

"Who the fuck are you?" he asked.

"This is my niece," said Jolita. "She came for a visit. But she's leaving now."

"I fucking hope so," said the bartender. "Some of us are trying to sleep."

He withdrew, slamming the door as he went. A few seconds later, the living room door was slammed with even greater force. The walls trembled slightly.

Sigita bent to retrieve the envelope. It contained eight five-hundred-litu bills and a few lesser bills Sigita couldn't be bothered to count.

"Four thousand litu," she said. "Was that the price?"

"No," said Mrs. Orlovienė. "At first he only wanted to pay three thousand, but in the end he agreed to five."

Jolita made a violent shushing gesture in Mrs. Orlovienė's direction.

"I don't quite see the reason for all this high-minded outrage," she told Sigita. "If some idiot is willing to pay five thousand litu for something you can look up in the phone book, why should I turn down good money?"

"He didn't know my last name till you told him" said Sigita, fishing three thousand litu from the envelope.

"What are you *doing*?"

"This is your contribution," answered Sigita. "I need it in order to get Mikas back." She let the envelope with the rest of the money fall to the floor. Mrs. Orlovienė was the one who snatched it up, ferret quick. Jolita remained where she was, staring at Sigita. Then she shook her head.

"You feel so put-upon, don't you?" she said. "Poor little Sigita who has had such a hard life. But did you ever pause to think what it's been like for your mother? You taking off like that, not even leaving a note? She lost a daughter. Did you ever think about that?"

The accusation hit Sigita like a hardball to the stomach.

"She knew where I was," said Sigita. "The entire time. They were the ones who turned their backs on me, not the other way around."

"Did you ever ask?"

"What do you mean?"

"You sit there in your fancy apartment, waiting for them to come to you, isn't that right? But you were the one who ran away. Perhaps you should be the one to make the first move if you want to come home again."

Not now, thought Sigita. I can't deal with this now. She glanced at her watch. Her plane would be leaving in two hours.

"Goodbye," she said. And stood there, waiting, even though she wasn't sure what she was waiting for.

Jolita sighed.

"Take the damn money," she said. "I hope you get your little boy back."

JESU HJERTE KIRKE, it was called in Danish. The Church of the Sacred Heart lay in Stenogade, squeezed in between a fashion shop and a private school.

Nina had asked an elderly lady in the Istedgade cornershop where she had bought fresh rolls for herself and the boy. They had struggled a bit over the translation; Nina had guessed herself that it might be Catholic, and the old lady's local knowledge did the rest.

Afterwards, Nina had called Magnus from a small, seedy bar on Halmtorvet. The bartender at The Grotto had let her use both phone and bathroom at no charge, but her conversation with her boss had been brief and unsatisfying.

"*Fan i helvete*, where are you? The duty roster is shot to hell, and Morten has been ringing us since seven o'clock. The police want to speak to you. Is this anything to do with Natasha?"

Magnus's tone had become very Swedish, and the words came pouring over her so quickly that she had no time to answer before he interrupted both himself and her.

"No. Don't. I don't even want to know. Only . . . are you okay? Morten wants to know if you're okay."

Nina took a deep breath.

"Yeah. I'm fine," she told him. "Although I won't be in today. Will you please tell Morten there is no need to worry."

It was a while before Magnus answered. She could

hear him exhale and inhale, big, deep barrel-chested breaths.

"Well, as long as you're not dead, I was to tell you . . ." Magnus hesitated again, and softened his voice so much that Nina could barely hear him.

"I was to tell you that this is the last time. If you come back alive, this is the last time."

Nina felt a sharp little snap in her chest and held the receiver at some distance, battling to control her voice.

"Alive," she laughed, too thinly. "How dramatic. There's really no need for such melodrama. Why shouldn't I be alive? I'm perfectly fine. It's just that there is something I need to do."

Magnus gave a brief grunt, and when his voice came back on the line, for the first time he had begun to sound angry.

"Well, fine. If you don't want anybody's help, Nina, you won't get it. But Morten sounded shit scared, I tell you. He says the police have found your mobile phone."

Nina felt a clammy chill along her backbone as he said it. She slammed the receiver down so abruptly that The Grotto's barman raised his eyebrows and grinned knowingly at the two regular patrons ensconced at the far end of the bar. Nina didn't care. Impatiently, she collected the boy, pulling him away from the old table soccer game he had become engrossed in. He yipped in protest as she half carried, half dragged him back to the car, but at that moment, she was too stressed to care. She started the car, turned the corner at Halmorvet and continued down Stenosgade while she followed the second hand on the dashboard clock: 13, 14, 15 . . .

Annoyingly, she caught herself moving her lips. She was counting the seconds under her breath. Sweet Jesus. How crazy was that?

Crazy. Insane. Mentally challenged. (Perhaps even so crazy that you did it on purpose?)

She managed to insert the Fiat into the row of cars parked by the curb in front of the church, in a slot too small for most cars. The boy in the back seat was staring out the window, steadfastly refusing to look at her. The sense of trust and familiarity from their morning bath had vanished, and it was clear that he had not forgiven her for the rough and hasty way she had bundled him into the car.

Sunlight made the digits on the dashboard clock blur in front of her. She leaned back, fumbling for the water bottle and a breakfast roll. She wasn't hungry, but she recognized this particular kind of lethargy from long hot days without appetite in the camps of Dadaab. If she didn't eat something now, she would soon be unable to form coherent thought.

She took tiny bites, chewing carefully and washing down the bland starchy meal with gulps of lukewarm water from the bottle. The she opened the car door and stepped onto the sizzling sidewalk.

Jesu Hjerte Kirke, Sacred Heart, Sacre Coeur. The English and French translations were posted helpfully below the Danish name of the church in slightly smaller letters. A very Catholic name, she thought to herself, full of dramatic beauty and signifying very little. The Lithuanian girl must be a Catholic, or she wouldn't have known about this church.

Mass was announced at 17:00 hours, she noted, but right now the doors were closed, and the huge cast-iron gate to the grounds proved unremittingly locked.

Nina got back in the car again, looking at the church with a vague feeling of unease. It looked like many other city churches in Copenhagen. Red-brick solidity and a couple of striving towers, squeezed in among tenement buildings. It looked cramped compared to the Cathedral grounds in Viborg (where they had buried him) and the small whitewashed village churches of the country parishes around it.

(*Goest thou thither, and dig my grave.*)

She blinked a couple of times, then scanned the street for any sign of the girl. Would she actually show? If she did, Nina was going to try to buy a few hours of her time. She turned her head, but the boy was still refusing to meet her eyes. Sunlight ricocheted off a window somewhere, forcing him to squint.

(*Alas, this world is cold, and all its light is only shadow.*)

Nina shuddered, and without thinking drew the blanket up to cover the boy's legs, despite the heat of the day. At that moment, she saw her. The girl from Helgolandsgade was peering into the car through the rear window, her face a pale outline. Nina jerked in her seat, then nodded, and leaned across to open the passenger door.

"I wil pay you," she said, hastily. "You just tell me how much you need, and where we can go."

It was 12:06.

The girl jackknifed herself into the passenger seat, looking quickly up and down Stenogade before closing the door. She smelled strongly of perfume and something sweet and rather chemical, possibly rinse aid. She fumbled in her bag and produced a stick of gum.

"It is five hundred kroner an hour, and three thousand for eight hours. How long will it take?" she answered, throwing a calculating look at the boy in the back.

Then she suddenly smiled at Nina, a crooked and unexpectedly genuine smile.

"He is so little," she said. "So cute."

She held out her hand, and Nina shook it, somewhat taken aback.

"Marija," said the girl slowly and clearly, and Nina nodded.

"I will pay for the eight hours," she said, offering up a quiet prayer to the bank. She had been uncomfortably close to the overdraft limit the last time she had checked, but she was uncertain whether this was before or after her latest paycheck had registered. She had never been very good at the money thing.

Nina turned the key in the ignition, and then sat in indecision, hands locked around the wheel. Where could they go? MacDonald's? A café?

No. Suddenly resolute, she turned left onto Vesterbrogade and headed for Amager. They could all do with a bit of fresh air.

THROUGH THE YELLOWED blinds, there was a view of the road, the parking lot, and the grimy concrete walls of some industrial warehouse or other. Every twenty minutes, a bus went past. Jan knew this because he had been sitting there staring out the window for nearly four hours now.

He hadn't considered that boredom would be a factor. But this was like sitting an exam at which one had offered what little one had to say on the subject inside the first ten minutes, and now had to repeat oneself ad infinitum. Even though the context was hideous, and he really shouldn't be *able* to be bored when talking about the brutal murder of someone who had been close to him, this was what had begun to happen. It felt as if his lips were growing thicker with each repetition, his mouth drier. The words wore thin. Concentration faltered. All pretense at naturalness had long since vanished.

"I met Karin Kongsted two and a half years ago, in Bern; she was employed by the clinic that performed my renal surgery. We probably grew more familiar than might otherwise have been the case, due to the fact that we were both Danes on foreign soil; it often works that way. After the operation, I needed fairly frequent check-ups and medical attention, but it was crucial that I didn't neglect my business any more than I had to. Karin agreed to return to Denmark and work for me in a private capacity, and this proved an excellent solution."

At the moment he was telling his story to an older

detective, a calm, almost flegmatic man whose Jutland roots could still be heard in his intonation. His name was Anders Kvistgård, and he was more rigidly polite than the others, punctiliously addressing Jan as "Mr. Marquart." In his white shirt, black tie and slightly threadbare navy blue pullover, he looked like a railroad clerk, thought Jan.

Mr. Kvistgård was the third detective to interview him. First there had been a younger man who had approached Jan with an air of comradery, as if they both played for the same soccer team. Then a woman, who to Jan seemed far too young and feminine for her job. Each time it had been back to square one, excuse-me-but-would-you-mind-repeating, how-exactly-was-it, could-you-please-tell-us, how-would-you-describe . . .

"A private nurse. Isn't that a little . . . extravagant?"

"My time is the most precious commodity I possess. I simply can't be stuck in a waiting room for hours every time I need to have a blood sample taken. Believe me, Karin's paycheck has been a worthwhile investment."

"I see. And apart from this, how was your relationship with Ms. Kongsted?"

"Excellent. She was a very warm and friendly person."

"How warm?"

Jan was jerked from his near-somnolent repetition. This question was new.

"What do you mean?"

"Were the two of you having it on? Playing doctor when the missus wasn't around? I understand you lived under the same roof?"

Jan could feel his jaw drop. He stared at this sixty-year-old Danish Rails ticket puncher lookalike with a feeling of complete unreality. This was bizarre. The man's expression of benign interest hadn't shifted a millimeter.

"I . . . no. Bloody hell. I'm married!"

"Quite a few people are. This doesn't stop around seventy percent of them from having a bit on the side. But not you and Ms. Kongsted, then?"

"No, I tell you!"

"Are you quite certain of that?"

Jan felt fresh sweat break out on his palms and forehead. Did they know anything? Would it be better to come clean and be casual about it, rather than be caught in a lie? Did they *know*, or were they just bluffing?

He realized that his hesitation had already given him away.

"It was very brief," he said. "I think I was taken by surprise at . . . Oh, I don't know. Have you ever been through a serious operation?"

"No," said the railway clerk.

"The relief at still being alive can cause a certain . . . exuberance."

"And in this rush of exuberance you began a relationship with Karin Kongsted?"

"No, I wouldn't call it that. Not a relationship. I think we both realized that it was a mistake. And neither of us wanted to hurt Anne."

"So your wife was ignorant of the affair?"

"Stop it. It wasn't an affair. At the most, it was . . . oh, it sounds so sordid to call it a one-night stand, and it wasn't, but I think you know what I mean."

"Do I, Mr. Marquart? I'm not so sure. What are we talking about? One night? A week? A couple of months? How long did it take you to realize that it was a mistake? And are you certain that Ms. Kong-sted understood that just because she was having sex with you, she had better not think this constituted an *affair*?"

Jan tried to remain calm, but the man was subjecting him to verbal acupuncture, sticking in his needles with impeccable precision, and observing him blandly all the while.

"You're twisting everything," he said. "Karin is . . . like I said, Karin was a very warm person, very . . . womanly. But I am perfectly sure she understood how much my marriage means to me."

"How fortunate. Is your wife equally certain?"

"Of course! Or . . . no, I didn't tell Anne about the . . . episode with Karin. And I would appreciate it if you didn't either. Anne is easily hurt."

"We will just have to hope it doesn't become neces-sary, then. Can you tell me why Karin Kongsted left the house so suddenly yesterday?"

"No. I . . . I wasn't there myself. But seeing that she went to the summer cottage, she must have decided to take a few days off."

"Am I to believe you haven't seen this?" Kvistgård fished out a vinyl sleeve and placed it on the table in front of Jan. Inside was Karin's note, with the brief, bald phrase clearly visible through the plastic: I QUIT.

"I didn't take it seriously. I think it was meant as a joke. She had been complaining that it was too hot to work . . . like I said, I think she was simply taking a few days off and had a slightly . . . untraditional way of announcing it."

"According to your wife, Karin Kongsted appeared upset and off balance when she drove off."

"Did she? Well, I can't really say. I told you, I wasn't there."

"No. But you did make a call to SecuriTrack in order to locate the car she was driving. Why did you do that, Mr. Marquart?"

There was a high-pitched whine of pressure in his ears. He was aware that he was still sitting there with a stiff smile glued to his face, but he also knew that any illusion of casual innocence had long since evaporated. There was no way he could make light of this, no way he could pretend it didn't mean anything, that it was just a routine precaution when a company car went missing. He couldn't do it. That bloody railway clerk had unbalanced him completely and nailed him in free fall, with no life lines left to clutch.

"I can see this needs a bit of mature consideration," said Anders Kvistgård. "Perhaps you wish to call an attorney? I'm afraid that I have to caution you that charges may be brought against you."

THE MILE-LONG, SURPRISINGLY natural-looking beach of the Amager Strandpark was only sparsely populated by bathers, despite the dragging heat. Weeks of drought and sunshine had apparently satisfied the city's hunger for beach life and first-degree burns, thought Nina. For most people, the holidays were over. In the spot Nina had chosen for them, they were alone except for a couple of students lying on too-small bath towels with open textbooks in front of them, and their only other human encounter had been with a sweat-soaked young man on rollerblades who had narrowly missed ploughing into the boy on the cement path.

Now here they were, sitting side by side on their brand-new soft towels, staring out across the mirror-smooth sea. Not a breath of wind rippled the surface, and the waves merely lapped the sand in soft, flat, nearly soundless surges. The silence among the three of them was equally noticeable, thought Nina. The boy sat still, with his head lowered, only moving his hand now and then to let the dry sand sift through his fingers in a steady stream. Marija reclined on her towel with half-closed eyes behind new shades bought at a local convenience store. She had taken off her tight jeans, revealing a pair of long, pale legs, as slender as the rest of her T-shirt-clad body. She hadn't said much in the car. A trip to the seaside would be okay, she agreed, as long as towels, sunscreen, sunglasses and a new bikini were part of the deal. Nina had had a brief flashback to negotiations with her own sulky teenage daughter, and had in the end secured a compromise that left out the bikini. For the boy, she had found a small dusty set of bucket, sieve, rake, and spade in red and yellow, languishing on a rack at the back of the store. Later, she had also bought them all ice cream from the kiosk. Marija had taken the boy by the hand and pointed to the faded pictures of cones and popsicles, and to Nina's relief the boy had answered her, opting for the biggest of the lot. After that encouraging breakthrough, silence had unfortunately descended, even though Marija had tried to encourage the child with soft, careful questions. Demonstratively, the boy sat with his back to them, working his fingers through the hot, white sand.

Glancing at Marija, Nina decided to break the silence. She and the girl, at least, could have a conversation. But what did one ask someone like Marija? Her work in Helgolandsgade? Her life before Copenhagen? Her hopes and dreams, if any had survived? The fact that Nina had bought her time and her presence here lay like a vague discomfort between them—it was a little too much like the selling and buying that went on between Marija and the men that sought her out at night.

"How long have you been in Denmark?"

Nina had meant to ask how she liked it here, but caught herself in time.

Raising her head, Marija looked at Nina with a faint smile that was at the same time amiable and distant.

"Seven weeks," she said, jerking her head at the city behind them. "It is a beautiful city."

Nina looked at Marija's long slender legs and feet, half buried in the sand. Two small round scars gleamed pinkly on her thigh, just above the knee. Cigarette burns, thought Nina mechanically, and the image of the small muscular man with the serpent tattoo flashed before her eyes. But it might not be him. Marija had, after all, only been here for seven weeks, and the scars had healed as much as such scars ever do.

Noticing her glance, Marija discretely slid a hand down her thigh, covering the scars. Then she suddenly leapt to her feet in a shower of loose sand.

"I go swim," she announced, indicating the mirror sea. "Just a quick one."

Nina smiled and nodded agreement, while Marija pulled off her T-shirt to reveal a soft, white cotton bra with wide straps. Another unwelcome image presented itself, this time of Ida and the way she had been standing in front of the mirror in her cramped little room last week.

She had bought herself a bra. One of the tight, elastic sport models that prevented abrasion and over-bouncing, which of course was quite sensible. It had to happen sometime, and Ida was way ahead of Nina in the bosom department. Nina and Morten had actually joked that Ida now, at thirteen, had bigger breasts than Nina would ever have, barring implants. Yet there was still something overwhelming about the sight of her, standing there with her narrow back turned, her shoulderblades sharply outlined under this new bra that she had to have bought with her own money and without consultation. Without asking Nina's permission, even.

Nina shook her head quickly. And just exactly what was it that Ida was supposed to ask permission *for*? Growing up?

Marija ran into the water wearing bra and panties, and dived in when it was up to her thighs, her arms describing a perfect curve over her head. She surfaced several meters away and swam back and forth at a practiced crawl for a while before flipping over onto her back. She kicked up a furious cascade with her legs.

"You come too," she called, with a grin that reached her eyes for the first time. "*Ateik čia!*"

The boy had left off his sand-sifting to look at her, and something was released in his expression, an eagerness, a yearning. He looked questioningly at Nina, causing a melting hot sensation somewhere behind her midriff. He was asking her for permission.

She nodded briefly and drew him close, so that she could help him out of his T-shirt and underpants. As soon as she let him go, he scurried across the firm damp part of the beach until the first ripples reached his bare feet. When a deeper surge lapped his ankles, he gave an enthusiastic shriek and continued a few steps forward, then stumbled and pitched onto his bottom, a mixture of elation and anxiety visible on his face. Marija reached him in a few long steps and helped him to his feet again, and Nina could hear them talking. Marija said something, and the boy answered her in the characteristic whine children employed when they were in need of help. Marija smiled, ruffling his short white-blond hair so that it stuck wetly in all directions. Then she said something else, taking his hands and towing him gently through the water. The boy was giggling and shrieking so that all his white milk teeth showed, and Marija was laughing too, now, a high-pitched girly laugh. She waved a hand at Nina.

"Come," she said. "Very nice."

Nina returned the wave but shook her head. She wanted the boy and Marija to be alone together in this. The boy had clearly missed having someone around who could understand him. The same might be true of Marija, thought Nina, watching the tall, skinny girl leaping joyfully about in the water. Hearing her own language spoken might not be an everyday occurrence, certainly not from someone as friendly and unthreatening as this. There was no reason Nina should butt in now. Marija knew what she was supposed to do—win the boy's confidence and try to find out where he came from. Anything would be useful, thought Nina. His name, the name of a town or a city, or of a street. Anything at all, as long as it helped pull him from the void he was floating in and anchor him somewhere, *with* someone.

Marija hadn't asked why, and Nina guessed that not asking questions had become a survival mechanism. That she had agreed to help, despite the man with the serpent tattoo, was little short of a miracle.

And another small miracle was taking place before her very eyes.

Marija said something to the boy, and he struggled free of her embrace with a scream of laughter. He splashed her with water, and then replied to her question, feet firmly planted in the wet sand. Instinctively, Nina understood what it was, even before the boy repeated his answer in a louder voice.

"Mikas!"

It was his name.

MARIJA AND THE boy whose name was Mikas stayed in the water until Mikas's lips were blue from cold and his teeth chattering like little castanets. Marija's long, dark hair hugged her shoulders wetly, and there was still laughter in her eyes as she let herself drop down onto the towel next to Nina, stretching so that she caught as much as possible of the hot afternoon sun.

Nina wrapped Mikas in the other towel, rubbing dry the narrow white shoulders, his chest and back, his legs. Then she helped him put on the T-shirt and the pants and liberated the spade-and-bucket set from their net bag for him. At once, he ran the few feet to the wet part of the beach and set to with an eager enthusiasm that made Marija and Nina smile at each other tolerantly, as if they were a married couple sharing a moment of pride in their offspring. Then Marija crouched forward, looking at Nina with a small sharp worry-wrinkle between her eyebrows.

"I know his name now," she said, in her heavy English. "He is Mikas, and his mother's last name is Ramoškienė. He remembered that when I asked him what the daycare staff calls his mama."

"Preschool?" said Nina, taken aback by the apparent normality of it. She knew precious little about Lithuania, she realized, and her ideas had run along the lines of Soviet concrete ghettos, TB-infected prisons, and a callous mafia. Somehow, preschools had not been part of the picture. "Anything else?"

Marija asked Mikas another question. He answered readily, without pausing or looking up from his work with the spade and bucket even for a second.

"He is from Vilnius. I am sure," said Marija. "I asked him if he liked riding on the trolley buses, and he does. But not in the winter when the floor is all slushy."

Marija smiled in triumph at her own invention.

"He said he is sometimes allowed to press the STOP button. But he has to wait until the driver says, 'Žemynos gatvė.'"

Nina rummaged in her bag and came up with a ball-point and a scruffy-looking notepad from some company of medical supplies.

"Will you write it out for me?"

Marija willingly took the pen and paper and wrote down both the name of Mikas's mother and that of the street near which she must live. Nina took it with a feeling of having brought home the gold. Then she realized that knowing his name and roughly where he came from was not actually enough. There was something else she desperately needed to know.

"Ask about his mother," she said. "Does he live with her? And why isn't he there now? What happened—does he know?"

Marija frowned, and Nina guessed that she was searching for the right words, comforting and unthreatening enough that she wouldn't upset the boy too much. A stab of outrage at Marija's own capsized life went straight through Nina's chest. She felt such rage at the thought of the Danish, Dutch, and German men who felt it was their perfect right to serially screw a young girl month after month until not the least remnant of the girly sweetness and the coltish awkwardness would remain. What do such men tell each other? That it is quite okay because it is her own choice? That they are offering her a way to make a little money and start a new life? How very grand of them.

With so many men, and such fine generosity, a national collection aimed at young Eastern European and African girls ought to raise millions. Why didn't Marija's customers keep their flies zipped and organize a fundraiser instead?

Marija had moved closer to the boy and was helping him turn the sand-filled bucket upside down. She ran her finger round the edge of the resulting cupcake shape, saying something with a reassuring smile.

Mikas was obviously uncomfortable with the question. He twisted, and began to fill the bucket with fresh sand, but the purposefulness had gone out of him, and after a few spadefuls, he dropped the little red spade and looked around, as if searching for something to hide behind. Then he looked directly at Marija, and answered her with a few soft words.

She nodded and put her hand against his cheek to keep his attention a little while longer. But at her next question, he struggled as if overwhelmed by a cold wave. His face closed, and with a thin frightened exclamation, barely audible, he tore himself free of her gentle grasp and ran towards the water.

Marija shot an accusing glance at Nina, blaming her, or, at least, her questions.

Nina got up quickly and caught up with Mikas in a few long strides. She swung him onto her hip and held him as gently as she could. At first he fought her, kicking against her shins and thighs with bare feet. Then he curled limply against her shoulder, not in trust but in resignation. Marija had risen too, and was pulling on her clothes with angry jerks.

"His mother?"

The question hung in the air between them while Marija buttoned her jeans, not looking up.

"Marija."

Nina put her free hand on Marija's arm, and finally the girl gave up her button battle and met Nina's eyes.

"Sorry." Marija took a deep breath. "It is just that he was so upset. I do not like it."

Nina shook her head slightly, but she had to know.

"What did he say about his mother?"

"I don't understand all. Children say what they like, no more," said Marija apologetically. "But he said he lives with his mama, she is nice, but he couldn't wake her."

Nina frowned. Couldn't wake her? She looked at Marija doubtfully.

Had Mikas's mama been ill? Or unconscious? And did it have anything at all to do with his involuntary trip to Denmark? As Nina recalled it, a three-year-old's grasp of the concept of time left something to be desired. She cursed her own linguistic inadequacies.

She needed to know if his own mother had sold him. Such things did happen. She knew that very well.

"What happened to take him away from his mother? Did he say?"

Marija raised her carefully plucked and penciled eyebrows.

"He said the chocolate lady took him. I do not know what that means."

"Does he miss his mother? Does he want to go back to her?"

Marija froze, and the look she gave Nina was completely naked.

"Of course he misses his mama. He is just a baby!"

SUNNY BEACH SOLARIUM AND WELLNESS, said the glass door leading down to the basement floor, with the added legend *New lamps!* Inside was a reception area with a dark-haired woman behind a desk. She was talking to someone on the phone, and Jučas could not make out which language she was speaking. Not Lithuanian, at any rate, but then that was hardly surprising. She was dressed in a white uniform as though she were a nurse or some kind of clinic assistant, and in Jučas's estimation, she was too old to be a whore. Perhaps it was actually possible to acquire a tan in this place.

The woman lowered the receiver for a moment and asked him something he didn't understand.

"Bukovski," he said, and then continued in English. "I have to see Bukovski."

"Wait," she said. "Name?"

He just gave her a look. Suddenly her gestures took on a nervous quickness that had not been there before. She rose and disappeared into the regions behind the reception, to emerge a few minutes later with the expected permission.

"You go in," she said.

It was surprisingly spacious, thought Jučas. There weren't any windows, but heavy-duty ventilation ensured that the air was cool and almost fresh. There were a couple of exercise bikes and two treadmills, but for the most part, the floor space was given over to numerous well-worn TechnoGym machines and a large free-weight area. This was no pastel-colored wellness center for fat-fearing forty-year-old women or middle-aged men with aspirations to a "healthier lifestyle." This was a T-zone. The worn gray carpeting was practically impregnated with testosterone and sweat, and Jučas felt at home immediately.

Dimitri Bukovski approached him with open arms.

"My friend," he said. "Long time no see."

They embraced in the masculine back-patting way, and Jučas endured the two smacking kisses Dimitri planted, Russian style, one on each cheek. Dimitri was an Eastern European melting pot product, a little Polish, a little Russian, a little German and a touch of Lithuanian. He must be over fifty by now, and balding, but he looked as if bench-pressing two hundred kilos was still no great challenge. Pecs and biceps bulked under his black T-shirt. Years ago, in a similar basement in Vilnius, it had been Dimitri who taught Jučas about serious training. Now Dimitri lived here in Copenhagen, and out of three possible Danish contacts, he was the only one who would not go squealing to Klimka the minute Jučas left.

"Nice place," said Jučas.

"Not bad," allowed Dimitri. "We're running it as a club, so we have some say in who gets admitted. Some people here do serious work. You want a workout?"

"God, yes. But I don't have the time," said Jučas with genuine regret.

"No," said Dimitri, "I understand this isn't just a courtesy call. Still working for Klimka?"

"Yes and no," said Jučas vaguely.

"Oh? Well, it's none of my business. Step into the office, then."

Dimitri's office was little more than a cubbyhole. A desk and two brown leather armchairs were squeezed into the narrow space, and the walls were covered with photographs, many of which were of Dimitri standing next to some celebrity or other, mostly singers or actors, but also a few politicians. Pride of place had gone to a picture of Dimitri, grinning from ear to ear, shaking hands with Arnold Schwarzenegger.

"Home Sweet Home," said Dimitri, with a vague gesture at his mementos.

Jučas merely nodded. "Did you find me anything?" he asked.

"Yeah." Dimitri opened a small safe bolted to the wall beneath the Schwarzenegger photo. "You can have your pick of a Glock and a Desert Eagle." He put the two weapons on the desk in front of Jučas.

Both were used, but in good condition. The Glock was a 9mm, the classic black Glock 17. The Desert Eagle was a .44, bright silver and monstrously heavy, and appeared to be somewhat newer than the Glock. Jučas picked them up one by one. Ejected the clip, checked that the chamber was empty. Worked the safety. Aimed at one of the pictures on the wall, and dry-fired. The pull on the .44 was somewhat stiffer than the Glock.

"How much?" he asked. "And are they clean?" He had no wish to acquire a weapon that could be traced to someone else's crimes.

"My friend. What do you take me for? Would I sell you a dirty gun? Two thousand for the Glock, three for the

Eagle. Dollars, that is. For an added five hundred, I throw in extra ammo."

"Which one would you choose?"

Dimitri shrugged his massive shoulders.

"Depends. A Desert Eagle is kind of hard to ignore. Very effective as a frightener. But if you actually want to shoot someone, I'd go for the Glock."

HE BOUGHT THE Glock. It was cheaper, too.

NINA DROPPED MARIJA off in Vesterbrogade at 4:47.

She noted the time specifically because the time on her own watch didn't match that of the clock on the arch by Axeltorv. Hers was two minutes ahead, and she couldn't help trying to calculate which of the two was correct.

The girl stood by the curb, hunched and uncertain, as if she wasn't sure where to go. There was sand in her damp hair, Nina noticed, but apart from that, not much was left of the girl from the beach. She was no longer smiling.

Nina watched her in the rearview mirror until the girl turned to walk in the direction of Stenogade, narrow shoulders tensed and raised as though she were cold. An acidic, heavy puff of exhaust and hot pavement reached Nina through the open car window, and for a moment she had to struggle with a burning compulsion to turn around and drag the girl back into the car. But Marija hadn't asked for her help, and Nina hadn't offered. Nina had written her name and phone number on a piece of paper, and afterwards got the money to pay Marija from an ATM in Amagerbrogade. That was all she could do at the moment.

She thought it was probable the police were monitoring her accounts and would make a note of the withdrawal, but she told herself it didn't matter. Not now.

She had sensed it at the moment she had heard the boy call for his mama at the summer cottage. Now she knew for certain. Mikas did not come from some orphanage in Ukraine or Moscow. He was not an orphan, he was not alone in the world. He had a mother, and from what little information Marija had gained from him, it seemed most likely that he had been abducted. Not sold, borrowed, or given away, but taken. And somehow he had ended up in the clutches of the man who had killed Karin. How and why, the gods only knew, but this was not Nina's concern.

If the boy's mother was still alive, she would probably have reported him missing to the Lithuanian police, and it should be a small matter to have the boy returned to Mama Ramoškienė, the daycare, and the trolleybusses of Vilnius. Even the Danish police ought to be able to handle that, she thought. They were usually surprisingly effective at getting people *out* of the country. They might even make an effort to investigate who was behind the abduction. If for no other reason, then because of Karin's death. No one could murder proper Danish citizens with impunity.

So. It really was that simple.

A smooth, warm feeling of serenity flowed from her diaphragm into the rest of her body.

She could take Mikas home to Fejøgade, and call the police from there. She might be allowed to remain with him while the police checked up on the information Marija had garnered from him. Nina knew that her perseverance could be quite convincing, and no one could claim it was better for Mikas to be in the care of some burned-out social worker he didn't know. She wanted to stay with him so that he wouldn't be left in the hands of strangers, until his mother could be flown in from Vilnius and he would finally be in her arms again.

Nina imagined how the boy's mother would arrive in a storm of smiles and tears, how she would take Nina's hands in wordless gratitude. Suddenly, Nina felt tears well up in some soft, dark place inside her. She didn't cry often, and certainly not in moments of success. Tears of joy were for old women.

But you don't see all that many happy endings, do you? a small cynical voice commented inside her. Nothing ever really comes out the way you want it to.

"This time, it will," muttered Nina stubbornly.

LARGE HOUSES MADE Sigita uncomfortable. Somehow, she felt that the people living in them had the authority and the power to decide, to denigrate, and to condemn. No matter how many times she told herself that she was just as good as they were, there was always some little part of her that didn't listen.

The house in front of her now was huge. So enormous that one couldn't take it all in at once. It was completely isolated, perched at the top of a cliff overlooking the sea, and buttressed by white walls on all sides. Sigita thought it looked like a fortress, and she was surprised to find the gate open, so that anyone could just walk in. What was the point, then, of building a fortress?

The taxi left. She was still shocked by the cost of it. How could she have imagined that the hundred kilometer ride would be more expensive than the flight from Lithuania to Demark? Now there was almost nothing left of the money she had taken from Jolita. I should have taken all of it, she thought. But taking only some had felt a bit less like stealing. And in the end, Jolita had, after all, consented.

Now she was here. She had no idea what she would do afterwards, and she wasn't even sure this was the end of her journey. The name on the brass plaque fixed to the white wall was the right one: MARQUART. This was where he lived, the man who collected her children. But she didn't know if this was where Mikas was.

Trying to make a stealthy approach was pointless—discrete surveillance cameras had already noted her arrival. She began to walk up the drive to the white fortress.

When she pushed the doorbell, a ripple of cheerful notes sounded on the other side of the door, a cocky little tune somehow out of sync with the tall white walls, the endless lawns, the heavy teak door. She heard footsteps inside, and the door opened.

A boy stood in the doorway. She knew at once who he must be, because of his likeness to Mikas.

"Hi," he said, and added something, of which she didn't understand a single word.

She couldn't answer. Just stood there looking at him. He was dressed in blue jeans and T-shirt, with a pair of shiny racing red Ferrari shoes on his feet, and a matching red Ferrari cap on his head, back to front, of course. He was slender and small for his age; no, more than slender, he was bonily thin. In spite of that, his face looked oddly bloated, and his tan couldn't conceal a deeper pallor, particularly around his eyes. One arm sported a gauze bandage under which she detected the contours of an IV needle that had been taped to his skin. He was ill, she thought. My son is very, very ill. What has happened to him in this alien country?

Again, he spoke, and from his intonation she thought it might be a question.

"Is your mother or father home?" she asked in Lithuanian, unable to absorb the sudden knowledge that of course he wouldn't be able to understand. He looked so much like Mikas, and she could see a lot of Darius, too, in his eyes and in his smile. It seemed absurd that she wasn't able to talk to him.

"Is your father at home? Or your mother?" she tried again, this time in English, though she thought he would be too young to understand any foreign language. But he actually nodded.

"Mother," he said. "Wait."

And then he disappeared back into the house.

He returned a little later with a delicately built woman who looked to be in her mid-forties. Sigita looked at the person who had become her son's mother. A pale pink shirt and white jeans underlined her pastel delicacy, and there was something tentative in her manner, as if she were uncertain of her bearings, even here in her own house. Like the boy, she was fair-haired and quite tanned; the superficial likeness was such that no one would ever question their relationship.

"Anne Marquart," she said, offering her hand. "How may I help you?"

But the moment she saw Sigita's face properly, she froze. There was clearly the same jolt of recognition Sigita had felt on seeing the boy. The genetic clues could not be erased. This woman saw her son's traits in Sigita's face, and was terrified.

"No," she said. "Go away!" And she began to close the door

Sigita advanced a step. "Please," she said. "I just want to talk. Please . . ."

"Talk . . . ?" said the woman. And then she reluctantly opened the door. "Yes, perhaps we'd better."

THE WINDOW STRETCHED the whole length of the living room, from floor to ceiling. The sea and the sky flooded into the room. Too much, thought Sigita, especially now that the wind was stronger, and the waves showed teeth. Had they never heard of curtains, here? Houses, after all, had been invented to keep nature out.

The space was huge and cavernous. At one end was an open fireplace, with a fire that Anne Marquart turned on with a remote control, like a television. The floor was some kind of blue-gray stone unfamiliar to Sigita. In the middle of the room, with several meters of empty space on all sides of it, was a horseshoe shaped sofa upholstered in scarlet leather. Sigita knew that this was the kind of interior that magazines begged to photograph, but it surfeited even her need for order and clean lines, and she felt ill at ease, sitting here in the middle of this stone and glass cathedral.

"His name is Aleksander," said Anne Marquart, in her neat British accent that sounded so much more correct than Sigita's. "And he is a wonderful boy—loving and smart and brave. I love him to pieces."

Something uncoiled itself inside Sigita. Ancient knots of guilt and grief came undone, and an instinctive prayer sprang to her lips. Holy Mary, Mother of God. Thank you for this moment. Whatever else happened now, at least she knew this much: that her firstborn child was not drifting in the dark, alone and bereft, like the naked fetus-child of her nightmare. His name was Aleksander. He had a mother, who loved him.

Aleksander himself had disappeared again, she knew not where to. Anne Marquart had said something to him in Danish; his face had lit up in a pleased grin, and an enthusiastic "Yesssss!" had hopped out of his mouth. Sigita had the feeling he was being allowed something that was otherwise strictly regulated. Video games? Computer? It was obvious that they were wealthy enough to provide him with anything he wished for. Sigita felt a peculiar pain. If Mikas ever found out what kind of life his brother was living, would he be envious?

The thought brought back all her fear for him.

"I am not here because of Aleksander," she said. "But because of Mikas. My own little boy. Is he here? Have you seen him?"

Anne Marquart seemed taken aback.

"A little boy? No. I . . . You have another child, then?"

"Yes. Mikas. He is three, now."

Something was going on inside Anne Marquart. She was staring into her teacup, as if any moment now a profound and essential truth would be revealed there. Then she suddenly raised her head.

"Same father?" she asked.

"Yes," said Sigita, not understanding the intensity with which Anne Marquart endowed the question.

"Oh God," said Anne Marquart softly. "But he is only three . . ."

Amazed, Sigita saw silent tears on Mrs. Marquart's face.

"It's not fair," whispered Aleksander's mother. "How are we expected to bear this?"

"I don't understand," said Sigita hesitantly.

"You have seen that he is ill?"

"Yes." One could hardly avoid it.

"He suffers from something called nephrotic syndrome. He has hardly any kidney function left now. He needs dialysis twice a week. We have a small clinic in the basement so that he doesn't have to travel all the way to Copenhagen for treatment, but still . . . he hardly ever complains, but it's tough on him. And . . . and eventually, it will stop working."

"Can't he get a transplant?" asked Sigita.

"We tried. My husband gave him a kidney, but . . . but we are not . . . biologically related, of course. And Aleksander rejected it, despite all the medication, and now he is worse than before . . ."

At that moment, Sigita finally realized why Jan Marquart had come looking for her. And why her son had disappeared.

THE BOY WAS sitting with his eyes half closed and showed no reaction when Nina parked the car in Fejøgade. The police car had gone, and the windows of the third floor flat were empty and closed. Morten might not be home yet, thought Nina distractedly, or he could have taken the children to stay with his sister in Greve. He liked to get them out of the way when a crisis was brewing. He didn't want them to see that there was anything wrong, didn't want them to see him losing control. And at the moment, he was probably half out of his mind.

Nina closed her eyes and felt the worm of conscience gnawing at the back of her mind. Tonight, she would have to put everything right. Rest her head against his shoulder and run her hands over his face while she told him why there was nothing more to be afraid of now. They could let the children stay overnight with Hanne and Peter and pick them up in the morning.

She lifted Mikas from the car and carried him up the stairs. He was awake, but tired and limp, as if he had spent everything he had on the beach. He didn't stir as she eased the keys out of her pocket. She could hear the muted roar of a video game the Jensen children were playing, and the rattle of pots and dinner preparations behind the Jensen door. But she didn't feel like answering her neighbor's curious questions—which would, no doubt, be endless—and so she unlocked her own front door soundlessly and slipped inside.

The flat was quiet and cool, and for the first time since

she had picked up the suitcase yesterday, Nina felt a genuine pang of hunger. She kicked off her sandals in the hall and walked barefoot into the living room. Mikas slid willingly from her hip onto the couch and subsided there in a small heap of three-year-old exhaustion.

The remains of breakfast were still scattered across the little coffee table in front of the television. Two bowls of souring milk and soggy cornflakes. An unopened, unread newspaper. A meal on the run, diagnosed Nina, taking the bowls into the kitchen where she pitched the contents into the bin and loaded the dishes into the dishwasher. She put fresh cereal into a new bowl for Mikas, adding an extra spoonful of sugar. The boy had eaten only a couple of ice cream cones, a breakfast roll, and a few slices of untoasted bread in the time he had been with her. He had to be just as weak at the knees as she was. And she was acutely aware, now, of the lightheaded feeling that came from not having eaten for too long.

She cut herself two slices of dark rye and sandwiched a thick wedge of salami between them. Cornflakes bowl in one hand, glass of milk in the other, and her solid sandwich clenched between her teeth, she returned to the living room. A strange flickering feeling of happiness settled in her stomach. Home. It felt fantastic. Now all that was missing was Morten and the children.

But there was no rush, just as there was no need to hurry the necessary call to the police. She placed the cereal bowl in front of Mikas and dropped into the armchair next to the couch with a muted thud. Slowly, she chewed her way through the soft rye and the sharp spiciness of the salami, eyes closed, mind gently drifting. When she was done, she climbed to her feet and went into the bedroom, where she pulled off the damp, dirty T-shirt and put on a crisp, clean shirt instead. From the living room, she could hear the rattle of Mikas's spoon against the bowl.

THE DOORBELL RANG.

It wasn't the muted scale of the door phone, but the insistent ring of the old-fashioned push-button on the door frame itself. Anton used it when he wanted to announce his presence, though his usual noisy progress up the stairs generally made any other signal redundant. No, it was probably Birgit next door, who must have noticed her arrival after all.

She might even know that the police were looking for Nina. Birgit was nice enough, really, but her curiosity was boundless, and sometimes Nina wished the walls between the flats were just a little thicker. Particularly now, when she could have done with a few more minutes on her own with Mikas.

Resignedly, she reached for the lock catch, but something made her hesitate. It was too quiet out there, she thought. Anton would have been bouncing off the floor, if not the walls, and Birgit usually had the door to her own flat open, yelling over her shoulder at her own children. It was silent out there. No scrabbling feet, no throat-clearing or nose-blowing. It was not a natural silence.

Automatically, she put the security chain on the door before opening it enough so that she could see whoever it was. A slender, fair-haired woman stood there on the landing, smiling politely, yet somehow reticently.

"Please," she said, bending forward slightly. "I think you know my son. I am Mikas's mother. May I come in?"

Instantly, Nina's mind was flooded with the fantasies she had entertained earlier, in the car. Mikas's mother, holding her hand and thanking her, as only one mother could thank another. Her happy ending. It was here, now.

But even as she slid the chain off the lock, she knew something wasn't right. The woman pushed open the door herself, with a smile that had grown oddly apologetic. As if she didn't really want to come in, thought Nina. And then she saw that Mikas had come into the hallway behind her. He stood there, still wearing his nice new sandals and holding the breakfast bowl, while a pool of dark yellow pee formed around his feet.

Smiling still, the woman held out her hand to him. He jerked from head to foot, and the bowl slid from his hands and hit the pine floor with a sharp clack.

There was a man behind the fair-haired woman. He must have been standing against the wall on the landing, out of sight until now. His massive shoulders in the too-hot leather jacket filled the doorframe, and she recognized him at once. The neo-Nazi haircut, the fury in his eyes, the huge, closed fists. In one hand he held a smooth black gun. There was no haste in the way he moved, noted Nina; it was all very calculated and precise, the routine actions of a man who had done this dozens of times. A single powerful stride brought him into the flat. He took the time to close the door behind him, and Nina heard the click of the latch with a peculiar lack of fear. She backed a couple of steps, and felt her foot slip in the puddle of warm urine, milk and cornflakes.

Idiot, she told herself, in the long stretched second that followed. Of course she's not his mother. You didn't have time to call anyone. Then the blow fell, and turned the world dark red and swirling. Then black.

BARBARA WAS CLINGING to his arm.

"Don't hit her anymore," she said. "Jučas. Don't do it!"

Jučas.

Not Andrius.

He lowered the gun. The boy-bitch lay in a heap at his feet, one side of her face completely covered in blood.

"Don't kill her!"

Barbara was as pale as a sheet. She didn't look young anymore, and for the first time he considered what the difference in their ages would mean in ten years, or twenty. When she turned fifty, he would be only just past his fortieth birthday. Did he really want to come home to a fifty-year-old woman then?

"Don't be silly. I'm not going to kill her," he said, wondering what the hell he was supposed to do with her if he didn't. He shook off Barbara's hand and stepped across the crumbled form. Where had the kid gone?

Barbara found him crouched next to the toilet, squeezed into the corner as if he was trying to push himself through the wall. A sound was coming from him now, a sort of squeaky whine, with every breath he took.

"But baby," said Barbara, kneeling down in front of him. "We're not going to hurt you!"

The child didn't buy that particular lie anymore. He screwed his eyes shut and whined even more loudly.

"Make him be quiet," said Jučas.

Barbara glanced at him.

"He's just scared," she said.

"Then give him some of that damn chocolate. Do you have any eyedrops left?"

"No," she said. But he thought she might be lying.

"Stay here," he said. "And keep the damn kid quiet!"

THE BOY-BITCH HADN'T stirred. He grabbed her shoulder bag, the only thing she had had with her apart from the child, and emptied it into the kitchen sink. Wallet, Kleenex, a fuzzy old roll of mints, car keys, two other sets of keys, and a dog-eared diary. No mobile. He took all the keys with him, and went quietly down the stairs to look for the red Fiat. He found it half a block away, hidden behind a big green-plastic container meant for recycling glass. On the backseat was a smelly blanket and two shopping bags, one containing kid's clothes, the other full of apple cores and bread and beach toys. That was all. The boot proved equally uninteresting; there was a plastic crate full of starter cables, sprinkler fluid, an aerosol can of puncture-repair foam, and other first-aid items for unreliable cars, a bin liner that turned out to contain empty bottles, a pair of gumboots, and a flashlight.

He took the blanket and left the rest, and locked up the Fiat once more.

She didn't have the money. He felt the certainty of it in his gut. And the other one, the blond one with the boobs, she hadn't had it either. She would have told him. In the end, she would have told him.

Which meant only one thing.

He was now completely sure that the Dane had lied to him.

There were still a number of things he didn't understand—what the boy-bitch was doing with the kid, for instance. And how and why the blond one was mixed up in it at all. But he knew enough. And he knew how he was going to make the Dane pay what was owed.

HE DROVE THE Mitsubishi onto the pavement and parked it right by the front door. Upstairs, Barbara had at least managed to extract the boy from the toilet. She was crouched next to him and had her arms around him, gently rocking him back and forth. It seemed to be working; he was quiet again.

The boy-bitch was still lying where he had dropped her. But she was breathing, he noticed.

"She's fine," he told Barbara. "I'm taking her down to the car."

Barbara didn't answer. She just looked at him, and her eyes were almost as wide and frightened as the boy's.

"I'm doing this for you," he said.

She nodded obediently.

He rolled up the bitch's limp body in the disgusting blanket and eased open the door with his hip. The stairwell was still deserted. What would he say if he met someone—she's had a fall, we're taking her to the hospital? But no one came. He maneuvered her into the back of the Mitsubishi and covered her completely with the blanket, then parked the car in a more legal and less noticeable spot. So far, so good.

When he got back to the flat, he could hear Barbara murmuring to the boy. In Polish, not Lithuanian.

"Stop that," he said. "He doesn't understand a word you're saying."

Jučas didn't either, and he didn't like it when Barbara spoke in her native language. It gave him a feeling that there was a part of her he couldn't access.

When they got to Krakow, she would be speaking Polish with everyone, he suddenly realized. Everyone except him. Why hadn't he thought of that before? But he hadn't. He had only been thinking about the house, about Barbara, and the life he imagined them having together.

The Dane would make it all possible. The Dane and his money. He could still recall the fizzy feeling of triumph when he had realized how easy it would be.

It had been Klimka who had told him to look after the Dane, and had emphasized that there would be no funny business. This man was a good client, with businesses not only in Vilnius but also a couple of places in Latvia, and he paid Klimka good money—very good money— to keep the other sharks at a distance. Now he was in Vilnius himself and wanted only a single bodyguard to follow him around. Discretion was essential.

And so Jučas had played the nanny from the moment the man got off the plane with his ridiculous little trolley that turned out to contain an unreasonable number of U.S. dollars. They had gone directly to some kind of private clinic, where the Dane tried to buy information about some Lithuanian girl or other who had apparently given birth to a baby. When Jučas had seen the sum he had offered the head of the clinic, he had begun to feel jumpy. It was as if the Dane had no idea what it was he was waving in the woman's face. A tenth would have sufficed; would, actually, have been too much. People had been murdered for less.

He called Klimka to ask for backup. Klimka refused—the Dane had specified one bodyguard. Jučas would just have to handle it for now, but if things looked tricky, he could call, of course.

Yeah right, though Jučas. If the shit really hit the fan, he needed his backup with him, not a couple of phone calls away. He walked around with his senses tuned to max all day, paying precious little attention to whatever the Dane was saying and doing, because he was too busy scanning the surroundings. When the nurse more or less slammed the door in their faces and they had to return to the hotel, Jučas heaved a sigh of relief.

Premature, as it turned out. In a bout of depression, the man downed most of the contents of the minibar, then went for the hotel bar, already so inebriated that the bartender refused to serve him. After which performance the idiot staggered out the door, without the dollar trolley, thank God, but still with enough of a wad in his wallet to get into every kind of trouble. There was nothing Jučas could do except curse and follow.

That proved only the beginning of a very long night. But as the booze went in, the story came out, little by little, mixed with the drinks. And Jučas listened, at first indifferently, but then with growing interest. Fledgling plans formed in his mind. And the next morning, when he poured a sizeable but unbruised hangover onto the small private Danish plane, it was with almost tender feelings that he buckled the guy's seatbelt for him and made sure a good supply of puke bags were in reach.

It had taken a little while to make the nurse tell him what she knew, but he had, after all, had some experience in making people do things they didn't really want to do. And when he discovered that Sigita Ramoškienė actually had a second child, everything had fallen brilliantly into place.

He had sent his first package to the Dane, and made him an offer. The price was easy to remember, and non-negotiable: one million U.S. dollars.

HE STILL DIDN'T understand why things had come apart the way they had. But one thing, at least, was very clear. The Dane was not going to put one over on him now.

"I'll take him," he said to Barbara, reaching for the boy.

She hugged the child even closer.

"Can't we take him with us?" she said. "He is so small. He could easily become ours."

"Are you insane?"

"He'll forget all the old stuff quickly. In a year, he will think he has always been with us."

"Barbara. Let him go."

"No," she said. "Andrius. It's enough now. We can take him and leave for Poland right now. You don't have to hit anyone anymore. No more violence."

He shook his head. The woman had gone completely insane. He should never have brought her here. But he thought she might get them into the flat without any fuss, and so she had. Now he wished he had just kicked in the door.

"The money," he said.

"We don't need it," she said. "We can live with my

mother, at least to begin with. And then you'll find a job, and we can get a place of our own."

He had to breathe very calmly and carefully to keep the rage at bay.

"You may want to live like a sewer rat for the rest of your life," he said. "But I don't."

Resolutely, he seized the boy's arm and tore him from Barbara's grasp. Luckily, the kid didn't scream. He simply went limp, as though he had suddenly lost consciousness. Barbara was the one doing the whining.

"For God's sake shut up," he said. "Not all the neighbors are deaf."

"Andrius," she begged. She looked as if she were dissolving. Tears and mucus made her look swollen, damp and unattractive. Yet some of the old tenderness returned.

"Hush," he said. "Stop crying, can't you? Go back to the hotel, and I will pick you up later. Once we get the money, Dimitri has a new car ready for us. And then we leave for Krakow."

She nodded, but he couldn't tell whether she believed him or not.

WHEN HE GOT back to the car, he saw that the boy-bitch had moved. The blanket had slipped, so that one could see a little of her face and shoulder. Damn it. But it was best just to get out of here, now. He could always stop later and cover her up again. He put the boy into the kid's car seat still fitted between the driver's seat and the passenger seat. Just as well he hadn't removed it yet. He fumbled with the straps and buckles—this had been Barbara's department until now—but luckily the child made no move to resist him. He turned his head away and wouldn't look at Jučas, but apart from that he was a life-sized doll, limp arms, limp legs, no more screaming defiance.

Barbara came out just as he was finishing, but he merely slid into his own seat and drove off, steadfastly ignoring her. He couldn't bring her.

He knew that he would probably have to kill someone. The boy-bitch at the very least, but perhaps also the Dane. And he didn't want Barbara to see.

JUČAS DROVE PAST the house twice just to get his bearings. There was a wall, but the wrought-iron gates were wide open, so there was really nothing to prevent him from driving straight up to the front door. Was it really that simple? It was hard to believe. In Lithuania, rich people had to guard their money better.

The third time, he turned into the gate and continued up the driveway. He let the car coast to minimize the noise of the engine and didn't stop in front of the main entrance. Instead, he followed the driveway around the house and into a huge garage at the basement level. Here, too, the doors were wide open. There was space enough for five or six cars, but right now the only occupants were a dark blue Audi stationwagon and a low sportscar silhouette shrouded by dust sheets. He parked next to the stationwagon and turned off his engine.

The kid had stayed quiet during the ride, never looking at Jučas. Every once in a while he cried softly, with barely a sound. No screaming and sobbing, just this timid, hopeless crying, which was worse, in its way. Jučas felt like assuring the boy that he meant him no harm, but he knew it couldn't be helped. He knew that from now on the monster in that little tyke's nightmares would be him. And what about Barbara? The look she had given him back in the flat . . . as though she, too, were becoming scared of him. Hell. I'm not the kind of bastard who would hit a woman or a child, he told himself.

Completely unwelcome, the memory of the other one

came back to him. The blonde. Crouched on the bed, with wide unfocused eyes that no longer understood he was in the room. The uncertain, labored voice, calling. "Ni-na. Ni-na."

He sat motionless for a moment, still with his hands on the wheel. What's the bloody use, he thought. What's the use of running from Klimka and his world, where fear is a bludgeon you use to batter people into compliance. What's the use of dreaming about Krakow and a house with a lawn and Barbara sunbathing on a quilt, when all this shit stays with you.

He got out of the car. Reached for the rage because it was the only thing that might get him through the next bit. He opened the rear door and looked down at the boy-bitch, still huddled in a boneless pile without any spark of consciousness. It was all her fault, he told himself. Her and the filthy swine who was trying to do him out of his money. It was them. They did it, and he was not going to let them get away with it. You don't fuck with me.

And the rage came. Like a wave of heat, it washed through his body, made hands and feet prickle and shake a little, but in a good way. It was best done now, while she was still just an object. He took the plastic shopping bag and emptied out all the stuff that Barbara had brought—bananas, lukewarm cola, some kind of soap she had liked because it smelled of roses and lily of the valley. Even though he didn't really feel like touching her, he climbed into the back of the car to the bitch. He grabbed her shoulders and rolled her limp body into his lap. She weighed nothing at all, he thought. No more than a child. He pulled the bag over her head and then realized he had nothing to tie it with. Instead, he tied the handles themselves into a knot under her chin, which would have to do. When he saw the plastic cling closer to her face with each breath she took, he knew it was enough. By the time he came back, it would be over.

He pushed her away with disgust and wiped his hands on his trousers, as if touching her had somehow contaminated him. The bitch got what she deserved, he told himself carefully, clinging to the strength the rage gave him. And as he went to pull down the garage doors, it wasn't her face that swam before his eyes. In the sudden darkness, other images forced themselves on him, the Pig, the Pig from the orphanage who pushed little boys up against rough, damp basement walls, down in the dim semi-darkness that smelled of pee and petrol and unwashed old man.

Filthy bastard swine, he thought, they were all filthy swine, and he was going to show them that nobody did such things to him. Hell, no. Not to him. He found a light switch and turned on the fluorescent overheads until he had found what he was looking for—the automated gate system that such a filthy rich bastard had to have. He yanked the wiring right out of the box with hardly any effort, leaving the bared copper threads bristling and exposed. So far, so good.

There was a door that had to lead into the house, but it was locked. He considered kicking it down, but decided that it was much simpler to ring the bell and wait for someone to let him in. He glanced back at the car. The boy sat there, still strapped to his little seat, staring at him through the windshield. Jučas slammed his palm against the light switch so that both boy and car disappeared in the garage darkness.

SIGITA WAS SHAKING all over.

"You can't!" she screamed, and for a few moments didn't register that she was screaming in Lithuanian. She searched desperately for the English words this woman would understand.

"You can't take a kidney from a three-year-old child! He is too small!"

Anne Marquart looked at her in astonishment.

"But Mrs. Ramoškienė. Of course not. We . . . we're not going to."

"Why did you take him, then? Why did people come to Vilnius and steal him from me, and take him to Denmark?" She didn't know for certain, but it had to be that way. Didn't it?

"I don't know where your little boy is, or why he is gone. But I assure you, we could never ever harm . . ." She broke off in the middle of the sentence and stared blankly out at the ocean for a while. Then she said, in a completely different tone of voice: "Would you excuse me? I have to call my husband."

These people are rich enough to buy anything, thought Sigita. They bought my first child. And now they have paid someone to steal the second.

"He's only three," she said helplessly.

Di-di-da-da-di-di-diiih . . . The unsuitably gay little tune from a different doorbell made them both freeze. There was the sound of child-light running feet from the hallway, and Aleksander's voice called out something in Danish.

"He always wants to get the door," said Anne Marquart absently. "With him in the house, there's no need for a butler."

Then, too quickly for natural speed, the door to the living room slammed back against the wall, and a man stood there, in the middle of the floor. He took up all the space, thought Sigita, and left no room for anybody else. It wasn't just that he was big. It was his rage that made everything around him shrink. He held on to Aleksander with one hand. In the other was a gun.

"Get down on the floor," he said. "Now!"

Sigita knew at once who he was, even though she had never seen him before. It was the man who had taken Mikas.

ALEKSANDER STRUGGLED AND tried to twist free of the man's grip. The man grabbed a handful of his hair and jerked the boy's head back, so the child emitted a thin sound of pain and fright and outrage.

"Don't hurt him," begged Anne Marquart. "Please." She said something in rapid Danish to the boy, and he stopped struggling. Then she lay down on the floor, obediently.

Sigita didn't. She couldn't. She stood there, stiff as a pillar, with the noise of her own blood crackling in her ears like a bad phone connection.

"Where is he?" she asked.

The man didn't like that she wouldn't do as she was told. He took a step forward, then raised the barrel of the gun against Aleksander's cheek.

"Who?" he said.

"You know damn well. My Mikas!"

"Don't you care about this one?" he said. "Is the little one the only one that matters?"

No. No, it was no longer only about Mikas. It had never been only about Mikas, she knew that now.

"Lie down, bitch," he said. "It will be better for all of us if I don't lose my temper."

He didn't say it in any menacing tone of voice, he was just offering information. Like the little signs by the predator pits in Vilnius Zoo: *Please don't climb the fence.*

Sigita lay down.

"What are you saying?" asked Anne Marquart in English. "Why are you doing this?"

The man didn't answer. He merely forced Aleksander down onto the floor next to them, then slid his hands over Anne's body, not in any sexual way, just professionally. He found a mobile phone in her pocket and bashed it against the stone floor till it broke. He then upended Sigita's bag, fished her mobile from the wreckage, and treated it to a similar destructive bang.

"He took Mikas," explained Sigita. "My son Mikas. I think your husband paid him to do it."

The man looked up.

"No," he said. "Not yet. But he will."

IT WAS NEARLY half past eight in the evening before they let him go. Jan felt as if he had been run through a cement mixer.

"Go home and try not to think too much about it," said his lawyer, as they shook hands in the parking lot.

Jan nodded silently. He knew it would be impossible not to think. Think about Anne, and about Inger and Keld. Think about Aleksander, and about an organ cooler box somewhere, with a kidney inside that had a maximum of twelve useful hours left before it became just so much butcher's waste. Think about the Lithuanian and Karin, who was dead whether he could get his head around it or not.

They had shown him pictures. They had meant to shock him, he knew, and it had worked. Even though he had seen her at the Institute of Forensics, it was somehow worse to see her in the place where she had died, crouched on a bed, blood in her hair. Crime scene photos. It made the violence of what had been done to her too real and unclinical. You could *see* the power behind those blows, the force that had killed her. He thought of the Lithuanian and his huge hands, and the words on the phone when he had tried to end it. *Not until you pay.* Fear tore at his stomach.

Nor had the police lost interest in him. He hadn't told them about the Lithuanian or about Aleksander and the kidney he so desperately needed. Even though Jan had rid himself of the stolen Nokia, the photo of the boy, and the blood sample with the perfect DNA match, he still clung to hope, irrationally and beyond all realism.

Perhaps they sensed the lie and all the things he left unsaid. Perhaps that was why they kept coming at him for such a long time, even after he had sacrificed his self-respect and told them about Inger's visit. And of course, they had sent someone to the villa in Tårbæk to check the usefulness of this alibi. Thinking about it was almost unbearable. He imagined Keld frowning and putting down his pipe. Getting up to perform polite handshakes with the cop. Hearing about Karin and the fact that Jan was a suspect. For a wild moment, he even thought that Keld might get into his old black Mercedes and drive directly to the house by the bay to take Anne away from him.

But of course, he wouldn't do such a thing. They were married, and Keld had a lot of respect for that institution. Which didn't mean he also had to respect the man his daughter had consented to marry, and Jan knew that that respect would now have evaporated. If it had ever really been there. In the midst of his general misery, that knowledge hurt with its own specific pain.

"You'll be all right," said the lawyer, patting him on the shoulder. "You have at least a partial alibi, and they have no physical evidence linking you to the scene. Almost the opposite, I believe. And the other thing . . . well, it will be very difficult for them to lift the burden of proof on that one."

Jan nodded, and got quickly into his car.

"See you tomorrow," he said, slamming the car door shut before the man had time to say anything else.

The other thing . . .

It was the man in the blue pullover who had said it. The one that looked like a railway clerk. "People like you, Mr. Marquart. People like you don't have to kill anyone themselves. After all, it's so much easier to pay someone else to do it."

That was an accusation that clung worse than a direct murder charge. Not least because it was much too close to the truth. He *had* tracked Karin. And he had offered the man money to go and get her. That he had never meant for the man to kill her—how does one prove that when she did in fact die?

THE WAY HOME felt long, even though he didn't actually want to get there. After several weeks of clear skies and sunshine, clouds had begun to roll in from the west, darkening the twilight. A strong wind made the pine trees sway so that it looked as if they were trying to fall on top of the house. The automated garage door failed to work, again. He was too tired to get annoyed and merely left the car on the gravel outside. He could smell the sea even though he had smoked three cigarettes during the drive. The sea, and something else—the ozone-heavy damp smell of rain that hadn't quite arrived.

He had barely inserted his key in the lock when the door slammed open, so abruptly that it tore the bunched keys from his hand. Something hit him in the face, and he was knocked backwards, ending up on his back in the gravel at the foot of the stone steps.

The Lithuanian stood there on the threshold, with the light at his back so that he looked barely human, a giant form towering above him, filling Jan's entire field of vision. He had a gun in one hand. The other clutched the back of Aleksander's head like the timber grab on a bulldozer. An involuntary sound shot up from the depth of his diaphragm. Please no. Not Aleksander.

"For God's sake," he whispered, not realizing that he was speaking Danish and that the giant would not be able to understand. "Let him go."

The Lithuanian was looking down at him.

"Now," he said, in a voice that made Jan think of rusting iron. "*Now* you pay."

ANTON WAS TIRED and surly. "Peepy" was Morten's mother's idiosyncratic term for it—possibly an amalgam of peevish and sleepy, and in any case a word that admirably covered the fit-for-nothing-yet-unready-to-sleep state with which his son struggled on a regular basis.

If only Nina hadn't taken the damn car, thought Morten. Today of all days he could have done without the trek from the daycare to the Fejøgade flat, dragging along an uncooperative seven-year-old. Anton considered it beneath his dignity to hold hands like a toddler, but he kept lagging behind if Morten didn't chivvy him along.

She had called her boss, but not him. Magnus had relayed her assurances, almost apologetically.

"She's okay," he said. "She said you shouldn't worry."

Of course it was nice to know she wasn't lying dead in a thicket somewhere in Northern Zealand, but apart from that, it wasn't very helpful. She was still out there somewhere, in that alternate reality to which he had no access, where violence and disaster always lurked just around the corner. He knew it was irrational, but he couldn't shake the feeling that Nina had somehow single-handedly managed to drag that world back with her to Denmark, disturbing the coffee-and-open-sandwiches tranquility of the family picnic he would have liked his life to be.

"I'm hungry," whined Anton.

"I'll make you a sandwich when we get home."

"On white bread?"

"No. On rye."

"I don't like rye," said Anton.

"Yes, you do."

"I don't! It's got *seeds* in it."

Morten heaved a sigh. Anton's pickiness came and went. When he was rested and happy and secure, he cheerfully wolfed down fairly advanced foods such as olives and broccoli and chicken liver. At other times, his repertoire shrunk alarmingly, and he would balk at anything more challenging than cereal and milk.

"We'll fix something," he said vaguely.

"But I'm hungry *now*."

Morten surrendered and bought him a popsicle.

THERE WAS A smell in the hallway that warned him the second he was about to cross the threshold. He stopped. Two floors below, Anton was making his way up the stairs by a method that involved taking two steps up and hopping one step down. Apparently, it was essential to perform the hops with maximum noise.

Morten switched on the lights. The semi-twilight of the hallway fled, and dark huddled silhouettes became coats, scarves, shoes, boots, and a lonely-looking skateboard. But on the worn wooden floor, there was an alarming pool of congealing blood. And a little further on, a cereal bowl lay on its side in a puddle of spilled milk and cornflakes. And something else—the something that caused most of the smell: urine.

"Anton," he said sharply.

Anton looked up at him from the landing below without answering.

"Go and see if Birgit is in. Perhaps you can play with Mathias."

"But I'm hungry."

"Do as I say!"

Anton's eyes widened in alarm. Morten wanted to comfort and reassure, but at the moment he simply couldn't. The fear that rose inside him left room for little else. He closed the door to the flat and rang the doorbell on his neighbor's side of the landing. Mathias opened, but Birgit was hot on his heels.

"Hi," she said. "Have you been burgled?"

"Why do you ask that?" said Morten, his fear still crouched right behind his teeth.

"I saw a police car parked outside this morning."

"Oh. I see. Er, could Anton stay with you for an hour or so? It's quite a long story, but I'll tell you all about it later." He deliberately dangled the tale in front of her like a steak in front of a hungry dog, because he knew that curiosity was one of the more powerful driving forces in Birgit's life.

She wasn't thrilled that she would have to wait for her titbit, but perhaps she sensed his curbed tension.

"Okay," she said. "Mathias, you can show Anton that new game of yours."

"Yessss!" said Mathias, and Anton brightened too. They scurried along the corridor to Mathias's room.

"Thanks," said Morten.

Birgit remained in her doorway, discretely trying to look past him and into the flat as he opened the door again, but he didn't think she saw much before he closed it behind him.

He avoided the bloodstain and stepped across the milk and pee puddle. Glanced into the kitchen and the living room. No one there. Ida's room was also deserted; she was with her classmate Anna this afternoon, he remembered. But in the bedroom a dirty T-shirt had been tossed across the bed. Nina's T-shirt. She had been here.

He stood very still, trying to collect his chaotic thoughts. What had happened? The bloodstain was ominously large. It could not have come from some trivial injury like a cut finger. And *pee*—where did that come from? Vague memories of a forensic TV series rose in his mind. Something about traces of urine and feces because all muscles let go at the moment of death.

Moment of death. No.

No.

He fumbled for his mobile. He had to call the police.

Then he heard a faint sound. A heave, or a sobbing breath. He tore open the door to the tiny bathroom.

On the lid of the toilet sat a woman he had never seen before in his life. She looked a wreck. She had obviously been weeping hard, and there was a quality of surrender about her. Her shoulder-length fair hair had slipped from what looked to be an immaculate chignon, but even under these circumstances, there was an unconscious elegance to the slender neck and the long legs.

Morten stood there gaping.

"Where is Nina?" he asked.

The woman looked up at him. Her eyes were swollen with grief.

"*Juz po wszystkim*," she said. And then in uncertain English, "Is over. Everything is all over."

Morten's pulse roared in his ears. *Nina.* What the hell had happened?

SHE WOKE BECAUSE she was drowning. She couldn't breathe. Something wet, black and sticky clung to her mouth, nose, and eyes, and with each breath she tried to take, she drew in only crackling darkness. No air. There was no air.

Panic had already seized her body before she had come completely to her senses again. Her hands clawed purposelessly at the darkness in front of her and encountered something soft and heavy. A blanket, perhaps. She tried to pull it off her body, but it tangled around her shoulders and arms, and she struggled like a trapped diver trying to get back to the surface.

Her chest hurt now. And still the darkness clung to her face. She gasped for breath in hard short heaves, and some part of her brain registered a perfumed smell of roses. An omen of death, it seemed. The smell of roses and lilies always reminded her of burials. Finally, she freed one hand from the blanket and raised it to her face.

A plastic bag.

First she tried to rip it. Then to claw holes in the plastic with her fingers, so that she might breathe. Air. Everything in her was screaming for oxygen, and her lungs cramped painfully. Again, she clawed at the bag, and this time, something gave. The bag loosened enough so that she felt a touch of air.

Easy. Breathe slowly.

Her thoughts slipped and wandered, and she had to

struggle to get a grip on them in the curious black and milky gray place that was her brain.

Someone had pulled a bag over her head. All she needed to do to be able to breathe again was pull it off. She reached above her head and yanked the bag all the way off, and finally, she could breathe freely, in long noisy gasps.

The darkness around her was still deep and black. For the first few dizzy seconds she was unsure whether she actually had her eyes open, and an absurd impulse led her to feel her eyelids, just to check.

"You're not dead, Nina. Take a breath, and get a grip."

It helped.

The words sounded real in the darkness, and Nina raised herself up on one elbow and turned her head a little. It hurt to move. Particularly one side of her face and head, which felt heavy and tender at the same time. Something wet and sticky lay like plastic wrap over her cheekbone and throat. Blood, she thought dispassionately, and recalled how the man from the railway station had stormed into the flat, gun in hand. She felt vaguely surprised that he hadn't killed her then, on the hallway floor. But for some reason, he must have decided to wait.

She turned her head the other way, and for the first time noted a slim crack of light in the middle of all the darkness. That, and a low, persistent whine, like that of a trapped animal.

Mikas.

She knew right away that it was him, but his crying was so muted that it sounded as if it was being transmitted to her from another planet. Where was he?

Nina fumbled with one hand in front of her, and came up against a smooth cool glassy surface. A car window. She was in the back of a van, she thought. The floor beneath her was covered with some kind of felt, prickly and new under her hands. She felt her way along the side of the van until her fingers closed around some kind of wire mesh. A dog barrier? Her eyes were getting used to the darkness, and she could just make out a seam of light around what looked like garage doors. A carpark or a garage, she thought, picking up the oily smell of tires and fuel. She had no sense that the man was here, but the sound of Mikas's crying leaked back to her through the mesh.

He was afraid.

"Mikas!"

Nina listened in the darkness. Waves of nausea rolled over her, and her tongue felt huge and shapeless when she tried to talk.

She called again, shaking the mesh testingly.

"Mikas, don't be scared. I'm right here."

She reminded herself that he wouldn't understand, but she hoped the sound of her voice would at least reassure him that he was not alone. Perhaps he did actually recognize it. He was silent for a few moments, as if listening. Then the faint, toneless weeping continued.

She got onto her knees and felt along the bottom of the car, probing and sliding her fingers into every space and crevice she encountered. A flattened ring caught her interest. She pulled at it, and felt the lining beneath her shift and move. There was a hatch beneath her, and she suddenly realized that this was the kind of car that had a spare wheel embedded in the bottom of the cargo space. She managed to pull back the lining and open the hatch, and there, beside the spare, was the folded plastic package she was hoping for. The car's tool set.

She felt a rush of triumph. If the man from the train station thought she was just going to lie there and die with a badly tied shopping bag over her head, he was much mistaken. And he was also mistaken if he thought locking her in the back of a van would keep her captive much longer. Nina felt a pang of contempt mixing with the fury that was growing in her belly. Weren't they all like that? The vultures that fed on the flesh of the weak. The pedophiles, the rapists, the pimps. All the damned lowlifes of this world. This was what they were really like. Such *stupid* little people.

This man was no exception. He wasn't getting Mikas. And he wasn't getting her.

She drew a wrench from the package and hefted it. She didn't know where the man had gone, but leaving Mikas here presumably meant he was coming back. The boy was what he had come for. The property he had come to reclaim. Smashing the window might be too risky, and too noisy. Instead, she made her way back to the mesh. The screws that fastened it to the car were easy to find even in the dark, and in the tool kit was a screwdriver that was a close-enough match.

Suddenly, light flooded the garage outside the van, and she instinctively cowered to the floor. She thought she heard voices. If help was within reach, she ought to bang and kick the sides of the van; but somehow, she didn't think that whoever was out there had come to rescue her.

If he came back, could she pretend she was still unconscious? She reached for the plastic bag, but couldn't bring
herself to pull it over her head again.

Then the lights went out, and darkness descended
once more. She crouched, still waiting. But no one came.

Loosening all the screws took a while, and she had to
pause twice to fight back nausea. But finally the mesh
came free, and she slid it to one side.

"Mikas?"

Silence reigned up there. She wormed her way past
the head rest of the driver's seat and tumbled forward
into the cabin. She could feel the boy move beside her,
in trembling jerks, but she couldn't see him properly.
Quickly, she opened the driver's door, and light from the
overhead bulb flooded the cabin and revealed Mikas's
face, frightened and blinking. Did he even recognize her?
She wasn't sure. He had been strapped into a child's car
seat, the way one would normally secure a three-year-
old child for a trip to visit a grandmother, or an outing
in a park. Nothing else was necessary. Mikas's soft short
fingers picked at the buckle, which he couldn't undo, and
his lips moved in a murmur of weeping.

She undid the buckle for him, with a soft click.

Then she heard the shot.

ANNE AND SOME other woman were lying on the stone floor in the living room with their arms raised like the victims of a bank robbery. One of Jan's own toolboxes had been upended on the coffee table so that pliers, bits of wire, screwdrivers and duct tape were scattered over the glass surface. It was only then he realized, in his daze, that Anne's hands and feet had been taped to the floor so that she couldn't move from her odd position. Her face was completely expressionless. She didn't look frightened or angry, just . . . he wasn't quite sure what to call it. "Determined" seemed too weak a word. Her eyes were the color of shadows on snow.

The other woman lay in much the same way, except that one arm was in a cast. That, too, had been forced to one side and stuck down with tape at a different angle. She looked a bit like Aleksander, he thought. And then a pounding shock went through his diaphragm as he realized who she must be. He had no idea how or why, but it had to be his son's biological mother who was lying there.

He felt a trickle of blood from one nostril on his upper lip and wiped it away reflexively. He had to get a grip. He had to get control of this situation, not just let himself be dominated. He turned to the Lithuanian.

"This isn't necessary," he said, slowly and carefully in English, wanting to make sure the man understood. "What is it you want?"

"What you owe me," said the man.

"Okay. But what about your end of the deal?"

The man stood still for a moment. Then he jerked his gun hand in the direction of the door. "That way," he said.

The other woman, Aleksander's Lithuanian mother, started to shout something incomprehensible. The man snarled at her, and she fell abruptly silent.

For a moment, Jan hesitated. But getting the man out of the room Anne was in had to be a good idea. If only he would also let go of Aleksander. He could see Aleksander was scared to the point of panic. His eyes looked huge in his pale, thin face, and there were tear tracks on his cheeks. Jan attempted a smile, but knew it came out wooden.

"It's okay, Sander," he said. "The man will leave in a minute."

"Shut up," said the Lithuanian. "Speak English. I don't want you to say things I don't understand."

"I just told the boy not to be frightened."

"Don't do it again."

"Okay. Okay." Don't anger him. Or . . . don't anger him *more*. The man's suppressed fury was vivid in every move he made.

They went into the hallway and down the stairs to the back door, which the man made Aleksander open. With his gun hand, he flipped the switch and turned on the light in the garage. There was an unfamiliar car in there, some kind of van. And inside, on the front seat, a child.

It was him—the boy from the photograph. Jan recognized him immediately. But what was he doing here? It wasn't the child Jan had paid for. Just one of his kidneys.

"What is he doing here?" he asked the Lithuanian. And

at that moment the truth began to dawn on him, like a series of flashes at the back of his mind. The Lithuanian had never meant to deliver a neat little transplantable organ. How could he? He didn't have access to the doctors or the technology for an operation like that. The suitcase Karin was supposed to pick up at the railway station . . . it had never contained an organ box. It had contained a living child.

Karin.

No wonder she had freaked.

A rush of pain went through him, and a bizarre image invaded his mind. It was as if he had ordered a steak at a restaurant and had been presented with a cow and a meat cleaver instead.

"Not like that," he said to the Lithuanian, hoarsely. "You didn't say it was a living child."

"Perfect match," said the Lithuanian. "Same father, same mother. Now you pay."

"Of course," said Jan, somehow managing to keep any sign of tremor from his voice. "Let's go upstairs again. You'll get your money."

The Lithuanian switched off the light. The child hadn't moved at all, and Jan felt a stab of pity for the poor kid.

"DOLLARS," SAID THE man. "Not . . . that." He pointed the gun at Jan's laptop.

"But I can transfer the money to an account only you have access to," tried Jan, but he could see that it was useless. Glowing numbers on a computer display wasn't *money* in the Lithuanian's world. "I don't have that much cash lying around!"

The man came closer, still with Aleksander in his grip. Casually, as though Aleksander were a toy he had almost forgotten about.

"You said you had the money ready."

"And so I did. But Karin took it."

"Karin?"

"The one you—" he stopped himsef short of saying "killed." It might not be a good idea to bring that up now. "The one at the cottage. She had it. It's not my fault that you couldn't find it."

Out of the corner of his mind, he saw Anne stir. Don't move, he thought, as if he could reach her telepathically. Don't make him see you, don't make him notice you right now.

The other woman said something in Lithuanian. She wriggled, trying to get free, he supposed. The man snapped something at her, and she stopped struggling. She too had been crying, he could see.

"She didn't know where it was," said the Lithuanian, facing Jan once more. "She would have said." He raised the gun and pointed it at Aleksander's head. "Last chance. Don't fuck with me."

Jan opened his mouth, but no words came, no sound. Aleksander may die because this idiot doesn't understand about money transfers, he thought, feeling his world shift beneath him. He crouched a little lower and considered a flying tackle; go for the gun, make him let go of Aleksander, something, anything, anything except this suffocating feeling of helplessness.

"I know where the money is," said Anne suddenly, in crystal clear and perfect English.

The Lithuanian looked at her rather than Jan now. Possibly considering whether Anne might be telling the truth.

Dammit, Anne, thought Jan. Can't you see that this is not the kind of man you can bluff?

"It's not true," he said quickly. "She doesn't know anything about any of this."

But the man had taken a box cutter from the tool box wreckage. He cut the duct tape so that Anne could sit up. Blood was trickling down one wrist from an accidental cut, but she didn't even seem to notice it.

"Show me," said the giant.

Anne nodded. "I'll get it," she said. "It won't take a minute."

A few moments later she was back with two heavy yellow manila envelopes. Jan looked on in disbelief as she upended them and let thick green bundles of thousand-dollar notes tumble out onto the floor.

Anne had taken the money. Not Karin. The discovery made the blood pound in his ears.

"Anne . . . what . . . why?"

The Lithuanian was staring down at the money, and for the moment, at least, didn't seem to care that they were speaking Danish.

"It's now been two years since I decided to leave you," said Anne. "Do you know why I couldn't go? Because of that bloody kidney machine in the basement. But when I saw that case on Karin's bed with all that *money* inside, things just fell into place. I had no idea what you needed so much cash for, but I had the feeling you wouldn't call the police if it disappeared. *I* could take it. And then I would be able to look after Aleksander without your help."

"But . . ."

"And you still don't get it, do you? Right now you're wondering if it is because of your pathetic little affair with Karin. Oh yes, I know. But that's not why. Don't you realize? You nearly killed Aleksander. *You* had to give him the kidney he needed. *You* would take care of everything. Because God forbid anyone should know. You nearly killed Aleksander *because you didn't want my father to know that you couldn't give me a child*. This marriage was always more about my family than about me, wasn't it? My father was the one you really wanted. Well, fine. You can have him. But I'm getting out."

Jan heard the words, but they didn't really register. He saw the Lithuanian let go of Aleksander. The boy gave a sob and ran to Anne, who put her arms around him without noticing that the blood from her wrist smeared his fair hair.

"Pick it up," ordered the Lithuanian. "Put it back into the envelopes."

It took a moment before Jan realized that the order was meant for him. His whole body felt alien to him, as if everything was dissolving, inside and out. He took a step forward, not toward the money but toward Anne. He saw the man raise the gun, but it had ceased to matter. Even when he saw the flash from the barrel and felt the impact to his chest, it still didn't really matter.

HE DANE FELL heavily, across the money. Jučas turned and raised the gun again, this time to aim at the wife. But she was gone. He could hear her running footsteps somewhere, in the hall perhaps. And, of course, she had taken her son with her.

He glanced down at the man to decide whether he should shoot him a second time, but he looked like a goner, and right now it was more important to get the wife and the kid before they succeeded in calling for help. Shooting the boy would be no fun at all, but he knew it was necessary now. He had to do some house cleaning here, make sure there was no one left who could identify him. The little one he could take with him, seeing that Barbara was so keen on it, but the older boy had to go. He had eyes in his head, he would be able to remember and tell others what he had seen. Jučas didn't want to wake up one morning in Krakow to find the police pounding on his door.

Four or five quick strides brought him to the door. The hallway was empty, the front door still closed and locked. Where had they gone? He opened another door and found a huge kitchen with shiny white cupboards and black marble work tops. But no woman and child. He withdrew to the hall again and wondered whether they had fled down the stairs to the garage. A good thing he had sabotaged the gate; they wouldn't be able to get out in a hurry.

Then he heard a soft bump overhead. Excellent. Now

he knew where to look. He headed up the stairs to the second floor.

The first room was a bedroom, probably the parents'. He switched on the light and looked under the bed. Checked the bathroom. Nothing. He continued along the landing to a sort of feminine office, with a blonde-wood desk and a small chintzy sofa by the window. Also empty.

In quick succession, he opened two more doors. A bathroom and a boy's bedroom. He had to spend precious time opening wardrobes and knocking over a playhouse shaped like a medieval castle, but still no sign of the woman or the boy. Then he attempted to open the second to last door along the landing.

It was locked.

He raised the Glock and aimed at the lock. The shot rang in his ears but did less damage to the door than he had expected. Despite his temporary deafness he heard a muted cry, but it sounded as if it came from above. Possibly he was shooting at the door to the attic stairs? He fired one more round, and this time the door began to give way when he put his shoulder against the woodwork. One more shot ought to do it.

At that moment, something hit him from behind. Something heavy, sharp-edged and hard. It drew a line of fire across the back of his neck and made him stagger briefly. He was turning as the second blow came, but he was off-balance, and he didn't even have time to raise his hands. The one shot he did get off went wild, smashing into the banister. Then the bloody toolbox hit him directly in the face.

He was lying on his back staring up at the little one's mother. Her eyes looked completely wild, and a strip of duct tape still dangled from her plaster cast. She could only hold the toolbox with one hand, but she swung it as though it were a handbag.

This time it smashed into his right arm, and he lost all feeling in his fingers and couldn't even feel the gun anymore. The crazy bitch dropped the toolbox and went for the Glock.

She'll bloody kill me, he thought. If she gets hold of it, she'll kill me.

He grabbed a handful of light brown hair with his left hand and pulled her all the way down to the floor. She wasn't screaming, but she fought like a woman possessed. She kneed him in the chest, and he still couldn't use his right hand. Then he felt something punch him in the leg, but it wasn't till the bang registered that he realized that she had shot him. He had no idea how bad it was. He only knew that if he didn't finish her *right now*, anything could happen. He rolled over so that his full weight held her pinned to the floor, and with his left hand—unfortunately more clumsy than his right—reached for her head in order to pull it sharply back and to one side, a swift jerk so that the neck would snap.

He didn't understand why it didn't work. He only felt another punch, this time on the side of the neck. From the wet heat he understood that he was bleeding. And from the manic racing of his heart, he understood that it was a lot. Strange. It felt almost like the throbbing pump he loved to feel in his body when he was training.

But the throbbing grew fainter. More distant. As though he was moving away from himself. Suddenly he saw the dream family quite clearly. The mother, the father, the two children. They were sitting around the dinner table, laughing. He wanted to call out to them, shout at them, but they couldn't hear him. He was outside, and he could not get in.

E VEN BEFORE NINA pushed open the door to the hall, she knew the house was enormous. The stairs winding up through the stairwell would not have been out of place at some corporate domicile built to impress, and yet there were enough domestic details to suggest that this was actually a private home—a collection of outdoor boots, neatly lined up on a rack, winter coats and scarves on pegs in the wide space under the stairs, two footballs in a net.

Everything else was white, including the staircase itself, and Nina stood for a moment, trying to adjust to the glare of a multitude of halogen spotlights.

There was a strange silence, as if the house had swallowed everything living and was now busy digesting. She sensed movement, but the sounds that did reach her were muffled and diffuse. Running footsteps, a door being opened and closed, the muted clicking of heels or toes against floorboards. But there had been a shot. Straining to hear, Nina felt adrenalin invading every single tired cell in her body.

Nothing.

Or, no . . . something. Something closer than the footsteps she had heard. She went up the stairs as quietly as she could, and listened again. A liquid moan reached her through a set of double doors leading off the hallway. She recognized the sound of human pain and felt automatic emergency reflexes kick in, forcing her own pounding headache into the background. Someone was injured.

She needed to know whether there was one or more, how critical the injuries were, the priority of treatment.

She checked her watch.

It was 9:37 P.M., later than she would have guessed.

She pushed open the door and entered an enormous living room.

A man and a woman lay on the floor. The woman was immobilized by wide strips of duct tape, but apart from an arm in a cast, which obviously had already been treated and was therefore irrelevant right now, she appeared to be uninjured. Frantic, but unharmed. Nina ignored her and focused on the man instead. He lay partly on his side, limbs outflung, like a fallen skater. Around him, a bizarre number of dollar bills lay scattered across the stone floor. Blood from the sternum area had soaked through his white shirt and run down to mix with the big wet stains of sweat under his arms.

ABC, she thought. Airways, Breathing, Circulation. She knelt next to him, tilting back his head a little to check his mouth. No blood, which was encouraging, and no obstructions. He blinked and gazed at her with eyes that might be unfocused and shocky, but still seemed reasonably present.

"What happened?" she asked, not only because she wanted to know but also to establish contact and to find out whether he could answer.

He didn't even attempt to reply, just closed his eyes again, but it seemed more dispirited than actually comatose. He wasn't unconscious, in her estimation; his breathing was fast and pain-afflicted, but unhindered, and his hands reasonably warm. There seemed to be no catastrophic hemorrhage going on, inside or out. She pulled the bloodied shirt to one side. He had been shot high in the chest, above the heart. The entrance wound was not enormous, but she could see no exit wound, which suggested that the projectile was still somewhere in his body, possibly lodged against the scapula. That, too, was to his advantage right now. Exit wounds were messy. Cautiously, she pushed back the lips of the wound. She could see splinters of bone in among the bleeding tissue. The man's collarbone had been shattered. The sharp fragments worked like shrapnel inside his shoulder, increasing both the bleeding and the pain, but the shot must have missed all major arteries, and he was not lethally wounded. He was beginning to rock back and forth, probably in an effort to escape what was no doubt a significant level of pain.

"Hold still," she said. "Moving makes it worse."

He heard her. He stopped rocking, even though his eyes stayed firmly closed.

Nina glanced around for anything that might be used as an emergency compress, but this was not the kind of home that had tablecloths and cozy plaids and decorative cushions on the couch. In the end, she took off her own shirt and used it for a makeshift bandage; there was nothing she could cover him with to alleviate the effects of the shock, and the only thing she could use to pillow his head were the blood-spattered dollar bundles.

She had done what could be done for him. She turned her attention on the woman.

She was struggling feverishly against her bonds. Her smooth brown hair stuck damply to her forehead, and she had obviously been crying. There was something familiar about her, but Nina couldn't quite pinpoint what.

Nina had pushed the cries of the younger woman from her consciousness while tending to the injured man, and this might have given her the impression that Nina didn't care and wouldn't help her. At any rate, she had stopped shouting. But now her eyes glittered wetly, and she spoke, in slow careful English.

"Please. Help me."

Nina spotted a box cutter in the jumble of tools, wires, and whatnots scattered on the coffee table from an upturned toolbox. She used it to cut the tape that held the woman down. The minute she was free, the woman catapulted off the floor and exploded into motion with a speed that seemed out of sync with her short, square, unathletic figure. She seized the toolbox with her good hand and ran out of room.

At that moment, shots rang out from above. Two shots, close together.

Nina suffered a brief moment of doubt. She glanced at the injured man. She wasn't sure how stable his condition was, but there was little else she could do for him now. She wiped both hands across her face. They were trembling, she noted, little sharp jitters she couldn't control. She checked her watch again to steady herself, and at that moment her subconscious finally came up with the answer, and she knew who the woman must be.

It was 9:39 P.M. Nina gave the injured man one last look, then she got up and followed Mikas's mother.

SIGITA COULDN'T GET clear. The man lay across her, pinning her to the floor, and one hand had closed around a handful of her hair. He was heavy. In a brief flash it reminded her bizarrely of sex with Darius, but this would not end in laughter and release. The gun had slipped from her hand, and she had no idea where it was. The massive body on top of her made it harder and harder to breathe. She knew people died in this way in nightclubs and football stands, but could one be crushed to death by the weight of a single person? It felt like it.

Where was the panicked strength that had driven her a moment ago? She had swung that toolbox at his head as if she meant to knock it clear off his neck. He had taken Mikas. And even though she had pleaded and begged, lying on the stone floor of that absurd ballroom of a living room, he had not told her where her child was. Not even when he took the Dane and returned so quickly that she understood Mikas must be nearby. He had just snarled at her that if she wanted the kid to survive, she had better shut up, and she had dared ask no more questions after that.

Now her head filled with the nightmare visions she had tried to keep at bay these last long days. What if Mikas had been hidden away in a box somewhere, or in the trunk of a car, every breath he took? Or worse. She saw his tiny body in the cargo hold of a refrigerated van, cold and blue and gutted like an animal. Who said he was even still alive? How could she trust anything the man had said? They only needed his kidney, they didn't care about the rest—his dark blue eyes, his bubbly laugh, the eagerness in his face when the words came tumbling out so quick and jumbled even she could not make heads or tails of them.

The man didn't move. Was he dying? She began to struggle again, even though she barely had breath left in her heaving lungs.

Then, suddenly, someone was helping her, rolling the heavy form to one side, so that she could sit up. She gasped and drew blessed air in long, shivery sobs, watching while the skinny short-haired woman who had cut her loose knelt beside the big man's trembling body. She had no shirt on, only a white bra, and it looked as is someone had sprayed her with red paint. No, not paint. Blood. There was blood on the wall, too, a long red arc like graffiti painted with a spray can. The woman was pressing her hands against the man's neck, but Sigita could see how the blood spurted between her fingers. One side of the man's neck had been torn open, and she slowly realized that this was something she had done. She had fired the gun blindly and felt it kick twice in her hand, but she had had no idea if she had hit him, or where. It seemed she had. In the leg, and in the neck. If he died now, she would have killed him.

"Mikas?" she asked, with what little breath she had.

"He is okay," said the dark-haired woman without looking up, and Sigita had no breath to ask what do you mean, okay, where is he, is he hurt, is he scared?

The battered door eased open a fraction, and Anne Marquart poked her head out. It looked almost comical.

"Was anyone else hit?" asked the dark-haired woman sharply.

"No," said Mrs. Marquart, staring at all the blood, and at the massive body on the floor. "We're . . . we're okay."

The dark-haired woman bent even further over the man who had taken Mikas, and said something Sigita didn't hear. He didn't answer. After a while, a sound did come from him, but it was just a sort of hissing sigh. The blood was no longer spurting quite so forcefully. Sigita got up slowly. She realized that she was smeared with blood, too, covered with it, in fact, in her hair, on her neck, down the front of her shirt. *His* blood. It made her skin crawl. Somehow, it was worse than if it had been her own. She felt dirtier. She could hear Anne Marquart saying something in Danish, possibly to Aleksander, who was still somewhere on the other side of that shot-to-pieces door and, Sigita hoped, couldn't see any of this.

"Is there anything we can do?" asked Sigita belatedly. The woman didn't answer right away, just crouched there with both hands pressed against the man's neck. Sigita could count every vertebrae in her curved spine, could see the effort that made the skinny, bare shoulders tremble.

Then the straining shoulders slumped, and the woman straightened.

"He is dead," she said.

Sigita stared at the big, heavy body.

"I shot him," she whispered. She wasn't quite sure how that made her feel. She suddenly remembered what she had promised herself if they harmed Mikas. *If you hurt my boy, I will kill you.* Does an act have to be conceived in the mind before it can happen? And once one had thought of it, did that bring it closer to reality? She had thought it. And now, she had done it. The calm she had felt then seemed very distant now.

"I think you are wrong," said Anne Marquart quietly, bending to pick up the gun. "I think I was the one who shot him."

Sigita stared at her in confusion. What did she mean by that?

Anne looked utterly calm. She raised the gun carefully.

"Watch out," she said. And fired a deliberate shot into the doorframe.

"It might be better that way," said the dark-haired woman thoughtfully. "The police will have no trouble believing *her* statement."

Finally Sigita understood. She was a stranger here, a foreigner without credibility, money, or connections. She remembered how hard it had been to make Gužas believe her at first, and they at least spoke the same language.

"I had to do it," said Anne, nodding at the big motionless body. "It was self defense."

Sigita swallowed. Then she nodded.

"Of course," she said. "You had to defend your child."

Something happened when they looked at each other. A silent agreement. Not a trade-off, more a sort of covenant.

"Not Mikas," said Sigita. "But me. He can have mine. If it's a good enough match."

"You had better leave now," said Anne. "But I hope you'll come back. Soon."

"I will," said Sigita.

Suddenly, the dark-haired woman smiled, a brief intense smile that made her dark eyes come alive and banished all the jagged seriousness.

"He is downstairs in the garage," she said. "In the gray van."

MIKAS WAS STANDING in the doorway with the darkened garage behind him. He was holding on to the doorframe with one hand, as if he had only just learned to walk. When he caught sight of her, an expression slid across his face that was neither happiness nor fear, but a mixture of both. She couldn't lift him, the stupid cast was in the way. But she squatted down beside him and pulled him into her embrace with her good arm. His little body was warm, and smelled of fear and pee, but he clung to her like a baby monkey and hid his face against her neck.

"Oh, my baby," she murmured. "Mama's little baby."

She knew there might be bad dreams and difficult times. But as she crouched here, feeling the warmth of Mikas's breath against her skin, she felt that something—life, fate, maybe even God—had at last forgiven her for what she had done.

THERE WASN'T MUCH time, thought Nina. In a little while, it would all begin—police, ambulances, paramedics, all the things that followed in the wake of death and disaster. They had exactly the time it would take for the first cars to reach them from Kalundborg.

Anne Marquart had made the emergency call, from her son's mobile. She had lent her own dark-blue station-wagon to Mikas and Mikas's mother. It would be better if they simply weren't here when the authorities arrived, she had said. Jan Marquart was still lying on the living room floor, but now as comfortable as she could make him, with pillows, blankets and proper bandaging.

Anne Marquart might look as if a rough wind could snap her in half, but there was an unexpected strength beneath the pastel-colored fragility. That she had a dead body in a pool of blood on her upper landing seemed not to shake her, and she stuck to her decision to claim responsibility for his death with no apparent effort. She and Nina had covered the body with a bedspread, mostly out of consideration for Anne's son Aleksander, and Anne had politely offered Nina the loan of a cream-colored shirt to replace the one that had served as emergency bandaging for her husband's gunshot wound. The label said Armani, Nina noticed with a pang of guilt as she stuck her haphazardly washed arms into its expensive sleeves.

Anne took her out of the house, around the corner, to a separate entrance at the back.

"This is it," said Anne, tapping a code into the digital lock. "Up the stairs. Just go in. I'll keep an eye on Jan until the ambulance gets here."

Nina merely nodded. The door to Karin's flat had been sealed with yellow POLICE tape, but Nina opened it anyway, ducking beneath the seal. The light in the small hallway came on automatically as she entered— there had to be a photo sensor somewhere. She located the switch and turned on the light in the living room as well.

This was Karin's home. Her coats and shoes in the hallway, her perfume still in the air. Her specific blend of chaos and tidiness. Piles of papers and books were allowed to grow abundantly, because Karin did not consider such things mess. But Nina knew that if she checked the laundry basket in the bedroom, she would find even the dirty clothes neatly folded.

She recognized Karin's old rocker, an heirloom that had followed her since their dormitory days. But apart from that, it was clear that styles had changed as her bank balance swelled. Conran and Eames rather than Ikea. A genuine Italian espresso maker in the open kitchenette. Original modern art on the walls.

On Karin's desk was a compact little printer, but no laptop. Presumably, the police had taken it away, along with some of the piled papers—you could tell, somehow, that there were gaps in the arrangement, and one drawer had been left slightly ajar.

Nina dropped into the rocking chair. She hadn't come to pry. She was here to say goodbye, as best she could.

Karin's fear. That was what kept coming back to her. It

had been obvious that Karin had been terrified during the last hours of her life, even before the Lithuanian found her. Had it been Jan Marquart who scared her? He hadn't seemed particularly terrifying to Nina, but then, that might be because she hadn't met him before a nine-millimeter projectile had made a mess of his shoulder and left him shocked and bleeding on his own living room floor.

Karin knew him better. Well enough for her to be shit scared of going against his orders. And it had even been she who had taken the dollar bundles still lying on the stone floor next to Jan Marquart. What had Karin imagined Jan would do? Why had she fled this lovely flat so precipitously, to hide out in an isolated summer cottage?

She was afraid of people who put little children into suitcases, thought Nina suddenly, and of the people who pay them to do it. She thought I might be able to save Mikas. And I suppose I did. But there was no one around to save Karin.

She heard distant sirens now. Time was running out. She got up to turn off the lights and leave, but as she reached for the switch, she noticed the various postcards, Post-its, and photographs that Karin had stuck to her refrigerator door.

There was an entire Nina-section, she realized. Top left was a picture of her and Karin, an ancient one taken at a concert at the Student Union Hall way back in a former century when they had been at nursing school together. Karin's hair looked huge, teased into a festive post-eighties pile on top of her head; her eye-liner would have done

Cleopatra proud, and her earrings almost reached her shoulders. Her eyes were laughing at the camera, with familiar sparkling warmth. Nina, of course, wore black, but for once she had been able to muster a smile for the photographer, albeit somewhat less exuberant.

She has kept this for seventeen years, thought Nina. I wonder how many fridge doors it has been stuck to?

Below it was Nina's wedding picture, somewhat hastily taken in front of the sow-and-piglets sculpture by the Registry Office. Nina had forgotten who had had that particular flash of artistic inspiration, but both she and Morten looked ridiculously young, eyeing each other with an earnest intensity that almost looked like somber premonition. Nina's dress could not quite disguise the four-months bulge that was Ida.

Still further down came the baby pictures of Ida and Anton. She and Morten had sent them out like picture postcards of holiday attractions, post-partum snapshots of rather purplish-looking wrinkled little creatures, supplemented by tiny black fingerprints.

My life is hanging here, thought Nina, and has been stuck to this door year after year, alongside pictures of nephews and nieces, dental appointments and holiday postcards. Here, where she might look at it every day if she wanted to.

A hodgepodge of feelings assaulted her, a sticky dark mixture of loss, grief, self-hatred, and guilt. It would take time to sort it out, more time than she had at the moment. She switched off the lights. Closed the door and heard the electronic lock click. As the sirens came closer, she plopped herself down on the front steps to wait. She really ought to go check on Jan Marquart, but right now she couldn't contemplate looking at him. It wasn't his hands that had beaten Karin to death, but he had paid the man who had done it. Karin's fears had been well-founded.

Her head hurt like hell, and she knew she probably should be hospitalized, but she just wanted to go home. At long last, and if at all possible. She had washed her arms and hands as best she could, short of soaking them in a tub for hours, but despite her scrubbing, she could still feel the Lithuanian's blood as a stickiness between her fingers and under her nails.

She hadn't been scared. Or not of him, at any rate.

He had been lying in a pool of blood that grew bigger and bigger around his head. He hadn't moved of his own volition, but faint spasms went through the big body, as though he were cold, and seeing him like that made it hard to feel anything except pity. That was how he looked—pitiful.

When she rolled him away from the woman, she had seen at once how the blood spurted in rhythmic jets. In that second, she knew he was dying. Yet she still instinctively knelt next to him, sticking two fingers into the messy neck wound. She had been able to feel the rubbery toughness of the torn artery, but although she tried to clamp it, blood still bubbled and spurted around her fingers, in a hot and uncontrollable flow.

The man had looked at her with a gaze already distant and milky. As if semene had drawn a curtain. She knew that look. She had seen it before. Of course she had. Nurses saw people die.

Yet this was different.

The smell of hot blood and the sticky, scarlet flow of it down her arms dizzied her.

(Don't let go of time, Nina. Stay awake. Don't forget time again.)

She'd shaken her head irritably and tried to catch the man's gaze once more. There was something she needed to know.

"Did you kill her?"

The man blinked, and his breath sounded wet and soggy. Perhaps the trachea had also been damaged? He wasn't looking at her, but she couldn't tell whether he had heard her or not.

"Karin. The woman in the summerhouse. Did you kill her?"

His lips parted, but it could be anything from a snarl of pain to an attempt at speech. His eyes were glazed, like dark dry rocks on a beach. He hadn't answered her. And yet she felt completely certain.

I could let him die now, she thought, looking down at her own hands. I could just let go and stop trying. He killed Karin, and he does not deserve any better.

But she didn't.

Instead, she slid her fingers further into the wound. Perhaps, if she got a better grip, if she squeezed harder . . . she was using both hands now, but blood still gushed up her forearms. And when it finally did ease off, it was not because she had succeeded in stemming it. It was because there was nothing left to pump.

The sternum heaved towards her, then fell in a sudden collapse of breath. She stayed as she was for a while, fingers still uselessly clutching, and an ache of ancient grief in her chest.

She would not have been able to save him no matter what she had done, she thought, and as the knowledge hit her, it eased a deeper and older pain inside her.

(He would have died no matter what she had done.)

NINA ASKED THE policewoman who had driven her home to leave her by the front door. She was sore and tired and hurt, and being polite to a stranger in her home was entirely beyond her. Pretty much everything was beyond her right now.

She knew Morten was waiting. The policewoman had told her as much. He had been notified right away and was reportedly "very happy and thrilled to have her back safe and sound."

Nina grimaced at the phrase as she took the first step up the stairs. No doubt Morten was relieved, but "thrilled to have her back" might be overstating it, and "happy" was not really a word that applied to their relationship right now. In fact, he looked anything but happy, confirming her worst fears.

He must have seen her arrive through the window, because he was waiting in the open doorway, arms crossed. Nina slowed her progress involuntarily.

"So there you are."

His voice was toneless and barely more than a whisper.

Not angry, not miserable. Something else she couldn't identify, and the look he gave her made her duck as if he had thrown something at her. She girded her tired loins and continued up the last few steps to the landing.

She was so close that they were nearly touching, and she had to fight back an impulse to put her face against his neck in the little hollow place by his collarbone.

"May I come in?"

She tried to make her voice sound casual and self-assured, but her throat was closing into the tight and tender knot that usually led to tears. She fought them. She didn't want to cry now; she needed to be the one to comfort him. She raised her head to catch his eyes, and in his gaze she saw something huge and dark come unstuck. His chest heaved in a single sob, then he grabbed the back of her head with both hands and drew her close.

Helplessness.

That was what she heard in his voice, and had seen in his eyes. The total and abject feeling of powerlessness that she knew seized him when something took her away from him.

"Don't," he said, holding her so tightly that it hurt, "don't *ever* do this again."

SEPTEMBER

THERE WAS FLOUR all over the kitchen. Flour on the kitchen table, flour on the floor, greasy doughy flour on one tap, and even a few floury footprints in the hallway.

"What are you *doing*?" asked Morten, putting down his laptop bag.

"Making pasta!" said Anton enthusiastically, holding aloft a yellow-white floury strip of dough.

God help us, he thought. Nina must be having one of her irregular attacks of domesticity. And it was typical of her that she couldn't just buy a package of cake mix and have done with it. He still shuddered to recall the side of organic beef that had appeared in the kitchen one day. The flat had looked like a slaughterhouse for the better part of twenty-four hours while Nina carved, filleted, chopped, packaged, and froze unsightly bits of bullock—or attempted to, because in the end they had to persuade his sister to take most of it. She lived in Greve and had an extra freezer in the shed.

Now here she was, hectic spots in her cheeks, running ravioli through a pasta machine he had no idea they possessed.

"Good job," he said absently to Anton.

"Hey you," said Nina. "What did they say?"

"Esben does it this time. But I've promised to take his next shift. I have to leave on the twenty-third."

Normally, his job required him to do a two-week stint on the rigs in the North Sea every six weeks, but this time he hadn't wanted to go. What he really wanted was for all of them to go on holiday. He had already managed to swap his way to a week's leave from the mud-logging. But Nina refused.

"What I need is a big dose of normal everyday life," she had said.

He had finally managed to drag her to the clinic so that Magnus could look at her. Magnus had stitched up the cut above her hairline, probed her battered skull with his fingers, and sent her on to the National for further check-ups.

"At the very least, you are concussed," he had said, shining his penlight into her eyes. "And you know as well as I do that we have to make sure it's nothing worse. What the hell were you thinking?" He looked at Morten. "If something like this ever happens again, don't let her fall asleep. People can slip right into a life-threatening coma without anyone noticing."

Dry-mouthed, Morten had nodded. Even though the doctors at the National later pronounced her skull uncracked, Magnus's words stuck in him, and it was more than a week before he could sleep normally beside her. It felt like the times he had needed to look in on the children when they were tiny, just to make sure they were still breathing.

Less than two weeks later, she was back on the job. And he had a strong feeling that Operation Ravioli had a lot to do with her need to prove that she was on top of it all. Could manage the job *and* her family, could be a Good Mother, could do it all and be *here* again.

He wanted to tell her that it wasn't necessary. That it

was okay if she was feeling irritable and tired, that it was okay to resort to easy fixes. If she had anything to prove, it certainly wasn't as a pasta chef.

He had been looking at her for too long. Caught, as he often was, by the sheer vitality and intensity of her eyes. He had once found a chunk of dolorite that reminded him so much of the storm-gray color of her eyes that he had dragged it all the way back from Greenland in his pocket.

"Is anything wrong?" she asked.

"No."

She held his face between her wrists so as not to get flour on his office shirt and gave him a kiss.

"We're making three kinds of ravioli," she said. "One with spinach and ricotta, one with prosciutto and emmentaler, and one with scampi and truffle. Doesn't it sound delicious?"

"Yes," he said.

MORTEN HAD STAYED up long after she had fallen asleep, and Nina woke to find him kneeling on the bed next to her. She reached for him, and drew him down. He let himself fall. Kissed her deeply and with a certain ferocity, pressing his fingers into her mouth, then down the curve of her neck, over her breasts, her arms, and wrists. His fingers meshed with hers, and he let the full weight of his body push her into the mattress.

His eyes were nearly invisible in the darkness. Nina saw only a vague glitter of reflected light, and she sensed something, some sort of melancholy grief, settle between them. Or perhaps it had been there the entire time, and she hadn't noticed.

She turned her head to look at the digital display of the clock radio.

"No." Morten's voice was hoarsely insistent. "Not now."

He tilted the clock so that the numbers were no longer visible. Then he caught her face and turned it towards his in the darkness, drawing her leg slowly but firmly to one side.

She let go. She let herself fall into him, into the feeling, into the warm zone where time meant nothing.

SHE RAN ALL the way home. She couldn't stop the panic even though she knew she was being hysterical, that he would no doubt be sitting at the kitchen table as usual, with an egg sandwich and a non-alcoholic beer in front of him and coffee brewing on the coffee machine. It was just the way it was—sometimes her father went home even though the school day wasn't over. It didn't happen often, three or four times a year at the most, and he was usually back at work the next day. Usually. But sometimes, when it was bad, two or even three weeks might pass by, and then it was "not too good." That's what her mother always said when people asked. "No, Finn isn't feeling too good at the moment." And then people didn't ask any more questions, not if they knew him.

EGGS AND CRESS, she thought. He'll be sitting at the kitchen table, and he has just cut himself a good helping from the somewhat shapeless cress hedgehog that Martin has made in kindergarten. And he is drinking non-alcoholic beer because he has taken his medication.

She looked at her watch. Twenty past eleven. If she could see him at the table, she wouldn't even need to go in. She could just turn around and make it back to the school in time for her next class.

BUT HE WASN'T at the table. And so she had to go in.

His furry green loden coat was on its peg in the hallway. His shoes were left neatly side by side in the shoe rack, with his briefcase next to them. She eased open the door to the bedroom, thinking he might be taking a nap, but he wasn't there. Then she noticed that the door to the basement stairs had been left ajar. And she heard the sound.

SHE WAS LATE both for her Danish class and for Geography, and the teacher took her outside and made her explain. At first she didn't know what to tell him.

"I had to change my clothes," she finally said.

And it wasn't till much later that anyone realized why, and then of course they began to ask different questions. Why had she just gone back to the school?

The school psychologist in particular asked that question, and a whole bunch of other questions, mostly beginning with "What were you feeling when . . ." or "What were you thinking when . . ." Those, she couldn't answer. She couldn't remember feeling or thinking anything at all. Or doing anything. It wasn't that she didn't remember being in the basement, and she remembered everything else too: her father, and how he had been lying in the bath tub with his clothes on, and that the water had been scarlet. She remembered seeing his mouth move when he saw her, but it was like a film with the sound off, she couldn't hear what he was saying. She was looking at the red stuff on his arms. And that was when time had disappeared, she thought, but she wasn't sure how. She remembered going over to Mrs. Halvorsen next door and telling her to call an ambulance. What she couldn't understand, what simply didn't make sense, was that more than an hour had passed. That it was now suddenly half past twelve, and that she had changed her clothes. I went over there right away, she kept saying, to herself and to others. I went over there right away.

THE TELEPHONE DREW her from her nightmare. She fumbled for it and managed to take the call before the ring woke Morten. Or so she thought.

At first, there was only a lot of hectic breathing at the other end. She was about to hang up, when finally a thin and panicked voice came on.

"Please come."

"Who is this?"

"Natasha. Please . . ."

Nina sat up abruptly and turned on the light. Still half asleep, Morten muttered something unintelligible. The word "Hell" could be distinguished, but other than that, she had no idea what he was saying.

"Natasha, what is it?"

For several long seconds she heard only the tear-choked wheeze of the girl's breathing.

"He touched Rina. Touched . . ."

"Report him," snapped Nina angrily. "Or I will!"

"I think maybe he is dead," said Natasha. "Please come. I think maybe I kill him."

There was a click as the connection severed. Nina slumped in the bed, remnants of her nightmare a blood-like taste in her mouth. Morten rolled over, away from the light, and went back to sleep. He had never really been properly awake. The sheet that covered him slipped to reveal the top of his buttocks.

Call the police, she told herself. Come on. 911. You know the number. God damn it to hell. The wound in her scalp had only just healed, and she still got random headaches.

She closed her eyes for a moment. Then she let herself slide carefully from the bed, put her arms into yesterday's T-shirt, and slipped into the bathroom for a quick splash of water to her face. She dressed as quickly as she could, and lifted the car keys from their peg by the door in the hall-way. It was still the summer that wouldn't die. Outside, the September darkness hugged the city in a close and damp embrace, the night hardly cooler than the day had been.

It was 4:32 A.M., she noted.

ACKNOWLEDGMENTS

Our sincere and deepfelt gratitude to:

Anders Trolle
Daiva Povilavičienė
Henrik Friis
Henrik Laier
Inger Laier
Joana Mikalauskaitė Nørskov
Juozas Mikalauskas
Justina Mikalauskienė
Kirstine Friis
Liudvika Strakauskienė and Žemyna Day Care Center
Lone Emilie Rasmussen
Pranas Povilavičius

and the many others whose help and support made this
book possible.

Lene and Agnete, August 2008

INVISIBLE
MURDER

LENE KAABERBØL AND **AGNETE FRIIS**

TRANSLATED FROM THE DANISH BY
TARA CHACE

SOHO
CRIME

PROLOGUE
NORTHERN HUNGARY

"**M**AYBE WE'LL FIND a gun," Pitkin said, aiming his finger at the guardhouse next to the gate. "Pchooooof!"

"Or even a machine gun," Tamás said, firing an imaginary weapon from his hip. "Ratatatatatatata!"

"Or a tank!"

"They took all the tanks with them," Tamás said with sudden, inappropriate realism.

"A grenade then," Pitkin tried. "Don't you think they might have forgotten a grenade somewhere?"

"Well, you never know," Tamás said to avoid totally deflating his friend's hopes.

Darkness had just fallen. It had been a wet day, and the smell of rain and damp still hung in the air. If the rain hadn't stopped, they probably wouldn't have come. But here they were, he and Pitkin, and even though he didn't really believe in the miraculous pistols, machine guns, or grenades, excitement was fizzing inside him, as if his stomach was a shook-up bottle of soda.

There was a fence around the old military camp, but the lone night watchman had long since given up trying to defend it against the hordes of scrap thieves and junk dealers. He stayed in his boxy little guardhouse now, the only building still boasting such amenities as electricity and water, and watched TV on a little black-and-white television set that he took home with him every morning at the end of his shift. Once he had actually fired a shot at the Rákos brothers when they had tried to steal his TV—something that had earned him a certain amount of respect. Now there was a sort of uneasy détente: The guard's territory extended from the guardroom to the gate and the area immediately around it; even the most enterprising of the local thieves did not go there. But the rest was no-man's land, and anything remotely portable was long gone—including some of the fence. György Motas had stolen long sections of it for his dog run.

Tamás knew perfectly well that the chances of finding anything of value were vanishingly small. But what else was there to do on a warm spring night if you were stone broke? And although Pitkin talked like an eight-year-old, he *was* almost eighteen and stronger than most. They might get lucky and find something that others had left behind because it was too heavy.

They ducked under the fence. That fizzing, tingling feeling of being somewhere forbidden grew, and Tamás grinned in the darkness. Around them still stood the bare concrete walls of what had been the officers' mess, shower stalls, workshops, and offices, looking like abandoned movie sets. Windows and doors were long gone and put to good use elsewhere, as were rafters and roof tiles, radiators, water pipes, taps, sinks, and old toilet bowls. The wooden barracks where the rank-and-file Soviet soldiers had once slept were gone, removed plank by plank so that only the concrete foundation remained. The largest and most intact building was the old infirmary, which at three stories towered over the rest of the place, like a medieval castle surrounded by peasants' cottages. For several years after the Russians had gone home, it had served as a clinic for the locals, run by one of the various Western aid organizations. But over time the English-speaking doctors and nurses and volunteers had left, and the scavengers had descended like a swarm of locusts. The first few weeks had been extremely lucrative—Attila found a steel cabinet full of rubbing alcohol, and Marius Paul unloaded three microscopes in Miskolc for almost 50,000 forints. But today even the infirmary was just a chicken carcass picked clean of every last shred of meat. Nevertheless, this was where Tamás and Pitkin were headed.

Tamás slid in through the empty door hole, turning on his flashlight to see where he was going. Patches of gray-blue moonlight filtered down from the cracks in the roof, but otherwise the darkness was dense, dank, and impenetrable.

"Boo!" yelled Pitkin behind him, loud enough to make him jump. The sound echoed between the walls, and Pitkin laughed. "Did I scare you?" he asked.

Tamás grunted. Sometimes Pitkin was just *too* childish.

There were still torn scraps of yellowing linoleum on the floor and remnants of green paint on the walls. Tamás shone the light up into the stairwell. Three floors up, he could make out a patch of night sky; the looters had stripped the roof of some of its tiles. The basement was inaccessible—the Russians had sealed it off by the simple expedient of pouring wet concrete into the stairwells, both here and at the northern end of the building.

Pitkin peered down the deserted corridor. He snatched the flashlight out of Tamás's hand, holding it as if it were a gun, and darted across to the first doorway. "Freeze!" he yelled, pointing the beam of light into the empty hospital ward.

"Shhh," Tamás said. "Do you want the guard to hear us?"

"No chance. He's snoring away in front of his TV, like always." But Pitkin lost a little of his action-hero swagger all the same. "Whoah," he said. "Something happened here . . ."

He was right. The light from the flashlight raked the flaking green walls to reveal a massive crack in the brick-work below the window. There was more debris than usual on the floor—parts of the ceiling had caved in and swaths of plaster and old paint were hanging down in strips. Tamás suddenly had the uncomfortable feeling that the floor above them might collapse at any minute, turning him and Pitkin into the meaty filling of a con-crete sandwich. But then he caught sight of something that made his greed unfurl like wings.

"There," Tamás said. "Shine the light over there again."

"Where?"

"Over by the window. No, on the floor . . ."

It might have been normal decay, or one of the small tremors that caused ripples in their coffee cups at home. Whatever the cause, the old infirmary had taken a big step closer to total ruin. The crack in the wall had made part of the floor tumble into the basement below—the basement that had been inaccessible since the day the Russians had sealed both entrances with concrete.

Pitkin and Tamás looked at each other.

"There must be tons of stuff down there," Tamás said.

"All kinds of things," Pitkin said. "Maybe even a gre-nade . . ."

Personally, Tamás would rather find a couple of

microscopes like the ones that had proved such a windfall for Marius Paul.

"I can fit through there," Tamás said. "Give me the light."

"I want to come down, too," Pitkin said.

"I know. But we have to do it one at a time."

"Why?"

"You idiot. If we both jump down there, how are we going to get back out again?"

They didn't have a rope or ladder, and Pitkin reluctantly conceded Tamás's point. So it was just Tamás who sat down at the edge of the gap and cautiously stuck his feet and legs through the irregularly shaped hole. He hesitated for a moment.

"Hurry up. Or I'll do it!" Pitkin said.

"Okay, okay. Just a second!"

Tamás didn't want Pitkin to think he was chicken, so he pushed himself forward and slipped through the hole. As he began to fall, there was a sharp stab of pain in his arm.

"Ouch!" he cried out.

He landed crookedly on a heap of rubble from the collapsed ceiling, but though it jarred his bones, the sharper pain still came from his left upper arm.

"What's wrong?" Pitkin asked from above.

"I cut myself on something," Tamás said. He could feel the blood soaking his sleeve. *Goddamnit.* A ten-inch wooden splinter was embedded in his flesh, just below his armpit. He pulled it out, but it left a jagged tear. The longer he waited for the pain to die down, the harder it throbbed.

"Well, is there anything down there?" Pitkin asked

impatiently, his concern for Tamás's wellbeing already forgotten.

"Can't see a thing, can I? Pass me the light."

Pitkin lay down on the floor and lowered the flashlight through the hole. Tamás was just able to reach it. Luckily the ceiling in the basement was lower than in the rest of the infirmary.

It was obvious right away that they had struck gold. Everything was still there, just like he had hoped. Two hospital gurneys, a steel cabinet, tons of instruments—although he didn't see anything that looked like a microscope. The radiators, faucets, and sinks were intact, there were books and vials and bottles on the shelves and in the cabinets, and in the corner there was a standing scale like the school nurse's, with weights you slid back and forth until they balanced. And this was just the first room. The thought of what it might be worth almost made Tamás forget the pain in his arm. *If* they could get it all out of here before anyone else discovered their treasure trove, of course.

"Any weapons?" Pitkin asked.

"I don't know."

He opened the door to the hallway—there were still doors down here. Thick, heavy, steel doors that squeaked when he pushed them. Tamás moved quickly down the corridor, opening them one by one, shining his light into the rooms beyond. This one was obviously an operating theater, with huge lamps still hanging from the ceiling and a stainless-steel operating table in the middle. Next came a storage room full of locked cabinets. Tamás's heart beat faster when he realized there were still unopened boxes of drugs behind the glass doors. Depending on what they were, and how they had held up, they could be worth even more than microscopes.

But it was the next room that made him stop and stare so intensely that Pitkin's impatient yells faded completely from his consciousness.

Once it must have hung from the ceiling, but tremors or decay had loosened the fat bolts, and at some point the whole thing had come crashing down onto the cracked tile floor. The sphere had been ripped off the arm in the fall and was lying by itself, cracked and scratched, its yellow paint reminding him a little of the bobbing naval mines he had seen in movies. He cautiously stretched out his hand and touched it, very, very gently. It felt warm, he thought. Not scalding, just skin temperature, as though it were alive. He could still make out the warning label, black against yellow, despite the scratches and the concrete dust.

He took a couple of steps back. The light from his flashlight had grown noticeably dimmer. The battery must be running low. He would have to get back to the hole while he could still see anything at all. On the way he smashed open the glass door of one of the medicine cabinets, blindly snatching a few jars and boxes. Pitkin was yelling again, more audibly now that Tamás was closer to the hole.

Tamás's mind was working at fever pitch. It was as if he could suddenly see the future so clearly that everything he would need to do fell neatly into place, almost as if he had already done it and was remembering it, rather than planning it. Yes. First we'll have to do this. And then this. And then if I ask . . .

"Did you find a grenade?" Pitkin interrupted his train of thought, less loudly now that he could see Tamás was back.

Tamás looked up though the hole. Pitkin's face hung like a moon in the middle of the darkness, and Tamás could feel a strange, involuntary grin tugging at his own mouth, turning it as wide as a frog's.

"No," he said breathlessly, still seeing in his mind's eye the cracked yellow sphere with its stark, black warning sign.

"Well then, what? What did you find?"

"It's better than a grenade," he said. "Much, much better . . ."

APRIL

LATELY, SKOU-LARSEN HAD been thinking quite a lot about his imminent death.

When he got out of bed in the mornings, he felt a certain amount of resistance as he inhaled, as if breathing was no longer something that could be taken for granted. He had to exert himself. The pains in his joints had long ago turned into a constant background noise that he barely noticed, even though it wore him out.

It was no wonder, he supposed. After all, his originally serviceable body had been in use since 1925, and some degree of decay was only to be expected. What bothered him wasn't so much the aches and the shortness of breath in itself; it was what they signified.

He looked across the shiny, white conference table at the lawyer sitting opposite him, duly armed with professional-looking case files and what was presumably the latest in fashionable eyewear.

"I just want to be sure my wife has the support she needs once I've passed on," Skou-Larsen said. That was what he had decided to call it, passing on. There was something graceful about the expression, he thought. It implied a smooth and civilized progress toward a destination, and for a moment he imagined himself aboard a tall ship, sails billowing in the breeze, flags flying, and the sunlight rippling on blue waves as the land of the living fell away behind him. He liked the image. It obscured the clinical reality of death, so he didn't need to think about fluid in his lungs, morphine drips and failing organs, lividity, and the moribund blood slowly congealing in his shriveled veins.

The lawyer nodded. Mads Ahlegaard, his name was. Skou-Larsen had picked him because he was the son of the Ahlegaard who had always been his lawyer. But now Ahlegaard the Elder was strolling around a golf course just outside Marbella in southern Spain, and Skou-Larsen was having to make do with this younger and somewhat less confidence-inspiring version.

"I can certainly understand that, Jørgen," Ahlegaard the Younger said, nodding again to add emphasis to his words. "But exactly what type of support do you believe your wife needs?"

Skou-Larsen felt a growing sense of frustration. He had already explained this.

"I've always been the one who looked after things," he said. "All the administrative and financial transactions, and . . . well, a lot of other things, too. I want Claus . . . that is, our son . . . to play that role in the future." The future. There. That was also a tidy, optimistic way of referring to it. The future—after the worms had had their way with him and moved on to their next feast.

"Yes, I'm sure he'll be a great support for her."

Skou-Larsen felt the muscles in his jaw and around his eyes tighten. The young man on the other side of the table simply *refused* to understand, sitting there in his shirtsleeves, with his jacket draped over the back of his chair like some high-school student. How old could he be? Not more than thirty-five, surely. Otherwise he would have learned by now that not everyone appreciates being addressed by their first name, in that overly familiar manner.

"But what if she doesn't ask him? What if she just . . . *does* something? She has no business experience, and I don't think she's a very good judge of character. She's a lot more fragile than people imagine. Couldn't we . . . take precautions?" Skou-Larsen asked.

"Such as?"

"If my son had power-of-attorney, for example. Then he would be in charge of her finances and everything to do with the house."

"Jørgen, your wife is an adult, with the right to make her own decisions. Besides, the house is in her name."

"I know! That's the problem!"

Ahlegaard the Younger pushed his thin, square titanium glasses higher up his nose with a tanned index finger. "On the contrary," he said. "This will make things so much easier for her tax-wise. Estate duties are no joke."

"That's as may be. But it also made it all too easy for her to borrow six hundred thousand kroner from the bank, and then blow it all on some Costa del Con-Artist project that I'm sure never existed outside the brochure's glossy pictures. Can't you understand I'm worried about her?"

"Jørgen, I think you should discuss it with her. Maybe you and Claus should do it together. Formally, the house is hers, and she can do whatever she wants with it. Legally and ethically, there is no document I can set up for you that will change that. Unless she's in favor of the power-of-attorney idea?"

"She is not," Skou-Larsen said. He had tried, but he just couldn't get through to her.

"No? Well, then . . ."

The meeting was over. That was clear from the way Ahlegaard gathered up his papers. Skou-Larsen remained seated for another few seconds, but all that did was draw Junior around to his side of the table to shake hands.

"Shall I ask Lotte to call you a cab?" he asked.

"No thank you. I have my own car."

"Really? Such a pain finding a parking spot around here, isn't it?"

Skou-Larsen slowly stood up. "So, you're saying that you won't help me?" he asked glumly.

"We're always here to help. Just call me if there's anything we can do, and we'll set up a meeting."

AN APRIL SHOWER had just been and gone when Skou-Larsen left the downtown offices of his unhelpful lawyer. In the park across the street, sodden forsythia branches were drooping over the gravel footpaths, and the narrow tires on passing bicycles hissed wetly on the bike path.

As his lawyer had predicted, he had indeed had a hard time finding a parking spot close to the firm's offices, and Skou-Larsen was quite out of breath by the time he made it back to the parking garage on Adelgade where he had eventually managed to park his beloved Opel Rekord. Perhaps that was why he didn't notice the black Citroën.

"Hey, watch out!"

He felt someone grab his shoulder, causing him to teeter backward and fall. Lying on the asphalt, he saw a car tire, shiny from the rain, pass within centimeters of his face. Grit from the wet road struck his cheek like hail.

"Are you okay?"

The car was gone. Skou-Larsen found himself staring up at a sweaty young man in a tight-fitting neon-green racing jersey and bike shorts, unable to answer his rescuer's question.

"Do you want me to call an ambulance?"

He shook his head mutely. No, no ambulance. "I'll just go home," he finally managed to say. Helle was waiting for him, and he didn't want her to worry.

He got up, thanked the neon-colored bike messenger, found his car keys, safely reached his Opel, and sat down in the driver's seat. Nothing had happened, he told himself, and then he repeated it to be on the safe side. Nothing whatsoever had happened.

But as he drove, he couldn't stop thinking about what might have happened. Not bit by bit, dragging out over months and maybe years, but *now*, in a single, raw instant, splat against the asphalt like a blood-filled mosquito on a windshield.

One could pass away like that, too.

"**G**OD, I WISH she had done it properly," Magnus said. "Finished him right off, the evil bastard."

Nina glanced over at Magnus. His smile seemed forced and his morbid humor as awkward as his large body. He looked tired, she thought. Tired and wan, completely lacking his usual aura of a corn-blond Viking crusader off to fight dragons, infidels, and bureaucrats.

"Check out the judge's hands," he hissed. "They look like they were made from Play-Doh. What a waste of space. Fucking paper-pushers. Fuck the fucking system." The last of the air inside him leaked out in an ill-tempered snort, and the flimsy chair groaned ominously under his weight as he slumped against the backrest, staring up at the ceiling in resignation.

Courtrooms had that effect on him, Nina knew. This wasn't the first time she had seen her boss despair at Denmark's foremost representatives of the "system." Dueling with red tape and lawyers always wore him out.

Her own rage was different. It stayed bottled up, lurking somewhere near her diaphragm.

It was 1:24 P.M.

Natasha had been sitting in the same position for more than an hour now, her elbows resting lightly on the edge of the table, a distant look in her dry, blue eyes. She looked vague and unfocused, her interest sharpening only briefly when the Russian interpreter broke into the proceedings to translate the stream of Danish phrases. The young Ukrainian woman had been in custody for almost seven months now. Her daughter, Rina, had been sent back to the Danish Red Cross Center at Furesø, more commonly known as the Coal-House Camp, to creep along the walls like a ghost among the other more boisterous children.

Sunlight flickered brightly through the courtroom's high windows, tiny motes of dust swirling in the warm columns of light. The prosecutor was about to make her closing argument. She was a small, energetic woman in her mid-forties, impeccably dressed in a dark-blue skirt, matching suit jacket, blouse, with a slender gold chain around her neck and matte, skin-colored nylons.

Nina focused on the plaster ceiling while the prosecutor slowly painted her way through the indictment and evidence. As if that were necessary. As if everyone in the courtroom didn't already know exactly what would happen.

"The defendant, Natasha Dimitrenko, walked into a hunting supply shop on Nordre Frihavnsgade . . ."

Restlessness was starting to spread through Nina's body. It lurked like a strange bubbling tension just below her skin, forcing her to stretch, slowly and silently like a cat. The Russian interpreter sitting next to Natasha droned on, slowly, in a monotone, below the shrillness of the prosecutor's voice.

". . . and bought a Sterkh-1, which is a twenty-four-centimeter-long traditional Russian hunting knife specially designed to efficiently gut and skin an animal . . ."

Nina turned and tried to look into Natasha's eyes below the wispy bangs.

". . . and it was with this knife that the defendant

stabbed her fiancé, Michael Anders Vestergaard, four times in his arm, shoulder, and neck."

Nina and everyone else at the Coal-House Camp knew that the man was a sadistic pig whose abuse had left Natasha with vaginal lacerations so extensive that Magnus had had to suture them. Even so, Natasha had gone back to him, choosing to put up with the abuse and the humiliation because he was the only thing standing between her and deportation back to Ukraine.

Nina had testified on Monday, as had Magnus, who had had the unenviable task of patching up Natasha at the clinic the previous summer after what the prosecutor chose to describe as "consensual sex with elements of dominance." Magnus had described Natasha's injuries in nauseating detail, while the prosecutor flipped distractedly through the medical records, doodling in the margins.

And, yes, Natasha had actually consented—or at least tolerated it. No, she hadn't reported anything to the police. Not even her suspicions that the man was starting to take an interest in Rina. When she caught him slipping a finger into Rina's light-blue Minnie Mouse underpants, she bought a knife instead. Natasha had called Nina, but not until afterward.

It was a foregone conclusion, and everyone knew exactly what was going to happen. Initially Natasha would be sentenced for assault with intent to kill. Premeditated, of course, since several hours had elapsed from the time she bought the knife to the moment it was actually lodged in Michael Vestergaard's neck, millimeters away from killing him. She would be stuck in a Danish prison cell while her application for asylum would plod along the winding paper trails of Danish Immigration Control toward almost inevitable denial. As soon as this occurred, swift deportation would follow, and Natasha would serve the rest of her sentence in a Ukrainian jail. Meanwhile, Rina would while away months or years of her childhood in the well-intentioned but inadequate care of the asylum system, most likely in the children's unit at the Coal-House Camp. Once her mother had been deported, Rina too would be returned to Ukraine, to wait for her mother's release, in whatever orphanage would take her. The whole nauseating story was as predictable as the prosecutor's monotonous account and the dry rustle of paper being turned, page by page, as the hearing wore on.

Vestergaard sat a little further back in the room, his Hugo Boss shirt open so everyone who felt like looking in his direction had an unimpeded view of the bright red scars on his neck and shoulder. His arm was around a young, dark-skinned woman—Nina guessed she was from South America. While the prosecutor spoke, Michael Vestergaard leaned against the young woman and tenderly held her chin. The woman pulled back slightly, but then looked at him and smiled as he ran his thumb over her lower lip, smearing a little of her lipstick over her chin.

He had stopped taking an interest in the proceedings long ago.

Magnus followed Nina's gaze.

"*God*, I wish she'd finished him off," he hissed.

RAGE WAS STILL running through her like a faint, pulsating current under her skin as Nina turned into the parking lot in front of the gates of the Coal-House Camp. Her shift was long since over, but this task just couldn't be left to anyone else.

She sat in her car for a second, listening to her own forced breathing. The April sun made the air shimmer above the black shingles on the roof of the children's unit. A couple of teenage girls lay on the lawn in front of the entrance, stretching their gangly legs in the sunlight as they casually flipped through a glossy magazine. Nina knew one of the girls was from Ethiopia. She hadn't seen the other one before, but judging by her almost bluish-white legs, she was probably yet another Eastern European dreaming of richer pastures in the West. They were unaccompanied minors. At the moment the Coal-House Camp had about fifty of them housed here in the former barracks. This was where Rina had been staying while Natasha was in custody. There had been talk of putting her into care elsewhere, but Magnus had kicked up such a fuss that he ended up getting his way.

"I mean, honestly," he had fumed. "The girl has been dragged halfway across Europe, then spends several months with that sick bastard. We're the only people she knows in Denmark. She's damn well staying here."

Nina found Rina in her room. The seven-year-old girl was sitting on a brand-new, red IKEA sofa surrounded by a handful of half-dressed Barbie dolls with hopelessly tangled hair. She was holding an old, broken mobile phone, punching its buttons with intense concentration.

I just have to get this over with, Nina thought, trying to catch Rina's attention.

"Hey, Rina. I saw your mom today."

Rina's nails were bitten down to the pink, fleshy tips, and her fingers kept rhythmically pressing the phone buttons as if she were working on an especially long text message. Nina cautiously laid her hand over Rina's.

"It worked out the way we thought it would, Rina. Your mother's going to be in jail in Denmark for a while. After that you'll both be going back to Ukraine."

Nina had been thinking she would make the Ukraine part of it into something good and hopeful—freedom and the future waiting on the other side of Natasha's prison sentence. But at the moment she couldn't think of a single word that would make the Ukraine sound like anything other than what she imagined it would be for Natasha and Rina: a bleak, poverty-stricken no-man's-land.

Natasha had never told Nina why she came to Denmark with her daughter, and Nina hadn't asked. She could have been fleeing anything from poverty or political harassment to the mafia or prostitution. Natasha had her reasons, and it would take more than an upbeat voice to convince Rina that Ukraine was the upside to this story. The girl sat motionless, her head lowered. Only her hands, still clutching the phone, quivered slightly.

"I know it's tough, Rina."

Nina scooted a little closer. She wanted to pick the girl up and carry her out to the car, bring her home to her apartment in Østerbro, and take care of her until . . . Well, yes, until when? Even if she mustered all her energy, Nina would be able to solve only a fraction of the girl's problems right now. Her mother was gone, and nothing in the world could change that. Natasha's sentence was five years, totally incomprehensible to a seven-year-old girl. And if her mother wound up in a Ukrainian jail, the time Rina spent in the children's unit at the Coal-House Camp might end up being the nicest part of her childhood.

Nina pushed the thought to the back of her mind. If it got to that point, they would have to think of something. Rina wasn't going to languish in a Ukrainian orphanage as long as Nina could prevent it. She cautiously tucked a long, soft lock of Rina's hair behind the girl's ear. Her blue eyes were wide open but seemed strangely dull and vacant. As if the girl wasn't seeing anything outside her own mind.

"You're going to live here at the center, Rina. Do you understand what I'm saying?"

The girl didn't respond.

"You'll live here and go to school here, just like you have been doing. Ingrid and the other adults here will take care of you and make sure you get to visit your Mom." Ingrid was the tough, middle-aged ex-teacher who ran the care program for the camp's underage residents. "But I'll be here, too. I'll come almost every day, I promise."

Now Rina finally nodded, but Nina had trouble deciding if that was because she understood what Nina was saying or if she just wanted to be done with this conversation. The girl pulled back on the sofa, reached for one of the Barbie dolls, and started dressing the doll with her clumsy fingers.

"Okay," Rina said. "That's okay."

THERE WASN'T MUCH going on in the camp this late in the afternoon. Most of the full-time staff were on their way home and would soon abandon the Coal-House Camp's six hundred resident souls to their own personal darkness. A small group of men and women were queuing outside Admin, waiting to pick up meal vouchers for dinner, and from the family units on the other side of the former parade ground came the quiet hum of voices and the muffled cries of children. While the days at the camp were strangely stagnant and sleepy, the nights were filled with a wary restlessness. Dinner was served at 6 P.M., and after that the doors to the office were locked. The employees returned to civilization. Only a few nighttime guards remained to patrol the hallways and make sure the Pakistanis, Indians, and Iraqis didn't kill each other overnight. The few single women hid, and families with children withdrew to their rooms behind locked doors with their TVs on loud enough to drown out the drunken cries of young men and their neighbors' incessant haranguing and bickering.

In the afternoon, people waited for night.

Nina looked at her watch. 4:04 P.M. She just had time to stop by the clinic. She asked the carer on duty to be a little extra attentive to Rina, knowing full well that the other children housed in the children's unit weren't in much better shape. Then she quickly walked across the grounds and up the flagstone path to Ellen's Place, the old, brick wing that housed the clinic and infirmary.

From the state of the waiting room, it was painfully clear that her and Magnus's absence during the week-long trial had left gaps in the clinic's defenses against chaos. Marie and Berit, the secretary and the other nurse, were both capable people, but running things on their own was an uphill job. Clearing away magazines, candy wrappers, and other debris came a poor second to registering complaints, monitoring sore throats and distressed mental states, and generally stemming the incoming tide of would-be patients, many of whom still had to leave dissatisfied because "the Doctor"—Magnus—wasn't there to see them.

The door to the clinic itself was locked, so both Berit and Marie must have left already. There was a yellow Post-it note on the doorframe, written in a hurried, nearly illegible scrawl that didn't seem to belong to either of them. Nina peered at the jumbled letters. It would seem that the family in Room 42 had asked for a doctor or a nurse to stop by.

She checked her watch again. 4:07 P.M. She had promised to buy Anton new soccer shoes on the way home. But if she scrapped any idea of catching up on her paperwork today, she could just fit in this one visit. She remembered Room 42 quite clearly. The family had arrived from Iran three months ago—the mother was a doctor herself, but at the Coal-House Camp that meant nothing. The past was erased, along with any pretense at skill, confidence, and independence. Nina had seen it happen many times before. Eventually, people could barely tie their own shoelaces.

The door to Room 42 was already ajar when she got there. A loud game show was flickering from the farthest corner of the dark room. Two preteens were glued to the screen, but the mother was sitting on the edge of the family's bed, stroking her husband's forehead. She looked up with a worried frown when she saw Nina standing in the doorway.

"Headache again," she said, pointing at her husband who was lying down with his eyes closed, panting dramatically. "I think maybe meningitis."

Nina pulled a chair over next to the husband and placed a hand on his forehead. Still no fever. The man's wife had also summoned her the week before. That time she thought it was a brain tumor, but Magnus had said it was more likely a migraine.

Nina shook her head and cautiously took the woman's hand. "It's nothing serious. Please, don't worry."

The woman shook her head skeptically.

"Do you have the pills the doctor gave you? Did you take them?" Nina asked.

"Yes," the man mumbled despondently. "I take them."

Nina sat there for a bit. She could get a new job, she thought suddenly. A job that didn't make her feel the way she felt right now. Mortal fear. That was what was wrong with him. Chronic anxiety that was turning into permanent state of panic. How could she be expected to treat that with a few platitudes and a couple of aspirins? It was wrong. No, it was more than wrong—it was reprehensible.

Nina forced a reassuring smile. "See you tomorrow, okay? Don't worry. Everything is just fine."

The woman didn't respond, and Nina knew perfectly well why not. Her husband probably didn't have meningitis, but apart from that, nothing was fine, or even remotely okay. While Nina went to buy soccer shoes for her son, night would soon be falling over the Coal-House Camp.

Nina tilted her head in a nod and shut the door a little too firmly behind her as she left.

WHEN THEY ASKED to be driven to Tavaszmező Street in Budapest's Eighth District, the cab driver locked all the doors. Sándor could clearly hear the click, and he noticed the look the driver flashed him in the rearview mirror—questioning, sizing him up. Good thing Lujza was with him. In spite of her penchant for weird shawls and flea-market finds—Boho chic, she called it—there was a down-to-earth, Hungarian middle-class respectability in her mousy-haired genes and sit-up-straight manners. For his part, even though he tied a perfect knot in his tie, polished his shoes, and ironed his shirts immaculately, somehow there would always be a question mark hanging over him: the doubt that he saw in the cab driver's eyes.

"Good thing you're here," he said aloud. But on the other hand, if it hadn't been for her, he wouldn't be sitting here. He never took cabs.

She looked at him in surprise—probably hadn't even noticed the doors being locked and the driver's suspicious looks.

"Why?" she asked.

He gave up without explaining. "It's just nice," he said.

She smiled, taking that as another compliment. "You're sweet," she said, kissing him on the cheek.

They had been to a baptism—Lujza's elder sister's little boy, her parents' first grandchild.

It was also the first time Sándor officially met the Szabó family. His nerves were still on edge, although it now felt more like fatigue than the tense stiffness he had experienced on the way there. He wanted to ask Lujza if it had gone okay, but he already knew the answer. It hadn't. Everyone had been pleasant enough, even friendly. Mr. Szabó had greeted him with a firm handshake and had chatted with him about his studies, about his upcoming exams and about what specialty he was going to choose—Lujza's father was a lawyer himself and had given criminal law an enthusiastic plug. Mrs. Szabó had been far too preoccupied with her small, screaming, tulle-bundled heir to pay much attention to him, but she had given him an absent-minded smile when he was introduced to her. There was nothing wrong with the way he had been received; it was more his own performance he was dissatisfied with. He had felt his facial muscles freeze, fossilizing with every passing hour. And as so often happened when he felt that way, his voice dropped to a scarcely audible mumble, forcing his conversation partner to lean in and say, "Sorry . . . ?" every other sentence.

He hadn't made a good impression. And he didn't understand how Lujza could sit there next to him, seemingly happy and content, and kiss him on the cheek.

They pulled onto Szív Street and suddenly had to slow down. A crowd of pedestrians was crossing without looking, as though normal traffic rules didn't apply. The driver edged the cab forward through the crowd and tried to pull out onto Andrássy Avenue, but that proved impossible. The entrance to the wide boulevard was blocked by a handful of police officers and a temporary barricade, and there were people everywhere, both in the road and on the sidewalks. When the driver tried to back up, it was too late. The crowd had closed around the cab like a fist. The driver opened his door a little and got halfway out.

"Hey," he called out to the closest officer manning the barricade. "What's going on?"

The officer glanced over his shoulder. When he noticed the taxi sign on the cab's roof, he raised his hand in a sort of semicollegial greeting between two professionals. "A demonstration," the officer yelled back. "We'll open up for traffic once it's passed."

The cab driver sank back into his seat again, shut his door, and re-locked it. "Sorry," he said. "We have to wait."

He rolled the windows down, just enough to let some air into the cab and then turned off the engine. "No point in wasting gas," he said. "We're not going anywhere for a bit."

Through the open windows, Sándor could now hear the sound of drums and rhythmic chants. He couldn't help speculating on how much the fare would be. Even though the engine was off, the meter was still running.

"Maybe we should just walk the rest of the way?" he suggested. "Or take the subway?"

"I'm wearing heels," Lujza objected.

The sound of the drums got louder; the demonstration was approaching. It was coming down Andrássy Avenue from Heroes' Square, he reckoned. He couldn't see much from inside the cab, but now he could hear what they were yelling.

"Save Hungary now! Save Hungary now!"

Involuntarily, Sándor slid down a couple centimeters in his seat. Jobbik. It had to be Jobbik, taking to the streets again to protest the Jews, Communists, and Romas "ruining our proud nation."

"Them," said Lujza, pursing her lips as though she had found something disgusting on the bottom of her shoe. "God spare us from any more racist, goose-stepping idiots."

The driver turned in his seat and gave Lujza the same suspicious look he had given Sándor at the beginning of the ride.

"Jobbik aren't racists," he said. "They're just for Hungary."

Oh no, Sándor thought. Please don't make an issue of it.

It was a doomed hope. Lujza straightened herself up in her seat and stared daggers at the driver, 128 pounds of indignant humanism versus 260 pounds of overweight-but-muscular nationalism.

"And what kind of Hungary would that be?" she asked. "A Hungary clinically scrubbed of all diversity? A Hungary where you can be arrested just because your skin is a different color? A Hungary where it's totally okay for Romas to have a life expectancy that's fifteen years shorter than the rest of the population?"

"If they want to live longer, they can quit drinking themselves to death," the driver said. "And spreading diseases to the rest of us."

"Where do you get that rubbish from? HIR TV?"

"Well, someone has to tell the truth if the government's not going to," the driver said. "I'd like to see you try driving a taxi in Budapest at night—the whole place is controlled by Gypsy gangs. They'll stab you if you so much as blink. They're worse than animals."

Lujza yanked a handful of ten thousand forint bills out of her purse and tossed them on the seat. "Here," she said. "We're getting out right now!"

The driver obviously agreed. The power locks clicked pointedly open.

"Bitch," he snarled. "Get out of my cab, and take your dirty Gypsy dog with you."

Lujza flung the door open and jumped out. Sándor remained paralyzed for a few seconds, his skin tingling as though the driver's words had struck him physically. His throat had closed up, and in any case, he couldn't think of anything to say.

"Come *on*, Sándor," snapped Lujza.

He fumbled his door open and climbed out into the middle of the street, into a throng of people pushing their way toward the police barricade.

"But your shoes," he managed to say. "Your heels . . ."

"I'd rather walk the whole way to Tavaszmezö in my bare feet," Lujza hissed. And then she burst into tears. He had to inch his way through the crowd around the now re-locked cab to reach her. He just wanted to get away—away from the yelling and drumming and red-and-white striped banners that were approaching. The shouts rumbled over their heads, from the demonstrators as well as from the scratchy loudspeaker mounted on a car in the demonstration:

"Save Hungary now! Save Hungary now!"

Lujza was obviously planning to follow through on her threat. She was standing on one leg, pulling her high-heeled shoe off her other foot. She looked so small and vulnerable in her sleeveless, cream-colored summer dress. Her white silk shawl had slipped down over one shoulder, and her neck looked strangely exposed because she was wearing her long, light-brown hair up with a couple of white silk flowers in honor of the day's festivities. Sándor wanted to stop her. He couldn't bear the thought of her small, naked feet among all the stomping, trampling boots and shoes. She had no idea how dangerous this was, and her fearlessness frightened him.

"Goddamn fascists!" she said, tears streaming down her lightly powdered cheeks. "It's unbearable that there are so many of them." She leaned on him as she angrily tugged off her second shoe.

"Put them back on," he begged. "What if you step on a piece of glass?"

She seemed not to hear him.

"Narrow-minded idiots who get their so-called information from nationalist TV propaganda. How can we let them march in our streets wearing their silly uniforms? Haven't we learned anything?"

"Shhh," he hushed her instinctively.

"You're *shushing* me?" She shot him an indignant look.

"You never know . . ." he began, and then stopped himself. It would only serve to enrage her even further.

"Are you scared?" she asked. "Are you scared of them?"

Well, yes, he was.

"He called you a dirty Gypsy." She pointed angrily at the cab driver, who luckily had stayed in his cab, entrenched behind the green Mercedes doors. "Just because you have dark hair! You don't even *look* like a Roma."

He just mumbled, "No."

"Well, you can't let them get away with that kind of thing."

"No," he mumbled, hoping his lack of opposition would end the discussion.

Suddenly the crowd stumbled in unison—a wave of people falling, people trying not to fall, and people who just wanted to get out of the way. Sándor pulled Lujza in against him, struggling to keep them both upright. They were pushed back against the cab, and that was probably the only thing that saved them from falling. One of the barricades had tipped over, and there was some sort of scuffle up ahead between the police in their neon-green vests and black helmets and a small group of young people trying to get onto Andrássy Avenue. They looked like disaffected teenagers with punk hair, hooded jackets, and torn and saggy pants that revealed too much of their underwear. They were carrying a banner that said, "NO RACISM. FUCK FACISM." Inside the O and the U, big round holes had been cut through the material.

Sándor could suddenly see the actual demonstration through the gap caused by the commotion. Long, straight lines of marching men and women dressed in white shirts, black pants and black vests, with red-and-white striped bandanas around their necks and garrison caps with red-and-white emblems on them. They looked oddly like folk dancers, harmlessly candy-striped and chubby-cheeked—not emaciated skinhead fanatics with brass knuckles and eyes brimming with hate.

"They look so damn *normal*," said Lujza, now standing so close to him that he could feel the warmth of her breath against his neck. "So orderly and law-abiding. But those Árpád stripes and double crosses . . . Who do they think they're kidding? Why don't they just wear swastikas or arrow crosses and be done with it?"

"That's not just Jobbik," he said, with a fresh spurt of foreboding. "That's Magyar Gárda, and they train with weapons."

Maybe a little of his fear had rubbed off on Lujza. Her outraged aplomb subsided somewhat, and she stood there next to him, letting herself be held.

"Let's go home," she said, finally.

IT TOOK THEM almost an hour and a half. The subway station at Kodály Körönd was closed, presumably for fear the protestors would vandalize its beautiful, historic interior. They had to fight their way through the crowd down to Oktogon and take a tram from there to Rákóczi Square. Lujza put her high heels back on and was quiet and withdrawn the whole way. She didn't say anything as they walked the last stretch, away from the wide József Boulevard and into the narrower streets of the Eighth District. The afternoon sun burned white against the cracked sidewalk slabs. A Roma family was arranged in their stiffest Sunday best on the stairs in front of Józsefváros Church on Horváth Mihály Street, ready to be photographed.

"Look," he said. "They just had a baptism, too."

She nodded but didn't perk up noticeably. Not even when he suggested coffee and poppy-seed cake from the bakery on the corner.

"I'm tired," she said. "I just want to go home."

Lujza lived with three other students in an apartment

on Tavaszmezö Street. He knew that didn't exactly thrill Mr. and Mrs. Szabó, who would have preferred to keep her at home a little longer in the somewhat more upmarket Second District where she had grown up. "But Lujza does what Lujza wants to do," Papa Szabó had said, resigned.

She didn't invite Sándor up, and he didn't push. But after he kissed her on the cheek and was about to leave, she suddenly asked: "Don't you ever get mad?"

"About what?"

"Them—those idiots—Magyar Gárda and all those other uniformed jerks."

"Of course. I can't stand extremists either."

But he could tell that wasn't enough. She felt betrayed. He had let her down, in a test that was far more important than making a good impression on her family.

She unlocked the front door to her building and disappeared into the dark foyer.

"See you later," he called loudly as the door closed behind her. But as he stood there outside the dilapidated townhouse, in his best suit and his neatly polished shoes, he had the disorienting sensation that she was slipping away from him, that the world was about to change, and not for the better.

MAY

MAY HIT **BUDAPEST** like a sledgehammer. You could practically see the pavement and the brickwork cracking under the oppressive heat. Sándor ran a finger under the collar of his shirt, trying to unstick the damp fabric from his back. He dropped the second-hand briefcase containing his most recent exam notes onto the top step, balancing it between his feet as he fished around in his pockets for his house keys. Then he discovered that a key was unnecessary because the door was already ajar. Home sweet home, he thought. Disgruntled, he pushed the sagging door open.

Szigony Residence Hall had a nice new sign, but that was the only new thing about the place. The university had taken over a couple of the old properties on Szigony Street, but since the demolition gangs were more or less waiting in the wings, no one saw any reason to waste money on maintenance and repairs. Some blocks had already fallen to the bulldozers, and soon this last, crumbling corner would also be part of the Corvin-Szigony project. Palatial office buildings, educational institutions, luxury condominiums, and exclusive shopping centers would rise from the ruins of what most Budapesti considered a "Gypsy slum." Unless the recession puts a stop to the whole thing, Sándor thought glumly as he tried to get the front door to close again. He had to lift it up a little and then give a sharp jerk . . . There! He heard the click.

"Waste of energy," called Ferenc as he came clomping

down the stairs. He lived on the same floor as Sándor and was studying music. "I'm going out. You want to try to shut the door behind me?" It was tricky to shut the door from the inside but near impossible from the outside; most people gave up without even trying.

"Okay," Sándor said.

Ferenc bounded down the last worn steps at an uneven canter. His hair stuck out wildly in all directions, and he was wearing his beloved double-breasted British blazer despite the summer heat. He had once confided in Sándor that women said it made him look like Hugh Grant.

"We're going out for a few beers at the Gödör," Ferenc said. "Why don't you join us?"

Sándor shook his head. "I've got to study," he said.

"That's what you always say. Come on, call Lujza. Don't you think that poor girl would like to get out a bit?"

Sándor could feel a numbness at the corners of his mouth. Novocaine-like. He had seen Lujza just four times since the baptism, and none of those dates had been particularly successful. He felt like he was under attack. She wanted to talk politics and human rights and fascism the whole time. It was suddenly terribly important for her to know what he thought, what he felt, where he stood. Was she afraid he was some kind of closet fascist? Up until the infamous baptism, they used to hold hands and kiss and chat and make love; now every date was like a damn debate. The mere thought of it made Sándor feel clumsy and uncommunicative.

"International law is hell," he said, because he had to say something. "I've only got a few more days to prepare, and it'll be a bloodbath if I don't know my stuff."

"Sándor, for crying out loud," Ferenc groaned. "You always know your stuff."

"Yeah, because I cram. It's called self-discipline."

"Okay, okay. But your dedication isn't much fun for the rest of us . . ."

Sándor held the door for Ferenc and repeated his door-closing ritual—lift and *jerk*, and wait for the click.

Then he just stood there.

Come on, he told himself. Go upstairs and study.

It was dark in the high-ceilinged stairwell. One of the windows facing the street was boarded up with sheets of plywood. The other still had most of its colorful stained-glass panes. At one time this had been a beautiful, classic Budapest property, built and decorated by the same crafts-men and artisan metalworkers who had created the mansions in the Palace District by the National Museum. The building had been in a state of disrepair for ages, but in recent years the pace of its decline had picked up as if the building was trying to beat the bulldozers to it. Like a man committing suicide to avoid being murdered, Sándor thought. The plasterwork was peeling off in sheets, and it reeked of dampness, brick dust, and dry rot. The rooms still had four-meter ceilings, but the electricity came and went, the water pipes were corroded and smelled like sewage, and after four months of empty promises and sheets of black plastic, he had ultimately given up and had repaired the window in his room himself.

He thought back to the yelling, stomping Magyar Gárda crowd who wanted to "save Hungary" and the newspapers and TV channels that were full of stories about hard times and unemployment and the risk of national bankruptcy. At the university, everyone was talking nervously about what would happen if the government stopped paying salaries and grants. Soon, there might be no such thing as free education. Or free medical assistance. Or pensions.

Everything is falling apart, he thought. We've struck an iceberg, and now we're sinking.

Couldn't this all have waited just a year or two? He was so close. Soon he would have his bachelor's degree. If things went to hell then, he might still be able to land a job with a law firm. Perhaps come back for his master's later or get it through one of the private schools. With a salary, he would be able to move. At least out of the Eighth District, to a place where the buildings weren't falling apart and people didn't mistake him for a filthy Gypsy all the time. "Just because you have dark hair," as Lujza had put it.

He trudged up the stairs, making sure to stay close to the wall where the steps were most solid.

A teenage Roma boy was standing there, leaning against Sándor's door—long, black hair and a macho attitude, skinny hips and tight jeans, dusty boots and an I-dare-you grin that was wide enough to reveal that he was missing one of his canines.

"Hey, *czigány*," the stranger said, and it was only when the boy actually grabbed his shoulders and slapped his back several times that Sándor realized it was his brother.

ON THE DAY of the white vans, Sándor had been eight years old. There had been four vans. One was an ambulance, the second a kind of minivan, and the last two were police cars. But all of them were white.

The vans followed the switchbacks in the road, zig-zagging their way down the hillside to the bottom of the valley where the village was. Reddish-yellow dust swirled up around them.

"Look," Tibor said, scratching his nose with his index finger. "Someone's coming."

Sándor gave his fishing line a little tug, but it was depressingly clear that there was nothing on the other end besides the hook he had fashioned out of bent wire.

"What do you think they want?" he asked.

"Don't know," Tibor said. "Want to find out?"

Sándor nodded. It wasn't often that strange cars came to Galbeno. He and Tibor left their fishing poles behind, hopped over the creek, and sprinted down the path that led back to the village.

"We can always come back later," Tibor said. "Maybe the fish will bite when we're not looking."

They weren't the only ones who were curious. People were craning their necks from the shelter of their porches, and the crowd of men in front of Baba's house stood up slowly and haphazardly and set down their guitars. Attila, who had been harnessing his gaunt, brown horse to the firewood cart, passed the reins to his oldest son and disappeared into the house. Shortly after, he was back with a couple of empty sacks, which he tossed onto the cart, and gave the horse a slap on the flank that sent it off at a bumpy, reluctant trot down the wheel ruts toward the woods.

The vans bumped their way across the dusty square in front of the school and the local council office and continued a short distance down the village street before they stopped.

"That's your house," Tibor said. "What are they doing there? Your stepfather isn't back, is he?"

"No," Sándor whispered. For the first time he felt a ripple in his stomach that wasn't curiosity or anticipation. His stepfather, Elvis, was in the district jail in Szeged and wouldn't be home for at least another six months. That couldn't be why the police cars were here. Unless he had escaped?

"Maybe we ought to stay put?" Tibor suggested.

Sándor shook his head. "It's only me now," he said. "When my stepdad is away, there's only me to look after Mama and the girls."

"And your little brother."

"Yeah, him, too." Sándor's feelings for his one-year-old baby brother weren't exclusively tender. It had been less obvious with the girls, but his stepfather had been unable to hide his excitement at finally having a "real" son. At his baptism they had let the stubby-fingered baby touch one instrument after the other, carefully watching for signs of excitement and familiarity, and when Grandpa Viktor had finally proclaimed that "the boy would be a great violinist like his father," his stepfather had been bursting with pride.

No one had made that kind of fuss over Sándor.

But now his stepfather was gone, and four white vans were parked outside the house. Sándor could see Grandma Éva telling off two of the men who had got out of the cars. She had positioned herself in the doorway and was trying to fill it completely even though she wasn't quite five feet tall, and the two men towered over her like giants.

Then more men climbed out of the cars, and Sándor couldn't see his grandmother anymore. They rolled a gurney out of the back of the ambulance and into the house. Sándor accelerated, sprinting the last few yards down the street. By now there were so many people, the men from the cars and villagers too, that he had to push and squeeze his way through.

His mother was lying on the gurney. The gurney was being rolled back to the ambulance.

For a second, Sándor stood stock still, his heart hammering against his ribs. "Mama," he said.

Even though he didn't say it very loudly, she heard him. In spite of the noise and the angry voices, in spite of the engine noise from the vans, whose motors hadn't been turned off even though they were parked.

"Sándorka," she said. "My treasure. Come here."

He ducked under the arm of a man in a gray EMT uniform and made it all the way over to the ambulance and the scratched aluminum gurney. He thought his mother looked the way she usually did. Yes, she had been sick, but why was it suddenly so bad that she had to go to the hospital?

When his other grandmother, Grandma Vanda, whom his oldest sister had been named after . . . when she had gone to the hospital, she hadn't come back. She died.

Sándor couldn't say a word. He couldn't even make himself ask. He just walked over to her so she could grab hold of his hand.

"Watch out," the ambulance attendant said. "We're lifting the gurney now. Don't get your fingers pinched."

His mother had to let go of him again.

"It won't be for very long," she said. "Then I'll be home again. You'll take care of the girls and Tamás until I get back, right? Along with Grandma Éva."

Then the doors closed, and the ambulance started driving away. The other cars stayed. And it quickly became apparent that the *gadje* hadn't come only for his mother.

IT WAS SO wrong to see Tamás standing here, outside Sándor's room, in the middle of a life that had nothing to do with him. Grown up, or almost—he still had a gangly teenager's body, and there was a softness to his features that didn't seem as tough-guy as the rest of him. Couldn't he at least get his hair cut? Did he have to look so . . . so Gypsy? If anyone saw him, they would assume he was here to steal something.

"Come in," Sándor said reluctantly. It was preferable to him hanging around in the hallway.

Tamás turned a slow circle in the middle of the room, checking it out. The proportions were a little odd because a dividing wall had been put up in what had originally been one large, well-lit room. Now Sándor and his neighbor each had half a window and a greater familiarity with each other's bodily noises than they would have liked, since the dividing wall was pretty much just painted plywood. But apart from that . . .

"This is nice," Tamás said. "You've got a lot of books, though."

"That's because I'm a student."

"Right. And which class did you get these for?" Tamás grinned broadly, pointing to a shelf full of well-worn paperbacks. He pulled one of them down, and Sándor instinctively reached out a hand to stop him.

"Morgan Kane," Tamás read. "*The Devil's Marshal*."

"Don't damage it," Sándor said. "They're really hard to come by these days."

He couldn't explain his fascination with the lonely, hard-hitting US Marshal. He was well aware that Westerns were not exactly what Lujza would call "literature," and he pretended he only ever read them to improve his English. But the books consumed him, and he had followed the entire course of Kane's life, from vulnerable, orphaned sixteen-year-old to aging, disillusioned killer. Or almost the entire course—there were eighty-three books in the series, and he only had eighty-one of them. He was missing *The Gallows Express* and *Harder than Steel*.

"Where's your computer? You have one, don't you?" Tamás asked, tossing *The Devil's Marshal* onto the bed. Sándor picked it up and returned it to its place on the shelf.

"Why do you ask?"

"Come on now, *phrala*. Are you my brother, or what?"

Phrala. He had heard people call each other that on the street in the Eighth District, their voices gently mocking, evoking a sense of community that he wasn't a part of. Hey, brother. Hey, Gypsy. No one called out to him, though. They could tell he didn't belong.

Take care of the girls and Tamás. But he had only been eight years old. What did she expect?

"What do you want?"

"There's just something I want to find out. Online, I mean. You have Internet access, right?"

"Yeah," Sándor admitted, reluctantly.

SÁNDOR HAD TO log him onto the university network with his own username and password, but otherwise Tamás needed no help. He clearly didn't want Sándor looking over his shoulder.

"What are you searching for?"

Tamás glanced at him briefly. "None of your business."

"Um, hello? That's my computer you're using, right?"

"Okay, okay. It's a girl. Happy?"

There was a fidgety energy in Tamás's compact body, excitement or anticipation of some kind. It worried Sándor and made him a little envious. He had never been young the way Tamás was young right now—there had always been so many rules for him to follow, so many unforeseeable consequences if he stepped out of line.

"You can't sit here and surf porn, just so you know."

"I'm not! It's not like that. I'm just going to chat with her a little."

"Is she Roma?" Sándor blurted out. Knee-jerk reaction, as if that were the most important thing. It would certainly be the first question his mother or grandmother would ask, he thought.

"No, she's a *gadji*."

"What does Mom have to say about that?"

Tamás straightened up and turned around. "Well, it's really more what Grandma would say. If they knew, but they don't."

Tamás's hands flew over the keyboard. But Sándor noticed that one of them was flying more slowly than the other.

"What happened to your hand?"

Tamás turned it over and studied it for a second,

almost as if he hadn't realized anything was wrong with it until now. The skin was peeling off in big flakes, like a freshly boiled new potato, and the surface underneath the old, dead layer of skin was strangely reddish brown.

"I burned myself," Tamás said.

"On what?"

Tamás flipped his hand back over. "A motor," he said. "Now get lost. I can handle this myself. Don't you have to study or something?"

Sándor did, but it was impossible to concentrate with Tamás in the room. He was a foreign body, and a fidgety one at that. He rolled around on Sándor's old office chair and drummed his fingers on the worn desktop, humming or whistling softly but constantly. Twice he pulled a mobile phone out of his pocket and spoke into it in a low voice, but it didn't sound like he was talking to his new conquest.

"You have a mobile phone," Sándor said, half as a question. Maybe that meant money wasn't quite as tight as the last time he had been home.

Tamás simply said, "Yes."

"Does Mama have one, too?"

"No."

It was quiet for a bit. Then Tamás said, vaguely apologetically, "Here. I'll write the number down for you. Give me yours, then she can call you, too."

Sándor gave Tamás his number, even though the idea that his mother could now call him at any time made him feel strangely uneasy. Going back to Galbeno for a few days a year when he thought he could cope with it was one thing. Being . . . *available* like this, whenever his Roma family felt like it . . . that was entirely different.

Added to that, there was the other increasingly urgent problem.

He needed to pee.

His computer was hands-down the most expensive thing Sándor owned. Scrimping to buy the Toshiba had been a struggle, even though it was secondhand and far from state-of-the-art. There was no bathroom on Sándor's floor. He had to go down two flights of stairs and partway down the hallway. But he didn't trust Tamás enough to leave him here, even though right now he seemed completely focused on typing and had just hissed a soft, triumphant "Yes!" which might mean his chat romance was paying off.

In the end Sándor didn't really have a choice. He set down his Roman law compendium and got up off the bed.

"Don't touch my stuff," he said. "And if you wreck my computer, I'll rip your nuts off."

That was the kind of thing he could never say to other people. To all his Hungarian friends and acquaintances who had no idea that he was half Roma. But Tamás just grinned.

"That would take bigger hands than yours, *phrala*."

SÁNDOR HURRIED. BUT of course the lavatory was occupied, and it wasn't until he had knocked on the door twice that one of his downstairs neighbors came out.

"Yeah, yeah! Give a guy a chance to pull up his trousers."

"Sorry."

He locked the door, pulled down his fly and relieved his sorely tested bladder. Someone had tried to improve the smell in the room with a pale-green air freshener hanging off one side of the toilet bowl, but as far as Sándor could tell, it just added an odd chemical sweetness to the considerable stench of sewage and urine.

He was too anxious to take the time to wash his hands properly, just quickly stuck them under the tap and dried them on his trousers instead of the damp, red towel hanging next to the sink.

When he got back, Tamás was gone. Luckily the computer was still there, unharmed, still on and logged in. He pulled the window open and looked down at the street. His brother's slender yet compact form was heading toward Prater Street.

"Hey!" Sándor yelled.

Tamás turned and danced a couple of steps backward.

"Thanks for letting me use your computer!" he yelled back at Sándor. "See you, *czigány*."

Then he turned the corner, and Sándor couldn't see him anymore.

SÁNDOR TURNED OFF the computer. Now that Tamás was gone, he suddenly wished he had asked more questions about how things were going and what kind of girl Tamás was so terribly in love with that he would travel for five hours on three different buses just for a chance to chat online with her. Surely there was a computer somewhere closer? Didn't they have Internet cafés in Miskolc?

Maybe the girl lived in Budapest. Maybe that's why Tamás was suddenly in such a hurry to leave.

Or maybe there was another reason. Sándor suddenly noticed that one of his desk drawers was ajar. It hit him like a punch to the stomach, because even though he had been afraid that Tamás would make a mess or knock something over or pour soda on his computer, at no point had he been afraid that his little brother would take something that was his. You didn't steal from your own people.

And his wallet was still there. It was his passport that was gone.

INSIDE THE SURVEILLANCE van, the smell of nervous sweat and coffee-induced flatulence had grown intense over the past couple of hours. Søren leaned forward, and then back, in an attempt to focus on the screen. Recently his optician had begun to mutter something about "bifocals."

"Any chance of a better picture?" he asked.

"Not while he's moving," the technician said. "It's not exactly broad daylight out there."

The image was jumping and shaking as the man outside made his way across the abandoned railway yard. Søren's eyes wandered over to one of the other screens, the one that gave him a bird's eye view of the area. They had two men stationed on the roof of the closest residential building on Rovsingsgade. The beat-up blue Scania refrigeration truck that was the object of the whole operation was parked more or less in the middle of the derelict triangle of no-man's land between Rovsingsgade and the old railway junction tracks. A little farther away, on the other side of the strip of straggling allotment gardens, a train rattled past in a flicker of lit windows. Darkness had given way to half-light. Luckily, a mass of leaden clouds delayed true dawn a little, but it was still light enough for the inhabitants of the refrigeration truck to spot Berndt if he wasn't careful.

But he was. Currently the little camera mounted on his headset was showing nothing except close-ups of stiff, yellow grass and nettle stalks from last year.

"Come on, come on . . ." mumbled a voice on the far side of the technician—Mikael Nielsen, an intense young man with a very high IQ, one of the new people Søren had personally helped recruit to counterterrorism from the surveillance force. With his crew-cut and ruddy complexion, he could be mistaken for the head of one of the more violent soccer fan clubs, and he gave off a vibe that made people reluctant to share a taxi with him. He had been part of Søren's group for a year and a half now, but Søren wasn't sure he would last. Yes, he had a sharp mind and a head filled with astonishing facts, but there was a restlessness in him that he struggled to control during moments like this, when all they could do was wait. And wait. And wait some more. Caution took time.

Suddenly the camera advanced with a bump. They could hear Berndt's breathing; it was very loud in the stuffy, oxygen-depleted atmosphere inside the van. The image got significantly darker.

"He's under the truck now," Gitte Nymand said, practically into Søren's ear. She was standing behind him and had leaned forward so she could follow the action more closely. He couldn't help noticing the feminine scent of freshly washed hair and deodorant. Hopefully the contrast with his own sixteen-hours-on-the-body shirt wasn't too jarring.

Suddenly an image popped up on a screen that had so far been dark. It cut in and out and bounced and pixilated before resolving into something Søren didn't need glasses to make out.

The bare interior of the truck's cargo compartment.

Spotlights from primitive work lamps fell stark and cold on a single, exposed silhouette on a chair. The man's hands were cuffed behind his back, and a black plastic package had been strapped to his bare chest with wide strips of metallic duct tape.

"Yes!" Gitte hissed softly, and Søren didn't begrudge her the small triumphant outburst. She had been right. She was the one who had gotten their captured activist to reveal his knowledge of the local area—surprisingly extensive knowledge, considering the man was a foreigner. She and Mikael had spotted the refrigeration truck and discovered that its registered owner had never heard of it. She had been in counterterrorism for only four months, and her self-confidence would undoubtedly benefit from a victory like this one.

"Contact on-site command," Søren told Mikael. "Tell him we have visual confirmation and that they have explosives on the hostage. We need to stop traffic on Rovsingsgade before we go in."

There were other more shadowy forms moving inside the Scania truck's cargo hold. Four of them, it looked like. Two were holding a video camera and debating quietly in English why it wasn't working.

"It's the batteries." The speaker was a woman, but the balaclavas and the shapeless bulletproof vests made it hard to discern much else.

"I just recharged them!" protested another, a youngish man by the sound of it.

"I can't believe that Berndt got us visuals," Gitte said. "I thought we'd be lucky to have sound. How did he do it?"

"The ventilation system," Mikael Nielsen said

absentmindedly, jabbing at his fancy new digital radio with an irritated thumb. "Come on!"

Finally he got a connection. He spoke quietly and moved over to the farthest end of the van so as to disrupt the surveillance as little as possible, and Søren refocused his attention once more on events in the refrigeration truck.

Two of the four kidnappers were holding automatic rifles; it was hard to see exactly what make, but there was something about the outline that reminded Søren of the Danish army's old Heckler & Kochs. Presumably the two with the video camera at least had handguns, even though he couldn't see them. But the explosives were by far the most critical factor in this situation.

All things considered, the hostage was remarkably calm. He was sitting quietly in the chair, watching his executioners with impassive equanimity. The spotlight bounced off his clean-shaven head and created sharp shadows below his chin and in the hollows beneath his collarbones. The mild shivers that made his naked shoulders tremble every few seconds seemed to be only a reaction to the cold.

Suddenly Søren felt Mikael's hand on his shoulder.

"It's not working," he said. "I can't get through to command. This crappy new system keeps transferring me to 911 instead."

Shit. Søren didn't say it out loud, that would only make the situation worse. He also suppressed the urge to snatch Mikael's radio in order to see if it made any difference that an inspector pushed the buttons. Sometimes you could get people to do what you wanted by pulling rank; technology couldn't care less.

"See if you can get him on his mobile," he said. "But be careful what you say. We aren't the only ones who can eavesdrop on the mobile network."

Mikael nodded, chewing the nicotine gum that kept him smoke-free in tense situations so vigorously that the muscles in his intimidating jaw bulged under his skin. "I'll try."

But a few seconds later he swore again. "He has turned it off."

That was per regulation, actually. Søren's own mobile was also off so it wouldn't jeopardize the operation.

"Okay," he said. "Input?"

"The clock is ticking," Mikael said. "At some point they'll notice that Blue 1 is missing or that Blue 4 is failing to check in." Blue 1 was the code name for the activist they had captured and interrogated; Blue 4 the guard that Berndt's unit had taken out.

"Can we still get in touch with our own lot?" Søren said.

"Yes. It's just the rest of the emergency services that have fallen off the map."

"Brave new digital world," Søren muttered.

"I think we should go in," Mikael said. "While we still have the element of surprise. Seize them before they can push the button."

"And if it goes wrong? You don't know how powerful those explosives are," Søren pointed out. "They're only about twenty to thirty meters away from the traffic on Rovsingsgade."

"And they could easily have a lookout outside—someone we haven't spotted," Gitte said.

"Well, if they do, then why didn't *he* spot Berndt?" Mikael objected.

"Because Berndt is Berndt."

"But it's every bit as dangerous to wait. They could kill the hostage at any time. With or without the explosives."

"No," Gitte said. "Because they haven't made the recording yet."

Mikael emitted a sound of frustration, half wheeze, half sigh.

"Terrorism is called terrorism because the goal is fear," Gitte said. "Isn't that what you're always preaching, boss?"

"Yes." Søren permitted himself the hint of a smile. Killing a man, however important, in a refrigeration truck in Copenhagen certainly wouldn't be the ultimate goal of any terrorist group. They would want the whole world to *watch* while they did it. To have the recording played on as many TV screens as possible, thus getting attention, instilling fear, and changing people's behavior. Without a video recording, there was precious little point to the act as far as the terrorists were concerned. They might even suffer the affront of having another group claim responsibility.

Suddenly Gitte sat up in her chair. She was a tall woman, as tall as most men and had the shoulders of an Olympic swim star. When Gitte straightened up, people noticed.

"What is it?"

"The traffic," she said, pointing to the screen that gave them the aerial overview. "It's stopped."

She was right. The sparse a-little-past-six-in-the-morning trickle of cars had completely dried up. Rovsingsgade was deserted.

"*Shit.*" This time Søren did say it out loud. What the hell was going on here? Who was the idiot that had blocked off the road without checking with them first? And how long would it take before the group in there realized it? Seconds, maybe, if they really did have another lookout outside the truck. "Now!" he said into the earpiece in Berndt's ear. "We're going in *now!*"

LIGHTS, COLD, MOVEMENT. The still-faint daylight felt like a birth shock after the dark incubator of the surveillance van. He hit the asphalt running, crossed the first parking lot, and jumped over the low beech hedge into the next. The refrigeration truck wasn't his goal; Berndt and the strike team would take care of that, and Søren had no intention whatsoever of getting in the way of people trained for that sort of thing. His goal was a man with a radio, standing on the roof of the four-story residential building their bird's eye view was coming from, a radio that could hopefully communicate with the rest of the emergency services, so he could find out what the hell was going on. He burst through the back door—considerably taped so the latch couldn't click into the strike plate—and sprinted up the smooth terrazzo stairs. First floor, second floor, third floor . . . past the fourth and up the last narrow service stairwell to the roof. There was an uncomfortable burn in his knee where he had had surgery on his cruciate ligament, and his lungs were on overtime. But he had enough breath left to snarl "Give me that radio!" at a startled young officer, uniformed police. In his own earpiece he could hear static and breathing and short, terse statements, but no shots. Thank God, no shots yet.

He snatched the radio—or "terminal" as they were supposed to call them now—out of the officer's hand and stood frozen for a second, staring at the unfamiliar keys. Then information he knew, but which had yet to become second nature, coalesced, and he entered the sequence that was supposed to put him in touch with on-site command.

At that moment a hard, flat bang resonated—both inside and outside his earpiece. In three quick steps, Søren moved over to the half wall that ran around the edge of the roof, and now for the first time in the cool, sharp reality of morning, he had the same bird's eye view of the area that he had had earlier on the screen in the surveillance van. The back end of the refrigeration truck was hanging open and a diffuse cloud of grayish-white smoke was wafting out over the railway yard.

"Berndt?" he said quietly into his microphone headset.

Twenty-eight seconds passed. Søren counted them. Then Berndt's voice responded with the unnatural intimacy that came with in-ear receivers:

"It's okay. We're in, and we have control."

BY THE TIME Søren made it down to the refrigeration truck, they had the handcuffs off the hostage and a blanket around his shoulders. Apparently Gitte was the one charged with the thankless task of removing the flat, black object that was attached to his chest. The man made a face as she tried to tug the wide tape off.

"Do we have any rubbing alcohol?" Søren asked. "That'll make it come off a little easier."

"Never mind," said the former hostage. "Just get it over with."

His naked torso was too muscular for him to be completely believable in the role of a captured head of state, and although Søren could see him flexing his fingers in a pumping rhythm to get the blood flowing to his hands again, he didn't otherwise look like a man who had been bound and helpless for more than four hours. Torben Wahl—deputy director of PET's counterterrorism section and Søren's immediate supervisor—was not a man who was easily rattled.

"How did it go?" he asked.

"Not that great," Søren admitted. "The intelligence side of things went okay, and Berndt and the SWAT team went in like they were supposed to. However, liaising with the rest of the emergency services was a total failure. Someone had better get a handle on that before the summit, because if this had been the real deal . . ."

"Well, that's why we drill," Torben said, but he didn't look happy.

DESPITE THE SHOWER, a fresh shirt, and four hours of sleep with the curtains drawn, the effects of the training exercise were still lingering in his body as Søren parked in front of PET's headquarters in suburban Søborg late that afternoon. He yawned on his way up the stairs. He could have used a couple more hours of downtime, but he had to check in to see what had turned up on his desk while he had been off playing cops and robbers in Rovsingsgade. His mood was not improved when he was forced to skirt around several young men in yellow T-shirts struggling with a giant, cube-shaped monstrosity and a plastic drum of drinking water that were apparently destined for the little niche in front of the lavatories farther down the hallway.

A water cooler. He had seen machines identical to this popping up throughout the building. They might keep the water cold, but they also gave off a constant irritating hum. Personally, he managed just fine with water from the tap in the men's room, but in recent years the younger people, especially the women, had insisted on the phthalate-saturated energy wasters. Now it appeared that their bit of the corridor would have one, too. Of all the frivolous, useless fads—and he could reel off quite a few without even trying—water coolers ranked among the very worst, on par with the spider catchers he had recently seen in Kvickly, followed closely by patio heaters and ceiling fans. But apparently this was what the younger people wanted these days. Søren sighed. "The younger people?" When had he begun to call them that? Of course the majority of the eighty men and women who worked in the Danish Security and Intelligence Service's counterterrorism branch *were* younger than him, but still—"the younger people"? He was going to have to stop using that expression. It made him sound like a world-weary old fart. Especially when he was also ranting about newfangled water coolers.

Søren ducked into the little kitchenette at the end of the hall and selected a mug from the cupboard. The coffee left in the machine was jet black and tasted like charcoal; it had probably been sitting there since lunch. A few other people from the group had also drifted in even though they weren't on duty again until the next morning. He could hear someone typing and quiet laughter coming from the large, open-plan office. Gitte Nymand was leaning over Mikael Nielsen's shoulder and pointing to something or other on the screen in front of them. She had a small wrinkle of concentration on her brow, but she was smiling, and her voice bubbled with excitement. Søren allowed himself to stand there for a moment longer than was strictly necessary, enjoying the view. Gitte wasn't beautiful in the traditional sense. Her short-cropped hair framed a face that was just as distinctive as her gold-medalist swimmer's shoulders and muscular legs. Wide cheekbones, strong jaw, bushy eyebrows that were astonishingly dark despite her standard Scandinavian blonde hair and blue-green eyes. But what rendered her one of his best personnel finds of late was the calm, natural authority she radiated, even though she was only in her late twenties. Also, she got along well with Mikael, who could be a little prickly to work with. Søren seemed to remember they had been at the police academy together. It did something to the cadets' relationships, those months of standing side by side in riot gear, in yet another interminable attempt to clear Christiania's cannabis market.

"Hi, Boss."

They had noticed him. Gitte straightened up and looked at him inquisitively, which gave him a brief and very irritating sense of being in the way. As if they were just waiting politely for their aging boss to clear off so they could once again immerse themselves in the details of their report on the training exercise. You could see the easy intimacy between them in the way they moved—Mikael, leaning back casually in his chair, Gitte with her hand still on his shoulder. Søren felt a ridiculous pang of jealousy. When had he last felt that kind of camaraderie with any of his colleagues? When had he last worked side by side with someone who had also seen him drunk? None of his supervisors ever leaned over his shoulder with bright eyes and eager voices, that was for sure.

"Hi," Søren grunted in response.

He raised his hand halfheartedly and continued into his own office, set the charred coffee down on the desk, and turned on his computer. He stared at the dark screen as the machine slowly whirred through its security protocol. His own face was reflected back at him dimly behind the blinking gray lines of text, looking rather more geriatric than usual. It was the lack of sleep, he told himself firmly, as if attempting to banish the specter of age by willpower alone. Normally, all he saw was himself—broad forehead, receding hairline, and the narrow, hooked nose which, along with his black hair, had earned him the nickname "Kemosabe" at the police academy. As far as he knew no one called him that anymore. Admittedly, the black hair had grayed a bit since then, and his promotion to inspector had probably put the kibosh on that type of linguistic creativity.

At least he was in good shape. He worked out in the gym in the basement every Monday and Wednesday morning before heading for his desk, and he ran two or three times a week, usually ten kilometers or more, and even though he didn't time himself, he knew he was still creditably fast. The physical that stopped any number of aspiring cadets every year because of excessive cigarettes and chronic puppy fat would still be no hindrance to him. No, there was nothing wrong with his physique, and he didn't feel old. But to everyone else, to the "younger people," he had already crossed the line into old-man territory. The most ambitious exercise program in the world couldn't change that.

Ding.

The computer had finally plodded its way through the startup process and automatically opened the most recently updated daily report. Leaning forward a little, Søren scrolled down the screen. It appeared that some wiretap equipment had been deployed the previous night without any hitches. He hadn't expected otherwise. The man they were supposed to be watching had gone to the derelict farmhouse he owned in Sweden. His mobile phone signal hadn't budged for three days, so everything indicated that he was standing thigh-deep in some river, happily catching salmon, while the tech boys were sneaking into his downtown apartment here in Copenhagen. At any rate, they had accomplished what they were supposed to. Aside from that, all seemed quiet on the home front. A couple of messages had come in from Hungary, Belgium, and Turkey. They had all been vetted by Communication, and none of them were priority matters. The Hungarian message had been tagged "Attn. Kirkegaard," though, so something in there must require his personal attention.

He printed the e-mail. He still preferred to read on paper—possibly another sign of age, he admitted grudgingly, but years of poring over typed reports had left him in the habit of doing his thinking with a pencil in his hand. It seemed a little late to change those spots.

He quickly circled the most important points of the mail. His colleagues from the Hungarian intelligence service, NBH, had a couple of websites under observation because they suspected these sites of trading in the arms, ammunition, and other military "surplus products" that poured over Eastern European borders in a steady stream. A neat flow chart showed that web traffic from a number of relatively legitimate forums and sites was being directed to a more hardcore inner circle of dedicated arms sites that in turn led to the object of primary interest to Hungarian Intelligence: the apparently innocent-looking hospitalequip.org, which served, according to the NBH, as a coded hub of exchange for customers looking to buy or sell arms, chemicals, and other dangerous substances.

Brave new World Wide Web. There were times when Søren felt sure there had to be a devil somewhere, gleefully contemplating the effects of his latest attack on humanity. In the past, people with shady, bizarre, or downright disgusting interests had had a much harder time locating each other. These days, even the most loathsome proclivities could find affirmation from likeminded nutters via the Internet, easily and more or less anonymously. And no matter what they wanted, it was out there—stolen antiquities, endangered species, illegal World War II souvenirs, pornography in all shapes and forms, weird drugs, and, yes, also arms, explosives, and dangerous chemicals.

"Fresh coffee, my liege?" asked Gitte, who was on her

way to the kitchenette, and Søren nodded gratefully as
he typed hospitalequip.org into his browser window. The
page appeared, bland, pale green, a simple layout with a
menu bar completely devoid of any graphic interest or
stylish Flash animations. There were currently five chat
rooms open. The discussion in one of them was apparently about "aggressive treatments for infections," while
another was simply about "equipment." He could see
which users were online—or, at least, he could see the
pithy little aliases they were hiding behind. In the last
three chat rooms, Søren couldn't tell what the topic of
conversation was or who was participating. When he
tried hitting the Enter Chat button, he was asked to enter
his PIN. He typed in four random numbers, and a few
seconds later an automated message popped up: access
denied. Please contact moderator.

He gave up trying to gain access. This was NBH's ball
game, and they hadn't asked him to play. Besides, he
could easily guess what was hiding behind the access
codes—hospitalequip.org was by no means unique. Like
other similar websites, it functioned as a marketplace
where buyers and sellers could find each other and
make that first contact. They announced what they
had for sale or what they were interested in buying,
anonymously of course, and then the hospitalequip
people took care of the rest. NBH believed they were
marketing their own stolen goods this way as well as
earning a hefty sum by steering customers into interest-
specific chat rooms that were set up and taken down
so fast that it was hard for the intelligence service to
keep up. The money flow was also hard to follow—the

hospitalequip people made creative use of gold-based Internet currencies like e-bullion and e-gold.

What was interesting from a Danish perspective was that a group of Danes appeared to have been poking around on the site. At least one of them had made a connection and then subsequently dropped out of the chat to continue the discussion more discretely via mobile phone. The trail petered out at that point because the telephone number obtainable from the chat records had only been used briefly, presumably to exchange more secure numbers that the NBH had not been able to trace.

The Hungarian end of the contact was an IP address associated with the university in Budapest. The Hungarian colleague who had written the e-mail, a man by the name of Károly Gábor, reported that in addition to hospitalequip.org the Hungarian user had also visited a number of other suspicious pages, including the Islamic hizbuttahrir.org. Thus, NBH were hereby giving due notification, according to instructions, etc., etc., etc. . . .

Søren sighed softly. The flag-burning and the riots might have subsided, but the Mohammed cartoons and Denmark's participation in Iraq and Afghanistan were still making the country a target. In the old days, e-mails like this would have slumbered gently in archives unless there were further alerts in the matter. Now they had to follow up on every single Islamist whisper that had Denmark's name in it. Especially now that the Summit was so close. His thoughts went to the morning's partially botched training exercise, and he suppressed a wave of irritation. The damned Summit was moving Copenhagen even further up the list of attractive targets, whether you were an Islamist terrorist, a swastika-waving neo-Nazi, or just an attention-seeking grassroots organization with a spare bucket of red paint.

It made him tired. The hatred that flowed in wide, black rivers across the Internet, venting itself at Danes, Muslims, Gypsies, gays, Jews, liberals, conservatives, women—at every conceivable and inconceivable minority, in Denmark and the rest of the world . . . it was more than just stupidity. It was evil. He wasn't a religious person, and he usually resisted such simplistic terms, but when he read what people wrote online on a regular basis about "stupid bitches" and "sheep fuckers" and "horny homos" who, according to vox populi, all deserved to be hanged or burned or mutilated, that was the only word he could think of: evil.

"Gitte!"

She had tiptoed into his office, set the coffee down, and was already on her way out again.

"Could you forward this to the techies right away?"

Gitte took the printout of the email and quickly scanned through it.

"These three," Gitte said, pointing at the first three addresses with a long, slender finger. "I think I can guess who they are without any help from the IT department." She smelled of apples and lemons now, Søren thought fleetingly, with a faint pang of emptiness somewhere in his abdomen.

"Yes," he said quickly. "It looks like our very own bunch of flag-waving White Pride idiots are at it again. These others, on the other hand, could be just about anyone. This one is probably the most significant." He circled the Danish IP address that had been in touch with what he quietly thought of as "the Islamist whisper." "But we ought to get them all checked out. Ask them to send us a list as soon as possible."

Gitte nodded briskly and left, and Søren turned back to the flickering pale-green screen on his desk. Despite Denmark's restrictive gun laws, it really wasn't all that difficult to get hold of an ordinary hand weapon if you knew where to go. Gun-shopping in Hungary seemed a bit extreme, what with all the delivery problems and border crossings it entailed, so maybe the buyer was looking for something a little more exotic. Søren scrolled down through the bare-bones layout one last time. "Buy now, good stuff, new needles, from Russia with love."

In my next life, he thought, I want to do something else. Something that actually permits the existence of love.

"**F**UCK!"

Nina jumped back a few steps, swearing, but it was too late.

The aerator from the kitchen faucet had come off. It shot down into the dirty pan soaking in the sink, and a cascade of greasy dishwater sprayed indiscriminately across the wall, the counter, the floor, and Nina's T-shirt and jeans. She turned the water off and gave the little piece of thoroughly corroded metal that should have been replaced a long time ago a dirty look. Now the kitchen floor was awash with water *and* dust bunnies, and on the counter, the parade of salad bowls, plates, cutlery, and cups remained unstacked and unwashed. Nina felt her already bad mood descend into a thoroughly foul temper. It wasn't really the water on the kitchen floor and the unappetizing onion skins and carrot peelings at the bottom of the sink, although none of that helped. It was Morten. Morten and the damn duffel bags in the bedroom.

Morten was packing.

He had done it many times before. He was a geologist and had been the resident "mud logger" at one of the North Sea oil rigs for years. Recently he had been promoted to project manager, which did mean fewer days at sea, but he still had to go on a regular basis, and every single time, Nina had the same aching anxiety in the pit of her stomach when he started packing. She missed him when he was gone, and once the door had closed behind him, Ida's hostile, brooding silence would hang over the apartment like a sort of teenage curse. It wasn't that Nina had much trouble from Ida while Morten was away. She went to her friends' houses most nights, but she also dutifully picked up Anton and did the grocery shopping a couple times a week. On the face of it, a fourteen-year-old marvel of daughterly obedience. But Nina knew she did those things only because Morten had asked her to do them and because doing them quietly was one more way of avoiding conversation. If Ida did deign to join them for dinner, her complete lack of expression squashed any attempt at small talk. Ida seemed barely able to tolerate Nina's presence, and Nina asking her to pass the potatoes was obviously a major imposition.

Nina would almost have preferred the arguments they used to have, and she felt sorry for Anton, who fidgeted in his chair as he tried to lighten the atmosphere with jokes and quotes from his favorite show on Cartoon Network. He did sometimes manage to wring smiles out of Ida or Nina, but God, he had to work at it.

Nina got out a cloth and mopped up the water from the kitchen floor while she tried to concentrate on the seven o'clock news. The police didn't have enough manpower for the Copenhagen Summit, and the far right was up in arms again because some new Islamic cultural center was building "what amounted to minarets," according to the professionally outraged spokesman for the party. As he went on about the importance of "upholding Danish values," Nina's ability to concentrate plummeted abruptly. She dried her hands, turned her back on the rest of the mess, and went into the bedroom.

He was almost done.

Socks, underwear, T-shirts, and a variety of electronic gear were laid out in small, separate mounds on the double bed, so that all he had to do was dump them into the waiting bags. He had done it so many times that he could now pack for a two-week absence in under half an hour.

"Have you seen my iPod?"

Nina shook her head. Morten put his arms around her and pulled her to him so her shoulders pressed against his chest. He was so tall that his chin rested naturally on top of her head, and it gave her a feeling of being tugged inside a big, friendly fur coat. He bent to give her a fleeting kiss on the back of her neck before he let her go and once again directed his attention to the piles on the bed.

"I lent it to Anton, so it could be anywhere."

Nina nodded. Anton scattered things throughout the apartment—and everywhere else, too—pretty much at random. In many ways it was like living with an eight-year-old Alzheimer's patient. Or maybe just with an eight-year-old, Nina corrected herself.

Morten began the process of transferring the piles into the duffel bags. He was working quickly and methodically now. He put his phone, train pass, and wallet in his jacket pocket, and that was pretty much it.

Nina felt the dull ache of longing already. It was her fault he had had to take this inconvenient job in the first place. It was all he had been able to get at short notice, and it would take time for him to work his way up from being an itinerant mud logger to a more family-friendly Copenhagen-based job. She hated it, and Morten probably did, too, although he was far too polite to complain about it to her face. Working on the rigs was a cross he had chosen to bear, like he bore everything else life had asked of him, or more accurately, everything else that Nina had put him through. Shaken, not stirred. James Bond-style.

"When are you leaving, Dad?"

Ida was standing in the bedroom doorway with an open book in her hand. She was reading *The Lord of the Rings* and had been discussing it with Morten as if she had personally invented the universe, or at least been the one to discover the books. The film version had, of course, been part of her classmates' stable diet since they were Anton's age.

Ida would say things like, "I'm not sure about Tolkien's view of women," and Morten would listen to her and answer her without batting an eyelid, never letting on that she had seized on the stalest of topics in one of the most endlessly debated books in the galaxy. James Bond teaching Literature. Nina was profoundly envious.

"I'm off in a minute," Morten said, casting a quick glance at his watch, "but call me on the train, and we can say goodnight."

Ida smiled, and planted a quick kiss on her father's cheek. She was wearing scent of some kind, Nina realized. Something sweet and a little too heavy.

"Keep your fingers crossed for my hockey match," she said. Then she waved and vanished back into her bedroom without even giving Nina a glance. The sound of muffled music seeped out into the hallway and on into their bedroom, and Nina knew she wouldn't be seeing any more of Ida tonight.

Morten didn't seem to have noticed any of this. He was leaning toward her so she could feel the warmth from his body.

"We still have our deal, right?" he asked softly.

Nina nodded. Their deal. Their Big, Important Deal. No underground work for the Network while Morten was away. She hoped no one from the ever-changing flock of illegal immigrants that Peter from the Network took under his wing would break an arm or a leg or come down with symptoms of appendicitis in the next fortnight.

"Of course," she said.

"And remember . . ." Morten whispered, pulling Nina in tight against him and kissing her mischievously on the nose. Feeling patronized, Nina wrapped her arms around his neck and stood with her nose right up against his throat.

"Remember *you're* driving the girls to roller hockey on Wednesday. It's our turn."

Nina nodded quickly. Roller hockey was one of the few of Ida's activities Nina was still allowed to attend. Maybe more out of necessity than desire on Ida's part, but Nina had to take what she could get. Morten gently maneuvered his way out of her arms and went to say goodbye to Anton.

NINA STOOD THERE for a moment in the hallway, listening to his light, energetic steps descending the stairs. Then she turned around and went back to the kitchen. Ida had turned up her music, and a significant amount of bass penetrated the wall, reaching Nina and the chaotic kitchen table that still hadn't been cleared. Anton had brushed his teeth and was in bed in his room with a comic book and his bedside light on, and Nina suddenly felt utterly miserable. Alone.

Two weeks, she thought, glancing at the calendar. Come on. The world won't fall apart in two weeks.

SÁNDOR HAD HIS half of the window wide open, but it didn't seem to do much good. There was hardly any draft, just lots of construction dust and street noise. He had taken off his shirt and trousers and was sitting on his bed in just his underwear, studying. Sweat trickled down his chest from his armpits, and the paper stuck damply to his fingers every time he turned a page.

He had left his door ajar to admit at least a trickle of cross ventilation; to Ferenc, that was obviously an invitation.

"When's your big exam?" Ferenc asked.

"Thursday." Sándor was hit by a surge of nerves at the mere thought. But he had it under control, he told himself. He knew his stuff. He just needed to take another look at—

His thoughts were interrupted when Ferenc suddenly grabbed hold of him. "Good. We of the Sándor Liberation Committee have officially nominated you the best-prepared student in the history of this university. And we've also decided that it's high time we intervene to prevent your body's ability to metabolize alcohol from atrophying completely. Put some clothes on, pal."

Sándor found himself standing in the middle of his room, still wearing only his underwear and desperately clutching *Blackstone's International Law.*

"Knock it off, Ferenc. I can't—"

"I'm afraid the Committee's decision cannot appealed. Please don't force us to resort to violen

Ferenc wasn't alone. Out in the hallway stood Henk, a Dutch exchange student who was studying music like Ferenc, and Mihály, who was in Sándor's class. And also Lujza.

Ferenc threw Sándor's trousers in his face.

"Here. Hop to it, or you're going as you are."

Sándor's whole body was stiff with passive resistance. It's just for fun, he told himself, relax. But he couldn't force the appropriate you-guys-are-crazy grin onto his face, and his lack of response gradually caused the others' broad smiles to fade.

"Come on, Sándor," Ferenc said.

He finally "hopped to it," as Ferenc put it. He could move again. He set *Blackstone* on his desk and then balanced awkwardly on one foot while he tried to stuff his other foot into his chinos.

"You guys are crazy," Sándor grumbled, and their smiles returned.

Ferenc patted him on the shoulder. "That's the spirit," he said in the fake British accent he was cultivating because it went so well with his Hugh Grant style. Lujza smiled at Sándor, candidly and warmly like in the old days before the baptism.

I can always get up extra early tomorrow, Sándor promised himself. After all, he *was* better prepped than anyone else he knew.

WHEN THEY GOT downstairs, there was a police car parked across the street from them. Two officers were just getting out.

Sándor was trying to close the defective front

door without much luck. The others stopped to wait for him.

"Just leave it," Ferenc said. "In five minutes someone else will come out, and then it'll be wide open again."

Sándor gave up. When he turned around, the two police officers were a few meters away. The older one, a muscular man whose light-blue uniform shirt had big sweat stains under his arms, checked a printout he had in his hand.

"Does a Sándor Horváth live here?" he asked.

Sándor froze. The other four also suddenly went still, their laughter faded, their faces stiffened.

"What seems to be the problem, officer?" Ferenc asked politely.

"That's him," the other officer said, pointing at Sándor.

"Turn around," the first one said sharply. "Hands up against the wall. Now!"

When Sándor didn't move, remaining rigid and mute, they grabbed his arm, spun him around, pushed him up against the wall, and kicked at his ankles until he was leaning against the sun-baked bricks at an angle. If he moved his hands, he would fall over. They frisked him quickly and matter-of-factly.

"What are you doing?" Lujza yelled at them. "Let him go! What is it you think he did?"

"None of your business, little lady," the one with the sweat stains replied.

"You can't just . . ." Lujza yelled. "Stop!"

Sándor couldn't see her. He couldn't see anything except a couple of square meters of crumbling sidewalk and the drop of sweat that was trickling down his nose.

"Sándor," Mihály said suddenly. "*You* ask them. If you ask, they have to answer. *The detainee must be informed of the charges* and all that."

But Sándor couldn't say a thing. His tongue was just a lump of flesh, his jaw was so tight he might as well have had lockjaw. The officers cuffed his wrists with plastic cable ties and bundled him across the street and into their squad car. He didn't put up any resistance.

"Sándor!" Of course it was Lujza who was yelling. "We'll file a complaint. Don't let them do this to you. There must be someone we can complain to . . ."

"Call 1-475-7100," the older of the two officers said placidly. "It's toll-free."

ONCE WHEN HIS stepfather Elvis went to record a CD with a band called Chavale, Sándor had been allowed to tag along. That was back when they were playing enough gigs to actually earn a little money, and his stepfather still believed firmly in his Big Break, as he called it. It was also before Tamás was born, so his stepfather would sometimes take him places without referring to him as "Valeria's kid from before we got married." Sándor could still remember the feeling of sitting quiet as a mouse on a chair that could spin around, but squeaked when you did it, so you couldn't. He could remember the men's concentration and laughter, the smell of their cigarettes, the multitude of buttons on the mixing board, and the pane of glass between the studio and the recording equipment.

The memory popped into his head now because the room they put him in reminded him of that studio. The gray, insulated walls, the pane of glass facing the hallway, and then of course the fact that they were recording everything he said.

"Where were you born, Sándor?" said the man who had introduced himself only as Gábor.

"Galbeno. It's a village near Miskolc."

"And your parents?"

Did he mean who were they or where were they born? Sándor's brain felt as thick as porridge.

"My father was born in Miskolc."

"Name?"

"Gusztáv Horváth. He's dead now." Gusztáv Horváth had keeled over in front of twenty-seven dumbstruck physics students at the Béla Uitz School on a warm day in September almost three years ago.

"And your mother?"

There was that stiffness in his jaws again, as if all his chewing muscles were in spasms. He was having a hard time opening his mouth, and every last bit of spit had evaporated. He didn't dare lie. This was the NBH. *Nemzetbiztonsági Hivatal*, Hungary's National Security Service. These days, they might have a fancy home page and a press secretary and even several ombudsmen who were supposed to keep tabs on things and ensure openness and protect the legal rights of the individual, but they were still the NBH.

"Ágnes Horváth."

The man whose name might be Gábor sat quietly, calmly, and expectantly, and the silence somehow forced Sándor to add the correction. "Or . . . well, she's my stepmother."

Gábor didn't reveal in any way whether he was satisfied

or dissatisfied with the response. He was still waiting. A man in his late forties with light, amber-colored eyes and graying, short-cropped dark hair. Shirt and tie. Strong, rounded shoulders, neck slightly too thick. His broad, calm face was almost gentle, and it wasn't physical violence that Sándor feared. This was not a man who would push people's heads into water-logged plastic bags.

"My biological mother's name is Valeria Rézmüves." The words tumbled out of his mouth one by one, oddly disjointed. It sound like one of those computerized phone voices, he thought. *You have. Selected. Zero four. Zero eight. Nineteen. Eight five.*

"Gypsy?"

"Yes."

Rézmüves was a typical Roma name, so it didn't take any secret archives or supernatural abilities to guess that. Still, Sándor felt exposed. Poorer by one secret.

There's no reason for people to know about that, Ágnes always said. You're mine now. That other thing—we don't talk about that. Do you understand?

He wasn't even nine yet, but he had already learned that silence was the only reasonably safe response, so he didn't say anything. And she had just nodded, as if that was precisely what she wanted from him. A child who could keep his mouth shut.

Gábor stood up.

"Excuse me a moment," he said politely. "We'll continue in a little while."

And then he left.

Sándor sat there on the gray, plastic chair with his elbows resting on the table. It was warm in the room, but not as hot as in his overheated room in the Eighth District. The temperature in here was not governed by such variables as sunlight and outside air. It was warm because a dial had been set to make it so.

Sándor felt strangely weightless. An astronaut with a severed lifeline, floating above the Earth. He could see it, could see life down there, knew there were people laughing, talking, working, making love, taking baths, arguing, living normal lives. He knew they were there, but he couldn't reach them. Just a few hours before he had believed he could be like them, but now he knew that would never happen.

He still hadn't asked them why he was here. Hadn't said a word that wasn't in response to their questions. He knew that wasn't normal. That if it had been Lujza sitting here, or Ferenc, or Mihály, they would have protested, kicked up a fuss, demanded lawyers and explanations. He also knew that if he wanted to *seem* like a normal person, he should do the same.

But he couldn't.

WELL OVER HALF an hour passed before Gábor came back. He had a piece of paper with him that he placed on the table in front of Sándor.

"Does this mean anything to you?" he asked.

It was a list of URLs. Some were Hungarian, others were various dot-com sites: unitednuclear.com, fegyver.net, attila.forum.hu, hospitalequip.org. He didn't recognize any of them.

"No," he said.

"That's strange," Gábor said. "Because we can tell from

your computer that you've visited all of them and spent rather a long time at each."

It took one long, freezing cold instant. Then the realization hit him like a bomb blast. Tamás. Tamás must have done it, that night when he was pretending there was a girl he was desperate to contact. Sándor looked down at the list again. United Nuclear? Fegyver.net? That must be some kind of gun site. Attila Forum sounded like one of those right-wing extremist pages Lujza would get so worked up over. But hospitalequip.org? What on earth was the connection there? And why had Tamás come all the way from Galbeno to Budapest to mess around with stuff like that?

"I . . . I don't really remember," Sándor said desperately. "I've been studying for exams lately. I use the web when I'm studying." It sounded pathetic and evasive, even to his own ears.

"I see. And which class are you trying to contact Hizb ut-Tahrir for?"

"What?"

"You also spent a fair amount of time on hizbuttahrir.org."

"Oh . . . that . . ." It stopped him in his tracks.

He knew that Hizb ut-Tahrir was an Islamic organization. But a connection between them and Tamás? They were hardly in the same galaxy, ideologically speaking. He wasn't even sure Tamás *had* an ideology, aside from a certain penchant for life's pleasures. Hedonism. Isn't that what it was called?

Gábor leaned in as if he were confiding something, in a way that also made Sándor's torso instinctively tip forward a couple of degrees.

"Sándor, listen up. I'm not one of those idiots who

believe that the Jews and the Gypsies have teamed up to destroy Hungary. And yet I have to wonder a little when a bright, young law student with a Gypsy mother starts researching right-wing nationalist and Islamist websites at the same time. That seems a little odd. And when that same bright young man suddenly becomes extremely interested in weapons and other potentially destructive items . . . well, a couple of alarm bells start going off, you know? But I'm sure we just don't understand. There must be an obvious, natural explanation. So, would you please be so kind as to set my mind at ease?"

Alarm bells going off? Sándor struggled to understand what kind of threat this NBH man was obviously envisioning. Jews, Gypsies, right-wing extremists, and Islamists? Only slowly did it dawn on Sándor that what Gábor really wanted to know was if Sándor was planning some kind of attack on Jobbik or Magyar Gárda, possibly as part of a Zionist conspiracy that might also hit an Islamic target. An armed defense or maybe even an armed attack.

He might as well have asked Sándor to explain his relationship with the little green men on Mars.

"It's research," Sándor flailed helplessly. "For a term paper."

And so it continued. Occasionally interrupted by lavatory breaks, polite offers of sandwiches and coffee, and a so-called "rest" when he lay on a thin mattress on a concrete floor in a basement room and stared up into the ventilation duct that was humming and flapping above him. No one hit him or humiliated him; in this respect, perhaps he was lucky that this *was* the NBH and not some random police station in Budapest's suburbs. But the intervals were brief, and then the questions started again.

When it became clear that they were planning on holding him overnight, he tried to tell them about his exam.

"We can legally hold you for up to seventy-two hours" was all Gábor said.

"How? Only under special circumstances. If the detainee is apprehended in the act of committing an offense . . ."

". . . or if the detainee's identity cannot be determined with certainty," Gábor said. "I used to be a law student, too, way back when."

"Identity? But there's no question about my identity!"

"Isn't there? The only record of your birth we can find is as Sándor Rézmüves. As far as I can tell, you've been living under a false name for more than fifteen years, and the passport you were issued under the name of Horváth . . . you don't even know where it is."

"It . . . was stolen."

"If your passport is stolen or lost, you're supposed to report that to the authorities. You appear not to have done that. Believe me, it could *easily* take us seventy-two hours to establish who you really are."

If you find out, please tell me.

That thought bubbled up from his subconscious along with a crystal clear memory that for some reason always came back to him in black and white. The headmaster's office at the orphanage. White stripes of light between the blinds. The dusty, dark-brown scent of books and stacks of papers, mixed with the strongly perfumed cleaner they used to wash the linoleum floors.

"Your father has come for you, Sándor."

But the man standing there in the stripy light wasn't Sándor's stepfather, Elvis. It was a man he had never seen before.

Sándor didn't say anything. You couldn't contradict the headmaster, he had learned that very quickly. But there must have been some mistake.

"Hi, Sándor," the man said, holding out his hand for an oddly adult handshake. "You're coming home with me now."

Then Sándor finally understood who the man was. His Hungarian father, his *gadjo* father, the man whose fault it was that he wasn't his stepfather Elvis's son, but just Valeria's-kid-from-before-we-got-married. And he also understood the rest—this man could take him, and he wouldn't need to stay at the orphanage anymore.

"If you would just sign here, Mr. Horváth," the head-master said.

"What about Tamás and the girls?" Sándor blurted out. "Aren't they coming?"

Mr. Horváth squatted down in front of Sándor, so that Sándor actually had to look down a little to look him in the eye.

"No, Sándor," he said in the tone that Grandma Éva used whenever she had to explain that something or other wasn't possible because his mother was sick. "They're not my children, but you are."

And so Sándor had gone with the man, out of the office, down the dark, wide staircase, and out into the parking lot in front of the main building where a little blue car was parked. He crawled into the back seat when he was asked to and let Mr. Horváth buckle his seatbelt with a click. Then Mr. Horváth got into the front seat, started the car, and smiled at him in the rearview mirror.

"We'll get to know each other after a little while," he said.

Sándor didn't say anything. He just sat there quietly as the car rolled down the drive and turned onto the paved road, leaving Tamás, Feliszia, and Vanda behind in the cold, gray buildings on the other side of the fence.

THE NBH INTERROGATED Sándor for three to four hours at a stretch, three to four times a day, for a little over forty-eight hours. He didn't tell them about Tamás. How could he?

"**W**E HAVE A problem."

Christian from IT had gone to the trouble of coming up to Søren's second floor office from the ground floor. Usually he just telephoned. He was standing in the doorway with a piece of paper that looked very small in his large hands.

"All right," Søren said, rolling his chair back from his desk and flipping a hand in an attempt to seem encouraging. "Tell me about it."

He liked Christian, but he needed to read at least two hundred more pages to prepare for the training exercise evaluation later that day, and he was meeting with a couple of visiting American police officers very shortly. Why was it that IT problems never seemed to fall into the solved-in-ten-minutes category?

Christian moved a little further into the office. He was a tall man, in his mid-forties, with wrists as thick as tree trunks and a solid barrel chest. He had been in IT for as long as Søren could remember, and he had recently taken over responsibility for most of their Internet surveillance.

"We've started tracing the IP addresses you sent down to us yesterday," Christian said, placing the piece of paper in front of Søren. "Three of them are familiar faces from the right-wing extremist scene, and they don't seem to have gone in too deeply. They were probably just drooling over the specifications for an M-79 or something. I've done a report on it that I'll send up later."

Søren nodded. All of this was what he had expected.

"Two of the IP addresses that visited the alleged hospital equipment page look like normal search errors. In
other words, people got there by accident and left again
as soon as they saw the trashy layout. The third, the
one you underlined . . . well, that one is a little more
problematic."

"And?" Søren glanced at his watch. He was supposed
to meet the American delegation in ten minutes.

"Well," Christian said and cleared his throat. "The
IP address belongs to a technical college in northwest
district and may have been used by any number of the
school's students, faculty members, and so forth. Luckily
the search was in the evening and during exams week, so
there weren't that many people on campus at the time. A
couple of teachers and four students, who were all identified from the school's surveillance cameras. We asked
all of them for permission to download the contents of
their laptops, but one of the students is refusing to give
us access to his PC."

Søren rolled his chair back up to his desk and looked at
the piece of paper in front of him. Khalid Hosseini, aged
nineteen, living in Mjølnerparken. Christian had bolded
the name, address, and civil registration number.

"And what's your impression?"

Christian shrugged. "He seems pretty normal. Young,
short hair, saggy pants, and T-shirt. Not your average religious fanatic, if that's what you mean. But he was clearly
shitting himself when we asked to see his computer, and
he wouldn't hand it over."

Søren stood up and grabbed his meeting papers off the
desk.

"Get a court order, then. I want a look at that computer."

Christian nodded, but remained next to the desk as if he were waiting for something more.

"I have to go now," Søren said, trying to hide the irritation that was starting to well up inside him. If the man had more to say, why didn't he just up and say it? Surely Christian could see that he was on his way out the door.

"There's a time issue," Christian said. "We're stretched to the limit right now in terms of manpower. We have three men off on the SINe course. Iben is down for the count with some virus, Martin is still on sick-leave with stress, and then there's the Summit and . . . well . . ."

Søren paused in the doorway. The problem was real, he knew that. Over the summer all of the civil defense and emergency services were supposed to switch their communication over to a common, coordinated digital communication system. Secure Information Net, or SINe for short. This way, it was hoped, they wouldn't be fumbling with outdated analog radios at the Summit. The switch was the main reason for the ill-fated training exercise. IT, in particular, were overworked and under pressure. Too many superiors were pestering Christian and his colleagues right now, and Søren was only one of them.

"Any idea what our young friend was doing on the site?"

"No. I mean, he was there for a while, and we can tell that he searched for 'radiation therapy' and 'cancer treatment.'"

"That could mean anything, given the content of the site."

444 **LENE KAABERBØL** and **AGNETE FRIIS**

"Yes. And the telephone numbers he used for the subsequent contact didn't give us anything either. Top-up disposables, probably dumped the minute he had used them. Possibly stolen in the first place. At any rate, they're not in service anymore."

"Okay." Søren drummed his fingers against the doorframe, then made up his mind. "How is this for a compromise? Get the computer off him ASAP, before he dumps it or makes some kind of switch. After that . . . if you get me the full report sometime next week, I'll get off your back. I'll talk to the young man tomorrow. See what he has to say for himself and put the fear of God in him while I'm at it."

"Um . . . maybe two weeks from now?" Christian's pleading face looked almost comical.

"Yes, okay." Søren nodded. So far, they were still just following up on the famous Islamist whisper. Pushing Christian past the point of collapse would get him nowhere.

Young men—and yes, some of them were Muslims—did routinely develop an unhealthy interest in recipes for explosives or suicide videos. The Service had had good results from nipping that kind of thing in the bud—often a little chat with the PET had a remarkable cooling effect on the hot-headed juvenile compulsion to fantasize about death, destruction, and things that go boom. It had been quite a while since he had personally done one of these wake-up calls, but right now that was the simplest solution. Most of his own people had been clocking overtime since the middle of March, and there wasn't a snowball's chance in hell that he would be able to pass it off to some other department. The ops teams were almost as run-down as IT, and most of Søren's colleagues were fighting tooth and nail to protect their own interests.

"Khalid Hosseini." Søren repeated the name to himself as he hurried off to the meeting room on the third floor. It was pretty damn ballsy to say no to the PET when your name was Khalid. Ballsy—and a little alarming.

SKOU-LARSEN HAD RESUMED his old habit of walking around the lake a couple times a week. It was a good, long walk that took him almost an hour these days. Back when they still had a dog he recalled being able to do it in half an hour, but then it had been almost fifteen years since Molly, last in a long series of fox terriers of that name, had died.

Helle was on her knees in the garden weeding among the perennials. She had recently acquired a pair of lined trousers with foam pads built into the knees so she didn't have to lug her weeding mat around the garden with her, although perhaps "garden" was too generous a word to describe their approximately 800-square-meter plot. The tough, dark-green fabric made her rear end look plumper than it actually was.

"I'm going now," he said.

She didn't reply right away. Instead she exclaimed in disgust and jumped up, quite nimbly considering her sixty-two years.

"They're here already!" she hissed.

"Who?" he asked, confused.

"The Spanish slugs!" She marched across the lawn to the shed on the property boundary abutting the neighbor's. Highly illegal nowadays, and during his time in the Buildings and Safety Department of the local municipality, he had helped to reject several planning applications for just that sort of thing. This shed, however, had probably been here as long as the house, or, in other words, since 1948.

She came out of the shed a few moments later, now armed with a dandelion knife, with which she proceeded to dispatch the offending gastropod by cleaving the gleaming brown body in two.

"I need you to get me some more slug bait," she said. "Preferably today."

"Why the hurry? It's just one slug."

She straightened up and used her wrist to push the hair out of her face. Her floral gardening gloves were dark from dirt and plant sap.

"It's an invasive species," she said with ruthless intensity in her blue eyes. "They don't have any natural predators here, and a sexually mature slug can lay up to four hundred eggs in one season. You *have* to keep them at bay."

"Yes, yes, all right. I'll drive over to the garden center when I get back."

"Where are you going?"

"Just around the lake."

"Take your phone."

He grunted. He didn't like the little metallic thingamajig. He struggled to read the numbers on the tiny buttons, and he had never grown completely confident in its use. But she was right, it would be wise to bring it. What if he fell and broke his hip? What if he had a heart attack out there on the lake path, and he keeled over into the reeds where no one would see him? Though whether he would be able to use this masterpiece of communication technology in that case was another matter.

He went inside, retrieved the phone from the drawer, and stuck it in the pocket of his dark-gray windbreaker.

"Okay, I'm going," he called out to the garden.

"Remember dinner is at five-thirty today," she called back.

Was it Wednesday again already? It must be. That was the night she had choir practice. Otherwise they always ate at 6 P.M.

IT WAS WINDY down by the lake, and he was glad for he wore his windbreaker. After a warm week when everything had blossomed all at once, it had gotten chilly again, and he had grown more sensitive to the cold with age. What with the dog walkers and the exercise fanatics there was a constant traffic on the lakefront path, and he stared at the joggers with envy as they pumped away with their muscular shorts-clad legs and carried on easy, smiling conversations with each other to demonstrate that they weren't winded by such a trifling little trot. Just you wait, he thought, just you wait. Someday you, too, will drag yourself out of bed gasping for breath, wondering whether you can make it to the bathroom by yourself.

He had barely reached the lake park when the symptoms started. The ache in his hip—he knew that one, he could get used to that one. But also a stabbing pain in his chest, like a stitch in his side, only worse. One foot in the grave, he thought, and was once again overwhelmed by frustration that he couldn't get that snotty-nosed puppy of a lawyer to understand that someone had to look after Helle.

She had just turned twenty-two when they got married; he had been forty-six. They had met each other at the Town Hall, where she worked as the mayor's secretary, a job she dispatched with a cool efficiency that made her seem mature and professional compared to most of the girls in the typing pool. Yes, that's what they used to call them, "the girls." Without any of the artificial political correctness one had to employ these days. This was back in the '70s when fringe purses and hot pants were starting to sneak into even the stuffiest of local government offices, but Helle stuck to classic pencil skirts, pearl necklaces, and cardigans with a Chanel-like elegance that always made him think of Grace Kelly. But it wasn't until he discovered that her father picked her up every evening because she didn't dare walk home alone . . . it wasn't until then that he realized the depth of the vulnerability she kept hidden beneath her professional façade. It touched him deeply, and it was for this reason that he began to cautiously suggest that he would be glad to drive her home any day her father found it inconvenient.

Occasionally, he had wondered, of course. A twenty-four-year age difference was quite a gap, objectively speaking, even in those days, but it didn't feel that way.

"My father is seventeen years older than my mother," she had said. "And they had me late. I'm used to older people." There had been no mocking glint in her eye, he recalled. As time went by, he discovered that she meant exactly what she said—she was more comfortable with his generation than with her own. Protest movements, bra burning, and mind-altering substances were absolutely not her thing. Young people scared her.

A man in his forties thinks only fleetingly about what will happen to his life partner when he is no longer around. His foresight then had been sorely lacking. Now he could hardly think of anything else. The savings, the house, her widow's pension would surely suffice if she refrained from stupid spending, but that was exactly what he could not count on. Costa del Castle-in-Spain. How could she do something like that without even talking to him about it? Over half a million kroner gone just like that. She might as well have flushed it down the toilet.

He stopped and clutched his chest. Yet another runner trotted past him, this time not one of the fit and well-trained casual lot, but a panting middle-aged jogger whose stomach was bouncing out of step with the rest of him in its own syncopated rhythm. The man's face was lobster red, and in his tortured expression, Skou-Larsen could see the fear of death shining, so he thought, with preternatural brightness.

When I turned fifty, no one expected me to buy a pair of trainers and start pounding around on park paths, Skou-Larsen thought, remembering the Georg Jensen designed cigar cutter his staff had given him to mark the occasion.

He decided his walk had been long enough. It was cold, and he wanted to go home.

He walked down Lundedalsvej instead of the parallel Ellemosevej because he couldn't help himself. It was unwise, particularly now when he wasn't feeling well. Also, he would be forced to lie to Helle if she asked, and she would ask, he was convinced of that.

The short access road still hadn't been paved. They had put down a bit of preliminary gravel, deeply rutted now from the passage of trucks and heavy machinery. The fence around the construction site formed a slipshod zigzag shape, tilting on gray concrete foundation blocks, and a man with a yellow hardhat and neon yellow vest was just closing the gate behind the last truck of the day. Skou-Larsen raised a polite hand in the kind of greeting you give someone when you don't actually want to shake their hand.

"How are things going?" he asked.

The man was pulling a thick chain through the gate. He half-turned and looked suspiciously over his shoulder, but when he spotted Skou-Larsen, he visibly relaxed. He obviously didn't consider older gentlemen in windbreakers and tweed caps to be threatening.

"How's what going?" he asked, not particularly courteously, Skou-Larsen thought.

"The construction. Are you making progress?" I've inspected hundreds of building sites in my life, Skou-Larsen thought, taking a steely, authoritative stance.

The man furrowed his brow and may have been having trouble deciding what to make of Skou-Larsen. After all, there was an outside chance that this senior citizen was not just a meddlesome nursing home candidate, but actually had some kind of influence in the chain of command above him.

"Pretty good," he finally responded. "Of course we're a little behind. And although we have a guard dog now, we've had trouble with vandalism at the site a couple of times. Not everyone likes this." He pointed his thumb at the big sign bearing a few lines of text in Arabic script and below that in somewhat smaller type, AL-KABIR ISLAMIC CULTURAL CENTER.

"Well, I suppose not," Skou-Larsen said in a neutral voice. "But do you still think you will be able to finish the building this summer?"

"We don't exactly have a choice," the man said with a wry smile. "Some Imam is coming from London to bless the whole thing for its grand opening, and obviously we can't just rearrange his whole schedule."

"Ah, yes. Well then, good luck with the project."

The man nodded and then snapped a heavy padlock into place on the chain.

"Have a good day," he said and jumped into a red station wagon with yellow plates.

Why doesn't anyone ever say goodbye anymore? Skou-Larsen thought.

He stood there for a bit peering through the fence. Nominally, it was a remodel, but apart from the foundation, there wasn't much left of the old factory building. White walls with arched windows had supplanted weathered concrete, and the old corrugated fiber cement roof was being replaced with shiny, glazed green roofing tiles. Farther back, behind the entrance hall, two slender towers rose on either side of a domed roof, still hidden under thick, red tarpaulins. The sign may have said Cultural Center, but the architecture clearly indicated that this was to be a proper mosque.

It was beginning to drizzle. He had to get home before it picked up; a cold could be the death of him at this point. That's how his old bridge partner Søndergaard had died. A runny nose, a couple of sneezes, and then suddenly it was the flu, pneumonia, a death certificate, and cremation. It hadn't even been Legionnaire's disease or anything else exotic, just a completely run-of-the-mill virus. And the man had been three years younger than him.

He gave the pseudo-minarets one last frustrated glance. If it had been twenty-five years earlier, the building permit for the project might have been his to give or withhold. But twenty-five years earlier, nothing like this would ever have been proposed.

If only the minarets were not so damnably tall. They were actually visible from the backyard of his home on Elmehøjvej.

He reached his own front door at quarter past five. Through the open kitchen door, he could hear the sound of sizzling margarine, and there was a pleasant smell of dinner in the making. He hung his windbreaker and cap up on the hook by the door, took off his shoes, and stuck his feet into the sheepskin-lined slippers Helle had given him for Christmas.

"What are we having?" he asked with a cheerfulness he didn't feel.

"Rissoles." Helle had a sharp, worried wrinkle on her forehead, like an inverted figure of 1, and he sensed the tension in her. Maybe she was afraid she would be late for choir practice, even small everyday appointments often caused her a considerable amount of anxiety. She stuck the spatula under a rissole and flipped it rapidly. "Did you walk past it?"

"No," he lied. "Why should I?"

"Remember you promised to get me the slug bait."

"I'll do that after we eat. The garden center is open until seven. If it can't wait until tomorrow, that is."

"I can't," she said, flipping the next rissole. "We need to finish them off before they have a chance to reproduce."

RINA WAS GONE.

The teachers had known about it since that morning, but Nina only found out about it when she came to spend her lunch break with Rina, a habit she had fallen into since the trial.

"She ate breakfast and grabbed her schoolbag, like all the other kids," Rikke said defensively. "But she never showed up in the classroom. The teachers have been out looking for her most of the day."

Nina looked at her watch. It was 1:45 P.M., and there was a chilly wind blowing over the Coal-House Camp. It took a certain amount of determination for a seven-year-old to stay out so long on her own, but that was still what she chose to believe for the time being—that Rina had left the camp alone and of her own free will. It was not completely unthinkable that Natasha's former fiancé had taken her, but Nina couldn't quite believe it. She pictured Michael Anders Vestergaard as he had appeared in court. Freshly ironed shirt, expensive cologne, and a broad, self-satisfied grin. He was a sadistic bastard, no doubt about that, but he went in for risk-free crimes. Women on the margins of society and possibly also their children; victims he could control without winding up behind bars with all those nasty Hells Angels thugs. For the moment, Rina was too big a risk for him now.

"We contacted the police," said Rikke, the carer. "They asked if there were any family members she might be with."

"They know damn well her mother's in jail," Nina said, pulling out her car keys. "Rina doesn't have anyone else."

"Well, you know how it is. They don't have unlimited resources."

Yes, Nina knew that quite well. Children ran away from asylum centers every single week, and it was true that some of them turned up with family members somewhere or other in the constantly migrating population that flowed back and forth across Europe's borders. But Rina wasn't that kind of child.

"She'll probably come back on her own," Rikke said, giving her best stab at a smile.

Nina couldn't even muster a response. Rina had been gone for almost six hours, and in Nina's opinion contacting the police now was too little, too late. Rina was seven. The world was a dangerous place for kids like her. This wasn't something that could wait until some duty officer could be persuaded to find the resources.

Magnus had apparently had the same thought, because when she returned to the clinic he was already ready to go, jacket and phone in his hand.

"I'll search the shrubbery behind the school grounds. Are you taking the car?"

Nina nodded, hastily typing a text message to Ida. *Delayed. Take 300 kroner from the kitchen envelope and call a cab. I'll be there as soon as I can.* It was roller hockey Wednesday.

"I took her to see Natasha last week," Nina said. "I think she made a note of the route. I'll try driving in that direction, anyway."

"It's is a long way for a seven-year-old," Magnus said. The district prison where Natasha was serving her sentence was on the other side of the city, nearly thirty kilometers away.

"Yes," said Nina."But if you were Rina, where else would you go?"

THE GIRLS WERE almost half an hour into their match by the time Nina found her way to the asphalt rink in one of the southern suburbs. They were playing outdoors today and had been lucky with the weather. The rink was dry and clean, and the air was cool. Nina settled next to the coach on the spectator side of the graffiti-covered boards, and looked around for her daughter. She caught sight of Ida's helmet, black and decorated with pink skulls. Ida had been playing on the Pink Ladies team for almost two years now and was small and lightning-fast and impressive to watch, out there in the thick of the action. Most of the girls Ida's age were taller and heavier, but that did not appear to bother her. Not even if it cost her bruises and countless scrapes.

Ida was playing the attack now. She crossed in front of a player from the other team and stole the ball with a couple of rapid jerks of her stick, then raced toward the goal at full speed, cannoning the ball into the net with an explosive and totally clean shot. She only just managed to evade the goal's metal bars and slammed into the boards with a hollow thud instead.

Nina had seen that kind of move before and knew it was part of the game, but it still seemed to her that Ida was playing even more offensively than she usually did. She glanced over at the coach, who nodded briefly at her and then turned back to look at the rink again.

Ida was on her way back to her half of the rink with her stick raised in a short victory celebration. Her hair shone wetly under the edge of her helmet; her face was clenched in concentration. Nina followed her with her eyes and felt a joyous tug in her chest at the sight of Ida surrounded by all the others.

Another face-off.

Ida was ready at the front of her own field, and as soon as the ball was in play, she hammered her stick between the legs of the other team's forwards. The sticks scraped and struck the asphalt until Ida finally got the ball free and continued, running amok in a new attack on their goal. She almost seemed to be alone on the court. The other players set out after her in a halfhearted job until she again hammered the ball in behind the goalie. This time she didn't manage to slow down properly; she stumbled, took a couple of quick tap-dancing steps in her rollerblades, and smashed onto the asphalt with her stomach, chest, and hands in a brutal smack. She lay there doubled over in front of the goal without making a sound, and the coach swore and hastily leapt over the sideboards.

"Goddamn it! No one was even on her."

Nina followed. She tried to ignore that distinctive jolt it caused because it was *Ida*. Of course nothing serious had happened to her. Of course not. She squatted down next to Ida in front of the goal. She probably just got the wind knocked out of her, Nina thought, her wrists and hands ought to be pretty well protected by her equipment. She cautiously touched her daughter's shoulder.

"Try to stretch out a little," she said. "It'll help."

Ida glared at her angrily.

"You keep out of this," she said, rolling away from Nina with a stubborn groan. "What the hell are you even doing here?"

The other Pink Ladies were there now. Anna and the new one, Josefine. They helped Ida to her feet, shooting awkward glances at Nina.

"We thought you couldn't make it," Anna said in a tone that Nina couldn't quite interpret. "It took forever to find a cab. And with all our equipment . . ."

"Look, I'm really sorry, but . . ."

With a jerk, Ida turned her back and skated slowly back toward her team's goal. Nina was left to deliver her apology to Anna and the empty space where Ida had been.

THEY HADN'T FOUND Rina until 3:45 P.M. The owner of an allotment garden in Gladsaxe called after seeing the girl sitting for more than twenty minutes, curled up next to the fence along the highway, her school bag still on her back. That was how far she had been sure of which way to go, Nina thought. At the Ring 3 overpass, she must have become discouraged. Rina cried when Nina came to get her, but apart from being generally exhausted from a day without food or water, there was nothing wrong with her. Nothing more than usual, as Magnus flatly remarked. He had volunteered to watch Rina for the rest of the afternoon, and Nina had driven off to the hockey rink as if her life depended on it, or at least as fast as rush-hour traffic would permit on the congested roads. Shit, shit, shit.

The girls won by a landslide, but Ida painstakingly

avoided meeting her eyes as she rolled off the rink and started taking off her gear. Nina wasn't even permitted to pack it up for her.

"My mom will be here soon," Anna said, talking to Ida. "We don't really have time for a shower."

Ida was still struggling with her shin guards, but Nina didn't need any help interpreting what was going on. Ida had arranged for another ride home.

"But it would be easier for you to ride with me since I'm here," Nina said.

Ida turned her head and looked at her.

"No thanks," she said and at first attempted an icy, arrogant stare. Then the corners of her mouth began to wobble and she looked away quickly.

"We were late for the match. Do you have any idea how embarrassing that was? For all three of us? They almost didn't let us play."

Nina quickly glanced at Anna. She wished that Anna would give them a little space, but Anna stayed where she was. She was obviously uncomfortable, but she stayed put.

"Come on now." Nina hoisted up Ida's equipment and jacket. "I need to have a look at those bruises anyway, once we get home."

"No."

Ida yanked her jacket out of Nina's hands.

"You're a shitty mother. You know that? Just a shitty mother. I'm spending the night at Anna's."

NINA WATCHED THEM go with annoyance.

Ida was bent over a little as she walked, as if she were

still in pain, with Anna and Josefine attending her like silent, slightly awkward squires. Anna's mom turned and gave a single wave before they drove out of the parking lot.

Nina hoisted Ida's equipment bag and tossed it into the backseat. She had heard from certain optimistic and bubbly colleagues that there was a life beyond the teenage years. She would, in other words, survive this. And so would Ida.

"**Y**OU WANT A drink?"

Søren gave the young man waiting for him at the café table a surprised look. Khalid had suggested the their meeting place, Café Offside, himself—a little sports bar awash with nicotine, crammed in next to Nørrebro Station, and clearly one of Copenhagen's few remaining smokers' sanctuaries. Also sufficiently Khalid Hosseini's home turf that he was the one to order the drinks. Søren decided to ignore this slightly provocative act and nodded briefly.

"Yes, please. A club soda."

Khalid, who had occupied the innermost corner of the booth, deftly got up and zigzagged his way through the busy café's crowd of standing patrons, laid a bill on the bar counter, and returned shortly afterward with a club soda in one hand. He slipped back into his seat and smiled at Søren with his eyebrows raised. A perfect saint, Søren thought sarcastically, wondering for a moment whether he should have turned up unannounced at Khalid's home address instead, just to catch him off balance. These young men were never quite so cocky when they had their gloomy father sitting next to them on the sofa. On the other hand, the family could also have been an extremely disruptive element, and Khalid had three younger siblings and a mother, who would presumably either lament reproachfully or dart back and forth with tea and sticky cakes that were far too sweet. Søren leaned

back in the flimsy café chair and tried to maintain eye
contact with his young host.

He was nineteen. Long-limbed, skinny, and smooth-
shaven if you ignored a pair of neatly trimmed sideburns.
He was wearing a tight, orange shirt that appeared to be
fairly expensive. The same was true of the dark, high-end
jeans and white sneakers.

It took a while, but finally he met Søren's eyes.

"What was it you wanted to talk to me about?"

Søren didn't answer. He waited, slowly pouring his
club soda into the glass and watched out of the corner
of his eye as the young man's façade began to crumble.
Young people weren't used to lulls in a conversation,
and certainly not to long periods of silence. Khalid's eyes
darted away from Søren's club soda before moving back
to the cola he had sitting in front of himself on the table.
He took a swig and was then inspired to fish his cigarettes
from his black backpack under the table. His fingers
trembled slightly as he pulled the cigarette out of the
packet, then he half-heartedly held out the pack to Søren,
but stopped midway through the gesture and let it drop
down onto the table between them instead, in a sort of
clumsy invitation.

"Feel free to . . ."

Søren impassively watched Khalid.

"I mean, if you want to smoke . . ."

Khalid tried his host's smile one last time, but it stiffened
before it made it all the way up to his eyes, and instead he
lit his cigarette with an uneasy glance toward the door. As
if he were considering his escape options.

This was all good.

Søren took a deep breath and calmly leaned in further over the table.

"We need your computer, Khalid. And our tech people are having a little trouble understanding your explanation as to why we can't see it. So I'd just like to hear it one more time."

"I didn't give them any explanation. It's my computer. That's why."

Khalid stuck his chin out in defiance and stared at Søren. A bright lad, Søren guessed. It wasn't so much what he had said so far, but Søren thought he could see it in his eyes, in the effortless way he had moved, and the reasonably civilized behavior he was exhibiting in the circumstances. That kind of thing required self-control and a certain mental capacity.

"Are you a Muslim, Khalid?"

"What business is that of yours?"

Søren gave a smile of acquiescence.

"I just want to know a little more about you. It's a straightforward question."

Khalid blew a narrow column of smoke out of his nose and for the first time turned to look directly into Søren's eyes with every indication of contempt.

"Look at me, man. What do you think?" Khalid challenged.

"Practicing?"

Khalid shrugged, fell back in the booth, and inhaled another batch of smoke into his lungs.

"Is that what this is about? Religion? Do you think I'm a fucking terrorist or something?" His shoulders sank a bit, and he smiled sardonically as he held his hands out to

Søren. "Hey, I love all Danes, man. I love Denmark. I'm totally harmless. Me tame Muslim."

He said that last line coldly, with a sneer and an exaggerated accent. He was more indignant than insecure right now, and Søren wasn't sure how to interpret that. If Khalid was up to something dangerous, shouldn't he be feeling scared?

Khalid turned restlessly in his seat, eyeing him expectantly with a mix of contempt and physical discomfort.

"You can't look at my computer, because you guys are fucking racists. I don't give a damn what you're looking for. You're coming after me because you think I'm a towelhead. Don't you think I know how it works? There were other people at school that night. But you pick on me because I'm Arab." Khalid's voice cracked several times from anger. "I've heard about all the crap you people get up to with the CIA. Sending innocent people to torture prisons in Egypt and wherever."

Søren shook his head slowly.

"We just want to talk to you about what you were doing on those arms sites you visited. Maybe you were just window shopping for a nice piece to put under your pillow. We're the PET. We don't care about trifles like that. If you have a good explanation, I just want to hear it."

"What the hell are you talking about?"

Khalid got up, stumbled a little over his black backpack before he pulled it out from under the table, and started edging his way out from behind the table. Søren could feel his control of the conversation slipping through his fingers.

"Khalid!" Søren calmly placed a firm hand on the

young man's shoulder. "A little more cooperation would be a smart move right now. For your own sake as well as ours."

Khalid stopped and directed a furious, icy look at Søren.

"Leave me alone. You can't have it."

Søren slowly removed his phone from his pocket and browsed through the menus. There it was. A text message from Christian, sent just ten minutes ago.

"We picked up your computer as soon as you left the apartment. Your mother even invited my colleagues in for tea while they took a look at your room."

Khalid stood there, swaying in the wind like a tree in a storm.

"What do you mean? It's my computer. You can't just take it. It's mine. I'm studying for an exam . . ."

Søren stepped past him and started to leave.

"You'll be hearing from us as soon as we've looked at it. It may take a little while."

He glanced back over his shoulder. Khalid stood frozen with one hand on the flimsy café table, as if he needed support. His black backpack hung heavy and motionless from his other hand.

OUTSIDE IN THE twilit street, Søren dialed a familiar number as an elevated train thundered by overhead. His first impression of Khalid was mixed. The boy could scream and shout all he wanted about racism and rights violations, but that didn't change the fact that he was hiding something. Søren had no doubt about that.

"Yes?"

Christian sounded grumpy and rushed on the other end of the line. From the background noise, Søren guessed he was still stuck in traffic somewhere on his way back to base.

"Did you get what you needed?"

"Yes, frightened mother, angry father, cute kids, and one laptop that at least looks like the one on the security footage. Everything went as expected."

"Check it out as soon as possible," Søren said. He glanced around before unlocking his car and slipping into the driver's seat, an old paranoid habit from his own days of working in the surveillance service.

"Yeah, get in line." Christian's grumpiness was uncharacteristic, but it was after all almost 9:30 at night, and he had two young children at home. Søren recalled seeing the family photos in Christian's ground-floor office.

"Just one more thing, Christian, then I'll let you go for the day. Khalid. You put a trace on that mobile of his, right? I want to see who he talks to tonight."

THEY RELEASED **SÁNDOR** four hours before his exam. He stood on Falk Miksa Street in the morning sun, outside the vast concrete beehive that was the headquarters of the NBH, and it felt like the sidewalk was swaying beneath his feet. He had been wearing the same clothes for almost three days, and he knew he reeked. People in suits and business attire rushed past him, skirting around the first meandering tourists with skill and irritation. The antique stores were just opening up. Traffic slid by, shrouded in a cloud of gas fumes.

He was an island in the middle of this stream of everyday activity and normality. No, not an island, an island was big and solid. He was just a foreign body, neither a Hungarian nor a tourist. A filthy Gypsy still stinking of the sweat of the interrogation room.

Pull yourself together, he told himself. But there wasn't much conviction to his internal voice.

He took the streetcar home. It was faster than a cab, despite the distance he had to go on foot on his wobbly rubber legs, but that wasn't why. He would have gladly sacrificed the extra minutes and also the money if he had believed he could sit in peace in the air-conditioned back seat and be treated like a human being. A paying customer, a member of society.

He didn't run into anyone he knew on Szigony Street. Even the bathroom was empty, and he stood there under the warm, yellowish stream of water for almost half an hour. The foam formed fleeting, white coral shapes around his feet. He lathered himself up again and rinsed, lathered and rinsed, and finally the drain couldn't handle any more. He had to turn the water off to avoid flooding the floor.

He shaved meticulously and splashed two handfuls of aftershave lotion onto his cheeks, chin, and neck. The alcohol stung as if the bottom half of his face were one big scrape, but that didn't matter. Then the deodorant. He lingered in front of the mirror and suddenly thought the crop of thick, black hair in his armpits and on his chest looked offensively beastlike. He quickly slathered himself with shaving cream and attacked it with the razor, clearing pale swaths through the thicket of hair, first one way, then the other, until there was only a shadowy stubble left. He cut himself twice, small stinging nicks because he was being too fast and too vigorous, but it didn't matter. He didn't want to look like an animal, not even under his shirt.

Then he got dressed. The suit he had worn to the baptism, a bright white shirt, a tie, black socks and shoes—despite the heat. He slicked his hair back with the expensive gel he used only rarely and looked in the mirror one more time.

You don't even look like a Gypsy, Lujza had said. But he didn't look like an average Hungarian, either. He looked like what he was—a mixture. Right now, his suit most of all ressembled a costume.

He thought about Tamás and the defiant confidence he radiated, from the pointy tips of his boots to his long, black hair. I don't even have that, he thought. Not even that.

There was a slip of paper on his desk. *CALL*, Lujza had written in big, desperate capitals. There were also more than twenty unanswered calls on his phone, but he wasn't up to that right now. Did she know they had released him? Otherwise she was probably on her way to the prosecutor's office with a loaded paint gun, or at least a letter of protest and a mass of signatures she had collected.

All that would have to wait, he decided. The most important thing now was passing his exam.

THERE WAS A pervasive smell of cheroots in the high-ceilinged office. Legal texts and books in tall mahogany bookcases, the heavy green velvet curtains, the moss-green carpet, everything was impregnated with cheroot nicotine. The professor was smoking with an arrogant disdain for the university's no-smoking rules. The office was his and had been for twenty years; any claim that it was actually public property was meaningless.

In honor of the occasion, there were a couple of folding tables and chairs for the students who were pre-paring for their oral presentation. The flimsy steel and plastic constructions looked completely out of place in the midst of all the sturdy mahogany, and none of the three examination victims looked like they felt particu-larly welcome either.

"Sándor Horváth."

Sándor gathered his notes and got up from his own plastic chair. There was no chair for the candidate being examined. He or she stood on the floor in front of the professor's desk, armed solely with the handful of sweaty

notes compiled during the preparation period. Mihály
had once said that he imagined himself pleading a case
in a courtroom when he took his exam. That made standing up feel different—it was a way of gaining authority
and rhetorical power, instead of a constant reminder that
you were worth less than the examining professor. Sándor tried to employ this pleasant concept, but without
much success.

Professor Lőrincz regarded him with hostile eyes,
Sándor thought. They hadn't had much to do with each
other before. Sándor was one out of maybe 150 students
who had attended a series of lectures, that was all.
Lőrincz was about fifty, a skinny man with long hands,
long fingers, and slicked-back, medium-brown hair
that was almost as Hugh Grant-like as Ferenc's, albeit
a version more advanced in graying. He had a habit of
holding his slender Spanish cheroot between the little
finger and the ring finger of his left hand, which was
apparent from the discolored condition of his skin. He
was good, but intellectually arrogant, and students who
faced him ignorant and unprepared received no mercy.

But you are neither, Sándor reassured himself. What
was it Ferenc had called him? The best-prepared student
in the history of the law school?

"Say what you have to say."

The order was short and sudden. No greeting, no
pleasantries, not even a question. Sándor was thrown
completely off balance. Say what he had to say? Of the
two oral exams he had witnessed while he was preparing
for his own, he had gotten the impression that Lőrincz
style was more of a cross examination.

A vaguely condescending grimace slid over the professor's face, as if silence was what he had expected. He raised his fountain pen and made a note on the yellow pad that lay in front of him. Sándor had the sickening sense that this was hopeless, that nothing he could say or do would alter the professor's verdict.

The man raised an eyebrow.

A tiny, defiant spark of rage ignited somewhere within Sándor. He had worked for this. And he knew he could do it. Or, at least some of the time he knew that, when he wasn't allowing himself to be reduced into a speechless, nervous wreck just because a man behind a desk looked at him with disdain.

He took a nervous, gasping breath and ventured into an explanation of supranational legal theory. His account was concise, well-structured, and laid out in order of priority. He put treaty law over common law, debated peremptory norms with himself, put forward hypotheses and arguments, drew conclusions. He talked and talked, and the professor didn't interrupt him even once. He spoke for so long that he lost his sense of time, but eventually he sensed a certain restlessness among his fellow students seated behind him. Was there anything else to add? Not without moving off-topic, he decided. He repeated a couple of his main points by way of a summary, and then fell silent. Relief had already begun to spread through his body, and he was not without admiration for the arrogant, old academic behind the desk. With his seeming indifference, he had forced Sándor to give an independent presentation at a very advanced level, instead of steering him around the circus ring with questions. Sándor's performance had been better for it, he conceded. But dear God, it had been uncomfortable in the beginning.

The professor made another note on his yellow pad.

"Fail," he said, without looking up.

Someone behind Sándor dropped a pencil. He could hear the crisp little smack as it hit the table, followed by a clicking roll.

"Excuse me?" Sándor said, thinking he must have misheard.

The professor ripped the yellow page off the pad, folded it carefully, made another note on a grading sheet that was waiting next to him, and placed both sheets into a manila envelope. He pushed the envelope across the mahogany desk toward Sándor.

"If you have any questions, please direct them to the guidance counselor," he said, his eyes already moving on to the next student. "Dora Kocsis."

The girl stood up. She was deathly pale, and her skin looked clammy. Sándor could see the disbelief he himself was feeling reflected in her face. Maybe she was wondering what you had to do to pass if Sándor had failed.

"Please leave the premises," the professor told Sándor. "Don't forget your envelope. It contains important information about your situation."

Sándor took the manila envelope with numb fingers.

"I don't understand . . ." he began, but he could tell from the steeliness of the arrogant face that his initial impression had been right: It didn't matter at all what he said or did today. The outcome had been determined in advance.

It wasn't until he reached the door that he received something that resembled an explanation.

"Horváth."

Sándor turned halfway around.

"A law degree is a weapon. The *law itself* is a weapon."

Sándor still didn't understand, not until the professor added:

"What makes you think Hungary wants to arm someone like you?"

HE DIALED LUJZA'S number and then found he couldn't force himself to speak.

"Sándor? Is that you?"

"Yes."

"Thank God. Are you . . . did they release you?"

"Yes."

"Are you okay?"

He didn't say anything. There was so much distance between him and those words, between her and him. Someone like you.

"Where are you?"

"Home."

"I'm coming over. Don't go anywhere."

"No. I mean, no, don't come."

"Sándor! Why not?'

"Because . . . I'm not going to be here by the time you get here."

Now it was her turn to be silent. He sensed her confusion, her hurt feelings.

"What's wrong?"

"Nothing. I just have to go home for a while."

"Now? Don't you have your exam?"

"No."

He hung up, because he couldn't bear to explain. She called back again right away, but he turned off his phone.

He sat on the bed, in just his underwear again. He had hung his suit neatly on a coat hanger; even now habit took over. He unfolded the three sheets of paper that had been in the manila envelope again.

One was a copy of the official grading sheet, where after *Evaluation* it succinctly said *Fail*. The second was the sheet with the professor's notes from the examination. It said only two things. In the name field, the professor had written *Sándor Rézmüves*, not *Sándor Horváth*. And underneath that there was just one sentence: *Has nothing relevant to say.*

The third sheet was an official letter from the university informing him that since he was no longer enrolled, they had to ask him to vacate his room at the Szigony Dormitory by May 15. The name *Horváth* was crossed out and replaced with *Rézmüves*. He wasn't sure if the administration office had done that or the professor himself.

He stood up and went over to his desk. All of his books and notes were gone, and the police had also confiscated his computer, but Tamás's mobile phone number was still sitting on the slip of paper he had tacked to his bulletin board. He turned his phone on again. He supposed he ought to be glad they had let him keep that.

Tamás answered after two rings.

"Yes?"

There was static and motor noise on the line, and Sándor had the impression Tamás was in a car or a bus.

"What the hell are you up to?"

"Sándor? Relax, *phrala*, it's just a bit of—"

"You little shit. I'm on my way to Galbeno. And when I find you, I'm going to wring your fucking neck."

Tamás just laughed and hung up.

"I mean it," Sándor said to the empty room, which was no longer his.

THE BUS HAD to slow down to 20 kph to maneuver its way down the pot hole-riddled road. Eventually, there seemed to be more holes than asphalt, Sándor noted. He leaned his head against the dusty windowpane, feeling the vibrations through the glass.

The rage he had felt when he spoke to Tamás two days ago had long since evaporated. Maybe it would come back again when he saw him, but right now he couldn't feel anything other than a thick, gray sense of failure. What the hell was he going to do when he arrived? Galbeno wasn't "home," even though that was what he had told Lujza. It hadn't been home since . . . no, he couldn't actually put a date on it, not even a year. He knew when he had been taken away, but he couldn't nail down the moment when his inner compass had stopped pointing to the green house in Galbeno whenever someone asked him where he lived.

Grandpa Viktor had roared and raged that day, and the policemen from the white cars had needed to restrain both him and some of the uncles. One of them had his hands full just trying to manage Grandma Éva. Sándor had also scratched and kicked and struggled when they put him in the minibus with Vanda and Feliszia and little Tamás, but it was no use. The door closed, and there was no handle on the inside. Finally they drove away, up the same road where the ambulance had taken his mother, and through the rear window he could see Grandpa Viktor running after the vans, but he couldn't run fast enough.

They had driven for a long time, without anything to eat or drink. There were two other children in the bus besides Sándor and his siblings, a boy and a girl. He had never seen them before; they must have been from another village. They held hands and didn't speak. Neither did Sándor. The boy had peed in his pants, and it didn't smell good.

Then the van drove through a gate in a fence and up the driveway to some tall, gray buildings. The door of the minibus was opened, and an adult stranger, an old bald *gadjo* in white clothes, pointed at Sándor and the other boy.

"Those two go to the blue wing," he said. "The girls go over to the red wing, and the little one needs an exam at the health clinic."

It took a second before Sándor understood that the *gadjos* wanted to split them up.

"No," he said then. "I'm going to take care of them."

"We'll do that," the bald *gadjo* said. "Now you just go over to the blue wing with Miss Erzsébet. That's where the big boys live."

Miss Erzsébet took his hand. She was young and pretty and also *gadji*, but he didn't want to hold her hand.

"No," he said. "I'm their brother."

But they wouldn't listen. A *gadji* lady, who was also dressed in white, had already picked Tamás up and was starting to walk away with him. Another woman had taken the girls by the hand, one on either side. Vanda's face was swollen because she had cried the whole way, but now she was quiet. Her eyes were dark and frightened. Feliszia just looked confused. She hugged her pink stuffed rabbit, filthy as it was.

He tore himself away from the Erzsébet woman, but she grabbed him again, this time by the arm, hard. Then he bit her.

He could still remember the feeling, the tiny little hairs on her arm poking softly into his tongue, the salty taste of her skin mixed with a soapy bitterness he later learned was moisturizer. As he bit, he felt the skin break, and the saliva and blood mixed in his mouth.

So many years and he could still remember that, maybe because that was his last true act of rebellion.

You'll take care of the girls and Tamás, right?

Mama, I was only eight.

The bus stopped at the end of the line, and he got out.

GALBENO WAS STILL Galbeno. Most of the houses had electricity now, but otherwise not much had happened in the past fifteen years. A small valley with a creek at the bottom, dusty grass and prickly shrubs, the odd fir tree that survived the quest for firewood because it was so full of resin that it would be foolhardy to toss it into the fireplace. Up on the eastern slope sat the cemetery with its crooked, white headstones, with a bigger population now than the village, which for a long time had been a dwindling cluster of houses along a road that didn't go anywhere.

His arrival was instantly noticed by at least twenty people. An older woman who was sweeping in front of her house. Seven or eight kids in the middle of a water fight at one of the village's three communal water pumps. Two men who were fiddling with an old, rust bucket of a car, three others who were watching and commenting. He knew they recognized him.

"*Szia*," one of the men by the car called out, raising his hand in a casual greeting.

"*Szia*," Sándor called back, without knowing who he was talking to. It could even be Tibor; Sándor wasn't sure he would recognize him now. He had forgotten so much. Only a few names lingered in his mind.

He hoisted his duffel bag over his shoulder and started walking down the road toward Valeria's green house. He hadn't brought his suitcase or the cardboard boxes he had packed his things in because he didn't want it to look like he was moving in. True, he had no idea where he would be living after May 15, but it wouldn't be here; he had made his mind up about that. He might have to spend a few weeks here until he found something else, but he wasn't moving in. Ferenc had been generous enough to store his boxes for the time being, though it meant he practically had to climb over the furniture to make it from one end of his room to the other.

Two little girls raced past him, giggling, and he knew he wouldn't make it to the house unannounced. He could already hear their high-pitched, excited voices: "Valeria, Valeria, Sándor's home!"

His mother appeared in the doorway. Then she came out to meet him, her arms outstretched.

"Sándorka! My darling."

She embraced him and pulled his face down so she could kiss him warmly on both cheeks. Then she did it again, just to be sure.

"Mama."

She was so small. It had come as a shock to him the first time he had seen her once he was a grown up—she was a tiny woman who didn't come any higher than the middle of his chest. She was thin and more sinewy than he remembered her, her face tauter. There was something birdlike about her lightness, as if she had air in her bones where other people had marrow.

He knew women in their forties in Budapest who looked like young girls, and often behaved like that, too. That was not the case with Valeria. Her hair was still black, and she was so small that her T-shirt and jeans would fit a twelve-year-old. But no one who saw her face would mistake her for a teenager. Life had left its mark on her. There was a determination and a will to survive in her that weren't the result of hours spent at the gym.

"Have you eaten?" she asked.

"Yes, yes."

"When?"

He couldn't help but smile in spite of everything that had happened.

"Mama, I *ate*." An apple and a sandwich from the kiosk at the bus station, but that was plenty. His stomach couldn't handle anything more.

"Well, then we'll have some coffee. And you can tell me why you've come."

Because naturally there had to be a reason for him to show up like this, in the middle of exams.

"Where's Tamás?"

"Tamás? He's not here." Her eyes darted away as she said it, and he guessed it was because she wanted to hide something from him. Did she know what Tamás was up to?

"Mama, where is he? Do you know what kind of a mess he is in?"

She didn't answer right away.

"Have a seat," she said, pointing to the bench by the door. "I'll make some coffee."

"Mama!"

"He left, Sándorka. He has to earn money, too, doesn't he?"

"Doing what?"

"The violin, of course. But there's no one willing to pay around here anymore. Do you know how many men in the village have jobs?"

Sándor shook his head. How would he know that?

"Fourteen. And eight of those are just doing temporary work paid for by the council."

He knew things were bad, but not that bad. From what he remembered from his childhood, nearly everyone had jobs most of the time.

"People used to have jobs," he said.

"Yes. When the Communists were in charge, the Roma had no trouble getting work. Now it's just the Hungarians. And hardly anyone hires musicians these days. So Tamás is abroad now."

"Where?"

"Germany, I think. No, wait . . . Somewhere up north. I think it was Denmark."

It would be nice to think that Tamás had only nicked his passport because he didn't have one of his own and wanted to go to Denmark to play his violin and earn some money. But Sándor remembered the interrogation room and the questions the ever-patient Gábor had asked him, over and over again. *Are you interested in weapons, Sándor? Why did you go to hizbuttahrir.org—you're not a*

Muslim, are you? Where does your money actually come from, Sándor? For seventy-two hours.

NBH wasn't in the habit of wasting their time on street musicians.

THE HOUSE'S ONLY habitable room was home to six people. Sándor's stepfather Elvis didn't live here anymore. He and Valeria had split up several years earlier. Both Sándor's sisters were married now, but neither of them had actually moved out. Vanda used to have an apartment in Miskolc, but then the building was renovated, and some of the apartments combined into something larger and more "in keeping with the times," as the property owner put it; when the tenants were due to move back in, for some reason or other there wasn't room in the lovely, remodeled building with tiled bathrooms, renovated kitchens, and steel balconies for the three Roma families. So Vanda was living with Valeria again with her two little boys while her husband worked as a painter in Birmingham to earn money so they could get another place. Feliszia, who was seventeen now, had married a boy her own age from Galbeno, just a few months ago; he and his father were putting a roof on one of the abandoned houses on the outskirts of the village "so the young people would have somewhere to live." Valeria quipped that at the speed those two were working; the young people would be middle-aged before they could move in. And besides, it wasn't what Feliszia wanted. She wanted to move to Budapest or at least Miskolc, but certainly away from Galbeno.

"There's nothing wrong with dreaming," Valeria said as she made a bed for Sándor in the spot that was actually

Tamás's. And Feliszia noticed the hint of sarcasm in her tone right away.

"Tamás promised he would help," she said defiantly. "He's going to lend me the money for that hydrotherapy course, and then I can work as a carer for people with disabilities until I can afford to start my own clinic."

Those weren't just dreams; they were plans. Sándor looked at the determination his suddenly grown-up little sister radiated and wondered where it had come from. A year ago she had been a quiet, mild-mannered girl who was the most cautious of all the siblings.

"It's easy for Tamás to make promises. And anyway, he doesn't have any money," Vanda said.

"He will. When he comes home from Denmark, he'll have money."

"How much does the course cost?" Sándor asked.

"Two thousand six hundred euros."

Sándor did a quick conversion. That was more 700,000 forints. Where in the world did Tamás think he was going to get that kind of money? Certainly not from performing on street corners. Not even if he were lucky enough to get a job in a restaurant. He usually just played for tips and maybe food—if he was lucky.

"And what does Bobo say to your big plans?" Vanda asked. Bobo was Feliszia's husband. "What does he say to a wife who wants to open her own clinic in Budapest?"

"He'd just be happy," Feliszia said with a defiant note to her voice which revealed that she wasn't entirely sure that was true.

"Why does Tamás think he can earn so much money in Denmark?" Sándor asked.

Valeria took the last quilt, unfolded it, shook it, and spread it out on the low built-in shelf, bench in the day-time and sleeping space at night, which ran around three of the room's four walls.

"You shouldn't talk about money right before bedtime," she said in a firm voice. "And it's bedtime now. Sándor, get out of here. Let the girls wash."

Sándor got up. It hadn't occurred to him that he would have to go out so his sisters could get undressed. God knows how long they had been waiting for him to leave of his own accord.

Outside it was so dark he was having trouble find-ing the path to the outhouse. There was a smell of wood smoke and a pig manure, as Valeria had bought a suckling pig that was being fattened up for the winter. He could hear it breathing, snuffling, and panting—presumably it was sleeping under its half roof of boards and plastic a few meters from the house.

Finally, there was the path. He made his way to the out-house wondering how he would know when it was okay to go back in again. He felt like a bumbling idiot. When had this happened? Was it because Vanda and Feliszia were married now? Did Tamás go outside, too, to give them some privacy? Or were the rules different if you grew up together? Nothing was simple or straightforward. Maybe it would be easier for all of them if he slept in the other half of the house, even if part of the gable and some of the roof had caved in. It was summer after all. But if the wind picked up, some of the loose tiles up there could come down on his head while he slept.

The instant he opened the outhouse door, he was

assaulted by yet another razor-sharp childhood memory. The darkness, the smell, the worn board with the hole in it that had been far too big for his little bottom. He had been terrified of falling in. So terrified that sometimes he would just squat down behind the chicken coop and hope no one noticed him. One time his stepfather had caught him in the act, with his pants down around his ankles. That had cost him a couple of sharp smacks.

"You're not a goddamned animal, you filthy little brat. Only animals shit in the street!"

"Yes, but this isn't the street . . ."

The story immediately became a favorite with the whole family, told and retold with laughter and giggles, especially among the grandparents: *There was the boy, squatting there with his butt hanging out, still as cocky as ever . . .*

Cocky. That was when you talked back to the grown-ups, when you were impertinent, and it was usually promptly punished. And yet there was always something ambiguous about the punishment. They didn't spare the rod, but nevertheless there was an acceptance behind it, bordering on approval. Boys were supposed to be cocky. Calling a little boy a "pet" was an insult, on a par with calling him a "sissy" or a "Mama's boy," and even though disobedience could earn you a beating, too much obedience just brought you scorn.

He sat in the stinking darkness of the outhouse, no longer afraid of falling in the hole. But other than that he was by no means cocky. He had had that knocked out of him, effectively and a long time ago, and fear had eaten its way into his life. There was no defiance left in him now, no rebellion. It had been a long time since he had dared to be disobedient.

He hadn't told Gábor and the NBH about Tamás. That was sort of rebellious, wasn't it? Or was that just obedience to an older law? One that had been beaten, yelled, drilled, and loved into him the first eight years of his life: You stick up for your own.

He was glad he hadn't ratted on Tamás to them. He was still furious at his brother, who had obviously acted like an asshole and a moron to boot, and the thought of the mess Tamás had landed them both in filled Sándor with a fear that was totally and utterly different in scope and extent than the everyday fear of messing up, failing, breaking written or unwritten rules, or being caught with your pants down. But in some small, overlooked, stubborn corner of his soul, he was still glad that he hadn't told them about Tamás.

He finished and stepped out into the somewhat fresher air outside. His eyes had adjusted to the May darkness now. Here and there it was punctuated by light from the village houses' small peephole windows combined with the bluish, white flicker of TVs. Maybe it wouldn't be so bad living here, he thought, without heat or running water or indoor toilets, if only you didn't see how other people lived whenever you turned on the TV. But there *were* TVs here, in almost every house. The antennas jostled on the decrepit roofs, their bristly metal branches jutting out in all directions to catch the best possible signal.

Valeria came out with a washbasin and tossed the soapy water out onto the stinging nettles behind the house. He took that as a signal that the coast was clear again.

"Do you want me to heat up a little water for you?" she asked.

"No," he said, because that would mean she would have to light the wood stove, and it was most certainly warm enough inside already. "I'll just rinse off down by the pump."

"No, do it here," she said, passing him the basin. "You don't wash in the middle of the street."

That was a subtle dig, he thought, noticing the hint of a smile in one corner of her mouth. Apparently there was more than one thing people didn't do in the middle of the street in Galbeno. He took the pink plastic basin but didn't move. Neither did Valeria, standing less than a meter away from him. The light from the open door etched deep shadows under her cheekbones and chin and made her look older and sharper. From inside the house, he heard a sleepy little boy's voice whining, and Vanda mumbled something reassuring in response.

"Mama, what's going on with Tamás?" he asked quietly. Maybe she would say more now that Vanda and Feliszia weren't listening.

"Why would anything be going on with Tamás?"

"Because the NBH is very interested in what he's up to. Mama, they arrested me because he had borrowed my computer and used it to visit some sites on the Internet." He faltered a bit, having no idea how much or how little Valeria might know about the Internet. It wasn't like Galbeno was crawling with laptops. Could you even get online out here? Apparently there was some mobile coverage, but the Internet?

Valeria raised her head, and the moonlight gleamed in her eyes.

"The police," she scoffed, sounding harsh and hostile. "They're always after us."

"It wasn't just police, Mama. It was the NBH, the security service!"

"They're still police," she said. "Stay away from them, Sándor."

"Well, I didn't exactly go and ask to be arrested," he said, unable to hold back a spark of irritation. "Mama, what I'm trying to say is that I think Tamás is mixed up in something dangerous."

She touched his cheek with a damp, soap-scented hand.

"Well then, Sándorka," she said in that Mama voice that went right to his gut. "You'll just have to get him out of it. Won't you?"

"**I**T'S MERCURIAL BY nature," Torben said.

Søren rested his paddle across the kayak in front of him and looked at his friend and boss with a certain impatience.

"What do you mean?" he asked.

"Islam. We're never going to be able to get the idea, because there isn't just one. There isn't any one thing to understand. That's why it's so hopeless to work with."

Torben ran both hands over his clean-shaven scalp. They had been paddling for almost two hours at a blistering pace, and there hadn't been a sound between them other than the soft whistle of the paddles as they sank down into the water, leaving swirling, black holes in the smooth surface. After the last sprint, they were both breathing hard, Torben of course half a boat-length ahead of Søren. Lake Furesø spread out smooth and dark beneath their kayaks. It was evening, and utterly still. Søren's fingers were reddened and chilled, but all the same, spring was in the air. The trees along the shore were displaying a light green mist of freshly budding leaves.

He didn't really want to talk shop right now, but Torben was relentless as usual. Did they ever really talk about anything else? Søren suddenly had his doubts. They had been friends since they were both junior officers in the Danish police force. Torben had been just that much faster and that much smarter. He had been made deputy director of the PET's counterterrorism branch at almost the same time that Søren had finally worked his way up to inspector. The ambiguous relationship usually worked out okay, but sometimes Søren wasn't sure if he listened to Torben because he was his boss or because they were friends.

Torben either hadn't noticed his lack of interest in the conversation or didn't care. Torben whipped out his water bottle, took a couple of swigs, and proceeded undaunted.

"Now take that Imam who's coming over for the opening of that cultural center in Emdrup. A highly educated man with honorary doctorates from several European universities. Of course we've had the analysts take a look at him, and apparently he's supposed to be an advocate of Euro-Islam. In other words, a way of practicing Islam that doesn't conflict with European values. That causes certain groups to accuse him of being too moderate or even a lapsed Muslim . . ."

Søren could feel the evening chill, even in his long-sleeved hoodie. He was ready to come ashore now and was thinking, with a certain amount of longing, about warm, dry clothes and maybe even a quiet, friendly beer. But Torben hadn't finished yet.

"But when Muslims who take an interest in Islam on a more intellectual level read his texts, the result is all over the place. They can be interpreted pretty much any way you want. Some people say he's an advocate of the hijab, total gender separation, sharia, the lot. Other people insist the opposite is true. And do you know what *I* say?"

Resigned, Søren shook his head.

"I say that no matter how hard these people look, they'll never understand what that man says or find the definitive truth about Islam. Because there isn't one. It's a rubberband. You can stretch it into any shape you like."

Torben grabbed his paddle again and started slowly paddling back toward the jetty.

Søren knew Torben was more than normally frustrated. To be fair, the politicians, particularly the parties on the right, had allocated plenty of resources to fighting terrorism since 9/11, but the demands placed on the PET were also sky high, and the upcoming Summit had gobbled up most of the annual budget. The government's decision to invest so heavily in the Copenhagen Summit certainly hadn't made the pool of potential terrorists any smaller.

"Do they have the Emdrup business under control?" Søren asked, thinking without envy of the five-man team that had been assigned to babysit the cultural center until the opening.

"Um," Torben grunted with a shrug. "We've had to cover ourselves on multiple fronts—the Muslims who think he's too moderate, Danish right-wing extremists, plus anyone else who might want to celebrate his arrival in an undesirable fashion. And now the minister has decided he wants to attend the opening ceremony. It's a bit of a nuthouse. But what about you? How are your own nutters coming along?"

Torben looked at him inquisitively, and again Søren had the uncomfortable sense he was meeting with his boss rather than out kayaking with a friend.

"We're having some trouble getting things through tech. That's the bottleneck for us at the moment. And then there's this little Hungarian affair . . ." Søren let the kayak nudge the jetty gently and held himself still for a moment, regaining his balance. Then he swung himself up onto the rough, wet boards. "The NBH picked up this student who has been searching in places he shouldn't and has also been in touch with someone here. They think it might be some kind of arms trade, but they didn't get anything definite out of him."

Torben was already carrying his kayak toward the cars, but Søren could tell from his back that he was still listening. Torben was in charge of the eighty people who worked in the counterterrorism center and investigation details that literally multiplied by the hour, but he could still remember every individual case and was able to pick out the main points whenever necessary. That was what had made him such an incredibly talented intelligence officer.

Brilliant career, loving wife, three strapping sons . . . wasn't that what Søren had once imagined his own life would contain, once he reached fifty? And Torben was actually a year or two younger than he was. He picked up his own kayak, feeling a heaviness weighing on his whole body as he followed Torben, barefoot on the rough wood of the jetty.

"What do we have on the Danish end?" Torben asked.

"A guy named Khalid. He wasn't all that cooperative, so I had a chat with him, and we've been keeping an eye on him and anyone he talks to."

"Aha?" A glint of interest in the deputy director's eye. "And?"

"And not much. He chats with a classmate from secondary school who's a sort of half-assed militant now, but not one of the ones on our black list. He has a broad assortment of acquaintances, including both Danes and immigrants, but mostly the latter. And an uncle who's well respected in the moderate Muslim community, one of the supporters behind the Emdrup project, as it happens. We confiscated his computer and are still waiting for the IT team to find the time to take a look at it. They're totally overworked. And so far there's nothing about this that would justify giving it top priority . . ."

"But?"

"There isn't one." They worked together to lift first one and then the second kayak up onto the roof rack of Torben's Audi. Since he lived significantly closer to Lake Furesø than Søren, they usually stored the kayaks at his place.

"Come on," Torben urged him. "What does your gut tell you?"

"Khalid is up to something. I just don't know what it is."

"So find out."

"Yes. Okay."

"Pressure him. Stress him. I mean, he already knows we're keeping an eye on him, so there's not much point in keeping a low profile, right?"

Søren couldn't tell if there might be a hint of reproach in that last part.

"You think it was a mistake to confront him so early?" Søren asked as he peeled off his Dri-Fit tights. Torben used to be an advocate of the so-called "pre-emptive interviews" that were supposed to stop young people from becoming radicalized before they got in too deep.

But maybe there was a new political wind blowing. After all, pre-emptive interviews didn't lead to trials, convictions, and deportations.

"Well, it's moot now, isn't it?" Torben said. "You did what you thought was right. We have to take it from there. And even if it is an arms trade, that doesn't necessarily make it grand-scale terrorism. Or terrorism at all, for that matter."

Torben had already changed into a pair of loose jeans and a red T-shirt with a cheesy design on the front. "Sugar Daddy." Probably from his wife, Annelise. Søren had always found Torben's wife to be slightly vulgar.

"True. But if all he wants is a can of pepper spray, he chose a pretty suspicious place to buy it," Søren said with a shrug. "Well, I'd better . . ." He carefully avoided finishing the sentence completely. He turned his back to Torben and sat down in the car, giving a half-hearted wave out the window.

He had been on the verge of suggesting that quiet, Saturday beer. The evening skies were still full of light, and his house in Hvidovre would be just as he had left it that morning at seven o'clock, complete with dirty coffee cup, cereal bowl, toast crusts, and the utensils he had not bothered to load into the dishwasher. But Torben would probably just turn the beer into coffee at his and Annelise's place, and Søren wasn't in the mood for Torben's idyllic coupledom or his three blond and almost ridiculously muscular teenage boys. Although, come to think of it, the oldest had moved out and was hardly a teenager anymore—he had just started medical school. But even so.

Torben grunted at him amicably. He was still resting his hands on the roof of his Audi, doing his stretches, as Søren pulled out of the parking lot and headed for Hvidovre.

Ah, well. There was more than one way to approach the big Five-Oh. Søren suppressed something that wasn't quite envy and called the night shift at HQ to have them step up the surveillance on Khalid Hosseini.

THE SHINY, POLISHED, black BMW was parked outside Galbeno's small church when Sándor and Valeria emerged from mass Sunday morning. It had already drawn a crowd of Galbeno residents, who had gathered around it, but kept a respectful distance.

Two men climbed out of the car. They were both Roma, but it was immediately evident that there was a world of difference between them and the Galbeno men. It wasn't just the expensive car or the black suits that Sándor instinctively thought of as "old-fashioned," even though he couldn't quite put his finger on why.

"Who's that?" he asked Valeria.

"Alexisz Bolgár," she said, her eyes trained on the older and more heavy-set of the two men.

"He isn't from Galbeno, is he?"

"No." Valeria's lips grew narrower. "He comes here a couple times a month. He wants to be *rom baro.*"

Those two words from his childhood were not in Sándor's active vocabulary, but now that he heard them, he remembered what they meant: the big man, the leader. He contemplated Bolgár with a certain nervous interest and was surprised when his curiosity was instantly returned.

"Mrs. Rézmüves. I hear your eldest has come home. Sándor, isn't it?"

Bolgár spoke with a formal politeness that seemed a natural extension of his less-than-modern suit. Sándor nodded guardedly.

"How do you do?"

They shook hands, again very formally. Bolgár's hand felt damp and fleshy, a rather unpleasant sensation. You couldn't call him fat, but there was a fullness to him, as if there were an excess of everything—strong hands, bulky shoulders, wide jaw, big ears. Shiny black eyebrows, sideburns, and mustache, and a hairline that teetered somewhere between receding and balding.

"We should talk, Sándor," Bolgár said. "Come visit me tomorrow."

Sándor hesitated. He didn't understand why Bolgár wanted to see him, but it seemed impolite to blurt out "Why should I?" Besides, it sounded more like an order than an invitation, and that troubled him.

"Mr. Bolgár . . ." he began as his mind was still flipping feverishly through the catalog of suitable excuses: I won't be here very long, I have to go back to Budapest, I promised my mother/my sister/an old friend . . .

"Of course you needn't take the bus, my friend," Bolgár added jovially, sensing Sándor's hesitation. "Stefan will pick you up, tomorrow at noon."

Then he turned to one of the men in the circle in a the-discussion-is-now-over motion and started a new conversation. Sándor felt ambushed, but unable to protest. He glanced over at the BMW and was far from tempted by the prospect of a ride in its lush, cream-colored leather seats. Maybe he should go back to Budapest now, right away, so he wouldn't even be here when Stefan came? He still had his dorm room for a couple more days. Maybe Ferenc would let him stay with him after that? He suddenly felt as if Galbeno was closing in on him and wasn't going to let him go, pulling him down and nailing his feet to the ground so he could never escape.

Valeria stuck her hand in under his arm and managed to maneuver him out of the crowd.

"Bolgár," she said in a tone that denoted more frustration than respect. "Uh, that man."

"Is he really *rom baro*?" Sándor asked.

"I just said he *wanted* to be, not that he was." Valeria waved her hand dismissively. Sándor couldn't tell if she was waving away a troublesome insect or if the gesture were meant for Alexisz Bolgár. "He's no big man. He's the man with the money, and that's not the same. But what are people supposed to do? When the house is falling apart or there's no food? What choice do they have? Bolgár lends them money. And then suddenly he owns them."

Sándor stopped. Valeria took another couple steps before turning around to see why he wasn't with her anymore.

"Mama," Sándor said cautiously. "Does he own you, too?"

Valeria's lips were thin lines now, and her face was hard.

"He loaned Bobo the money for the roof," she said. "And he's the one who helped Tamás get to Denmark."

"What does that mean?" Sándor asked. "How much do you owe him?"

But he already knew what that meant. It meant, for example, that tomorrow he would have to get into that BMW when Stefan came to pick him up.

NINA FOUND **A**NTON behind the school gym. He had taken off his sweatshirt and T-shirt, and his blond hair was sticking out in damp, sweaty spikes as he concentrated on pounding a heavy, green plastic ball against the wall. He kicked it, changed direction, kicked it again. The ball sang through the air with each well-aimed kick, and even though he had his back to her, Nina could tell right away that he was in a good mood.

She let her bag flop down on the ground and ran up to him just as he was about to whack yet another volley at the wall.

"I've got this one," she yelled, and just managed to catch Anton's grin of satisfaction before she kicked at the ball, striking it at an unfortunate angle and sending it careening past the corner of the gym out onto the playground.

"Hi, Mom."

He was panting happily, and he cast one last wistful glance at the ball before he pulled his yellow T-shirt over his head and ran a hand through his sweaty hair. He's getting so big, Nina thought, a warm wave of tenderness sloshing around pleasantly somewhere in her stomach. Occasionally she still had that feeling when she looked at Ida, as well, but these days it was mostly when Ida was asleep, her face resting childlike on her pillow. The rest of the time, words seemed to fall flat between them in a heavy, tangled mess, if they spoke to each other at all. The unfortunate roller hockey fiasco was just the latest example.

Things had always been more difficult with Ida, Nina thought, recalling Ida's contorted little face in the highchair that terrible panicky day when she had dumped everything on Morten—including Ida—and had run away to foreign parts for several months. It was hard for her to explain why she had done it, even now, except that Ida had seemed so fragile, and she had become convinced that she would damage this tiny, helpless being with her own damaged life if she stayed. They had got off to a bad start, and though they had had a couple of peaceful years of something that had felt like normality with pasta necklaces, mother-and-daughter trips to the movies, and help with homework at the kitchen table, Nina had always had the sense that it was the calm before the storm. As if Ida were only waiting for a chance to relegate Nina once and for all to where she really belonged: Mom Hell. The place reserved for bad mothers, career women, alcoholics, and mentally unstable women where they might suffer for all eternity because they had dared to reproduce despite a complete absence of maternal qualifications.

They went inside the after-school club, where Anton crossed himself off the list as usual, and Nina quickly raked the contents of his locker into his backpack.

Her mobile phone rang.

Nina looked at the display and recognized the number just as she pressed the green button. Oh, hell. Peter from the Network.

It had been a while since she had last heard from him, and for once that had suited her just fine. There had been plenty of crises at the Coal-House Camp in the past few months, and after that whole business with the boy in the suitcase last year, Morten had been adamant about putting the brakes on her Network involvement. They had had the Big Important Talk—she had permission to continue her work with the Network, but on the condition that she stayed home when Morten was away on the rigs. Anything else would be "treating her own family like shit," as Morten had so poetically expressed it, and even though their marriage was going through an unusually good patch, Nina still had the sneaking suspicion she was being forced to resit an exam in Virtues of Danish Family Life 101. She didn't want to find out what would happen if she flunked.

"We need you in Valby. If you make it before 4 p.m. I can meet you there."

Peter spoke with authority in his voice, as if he were Barack Obama personally shutting down Guantanamo. He hardly even waited for her to say hello.

"No go, Peter," Nina said, noting the time automatically: 3:44 p.m. exactly. "I can't today. Morten is away in the North Sea, and I'm literally up to my ears in my son's leftover lunch. You have to find someone else."

Peter was quiet for a moment on the other end of the line.

"Can't you leave him on his own for a while? It won't take more than an hour."

Nina tried to quell her rising irritation. Although she had never actually said so, Peter should know by now that saying no was not an easy thing for her. She felt an unreasonable burst of resentment that he wouldn't just accept it when she actually did decline a request.

"No, I can't just leave him," she hissed. "He is eight years old, for God's sake. What's the problem, anyway?"

"This guy from Hungary," Peter said neutrally. "Not that old, maybe sixteen or seventeen. He just arrived and is staying with about fifty other people in this derelict garage in Valby, and he's sick as a dog. Vomiting and diarrhea. I think it must be some kind of food poisoning, and I could really use a little help."

Nina breathed a little easier. Peter painted the picture with irritating clarity, and of course someone should probably try to figure out if it was food poisoning or just an ordinary case of the trots. But all things considered, it didn't sound like anything she needed to be involved in.

"Hungary is part of the EU," she said. "No one is going to deport him. Send him to the doctor with a stool sample, and buy some rehydration powder, cola, and lots of mineral water. He'll be back on his feet in a couple of days," she said quickly.

"You know damn well he won't see a doctor," Peter said, raising his voice a bit. "He would have to pay for it himself, and these boys aren't exactly loaded. They're Roma, most of them. They don't understand a word of English, German, or French, and they're totally paranoid about any kind of authority figure. They made me hide in the goddamn inspection pit just because someone knocked on the door. I couldn't get through to them at all." Peter didn't usually swear, and it sounded almost comical when he did. Nina guessed his visit to the inspection pit had put a couple dents in his dignity. "You simply have to help," he continued. "I have no idea what to do with them."

"I'm sorry, Peter." She gave Anton a quick smile,

realizing that last part had eased her guilty conscience further. Even she, Save-The-World Woman, as Morten sarcastically referred to her, sometimes found the Roma hard to love. She had once stood in the middle of a crowd of Roma trying to examine a boy with a fever and a tooth abscess the size of a ping pong ball. Aman—presumably the boy's father—had alternately begged and threatened her, and ultimately the whole crowd had stormed off in a huff, spluttering and gesticulating, dragging the sick boy with them. She had been more nervous than she usually was when she was called out at night, and the thought of fifty Roma packed into a repair shop in Valby gave her an unexpectedly uneasy feeling. They had presumably traveled up to Denmark by bus, hoping to scrape together some money over the summer through begging or trickery. It didn't make their physical ailments any less uncomfortable, but damn it . . .

"I'll call you later," Peter said, his voice icy. "And in the future it would be helpful if you could send me Morten's schedule so I'll know when we can count on you."

Then he was gone.

Nina let her phone slip back into her jacket pocket and hoisted up Anton's bag. Did he really need to be so bossy? But she knew Peter had trouble finding both people and funds at the moment. The Network had a limited circle of supporters, and the financial crisis hadn't exactly helped their bottom line. Also, the new nurse Peter had found in the autumn had recently moved away from Copenhagen to settle on the West Coast with her husband and kids and a German shepherd puppy. Peter would calm down eventually. He had no other choice.

SÁNDOR WAS STARING at the piece of paper Bolgár had put down on the table in front of him. It didn't exactly look official, and he doubted the document would ever be presented to the tax authorities or any other official for that matter, but the mere fact that it had been written down gave it a certain, unarguable weight.

It was an IOU. And the amount was a staggering two million forints.

Tamás! he protested silently to himself. How in the hot, stinking bowels of hell could you sign this? But that was just what he had done—*Tamás Rézmüves*, with big adolescent swoops to the T and the R.

"Tamás isn't eighteen yet," Sándor said in a sort of legal reflex. But he also knew that didn't matter here. The IOU in front of him had nothing to do with Hungarian law.

Bolgár leaned back until his wicker chair creaked under the pressure. They were sitting on the patio at Bolgár's house, in a village that wasn't so terribly different from Galbeno apart from the fact that the cars were bigger and newer. Only Bolgár's own house stood out, and then some—it must be five or six thousand square feet, Sándor thought, with a two-story central core and two lower side wings surrounding the patio. Facing the street there was a tall wrought iron fence with so many curlicues and flourishes that it made his eyes swim when he tried to look through it.

"Sándor, my friend," Bolgár said slowly. "Your brother is a man, and this here is his signature. Do we agree on that much?"

Sándor thought about Valeria and the girls and about the money for the new roof. He nodded.

"Yes."

Bolgár smiled.

"Good. Then we can work out the rest." He gave a curt, brisk wave with one hand, and a teenage girl came out of the house with a tray of bottles and glasses. "It's hot," Bolgár said. "I'm sure you would like a beer."

The girl set the tray down on the little wrought iron table between them with a bang. Her sullen face radiated antipathy; she obviously wasn't thrilled to be waiting on the men.

"My daughter," Bolgár said proudly, completely disregarding her rebellious glare. "Give your daddy a kiss, girl."

The girl leaned forward and kissed him on the cheek without the slightest change in her facial expression. Then she disappeared back into the house. Bolgár raised his glass, and Sándor's reflexive politeness forced him to do the same even though he actually had no desire to drink with this man. The beer was so icy-cold that he felt it all the way down his esophagus; it was almost painful.

"Why did Tamás borrow so much money?" Sándor asked.

"Business," Bolgár said. "Your brother had an item to sell, but he had to borrow money for the trip, transportation, room and board. It all adds up, you know."

"But . . . two million?" You could buy ten airplane tickets for that kind of money, Sándor thought.

"Shall we say there was . . . a certain element of risk. Your brother couldn't just take the bus."

Sándor felt a shiver in his gut that had nothing to do with the chilled beer.

"What kind of item?" Sándor asked. "And where did he get it?"

Bolgár shook his head.

"Your brother was extremely tight-lipped about the details. Still, I trusted him, which is why I invested such a large sum and put him in touch with some men in Denmark who could help him. But now I'm starting to have doubts. I haven't heard anything, you see. From him or the Danes. And so now I'm asking myself: Who is going to pay me back my two million forints?"

Bolgár's eyes came to rest on Sándor with a weight that made it clear it wasn't actually a question.

"FELISZIA. CAN I ask you something?"

His little sister was standing in front of the house with her forearms immersed in an orange plastic basin, washing clothes. The front of her pink T-shirt was covered with wet splotches.

"What?" she asked.

Sándor looked around. One of Vanda's two boys was chasing the other with a little, yellow squirt gun. Both of them were screaming with delight. Vanda was nowhere to be seen, and he couldn't spot Valeria either. Probably just as well.

"The money Tamás thinks he's going to earn in Denmark. I know it's because he has something to sell. But do you know what it is?"

She shook her head. "No. He didn't say anything about that."

"Feliszia, it's important. I think he's in trouble, but I can't help him unless I have some idea what it's about."

Feliszia regarded him with calm, dark eyes. She had become so beautiful, he thought. So very much alive.

"What kind of trouble?" she asked.

"Well, Bolgár for starters." He didn't want to bring up the NBH just now.

"That man," she said in exactly the same tone Valeria had used. "I didn't want Bobo to borrow the money from him. But he did it anyway."

"Tamás borrowed two million forints."

"Two million?" Feliszia looked startled. "But why?"

"That's what I'm trying to find out."

"That idiot," she whispered. She had tears in her eyes now.

"What is it?" He placed a hand on her arm awkwardly. "Feliszia, what's wrong?"

Suddenly she wrapped her soapy arms around his neck and hugged him tight. It took Sándor so much by surprise that he just stood there like a peg doll with stiff, mechanical joints. Feliszia let him go again and looked at him with the same confusion he had seen before in both her and Vanda's faces. He was their brother, and yet he wasn't. The distance between them suddenly hurt; he didn't want it to be there. He wanted to belong.

"I really want to help," he heard himself say. "I just don't know how." And this time he meant it; he was no longer just trying to persuade her to talk to him.

"He was so angry," Feliszia said. "About that business with Vanda's apartment, about what happened in Tatárszentgyörgy."

Sándor bit his lower lip. He remembered his own feeling of impotent shock when he heard about the tragedy in the little village forty kilometers from Budapest. Someone had set fire to a house where a Roma family was living. When the inhabitants tried to escape from the flames, they were gunned down. A father and his five-year-old son.

"Was it someone you knew?" he asked.

"No," Feliszia said. "But it doesn't matter. They were Roma."

"You're angry, too."

"Yes, I am. So you see, I understand Tamás."

"What do you mean?"

"He said the only thing that could save us was money. Lots of money. So we could get out of here, and no one could hurt us."

"Feliszia, this isn't going to save anyone. Tamás is up to his neck in it, and so are we. And everything is just getting worse."

She shot him a furious, betrayed look, which pierced him to the soul. *A little girl with a filthy pink stuffed rabbit on her lap, confused and afraid and surrounded by strangers . . .*

"Well, it's not *my* fault," Sándor said defensively. "I'm just trying to help . . ."

She plunged her arms back into the basin so abruptly that soapy water splashed out in all directions and began to scrub at the wet clothes with quick, fierce jerks.

Then her motions slowed. She pulled up one shoulder and used it to rub a soapy smear off her cheek.

"I don't know what he wants to sell," she said. "And I

don't know where he got it from either. But you could try asking Pitkin."

THE DOG WAS barking, very loudly and insistently with just a split second between each deafening woof. Its lips were pulled so far back that every single tooth was visible and most of its glistening pink-and-black mottled gums, too. Sándor remained motionless, standing in the relative safety on the other side of the ramshackle fence. It was bigger than most of the village dogs, and he rather thought a German shepherd had been added to the mix not too many generations ago.

"Hello?" he called, tentatively. "Is Pitkin home?"

Pitkin lived in "the old village," as people in Galbeno called it, even though only three buildings there were still even marginally habitable. It was a collection of wattle and daub huts a little farther up in the hills, closer to the source of the spring, but otherwise just a little farther away from everything. No road, just a winding path. No electricity. Roofs that were patchworks of rusty metal plates, plastic, and straw. Galbeno wasn't actually the end of the road, Sándor reflected. There was a back of beyond beyond the back of beyond.

A man came out of the house. His back was so stooped that his head with its plaid cap jutted out between his shoulders like a turtle's. His trousers were being held up by a pair of black suspenders, and his torso was clad solely in a yellowing vest.

"Who are you?" he asked.

"Sándor. My mother's Valeria Rézmüves."

"Valeria's boy? How tall you've grown!"

Sándor shrugged. "Is Pitkin home?" he asked.

The old man nodded. "Come in," he said. "Shut up, Brutus."

The German shepherd mix stopped barking immediately. It wagged and danced over to the old man, who patted its head with a calloused, gnarled hand. Sándor ventured inside, closing the gate behind him by the simple expedient of looping a bit of dark-green binder twine over the top of the post.

Inside the hut itself it was so dark that at first Sándor could barely make out the details. The floor plan was the same as in Valeria's green house. One room, a shelf for sleeping and seating along three of the walls, a wood stove, and a door. No TV here, of course, since there wasn't any electricity. Also lacking was the cleanliness and order Valeria insisted on.

A moped was parked in the middle of the room. A blue, three-speed Kreidler Florett, Sándor noted, recollecting specifications picked up in his teenage years that he hadn't realized he still remembered. The smell of gasoline mixed with the pungency of dirt and human body odor. The moped was definitely the cleanest thing in the room. New wasn't quite the right word, but maybe newly purchased? There was something about the way it was polished, and probably also the fact that it was parked in the middle of the house, that suggested that the joy of ownership hadn't lost its luster.

"Pitkin, this is Sándor," the old man announced. "Valeria's boy."

A pile of blankets in the corner moved, and a large, droopy form sat up.

"Tamás?" Pitkin said. "Is Tamás home?"

"No," Sándor said. "Not yet."

"He's been a little under the weather lately," grunted the man who must be Pitkin's grandfather. "He must have eaten something that doesn't agree with him. But if you'll sit with him for a bit, then I can go down to the council office."

"Are you going, Grandpa?"

"Yes, Pitkin, but Sándor's here now. So it's okay if I nip out for a bit."

You would have thought Pitkin was eight rather than eighteen, Sándor thought. How sick was he really? But then it dawned on him that it wasn't just this momentary discomfort making Pitkin seem like a child. Feliszia had mentioned it, too; she had described him as "a little immature," and that was no exaggeration.

"You will stay, won't you?" the old man said, and even though his voice sounded casual, there was an intensity in his eyes that made it clear that it was a plea. "I also have to pick up a couple of things at the store."

Dear God, Sándor thought, how long has Pitkin been sick?

"Of course I will," Sándor promised, sitting down on the bench to demonstrate that he wasn't about to run off. "Take your time."

Pitkin followed his grandfather with his eyes as the old man put a jacket on over his yellowing vest—despite the heat—and straightened his cap.

"I'll be home again soon, boy," he said, and Sándor was a little unsure whether the boy being referred to was him or Pitkin.

"When's Tamás coming back?" Pitkin asked once his grandfather had gone. "He said it wouldn't take that long."

"I don't know, Pitkin. What was he was going to do?"

But Pitkin wasn't that gullible. His face suddenly went blank, and he blinked a couple times.

"He was just going to earn a little money," Pitkin said. "With his violin."

Sándor stifled a sigh. Pitkin was clearly smart enough to lie, he thought, just not smart enough that the lie wasn't obvious.

"That's a nice moped," Sándor said. "Have you just bought it?"

Pitkin's face lit up like a sunrise.

"It's a three-speed," he said. "It can go seventy on a flat road."

"That's great. What did you have to pay for it?"

"Tamás bought it for me. He said . . ." Pitkin stopped.

"What did he say, Pitkin?"

But Pitkin just shook his head.

"I wish he'd come home again," he said. "It's so boring here without him."

"You're good friends, you and him?"

Pitkin nodded so his dark hair danced.

"He's my best friend."

"So you would want to help him, if he needed it?"

"Of course!" Pitkin's serious face practically radiated indignation. "He's my friend."

"Yes, and he's my brother. And I really want to help him."

"Help him with what?"

Sándor hesitated. He suddenly found it hard to lie to this big, vulnerable child-man. So he chose some words that were actually true.

"Help him come home," Sándor said. "He's been gone too long."

Pitkin nodded. "That's right."

The dog came into the house. What was its name again? Brutus? Very apt. It gave Sándor a suspicious look just to let him know that it was keeping its eye on him. Then it lumbered over to Pitkin and nudged its head under Pitkin's hand to entice him to stroke it. Pitkin scratched the dog behind the ear so it closed its eyes and moaned in pleasure.

"Do you know where exactly he was going?"

"Denmark. He said Denmark."

Sándor knew that much already.

"What was he going to sell?"

"Just something we found," Pitkin said.

"Where?"

"The hospital in Szikla." Pitkin bit his lip. "He told me not to tell anyone that."

"It's okay, Pitkin. It's just me."

Suddenly the look on Pitkin's face changed. He stood up abruptly, fumbling his way past the moped to the door. He barely made it out before the first wave of vomit splashed onto the ground.

Sándor got up instinctively without knowing what to do. Hold Pitkin's forehead? Clean up the mess? The dog whined and bumped Pitkin with its nose, and when Sándor took a step closer, it turned its head and growled. Sándor sat down again.

Pitkin wiped his mouth on his sleeve.

"It won't stop," Pitkin said, his voice making it clear he found this unfair. "I haven't eaten anything at all today and still it just keeps coming."

He sank back onto the bunk, on a pile of quilts and pillows. The dog was sniffing at the pool of vomit outside, but when Pitkin snapped his fingers, it obediently came back in and sat down next to him.

"Do you want a glass of water or anything?" Sándor asked awkwardly.

Pitkin shook his head. "I'm tired," he said. "I think I'm going to take a nap."

"What was it you found?" Sándor tried one more time.

"I can't talk now," Pitkin grunted and lay down.

"Not even to help Tamás?"

But that appeal no longer had any effect.

"He said I couldn't tell anyone," Pitkin said, closing his eyes.

Sándor sat up straighter. The dog followed his every move.

"Pitkin . . ."

A fake snore was all that came from Pitkin.

"You're not really asleep . . ." Sándor tried. But all he heard was more snoring, and he began to realize that he wasn't going to get anything else out of this conversation. He got up slowly so as not to alarm the dog. Pitkin opened his eyes.

"You're not leaving, are you?"

"Well, you're just going to go to sleep, right?"

"But you promised my grandpa."

The fear shone out of Pitkin's eyes. Sándor didn't know if he was always afraid of being alone or if it was just because he was sick. Either way, he couldn't resist the boy's obvious terror.

"Okay, I'll stay for a bit," he said.

Pitkin grunted in satisfaction and made himself more comfortable. Sándor sat quietly next to him until the old man came back.

THE NEXT MORNING Bolgár's BMW was parked outside Valeria's house when Sándor went out to pee. Stefan was leaning against the front door with his arms crossed. When he spotted Sándor, he straightened up and started moving.

"Mr. Bolgár wants to talk to you," he said.

Sándor had pretty much guessed that.

"So early? Can't it wait until I've had a pee?"

Apparently it couldn't. There was a certain inevitability to the way Stefan was blocking his way.

"Now," he said.

A few hours later Sándor was once again sitting on a bus. Not the local one this time, but an old, blue Ford Transit minibus. All seventeen seats were occupied, and the aisle between the seats was stuffed full of luggage in suitcases and plastic bags. He was the only one from Galbeno, but most of the others were from similar villages or from Miskolc's Roma ghetto. Three women had their own section at the very back of the bus where a couple of sheets could be rigged up as a curtain at night. One of them was traveling with her little daughter, a girl of about four. The rest of the passengers were men.

Sándor was sitting on a worn, gray imitation leather seat that was already sticking to his thighs, with his feet awkwardly wedged on either side of the cardboard box of food and water that Valeria had presented him with, and his feeling of unreality grew until he was seriously considering banging his head against the window a couple of times just to check if it hurt. Outside the window Miskolc's industrial district slid by, a gray and rusty brown landscape of fences and crumbling concrete, dented steel containers, and high smokestacks from the time when smokestacks were a symbol of progress, growth, and jobs.

Ten days ago, he thought. Ten days ago I was a law student. I was living in Budapest. I had a future.

Back then he had enjoyed the illusion that he was the master of his own life, that he could steer it in whichever direction he wanted. With a few limitations, of course, and as long as he was good and careful about not breaking the rules. Since then he had been jerked this way and that, first by Tamás, then by the NBH, the university, his professor, his mother, his family, and now most recently Bolgár.

"We've heard from Denmark," Bolgár had said when Stefan deposited Sándor on the patio like the previous time. "Your brother needs you."

"Tamás? What for?"

"Who asks why when his brother needs help? He just wants to talk to you, he says. Don't worry, Sándor; we'll take care of everything. At no extra charge. You're leaving this afternoon."

Again it wasn't a question. Not even a demand for his consent. His compliance was taken for granted.

But Bolgár might not have trusted completely in his obedience after all; as he was put on the bus, Stefan took his wallet, removed his Visa card, and gave it to the driver before handing Sándor back his money.

I'm going to Denmark, he told himself. It didn't really make any sense. If he had been the cowboy in one of the two tattered Morgan Kane novels he had in his bag, he would have a clear mission at this point: someone who needed to be found, rescued, or avenged. Of course there would also be bad guys and trials and tribulations, and a dynamic hero who would see things through to their conclusion and emerge victorious in the end.

Sándor had a hard time seeing what his mission was. And an even harder time picturing the victorious hero.

Bolgár wanted him to help his brother. But with what? he wondered.Presumably with selling whatever the heck he and Pitkin had found, on some ultra black market to a buyer who was no doubt a criminal and possibly worse. What an outstanding start to his law career that would be.

But you don't have a law career anymore, an icily sarcastic voice jeered in his mind. And if you don't get Bolgár his damned two million forints, you might not have a family anymore, either. Because that was what this was about. It was never said out loud, but that was the implication. It was the reason he hadn't refused to go, the reason he hadn't even protested when Stefan took his credit card. Valeria and the girls. Their lives and ability to survive in the village. He didn't even dare contemplate what consequences it might have for them if he stood up to a man like Bolgár.

He rubbed his forehead with his wrist and suddenly felt like talking to Lujza. Not to tell her where he was going or what had happened so far. Just . . . because. Because she was his real life, the one he had had before he became hopelessly trapped in this web of family and past and veiled threats.

He pulled his phone out of his jacket pocket. If he was going to call, it made the most sense to do it while it was still a domestic call. But when he tried to turn the phone on, it shut off right away. The battery needed to be recharged.

He sat there for a while with the phone in his hand. Then he let it drop back into his pocket.

Maybe it was better this way. He had no idea what he would have said to her anyway.

R INA DIDN'T WANT to talk to anyone anymore.

They had called from the children's unit that morning while Nina was leading her class for new mothers, Infant Health. That was one of the more pleasant jobs at the Coal-House Camp. Women who had just given birth had an astounding ability to shut out the rest of the world. The five women sat on the floor of the clinic's little waiting room with their babies in front of them on soft, brightly colored baby blankets as they followed Nina attentively with their eyes.

"Put your baby on its tummy as often as possible. After each diaper change, for example."

Nina squatted down and carefully rolled a three-month-old boy onto his stomach, and couldn't help but smile. The boy struggled to hold his big wobbly head, but gave up after a few seconds, resting his forehead on the blanket in front of him and squawking shrilly and angrily. The women laughed. The boy's mother, a very young woman from Sudan, stroked him soothingly over his dusting of curly hair. Then she turned him around, picked him up in a quick and secure grip, and snuggled his little body to her chest. The boy instantly stopped his screeching, but was still whimpering at the affront when the phone rang. Rikke from the children's unit made her brief report. Rina wasn't sleeping, wasn't eating, and refused to talk to anyone. Including the kids she actually knew well from the family section at Unit B.

They didn't need Nina to come back, because as Rikke

said, "the positive effect of Nina's daily visits was obviously limited." She was actually just calling because she wanted to talk to Magnus. He was going to have to get the girl some kind of psychiatric evaluation.

"Damn and blast it," Nina said, aware of how her loathing of the system came sneaking in. She pictured Rina, sitting in the office in the children's unit, spinning around hesitantly on a stool in front of the camp's child psychiatrist. He was actually pretty good, a friendly middle-aged man with a little pot belly and a pair of narrow glasses mounted on his nose. But she wouldn't be given more than an hour of therapy a month. Which was hardly better than nothing at all.

"What she needs is her mother," Nina said, trying to rein in her frustration. After all, it wasn't Rikke's fault. But still . . . Nina wasn't sure she liked the tone of Rikke's voice. Wasn't there a touch of blame in it?

"I'm not disagreeing, Nina," Rikke said. "But neither you nor I can give her what she needs most of all now. You're wasting your time over here. She's totally out of it. I need to talk to Magnus. Now."

"He's not here."

"Then ask him to call when he gets in."

Nina said an overly hasty goodbye and put the phone back down on the desk with a hard bang. The babies' mothers were still sitting on the floor in the next room, and she could hear their soft, cooing voices, their laughter, and the babies' little grunts of satisfaction at the attention.

She waved a quick farewell to the women and then walked rapidly down the hallway toward the exit. She needed a break. It had started raining outside. Soft, heavy drops were falling from the gray May sky and had already soaked the lawn in front of the main building. Nina stood in the doorway watching the water run in little rivulets over the paved walkway, which was lined with old cigarette butts and gum wrappers. Spring spruced up the Coal-House Camp, no question. But there was no hiding the fact that both the residents and the Danish government were basically indifferent to the place. It was ugly and uncared for. Scratched up, scuffed, worn out. Being here made people gray, no matter how much paint they sloshed on the outside and how much IKEA furniture they stuffed inside.

She took a deep breath. The scent of wet dirt and grass and asphalt and summer. She made a decision. She would bring Ida, Anton, and Morten to Viborg with her this year, to stay with her mother. The kids really ought to spend a little time with their grandmother. Nina would just have to grit her teeth and smile her way through it.

Her phone's protracted trills interrupted her, and she just managed to get it up out of her pocket before the ringing stopped.

"Nina?"

It was Peter. She recognized his voice after a brief delay. He didn't sound the way he usually did. "Nina, I know Morten isn't home yet, but I was really hoping you could make an exception. I'm . . ." Peter was cut short by a protracted coughing fit, followed by long, labored gasps for breath. "I've come down with something," he said. "I'm sure it's the same thing the young Roma boy has. It's really nasty. I'm so . . ."

Again a protracted rattling cough that almost made Nina hold the phone away from her until the worst of the fit had passed. She lowered her voice.

"What were you hoping I could do?"

Peter laughed hollowly into the phone.

"Nothing fancy. I've gathered a few supplies for that young man at the Valby garage. You know, fluids, Imodium, seasickness pills, and that rehydration powder you said he should have. What was that stuff called . . ." Nina could hear Peter rustling around in some packages. "Well, it doesn't matter." He called off the hunt. "Now the problem is that I'm not up to driving out there to drop them off. I've been throwing up nonstop."

His voice became high-pitched, almost childlike, as he said that last bit, and that made Nina hesitate with her refusal. She looked at her watch and considered her options. Anton was going to spend the night next door at Mathias's. They had been planning that for a few weeks, so she wouldn't need to feel guilty about defending that to Morten, and it was pretty much standard routine that Ida disappeared into her room the instant Nina walked in the door.

"I'm not driving out to Valby, Peter," Nina said. "But I'll come over and check on you. You shouldn't be lying there all by yourself." That wasn't breaking her promise to Morten, she thought, painstakingly suppressing the sudden sense of relief she felt at not having to spend the evening ignoring Ida's coldness.

There was silence on the other end of the line.

"Peter?"

"Thanks, Nina. That's really nice of you." Peter's voice

caught a little over his own unaccustomed politeness. Peter didn't usually thank people, Nina mused. Peter usually demanded her assistance for the Network and took it for granted that she would say yes. Nina furrowed her brow and let her phone fall back into her jacket pocket. Only then did the penny drop. Peter didn't care if she went to Valby tonight. This time he had been calling to get help for himself.

PETER'S HOUSE WAS on a long, flat street on the borderline between two of Copenhagen's less fashionable suburbs, Vanløse and Brønshøj. She had never been there before and had to double-check the house number on the little yellow slip of paper she had sitting next to her on the passenger's seat. The street was lined with light-green beech hedges, and behind them she caught glimpses of gardens tended with varying degrees of enthusiasm, with small, crooked fruit trees, lilacs, birches, and chestnuts. The houses looked like they were from the 1950s, originally small, but now with add-ons and remodels on all sides and of generally doubtful aesthetic merits.

Peter's house was no exception. A small, red-brick bungalow surrounded by a lawn, a couple of bushes, and a narrow garage at the end of the driveway. Peter had his own alterations underway, Nina knew. A little annex that would connect the garage to the bungalow. He had been talking about it for several years. Being able to bring people, unseen, into the house from the garage would make some of his work for the Network easier, but of course that hadn't been an option while he was married. No self-respecting woman would have allowed the monstrosity

Nina saw being added onto the end of the house. Not even if it was going to help save the world.

The foundation had been poured for the little add-on, and a hole had been knocked through the wall. That was as far as he, or the workmen, had gotten, and a perfunctory tarpaulin now covered the opening, flapping gently in the cool May breeze. Small, shiny pools of water sat on what would be the floor of the annex someday.

The divorce had taken its toll on him, Nina thought. He never mentioned it when they saw each other. He rarely talked about himself, just the "cases" and the "clients." But Nina felt she could see the grim contours of the divorce in the construction mess—the sagging sacks of building rubble slumped at the corner of the driveway and the windows gaping emptily out at the garden. His wife must have taken the curtains, she thought with disapproval. That was the kind of thing women did to their ex-husbands, knowing full well that the poor slobs would never get around to fixing new ones. And on top of that, Peter now obviously didn't have anyone besides her to call when he was sick.

It took Peter a while to open the door.

He was fully dressed, but unmistakably sick. His eyes were bleary and bloodshot, his face unshaven, and his hair was sticking out every which way, sweaty and disheveled. There was no mistaking the sour smell of sweat and vomit as he stepped aside and invited her in with a sarcastic, stewardess-like gesture.

"Welcome to my humble abode," he chimed with a wan smile.

Nina smiled back, setting her grocery bag of fresh

supplies—a loaf of bread, cola, and oatmeal—on the floor in the hallway.

"How bad is it?"

Peter sighed. "Well, I think it's a little better," he replied evasively. "I haven't thrown up in over an hour, but I'm just completely wasted."

Nina nodded.

"Well, let's look on the bright side. Did you eat or drink anything when you were at the house?"

"Oh, it's hardly a house. It's an old auto mechanic's shop. But, no. I don't think I did. A cup of tea at the most."

"Good. Then I don't think it's food poisoning. It sounds more like a stomach virus. They can be ridiculously contagious."

Peter turned around and slowly made his way into the sparsely furnished living room, where he collapsed onto a faded sofa. A bucket and mop were in position next to him, and on a low table he had a stack of hand towels, a roll of paper towels, and a pitcher of water.

"I'm really sorry I called you like that," he said. "But at one point I just got so . . . scared. I damn nearly blacked out when I tried to stand up, and I really freaked that something was seriously wrong. But now I risk infecting you, too."

Nina shook her head dismissively.

"You help so many people, Peter. If for once you need someone to cool your fevered brow for you, that's only fair."

She quickly gathered up the used towels and located the washing machine in the bathroom. There wasn't much that you could say about stomach bugs that was good, but at least it usually cleared up on its own.

"Have you had any diarrhea?"

"Not yet."

"Fever?"

Nina snapped the washing machine closed and set it on hot. Peter responded something or other from the living room, but she had to go back in to hear what he said. He was lying back with his eyes closed and a limp hand resting on his forehead.

"No, no fever," he repeated. "But blood. There was a little blood in my vomit."

Nina was puzzled. Blood didn't necessarily mean anything. It could have come from some small lesion in his esophagus or pharynx. It could easily happen if the vomiting was intense. And since he was improving . . .

"How long have you been sick?"

Nina looked around the room. There were two empty 1.5-liter Coke bottles on top of the TV. Peter had amassed a whole little pile of mail on the shelf over by the door without apparently having had the strength to open it.

"Since last night," he said with an uneasy, drawn out sigh. "I was supposed to head out to Valby with fresh supplies today."

He nodded tiredly toward a couple big bags in the corner of the living room.

"Isn't that a lot of shopping for one person?" Nina asked, recognizing an all too familiar sense of anxiety starting to move around somewhere in her stomach.

"Yes, plus now I've gone and drunk all the Coke myself," Peter said in a voice that sounded a little choked up. "But they called me again after I talked to you. More people are sick now. They were worried about the little ones. The kids. So I bought a lot. They also called while I was sick, I could see. But I just wasn't up to answering. I was throwing up nonstop."

Peter sounded almost ashamed now, and Nina's mild flutter of concern picked up. What if she were mistaken? Young children could get very sick very fast, and a group of Roma in Valby wouldn't have any idea what to do here in Denmark if something went seriously wrong. Peter was probably their only Danish contact, apart from the bloodsuckers who were no doubt charging the group an arm and a leg for "rent" and other "extras" while they were in the country.

Nina quickly glanced at her watch. It was only 7:32 P.M.

THE OLD GARAGE sat in a long, narrow lot between a barn-like production shed with bright-red corrugated steel walls and a low, white building with a peeling sign that filled most of its façade—Bækgaard Industrial Technology. There were no signs of life in either of the neighboring buildings, but then it was well after closing time, Nina thought. 7:57 P.M. to be precise.

She got out of the car. The breeze had picked up. Small, strong gusts seemed to be coming from all directions at once, blowing cold cascades of rain at her. You could hear the faint whoosh of cars on the old south-bound highway. A solitary blackbird sang softly and melodically from its perch in a stubborn elder bush that had found a way up through the cracked slabs of concrete right where they met the boundary wall. Apart from that, the silence outside the garage was total.

Nina picked up the bags of groceries and the first aid kit she kept in the car and quickly crossed the little parking lot in front of the garage doors.

They must have seen her coming.

The door to the garage was already ajar before she had a chance to knock, and a youngish man in a worn turquoise sweater was eying her suspiciously.

From the darkness behind him now came the sounds of muffled voices, children crying, and women shushing the littlest ones in soft voices.

"I am a nurse," said Nina in careful English, enunciating each word slowly and clearly while pointing to her first aid kit with its discrete red cross on the white background. "Peter told me to come."

The man, joined now by a slightly older, unshaven man in baggy sweatpants and shoes flopping open at the toes, peered at her skeptically. The older one said something that made the one in turquoise shrug. Nina peered up at the cloudy gray sky as she waited for the two men to reach some sort of consensus. It was by no means clear that they had understood what she had said, and even more doubtful whether they recognized Peter's name. A child cried weakly in short bursts somewhere in the darkness. Nina fidgeted uneasily and gave the man a stern look.

"Please, if the child is sick . . ."

Again the older man said something to someone in the shop, a couple of voices replied, and after yet another uncertain glance at Nina, both the one in turquoise and the older man stepped aside and let her into the semidarkness.

At first she couldn't see much. The only source of light in the garage was a single fluorescent tube at the very back, which cast a weak bluish gleam over the room. The rest of the light fixtures hung empty under the rafters in the ceiling.

The older of the two men blurted out some kind of warning and pushed Nina a little to the side on the way in. She had been about to step into a splintered hole in the rotten plywood boards that covered the long inspection pit, which ran from the doors in front toward the rear wall. There were mattresses and sleeping bags on either side of the pit, and the heavy odor of cigarettes and too many people in too little space had mixed with the original smell of oil and rusty iron.

There were people everywhere. At least that was how it looked once Nina's eyes finally adjusted to the dim light. Some of them were curled up on mattresses and seemed to have gone to bed early. Others were sitting in small groups on the floor, talking and smoking. The ends of cigarettes glowed orangey-yellow among the men. And they were mostly men. Nina counted about twenty of various ages. There were a handful of women and, Nina guessed, a small number of children. It was hard to see exactly how many people were sleeping between all the sleeping bags, mattresses, and backpacks. Peter had said there were about fifty people living in the shop, the rest were probably still downtown begging, collecting bottles, selling flowers, or running shell games among the crowds on the pedestrian streets.

"Ápolónö."

The man walked over to a skinny young woman who

was sitting, holding a child in her arms, and pointed at Nina.

"*Ápolönö*," he repeated. The woman looked at her. The child in her arms whimpered, writhing in spite of her constant rocking motions. She looked tired, and when Nina got closer, she could smell vomit lingering in the air.

Nina cautiously eased the child away from the woman and laid him on one of the thin, shabby mattresses next to the inspection pit. She guessed the boy was about three. His face looked like a three-year-old's, but his body had been small and light as a feather in her arms. He had probably eaten too little and too poorly most of his life, she was guessing. The boy winced a little when she pulled his shirt up and slid her hand over the taut skin on his belly. He didn't have a fever, but his skin felt warm and dry, and when she gently pinched his skin between her thumb and forefinger, a soft little ridge remained on his arm for a second too long.

"How long?" Nina asked, looking questioningly at the mother. The woman was surely no older than twenty-five herself but was missing two of her top teeth. She nodded as a sign that she had understood the question and held up three fingers.

"And you?"

The young woman suddenly looked embarrassed. Then she nodded and made a gesture with her hands in front of her mouth. Vomiting, Nina interpreted.

"Throw up."

One of the young men, who had been following along nosily, now stepped in to contribute his meager English vocabulary. The woman had been sick, like her child, he explained, but it hadn't been quite as bad. It was the kids who were really sick. They fell ill a couple of days ago. Throwing up, having nosebleeds. The man pointed meaningfully at his nose and stomach.

"Yesterday . . ." The man began, his eyes lighting up as he put on a theatrical smile. "Yesterday everybody fine, happy, eating. Today everybody sick again."

He shrugged and pointed to the little boy on the mattress. "My son. Yes. Very sick again."

The boy on the mattress moaned slightly but continued to follow Nina with his wide, wary eyes.

Nina stood up and peered further into the room. Two heavy, yellow tarpaulins were hanging from the ceiling so they served as a makeshift curtain in the middle of the room, maybe in an attempt to make some sort of division between women and men, but right now the two tarpaulins were pulled to the side so that what little light there was could reach both sections.

She spotted a couple of doors at the back of the room and guessed one of them must be a lavatory and maybe even a shower room. They might well have had something like that in an auto repair shop. She started walking back along the edge of the inspection pit.

The men went quiet, and she could feel their hostile eyes peering at her from all sides, following her as she moved through the room. The young man who had let her in when she arrived slid up next to her, so close that his shoulder touched hers with each swaggering step he took.

"I need to wash my hands." Nina held her hands up to illustrate. Irritated, she maneuvered herself a little farther away from him and sped up. She didn't understand why they needed to get all macho on her right now, but it wasn't the first time she had been forced to put up with puffed up chests and threatening gestures before she was permitted to do her job. Sometimes there was a whole pantomime to get through, complete with jutting chins, bumping chests, heated discussions, and ultimately an ostentatious granting of permission to approach their child, sister, mother, or little brother. Nina had long since realized that it rarely had anything to do with her or what she did, it was more that to certain men she provided a welcome opportunity to demonstrate their glorious manliness and the accompanying ability to defend their family. However crude it might be.

All the same, she had started sweating a little.

No one, apart from that young mother, had seemed particularly pleased to see her, and she didn't like the way the men were starting to fill the space behind her. As if they were moving in on her. She didn't want to turn around to see if she was right.

She opened the door and stepped into a white-tiled lavatory. There was a toilet on the back wall that was missing its seat and lid. There was also a sink with a cracked mirror and a small shelf for the soap, and in the back corner there was a shower coated in lime scale, shower head barely attached to the wall. Otherwise the room was cold and bare. Nina cast a quick glance into the toilet bowl and noted that it was actually clean despite this being the only facility for the large number of people out there in the shop. Someone had employed soap and scrubbing brush with a will.

She washed her hands slowly, making a show of it for the young father, who had hung back in the doorway. Like a watchdog behind a fence, Nina thought, and felt it again. The anxiety. Something wasn't right. They were the ones who contacted Peter for help, but now it almost seemed like they couldn't wait to get rid of her. The child she had seen was very obviously sick, but so far everything still indicated it was a relatively benign stomach virus.

"Please," the young man said, now adding a smile and an urgent hand motion. "More children sick. Please look."

He remained there while Nina carefully edged past him through the doorway back into the garage. She hesitated. Where was Peter's sick young man? After all, he was the one the whole thing had started with. She tried to ask, still in slow, clear English.

"What about the young man? The one who was sick. Where is he?"

The young father smiled, revealing a row of teeth marred by little black flecks.

"Fine," he said. "He fine." He looked away, and his eyes lingered a second too long on a door to the right of the bathroom.

"Where is he?" she asked again. "In there?"

"No, he fine. Gone now."

He exposed his teeth again in a wide smile that finally convinced Nina that he was lying. They must have the room stuffed full of stolen flat-screen TVs, she thought, which would also explain the strange mix of aggressive macho attitudes and faint, shivery nervousness that filled the room. It was possible that the sick man was still in the garage somewhere, but they clearly weren't interested in letting her talk to him, and that was all there was to it. She would be allowed to see the children, and that was also the most important thing. They were the only reason she had come.

She nodded quickly.

"Where are they? Where are the children?"

NINA DROVE HOME at 8:52 P.M.

There was almost no traffic on Jagtvej, but the rain ran down the windshield in thin, gray rivulets and made everything inside the car fog up. The de-mister no longer worked in Nina's old Fiat, and she had to lean forward at regular intervals to wipe the inside of the windshield with her sleeve.

There was a certain sheepish feeling lurking in the back of her mind. Like an alcoholic on the wagon who had snuck a drink after work, she thought. It had almost been okay, what she had done. Visiting Peter wasn't strictly speaking part of her work with the Network. The fact that she had gone out to Valby afterward was harder to justify. And now she felt strangely cheated. The children she had examined had stopped vomiting. The biggest ones, who were around Anton's age, had been sleeping peacefully on the thin mattresses, and she hadn't even needed to wake them up to determine that they were getting better. Their color was good, they were breathing calmly and steadily, and there were no immediate signs of dehydration. The smallest ones, the three-year-old boy and two twin girls who were slightly older, had moaned a little when she pressed on their stomachs. She had instructed the mothers thoroughly on how to add sugar and salt to bottled water and make sure the children got plenty to drink, and she had left a few packets of antiemetics that could help a little with the nausea. All in all there was nothing to worry about, and maybe there never had been. She had gone there out of her usual irrational anxiety, knowing full well that Morten wouldn't be very understanding about her breaking her promise because of a couple of half-sick kids in Valby. Nina wasn't sure if the severity of their condition made any difference to Morten, but it mattered to her.

Nina pulled into Fejøgade and glanced up at the windows on the second floor. The living room lights were on, so Ida must have crawled out of her cave while Nina was out and was probably happily enjoying the brand-new flat screen and having the whole sofa to herself. Nina had sent her a text message that she would be home late from work. She hadn't given a reason, and Ida hadn't asked. Just sent a laconic "OK"—without a smiley, of course. Ida considered emoticons tween, and if she ever did use them it would never be in a text message to Nina.

Nina left the first aid kit on the back seat and slammed the car door. She had no desire to go inside. Damn it. How had they ended up like this?

She left the question unanswered in some corner of her mind as she carefully pushed open the door to the apartment. The TV or stereo was on in the living room. "Let me rot in peace," thundered the lead singer from Alive with Worms, an iconic Copenhagen Goth-rock group. Nina recognized both the singer and the Goth style from her own distant youth and felt

LENE KAABERBØL and AGNETE FRIIS

annoyance starting to boil in her. Why did teenagers have to be such damned clichés? Did parents really only get to choose between pop chicks who wore lip gloss that reeked of strawberry, watched Paradise Hotel on TV, and had a stack of glossy magazines on their desk, or self-pitying mini-Goths who painted the insides of their heads black, romanticized anarchy and evicted squatters, and dug around in small, obscure shops for tattered clothes and narrow-minded music that would put them in an even worse mood? The latter was perhaps marginally better than the former, but hardly original, and it was ridiculously difficult to take it seriously while it lasted.

"Hi."

She opened the door into the living room and stood there reeling slightly at the unexpected sight.

Ida was sitting on the sofa. Nina's guess had been right about that part of it. However, there was a young man sitting next to her, holding one of Ida's oversized teacups in his hands. He had just been saying something to Ida, but now they both turned around to face her. The guy smiled, hurriedly placed his cup on the table, and shyly ran a hand up over his clean-shaven scalp.

How old was he? Sixteen, maybe seventeen?

Nina looked over at Ida, who stared back with a mix of defiance and embarrassment. Then she obviously decided that offense was the best defense. Her posture became professional and self-assured.

"I thought you said 'late.'"

"Uh, yes," Nina mumbled, reminding herself how easy it was for mothers to stumble and turn into clichés right alongside their teenage daughters. "It's almost nine o'clock."

The boy on the sofa stood up and quickly wiped the palms of his hands on his trousers, which were hanging dangerously low on his hips.

"Hello," he said politely. "I'm Ulf."

Nina tamely extended her hand to him, weighing her options. When it came right down to it, she really had only one, she decided.

"Hi, Ulf," she said. "Nice to meet you."

THE BUS BROKE down a little north of Dresden, near a place called Schwartzheide. The driver managed to get the bus to limp along to the next motorway exit and partway down the ramp before the old Ford Transit conked out completely.

The driver tried without success to get everyone to stay inside. Within five minutes Sándor was the only one still obediently sitting in his seat. The rest were spread out like a motley human blanket across the grassy slope, peeing, talking, stretching, and arguing. Some of them started walking toward the highway rest stop cafeteria they could see a few hundred meters away. The arguments centered on the driver, who was by turns yelling futilely at the passengers, staring probingly at the engine, and trying to reach someone on his mobile phone.

Finally Sándor got up, too. His knee hurt after having been wedged in the same position for more than twenty-four hours. He felt greasy and unkempt, and every cell in his body was screaming for coffee. His phone also really needed a charge. The cafeteria was tempting, but he didn't have any Euros or his credit card. Or . . . did he? The driver's jacket was hanging on a hook behind the driver's seat.

He felt oddly delinquent, sticking his hand in another man's pocket, even though the only thing he was planning to steal was something that belonged to him. He glanced out the windscreen, but no one seemed to be paying any particular attention to him. His card was in the middle of a bunch of others in a plastic pouch—he obviously wasn't the only one whose finances the driver was "looking after."

Sándor stuffed the pouch with the other cards back in the pocket of the unattended jacket, pulled the charger out of his bag, and exited the minibus. Outside, the morning traffic was edging its way around the broken-down bus by driving partly on the shoulder, and the mist over the road was so heavy it almost felt like rain. The cafeteria sign, a big yellow coffee cup with wisps of white steam in artistically swooping neon, shone like a light-house through the fog.

Sándor got in line at the checkout and splurged on a cellophane-wrapped croissant along with his coveted cup of coffee, placing both on his plastic tray. He realized a little late that he didn't have any ID if the girl at the register didn't automatically accept his Hungarian Visa card, but luckily she did. Given that they were right off the E55, they probably saw a little of everything here, and even at German autobahn prices, the price of his break-fast was small change to them.

He spotted a free table with—hallelujah—an available socket, and gratefully slid onto the red vinyl seat. The coffee smelled amazing. The croissant tasted like cotton.

As he sat there imagining he could feel the caffeine rushing to his deprived cells and filling them up, a text message appeared on his resurrected phone with a beep. At first he couldn't tell who it was from, because the number was a different one from what Tamás had given him that evening on Szigony Street, and there was no sender name. *WHY AREN'T YOU COMING*, it said in desperate all caps. "Didn't you see my e-mail? Help me. I'm dying!"

The last part was in Romany—"*Te merav!*"—and that was what made him realize the message was from Tamás. He stared at the phone's miniature bluish-white screen. He had heard the phrase so often, in Galbeno and also in the Gypsy neighborhood in the Eighth District. *Te merav, te merav. It's so hot, I'm dying. I'm so tired, I'm dying. Give me a cup of coffee, I'm dying . . .* A hyperbolic expression his Hungarian stepmother would have found inappropriate, if she could've understood it, that is. But was this hyperbole, or did Tamás really mean it? There was a desperate quality to the rest of his message that made Sándor think this was more than merely an expression.

He tried calling the number, and it rang, but no one answered.

He hadn't checked his e-mail in almost a week now, since he no longer had a computer. The NBH had it. He was going to have to find an Internet café somewhere if he wanted to read the e-mail Tamás had apparently sent him.

Te merav. He hoped Tamás was just being melodramatic.

SKOU-LARSEN WAS STANDING in his garden, looking at those damned minarets. He couldn't believe they had been allowed to build them that tall, right next to a residential neighborhood. Someone in his old office had completely dropped the ball, he decided. The zoning laws called for low residential structures and scattered recreational areas. Not a word about prayer towers.

Maybe he could call and complain? After all, he still knew a few people at the planning office.

"Jørgen?" Helle called.

"Yes?" he replied.

"Coffee."

He obediently slunk back in through the sliding glass doors—the trim around them needed painting again, he noted—and took his place by the coffee table. There was marble cake, but it didn't look homemade. And Helle seemed a little absent-minded, pouring their coffee into their everyday mugs from the Arabia set.

"I talked to the lawyer," he said. "That young Ahlegaard. He says he knows a decent law firm in Marbella if we want to sue."

"Why would we?" she asked.

"To get the money back," he said patiently.

"But I'm happy about the apartment."

Skou-Larsen gave up. He couldn't make her understand that there was no apartment and there wasn't going to be one, at least not at the address specified in that fancy brochure she had. He poured cream into his coffee and took a sip. It tasted strange.

"What's in the coffee?"

"Nothing," she said.

"It doesn't taste the way it usually does."

"That's because it's decaf. And that's fat-free milk, not cream."

He felt oddly deceived.

"Decaf?"

"Yes, it doesn't cause as much stomach acid."

Lately he had been having a little bit of a burning sensation just behind his breastbone, and the doctor had said it was something called reflux. He thought that sounded like some kind of cleaning product. Reflux: cleans like a white tornado! But it turned out it was the acid in his stomach rising up and irritating his esophagus, and he had been instructed to cut back on coffee, tea, alcohol, chocolate, and orange juice. And what was that other thing? Peppermint. He never ate peppermint. Who the heck ate so much peppermint that it could be a problem? And in the bedroom they had put wooden blocks under the legs of the bed at the headboard to elevate it, so now he felt like he was constantly sliding down toward the foot of the bed.

"It doesn't taste like real coffee," he said, setting down his cup.

She stood up abruptly.

"Well then don't drink it," she snapped, disappearing into the kitchen.

He sat there for a bit, looking at the coffee table. At the meticulously arranged slices of marble cake and the bowl of currant cookies, the cream jug, which had now become a skim milk jug instead, the napkins, the cake plates. It had been wrong of him to complain about the coffee. She had only done it because she cared about his health.

So go out and apologize, he told himself. But he just couldn't make himself do it. It wasn't just Helle and the decaf. It was the damn minarets in the garden, the scam artist brochures on the nightstand, those darned wooden blocks that made him wake up with a sore back, and then of course the biggest injustice of them all, death.

Just when exactly had he stopped calling the shots in his own life?

Maybe he never had. Maybe free will had been an illusion the whole time, the biggest scam of them all.

He got up and went into the hallway.

"I'm going for a walk around the lake," he called, in the direction of the kitchen door. He waited for a while to see if there would be a response. There wasn't.

HE DIDN'T GO down to the lake after all. He wasn't in the mood for all those joggers. Instead he walked defiantly over to the construction site. They were pulling the tarpaulins off the domed roof now. The gate was ajar, and there was no one in the little trailer that served as a kind of guard hut by the entrance. It didn't make much of a difference, anyway. Skou-Larsen had noticed that holes had been cut in the wire fence in two different locations on the side facing Lundedalsvej. There was a sign that said NO TRESPASSING, but he didn't feel like he was trespassing. This building was very much his business. It was marring his view and upsetting his wife.

"Well, I'll be damned. It's Mr. Skou-Larsen, right?"

He turned around, feeling a little guilty in spite of the justifications he had just been reviewing in his mind. An alien in a cylindrical helmet and hazmat suit that covered his entire body stood before him.

"Ah, yes, excuse me," the alien said, flipping off his helmet. "It's not easy to recognize someone in this getup. We're just removing asbestos panels from the old ceilings."

Skou-Larsen contemplated the ruddy face and the thinning flaxen hair that came into view. Everything about the face was a little plump and round, like those cartoons of hysterically happy pigs that used to decorate the sides of butchers' vans in the old days. As if nothing could be funnier than being strung up by your hindquarters and having your throat slit.

"Ah, yes. Hello," he said tentatively. "It's been a long time."

"It certainly has. Are you still working in the planning office?"

"No. I've been retired for several years."

"How time flies! I switched over to the private sector myself. Have my own company now. We specialize in asbestos removal." The man gestured toward one of the cars haphazardly parked in the area in front of the future cultural center. Jansen Enterprises, it said, which finally jogged Skou-Larsen's memory. Preben Jansen, he worked in maintenance and engineering. Or at least he had back when Skou-Larsen used to occasionally run into him in the course of duty.

"Congratulations," Skou-Larsen said.

"Thanks. To what do we owe the honor?"

That was, of course, a polite way of saying, "What are you doing here?," but then Skou-Larsen valued politeness.

"Uh, I live nearby," he said, pointing toward Elme-højvej. "So I'm curious to see what all this is turning into. I mean, when you've worked with construction and building permits your whole life . . ." A thought suddenly hit him. What if they didn't have a permit to build this high, after all? It had happened before. People sometimes thought absolution was easier than permission. Or maybe they had broken other rules—fire safety or some such, anything at all that could be used to file a complaint . . . Maybe he could still find some grounds for objection that would stop the project, or at least delay it. "Do you think I could come in to see how it's coming along? People say it's going to be really stunning. A little multicultural gem." Was he laying it on too thick? No, Jansen just nodded.

"The architect is brilliant. He's done several mosques in Europe." His round, hurray-I'm-about-to-be-slaugh-tered pig face was still furrowed with hesitation, but then he appeared to make a decision. "Oh, sure, why not. It's about time for us to call it a day anyway. Just follow me, Mr. Skou-Larsen, and I'll see if we can't give you a little tour."

THE OLD FACTORY building formed the flat-roofed reception area, now significantly renovated with arched windows, gleaming pine woodwork, and ornamental tiles. The cloakroom and lavatories were being installed at one end of the reception hall; at the other end was quite a plain-looking meeting room with a small kitchenette.

Skou-Larsen inspected and made mental notes. They weren't done with the ceilings yet, and there were still drop cloths and plastic covering the tile floor.

"We're a little behind on the ceilings," Jansen said. "They didn't realize there was asbestos in the old panels until quite late—they hadn't been properly registered, I guess. And that's when we were called in."

"Did they do an expanded workplace health hazard evaluation?" Skou-Larsen asked automatically. As soon as asbestos was involved a special workplace evaluation was mandatory.

"Hey, I thought you were retired?" Jansen said with a smile, which Skou-Larsen hurriedly returned.

"Old habits," he said. "Sorry. Of course it's none of my business." But now the asbestos rules were swirling around in his head; there were so many potential oversights and minor legal violations. If a seventeen-year-old apprentice so much as walked through the site, for example . . .

"I understand. But you can sleep soundly. The site manager knows his stuff, and . . . well, I'm not exactly an amateur, either."

"No, of course not . . ."

They walked down a long, dark passage, where the windows were still covered by black plastic sheeting, and into the dome itself.

Skou-Larsen loved buildings. Even though his job had mostly consisted of making sure they obeyed local plans and regulations, he had a love of bricks and mortar, too, of space and architecture and craftsmanship. Maybe that was why it hit him so hard.

He stood still. And remained still. For a small eternity.

The dome was the heavens. It soared above him as if stone and copper weighed nothing at all, and the mosaics on the walls glowed with the bright colors of creation itself. He tried to make himself think about emergency exits and soil pipes and ordinances, but it was no use. The light enveloped him, and his aging heart swelled in his chest so that in that moment awareness of his impending death left him.

Oh, he sighed. They have built a cathedral.

"Mr. Skou-Larsen? Is something wrong?"

He shook his head. "It's just . . ."

"Yes, it's nice, isn't it? Makes you envy those Muslims, huh?" Jansen grinned knowingly, with an admiration that Skou-Larsen assumed he otherwise reserved for expensive cars or the highlights of the soccer games he watched on TV. There was no sign *he* was having his foundation rocked.

"What are you doing here?"

The man's voice was angry and tense, in a stressed-out way that might also be covering a certain amount of fear.

When Skou-Larsen turned around, he spotted a well-dressed older gentleman—well, twenty years younger than you are, he corrected himself—clutching a length of copper piping in one hand and a mobile phone in the other.

"Everything's under control, Mr. Hosseini," Jansen said quickly. "My firm is responsible for the ceilings in the entrance hall. Preben Jansen. We've met."

"And him?" The suspicion had not completely left the man, but his grip on the pipe relaxed somewhat.

"This is Mr. Skou-Larsen, from the city," Jansen said, conveniently forgetting to mention that Skou-Larsen's tenure in that role had ceased a number of years ago. "We're just taking a look around."

The man set down the copper pipe and held out his hand.

"Forgive me," he said, formally. "But the site is closed now, and we've had our fair share of vandalism and the like . . . It puts one on one's guard."

"Of course," Skou-Larsen said, clasping the outstretched hand.

"Mahmoud Hosseini. I'm the chairman of the organizing committee."

"Jørgen Skou-Larsen," said Skou-Larsen, and then added, because it had to be said: "You are building a beautiful place, Mr. Hosseini."

Back home the coffee still sat untouched and a sugar-drunk housefly was crawling around on the marble cake. Helle wasn't home. He didn't know if he should take that as a good sign. It was hard for her to go out alone, even in the middle of the day when her anxiety was at its lowest ebb. On the other hand, it probably meant she was still mad at him about that business with the coffee. He started clearing the table, and while he was rinsing the Arabia cups before loading them into the dishwasher—she always insisted on that, as if they needed to avoid sullying the inside of the dishwasher—she came slowly up the garden path with her old Raleigh bicycle. He could just make out a grocery bag in the bike's basket.

"Where have you been?" he asked when she walked in the front door.

"Out buying slug bait," she said grumpily, setting a five-kilo package of Ferramol on the kitchen counter. "You keep promising, but you never actually manage to get anything done, do you?"

"**H**ORVÁTH IS ON the move."

Károly Gábor spoke excellent, but slow, English, and that gave Søren's brain time to leave its vegetative state and come up to speed. Horváth. That was the name of the Hungarian student, the one the NBH had hauled in for questioning. He fished around in his bag, flipping through the case folders he had brought home, and found his Hungary notes. Yep. Sándor Horváth.

"Where is he?" he asked.

"Germany. His phone was activated near Dresden yesterday and again this morning in the Potsdam area."

Søren knew that the NBH had let the young man keep his phone so they could keep track of his whereabouts if he should happen to use it again. Which he obviously had. Not exactly a hardened, professional operative, this Horváth.

Dresden and then Potsdam.

"You think he's on his way to Denmark?"

"Could be."

Søren looked at the sickly house plant in the pot on his kitchen windowsill without actually seeing it. Gábor had caught him right in the middle of his muesli, with a shoe on one foot and just a sock on the other. After having worked eleven days straight, he had treated himself to a calm, quiet morning and hadn't actually been planning on going in until around noon. That might have to change now.

He thanked Gábor for the message and called Mikael

Nielsen, who was keeping tabs on the surveillance of Khalid Hosseini.

"Where is he now?" Søren asked.

It took just a second too long before Mikael answered.

"Um. He's actually sitting in Bellahøj police station."

"He's *what*? What's he doing there?"

"He was arrested an hour ago. For assaulting and threatening an officer on duty."

"What happened?"

"Apparently he got into an argument with one of our surveillance people. I was just about to call you. Bellahøj wants to know what they should do with him."

KHALID HOSSEINI SAT low in the chair, with his jeans-clad legs stretched out in front of him and his hands buried in the pockets of a black bomber jacket. When he saw Søren, he leapt up like a spring being released.

"I knew it was your lot," he hissed. "This is fucking harassment, that's what it is. I bet it's not even legal!"

"As far as I've gathered," Søren said, "you attacked a police officer, who is now receiving treatment at the ER."

"No!" The denial came instantly and with the force of conviction. "It's a fucking lie, man. I didn't even touch that guy. You should be asking him why he ran over my little brother in his fucking car!"

What? There hadn't been anything about a traffic incident in the reports Søren had received from Bellahøj's uniformed officers. According to them, they had gone to Mjølnerparken in response to a distress call from the officer tailing Hosseini and had found the officer holed up in his patrol car, bleeding from a laceration over one

ear and surrounded by a crowd of enraged residents
who were rocking the car, hitting its roof, and screaming insults in a mixture of Danish, Arabic, and Urdu. The
shocked police officer had been taken to the emergency
room at Bispebjerg Hospital for treatment for the cut and
a possible concussion. There had been no mention of a
younger brother.

Søren put a neutral look on his face and hoped his surprise wasn't visible.

"What I would really like to hear now . . ." he said, sitting down on one of the desk chairs, ". . . is *your* side of the
story. What happened out there?"

His neutrality actually had a soothing effect. Khalid
flopped back down in the chair again and stared at him
with obvious, but controlled, aggression.

"Like you give a crap," he said. "This is a set-up. Don't
you think I've figured that out? Now you've finally got the
towelhead where you want him, right? Well, what the hell
do I care? Go ahead—lock me up. No fucking cop has a
right to run over my little brother!"

Søren said nothing. He just waited. He avoided Khalid's
aggressive stare, studying the domestic clutter on the
borrowed desk instead, the stack of folders and loose
papers, a mouse pad with the AGF soccer team's logo and
the slogan, "Stay loyal!"—the desk's usual occupant must
be from Aarhus—and a picture of a remarkably beautiful,
blonde girl fondly embracing a golden retriever.

"I didn't touch him," Khalid finally said in a different
voice. Higher, more childlike. Plaintive. "Or, well, okay,
I pushed him, but what would you have done? Kasim
was sitting on the pavement sobbing. He was just trying

to give me my phone, for fuck's sake. He ran after me because I forgot it, and then that fucking idiot ran him down."

He was starting to get angry again in order to keep up his courage. Because underneath the aggression and attitude, Khalid was scared now, Søren guessed. He was nineteen years old, and this was the first time he had been arrested.

"Then what happened?" Søren asked, still completely neutral.

"Then the police came and dragged me in here."

Something was obviously missing from that chain of events, Søren thought. But right now he sorely needed to hear what the wounded officer had to say. Khalid wasn't going anywhere.

"I DIDN'T HIT the kid!" the police officer insisted. He was twenty-six years old, new to the surveillance unit, and his name was Markus Eberhart. He had a shaved spot on one side of his head that made his otherwise stylish haircut look sadly asymmetrical. They had managed to fix up the scalp wound with just skin glue and butterfly bandages, and according to Bispebjerg Hospital, his pupils were normally responsive and he had displayed the ability to orient himself with regard to time, place, and personal particulars. In other words, things weren't so bad.

"What happened?" Søren asked with more or less the same neutrality he had used with Khalid.

"The boy ran out the front door without looking right or left. I slammed on the brakes. But I didn't hit him!"

"And then what happened?"

"Then the kid plunked down on his rear end on the asphalt and started bawling his eyes out. I think he was pretty shocked."

"And then?"

"Then the suspect and his cousin jumped out of their car and came running. I got out to try to comfort the child, but they pushed me up against the hood and were acting menacing, and then all the neighbors came running, and . . . then I was struck by an object."

The officer was struggling to report this using professional terminology, but Søren noted the switch to passive voice—it started out *I* got out, *they* came running, *they* pushed, but then "I was struck."

"Do you know who struck you?" Søren asked.

The officer hesitated. Then he said, "No. I can't say with certainty. At first I thought it was the suspect, but . . . I think actually someone threw something. And Khalid was standing right next to me."

"And then?"

"Then . . . I managed to get into the car and secure the doors. And call for backup."

Søren could just picture it. The crying child, the irate men, the neighbors and family members crowding round. And in the middle of the whole god-awful mess, a young police officer ready to shit his pants and not without reason.

"How close were you to the front door?" Søren asked.

"I was parked almost right in front of it. Ten or twelve meters away max. I had just started the car to follow the suspect when the accident happened. Or . . . nearly happened. I slammed on the brakes right away, and there's no way I was going more than ten kilometers per hour."

"Why were you parked so close?"

"We had been told . . ." The officer hesitated again; it seemed like he felt he was being tested in some way and was afraid he would give the wrong answer. "Well, it was a close-tail surveillance assignment, right? They said it didn't matter much if we were seen. That it was more important that we didn't lose him."

"How long have you been working in surveillance?"

"A little over a month."

Søren painstakingly avoided sighing. The assignment had been to put pressure on Khalid with surveillance that was fairly obvious at times. That was probably why the surveillance unit had decided to use it as a sort of training exercise for newbies. And that was why an insecure, young policeman had ended up in a situation that could have been dangerous to all involved. He could have hit the child. And he could have been seriously hurt himself.

"But the child wasn't injured?"

"No. He was just crying because he was scared."

"And Khalid Hosseini didn't hit you?"

"No. It . . . I can't say that he did."

"Good. Then I think we should let this whole incident die as quiet a death as possible. Agreed?"

Markus Eberhart nodded. The gesture made him wince, and he carefully touched his head.

SØREN CALLED BELLAHØJ from the parking lot in front of the emergency room entrance.

"Release him," he told the desk officer, repeating Eberhart's explanation. "We don't have any actual grounds to hold him on."

"The father and the uncle are here already" was the response. "Looking appropriately aghast and appalled. They say he's a good boy, and that we're hounding him for no reason."

"Yes, I'm sure they do." But somewhere or other north of Potsdam, Sándor Horváth was on his way to Denmark. And Søren was eager to find out what was going to happen when he met with Khalid Hosseini.

So when Khalid left Bellahøj police station a half hour later with his father and uncle, there were not any surveillance newbies tagging along. But that didn't mean he was unobserved.

NINA PULLED INTO the parking lot in front of the Valby garage at 1:37 P.M. Peter's emergency call had come in the middle of the clinic's drop-in hours. Snotty noses and infant vaccinations. Peter was his usual grouchy self as he outlined the situation. The young man had apparently disappeared, but the children were sick again. All of them. He needed a "professional on site," as he put it, and Magnus had just thrown up his hands in exasperated acceptance when Nina asked for permission to pop out for a couple of hours.

This time it actually seemed she was welcome. The door opened before she had a chance to knock. They had been waiting for her, she could tell. The young mother with the missing front teeth was perched just inside the doorway and eagerly grabbed hold of her arm as soon as Nina crossed the threshold. The other women and a small group of men were behind her, and they followed Nina and the young mother with their eyes. Nina thought she could sense a new tension that didn't have to do with her presence. Illnesses that didn't go away on their own were poor people's worst nightmare.

"Ápolónö. Jöljön be, jöljön be!"

Nina didn't understand the words, but their meaning was clear enough. The woman pulled her into the garage so quickly that she almost tripped on the mattresses, stuffed plastic bags, and duffle bags.

The boy was lying totally motionless on a filthy foam mattress pushed up against the wall, and when she cautiously squatted down next to him, his whole body jerked. A stream of yellowish vomit welled out from under his head; he opened his eyes, looking vaguely about, and then disappeared back into a fog. The young woman emitted something between a sob and a sigh and ran to get a new cloth. She must have had to do that quite a few times, and Nina could see the fatigue and worry in her eyes when she came back and started wiping sweat and vomit off the boy's face. She gave up on doing anything about the mattress, just pushed a clean towel in under his head.

"*A fiam rosszul. A fiam rosszul van.*"

She looked up at Nina with a question in her eyes, and Nina cautiously began her examination. The boy was considerably worse than a couple of days ago. He still didn't have a fever, but he was exhausted from all the vomiting, and though Nina managed to get him to sit up for a couple of minutes, he kept falling asleep leaning against his mother's shoulder. His belly wasn't distended; his biggest problem was probably dehydration. His skin was bone dry, and he was either going to need IV fluids here—or, better still, a hospital.

Nina pulled out her phone, found Allan's number in her address book and wedged the phone between her shoulder and cheek as she scanned the garage. The boy's English-speaking father had taken refuge in the group of men over by the door, away from his son's illness and his wife's worried looks. Now she waved him over, Allan's ring tone still chiming away in her ear.

"The other children," she said, pointing around the garage. "Where are they?"

He pulled her further back toward the rear of the garage, where to her relief she saw the other children sitting with sleeping bags wrapped around their shoulders. Weak and pale, but clearly healthier than the boy on the mattress.

Allan finally answered his phone. "Hi, Nina."

He sounded like he was in a relatively good mood, which was a plus. She hadn't spoken with him since the previous August. Allan was a doctor with a practice north of Copenhagen, in fashionable Vedbær. He had also been moonlighting as part of Peter's standing team when their "clients" had problems that required prescription medication or an emergency house call. But that was over now. He was no longer part of the Network, and the last time she had seen him he hadn't been mincing his words when he told her to shove off and never come back.

"I need your opinion," Nina said, trying for Peter's crisply managerial tone of voice. "I'm standing in an old auto repair shop in Valby with a lot of very sick children. One of them in particular is dehydrated, and I can't really figure out how bad it is. I think it's a stomach virus of some kind, but they've been sick for several days now and apparently it's mostly the children who are getting sick."

Allan sighed.

"Tell me more. Vomiting, diarrhea, fever, blood?"

Nina summed up the situation and waited patiently while Allan chewed on a pen on the other end of the line.

"Hmm. It's a little odd that they're having multiple bouts of it," he said. "Maybe it's some kind of poisoning. Industrial waste, heavy metals, or gasoline fumes could cause those kinds of symptoms if they were exposed to them for long enough. Might also explain the pattern of recurrences. Did you ask where the kids have been playing?"

"Thanks," she said quickly. "What else?"

"Virus, bacteria, it could be anything. Make sure you wash your hands really well and get yourself some gloves and a face mask. You know the drill. Obviously the boy's going to need fluids, and then I think it would be good for all involved if the group left the repair shop if there's any way to make that happen. And be careful yourself."

Click.

He was gone before she had a chance to say a proper goodbye. Allan really didn't want to know, and he also wanted to avoid any request for impromptu house calls. And he was right. She might have asked if he hadn't wrapped up the conversation so quickly.

Poisoning. Nina didn't have much experience with that kind of thing, but this was an old auto mechanic's garage, and there could still be gasoline or other organic solvents stored on the premises. The children might have drunk or inhaled some toxic substance by accident.

She looked at the child's father who was standing next to her expectantly. His forehead was wet with sweat.

"What did the children do yesterday? Where were they?"

"Big children work. My son here. To rest. Get stronger."

Nina started her exploration in the room that had probably been the foreman's office. The walls were bare with holes in them and faded areas in the paint where there used to be shelves. There were mattresses and sleeping bags here, too, maybe a couple had managed to win themselves a little privacy. Apart from that there was nothing. The same was true for the actual garage, if she ignored a pile of worn-out tires in one corner and a couple of rusty cans of paint and a container of motor oil sitting on a rickety shelf down by the far end. Nina tried to unscrew the lid off the motor oil, but it only budged reluctantly and greasy dirt and cobwebs fluttered down to the floor in clumps and flakes. It hadn't been opened recently, and the spray cans of paint were also a non-starter since the valves were so rusty that they couldn't be pushed down. Nina continued toward the door next to the foreman's office and the little kitchenette. It was still closed, but this time no one tried to prevent her from going in. She stepped into the small, dark room and turned on the fluorescent ceiling light. The window was wide open, and a couple of tattered, red curtains fluttered in the faint breeze. A bed frame with no mattress and a scratched, old laminate table were the only furniture in the room. The linoleum floor was worn to a thread, but clean, and there was the faint odor of dishwashing soap and chlorine. There was nothing to see.

Nina returned to the boy and his mother. She wanted them out of here. She didn't need to be an expert on poisoning to know that Allan was right—it was potentially hazardous for them to stay in this place.

"Chemicals," she said. "Poison. Dangerous for children." She looked at the boy's father and waved her hand at the interior of the garage. "You must go somewhere else."

The man shook his head.

"No poison. We stay."

He wasn't a tall man, Nina noticed. One of his shoulders drooped a little, and like his wife, he revealed a number of cavities in his teeth when he spoke. But there was a massive dignity in his refusal. Presumably he was well aware that the garage wasn't the healthiest place in the world for a child. He may even already have had an inkling that it might be a contributing factor, but he had to reject her suggestion out of hand simply because he had nowhere else to go. Not without risking exposure and losing everything he had gambled when he decided to bring his family to Denmark this summer—the money for the trip, the rent they had already paid for this sorry place, and god knows what other expenses he might owe to people who did not deal kindly with debtors. He had to hope the illness would pass on its own—he had no other option.

She took a deep breath and studied the boy. She would have to treat him as best she could for now and hope he improved over the next few hours. If not, she really would have to call an ambulance, no matter how much the parents protested. But she wouldn't fight that particular battle until it was absolutely necessary.

She pulled a saline drip out of her bag and kneeled down next to the sick boy. The light wasn't good, but thankfully his mother helped by lifting the boy up and rotating him so she had better access. Nina found the vein in the soft crook of his elbow with her fingertips and hit it on her first try.

A car door slammed in the parking lot outside.

The boy's mother cowered, casting a furtive, pleading glance at her husband, who was on his way over to them in long strides. Without a word he swept the boy up into his arms and carried the boy and the drip bag away in rapid, sturdy steps. The boy's mother followed, and before Nina had a chance to react, someone shoved her adamantly in the back. The man standing behind her pointed meaningfully to the middle of the garage, where a couple of the other men had quickly and silently pulled one of the worn plywood boards to the side. The father helped his wife and child down into the inspection pit while one of the others ran over to the door and disappeared out into the parking lot. Nina could hear him talking to someone outside. She could only discern the occasional English word and had no idea what the conversation was about. The man next to her pointed into the inspection pit again and tugged at her arm impatiently. Nina pulled herself free in an irritated motion. She got it. For some reason or other, she and the children were supposed to hide, presumably just the way Peter had needed to. The voices outside had moved closer now, and Nina walked over to the edge and hopped down to the bottom of the inspection pit on her own.

She stepped on something soft that moved, looked down and discovered the sick boy's mother, who was already sitting on the sunken floor with the boy in her arms. She cradled the hand Nina had stepped on for a brief moment, then moved deeper into the pit to make room for Nina. The rest of the children from the garage followed in quick succession, and Nina tried automatically to receive the small bodies as they were lifted down to her one by one.

The board was pushed back into place with a heavy,

grating sound. The darkness was absolute. Nina could hear the children breathing softly and quickly, but no one said anything. They just sat and listened to the sound of heavy footsteps and voices from the world up above.

Nina tried to calm her breathing. The whole thing had happened so quickly that she hadn't had a chance to feel scared, but now she could feel her heart pounding fiercely. The pit she was sitting in was easily a meter and a half deep and only just wide enough that she could sit with her legs bent and her back up against the wall. The darkness around her felt dense and suffocating, and the smell of old motor oil tore at her nostrils. A small, warm body touched hers, and she pulled away, startled. But even here in the pulsing darkness, the children were still completely quiet. She got the distinct impression that they had done this before.

The boy with the drip. She had to make sure the mother understood that the infusion bag needed to be held high so the flow wouldn't be reversed. Nina crawled noiselessly on all fours past the sitting children toward the rear of the pit. It was slow going because apparently the ever-changing inhabitants of the garage had been using the inspection pit for trash disposal for a long time, and the floor was covered in rubble, paper bags, and old plastic bottles. The darkness was dense around her, but now she could make out gray cracks of light between the plywood boards overhead, and about halfway to the back, she finally found the boy's mother, sitting in complete silence with the child in her arms.

He was asleep. His soft breaths faltered a little each time as he breathed in, and he didn't respond when she felt her way to the drip in his right arm. The IV tube was positioned correctly despite their rough and rapid retreat into the inspection pit, and Nina felt her way to the bag of saline which was in the woman's lap—way too low. Nina crawled around to the other side and perched the bag on the woman's shoulder so it was at least a little higher than the boy.

It seemed as if the mother understood what Nina was trying to do. She lifted the bag in her outstretched arm and held it there, though it must be uncomfortable for her. Everything was still being done without a sound. Above them the boards groaned whenever someone walked over them, and Nina could hear voices. There was some kind of argument, but the sound was muffled and subdued, and she couldn't understand what was being said.

"*Ápolónö.*"

Nina turned in the darkness toward the whispering voice. She had heard the man who had let her into the garage call her the same thing. *Ápolónö*, nurse. The woman's voice was so soft and trembling that it almost disappeared in the darkness.

"*Rosszul.* Sick. Why?"

The woman flitted like a black shadow just a couple of hand-widths away. She moved nearer.

"I don't know," Nina admitted.

She tried to sound calm and soothing. She wanted the woman to shut up. She didn't know what would happen if they were discovered, but something told her it wouldn't be good.

"*Ápolónö!*"

The woman whispered again and was now so close that Nina could feel the warmth of her breath on her cheek. A thin, boney hand grabbed her arm.

"Please, *ápolónö*. He die. Please. He die."

An image from one of the Coal-House Camp's claustrophobically small family rooms popped into Nina's mind. Paracetamol to treat mortal fear, she thought. Paracetamol and a saline drip.

"He'll be fine. Nothing serious."

Nina tried to sound calm and cheerful and put a reassuring hand on the boy's stomach. There was a multitude of reasons to fear death in the half-lit world of poverty in which these Roma lived. It was human and totally understandable. Still, Nina could feel the woman's terror, the darkness, and the cramped space starting to close in around her. The woman's gaunt hand rested heavily on hers and held on tight. Squeezing her fingers too hard and for too long.

Nina twisted free and pulled away, away from the warm crush of human bodies. She crawled father back into the inspection pit, over heaps of trash, a broken bottle, nuts and bolts, old newspapers, and finally found a small patch of unused floor space all the way down by the wall at the far end. Beneath her sand grated against the concrete floor, and although the fine, small grains dug into the palms of her hands, it was better here.

It had grown quiet up in the garage above them. A door slammed somewhere far away, and after a few minutes, the plywood boards were pulled aside. The light from the lone fluorescent tube fell down into the inspection pit and one by one the children were pulled up. The woman with the sick boy cast a quick glance into the darkness for Nina before she passed the boy up to his father and was herself helped up and out shortly thereafter. The men waved Nina toward the opening.

"Come, *ápolónö*. Boss men gone. Is all OK now."

NINA STAYED AT the garage for a few hours.

The boy improved on the saline solution and was awake long enough to eat a couple of crackers and drink half a bottle of juice. He was still pale as a corpse, and the bigger children were complaining of headaches. But all things considered Nina thought the situation was under relative control. She had even managed to clean the trash out of the inspection pit, although she had had to do most of the work herself; she had more luck getting the garage's residents to help clean up the grounds, which she also insisted on. Maybe they didn't want her hanging around outside too much; they obviously thought it were best if no one found out she was here.

"Don't let the children play where the garbage is," she said, miming and pointing. "Don't let them put things in their mouths." She wrote her mobile number on a piece of paper for the boy's mother. "Call me if he is still sick tomorrow, okay? I have to go now."

She tried to get the woman to look her in the eye, but whatever connection there might have been between the two of them earlier was gone. The boy's parents had had a big argument about something, and ever since, the mother had just sat there with the child in her lap, whispering into his soft, dark hair, a low-pitched stream of words that seemed more complaint than comfort.

Nina stood there holding out the slip of paper for several seconds. She felt her old irritation welling up again. Why was it so hard to help these people? They were treating her as a stranger once more, someone to be eyed with mistrust. But just as she was starting to think she would have to leave the note on the ground, the woman took it after all, in a quick, snatching motion, and stuffed it in the pocket of her fleece jacket.

THERE WAS A kind of Internet café on the ferry to Denmark. Or a computer, at any rate. It had been crammed into a minute glass enclosure that served as a business lounge, and Sándor sat down with the sense of being in forbidden territory. Lord knows there wasn't much about him right now that was business class. It had taken them two days to hobble their way north through Germany—with a radiator that was being kept artificially alive by Wondarweld cylinder block sealant and frequently adding water—and that had been more than his scant travel wardrobe had been prepared for. He was wearing a pair of recycled underpants that he had been forced to wash in a gas station restroom outside of Teupitz. Under his shirt he was itching incessantly, possibly because of the hair that was growing back after the shaving binge caused by his exam nerves. At any rate, he hoped that was all it was.

He was so tired that at first he couldn't remember the password for his webmail. Eventually he turned off his mind, hoping his fingers would remember better than his brain cells.

There was a long e-mail from Lujza. Even though he didn't know how much time he would have before he got kicked out or the ferry docked, he couldn't help but read it. *Dearest Sándor, I don't know what's going on in your life, and you won't tell me,* it began. And then it continued with an in-depth description of her feelings, her confusion and

powerlessness, her anger at being shut out. And worst
of all: the feeling of betrayal she was left with because
you haven't let me get to know you. The conclusion was, of
course, unavoidable. Lujza wasn't the let's-just-be-friends
type, nor was she the kind who dabbled in restrained
platitudes like "It's not you, it's me." *I don't think I have
the strength to love someone who hasn't got the courage to be
himself,* she wrote. *And I can't be with you without loving
you. I would have rather said this to your face, but you didn't
give me that chance.* And then just: *Goodbye.* No affection-
ate greeting, no hopes for the future, no cracks in the
wall of her rejection.

His whole body was trembling. He didn't know why it
came as such a shock, since he knew very well that he had
done it to himself, that he was the one who had severed
his ties to her and not the other way around. Suddenly
he missed her scent, her hands, the heat of her body,
missed her so much he felt hollow inside. Even missed
the frightening feeling of being carried along when she
latched onto some preposterous cause, sinking her teeth
into it and shaking it half to death. But how could he go
back? Even if he found Tamás now, got the money one
way or another, if he made it back to Budapest again . . .
he still wouldn't be going back to the same life.

He scrolled down through the list of messages in his
inbox until he got to one from tamas49 at a Hotmail
address. The e-mail was longer than the text messages
and just as desperate.

Phrala, *I don't know if you will help me. Maybe, maybe not.
But you will help Mom and the girls, won't you? It's for them,
all of this. I would do it myself if I could, but I'm sicker than*

a dog. I can't stand. Having trouble seeing. Don't respond,
just come. I'll try to hide my phone once I'm done writing this
message, but if they find it and you have responded, then they
might see what you write. I don't trust them. I only trust you.
Write this down and delete the message. You'll find out the
rest when you get here.

There was an address and some columns of numbers.
One column was dates, he was pretty sure, but he didn't
know what to make of the second. Phone numbers,
maybe? They looked a little short, only eight digits. But
they must be phone numbers after all because Tamás had
added underneath: *Only texts, no calls. Hurry.*

Someone had courteously provided a little notepad
and a pen with the ferry company's logo next to the
computer. Sándor wrote down both the address and
the series of numbers. He checked to make sure he
had it right and then obediently deleted the e-mail. *I*
can't stand. Having trouble seeing. Tamás, what the hell
is wrong with you? And who are "they"? Who don't
you trust?

He sat for a while staring at the pale gray computer
screen. He had to find Tamás *now*, as quickly as possible.

"The ferry will be docking in a few moments. We
kindly ask passengers to return to the car deck . . ."

Sándor stuck the slip of paper in his jacket pocket and
stood up.

DOWNSTAIRS IN THE car deck, the driver was standing with one foot on the bottom step of the bus, forcing
Sándor to edge past him to get back on again. While he
still had one foot on the briny and slippery oil-spattered

deck, the man suddenly shifted forward, trapping Sándor against the door.

"Your card," he said.

It took Sándor a second to understand what he meant. It felt like several weeks since he had stood on the highway ramp outside Schwartzheide and stolen his own Visa card from another man's pocket. But now apparently the driver had discovered his "theft."

"But it's my card."

"Did you go to the duty free shop on the ferry?"

"No . . ." Sándor said, confused.

The driver stuck his hands into Sándor's pockets, both his jacket and his trousers, frisking him like a nosy customs agent.

"What are you doing?" Sándor protested.

"What do you think? If even one of us smuggles so much as a carton of cigarettes, they'll detain the whole bus. And believe me, they're going to check us. Thoroughly, if you catch my drift. People like us, we always get checked."

It hadn't occurred to Sándor that the reason the driver had confiscated their credit cards was that he had to maintain this kind of discipline. Sándor stood passively as the man patted him down, running his hands inside his waistband and then sliding them down his thighs. He just hoped they were far enough inside the bus that this humiliation wasn't providing a moment of entertainment for all the other ferry passengers. Finally the driver loaded everything he had found—a handkerchief, wallet, comb, the slip of paper with Tamás's numbers on it, the Morgan Kane book he was currently rereading—back into Sándor's arms.

"OK," he said. "But when it's time to go back, I'm going to need your card again. Are you coming?"

Sándor nodded, stuffing his possessions back into his various pockets. Just at that moment, the bow doors began to slide open, and the driver hurried to take his seat and get his ailing bus started.

"When will we be in Copenhagen?" Sándor asked.

"In an hour and a half, if I can get this rust bucket going. If not it might be faster to walk."

"Is Valby close to Copenhagen?" That was the name of the town in the address Tamás had given him.

"It's *in* Copenhagen, dimwit. That's where we're going. Go get in your seat, and shut the fuck up."

THWACK!

Nina aimed a quick, precise blow at the vicious little gnat that had been hounding her for the past thirty seconds. First it had gone for the back of her neck, then it had changed tactics and tried her lips, eyes, and ears. Now it was smeared across her bare shoulder, a small disgusting streak of blood. She brushed the worst of it away and looked around at the crowd of happy people with the growing sense that she had landed on some alien planet. Class 2A's first big overnight field trip. When Nina was a kid, that kind of thing was between the kids and the school. These days the parents were supposed to come along to "get to know each other." And that was just one horror on a long list of social activities requiring creative costumes, fake smiles, and liters of mediocre coffee. Thank god the school year was drawing to an end; she was completely and utterly fed-up. But here they were, in one final binge of get-togetherness, in an old Boy Scout cabin near Solrød Beach, and everything was exactly the way she had pictured it. It was dark and dank and smelled of damp wood and sweaty feet. The kitchen was a grease pit, and a quick glance at the sleeping facilities revealed that, just as she had feared, everyone was supposed to sleep in one common bunkroom, which meant getting a whole lot better acquainted with the other parents than she was prepared to. The fact that she had had a pounding headache ever since she returned from Valby the previous evening did nothing to improve her mood. She had taken a cocktail of aspirin with codeine and Paracetamol that usually worked for most kinds of pain, but without much success so far. The low evening sun pierced her eyes, and invisible knives stabbed into her temples every time she turned her head toward the light.

But Anton was loving it.

He was standing over by the campfire with Benjamin poking the embers with a long stick. They had finished their twist bread long since, and Benjamin's mother had chased them away from the flames several times. Nina had given up without even trying. Boys had been playing with campfires since before recorded history, and it was presumably part of their DNA. They poked at the coals, pushing twigs into the flickering, orangey yellow flames, sending little clouds of sparks and ash up into the blue sky at regular intervals.

Nina knew she ought to be doing something. Clearing the table, making coffee, or at least chatting with the other parents. But right now she didn't have the strength for anything other than nursing her headache and holding it together. She missed Morten. He would have been so much in his element. Right now, he would have been laughing and talking with the other dads, and no doubt he would also have had the energy to bake a proper cake for the group instead of the hastily purchased store-bought version she had brought along. He would have loaded the car full of balls and bats and got a pickup game going on the lawn in front of the cabin. Morten was good at this kind of thing, and when he was along, he provided a peaceful refuge from all the socializing whenever she got tired of smiling.

Behind the cabin there were newly grown, knee-high stinging nettles under the beech trees. She walked a few steps farther away from the cabin, carefully bending the nettles to the side with her feet, and sat down on a large boulder with her phone in her hand.

An international number had called. Twice. Nina guessed it was the little boy's mother out in Valby even though there was nothing on her voicemail aside from white noise and a faint murmur.

She sat with her phone in her hand and listened to the raucous drone of the kids and grownups on the other side of the building. A woman laughed shrilly, and Nina again noticed her headache, which came rolling in like a heavy wave from somewhere in the very back of her skull, moving forward toward her eyes.

She had promised to return to the garage if they needed her. The forest floor swayed very slightly as she stood up and started walking back toward Anton. Hopefully he would insist on staying.

The boys were still standing by the fire with their sticks, and Nina decided to exploit her casual acquaintance with Benjamin's mother, a short, sympathetic looking woman who looked to be no older than thirty.

"Excuse me." Nina attempted to smile weakly, but bravely. "I think unfortunately we're going to have to head back home. I'm coming down with the worst headache."

Benjamin's mother stepped out of the little cluster of parents she had been standing in and looked at Nina with compassion.

"Oh, that's too bad," she said. "The boys are having

such a good time. Don't you think Anton would like to stay? I'd be happy to watch him."

Nina smiled gratefully and glanced quickly over at Anton.

"Oh, would you? That's so sweet of you," she said. "I'll just go ask him."

"Yes, by all means." The woman gave Nina a serious look. "But are you sure you can drive? You don't look well."

When Nina climbed in behind the wheel of her Fiat seven minutes later and glanced in the rearview mirror, she saw what Benjamin's mother had meant. She was pale and her skin gleamed damply in the light refracting through the windshield, painting rainbow-colored stripes on the dashboard. She waved to Anton as she backed down the narrow drive, her skull feeling as if it was about to explode. He waved back with a cheerful grin and then took off, galloping after Benjamin into the trees. She couldn't see him anymore as she pulled out onto the paved road. Just before getting on the highway, she stopped the car, walked all the way over to the drainage ditch and threw up the sausages, twist bread, and mediocre coffee onto the fresh green dandelions.

WHEN NINA PARKED the Fiat in front of the garage, a man was standing by the chain-link fence by the road. The sun had sunk farther in the sky and hung behind his head like a glowing halo that made it impossible for her to make out his facial features. All the same, she had the sneaking sense that he was watching her as she walked across the cracked asphalt.

A muffled bass line with a techno beat hammered at her as she opened the door into the shop. There were only a handful of men in there. The nice weather apparently meant longer workdays in the city. The few that had returned home were sitting on a set of rickety lawn chairs just inside the door and were so preoccupied with their card game that the only scrutiny she received was a scowl as she scooted around them. At the back of the room, there was a slightly overweight teenage girl in pale blue jeans that were far too tight, a bright-yellow top and ponytail leading an impromptu chorus line of younger girls. Nina saw two little girls who hadn't been at the garage the previous evening. They must be seven or eight, she guessed, as she saw them carefully copying the teenager's not- entirely-unrefined dance steps with dark-eyed concentration. A couple of the boys, slightly younger, were fiddling with the source of the noise, a greasy ghetto blaster that had been plugged into a socket next to the door to the kitchenette. One of them was trying to sabotage the girls' dance with a big, impudent grin, swaying hips and holding a chocolate cookie in his right hand, but the rest of the group gathered around the ghetto blaster looked wan and limp.

The little boy was nowhere to be seen.

Nina proceeded down the length of the garage, her steps wobbly. Objects kept floating off to one side whenever she tried to focus on them. The cold, blue light from the fluorescent tube blinked irregularly as she made her way back down the rows of mattresses, rolled-up bedding, and sleeping bags. Then she spotted the boy's mother. She was huddled up against the wall, tiny. The boy was lying next to her, and when Nina got close enough, she saw that he was awake. His eyes were big and dark in his pale face, but it reassured Nina to see that he was conscious. His mother looked like someone who hadn't slept in days, which she probably hadn't. She was pale and colorless in a pair of worn jeans and a pink fleece jacket that looked too warm for May. She pointed to a little phone she wore hanging around her neck and flashed her cavity-ridden teeth in something that was meant to resemble a smile.

"*Ápolónö, telefonál!*" she said.

Nina nodded and slid down beside the woman. The nausea, which had been lying in wait the whole way to Valby, came back when the stench of the boy's sickbed hit her nostrils. What is this damn thing, she wondered, aware of how the question drifted around inside her aching head in an oddly aimless way. The boy's pulse was a little too high, but that wasn't a big deal. He could definitely use a new unit of saline, but his mother had apparently succeeded in getting him to drink some fluids. There were a couple of empty half-liter water bottles rolling around next to the mattress. Not critical, Nina thought, but the boy wasn't healthy either. Far from it. The boy's mother looked like she had read Nina's thoughts.

"*Kórház,*" she said. "Hospital?"

Before Nina had a chance to respond, the woman stood up in a wobbly, exhausted motion and gestured to Nina to follow her outside. They walked past the men playing cards and out into the parking lot, where darkness had now settled over the industrial neighborhood. The woman continued around the corner of the garage and down the uneven concrete pavers of an overgrown walkway that led to the garage's boarded-up office shack. A tall, untrimmed beech hedge was leaning across the path from the neighboring property, and Nina was on the verge of losing her balance as she ducked to pass underneath the branches. The pavers were wobbling. The whole world was wobbling now. The woman stopped about halfway down the path, squatted down, and separated the leaves in the hedge. Then she pulled out an old, plastic bucket that she held with just two fingers on the handle, cautiously placing it on the cobblestones between them.

The stench from the sloshing plastic bucket revealed its contents even before Nina looked into it. Vomit. The woman pointed into the bucket and looked at Nina with bare, black fear in her eyes.

"*Vér*," she said. "Much sick."

Nina held her breath and cautiously leaned over the bucket. The contents were grainy and dark, like coffee grounds.

Hematemesis. The person whose vomit this was had a seriously bleeding ulcer. It couldn't be the boy, Nina told herself. It couldn't. Not when he was sitting in the garage eating cookies, looking sick, but not deathly ill. It must be someone else, maybe the young man who had disappeared. Either he had consumed something that had eaten away the mucous membrane in his stomach or his stomach was totally ravaged by the effects of the disease. Hematemesis didn't just stop on its own. It was a potentially lethal condition.

"Where did it come from? Where is he?"

The woman hesitated.

"*Mulo*, much sick. Gone. Now, my son same sick." Fear pulled at the woman's mouth.

Nina moved, as quickly as her wobbly state permitted. If the vomit had come from Peter's "sick young man," he was in serious trouble. But she had no idea who he was or where in the world he was, and the children had to be her first priority now.

She yanked open the door of the garage and went across to the boy on the mattress. She was still far from certain that this was the same thing the young man had been suffering from. But she couldn't let herself run that risk any longer. The boy had to go to the hospital.

"Hospital. Now."

Nina gave a friendly smile and went to great lengths to act calm. There was no reason to scare the wits out of the boy's mother. On the other hand, it was important that she understood what had to be done. Nina could leave no room for doubt.

The woman glanced anxiously over at the men on the rickety lawn chairs. Then she took out a crumpled white plastic bag and started gathering up a few of the boy's clothes. It said "Ticket to Heaven" on the bag in big, attractive, swoopy letters. Below that was a drawing of happy stick- figure boys and girls in colored shorts and dresses. The woman's hands had started shaking.

One of the men got up. Nina could hear his footsteps approaching on the bare concrete floor but didn't turn around. She kneeled down next to the boy and smiled at him.

"Do you want to go for a little trip?" Nina asked, picking him up. Then she nodded quickly at the woman. "Let's go."

She started walking toward the door, and the boy's mother followed. He was heavier than she remembered him being, or maybe she was weaker. It felt like she was walking on pillows.

"*Abbahagy*. Stop."

The man hadn't even raised his voice, but Nina sensed the woman behind her stiffen. Now all of the men stood up and came over to block their way, arms crossed and eyes narrowed. The boy's father took a step forward and grabbed his wife's arm.

"*Örült éu vagy?*"

A shower of Hungarian words hailed down on them. The man gestured in Nina's direction, and the woman responded quietly and fervently. Then she pulled herself free, walked over to Nina, and tried to clear a path for them through the little group of men.

"*Né!*"

The man jumped forward and grabbed her again, this time so hard that it was obvious it hurt. Then he looked over at Nina.

"My son stay here."

The woman protested, clearly trying to explain something to him, but still without luck. The men had begun to close in around Nina, who stood motionless with the boy locked in her arms.

"The boy is very sick. We must take him to the hospital," she said calmly. "Please let me through."

She expressed her desire to proceed with her face, and

a very young man with a ponytail and youthful peach fuzz on his chin moved just enough to allow her to proceed toward the door. If she made it out with the boy, presumably his mother would be allowed to follow. Otherwise Nina might have to come back for her later.

With a quick yank someone spun her around, and she was now face to face with the boy's father, who looked like a man ready to fight to the death. He was furious, and behind the fury lurked something that resembled panic. As if he were afraid of her.

The man made a grab for the boy and tried to lift him out of Nina's arms with harsh, vigorous yanks, which caused the boy to emit an ear-splitting shriek. Nina let go of him. They couldn't stand there each tugging on either end of the child like two dogs with a piece of meat. But it was too late. The boy's shriek made the man yell something, first at Nina and then at the boy's mother, who had begun to cry. Nina looked at the men's faces, backed over to the door, grabbed the handle, and left. They let her do that.

She stood in the parking lot and took a deep breath, mouthful after mouthful of cool evening air. Her headache, which had receded slightly during the scuffle, returned as if her head were being bludgeoned.

She wasn't physically up to taking the boy away herself and would now have to notify the authorities. There was no way around it. Nina decided to start with Magnus, who had a detailed list of contact numbers for the police and the various welfare agencies. No matter who came out here now, they were going to need police assistance if they were to have any chance of taking the boy.

LENE KAABERBØL AND AGNETE FRIIS

Magnus's number was in her fingers, but she didn't manage to finish dialing it. A hard blow struck her hand. The pain in the back of her hand made her lose her grip on her phone. The phone hit the asphalt with an ominous crack, and when she spun around, she saw the young man with the ponytail standing there holding a broomstick. That was what he had hit her with. He put his heel on her phone, and there was a crunching sound as he crushed it. He raised the broomstick yet again and yelled something or other, either at her or to the men who had stayed behind in the garage.

Nina turned around and sprinted the few remaining meters to her Fiat, flung herself into the driver's seat, and jabbed her key into the ignition. Someone tried to open the door on the passenger's side. She couldn't see who it was and didn't care, either. She leaned across the passenger's seat as best she could with the steering wheel in her way and tried to force the door closed again. Without success. Whoever was holding the handle was stronger than she was, and in the rearview mirror, she could see a bunch of angry men closing in. A rock hit her rear windshield with a dull crash. The door handle slid out of her desperate grasp, and a man slipped into the front seat next to her.

"Drive," he said. "Please . . ."

It wasn't until then that she realized that he wasn't one of the pursuers but appeared to be pursued like herself. His face was red and swollen. He had a busted eyebrow, dark with clotted blood. As if he had just come out of a bar fight. Yet another shower of rocks hailed down over the car.

Nina turned the key in the ignition, and the Fiat started miraculously and immediately. She backed up so fast that the men behind them had to jump to the side, then sped ahead and threw the car onto the deserted industrial road, still with one door wide open and the stowaway clinging to the seat and the handle of the glove compartment. He managed to get the door closed again before they merged into the steady evening rush hour traffic on Gammel Køge Landevej.

THE CAR'S FRONT wheels hit the curb by the sidewalk in Fejøgade with a soft bump, and Nina heard the scraping sound of the undercarriage against the concrete. She was starting to feel dizzy again, and small black spots were dancing in front of her eyes as she turned her head to look at her uninvited passenger. He was pressing a handkerchief against the gash in his eyebrow. It was already soaked with blood, and a couple of big, dark drops had seeped through the fabric, dripping onto his arm. He noticed and folded the handkerchief carefully, trying to avoid further mess on himself or the car seat. It was almost touching, Nina thought, with a glance at the Fiat's shop-soiled upholstery. She opened the glove compartment, pulled out a roll of paper towels, and handed it to him.

"Thank you," he said politely.

They hadn't said anything to each other the whole drive. She hadn't had enough breath for anything besides maneuvering them in one piece through the city traffic despite her headache, and he had just sat there, motion-less and silent, as if he felt that any movement on his part would be interpreted as a threat.

He fumbled the paper towel into place over his gash and continued to sit there with the bloody handkerchief in his other hand as if he didn't quite know what to do with it. It wasn't until now that Nina had a chance to size him up. He was a long way from home, she thought, and young, probably somewhere in his early twenties. At first she had assumed he was Roma, but now she wasn't sure. There was something about the way he was dressed, his mannerisms, his reserved politeness—something that somehow set him apart from the other men out there at the garage. And then of course there was also the fact that they had beaten him . . . His breathing was unsteady, and he was holding his elbow awkwardly against his ribcage on one side. The split eyebrow clearly wasn't the whole story.

"What happened?" she asked, grateful that he spoke at least a little English. "Where does it hurt?"

"My side," he said. "I got kicked . . ."

At least it wasn't a knife or a baseball bat. Her eyes wandered up to his mouth, but there were no blood bubbles, and the blood that was there all seemed to have come from his eyebrow. A kick could easily break a rib, and a broken rib could perforate a lung. The eyebrow would have to wait; it wasn't life threatening. Chest pain could be.

"Take your jacket off. No, wait. I'll help you." She didn't want him to move his torso too much until she had an idea of what was going on with his ribs. The need to call on her professional skills once again pushed her own nausea into the background, and she was grateful for that. She turned on the overhead light to see what she was doing and pulled the now blood-splattered white shirt to the side to expose his torso. There was a round red mark along the third rib on his left side, and he inhaled sharply when she touched it. But the bone felt intact; at most it was cracked, which was still enormously uncomfortable and would make breathing an unpleasant chore for a few days, but nothing worse.

"Are you a doctor?" he asked.

"Nurse."

A flash of eagerness and hope lit up the eye that wasn't stuck shut with blood.

"My brother," he said. "Have you seen him? He's sick . . ."

"How old is he?" she asked.

"Sixteen."

"No. Then I haven't seen him." Was he the sick, young Roma man who had disappeared from the garage? Should she ask? But she didn't know anything other than that he was gone and that he might not be just sick but critically ill.

The man's shoulders sank. She cautiously moved the hand protecting his eye so she could see the gash. It was what she had been expecting, a classic boxing injury. It bled a lot, but the gash wasn't all that long, and Nina could have fixed it up with a drop of skin glue from her first aid kit if she had had a chance to grab it when she left Valby. Now she would have to make do with the car's first aid kit, which wasn't ideal, but better than nothing.

"Do you know the people out there?" she asked.

"No," he said.

He sat perfectly still while she worked, almost as if

he wasn't completely present. As if he had disappeared into himself, to some place where the pain couldn't reach him. It gave her a jolt of discomfort because that was a reaction she was more used to seeing in exhausted or abused refugee children, but at least it made him an easy patient. She cleaned the wound with a splash of iodine and closed the gaping gash with small pieces of surgical tape. Finally she turned the rearview mirror so he could view the results. The look in his eyes became more alert, and he thanked her again, just as politely as the first time.

"You're welcome."

Nina forced herself to smile as she felt the nausea come roiling back up from somewhere low in her abdomen. It was that refugee child's reaction in him that made her continue:

"Are you in trouble? Is there anything I . . ."

She only made it halfway through the question. It felt as if the car were sailing across the black asphalt, like a ship in rough waters. She opened the door, but only made it halfway out before she threw up, hanging out of her seat. Warm vomit spattered her sandal, her foot, and her bare leg. When the heaving stopped, she sat there for several seconds with her eyes closed and her forehead resting against the steering wheel, gasping the cool evening air.

Then she felt a hand on her shoulder and looked up. He had gotten out of the car and come around to her side to help her out. He looked scared, she thought. Worried and scared, in a way that looked wrong for someone that young. People his age usually lived secure in their faith in their own immortality.

He supported her gently under the elbow as she awkwardly straddled the little pool of vomit next to the car. There were small bright red splotches in the grayish yellow. Blood. That put paid to any lingering doubts. She was suffering from the same thing as the children at the garage.

Nina instinctively pulled her arm back and took a step away from the young man. If this was contagious, and she was a carrier, then she had already spent too long with him in the car, not to mention with Anton and all the kids on the field trip. She wasn't too worried about herself or Anton. A well-equipped hospital would have no trouble curing this thing, whatever it was. It was a different matter for the Roma at the garage and for her injured passenger. She had no idea where he was going and if he would have access to a hospital if he got sick.

"This is just first aid," she told him. "Get back in. I'll drive you to the emergency room just as soon . . . just give me a moment."

"No." He shook his head vehemently.

She stared at him and felt an intense exasperation spread like heat through her chest. What was it with these people? Why couldn't they just do what she said?

"You need more treatment. And the children out there. They need to go to the hospital. Why won't any of you see that?" Her voice had become hard and flat with suppressed rage. But not sufficiently suppressed, it seemed.

"I'm going now," he said, taking a step back, as if he was backing away from a vicious dog. "Thanks for your help."

She wanted him to wait. To at least stay long enough

to get her phone number so he could call if there were problems. If he got sick. Or if he found his sick brother. But he was already walking down the sidewalk. The muscles in Nina's legs trembled as she tried to take a couple of swaying steps after him. She didn't even have the strength to call out. She was afraid she would throw up again if she so much as flexed a single muscle in the region of her neck. But when he got to the corner, he turned around spontaneously. He hesitated for so long she thought maybe he had changed his mind after all.

"The children," he said then. "In Hungary, Roma children are often removed from their homes. For example if someone in the family is seriously ill or . . . or something. That's why they're afraid. That's why they don't dare go to the doctor here. Because the children don't always come home again."

He looked as if he wanted to say more, but then he turned his back on her again, lengthened his strides, and disappeared down Jagtvej. She stood perfectly still for a while, waiting for her nausea to subside.

HIS HEAD HURT like crazy. Sándor cautiously fingered his eyebrow, tracing the edges of the wound under the bandage, but that wasn't where most of the pain was coming from. When the blow hit, his head had slammed back and something in his neck had dislocated, or at least that was how it felt. And the ribs on his left side ached with a steady, dull pain with every breath he took.

Traffic churned past on both sides of a narrow central strip of trees. It wasn't very dark yet even though it was past ten, and though he felt like sitting down on the sidewalk and leaning against a wall, there were limits to how weird he could act out here in the open where everyone could see him.

It was no longer hot. There was a sharpness in the air, and a shiver ran through him when he breathed, partly because of the cold, partly because of the shock. Someone had hit him. Someone had kicked him while he was down. Someone had thrown rocks at him. There was a tumultuous, injured humiliation inside him. He felt *picked on*. The entire Hungarian part of his upbringing was in offended uproar—"You can't just hit people, you know!"—while at the same time he could hear his stepfather Elvis's sarcastic scorn when he had been stupid enough to complain that someone had pushed him at school. *Crybaby. Push back!*

He hadn't found Tamás.

Even though the place was at the address Tamás had

given him, Tamás wasn't there. No one would admit having seen him. No one would say where he was. And when Sándor had kept asking, insisted . . . it had happened in a flash. There hadn't been any introductory pushing or bumping chests, they had just . . . let him have it. Three or four quick blows and, when he fell down, a kick to the kidneys and one in the side. He wasn't even sure which of them had hit him, after the first man, that little square guy with the mustache, the one who sounded like he came from Szeged. He was the one who had busted Sándor's eyebrow.

As he lay doubled over on the filthy, gritty concrete floor of the repair shop, he heard the sound of breaking glass. Then they hauled him up onto his feet and pushed him up against the wall, and the Szeged man stuck something right up in his face, so close that Sándor had to squint to see that it was a broken bottle.

They're going to slit my throat.

He had time to think that thought, disjointed and panicky and yet strangely matter-of-fact. A noise came out of his throat, a squeak that was both pain and fear. And that very instant there was a *pling!* from his mobile phone, an absurdly everyday sound in the midst of impending death. That didn't stop the man with the broken bottle.

"Get lost," he said coldly. "If we see you here again . . ."

He didn't need to say any more. The edge of the broken glass rested sharp and cold against Sándor's cheek, and Sándor could feel his pulse throbbing in his carotid artery a few centimeters down.

"You and your *mulo* brother . . ." one of the other men whispered. "*Mamioro*, scram."

And Sándor had run away. His tail between his legs, his throat full of bile. But when he got outside, there was nowhere to go. After all, he *had* to find Tamás.

Mulo. He remembered that word because ghosts and evil spirits were staples of his grandmother's bedtime stories. *Mamioro*? Wasn't there a story about . . .

But the memory slipped through his fingers like a fish squirming its way out of the fisherman's grasp. And *mulo* was ominous enough on its own. Why were they calling his brother an evil spirit?

He shuddered and suddenly noticed that he was in his shirtsleeves, leaning up against a wall whose cool stone façade was sucking the heat out of his body with each second. His jacket. What happened to it?

Damn it. That's right, the nurse had helped him to take it off.

He swore softly and starting walking back toward the street where she had dropped him off. It wasn't far; it couldn't be. A quiet side street off the noisy boulevard he was on now with three- or four-story residential buildings on both sides and some fragile, freshly planted trees in pots here and there . . .

Was it here? FEJØGADE the sign said, a collection of letters that refused to make any kind of sense in his head whatsoever. And people said Hungarian was hard . . .

The little, red Fiat was parked next to the curb, with a spider web shaped pattern in the rear window where the rock had hit it. He put his hands on the roof and peered in the side windows. Yes. There it was, tossed on the back seat with the first aid kit she had used when she patched him up. He grabbed the door handle, but of course the car was locked. The locking reflex was apparently so ingrained in city dwellers that it would take more than a stomach bug to defeat it.

He tried to figure out which building was hers. Surely she had parked as close as she could, but there weren't very many free spots to choose from. He stared doubtfully at the big entry door closest to the Fiat. Was that it? He couldn't be sure. And which floor? He stared at the row of lit buzzer buttons with neatly typed names behind Plexiglas. HANSEN, KRONBORG, H. SKOVGAARD, MALENE HVIDT & RASMUS BJERG POULSEN . . . She hadn't said what her name was. He tentatively pressed the button next to HANSEN, but there was no answer. KRONBORG turned out to be a man's voice, speaking Danish, of course. Or so Sándor assumed anyway. He couldn't make out a single word.

It's just a jacket, he told himself. But he felt still further reduced. Going from a room full of possessions to a duffel bag of just the most essential things. Then the bag was gone—he hadn't brought it from Valby. And now his Studio Coletti jacket, which with a little generosity could be mistaken for something more classic. What would it be next? For a brief nightmarish moment, he pictured himself roaming the streets of this foreign city stark naked. But he still had his wallet in his trouser pocket, his mobile phone, and the keys to the dorm room that was no longer his.

The phone. He had received a text message, hadn't he? While he'd been pushed up against the wall with the sharp edge of the broken bottle at his throat.

The message was empty. But it had come from Tamás's number.

He feverishly pressed "call." How long had it been since the message had arrived? A half hour? More? Less? He had no idea. He just had to desperately hope his brother was still by the phone.

"Yes?"

"Tamás. Where are you?"

"Who is this?"

Only when the voice began speaking English did he realize it wasn't Tamás.

"Could I please speak to Tamás?" he tried.

"Who may I say is calling?" said the man on the phone, very correctly, but in some accent that Sándor couldn't identify. Maybe that was what it sounded like when Danes spoke English.

"I'm his brother."

"Oh, good. He's been asking for you. He can't come to the phone right now, but he really wants to talk to you. Where are you?"

The alarm bells started going off in the back of Sándor's mind. *I don't trust them. I only trust you.*

"In Copenhagen," he said vaguely. "Where's Tamás now?"

"He's here with us. He's sleeping right now. He's been very sick, and he's not doing so well. But I know he'll be really happy to see you when he wakes up. Where are you? We'll just come pick you up. It's no problem."

I don't trust you either, Sándor thought. But I don't have any choice.

"It says FEJØGADE on the sign," he said and spelled it out for them.

IT TOOK A while for her to make it up the stairs. Nina's legs were sluggish and sore, and she was forced to stop on the landing halfway up to gather her strength for the last flight. Then she let herself into the apartment and stood for a moment, on wobbly legs, contemplating her next move.

Leaving the boy and the other children at the garage was no longer an option. She wanted to get them all over to Bispebjerg Hospital and have them checked out, but her powers of persuasion had been woefully insufficient, and she had a serious bruise on the back of her hand to remind her of that fact. It would take both the social welfare authorities and the police to get the children out of there. What this would mean for their parents was no longer a concern she could afford to be influenced by.

She called Magnus's mobile, her fingers feeling like oversized gummy bears. He sounded like his usual calm, overworked self when he answered. It was 10:10 P.M., but he was still at the Coal-House Camp waiting for the medical transport he had just ordered for one of the camp's elderly residents. Of course Valby wouldn't shock him either.

"You could call one of the pediatricians at Rigshospitalet," he said. "They have details of all the agencies you'll need. They are the ones who pick up the pieces when little kids get beaten by mom and dad. They know what they're doing."

Nina sighed. Damnit, this wasn't the same thing at all. Magnus was quiet on the other end of the line.

"Are you okay?" he asked.

Nina had no idea how he did it, but Magnus had something like a sixth sense when it came to illness. As if he could hear it, even over the phone, even when the call was routed via satellites.

"I'm not one hundred percent," she admitted, sitting down on the edge of the sofa.

Someone said something to Magnus in the background. The medical transport team must have finally arrived, and Nina waited, supporting herself with her hand on the coffee table, while Magnus directed them down the hallway. Then he was back on the line.

"Right," Magnus said. "Here's what we'll do. You come out here now. Take a taxi. We've got to have a look at you, too."

Nina smiled weakly at the phone.

"I've got to get the boy to a hospital first."

Magnus snorted. "Now you listen to me. I'll take care of the Valby kids, but only if you come out here. Now. Besides . . ." Magnus exhaled heavily into the phone, and Nina guessed he was on his way over to the clinic. ". . . the faster we run some tests on you, the faster we'll figure out what's going on with those children. It can be difficult to get the social welfare authorities off their backsides, so it could easily take a few hours before anything happens in that department. You're sick. Let's start with you. I'm sure you're suffering from the same thing."

"You're just saying that to get me to do what you want," she said. "So I'll quit being a nuisance."

His warm, rural Swedish laugh resonated into her telephone ear.

"Perhaps," he said. "But I'm right, aren't I?"

SHE DIDN'T TAKE a cab. She wasn't completely helpless, even though it was surprisingly hard to turn the key in the ignition.

Her fingers trembled, and to her intense irritation after two fruitless attempts she was forced to rest her hands on her thighs, take a deep breath, and try again. This time the motor started. Fucking hell. Nina swore softly in a mix of relief and frustration. She sat still for a moment, trying to get control of her body before she put the car in gear and backed out onto the road. So far, so good. She cast a quick glance in the rearview mirror just before she turned onto Jagtvej and caught a glimpse of a lanky, girlish figure on a clunky old lady's bicycle. Then the cyclist disappeared from view. Ida? Nina tried to turn her head and catch sight of the cyclist again, but the movement made her head pound, so she gave up. No, of course it wasn't. Ida was at Anna's.

Nina suddenly felt miserably alone. Her thoughts drifted off into the darkness around her. She pictured all of them, Anton, Ida, Morten, and herself, as small, illuminated fireflies surrounded by black nothing, each heading off in its own direction.

THE CAR THAT had come to get Sándor was a dark-blue Volkswagen Touareg. A chocolate labrador was sitting in the back. It breathed on him the whole way, heavy and wet down the back of his neck. Mounted in the back seat next to Sándor was an infant's car seat, which reassured him. One of the two men seemed perfectly ordinary, unthreatening and reasonably trustworthy. Probably in his mid-forties, blond, casually dressed in deck shoes, khaki chinos, and a thin, navy blue wool sweater with a little Ralph Lauren polo player embroidered on the chest.

"Frederik," he said, holding out his hand.

"Sándor Horváth."

"So you're Tamás's brother?"

Sándor nodded. The driver hadn't greeted him. He was a skinny, not particularly tall man whose face was partly hidden in the shadow of a cowboy hat that would have made John Wayne jealous. So far he had completely ignored Sándor.

"We're glad you came," Frederik said. "Has Tamás filled you in on the situation?"

"Not really," Sándor replied evasively. "He just said he was feeling terrible and needed help."

"Yeah, unfortunately that's true. Don't really know what he's got. It would probably be best to get him a doctor."

Sándor thought about what Tamás had written: *I can't stand. Having trouble seeing.*

"Shouldn't he go to the hospital?"

The man turned around so far that Sándor could see his whole calm, neatly shaven face.

"Let's just cut the crap," he said. "Your brother can't go to a normal hospital. But we know a doctor who'd be happy to treat him, discreetly, you understand."

"Well, do that then."

"That's what we want to do, but it's not cheap. And his sponsor has put his wallet back in his pocket."

Sponsor? What did they mean by that?

"Bolgár? Do you mean Bolgár?"

The man in the Ralph Lauren sweater smiled guardedly.

"We don't need to mention too many names now, do we? But yes. He paid for your brother's trip and room and board, but he drew the line at the expense of a private clinic. That kind of thing is expensive."

"How much?" Sándor asked, feeling the rage smoldering just below the surface. His brother was sick, very sick, and now this man was sitting here saying, sure they wanted to help him—just as long as they were paid for it. Money Sándor didn't have.

"A considerable sum. Several thousand Euros."

Sándor's heart sank.

"I don't have that much."

"No, we realize that. But luckily your brother has a valuable item that he can sell. As you well know."

Sándor didn't say anything. He didn't want to say yes, but it also didn't make much sense to deny it.

"So sell it," he said hoarsely. Preferably without involving me . . .

"What we're missing," Frederik said, "is the contact

information for the buyer. Your brother entrusted you with that particular key, he said. So we thought that if we helped your brother get some medical attention now, then one favor could repay the other, if you catch my drift. It's a very nice place, private clinic and all that, better than a big public hospital."

"I would really like to talk to my brother first," Sándor said insistently.

There was a little pause. The streetlights alternated in a Morse-like rhythm as the car slid through traffic, light-dark, light-dark, light-light-dark. Sándor cautiously leaned his head back against the cream-colored headrest and was suddenly dead tired of sitting in big German cars and being blackmailed.

The driver pulled something out of the chest pocket of his fringed cowboy leather jacket and handed it to Frederik. A mobile phone, it looked like. One of those ones that was practically a small computer, with a flip out keypad and double-sized screen.

"I have a video I think you should see," Frederik said. He held the phone's screen up so Sándor could look at it.

It was Tamás, of course. A close-up of his face, grainy and overexposed, but still frighteningly clear. His eyes were closed; no, more than closed, glued shut by some kind of goopy, yellow infection that stuck to his eyelashes in clumps. A tear track that was reddish from blood and pus ran down along the side of his nose. Little reddish-brown splotches covered the skin around his eyes like freckles, and he could hear a wheezing, gurgling sound that must be Tamás's breathing. His lips were cracked and bloody, and it didn't seem like he was aware of what was going on around him.

It was at that instant that Sándor remembered what *mamioro* meant: a spirit who brings deadly disease.

Frederik turned off the phone's video function and passed it back to the driver.

"I don't think there's a lot of time for the doctor," he said, sounding just as friendly and calm as before. A *thump-thump-thump* came from where the dog was sitting. The Lab was wagging because he had heard his master's voice.

"I don't have any keys," Sándor said desperately.

"Well, I hope you do," Frederik said. "It's a short list, I believe. With some phone numbers and dates on it."

Sándor closed his eyes. Oh, yes, I had one of those. In the pocket of the jacket that's in the nurse's car.

MAGNUS SWORE WHEN he saw her.

It had taken her more than half an hour to reach the Coal-House Camp because she had had to pull over by the Gladsaxe exit to throw up. After that she had sat for almost seven minutes with her forehead resting on the wheel before she had summoned up enough energy to drive on. Magnus had met her in the parking lot, stuck a long bear paw into the car, and practically scooped her out of the Fiat.

Now she was lying on the clinic's examining table while Magnus, still cursing, tended to her.

"You have quite a high fever, thirty-nine point one, and your pulse is through the roof. I don't understand how you even made it out here. I told you to take a cab. You're acting like a goddamn idiot, but I suppose there's nothing new about that. Goddamn it all to hell."

Nina didn't respond. Magnus swore when he was worried, usually in his native Swedish; she was used to it, and even if she hadn't been, she was beyond caring. She had spent the last of her energy getting here. Now she lay still, feeling the nausea settling over her like a heavy, cloying duvet.

"I could do some of the tests here, but we really need to get you into a hospital. I know someone in the infectious diseases ward at Rigshospitalet. I'm sure I could get her to admit you. She isn't such a stickler for the rules, and if she can figure out what this is, she could probably do something for those children very quickly."

Nina nodded and rolled over on her side. That reduced the nausea for a brief moment; then it came back with renewed vigor. She sat up and vomited into the basin Magnus had placed in front of her. He wrinkled his nose and took the basin away with a new torrent of cussing and swearing.

"As quickly as possible, Magnus."

She lay there with her eyes closed while Magnus made the call. He talked for a long time, his voice was quiet and strained. Persuasive. But she wasn't paying attention to what he was saying anymore. She drifted off for a few minutes but was forced to wake up again almost immediately as Magnus began the awful process of getting her to her feet and into his Volvo.

Some oversight must have occurred to him then, because he tossed her bag and jacket into the driver's seat and left her sitting unsteadily in the other front seat, while he sprinted back into the clinic.

Only then did she notice that there were two jackets. Her own windbreaker and a man's jacket that had definitely never been hers. The young man must have forgotten it in her car.

Magnus came back with his arms full of emesis basins, which he piled into her lap.

"Yeah, sorry," he said. "But . . . you know. It's the Volvo."

Nina couldn't help but laugh even though it mostly sounded like a long, hacking cough.

"My valiant hero," she said weakly, feeling the fierce, familiar undertow of her longing for Morten. "What would I have done without you?"

HE FIAT WAS gone when they got back to FEJØ-
GADE. Sándor stared at the empty parking space on
the curb where it had been an hour before.

"It's gone," he said.

If only he had just smashed the damn window and
taken the jacket while he had the chance. But the thought
hadn't even occurred to him. That would have been
Against The Rules. Of course at that point, he hadn't
known that Tamás's life might depend on it.

"Then I suppose we'll have to wait until it comes back,"
Frederik said. "Because this is where she lives, right?"

"I don't know," Sándor said. "I think so. She went into
that building there." He pointed to the front door he was
most convinced was hers. No reason to mention that he
wasn't a hundred percent sure.

"Find another place to park, Tommi," Frederik told the
driver. "So her spot is still free."

Tommi nodded and slid the Touareg in between a Kia
and a Škoda Felicia a little farther down the street. He
turned on the radio and shoved a CD into the slot, and
soon Johnny Cash was rasping through the speakers:
"Saint Quentin, you've been living hell to me . . ."

They sat in silence. Sándor had stopped asking them
about Tamás, and there wasn't anything else he wanted
to talk to them about. The driver lit a cigarette.

"Open the window," Frederik said, irritated.

After half an hour, during which Johnny Cash had
sung "Folsom Prison Blues," "The Man in Black," "Ring of

Fire," and several other classics, Tommi suddenly opened the driver's door.

"Can you see the Fiat?" Frederik asked, still in English, which suddenly puzzled Sándor. Why weren't they speaking Danish to each other?

"She obviously didn't just pop out for cigarettes," Tommi said. "And we don't have all night."

Frederik sat there for a brief moment. Then he nodded.

"Okay. We'll go in and have a look. Come on." That last part was to Sándor.

"But I don't even know her name!"

"You said she was a nurse, right?" Tommi said. "I'm sure we can figure out the rest. Get off your ass."

Tommi tossed his ten-gallon hat onto the seat and took off his fringed cowboy jacket. He pulled two black sweatshirts out of the trunk, gave one to Frederik, put on the other, and stuck a couple of screwdrivers in his pocket. The Lab whined, wanting to go with them, but Frederik commanded it to "Lie down!" and at the same time cracked the window a little to let air into the car for it.

Frederik pressed the doorbells one by one and said a few words each time, completely incomprehensible to Sándor, until there was a buzz and a click and they could enter. Ten or twelve identical mailboxes were mounted just inside the door. With a quick, practiced wrench of the screwdriver, Tommi broke the first one open and passed the contents to Frederik, who quickly skimmed through it while Tommi set to work on the next mailbox.

"Bingo," Frederik said of mailbox five, waving a window envelope. "Nina Borg, RN. Second floor on the right."

Tommi carefully returned the mail to the appropriate boxes even though the doors were hanging open and could no longer be closed.

Frederik rang the doorbell for the second-floor apartment on the right, but no one came to the door. They could hear music from inside, something loud and heavy and apocalyptic, and when Tommi opened the mail slot, they could see that the lights were on. Frederik and Tommi exchanged glances, and Frederik nodded. Tommi pulled a floppy, crumpled nylon stocking out of his pocket and handed it to Frederik. Frederik sniffed it and made a face.

"For fuck's sake," he said. "Don't you have any that haven't been worn?"

Tommi just shrugged. He had already pulled a stocking over his head so his facial features were grotesquely smushed and camouflaged.

"No," Sándor said, aghast. "You can't just . . ."

Crunch. The doorframe splintered under the pressure from two screwdrivers at once. The door opened.

Sándor just stood there on the landing until Tommi grabbed hold of him, pulled him inside, and shut the door behind him. The music pulsed out to meet them on heavy bass feet.

"But . . ."

"Shut up. You want to get your brother to the doctor, right?"

Sándor closed his mouth again.

"Is it one of them?" Frederik asked softly, pointing to the overloaded coat hooks on one wall. Tommi had begun opening doors, quickly and quietly—or at least quietly enough that the clicks were lost in the bombardment of death metal. Sándor obediently flipped through the untidy collection of raincoats, windbreakers, and jackets but couldn't find anything that resembled his Studio Coletti.

Suddenly there was a feminine shriek and an outraged yell from an only slightly less shrill but still unmistakably masculine voice. A shudder ran through Sándor's entire body, and he involuntarily took a couple of quick steps back toward the door.

Tommi was standing in the doorway to what was obviously a teenager's room. On the bed that occupied most of the space lay a young couple, a girl with short, wispy, tar-black hair and a young guy with tattooed shoulders and a shaved head. They were both more or less naked, and the girl was trying to pull the blanket up to cover her breasts.

Sándor hurriedly looked away. Tommi didn't.

"Keep going," he told the shocked couple, clicking the record video button on his fancy phone. "They're crazy about this kind of thing on the Internet . . ."

SOMETHING WAS BEEPING.

Nina detected it somewhere at the outer limits of her consciousness. First she tried to get away from the noise, burrowing back into the dim, gray semidarkness she had been inhabiting, but someone was moving around in the room again, and she reluctantly opened her eyes. There was a nurse next to her bed, fiddling with the machine that was beeping. She was wearing an aggressively yellow lab coat with a matching face mask of the type that meant "contagious," but when she turned around Nina could see that she was smiling reassuringly behind the mask. Dawn was underway outside. A subdued, gray light filtered into the room through the voluminous, brightly patterned curtains.

"False alarm," the nurse said. "Your pulse has just been a little too high for a little too long. It's all over the place at the moment."

Nina nodded and looked away. The nurse's yellow coat made her feel sick to her stomach, or maybe she was just starting to notice the nausea again after her interval of dozing. She shifted uneasily, trying to see if she could move away from the discomfort, rolling halfway onto one side. That was as far as she could go because of the IV drip and the Venflon catheter in her left hand. She sincerely hoped the next round of vomiting would hold off for a while. She was unbelievably tired, and she didn't know if she had the strength to sit up properly. It felt as if she hadn't slept a wink, and that might not actually be an exaggeration. Since she had been admitted, she had thrown up twice every hour, on the hour. At least. She had stopped counting after 2 A.M. They took new blood tests, and two doctors had asked her the exact same questions. They had pressed on her abdomen, turned her over, made her stand up and sit down, and pulled up her hospital gown so they could study her skin. The piercing beeping from the machines in the room hadn't made it any easier to sleep. They were monitoring her pulse, and the device made a noise as soon as it went over one hundred, which it frequently did. She had wanted them to turn all this crap off, but their response was a firm no, and she had given up arguing with them at 2:24 A.M.

Now it was 5:32 A.M. Nina could follow the minute hand as it staggered its way in loud clicks around the clock over the door. She had established that she wasn't allowed to leave the room, at the moment a completely unnecessary admonition. She couldn't even get out of bed by herself.

Magnus's unshaven face appeared in the doorway. He didn't look so good either, Nina thought, adjusting her position again. He was wearing the same clothes as the night before, a tattered plaid flannel shirt and Bermuda shorts. He had also been equipped with a toxic-yellow face mask, which made Nina consider a snide comment. But she decided against it. It might well make her throw up, and Magnus didn't look like he was in the mood for banter, either. His eyes looked tired and worried, and probably not only because of her. Magnus worked himself ragged both at home and at the Coal-House Camp.

"First, the good news." Magnus sat down on her bed,

and she could tell from his eyes that he was smiling behind his face mask. It didn't have quite the same reassuring effect as when his mouth was visible as well. "Your friend Peter called me a couple of hours ago just as I was about to send in the cavalry. The mother of the sick child was able to sneak out with the boy while the father was asleep. She called Peter, and he picked them up somewhere along Roskildevej. I got them set up at Bispebjerg Hospital. The boy is doing reasonably well. Better than you in any case. I'm not too worried."

"You could have fooled me," Nina said, attempting a wry smile. Magnus didn't smile back.

"Nina, I'm sorry to have to tell you this while you're ill. Don't be alarmed, but . . ." Magnus moved in closer and cautiously rested a hand on her shoulder. "Morten just called me. Something happened. There was a break-in at your apartment. Ida was home at the time."

It took a second before the words sank in. Then Nina straightened up with a jerk that made her IV stand teeter dangerously next to the bed. What was Magnus saying? She couldn't make sense of it. A break-in. But Ida was spending the night at Anna's. She wouldn't have been home at all. Magnus must have made a mistake.

"Nothing happened to her, and Morten is on his way home."

Nina sat there for a while, struggling to process the information she had been given. Then she remembered seeing the familiar-looking figure on the bicycle just as she had left Fejøgade. Maybe it had been Ida after all. She gave Magnus a questioning look. He wasn't normally the type to mince words. He neither could nor wanted to sugar-coat things, and she was grateful for that when they were working together at the Coal-House Camp. But now that she had been reduced to a poor, pathetic invalid was there something he wasn't telling her? What had happened to Ida? And where was she now?

"Morten's sister picked her up, and Morten will be home in a few hours. There's nothing to worry about."

It was as if Magnus had guessed what she would be thinking and had already prepared an answer. Nina felt her short, labored breaths, and the machine started emitting a small, warning blip. Her pulse was on its way up again.

"Can I call her?"

Magnus looked away, a little too fast, and shook his head.

"She doesn't want to talk to you. She's waiting for Morten. But I was supposed to give you her best and tell you she hopes you get well soon."

That last part was a lie, Nina thought dryly.

"Could I at least call Morten?"

Again Magnus's eyes were strangely evasive.

"Nina, he's probably sitting up on top of an oil rig, waiting for the next available helicopter. That kind of thing requires a man's full attention. Give it a rest, and concentrate on getting better."

Magnus's voice was disturbingly light-hearted and devoid of swear words, but Nina was too exhausted to break through the Teflon surface of his concern. For the time being she was forced to let Morten handle it.

"And what else? Have you heard anything from the lab?"

Magnus nodded, visibly relieved at the change in topic.

"Some of the results came back, and they're looking at them now. They'll let you know as soon as possible, and apparently there's also a team from the radiology department on its way up. I guess they're not wild about the idea of moving you around right now."

No, they didn't want her potentially plague-inducing bacteria to contaminate the entire hospital. Nina knew the drill. They would X-Ray her thorax to assess the state of her lungs. Maybe there were signs of some kind of infection in the tests they had already done.

"Have you seen my numbers?"

Nina tried to pull herself together as much as she could and give Magnus an authoritative look. The feeling of being cut off from the information that was available to her doctor made her fidgety.

"Your infection counts look a little suspect," Magnus said, sitting down next to the bed. "They did a differential count, and your lymphocyte numbers look odd. They're coming to ask you a few questions again in a half hour. I'm going to hang around until then."

Nina sank back in the bed. A half hour didn't give her enough time to sleep but was too long to stay awake. The nausea kept churning in her stomach, and small, flashing spots danced up over the white ceiling. And then it seemed she was, after all, able to fall asleep; the last thing she was aware of was Magnus's heavy, dry bear paw on her forehead, cautiously stroking her hair.

SHE WOKE UP because someone was shouting. It was a woman, and her voice was high with surprise. Nina opened her eyes, her head still pounding, and looked at the clock over the door. 6:24 A.M. Everything was a little blurry. But it must still be morning, and there was a cluster of toxic-yellow gowns converging around her.

"Nina."

Magnus's voice sounded like he was standing on the other side of the room, but she saw him right beside her bed and moving in closer to bend over her.

"Nina. You're going to have to wake up, sweetheart."

She sat up too fast and felt a flood of vomit forcing its way up her throat. Someone held a basin for her, while Magnus patiently waited. When she was done, she looked up and met his eyes.

"There was a blip on the radiology nurse's dosimeter."

Nina shook her head. It was like Magnus was starting to slip out of focus again. What he was saying didn't make any sense.

"You've been exposed to radiation, Nina. You have radiation sickness."

THERE WAS FRENETIC activity in Nina's room. At least three doctors, each with an entourage of medical students, had been by over the course of the morning, and they had all looked at her with a mixture of concern and professional excitement. The team from the Danish National Institute of Radiation Hygiene in particular had a hard time hiding their enthusiasm as they filled out their paperwork, consulted, and issued instructions for the rank-and-file staff. Nina saw it happening, but didn't have the strength to get worked up over it. She recognized their response. Professionals were always fascinated to encounter in real life things they had only read about in books. She was probably one of the few patients—if any—with radiation sickness they had ever seen, and she could hear their whispered, animated discussions out in the corridor. If she hadn't been feeling so dreadful, she would probably have been just as curious, but she had other things to worry about.

It was a relief to be able to see people's faces again. The staff no longer wore face masks—you couldn't catch radiation sickness through inhalation.

An investigator from the Danish Emergency Management Agency had already been there at 7:40 A.M. He was middle-aged, short, and balding and had smiled politely as he opened his bag and took out a pad of paper and a pen. Then, without warning, he had launched into his barrage of questions.

Where had she been, who had she talked to, what had she seen?

She answered as best she could. She had told the hospital staff about the repair shop right away, and the Emergency Management Agency was presumably already turning the place upside down. She had every possible reason to cooperate. The boy was receiving treatment now, but the rest of the residents from the Valby garage had potentially been exposed to amounts of radiation that were just as serious as her own exposure, and they would have to be examined. Beyond that, of course there were other and very obvious reasons the Emergency Management Agency had turned up less than half an hour after the radiology team's dosimeter had started beeping. A source of radiation in central Copenhagen must be Nightmare Scenario Number One for the PET, the police, and the Emergency Management Agency.

The man's ballpoint pen scribbled things down on paper at a furious pace as Nina responded to his questions. Beyond her own address, he also asked for Peter's and that of the Coal-House Camp.

"As far as I can tell," she said, "everyone who got sick was down in the inspection pit, either briefly or for perhaps as long as an hour at a time. Maybe that's where it came from?"

"Yes," he said, with a single quick nod. "That's what our people at the site reported. The radiation level down there is significant, and they found small amounts of radioactive sand."

She remembered the feeling of small, sharp grains of sand digging into her skin, and instinctively rubbed her palms on the sheet, as if to brush them off. Her hour-long hunt for a possible source of poisoning, the cleanup she had done with such determination—it had all been in vain. Radioactivity. While she had been removing plastic bags, moldy cardboard, and old oil drums, there had been an invisible, imperceptible enemy down there the whole time.

"Where did it come from?" she asked.

"The main source had been removed by the time we arrived," he said. "We can only speculate." Then he started cross-examining her about the residents of the garage. She patiently listed everyone she had spoken to, but that wasn't that many, and she hadn't taken their names or collected any other useful information while she'd been there. The man smiled at her with a trace of contempt.

"A lot of things would have been easier if you had informed the authorities about the outbreak of a suspicious illness right away," he said and started packing up his things. "Sometimes you need to think with your brain instead of your heart."

Nina didn't answer but sank back in the bed, silently fuming. There hadn't been anything particularly suspicious about the outbreak until she herself had fallen ill, and as for the Danish authorities' response to a group of Roma in Valby, not much thinking was likely to have been involved—with their brains *or* their hearts. Their Pavlovian reaction would have sent the whole lot back across the border, to scatter themselves and their contaminated luggage across half of Europe. Still, he had touched a nerve. How much radiation had they been exposed to? And what about her?

She threw up again, and there was no sign she was improving. They were treating her with a drug called ferric ferrocyanide, more commonly known as Prussian Blue, which was supposed to bind to any unabsorbed radioactive material inside her, which of course she was totally in favor of. The only snag was that it had to be administered through a thin, plastic tube that was inserted through one of her nostrils and then fed all the way down to her duodenum "to prevent any irritation of the stomach lining." She could certainly have done without the effect the tube had on her already hypersensitive gag reflex.

The doctors said she was going to have to be patient. It was "unlikely" she had received a life-threatening dose, but "the course of the sickness could be extremely unpredictable." She might feel better now or be sick for several days. After that she would recover quite quickly, they thought, but her fertility would be "problematic" and her immune system would be seriously compromised for a long time to come.

She believed them, especially on that last point.

She was so tired she could hardly feel her body anymore, and she desperately needed sleep, but the vomiting forced her to wake up several times an hour, and the traffic of people in and out of her room kept increasing. Unknown faces ebbing and flowing past the foot of her bed. Poking her, taking her blood pressure, pulling up her all-too-short hospital gown and letting their fingers run down over her ribs. Spreading her legs to look for any sign of a rash around her groin, on her buttocks, and on her back, as if she were a piece of meat on an autopsy table. As if she were dead.

And in the middle of all this, she missed Morten so much she couldn't think straight. She imagined how he would enter the room and chase away all those toxic-yellow gowns. She would ask him to lie down on the bed next to her so she could bury her nose in his T-shirt and inhale the safe scent of North Sea winds and water and salt and Morten, instead of the smell of disinfectant soap and vomit. Maybe then her stomach would finally settle down a little.

The hospital had provided her with a phone next to her bed, but it remained silent. Morten hadn't called, and he hadn't answered his phone on either of the occasions she had tried calling him. On Ida's voicemail she heard Ida's soft, cheerful voice asking her to leave a message. It almost hurt to listen to that now, and Nina felt herself cringe inside as she contemplated a short message in a casual voice. "Hi, it's Mom. Call me," or "Hi, honey, just wanted to see how you were."

She gave up, hanging up and setting the phone back down on the nightstand. She didn't want to leave a message. She shouldn't have to. Her family knew exactly where she was, and a friendly nurse had made sure that Morten got a text message with her direct number.

Nina tried to breathe slowly and calmly. The sun colored the darkness a flickery red whenever she shut her eyes, but it helped. She would rest now, just a little. When she woke up again, Morten could come pick her up, and she could sort out this business with Ida and the break-in.

S KOU-LARSEN WOKE UP slowly, disoriented. The
TV was on, and the curtains in the living room
were drawn. He was lying on the sofa with the crocheted
blanket over him, but he couldn't remember having put
it there. His mouth and throat were dry, and he felt like
he had been snoring.

He stared up at the wood paneling of the ceiling. Helle
had had it whitewashed a few years earlier, it brightened things up so nicely, she said. He thought it looked
strangely half-finished, as if someone had started painting and then hadn't bothered to give it a second coat so it
covered properly.

"Helle?" he called.

There was no response. Maybe she was out in the garden? No, probably not now, it must be dark outside. Or
was it? He tried to focus on his Tissot watch with the
nice, wide-linked watchband—a retirement gift from
the office—and when he saw that it was a few minutes
to eight, he was genuinely puzzled as to whether it was
eight in the morning or eight at night.

But that was the local news on the TV, wasn't it? So
it must be evening. How long had he been lying on the
sofa?

"Helle?" He slowly swung his legs out from under
the blanket and sat up. How come he felt so weak and
dizzy? And Helle still didn't answer. Was she mad at him
again? No. That wasn't it. The house seemed empty;
there weren't any noises other than those of the house

itself—the door upstairs that always banged if the bathroom window was open, a subtle gurgling from the water pipes every now and then, the lilac branches scraping against the windowpane in the office.

He felt abandoned. For a brief instant he had the absurd notion that maybe Helle had decided to leave him. Despite their age difference, it wasn't a thought that had ever occurred to him before. After all, she was the one who needed him, not the other way around.

Or did she? As he had aged, had there not been a shift in the balance of power between them, so gradual and indiscernible that he had barely noticed it? She had begun to go out on her own lately. Had left the house and the garden without having him by her side, something that had always been hard for her. She had also learned how to use the computer Claus had given them, so she could send e-mails and be in touch with other people that way. He had taken it as a good sign, but perhaps it wasn't.

Maybe that was how she had ended up buying that idiotic condo in Spain.

This new, unwelcome realization struck him with a burst of small, cold prickles. Of course that was why. She hadn't been planning it as a surprise, as she had claimed. She had never intended for them to travel there together in the winter months to help his arthritis. She would never have told him about it if he hadn't found the bank statement himself. Maybe he should count himself lucky that it had turned out to be a scam. If the condo had existed, she might have been down there already, on one of those ocean-front balconies they showed in the pictures in the brochure, enjoying a sangría while her swimsuit dried on the railing. Probably with . . .

Who? This was where his foggy imagination faltered. He had a really, really hard time picturing Helle with another man. Not that she wasn't still attractive in that classic Nordic way, with high cheekbones and silvery streaks in her sun-bleached hair. She had never been an aggressive sunbather; she usually wore a hat in the garden so her skin wasn't scorched and ravaged like so many other women of her generation. But she had never been an enthusiastic partner when it came to sex, and in recent years . . .

Or was it just him? He had always been patient, considerate, carefully awaiting her response before proceding. Had that been a mistake?

He stood up. Even though he was aware that his actions were paranoid, he went straight to the bedroom and flung open the closet. Not to see if there was a young lover hiding inside, but to see if all her clothes were still there. She hadn't packed anything. Their suitcases were sitting in their usual spot on top of the white cabinets, and as far as he could tell, nothing was missing.

He proceeded into the bathroom, dumped his toothbrush out of its glass and drank from it, even though the water tasted faintly of Colgate. His mouth was so dry that a cactus would feel at home. He filled the glass again and brought it back out to the living room. Some hairy-chested macho type with sideburns, someone who didn't wait for permission. Was that the kind of man she had fallen for?

No. Not Helle. He smiled despite his general despondency. She was the last woman in the world who would do something like that.

SHE CAME HOME a little before 9 P.M., while he was waiting for the Danish Broadcasting Corporation's evening news to start. She hung her cotton coat in the hall and came in as if nothing had happened.

"Ah, you're awake," she said.

"Where have you been?" he asked.

"At Holger and Lise's, of course. True, we couldn't play bridge without you, but we had a nice time anyway. Lise made Cordon Bleu. It's a shame you missed it."

Holger and Lise. Bridge. Now he remembered.

"Why didn't you wake me?"

"Darling, I tried. I did, but you were completely out. Do you think maybe you've got your pills mixed up again?"

"Pills?"

"Yes. You do know that the Imovanes are the sleeping pills and Fortzaar is for your blood pressure, right?"

"Of course I know that," he said. "I've been taking them for years. The blood pressure pills, anyway." The Imovanes were relatively new; he had started taking those after complaining about insomnia and restless legs. Just a half pill, his doctor had said, and he had stuck to that.

"Maybe you should let me fill your pill case for you," Helle suggested.

"I'm perfectly capable of doing it myself," he snapped, picturing the plastic case he loaded his pills into every Sunday, labeled MORNING, NOON, EVENING, and NIGHT along one side and all the days of the week on the other, in clear, blue capital letters. "I'm not an idiot!"

But she wasn't listening anymore. She was staring at the TV instead. Then she grabbed the remote control and turned up the volume.

". . . officials believe that up to fifty people have been exposed to radioactive contamination, and they ask that anyone who has been in the proximity of this address within the past few weeks to report to the Danish National Institute of Radiation Hygiene for a screening. Further information can be found on our website."

Radioactive contamination?

Skou-Larsen forgot all about the pill organizer, side-burns, and bridge games for a moment.

"There was something about that on the news at six, too," Helle said. "But they haven't figured out where it came from. Have you heard anything?"

"No," he grunted, watching as an expert who looked more like a professional soccer player than a nuclear physicist explained about background radiation and radon, which was "the most common source of radioactive contamination in buildings." A fence and a couple of gas pumps and two men in bright-yellow protective suits were visible, walking around holding devices he assumed were Geiger counters. And then of course they showed the footage from Chernobyl again, even though Skou-Larsen couldn't see what that had to do with any of this. There was a world of difference between a nuclear reactor melting down and radon contamination, but as soon as anyone said the word "radioactivity," the media always went into a frenzy.

"I'm sure it's just underground seepage or emissions from construction materials," he said, irritated that the cameraman was focusing on the protective suits instead of on the buildings, which were somewhat more relevant.

"Seepage?"

"Yes. It can be a real nuisance if the building is built on moraine clay. All the way up to six hundred becquerels per cubic meter. That could easily make you sick."

The camera moved to a new expert, this time a less photogenic one from Risø Laboratory.

"Then why are they suddenly talking about cesium now?" Helle asked. "That's not the same thing as radon, is it?"

"No," Skou-Larsen mused.

"Does that seep up from underground, too?"

Skou-Larsen shook his head slightly. His mouth still felt pasty and terribly dry.

"No," he said. "It doesn't."

NINA **WOKE UP** to the sound of trays clattering in the corridor outside. Nurses' heels striking the floor with a rhythmic clack. What time was it? She must have been asleep, but for how long? They had packed all her clothes and other possessions into a yellow plastic bag, her watch included, and it took her a few seconds to focus on the clock over the door. 9:10 P.M. Her head felt better. Razor sharp, actually. Nothing hurt anymore, and she could stretch out to her full height without being afraid of throwing up. They had also finally removed the tube from her nostril. The nausea was still there, lurking, she noted, but distantly. She decided to pretend it wasn't there anymore.

Nina swung her legs over the edge of the bed and tentatively put her feet on the floor. She felt her pulse explode in a wild frenzy as she slowly transferred her weight onto her feeble legs and took a couple of steps into the room. Things worked, she thought, relieved. She was functional again. She cast an irritated glance at the IV bag and stand she was still tethered to. Then she turned off the drip and pulled out the Venflon mechanism taped to her left hand. She didn't have any Band-Aids and had to make do with pressing a paper napkin from the nightstand drawer against the back of her hand until the bleeding stopped, but now she was free.

She walked across the floor with faltering steps to the bathroom and peed with the door open. She felt a single drop of sweat trickle from her temple down her cheek and neck. Her heart was racing, and she sat for a few minutes fighting the nausea churning in her stomach. But so far so good. She had conquered the bathroom, she thought, doing a sarcastic little fanfare for herself in her head. Now all that remained was the rest of the world.

She got up, washed her hands and face in the cold jet from the faucet and slowly started staggering back across the floor. It felt like walking on cotton.

Then she stumbled.

One of her feet simply gave way beneath her as she went to take the last step over to her bed. She landed hard on her hipbone on the mottled gray floor, and the sudden pain made her hiss between her teeth. She pulled herself up into a sitting position and glared furiously at her right foot, cursing her own clumsiness. She had seen plenty of patients do exactly this. Flail around on their own before they were strong enough, fall, and end up in an even worse state than when they first arrived at the hospital. Luckily her hip still worked. The pain had already faded to a dull throb, and the fall would result in a bruise at most, but still hurt. Nina took hold of the bed and hauled herself to her feet, with her heart pounding frenetically beneath her hospital gown. A sound from over by the door made her stop in mid-motion. A sort of drawn-out sigh. She turned her head and saw Morten.

He was standing in the doorway with his arms dangling weirdly, hanging too straight from his shoulders, as if they had stopped working. She hadn't even noticed the door opening. How long had he been standing there and had he seen her fall? There was something about the look on his face that made the last of the strength in Nina's

legs give way, and she plopped down onto the edge of
the bed and pulled her arms around herself and the limp
hospital gown.

"Let me help you."

Morten came over to her, carefully raised her legs onto
the bed, and tucked the blanket in around her.

"I tried calling you," she said, reproachfully. "Several
times."

She followed his movements with her eyes. He didn't
look at her, and his hands kept stroking the blanket as if
he were smoothing out invisible wrinkles in the bedding.
He was trying to smile, she could tell, but it wasn't really
working. Suddenly Nina felt afraid. What had happened?
Was there something Magnus hadn't told her after all?

"Is it Ida?"

Morten looked up for a brief instant.

"She's upset, but . . ." He cut himself short. "How are
you doing?"

Nina felt a sense of relief along with a touch of confusion. Why was he asking her about it like that? Politely.
As if he were a co-worker, or a distant relation. She
reached out with her hands and cautiously tried to pull
him a little closer, but he resisted. At first it was subtle, a
faint counter pressure, a tension in his neck muscles, but
when she didn't let go, he suddenly yanked himself free
and backed away. And then he made eye contact for the
first time. He looked tired and haggard. As if he had been
crying, but Morten almost never cried. He got mad and
swore, but he didn't cry.

"Excuse me."

A health care assistant in a white coat slid into the

room with a broad smile. She closed the curtains, then stood by the window for a minute, shuffling her feet before she decided to fill Nina's water glass. She took the glass and went to the small bathroom, and Nina could hear the water running. Morten didn't say anything. He glanced impatiently at the open bathroom door in irritation.

"They don't usually fill the patients' water glasses in the bathroom."

Nina said that more to herself than to Morten, and he didn't respond. The assistant made a clattering noise with something or other in the bathroom, and Nina and Morten sat for a long moment waiting for her to finish up and leave. Then Morten gave up and started up the conversation again.

"I'm going to say something now," Morten said, looking resolute. "And afterward I'll leave so you can have some peace and quiet to . . . rest."

Nina nodded slowly, attempted to smile, but a chilling fear begin to spread beneath her breastbone. This didn't seem like one of the dressing-downs that Morten usually dumped on her when he was angry. This wasn't like anything she had seen before.

"Ida was home by herself Saturday night," Morten said, and his voice trembled a little. "She was home alone in the middle of the night in an apartment in Østerbro because her mother was in the hospital."

Nina raised her hand halfway to protest. It wasn't correct that Ida had been home alone because Nina was sick. If Nina hadn't gone to the Coal-House Camp, she would have been spending the night in a foul-smelling scout cabin with Anton. Ida was supposed to be spending the night with Anna. That was the agreement.

Morten brushed her aside with a tired motion.

"Ida's mother wasn't home because she had come down with radiation sickness. On multiple occasions, as I have learned, she visited a flock of sick Eastern Europeans in Valby even though she had promised not to do that kind of work while I was in the North Sea."

Morten's tired eyes, red from crying, caught hers and held them.

"I'm sorry," he said. "Not Ida's mother, you. *You* promised, Nina."

She cringed under his gaze. The nausea was coming back now, and there was a faint rushing sound in her ears.

"While you were in the hospital, three men broke into the apartment, where Ida was alone with a boyfriend I've never heard of. They beat him, and Ida, who was half naked . . ."

Nina looked down at her hands. Please, would he stop soon? Could she stand to hear any more?

"They took pictures of her. They humiliated her. Our little girl."

Morten's eyes looked exhausted, lifeless.

"I have no idea if the break-in was related to what you were doing in Valby. But, do you know what? I couldn't care less, Nina. It doesn't interest me anymore. Our apartment has been sealed off because of potential radioactive contamination. As has our car."

Morten flung out his arms, almost helplessly, Nina thought, feeling something hard and painful lodge itself like a lump in her throat. Then he took another step away from the bed.

"If it was just you and me . . ." he said. "But it isn't. And I simply can't understand . . . I simply can't let you bring Anton and Ida along with you into . . . into that permanent war zone you insist on living in. We've moved down to my sister's for the time being. That's what I came to tell you."

For the time being, she heard. For a while. Maybe he *could* live with this, maybe they would be okay again.

But he kept moving toward the door, and then he opened it, and he was almost all the way out in the corridor before he turned around and looked at her with an unrelenting determination that destroyed her illusion.

"This is it for me, Nina," he said quietly. "It's over."

NINA WOULD HAVE called out to him, but she couldn't think what to say to make him stay. He stood in the doorway for a microsecond. As if he wanted to give her a mental snapshot for the family album. His long, slightly stooped silhouette. His shoulders, which along with his narrow hips formed a perfect V under the loose T-shirt. She knew that body down to the smallest detail, and images of Morten from their sixteen years together flickered through her mind. How he had stood at the foot of their bed a thousand times, tiredly pulling his T-shirt up over his head. The birthmark under his right shoulder blade, the soft armpits, the long muscular legs, and the soft, dark hair that covered his chest, arms, legs, and groin. His smile when he turned around and looked at her. But this time he didn't turn around.

He didn't even look back once as he turned down the corridor. Her diaphragm contracted painfully. As if she had been smacked in the stomach by a ball Anton had kicked. The realization that he was leaving her, that he had already left, struck in a single brutal blow.

In the bathroom the laggardly assistant clattered around, cleared her throat, and then finally reappeared with a full water glass in her hand that she passed to Nina.

"They don't fill patients' water glasses in the bathroom," Nina said mechanically, and turned her sluggish eyes toward the assistant's freckled face. She looked strangely guilty, Nina thought. As if she knew she was doing something she wasn't supposed to. And her coat was white, not yellow. A faint suspicion crept to the front of Nina's consciousness. Why was she even in the room? There was no reason for her to close the curtains. Nina hadn't asked for any water.

The woman cleared her throat and pulled the corners of her mouth up into an expression that was supposed to resemble something halfway between perky and kindhearted.

"I'm sorry," she said. "My name is Lone Walter, and I'm a journalist with *Ekstra Bladet*. Would you mind if I asked you a couple of questions?"

A little red spark of rage shot up through Nina. A journalist! Of course. No real health care worker had time to waste the way this woman had just done. Nina looked over at the empty doorway where Morten had disappeared.

"Did you get all that?" Nina tried to make her voice sound cool and collected as she turned her eyes back to the woman by her bed.

"I don't know what you mean."

The woman's fake smile persisted, unflappable, and Nina finally felt the nausea regaining the upper hand. She reached for the basin next to her bed and vomited in long, pink jets. Blackcurrant juice, Nina thought, and looked up at the now slightly flustered journalist.

"Get the hell out of here," she said. "I don't want to talk to you. I don't want to talk to anyone."

SÁNDOR DIDN'T UNDERSTAND a word of what the nervous looking television commentator said, but his two captors obviously did.

"Fuck," Frederik hissed, slamming his can of beer onto the glass top of the coffee table with a bang. "Shit, shit, shit." In a flash he snatched the can back up again and hurled it at the window, where it hit the plastic covering the window with a soft, dissatisfying sound before clattering to the ground. The smell of top-fermented beer filled the room.

Tommi didn't say anything. He just kicked the TV console so hard that the flat screen tipped over backward and hit the floor with an ominous crunch. Despite the fall, the TV kept displaying footage of the garage in Valby surrounded by yellow-and-black striped tape and people in yellow spacesuits.

Sándor remained motionless in his black leather recliner without saying anything, without drawing any attention to himself, without providing any provocation.

They weren't in the city anymore, but some distance outside, Sándor didn't have any real sense of where. The sound of planes taking off and landing could be heard at regular intervals not that far away, but when they arrived in midmorning after a long and frustrating night, he had seen grazing horses and flocks of wild geese. From the outside it looked to be just a fairly ordinary, red-brick farmhouse sitting alongside a derelict stable, and a dilapidated garage structure. Sándor didn't know what they were doing here, and no one told him. Tamás wasn't here.

"You don't get to see him until we have the jacket," Frederik had said.

The inside of the house was bizarre. The wallpaper, in what must at one time have been the living room, was painted a lurid eggplant purple, and on the walls was a series of equally lurid posters in clip frames. They weren't there just for their entertainment value, they were a sales catalog. The girls, holding their breasts out provocatively at the viewer with both hands or suggestively rubbing their crotches, were accompanied by texts in German and English and a third language he assumed was Danish. "Russian Katarina, twenty-three, loves oral, anal, and gentle dominance; Anna from Riga, only fifteen years old—do you want to be her first?" But neither Anna nor Katarina nor any of their colleagues were in evidence, and some of the frames had already been taken down to make room for a half-hearted normalization of the room involving a lot of white paint, some wood paneling, and several plastic-wrapped bales of rock wool insulation.

In the middle of all that, there was an arrangement with a three-seater sofa, love seat, and armchair, as well as a glass-topped coffee table and TV console, a little island of bourgeois conventionality in the midst of the brothel ambience. Frederik had slept on the longer sofa for a few hours, Tommi on the shorter one, while Sándor had been left to curl up in the armchair.

In the twenty-four hours that had elapsed since the break-in on Fejøgade, Tommi and Frederik had become increasingly frustrated. They hadn't been able to find the nurse or her car, in spite of all the information they had frightened, threatened, and shaken out of the teenage girl and her boyfriend. Sándor still felt a deep stab of guilt when he thought of those terrified teenagers; of the boy's pretended cockiness as he nerved himself up to defend his girlfriend, of the sound it had made when Tommi nonchalantly whacked his head into the doorframe. Of the girl who had let go of the blanket and tried to kick Tommi with her bare feet, of how she yelled and screamed and lashed out at him even though all she had on was her panties. Of Tommi who had held her, just held her from behind, while Frederik grabbed the mobile phone and took pictures of her both with and without her panties on.

"Sweet little pussy," Tommi had whispered in the girl's ear, but loud enough that they could all hear it. "Just let us know when you get tired of the boy wonder over there, and we'll get you a real man."

Then she got scared, Sándor could tell. Until that point she had been shocked, anxious, upset, and furious, but only then did terror set in. She curled up in his grasp, trying to protect her body from the violation of the camera.

Don't give up, Sándor had wanted to tell her. Don't let go of your defiance and your rage. But to her he would have just been one of the attackers, the only one of her assailants whose face she could describe. My God, how old had she been? Fifteen? Sixteen? Maybe even younger. She was definitely still in school; Tommi had stolen her school bag.

And you did nothing, Sándor told himself caustically.

You just stood there and did nothing. His passivity was a crime, and he couldn't think of any way he could atone for it.

Frederik stood the flat screen back up. The picture flickered a little and disappeared, along with the sound, in a storm of multicolored pixels.

"Can they trace Valby to us?" Tommi asked. Still in English, in that strangely broad, rolling accent that sounded so wrong to Sándor's ears.

"Not right away," Frederik said. "It depends on how long Malee keeps her trap shut."

"She won't say anything," Tommi said.

"They always do at some point or other."

"Not Malee. She was one of the strong ones. She was in the tank three times before she gave up."

"And you think that is going to make her love you?"

"No. But she remembers me. And after that lot, she won't cave just because the police ask her a couple of polite questions."

Frederik grumbled. "What are we going to do?" he said. "We can't leave that thing out there for ever. And the car. You think it's radioactive, too?"

Tommi shrugged dubiously.

Suddenly Frederik jumped up and went outside.

"Where are you going?" Tommi yelled.

"To get Tyson. He shouldn't be out there."

Tommi rolled his beer can back and forth between his palms.

"He spoils that mutt," he told Sándor. "A wife and two point five kids in Søllerød, but sometimes I think he loves the dog more."

Quit telling me stuff like that, Sándor pleaded silently. I don't want to know that he's married or where he lives. I don't want to know anything about you two at all. I just want to get my brother and go home.

But Tamás . . . How could he even find out if Tamás was still alive? He had asked to see him, be allowed to speak to him, even if just by phone. But aside from that repulsive video, they hadn't given him any sign of life.

"You're from Hungary, aren't you?" Tommi asked suddenly, leaning forward.

Sándor stiffened. Sat even stiller, if that were possible.

"Yes," he said, without looking Tommi in the eye. No opposition, no provocation.

"How do you say 'house' in Hungarian?" Tommi asked, making an expansive gesture with his hand to illustrate what he meant by drawing Sándor's attention to the derelict farmhouse they were sitting in.

"*Haz.*"

Tommi looked disappointed.

"Huh," was all he said.

Frederik came back in again, now with an enthusiastically barking Labrador dancing around his feet.

"Okay, down! No jumping," he commanded, with a certain lack of impact. "Go lie down, Tyson." He pointed authoritatively to the shag rug under the coffee table. Tyson jumped up onto the sofa next to Tommi instead and settled there. Tommi shot him a dirty look.

"Okay," Tommi said. "So, we have this damn thing out there in the shed. And apparently it's leaking like crazy. What are we going to do about it?"

"Call the authorities, and get the hell out of here," Frederik said. "Well, in the opposite order obviously."

"Fucking brilliant," Tommi said. "Then they have both Valby *and* this place. How long do you think it'll take before they figure out we actually own them both? And what about the money?"

"Okay, so we dump it somewhere."

Tommi held up his hand defensively, more or less in front of his crotch. "No way I'm going to have *my* onions toasted. I'm not touching that shit. Not again." Then he suddenly looked pale. "You think we've already been affected? Fuck. That little shit. I would strangle him if he weren't already dead."

Frederik sliced his hand through the air as if he wanted to cut off the torrent of words. But it was too late. Sándor had heard and understood. If he weren't already dead.

Something churned deep down inside him. Hot, fluid, and alien. He sat there in complete silence, noting the feeling, observing how it rose and rose, pouring like lava into every part of his body. He was looking at the two men who had let his brother die. Who had watched while he got weaker and sicker. As he lost the use of his limbs and his vision and finally his ability to breathe or make his heart beat.

Sándor split into two. One part of him was still sitting in the chair, watching, passive, neutral. He had never had an out-of-body experience before, but that was what was happening now. His rage *was* his body, and as he hurled himself across the coffee table and jabbed his elbow horizontally into the face of that little psychopathic wannabe cowboy, it was as if he could again taste the mixture of blood, saliva, and moisturizer from the *gadjo* woman who had once tried to take his siblings from him.

He only heard the screams from a distance. To begin with he didn't even feel the pummeling blows he was receiving. He bit into something that felt cartilaginous and earlobe-like, hammered the base of his palm into a throat, thrust his elbow into a soft abdomen. Something struck him on the back of the head, making the sounds even more distant, but he didn't stop hitting and kicking. Not even when he was picked up and hurled to the floor or when it got hard to breathe because someone was sitting on his battered ribcage.

The first thing that penetrated through the fog was a searing, white-hot pain in one of his hands. He instinctively tried to pull it toward himself, but that only made the pain worse. He was stuck. And suddenly he was back in the painful shell of his body, excruciatingly aware of every single blunt protest from his ribs, kidneys, and head, but especially the screeching, unbearable pulse pounding in his left hand.

"Fuckhead," Tommi said testily. "Now look what you've done."

Blood was pouring down the lower half of the pseudo-cowboy's face, but Sándor didn't care about that right now. He turned and stared at his left hand, which was stuck securely to the floor with two nails from a nail gun.

Frederik must have fired the gun, since he was still standing there holding it in his hand.

"Give me that," Tommi said, yanking it out of Frederik's grip. He put one knee on Sándor's chest, forcing him onto his back again, and pressing the cold tip of the nail gun against his forehead just above the bridge of his nose. Sándor instinctively tried to focus, squinting at the green Bosch tool.

"No . . ." he said, in Hungarian, *Nem!*, but it didn't really matter if that psycho cowboy understood him or not. The inevitability was palpable in the weight of the tip of the nail, in the pressure of the knee on his chest.

"Cut it out," Frederik said.

"Why? He broke my nose!" Tommi said.

"Yeah, but you said it yourself. *You* don't want to fry your onions."

"What are you talking about?"

"Someone's going to have to move that thing out there. Are you volunteering?"

The nail gun vanished from Sándor's squinting field of vision. The weight was lifted off his rib cage.

"Fuck," Tommi said. "Fucking hell. Goddamn it!"

"Find a hacksaw or a pair of pliers or something and get him up off the floor. I'll go get the first aid kit from the car so he doesn't bleed out on us."

Sándor lay there on the floor like a half-crucified sinner, his sense of relief struggling against the nausea. But maybe there was no cause for relief. If only that guy had fired, it would all be over now. No more pain, no more guilt. Then he would just be dead.

Like Tamás.

"WHITE AS SNOW, red as blood . . ."

For some reason that fairy tale line was the first thought that struck Søren as he pulled the blanket away from the young man's face. Even through his mask, Søren thought he could smell the sweet, rotten stench.

"And hair as black as ebony."

Snow White from Hell, Søren thought, looking at the long, greasy strands of hair that stuck to the boy's forehead. His narrow face gleamed white under the floodlights the Emergency Management Agency had set up at the crime scene, and his chin was covered with dried brownish streaks of blood that had apparently come from both his mouth and nose. Just under his hairline at one temple there was a crater of a wound that shimmered in shades of green and white, and a fresher sore on his cheekbone appeared to be the source of the broad reddish-brown streaks that ran across his cheek like war paint. Søren couldn't help but wonder if it had been smeared like that before or after his death. He looked down into the dark, underground metal tank from which the body had just been pulled, and shivered.

"Can you say anything about the cause of death?"

One of the forensic technicians who had placed the young man on the stretcher shrugged his shoulders. The man's nose and mouth were covered by his black respirator face mask, and the reflection of the lights in the glass visor meant that Søren only got a rather blurry view of his eyes. But his arms were drooping, and he looked tired. They had been working out here for almost twenty-four hours, Søren knew, even though they hadn't opened the cover to the repair shop's old gas tank until about 3 A.M.

"It's too early to say, but at first glance he doesn't seem to have been shot, strangled, or beaten, so I'd guess it's either radiation sickness or suffocation that killed him. Personally my money's on radiation."

Søren raised his eyebrows behind his own protective mask. The tech leaned across the dead body and cautiously peeled back the shirt so Søren could see the top of the boy's torso. He instinctively took a step back. The chest was mottled with blackish-brown hematomas. Like enormous blood blisters, Søren thought, feeling the nausea kick in his gut. In several places the hematomas had turned into open sores that stuck to the plaid fabric of the shirt in patches.

"I'm no doctor," the technician said. "But that doesn't look healthy. The coroner's on his way."

Søren looked at the bloody streaks on the boy's cheeks again, and the half-frozen bread roll he had managed to wolf down in the car on the way out to Valby churned in his stomach. The boy on the stretcher under the floodlights looked like he had cried blood and then smeared it across his own cheeks, like a snotty five-year-old might have done with his tears. Søren had been a policeman for almost twenty-five years, but he occasionally still saw things he wished he could unsee. He caught himself hoping the boy had at least been dead before he was entombed in that damn gas tank. To think otherwise was near unbearable.

As far as Søren had been informed, it had started as a case for the police and the Emergency Management Agency early yesterday morning, but the investigation had been triggered because they thought the Hungarian Roma who had been staying at the garage had suffered an accidental contamination, perhaps from radioactive scrap somewhere back in Eastern Europe. That theory had crumbled when the Geiger counters started howling hysterically down in the covered inspection pit. They hadn't found the actual source, but small amounts of radioactive sand were still there, revealing where the material had presumably been stored. And when they found the body in the tank, the alarm bells really started going off. Especially because of the passport they had found in his shoe. The police had run a routine check on the computer and called the PET.

Søren ran a hand through his hair, as if to brush the last remnants of sleep away. Morning fatigue still sat heavily in his body, but he could also feel his hunting instincts sending small surges of eagerness and heightened attention to his brain and muscles. Because the name in the Hungarian passport was Sándor Horváth, which tied the find in Valby to the investigation of Khalid Hosseini and the weapons trail in a particularly ominous way.

Søren started walking back toward the barriers a few hundred meters away. His yellow protective suit was cumbersome and crinkled stiffly as he walked, but it was only once he had made it all the way out to the other side of the flashing cars that he was finally allowed to undo the silver-colored duct tape that sealed the suit at his wrists and ankles. He handed the gloves, suit, and mask to yet another spacesuit-clad younger man, whom he assumed was from the Emergency Management Agency or the National Institute of Radiation Hygiene and allowed himself to be taken to a hastily set up trailer with showers.

Once he was back in his own clothes, his hair wet in the morning chill, he was directed to the green minivan that was parked a little farther down the road. Outside the van, surrounded by a group of police officers in a heated discussion, stood a short, angular man with a phone in one hand and a heavily laden clipboard in the other.

"He certainly can't," the man barked into his phone. "He'll have to do that later. I need him now!" He looked up as Søren approached. "This is hopeless. Half the people we need are off on that Secure Information Networks course. Are you one of the people from Radiation Hygiene?"

"Sorry. Søren Kirkegård, PET." He stretched out his hand, and the man gave it a skeptical look as if he thought it might be contaminated. Eventually, though, he held out his own hand to complete the handshake and nodded curtly.

"Birger Johansen. Yes, I can see why you might also have an interest in this case. What do you need to know?"

"First and foremost, what substance are we dealing with, and what can it be used for?"

"Cesium chloride. I thought you knew that."

"Yes," Søren said patiently. "But what does that mean? For example, can it be used to make a bomb?"

The man snorted, clearly disgusted at Søren's abysmal ignorance.

"Not an atomic bomb. That's completely out of the question."

Søren nodded. So far his conjectures were proving correct.

"But an ingredient in a dirty bomb?" Søren suggested. "Could it be used for that?"

It was as if Birger Johansen were yanked down out of his pulpit of know-it-all arrogance for the first time.

"Well, ultimately any kind of radioactive material could be used for that," he said. "The explosive force comes from a conventional detonation, of course. The radioactivity is just a . . . way of making the effects more unpleasant for longer."

"And how effective would cesium chloride be at that?"

"Unfortunately it's one of the most suitable substances available, if widespread contamination is the goal. It enters the environment very easily because it's a powder, not a metal, and it reacts with pretty much any form of moisture."

Søren felt something tighten in his chest and thought about Snow White's bloody tears. Personally, he would rather be blown sky-high than end up like that.

"But you haven't been able to track down the main source?"

"No. We're assuming it was stored in the inspection pit for a few days. We found a small amount of radioactive sand, and the radiation level in general is extremely high right around there."

"What did it take to move it?"

"What do you mean?"

"What kind of equipment? How big a vehicle? What

are we searching for? A lone idiot with a wheelbarrow or a well-organized group with forklifts and trucks?"

Johansen raised a pair of thin, colorless eyebrows. The reflected glare from the windows of the minivan made the thinning hair on the top of his head glow strangely.

"Impossible to answer that one."

"Why?"

"It depends on what kind of containment shielding they used. It could be anything from seventy to eighty kilograms of lead to a couple of bags of sand. The source itself isn't very big on its own."

Søren struggled to suppress his irritation. Presumably the man didn't mean to be unhelpful, it was just his general condescending style that made him seem that way.

"The radioactive sand you found. Could that have come from the containment shielding?"

"It's possible. Lead or concrete are better, but then there wouldn't have been such severe contamination if we were dealing with professionals, would there?" Johansen said. "Whoever did this obviously had no idea of the correct way to store this kind of material."

Based on what Søren had seen so far, neither Horváth nor Khalid seemed like professionals. Nor did they need to be, unfortunately, to set off a dirty bomb, he thought. Besides, he had a strong feeling that the overall picture was going to include something else, something more than those two. If Horváth was the guy they had just hauled out of the gas tank, then he certainly didn't have the cesium now. And based on their surveillance, Khalid had never been anywhere near the Valby address.

"How many of the people living here have you found?" Søren asked.

Birger Johansen looked at him with a weary expression and turned an expectant face to the two nearest police officers. They weren't wearing uniforms, and Søren guessed they were the local detectives who had been assigned to the operation.

"A dozen adults, plus a couple of kids," one of them said. "But we haven't been able to question them all. They speak neither German nor English, so we're still hunting around for interpreters."

"And how many people were staying here?"

Birger Johansen pushed a pair of narrow reading glasses into place on his nose and flipped through the papers he was holding in his hand.

"Based on the number of makeshift beds, we're missing at least thirty of the tenants, if you can call them that. I don't know how those Gypsies do it, but they weren't here when we moved on the address, and they haven't been back since. Someone must have tipped them off. They aren't exactly keen on the police, you know . . ."

Frustrated, Johansen rolled a pen between two fingers and tipped it toward the two detectives.

"The police have asked all officers to be on the lookout for Gypsies in town, and so far they've picked up about sixty of them from locations such as the Central Railway Station, Vesterbro, and Strøget, but then that's twice as many as we're looking for, and we have no way of knowing if we've got the right ones. I don't even think they're all from Hungary. Some of them are sitting in the police station downtown right now, but of course they won't say boo in any language any of us can understand. It's a little like herding cats."

Søren nodded.

"Then I suppose we'd better start with the Danish witnesses," he said. "I understand there was a woman who tipped you off about the radioactive material."

"Tipping off is perhaps not quite the word," Birger Johansen said crossly. "She was admitted to the hospital with radiation sickness Saturday night and was then gracious enough to tell us where she'd been. A nurse. Apparently, she had been attending some of the children. Not entirely legit, you know. She's pretty sick because of the radiation so it wasn't all that easy to talk to her. If I were you, I'd start with her 'colleague.'" Birger Johansen made air quotes with his fingers with a condescending smile, which for some reason or other particularly pissed Søren off. He ignored the sarcasm.

"And his name is?"

"Peter something-or-other. It's all in there." Birger Johansen detached a couple of sheets of paper from his clipboard and grudgingly offered them to Søren, then pulled out his phone again and entered a number. "If you have questions, just call me later."

Søren folded the papers in half and started walking back to his car.

"I doubt you'll get much useful information out of those two." Birger Johansen was standing behind him in a jaunty position, his stance wide, phone held rather abortedly at head height. "They're both bleeding-heart liberals. The kind who think they can save the whole world."

Søren smiled as politely as he could manage. Farther

up the road, he could still see the cluster of flashing police cars and fire trucks, and the image of Snow White from the gas tank flitted ephemerally through his mind. The edges of those weeping, crater-like sores, the yellowish fluid that had soaked the boy's shirt, and the bloody tears. The ironic cynicism of Birger Johansen's comment was wasted on Søren this morning. If anyone was volunteering to save the world, that was just fine with him. It certainly needed doing.

HE CALLED GITTE and woke her up.

"Yes?" she said in that aquarium voice people had when they've just been hauled up from the depths of sleep.

"Drag Khalid Hosseini in and get one of the real pros to interrogate him. HC or someone like him. And tell Christian that I need everything he can get out of that computer *now*."

"HC is in the middle of a training exercise for the Summit," she said.

"So call him back in. Right now there's nothing out there more important than this. No, wait. You're going to have to clear it with Torben first. Tell him I'll call and explain. But bring Khalid in now. And make sure there's a fresh report summarizing everything we have on him—phone contacts, surveillance, the works. Plus, I want to know everything we can dig up on this address in Valby. Gasbetonvej 35. Who owns it, who uses it, and for what."

"Yes, sir. Will that be all?"

She wasn't being sarcastic. That was just Gitte.

"No. Also . . . the Emergency Management Agency

removed some Hungarian Roma from the Valby property. Find out where they are now, and see if you can get anything out of the women. You're good with languages."

"Um, not Hungarian."

"I'm sure it's just as important that you're good at winning people's trust. Get as much information on this group of people as you can. And ask them if they've seen the damned cesium. Birger Johansen from the Emergency Management Agency can tell you a little about what it might look like. Just keep pushing him until you get a real answer."

He gave her Johansen's number.

"Okay. Anything else?"

"We need to get in touch with Hungary and get the NBH to give us some more about Sándor Horváth's background. But I suppose I'll put Torben on that. No, nothing else for you. And, uh, sorry I woke you up."

"*De nada*," she said with a very authentic sounding Spanish accent. "Uh, but, boss . . . what exactly is going on? I mean what's the big picture?"

"The fat's in the fire," he just said. "See you at the briefing at noon. I just have a couple of witnesses to grill first."

"**D**EAD?"

The tall, bony man in the yellow hospital gown stared at Søren in disbelief. He was a little disheveled to look at. In Søren's opinion, his thin, blond hair should have been cut a few weeks ago. It stuck out in flat, greasy tufts, and below that he could just make out the man's pink scalp, so that he looked vaguely like a newly hatched chick. Peter Erhardsen had already been in a nervous sweat when Søren entered the room, and when he heard the news about the body, he looked as if he had been punched in the face.

"Are you sure?" He shook his head. "I mean . . . what did he die from?"

"We don't know yet, but his body was so radioactive the Geiger counters found him."

Peter Erhardsen made a strange hiccupping sound and stared fixedly down at the palms of his hands, as if he expected to find some sort of explanation there.

"The first time you went out to the repair shop was May eleventh. Is that correct?"

Peter nodded, cleared his throat, and rested his apparently unhelpful hand on the table between them. He had positioned himself in the seating area by the window instead of in the hospital bed and had tried to make the situation seem normal by offering coffee that he was then unable to produce when Søren accepted it. The man had nearly recovered and was mostly in the hospital for follow-up treatment, but he wasn't allowed to leave his room. At the moment it looked like he desperately wished he had a coffee cup to fiddle with.

"I got a call from one of my acquaintances who'd met some Roma on Strøget," he explained. "My friend is one of those . . . well, he really wanted to help them. Asked them if they needed clothes or medicine or that kind of thing. Everyone knows they have a hard time in Denmark. I mean, that's why they're always out begging."

Peter looked over at Søren as if he expected some form of protest. Peter's eyes were very light blue, and Søren thought he detected an almost aggressive obstinacy beneath the disheveled exterior. He was also guessing that Peter was unlikely to be an entertaining companion at a dinner party.

"But these Roma . . . At first they didn't want anything to do with him. They almost got angry even though my friend was just trying to help. Then suddenly, just a few days later, they called him in complete panic. Something about a young man who'd gotten sick, and they wanted someone to take a look at him. That's why I went out there, and then I also called a nurse I know from . . ."

Peter stopped and got that vacant look in his eyes again.

"The young man, was this him?"

Søren pulled out an enlarged copy of the passport photo from the dead man's shoe and passed it to Peter. He shook his head doubtfully as he looked at the picture with his brow furrowed.

"I don't know. I was never allowed into the room where he was. My friend called me in the morning when I was at work, and I didn't have a chance to go out there until the afternoon, and by then they'd already had second thoughts. Or at least they wouldn't let me see him properly. He was lying in a sort of back office. I was allowed to look in there from the doorway, that was all, but it was totally dark, and it stank to high heaven. Vomit and shit, to put it bluntly. So I called Nina. She's the nurse I mentioned."

"So you didn't get a good look at him?"

"Well, I could see that there was someone lying on a mattress in there. Like I said, it was really dark because the windows were boarded up, but I could see a figure in a fetal position, I could hear him, too, of course. He was moaning, and every once in a while he would start to call out, but I couldn't tell what he was saying. They said he was just sick to his stomach, and I didn't think it was that serious, and Nina, well, she also said . . ." Peter suddenly looked distraught. "Maybe he was already dying when I looked in at him."

He hid his face behind his hands and sat in silence for a moment. Then he straightened himself up and looked at Søren again.

"I'm sorry," he said. "It's just been a hard week."

Søren nodded but didn't offer any words of comfort. He had no interest in soothing the man's guilty conscience.

"So you couldn't say if it was the man in this picture?"

"No." Peter raised a hand in a tired, apologetic motion, pushed his chair back, and got up on unsteady legs. "I have a meeting with the engineering department at eleven this morning," he said, pointing to his watch with his long, bony index finger. "If we're done here, couldn't you just give me the okay . . ."

He stood there with a slightly nervous, beseeching smile. Ran his hand through his thin, tousled hair. He must be almost six foot seven inches, Søren thought. Tall and gangly like a pubescent boy and apparently with the social graces to match. This man had been at the garage while the source was presumably still in the inspection pit. He had seen the people who were there at the time. And now he wanted to run off to a meeting.

"Sit down," Søren said, knowing he was failing to hide his irritation. "We need to know who your friend is."

Peter's nervously optimistic smile visibly faded as he slid back down into the chair again.

"I'd rather not . . ."

"Your friend, the people you talked to out there, the phone numbers you were given . . . everything. And we would also like access to your house."

Now there was something akin to panic in Peter Erhardsen's eyes.

"This is serious. For you, too," Søren said. "We suspect potential terrorist activity on Danish soil, so if I were you, I would be bending over backward to explain exactly how you got it into your head that you and Nina Borg were going to help a bunch of Roma in Valby."

THE WARD NURSE had lent Søren an office and a coffee mug, the side of which was adorned with an amateurish photo of an irritable looking gray Persian cat. Søren gratefully downed the coffee, stale from sitting in the thermos too long, without a thought to its quality—it was the caffeine he was after—and flipped through the notes he had made and the inept descriptions he had managed to coax out of Peter Erhardsen. Maybe the man had done his best, but it was still a pretty poor performance: Roma male, about fifty years old, possibly missing one of his upper teeth, dirty wine-colored shirt. Speaks a little English. Roma female, twenty to thirty years old, has one or more children, average height, very thin . . .

There were eight people and two phone numbers, which he had Mikael Nielsen check right away. One turned out to be a pay-as-you-go phone that was turned off. The other had apparently been canceled a week ago. Neither was going to get them any further right now, and the descriptions couldn't be used for more than a preliminary sorting of the seventy Roma who had been rounded up and were now being held downtown. The border police had also picked up a few on the Øresund Bridge heading for Sweden, so there were plenty to choose from. In the best-case scenario, it would take a few hours, but more likely days, to establish who had been at the garage. And even if the police managed to bring in most of them, it was far from certain that that would get them any closer to the source.

The initial report from Gitte was also very discouraging. The Roma they had picked up at the repair shop all denied seeing anything, no matter which language they were asked in. The police had been forced to use physical force in order to send the children to Bispebjerg Hospital to be examined, and according to Gitte, the adults who had accompanied them had been panicky and terrified to let the children out of their sight.

"They clammed up as if their lives depended on it," as Gitte put it. Søren sank a little farther back in the desk chair, wondering whether the Roma were afraid because they had something to do with the source of the radioactivity or if they were just scared to death whenever they had any kind of official interaction. The latter was at least as likely as the former. There were places in Eastern Europe where Roma women who gave birth in the hospital risked leaving with their fallopian tubes tied. And wasn't there something about Sweden forcibly taking Roma children into care well into the 1970s as standard practice? He had read something about that a few years earlier when the police were trying to get a handle on the integration problems in Elsinore. And then there was Peter himself, who had flatly refused to give them the name of this friend of his who had put him in touch with the Roma in Valby. Søren was increasingly convinced that the "friend" was Peter himself. He only had a vague idea why Peter would make such a bumbling attempt to distance himself from the first contact with the garage in Valby, but it would certainly have to be looked into more closely, and Søren had arranged a search warrant for the man's home address.

He didn't look like your classic terrorist, but then again you never could tell. Looking up Peter Erhardsen in the POLSAG register revealed that he had been arrested a couple of years earlier at a demonstration at the Sandholm refugee camp, where the fence had been cut and several hundred activists had stormed in. Probably to improve conditions for the asylum seekers, which did not necessarily mean that Peter Erhardsen was anything more dire than a soft-hearted humanist. He was, how-ever, definitely an activist, and Søren hadn't felt entirely comfortable with the near-religious zeal he thought he glimpsed beneath Peter's pale-faced nervousness.

The timer on his phone beeped. A quick shave with borrowed amenities and fifteen minutes for coffee and contemplation was what he had allotted himself. Now it was over. It was time to meet Peter's partner-in-activism, the nurse, Nina Borg.

THE MAN FROM PET looked surprisingly ordinary. Nina didn't know exactly what she had been expecting, but certainly someone more mysterious and secretive. A black suit maybe, a crew cut, and black sunglasses. Instead the man who turned up in her hospital room looked amiable enough. He was probably about fifty, wiry, and in good shape under his black T-shirt, with dark, slightly graying hair and a pair of narrow glasses that slid down his curved nose at regular intervals. She hadn't caught his name, but she also didn't care. He was here to learn something from her. Not the other way around. And now he was seated in a chair by the little table in the corner of the hospital room. Someone had brought coffee, a plastic mug, and a bowl of pale yellow Coffee-mate, and he had already started on his first cup before he sat down across from her.

"Is this okay?" He pulled out a shiny little digital recorder, pressed record, and set it on the table without waiting for her response. Then he cleared his throat and aimed a pair of surprisingly Paul Newman-blue eyes at her.

"Valby . . . You told the Emergency Management Agency that you thought the source was in the inspection pit. What gave you that idea? Did you see something?"

Nina's mouth felt strangely dry, but she was no longer sure if the radiation was to blame. She had spent most of the morning sitting in bed, staring mutely at the hospital phone even though deep down she knew Morten wasn't going to call. She could still taste her tears at the corners of her mouth. She forced herself to look the PET man in the eyes.

"Before we talk about this, I just want to ask how the children are doing."

He looked puzzled. Then he pulled a folder out of his bag and flipped a little through the papers in it.

"Yesterday, Sunday, May seventeenth, the Emergency Management Agency evacuated a defunct auto repair shop at 35 Gasbetonvej, in Valby. The evacuees totaled twenty men, five women, and seven children between the ages of three and eighteen. All seven children were taken to the Infectious Diseases Ward at Bispebjerg Hospital. Four of the children presented mild to moderate symptoms of radiation sickness, but were evaluated and found not to require any treatment. One child was slightly dehydrated because of several days of nausea and vomiting. The boy is being given fluids now. They're all expected to make a full recovery."

Nina felt a flood of relief rush through her. Since she had been diagnosed with radiation sickness, she hadn't been able to find out anything about the children. The nurses knew nothing, and the doctors from the National Institute for Radiation Hygiene had acted like it was top-secret information of the most confidential nature. Even Magnus hadn't been able to drag anything out of his colleagues at Bispebjerg.

The PET man regarded her calmly.

"In other words there's nothing to indicate that the children were seriously harmed. So, if we could turn our attention back to the question. Did you see the source of the radiation?"

"No. It was pitch black down there. And, besides, I wouldn't have any idea what something like that looked like."

"I'm assuming you guessed it was in the inspection pit because you and the children were down there?"

Nina nodded, squirming in the chair. It was hot in the room, and her thighs were sticking damply to the plastic seat. She felt uncomfortable in the floppy hospital gown, granny underwear, and bare legs. Her own clothes had been thrown away, and there was no one at home to bring her new clothes. They sealed off the apartment, Morten had said. The image of his back framed in the doorway flitted through her mind. She pushed it aside with a deep breath and forced her attention back to the conversation. The inspection pit.

"Yes. When I was out there Friday night, the children and I were ordered into the inspection pit. And I think the children had been down there many times."

"Ordered, you say. By who?"

"The people at the garage."

"And why? Do you know?"

Nina shrugged. "Someone came. The Roma called them 'boss men.'"

"More than one, then."

"Yes. I heard them arguing up above, but I couldn't hear much of what they were saying. It sounded like it was about money, maybe rent. I'm assuming there weren't supposed to be children or people like me at the repair shop. Peter . . . uh, Peter Erhardsen that is . . . he experienced something similar."

"And you didn't see these 'boss men?'"

"No."

Despite the recorder, he still made a note in his papers. He pulled out a plastic folder from his briefcase and pushed it over in front of her. It contained a single, letter-sized printout of what looked like a passport picture.

"Do you know him?"

There was very little personality in the stiff, over-exposed face. But yes, she was absolutely sure she had seen him before. Was he one of the men from the repair shop? She tried to remember the faces from the cold, flickering glare of the fluorescent light, but they all merged into one. Turned into frozen masks with hostile eyes.

Then it clicked. The gash over his eye. She had seen his face half covered in blood, in the yellow glow of the light in her car. She didn't know his name, what he had done, or where he was now. Just that the left side of his rib cage must still be fairly sore.

"He . . . he was out there," she said. "Who is he?"

"We were hoping you knew that."

"No. He'd been in a fight, and I patched up a gash on his eyebrow for him. That was all. He was polite. Spoke very good English." And then it hit her. He had been in her car. She had brought him home to Fejøgade and let him out there. And then a few hours later . . .

"Oh, God."

The PET man didn't ask right away. He just waited, with relentless serenity.

"My daughter," Nina said then. "My daughter was attacked. They broke into our apartment. Was he one of them?"

The man's hawk face gave nothing away. Damnit! Couldn't he just be human?

"When did the attack take place?" he asked.

"For God's sake, you should know that better than me. My husband reported it. The police were there, they questioned her . . . Was it him?" Her voice rose, becoming shrill and edgy. She could hear it, but she couldn't stop herself. And that damned iron-faced robo-cop just sat there watching her, clearly making mental notes.

"We don't always get every bit of information right away," he said. "So when did this attack take place? And where?"

"Saturday night. In our apartment on Fejøgade. I just told you!"

"Thank you" was all he said, and then continued as if nothing had happened. "Tell me a little more about why you went to Valby."

Nina tried to breathe calmly. If she didn't relax, she was going to throw up again.

"I went to see a friend who was sick," she said. "He said there were some sick children living under poor conditions, so I went to have a look at them."

"Was this friend of yours Peter Erhardsen?"

"Yes."

"Is this something you and Peter had done before? Tending to the sick and needy?"

Nina swore to herself. The Man in the Iron Mask was intent on digging around in the past, and she didn't know how best to worm her way out of it. Luckily the Hungarian Roma were EU citizens and thus not as illegal as many of the Network's "clients" were. Helping them with a little over-the-counter medication was hardly a hanging offense. It was another matter for Peter, who regularly hid illegal refugees at his house. If the police really looked into that, it could very easily turn into a criminal case. And all his damn lists and three-ring binders and budgets . . . How many poor slobs would they find based on that treasure trove? Fuck. What if they had already ransacked his house in Vanløse . . . ?

"We just think people ought to be treated properly," Nina said vaguely. "Sorry. I'm not feeling so good." She had no trouble at all pretending she was ill. She had been out of bed for half an hour now and was sweating hot and cold from exhaustion. When had she last eaten anything that didn't come in a drip bag? She remembered the twist bread and the grilled sausage she'd chewed her way through outside the scout cabin Saturday evening. Back when she was still married and a mother, albeit not a perfect one, with an apartment in Østerbro. Today it was Monday, and Morten had left her. The nausea came all on its own now, and small black spots started to dance in front of her eyes.

The PET man sat motionless in front of her. The glasses on his curved nose caught and reflected the light from the window.

"I have neither the time nor the patience for your little games," he said. "If you're going to throw up, then throw up. But cut the crap. Someone brought radioactive material to Denmark, and at the moment we have every reason to believe it was done with malicious intent. People—a lot of people—may get hurt if we don't stop this. Which is why we are prepared to go further than the police normally go when faced with a hostile witness. I can have you remanded for up to six months. And I will, if I have to."

Nina stared at him in disbelief. No kid gloves here apparently—it was an iron hand in an iron glove.

"What I and Peter Erhardsen may or may not have done in the past has absolutely nothing to do with the repair shop in Valby," she said. "I've already told you everything you need to know."

For the first time his irritation was visible. His movements were still calm and completely controlled, but his eyes grew a shade darker as he spoke.

"In cases like these, the witness doesn't decide what I need to know. I do," he said coolly. "I ask a question, and you answer it to the best of your ability. Those are the rules. If you have a problem with that, as I said, I can lock you up."

Nina noted a sour taste spreading through her mouth. She was wearing a gown so short and thin that it barely covered her high-waisted mesh underwear, stamped COPENHAGEN HOSPITAL AUTHORITY in bold, dark-green letters. She had been vomiting for two days, her apartment was sealed, and she had no idea where she would go if she ever got well enough to leave this sterile, gray room with its ugly '80s-colored curtains. And now he was sitting there smelling of aftershave and everyday reality and threatening to put her in jail. As if she were a criminal.

"Peter Erhardsen works as an engineer for the City of Copenhagen." The PET man didn't seem to have noticed her stony facial expression and ploughed on, unperturbed. "It's not an obvious place to run into Hungarian Roma. We suspect that Peter Erhardsen might be systematically working with illegal immigrants. Is this something you're aware of?"

Was he bullshitting her? A single look at the man's calm, resolute face made clear he wasn't, and now to her annoyance she noted a hard, sharp lump in her throat that made it difficult to swallow. She was about to cry for the second time today. The first time had been right after she woke up and remembered Morten and Anton and Ida in Morten's sister's house in Greve. She had thrown up on the floor. The nurses had scooped it all up and packed it into the bright-yellow hazardous waste bags, but at least after that she had been left alone to cry into the enormous, bouncy hospital pillow. But sobbing hysterically in front of this imperturbable PET man, studying her right now over the rim of his glasses with that oh-so-patient look of his . . . Nina resolved to buck up and fight her tears, and with a certain sense of relief, she felt the rage starting to grow somewhere inside her.

"Who the hell do you think you are?" she hissed, slowly getting up from her chair. Her knees wobbled beneath her as she straightened, and she was forced to support herself with one hand on the wall behind her to regain her balance, but that didn't matter. "I haven't done anything to you or to anyone else for that matter. All I did was buy some diarrhea pills, salt, sugar, and bottled water for a couple of Roma children who really needed it." Nina was forced to pause for breath. Exertion and rage sizzled and throbbed in her temples. "I hope you find what you're looking for out there in Valby, but the rest of my life is none of your damn business, and I'm not going to trot it out for your inspection, so you can just get the hell out of here and leave me alone. If you want to haul me off to jail for that, you're more than welcome. It just so happens I don't have anywhere else to stay right now."

She tried to forget the gown, the mesh underwear and the white legs as she pointed to the door with a trembling finger. Even if he tried to act on his threat, he probably wouldn't be allowed to yank her out of a hospital bed. Happily the PET man seemed to have drawn the same conclusion.

"My card," he said, handing her a small, white card with tasteful black lettering. *Søren Kirkegård*, it said. *Inspector*. "In case you change your mind."

He stood there for a moment with his arm out-stretched, holding the card out to her but ended up leaving it on the table next to his empty coffee cup. Then he loaded his things back into his briefcase, calmly and methodically, nodded briefly, and left. The door closed behind him with a subtle click, and Nina stood there for a second, glaring at it with the remnants of her anger. Then she staggered over to her bed and sat down while she tried to get control of her breathing.

"It'll be okay," she told herself. "This will all work itself out."

But as she said it, she realized she wasn't quite sure what was going to work out. The trouble with the PET, the apartment, the nausea, or Morten. Just all of it, she thought. Please make all of it turn out all right. And hopefully soon.

SÁNDOR'S LEFT HAND was the only thing tying him to reality. He wanted to disappear into the black fogs that shrouded his consciousness, but the aching pulse in his hand was an anchor that wouldn't let go. He was stuck, even though it had been hours—he had no sense of how many—since Tommi had grabbed hold of his hand and yanked it free from the nails which were still lodged in the floorboard. No messing around with pliers or a hacksaw, just a hard, wet yank that unfortunately hadn't even made him faint.

He was in a room next to the eggplant-colored one, lying on a rug that smelled strongly of brown Labrador retriever. In the adjoining living room he could hear Tommi and Frederik arguing over breakfast. He had figured out why they spoke English together. Tommi wasn't Danish. According to Frederik he was a "Finnish pea brain." *Can't you get it into that Finnish pea brain of yours that . . .*

Frederik had showed up again an hour ago with pastries, Nescafé, juice, and newspapers, after having been home to spend the night with his wife and those two point five kids in Søllerød.

"Right, let's plan this," he had said in an enthusiastic tone, as if they were going to organize an orienteering activity for the local Boy Scout troop. But the "Be Prepared!" mood had quickly turned belligerent.

". . . of course I want the money," Frederik snapped at Tommi. "I've got bills to pay, the Valby place is a dead loss now, and this dump is useless as long as that thing is out in the garage. And in case you hadn't noticed, we're having an economic downturn."

"So what's the problem? We can dump the damn thing in a creek somewhere and be left with fuck-all, or we can dump it on the buyer and walk away with a cool half million. And if you really need to play the good citizen, we can always just call the cops later."

"The problem, you dimwit, is that we don't *have* a buyer. I drove past that nurse's building, and the whole street is full of police and cordons. She's the only one who knows where that Gypsy's stupid jacket is."

"Couldn't we just sell it to someone else?"

"Do you know anyone who wants to buy a can of hot cesium? By all means, speak up if you do."

It was quiet in the living room for a few seconds.

"Why didn't you get milk?" Tommi complained. "You know I don't drink it black."

"Shut up, Tommi. You should be happy I even brought food."

Silence again. Then a newspaper rustling.

"Holy shit," Frederik said.

"What?"

"That's her. It has to be!"

"Who?"

Frederik didn't answer him. Instead there was a scraping sound from a table or a chair, and a few seconds later, Frederik was bending over Sándor.

"Look!" he said and thrust the front page of the newspaper right in Sándor's face. "Is that her?"

Sándor reluctantly opened his eyes. The front page of

the paper proclaimed something or other dramatic in big red letters, but it was the picture next to the headline that Frederik was frenetically jabbing at with his index finger.

An official looking photo of a serious woman with short, dark hair and intense gray eyes. It *was* her. The nurse who had patched up his eyebrow. The nurse who had his jacket.

"Well?" Frederik poked him insistently on the shoulder. It sent a wave of pain all the way out to his fingers and back again.

"Uh, maybe. Yes," he said, just to make the man go away.

Frederik went back to the living room and slapped the newspaper down in front of Tommi.

"Well, at least now we know where she is," he said.

SØREN MARCHED INTO the meeting room with a seething sense of rage and no real target for it. The fact that he hadn't heard about the attack on Nina Borg's teenage daughter until he was in the middle of questioning her was an almost unforgiveable mistake, and yet the explanation was so simple that he couldn't rake anyone over the coals for it.

"The attack in Fejøgade was reported by a Morten Sindahl Christensen" was the explanation provided by the young detective he had phoned while driving back from Rigshospitalet. "It doesn't say anything about a Nina Borg." Søren could hear her fingers flying over the keys. "I'll send you the case file right away."

He had printed out the report as soon as he got back to his office in Søborg and managed to skim through it before the group meeting. It made unpleasant reading. The three men who had broken into Nina Borg's apartment Saturday night hadn't exactly raped and pillaged, but it wasn't far off. And the girl was only fourteen years old. In addition to the violence and the sexual aspects of the attack, it was very clear that this wasn't your ordinary break-in. Nothing was stolen, apart from the girl's school bag and some personal papers, and one of the three English-speaking men had repeatedly asked for Nina, which made it all the more irritating that the officers investigating the case hadn't flagged it right away. Nina's husband stated in the same report that his wife was in the hospital and would no longer be living in Fejøgade because they had decided to separate and, moreover, he had no idea why three angry foreigners were looking for his wife. If only the investigating officers had taken the trouble to dig a little deeper . . . He left a message asking Mikael to drive over and see if the daughter could recognize Sándor Horváth's passport photo and asked the crime team to prioritize the case. There was nothing more to be done, and there was no reason to waste time apportioning blame. Yet his anger wouldn't abate.

He surveyed the meeting room grimly. In addition to the people from his own group, there were now four extra investigators who had been assigned to the case first thing that morning, plus an analyst sent by Torben "to fill everyone in on the bigger picture."

"Go ahead, Gert," Søren said. "Let's hear it."

Gert Sørensen was a mild-mannered man in his early forties, with curly, flame-red hair that somehow seemed misplaced given his natural reserve and discreet tweed-gray appearance. He hadn't gone to the police academy but had a degree in political science, and he managed the more academically gifted members of the PET's ranks, the Terror Analysis Department. He stepped over to the projector and pulled up the first PowerPoint slide on his computer.

"November, 1995. Chechen separatists bury a cesium-137 source in a park in Moscow. The cesium source was equipped with a detonator, but it was never triggered. There were no injuries in connection with this event."

Click.

"December, 1998. The Chechen Security Service finds a container filled with a mixture of radioactive materials.

An explosive mine was attached to the canister, which was placed in Argun, a suburb of Grozny. No injuries."

New click.

"June, 2003. Thai police arrest several men in possession of a large amount of cesium-137 intended, as far as could be ascertained, for the manufacture of a dirty bomb."

Gert turned off the projector so as not to have to talk over the fan noise. Søren switched on a couple of the overhead lights.

"We also know that al-Qaeda tried to make a bomb with the substance in the United States at least once. Dirty bombs are obviously a part of the contemporary terrorist's arsenal that we're going to need to deal with. The world has been spared a full-on attack of this type so far, but in a case like ours, where we have positive affirmation that a radioactive source has been and probably still is active right here in Copenhagen, we have every possible reason to take this seriously. The National Institute for Radiation Hygiene says they found traces of cesium chloride, and that cesium is currently one of the most easily accessible radioactive materials, especially in the former Soviet bloc. Based on the traces, it is not immediately possible to determine how much radioactive material was at the address in Valby, since the extent of the contamination largely depends on how well the source was shielded."

"And what exactly can a dirty bomb do that other bombs can't?"

Gitte Nymand's dark eyes gleamed with something that looked like equal parts professional curiosity and concern.

674   LENE KAABERBØL AND AGNETE FRIIS

"Aside from the fact that they explode, which can obviously inflict serious injuries and damage depending on the force of the explosion, the goal is to spread radioactive material throughout the area," the red-headed analyst said. "Which doesn't necessarily have a significant impact on the fatality rate. It's more the *nature* of the fatalities that causes the concern, and the long-term effects. And especially the psychological effect it can have on the civilian population."

Søren was on his feet now.

"I don't need to give you my whole terrorism lecture again, do I?" he asked, and an only partially stifled groan spread through the room. "Terrorism is called terrorism because . . . ?"

"Because the goal is fear," a couple of them said almost in unison.

"Yes. And that's exactly what makes a dirty bomb an effective weapon of terror. It's exceptionally well suited to spreading fear."

"Decapitated heads," Mikael said suddenly. "At Antioch the crusaders chopped off enemy heads and lobbed them into the city with the trebuchets. It's nothing new."

Sometimes that man knew the strangest things, Søren thought. Mikael had had the dubious honor of escorting the corpse from the gas tank to the medical examiner's and observing the autopsy, which might explain why his thoughts were a little gorier than usual.

"Let's just get it over with, Mikael," Søren said. "The autopsy report?"

Mikael stood up. He looked tired, but then he had been on his feet since 4 A.M. like the rest of the team.

"According to the preliminary report, the guy died of radiation sickness, presumably Thursday or early Friday."

"Not later than that? Maybe Saturday night or Sunday?" Søren asked.

"No." Mikael cleared his throat and reached for a water glass. Jytte from the cafeteria had also stocked the meeting table with a plate of open-face sandwiches, but apparently Mikael had lost his appetite. "The pathologists and the staff at the National Institute for Radiation Hygiene pretty much agree that he was exposed to very powerful radiation two to three weeks ago. From accidents elsewhere in the world, we know that the illness typically begins with nausea and vomiting, fever, and in serious cases diarrhea. After that people often improve, but if the exposure was significant, for example four to six grays, the immune system is so compromised that, after a few days, the patient starts to develop infections, another fever, hemorrhages, sores . . ." Mikael caught Søren's eye. "Well, you saw him yourself. When they opened his mouth, his gums were almost gone. God-awful sight."

Mikael's last statement hung in the air for an uncomfortably long time, and again Søren had to wave the disturbing images from Valby out of his mind.

"Can they say anything about how he was exposed?"

"Yes. He presumably took in the brunt of the radiation through his hands. The pathologists found wounds there that were reminiscent of burns. There were also a number of other signs that suggested he might have handled the radioactive source."

"What about identification?"

"Wasn't there something about a passport? Sándor

Horváth, right? Isn't that why they woke you up in the middle of the night?" Gitte asked.

"I don't think it's him," Søren said. "The nurse recognized the passport photo. The man in the photo was still alive Saturday night when the nurse treated him for a minor eye injury. Alive, and in Denmark. Besides, Sándor Horváth is in his early twenties, and I think our corpse is younger than that. An overgrown boy, no more."

"Our John Doe was missing a canine in his upper jaw," Mikael said. "The pathologist thinks he had probably never seen a dentist, unfortunately. At any rate he had no fillings. That's typical for some of the poorest of the Eastern European Roma."

"So there won't be any dental records," Søren said. "But there must be a link between him and Sándor Horváth. If we haven't done it already, send a picture of the body to the NBH."

"It's been done," Gitte said. "They were actually very helpful. A man's on his way up here to assist us in our search for Sándor Horváth, and they also assigned a couple of people to dig up a little more on his family and friends in Budapest. They're going to keep us up to date."

"And how's it going with our friend Khalid?"

"Not so well."

That response came from Bjørn Steffensen, a generally unshaven and insolent aging homeboy from the rough part of Amager. He normally worked with the Organized Crime Center. He was one of the team members Torben had managed to borrow, and he didn't look too happy that his first job here was to be the bearer of bad news.

"This whole line of enquiry is a ticket to Shitville" he said, having apparently decided that offense was the best defense. "The technicians have been working on the kid's computer since 5 A.M., and we have fuck-all on the guy. To begin with, it wasn't even his computer that was used to contact Sándor Horváth. Or at least not the one we confiscated. I suppose he could have another one stashed somewhere."

Søren felt an uncomfortable sinking sensation somewhere in that part of his mind where he was trying to keep all the facts in the case straight. "What do you mean?" he said. "I thought that we'd at least established that much?"

"The MAC address doesn't match. You'll have to ask IT about the details," Bjørn said. "And when we sent one of the tech guys to look at the school's network, he reported that the security system has more holes than a Swiss cheese. The head of the school's IT department has apparently been busy with more important things. He teaches Danish and English as well." That last bit was said with a snide curl at the corner of his mouth, as if nothing could be more laughable than a literature teacher being in charge of the school's Internet security.

"Christian was able to get onto the school's wire-less network from his own laptop without any trouble," Mikael added. "The security was so bad that he didn't even need a username or password, and that means that anyone within a radius of thirty meters of the school could have used the school's IP address to visit those shady sites."

"So I high-tailed it out there to pick up the footage

from the surveillance cameras that cover the schools' outdoor areas," Bjørn said.

Søren listened with a growing sense that everything was falling apart.

"But if Khalid didn't do it, why wouldn't he let us look at his computer?" Søren asked.

Bjørn smirked.

"As I said, it's possible that he has another computer and needed to win himself a little time so he could swap the two machines. But personally I think he was just worried about his little side business. I've never seen so many pirated music files in one place before. He could get in real trouble for that, and I guess that would be reason enough."

Søren curbed his desire to kick something. Bjørn, preferably. Don't shoot the messenger, he admonished himself. But couldn't the man control his gloating just a little?

"And what do the surveillance cameras say?"

"We know that our potential buyer went online Saturday, May second, at 8:52 P.M. and was logged on for about forty minutes. We can see only one car that was parked at the school for that entire time frame, and it left the site immediately after. It's impossible to read the license plate, but luckily it's an old banger, an Opel Rekord E, probably from the early '80s, and there aren't that many of them in the motor vehicle registry. About two hundred or so in the whole country, a hundred and eighteen of which are in the Copenhagen area."

Okay, thought Søren. At least that was something. A start.

"Check it out. But I also want people out canvassing the area around the school. Find out exactly where he might have been holed up, aside from in the car. What about the neighboring properties? Can you go online from them? Talk to the residents. And find out if they noticed the car or any other cars that spent a long time in the area on the evening in question. The surveillance cameras have blind spots." Like people, he thought. Admittedly, Khalid had been an obvious suspect with his nervousness and his little display of civil disobedience. But they couldn't afford to make another mistake like this.

"HC wasn't happy," Gitte remarked. "He was pissed off when he found out we'd called him out of his training exercise to question a smart-mouthed teenage bootlegger."

"HC's mood is not our biggest problem," Søren said. "But okay. I suppose I could offer him an apology. I'm assuming we've already released Khalid?"

Gitte nodded. "At 11:23 A.M. His uncle threatened to sue us for false arrest, but Khalid talked him down. He doesn't want to have to discuss his pirated files with the prosecutor."

Exit Khalid, thought Søren, picturing the cocky, young café shark who had so familiarly offered him a drink and a smoke at their first meeting. Hopefully HC hadn't managed to shred his self-confidence too much before the word came from IT to stop the interrogation.

"What about the property in Valby? Anything on that front?"

"They just called up from reception," Gitte said. "A Birgitte Johnsen from the NEC is on her way up to talk to you."

"The NEC?" Søren looked at her over his reading glasses. The NEC was the Danish National Police Investigation Center. "What the hell do they have to do with this case?"

Gitte shrugged her broad swimmer's shoulders. "She's in the sex trafficking and immoral earnings division," Gitte said.

BIRGITTE JOHNSEN WAS unbelievably navy blue, Søren thought. Navy blue skirt, navy blue jacket, navy blue nylons, and navy blue shoes with oversized gold buckles. The blouse under her jacket was white, but otherwise she was an unbroken vision of blueness.

They shook hands, and Søren showed her into the external meeting room that was located right off reception. Unauthorized visitors were not allowed to wander the PET's corridors, not even unauthorized police employees.

"I understand that you have some information on 35 Gasbetonvej?" Søren said, gesturing with his hand. "Have a seat. Coffee?"

"No thanks," Birgitte said. "But if there's a mineral water?"

"Of course." Søren opened a Ramlösa for her. The writing on the label was, very appropriately, printed in navy blue.

"The property is owned by a Malee Rasmussen. And we know her quite well over in our section. She's originally from Thailand and is married to a former factory worker named Hans Jørgen Rasmussen, who is on disability allowance. We presume the marriage is just a sham, but we haven't been able to prove it. She, however, has a conviction for living off immoral earnings and has been part of the local prostitution scene for many years now."

"Prostitution? But surely . . . the property in Valby could hardly have been used for that?"

"You'd be amazed if you saw some of the places people are prepared to go to buy sex," Birgitte said. "But no, regardless of sexual predilection, concrete floors and inspection pits are not particularly well suited to running a brothel. We have no reason to believe that that's what they've been doing out there. It probably is what it looks like: a flophouse for Roma and other Eastern Europeans who come up here during the summer months and pay about eighty to a hundred kroner a night for permission to sleep under conditions that would make the inmates at Vridsløselille State Prison riot."

"Then that's a bit of a career change for her, isn't it? Is the property really hers, do you think, or is she just the front for someone else?"

"I think she has a backer. But the career change, as you call it, isn't actually that unprecedented. Earnings are way down in the prostitution business due to the financial crisis."

"Do you know why?"

"Fewer courses, conferences, and fringe benefit trips. Greater need for security. The average John can't really afford trouble with Mrs. John right now. And while the demand is falling off, the supply is increasing. In the wake of the social hardship that has spread in countries even worse affected by the financial crisis than Denmark, more and more girls flock to the trade. Malee and her backer aren't the only ones who've had to restructure their businesses."

"Okay. Any guess who this backer is?"

"We've asked her, of course. I brought a recording for you to watch. But first I want to show you a previous clip, from when we were investigating the immoral earnings case. That was five years ago now, and she's in her late thirties in this recording."

Birgitte slid a DVD into her laptop and rotated the computer so he could see it better. A woman with jet-black hair and spirited dark eyes appeared. Vital. Expressive. There was a self-awareness of her appearance and attire, jewelry, and the heavy but stylish makeup. And her eyes twinkled as the questions hit her.

". . . she said that?" The lilting Thai accent was obvious; her eyes were bright and ready for a fight. She laughed a short, hard laugh and snorted disdainfully. Clicked her tongue when the lead interrogator asked about one of her acquaintances. "She's full of lies. Lies. And she's jealous!"

Birgitte stopped the DVD and clicked on another file.

"Now watch this. This recording is from this morning."

At first Søren thought she had selected the wrong file. It wasn't the same woman. And yet it was. But Malee Rasmussen's smile was so strained that her face resembled one of those grotesque grinning Balinese masks that his ex-wife Susse had bought on a trip back in the '90s. If she was in her late thirties in that first clip, she must be forty-two or forty-three here, but she looked ten years older than that. Her makeup was so very cliché for the prostitution world that it looked like stage makeup, and although her voice was still light and lilting, there was no trace of vitality left in that hardened face.

"What happened to her?" he asked. "She's . . . is she sick or something?"

"Not that we know of. But there are rumors that she has a new backer. And that he's taught her some new tricks. The hard way. As you'll see, she's not very forthcoming these days."

The camera zoomed out a bit, and Malee's whole body could be seen. Her short, sturdy silhouette was dressed in a mint green dress with flowers around the neckline and matching stiletto heels. Her legs were crossed. Her hands lay motionless in her lap, but she was rapidly whipping her foot back and forth as the questions were repeated interminably. Who was using the repair shop? Who had the keys? Why had she bought it anyway? Where had she gotten the money from?

Malee's forehead glistened damply under her elaborately arranged black hair. She was still smiling, and at regular intervals, she chose to respond but only to repeat what she had already said.

"I didn't know there was anyone at the repair shop. It was an investment. I haven't been there since February. I didn't know there was anyone there. The repair shop is just real estate. An investment."

"Try to catch her eyes right there."

Birgitte rewound a couple of seconds and started it playing again. Søren looked at the woman again. Her eyes flickered nervously in the midst of the hardened mask of her face.

Birgitte shook her head.

"I don't know who or what she's afraid of now, but it certainly isn't us. I don't think we're going to get anything else out of her, but I've asked the Fraud Squad to dig a little deeper into her finances. Maybe that will give us a few names."

"Something happened to her," Søren maintained. "It would be good to know what."

"Yes. She wasn't exactly a lovey-dovey person before, and she's always been quite tough on her girls. But now . . ."

Søren looked at the pale, fossilized face on the screen. "What now?"

Birgitte snapped her computer shut and placed it in her briefcase.

"We don't know. But we've talked to girls who've worked for her, and they refuse to testify. There's a whisper that you get buried alive if you don't do what Malee says. That you wind up in the 'Coffin.'"

Buried alive . . . Søren thought of Snow White.

FREDERIK WASN'T TAKING any chances. There was no more pretense of civility left, no more armchairs and offers of beer—now Sándor was sitting on the floor next to the radiator, with his healthy hand strapped to the water pipe with two narrow black cable ties that reminded him of that paralyzing moment outside his dorm when he was arrested. He felt less dazed now, but also . . . more distant. As if he were standing on the other side of a border and looking back at a life he couldn't get back into. His left hand throbbed heavily, like the bass line from a bad speaker, a rhythm he couldn't ignore but also couldn't quite accept as part of him. His own pulse. Which shouldn't be there.

Frederik was leaning over the slightly too-low coffee table, working on a laptop, surrounded by folders that appeared to contain various corporate accounts. Now and then he would set down the computer and punch some numbers into an old-fashioned pocket calculator with rapid, practiced fingers.

"Could I have a little water?" Sándor asked.

Frederik lifted his eyes from the computer screen.

"I don't think so," he said. "Not until Tommi gets back."

"I'm thirsty."

"Sorry. I'm not getting close to you. Not as long as we're alone here." He started typing again, but just for a few seconds. Then he glanced at Sándor and asked him, "Where did that come from?"

"What?"

"That . . . outburst. Most people, they're sort of . . . you can sort of see it in them. They have to gear themselves up. There are signs. You seemed totally calm and laid back, right up until—boom. Like those pitbulls that just attack without any warning." Frederik looked absurdly well-shaved and normal—today in a freshly pressed light-blue shirt, light linen pants and yet another Ralph Lauren sweater, which was now draped effortlessly over his rounded shoulders. Mr. Clean, thought Sándor. Respectability itself. But Mr. Clean had sat by and watched Tamás die.

Sándor didn't reply. Frederik shrugged and pulled a plastic water bottle out of his computer bag.

"Here," he said, and rolled it across the floor to Sándor.

Sándor looked down at the bottle. He could just reach it with his zip-tied right hand. But he couldn't unscrew the plastic lid with his injured left hand.

"I can't open it," he said.

"Oh, right," Frederik said. "I don't suppose you can." But he didn't do anything to help.

Having a bottle of water in his hand without being able to drink it was worse than just sitting there being thirsty. Was that intentional on Frederik's part? Sándor didn't know. They sat there looking at each other for a bit, two quiet, respectable men who were both a lot less respectable under the surface.

AT THE ORPHANAGE they didn't hit the kids. But they did believe in calm, cleanliness, order—and consistency. "They might as well learn it now" was the pervasive pedagogical principle.

That was why they had the Yard.

It was actually just a glorified air shaft, about eight meters on each side, with a floor of frost-ravaged paving and a scrawny rowan tree in a concrete planter in the middle. The four-story orphanage buildings towered around it, but there were only windows from the second floor up. On the ground floor, the only openings were for the ventilation ducts from the kitchen and bathrooms, and one lone, solid door.

"Tell Miss Erszébet you're sorry," said the tall old *gadjo* who was apparently the Big Man here. But Sándor didn't want to say he was sorry.

"You can't take them," Sándor yelled instead, as loudly as he could. "I'm their brother!"

"Look at me, Sándor," the *gadjos'* Big Man said. "You have to learn not to lose your temper. Here at the orphanage, we behave properly. You may come back inside when you are ready to apologize. Calmly, quietly, and politely."

And then the door was shut and locked.

It was getting late. Sándor wasn't afraid of being out in the open air; it wasn't even dark yet. In Galbeno, people tended to be inside their houses only when it was time to go to bed or when the weather was bad. What else were you going to do in them?

But this wasn't "the open air." This was just a brick and concrete room without a roof.

He screamed and cried in rage and kicked the door, but there was already something half-hearted about his kicks. Some of the man's calm relentlessness had stuck with him, a little it-won't-do-any-good-anyway parasite that invaded his eight-year-old's determination and sapped his strength.

Once the sun had disappeared from the courtyard and there was just a faint orange reflection in the uppermost windows, the Big Man came back. Sándor ran over to the door as soon as it opened and tried to push his way past the grown-up body. He was stopped by a strong arm, and when he tried to twist himself free, he was pushed back into the Yard again in a restrained, but firm, way. Another escape attempt was blocked in the same manner.

"I can see that you haven't calmed down yet," the man said. "Now I will slowly count to ten. While I do that, I ask that you take time to reflect. If we can't speak properly to each other when I'm done, you'll have to stay out here all night."

The man started counting, slowly and deliberately. "One. Two. Three. Four."

"I want to go home," Sándor yelled.

"Five. Six."

Sándor raised a fist in frustration, but he didn't strike. He didn't dare.

"Seven. Eight. Nine."

"We want to go home to our mother." Sándor's voice cracked, hoarse, and resigned.

"Unfortunately that is out of the question. Ten. Now. Are you ready to say you're sorry?"

Sándor shook his head mutely.

"I'm their brother," he repeated, somewhat less vehemently.

"Good night, Sándor."

And then the man closed the door again.

It got cooler, but not freezing cold. After all, it was spring, the rowan tree was sporting delicate new leaves.

Sándor discovered that there was a water spigot you could drink from even though the water had a very definite muddy and metallic taste. But he was alone. Sándor couldn't remember the last time that had happened. There was always someone *there*. If his mother didn't happen to be around, then his Grandma Éva was. Or one of the other grandmothers. Or Aunt Milla who lived four houses away. Or Tibor, or Feliszia, or Vanda, or . . . there was always *someone*.

Now there wasn't. Just the darkness and the walls and the sky, those rough, cold pavers and the seeping steam issuing from the bathrooms' ventilation ducts, although he didn't know that then. That first night, he just huddled up next to the door and stared at the gray column of condensing vapors and hoped it wasn't a *mulo*. At some point he started crying again. At some point he stopped. And when they came back the next morning, he told Miss Erszébet he was very sorry and began to learn the rules of the *gadjo* world. There was still trouble now and then, and he came to know the Yard well. But he never spent a whole night there again. It was like he once heard the Big Man tell one of the municipal inspectors: "Roma children are no more troublesome than other children. You just have to nip them in the bud."

A CAR PULLED up outside. Frederik stiffened and reached into his computer bag. The gesture so much resembled a movie cliché that Sándor wondered whether he had a weapon hidden there. Then a car door slammed, and Frederik let go of the bag and visibly relaxed.

"He got her," he said. "He really got her."

But it wasn't the nurse Tommi shoved in the door a few seconds later. It was the girl from the apartment. She looked like a disfigured Pierrot, with her chalky white face and black eyes smeared from a mixture of tears and cheap mascara. The sight struck Sándor like a bludgeon.

"What the hell," said Frederik, who obviously wasn't pleased either. "Why did you take *her*?"

"Piece of cake," Tommi said with a triumphant grin. "Just had to check the girl's school timetable, right?"

Oh, that's why, Sándor thought. That's why he had snatched her school bag. Because he wanted to be able to find her again.

Frederik shook his head in disbelief. "You were supposed to get the goddamn mother, not the kid."

"This," said Tommi, "is even better. And more fun . . ."

1

T HAD BEEN strangely quiet inside Nina's head since the PET man had left. Her head still ached a little and there was a very faint, whooshing throb, like in the water pipes she used to listen to before she fell asleep in the room she had had as a teenager back home in Viborg. Nina pushed the tray of uneaten rissoles and overdone cold carrots aside, leaned back, and closed her eyes. She couldn't sleep, but she didn't have anywhere good to send her thoughts, so instead she allowed herself to slide into the gray throbbing, whooshing semi-darkness inside her eyelids instead.

She heard the sounds a second before it happened.

The door that slid open almost imperceptibly, soft rubber soles padding across the gray linoleum, first by the door, then a little closer. The little click as the door closed automatically behind the intruder. Then, abruptly, something big and warm was pressed against her mouth, and Nina's eyes flew open. Her head was being pushed so deeply into the pillow that it almost closed around her face, and the sense of being suffocated caused panic to explode through her for a second. Trying to move her head was hopeless, the man crouched over her was now putting his weight behind the outstretched arm and hand while Nina frantically batted at the air around her. She grabbed for the face, the hair, the neck, and arms of her attacker, but he moved quickly and avoided her blows. The man's little finger had been pushed up under her nose, and she had to fight for every single scrap of air for her lungs. As if she were breathing through wet gauze. And in the middle of her frenzied panic, she could see a gaunt face with a wide grin swaying back and forth over her. The eyes gleamed, distant and exhilarated. He's on drugs, Nina managed to conclude. An addict looking for morphine or maybe someone who was mentally ill, lost in the wrong part of the hospital. His breath was heavy and sharp and smelled of cigarettes and peppermint. The man was making an effort to catch her eyes, and for some reason or other, that made her slow down. She tried to aim her blows better. Make them harder. But the hand that was pressed so solidly over her mouth didn't budge a millimeter, and eventually she lay perfectly still as she tried to breathe through the one, almost free nostril.

It seemed like that was what he had been waiting for.

The man eased up on the pressure on her mouth a little bit and reached for something with his free hand. Nina tried to follow his movements with her eyes, but her head was still being pushed so far down in the pillow that it obscured her view like a white mountain range. She couldn't see much besides the ceiling, the man's arm, and little bits of his head and upper body. All that smothering softness drowned out even the sounds. Some notion of escape occurred to her. The man still had a hand over her mouth, but he was only holding her with one arm. Maybe she could slide free and pull the alarm cord that was hanging right over her bed.

Then a black object appeared right over her face. It took a couple of seconds before she was able to focus on it, and yet another moment before she realized what it was. A mobile phone. It was on, and the screen showed a picture with a dark, almost-black background. In the foreground there was a person who had been photographed from above. The girl's pale face glowed white in the darkness. The eyes were slightly narrowed and the facial expression frozen in that defiant face she always made, when she was trying not to cry.

Ida.

Nina didn't scream.

She could tell he was expecting her to, because he clamped his hand down tighter over her mouth before he pushed the button. But Nina couldn't scream. Nothing inside her was working. There was only silence and cold and the picture dancing on the black phone in front of her. Something started moving on the tiny screen. The sound of footsteps on a floor that echoed in a strangely hollow way. The man doing the filming said something or other, but Nina couldn't hear what it was, and now she could see Ida take a step back. As if she were trying to disappear into the darkness. Where? Nina desperately tried to gauge the location of the recording. It wasn't home in their apartment—the wall behind Ida was a hideous dark purple color—but otherwise there wasn't anything that revealed where she was.

The angle changed. Now the photographer was standing over Ida, speaking once more.

"Say hi to Mommy. Smile."

Ida's eyes flitted toward the camera, then she looked directly at the man holding the phone and angrily jutted out her chin.

"Smile."

Ida shook her head, took two steps farther back, and

bumped into the purple wall. The phone was right up against her face now. A finger slid slowly over her chin, pushed its way tentatively between her lips, and made its way over to the corner of her mouth. Pulled it upward into a grotesque, crooked grin.

"Smile for Mommy."

The picture went black, and Nina felt the man slowly ease up on the pressure on her mouth. He pulled his hand away completely. She turned her head, and it was only now that she could really see the man next to her bed. He wasn't that much taller than her, she thought, and skinny under that loose T-shirt. He was wearing a pair of very light-blue Levis that were cinched in at the waist with a wide, studded leather belt, its oversized belt buckle featuring a shiny, pale skull. His hair was shoulder-length, dark blond, and looked freshly washed. The rest of him was worn and scruffy and cigarette-ravaged, even though he could hardly be older than thirty. His nose was swollen and bruised on one side, his eyes wide and feverish. Probably snorted a line of crystal meth a few hours ago, Nina thought hostilely, and felt a glint of satisfaction at the thought of how short and miserable this man's life would be. How his body would be covered with oozing sores from the crank bugs, how he would scream and call for mercy, and how he would die alone and in pain. She would kill him herself right now if she had the slightest opportunity. For what he had done to Ida. She lashed out at him, but there was no strength in her blow, and it only grazed his throat before he grabbed her hand and held it securely.

"Easy, girl." He spoke to her in accented English.

His voice was quiet and arrogant, as if he were talking

to a child, and then he let go of her entirely and let her sit halfway up in bed. He pulled a clear plastic bag out of a duffel bag that was on the floor next to the bed and set it on the covers.

"Put them on," he said, still in English.

Nina peeled the crackling plastic aside with two fingers and glanced quickly at the contents. It looked like some sort of tracksuit. The price tag was still on, fluttering from the waist of the dark-blue pants.

"Where is she?"

The man looked at her and smiled.

"Really cute daughter you've got. She looks like you. Just a little firmer in the flesh. Delicious young cunt. Totally soft to touch."

His accent might be thick, as if he had a mouth full of gravel, but his vocabulary was convincing.

Nina felt defeated. His words were so harsh. So evil. She could feel her defenses washing away. A floodgate had been opened. The fear that had started to seep into her body at the sight of the first picture of Ida on the phone roared through her now, full strength. It slid into every single thought, formed unwelcome images, and little film clips that churned and rattled and played over and over again in endless loops. Ida in the apartment in front of her three attackers without her clothes on. Ida naked in some basement. Ida in the rearview mirror, a thin, black silhouette on a bicycle in the dark on her way up Fejøgade. That was the last time she had seen her.

Nina tried to inhale again. Tried to think. Should she try to stall for time? Pull the cord to call the nurse? He wouldn't be able to stop her. All she needed to do was to reach up.

They heard footsteps out in the hall, and the man sat down on the chair next to her bed. He quickly pulled a small, tired-looking bouquet of tulips out of his bag on the floor and placed it on the covers. Water seeped out of the plastic wrap surrounding the green stems, making a big, wet stain on the white bedding. He wasn't nervous, Nina thought. Everything he did was so calm and effortless. As if this were a totally normal day in his life.

A nurse came into view in the little window in the door just as the man leaned over the bed and placed his free hand over hers. His smiling face had moved in very close to hers, and he had even managed to adopt something that resembled a concerned smiled. A couple of long, bright- red lines stretched from his ear down over his cheek and Nina couldn't help thinking of Ida's black-painted fingernails.

"My poor baby," he said, and behind him Nina could see the nurse's face disappearing again. Her white clogs clicked quickly on down the hall, and Nina knew that the woman was probably already reporting the latest gossip on the odd patient in the isolation room. By now everyone had probably read about her marital problems in *Ekstra Bladet*. The news of a man in her room with flowers would add some excitement to the staff's lunch break.

Nina looked at the man and knew that she wouldn't put up any resistance. She didn't dare. He had Ida.

He stood up, pulled Nina's covers aside, and threw the tracksuit at her with an impatient grunt.

"Put it on. Now!"

Nina pulled the clothes on over her hospital gown without protest and without looking at the man. A feeling of disgust crawled across her skin when she thought of him holding Ida down, touching her. Whatever plans he had for her were immaterial compared to what he planned to do to Ida. Out of the corner of her eye, she could see that he had opened the cupboard next to her bed and was rummaging around in the white hospital linens on the shelves. He swore quietly.

"Where the fuck are your shoes?"

Nina leaned against the bed, exhaustion from the effort of putting on the clothes making the room swim around her.

"They threw them away," she said. "Because of the radiation."

He swore again, pulled some long, white socks out of the cupboard, and threw them at her.

"Put these on and don't try anything clever."

Nina obediently pulled on the socks and found herself standing there in white socks and a pair of dark-blue tracksuit bottoms that were slightly too big. He moved over behind her. She could feel his sharp, warm breath against her ear.

"And now, we go. Pretend you're healthy and have shoes on," he said. "And pretend you're not you."

SØREN RINSED THE coffee cup in the sink in the men's restroom, filled it with cold water, and drank. Tomorrow, or next week, or whenever this goddamn case was over and he had time to catch his breath again, he would take the time to find that article he vaguely remembered about bacteria in water coolers and send it out over the intranet. He knew his little act of protest against the tyranny of water coolers was a waste of energy, but surely a man his age was allowed to mount his moth-eaten warhorse and attack a windmill now and then.

He was holding the cup under the tap one more time when it slipped through his fingers. He grabbed for it with both hands and managed to stop it from crashing to the terrazzo floor, but water splashed onto his shirt and trousers, leaving a trail of drip marks near his fly that was not very flattering.

Oh, crap. It wasn't so much the accident—the water would dry quickly—it was what it told him. That he was tired. That he ought to go home, or at least down to the basement to crash in one of the bunks for a few hours. He had only slept three hours the night before and had been working for more than eleven hours since then. And, well, he wasn't eighteen anymore. But his young Hungarian colleague would be landing at Copenhagen Airport in an hour, the results from the Opel registration list would be back soon, and he really wanted to talk to Malee himself and see if he could get anything out of her that Birgitte and her colleagues in the NEC hadn't been able to. A video wasn't enough.

A shower. A clean shirt. And yes, an hour's downtime. But not home in Hvidovre, that would take too long. And not in the basement either. He'd always hated those small, cell-like rooms.

He poked his head into Torben's office. Torben was staring intently at his computer screen as he scrolled his way through some document long enough to induce cramps in anybody's index finger.

"I'm going over to Susse's if that's okay," Søren said. "Just for an hour."

Torben nodded without looking up from his screen.

"Good idea," Torben said. "See you later."

Why did he suddenly feel like a loser who couldn't go the distance? Torben hadn't been up since a little past 3 A.M. And this wasn't a competition to see who could stay awake the longest.

"Call if there's anything," he said.

Torben waved his left hand in a get-out-of-here fashion, and Søren ducked back into the hallway.

SUSSE LIVED SO enticingly close by, less than a kilometer away, in an old bungalow right next to the railway. There was a solid, white-painted wood fence around the yard to keep children and dogs in, and the garden was disheveled in that pleasant way, with narcissi in the overgrown lawn and lanky roses in need of a good pruning. The two pear trees he had planted too many years ago were still there, currently sporting delicate pink blossoms.

The children had mostly left home, one of them for

boarding school, the other more permanently, but the dogs were still there. Two of them, a couple of black-and-white cocker spaniels, who barked enthusiastically and stuck their wet noses and long-haired paws up against the pane of the glass door when he rang the bell.

Susse opened the door with her phone to her ear and mimed "Come in," continuing her conversation. "Yes, I understand that, but I still think it's stressing Linus out that Karl is so rowdy in the classroom. I think we ought to separate them, at least for a few weeks, and see how it goes. Yes. Yeah, okay. I'll see you."

She lowered the phone and smiled at him.

"Do you want a cup of coffee or are you just here to lie down? You look tired."

"No more coffee." He made a face at the mere thought. "But do you think it would be okay if I took a shower first?"

"Of course. You just do what you need to do. I'll be in the sunroom grading papers if you need anything."

They exchanged a civilized peck on the cheek. She looked good, he thought. Or more to the point, she looked like a woman who was feeling good. She wore her copper-red hair in a shoulder-length pageboy, which was probably not the height of fashion. But she'd been wearing it that way for a really long time, and it suited her heart-shaped face perfectly. She was round and comfortably plump all over, and her eyes were calm, clear, and warm. He had known her for more than thirty years. They had been high school sweethearts. They got married. They bought a house together—this house, where she still lived. But the children she had had weren't his, and the man she was co-habiting with in lifelong devotion wasn't him either. And even though she opened the door to him time and time again with the generosity that was one of her most pronounced character traits, there wasn't the slightest risk she would be unfaithful to Ben.

Nor did he want her to be. That wasn't why he came. It was more just for the . . . peace. A little dose of calm and normality before he returned to a world where people buried young men like Snow White in underground gasoline storage tanks and went around planning how to deploy a package of explosives contaminated with radioactive material so it caused the greatest possible number of fatalities.

He took a long shower in the bathroom in the basement. Then he lay down on the bed in the guest room that was actually Ben's practice room—rows of vinyl records, amps everywhere, three different guitars, two keyboards, and a double bass in one corner—and fell asleep as if someone had just turned off a light.

SUSSE WOKE HIM up.

"Your phone is ringing," she said.

And it was. Again and again, louder and louder. But he hadn't heard it. Not until she shook his shoulder.

He grabbed the phone.

"Yeaaaaah," he said, his throat feeling as if someone had tried to scrub it with a toilet brush.

"It's Gitte."

"Yes."

"Jesper Due called from Rigshospitalet. The nurse is gone."

"What do you mean gone?"

"We're checking the video from the hospital security system. But it sounds like she left the hospital with a youngish man without saying anything to anyone. A nurse saw them together."

He swore.

"And it wasn't her husband? Or ex-husband, or whatever he is?"

"No. We called him."

"And we don't have anyone watching her?"

"No. By the time Jesper got up there, she had already walked out."

Fuck. Fuck, fuck, fuck.

"And the flight from Budapest is late so the NBH guy isn't here yet."

Well, that's something, he thought, though he would still have to find time for him eventually. International cooperation was important and good and necessary and all that, but it also required a certain amount of diplomacy, and at the moment they just didn't have the resources to be polite on top of everything else.

"I'll be there in fifteen minutes," he said.

THE VIDEOS FROM the hospital were a grainy mess. But there was a sequence, from the front entrance, where you could clearly identify Nina Borg. She was wearing a dark tracksuit, and yes, she was with a "youngish man." They were walking side by side, with slightly more than a meter between them. The only thing he could see for sure was that it wasn't Sándor Horváth.

"Is she leaving of her own free will?" Gitte asked. "What do you think?"

He shook his head faintly.

"If she is under duress, he's too far away," Mikael said. "That's a public area, lots of people around. If he wanted to control her, he should be closer. And there aren't any obvious signs that he has a weapon."

"Well, a weapon could be any number of things, of course," Søren said. "Get as good a still of him as you can, and send it around to all divisions. The NEC, too, you never know. Maybe somebody out there knows him. Did you get hold of the daughter? And her boyfriend, who was attacked?"

"She wasn't at school," Mikael said. "She had been, despite the attack. But of course they understood her wanting to go home again. I'll head over to that address in Greve and talk to her."

"Also the boyfriend, Ulf. Bring them in here. I want to talk to both of them. And Gitte, could you make sure someone from Transportation heads over to the airport to pick up our colleague from the NBH?"

"Transportation?" she said. "They're at a training exercise. It's going to have to be the cafeteria lady or me. Couldn't he take a cab?"

"**V**ERY BEAUTIFUL."

The man nodded, looking out over the pancake-flat countryside, in rolling greens with small strips of brackish gray water in between. The sky hung low and dark over the water, and the clouds on the horizon painted dark-blue stripes across the sky.

Nina looked over at the man next to her. He seemed to be in a good mood and only had one hand on the wheel as they rumbled their way up the rough gravel road. He gesticulated with the almost finished cigarette in his other hand whenever there was something particularly exciting he wanted to show her. There and there and there. He had caught a sea trout on the other side of that strip of trees over there, with a lure. Just like back home in Finland. A bunch of wires were hanging out of a dangling plastic panel next to the steering column, presumably because he had stolen the green van, and the black phone with the pictures of Ida was on the dashboard, but the man acted as if he had already forgotten all about that. His mind was on other things now.

Nina felt strangely outside her body. It wasn't just from the exhaustion and the recurring nausea. It was also the indiscriminate small talk that had been flowing unchecked from him from the second they got into the car and pulled out of Rigshospitalet's parking lot. In the beginning she had tried to find out more about Ida. She'd asked how Ida was doing and where she was, but the man had either ignored her questions or told her to shut up.

Eventually she just stared out the window and let him talk. She didn't recognize the whole route, but right now she was guessing they were somewhere on the south end of Amager Island on the outskirts of Copenhagen. Farther up the gravel road, she could make out some kind of small holding. The skinny Finn sped up for the last few meters and gave Nina a friendly smile as he spun his wheels in the smooth gravel. The 1970s-style windows of the farmhouse stared emptily out the U-shaped gravel drive in front.

The Finn jumped out of the van, letting the rest of his cigarette fall onto the gravel. Then he continued around the car, opened Nina's door and yanked her out of the car so hard that she almost landed on her knees. The pea-sized gravel stung cruelly under her white sock-clad feet, and she still didn't have any strength. Nothing to fight with, she thought. It was painfully obvious that the Finn had come to the same conclusion. He had already disappeared in the front door where he was impatiently banging doors and yelling something at someone. Of course he wasn't alone, Nina thought sluggishly. There had been three men in their apartment, and now wherever they had Ida . . . maybe she was here.

Climbing the steps to the front door of the farmhouse was like climbing a mountain, and with each step she felt her pulse race at an insane tempo. The hallway, like the windows, was a relic from the '70s. There was a pair of worn-out plastic clogs with no heels sitting on the threadbare green indoor-outdoor carpet. The door to what must have been the kitchen was open. The floor was crumbling yellow linoleum with a brown floral pattern, and all of the old kitchen cupboards and cabinets were missing. All that was left were faded patches along the walls where they used to be. Now there was just a card table pushed against the wall with an electric kettle and a stack of rolled up newspapers. A smashed picture frame was lying on the floor containing a picture of a naked girl, in a spread-eagle pose. She was pushing a pair of enormous breasts with pale nipples all the way up to her open lips. *Sabrina, eighteen years old*, Nina read. *Loves it rough, doggie style*.

Nina carefully stepped around the small shards of glass, which were strewn across the kitchen floor, and proceeded into the living room.

The first thing she saw was Ida.

She was sitting against the far wall in a weird, floppy position with one arm crooked, raised awkwardly over her head. A rag doll tossed aside by a bored child. Her dark eyes looked even darker than they usually did. Her mascara had run in long black smears so her eye sockets had turned into deep, black pits. But she was there, and she was looking at Nina with watchful eyes that were somehow still intact and defiant and teenagery. She was still Ida. Nina felt the ground disappear from under her feet in a brief giddy second of relief. Then she sank down next to Ida, carefully running her finger over Ida's black-striped cheek.

"Mom?" The wariness left Ida's eyes, and she leaned her disheveled, black-haired head against Nina's shoulder. "He came over during my free period. We just went to the bakery, and then suddenly he was there, and I didn't have time to . . ." Ida was talking so fast she was tripping over her own tongue. "I'm sorry, Mom, I'm sorry. So sorry . . ."

The sobs came like an earthquake, causing Ida's whole body to tremble, and Nina tried to pull her in closer and enfold Ida's gangly teenage body in her arms. But something was in the way. Only now did Nina realize why Ida was sitting so awkwardly on the floor. Her left arm was attached to the pipe feeding the radiator behind her with black plastic ties, but she clung to Nina with her free arm and kept mumbling about Ulf and Morten and school. Nina had stopped paying attention. She let one finger slide along the edge of the strip of black plastic around Ida's wrist. It was tight, but not dangerously so.

Only now, as she stroked Ida's hair, did she take in the rest. A young man was sitting on the floor on the other side of the radiator, tied to a pipe the same as Ida. Nina was startled to recognize him—the young man from Valby. The gash over his eyebrow still gaped a little, and he looked like he had taken several more blows in the interim. His right cheek was almost the same dark purple color as the wall behind him, and he had a deep, oozing sore on the hand that wasn't tied to the radiator.

She didn't feel sorry for him. Not anymore. No matter why he was sitting here on the floor with her daughter now, he deserved whatever beatings he'd gotten. She was only sorry that she hadn't actually been the one to give them to him.

The Finn seemed to have completely forgotten about her. He'd pushed a cowboy hat down over his forehead, adopting at the same time a more swaggering gait. He opened up a can of beer, drank, and made a slightly disgruntled face when the beer can accidentally bumped his swollen nose.

"You. Gypsy boy. Sándor—isn't that your name?" The Finn pointed to the Valby man with his beer can. "How do you say 'cunt' in Hungarian?"

The young Hungarian raised his head very slowly, but didn't respond. The Finn casually kicked one of the guy's legs.

"Come on, pal. How do you say it?"

"*Cuna*," the Hungarian said, his face completely devoid of any expression. The psychopath in the cowboy hat furrowed his brow.

"How do you spell that?" he asked, as if it were an important detail he needed for a thesis on the Hungarian language.

Beyond the Finn there was another man, sitting on a black leather sofa in the middle of the room. A slightly overweight chocolate Lab was lying on the sofa next to him, hesitantly wagging its tail as it followed the Finn around the room with its eyes. The man on the sofa slowly shut the laptop in front of him. His shoulders were pulled all the way up to his ears, and he was scowling in irritation at the Finn, who had already fished a new cigarette out of his pocket and was pacing around the leather sofa with his beer can in his hand.

"Damnit, Tommi. Can't you shut up and stand still for even a second?"

The Finn grinned. "Goes against my philosophy of life," he said. "Moss and rolling stones and all that." Then he suddenly stopped after all, eyeing Nina through narrowed eyes.

"Okay. Mother and daughter, touching reunion, cool, cool. Now we get down to business."

Nina had a strange feeling of having gone straight from small-talk recipient to being a daddy longlegs in the hands of a boy armed with a magnifying glass and the desire to take revenge for a bunch of lost fights. She had no idea what kind of "business" he might have with her, but she had a chilling sense that it was going to be horrendous.

And she still couldn't do anything. There was no chance she would be able to free Ida and slip out of the house. Even if by some miracle they managed to get that far, they were surrounded by fields and miles of unpaved roads, and the muscles in her thighs were trembling just at the effort it took to kneel down next to Ida. She was thirsty now. Her jaw clenched too tight, and her mouth felt both dry and pasty at the same time.

"What do you want?" Nina asked. She deliberately ignored the restless Finn—Tommi, the other guy had called him. Instead she looked directly at the man on the sofa. He looked more normal than the Finn. Actually he looked like he would fit seamlessly into any suburban Danish neighborhood, armed with a dog and a stroller and a sports bag and whatever else your average dad carried around. But some dads evidently dreamed beyond little league soccer practice with their sons. She had no idea what connection these two men had to the source of the radioactivity in Valby. It was hard to imagine that either of them would personally go and set off a bomb; there was hardly a seething religious or political undercurrent to them or to this house. So what *did* they want?

Maybe something to do with money and eighteen-year-old girls like Sabrina.

The man on the sofa didn't answer her. He hardly seemed to see her. His pale blue eyes only rested on her for a brief instant before he looked back at Tommi.

"Okay, then. But you handle it." The man spoke English with a heavy Danish accent. "I don't want to have to deal with stuff like that right now."

He opened his computer again and took a drink from a ceramic mug that was painted red and decorated with big, clumsy black letters. FOR DADDY, it said. Then she felt Tommi's hard, thin fingers closing round her upper arm.

"THE JACKET?"

The room he dragged her into was painted baby blue with little, white stars scattered over the walls and ceiling. A double bed covered with a worn quilt with a big floral pattern took up almost the entire room, but a rickety, white plastic lawn chair and some empty paint cans jostled for space in one corner. A flat screen TV was mounted over the bed, casting a blank blue glow over the room. The room had a faint barn-like smell, mixed with mildew and those little air fresheners people hung from their rearview mirrors. Tommi had taken up a straddling stance in front of her, and his face wore the same slightly indulgent look he had had when he pulled out his phone in the hospital.

Nina didn't understand what he meant. "What jacket?" she asked.

"Saturday evening you gave that little Gypsy shit in there a ride. He was wearing a jacket. Where is it?"

Nina began to see the light. The young Hungarian. She had taken off his jacket to check his rib when they were sitting in her car outside her apartment. And then what had happened to it? That evening wavered in her memory, half hidden in green clouds of nausea.

"In the car," she said. "It's in the car."

"You're lying," the Finn said, staring at her expressionlessly. "I don't believe you."

Nina waited a few seconds for an explanation, but none came. The Finn slowly shook his head. Then he hit her. He struck her with the palm of his hand on her left cheek, but the blow wasn't actually that hard. Just unexpected. Nina took an involuntary step back and bumped into the light-blue wall. The Finn's eyes had that same glassy look they had had when he pushed her head down into the pillow. She was shaking both from exhaustion and anticipation of the next blow, but instead he suddenly turned his back on her and picked up the Mac laptop connected to the TV and put it on the bed. The big screen mounted on the ceiling flickered obediently and opened a page with a list of choices. *Hotel whore gets pounded. Schoolgirl and teacher.* And of course more *Sabrina, eighteen years old*, who apparently liked it all the time and in every conceivable position. He took his time, appearing to surf aimlessly around between the numerous flashy ads but finally ended up choosing a video with two Asian girls on a beach.

Nina had moved into high alert ages ago. The door behind her was still open and every single cell in her body was tensed for flight. She wanted out of here. Now. She wanted to go to Ida, get her free, and get her away from this place. From this man. What did he want that jacket for?

"If it's not in my car, then I don't know where it is."

Tommi didn't even look up from his computer. The sound of his rapid fingers on the keys was the only thing audible in the light blue room. Then a new picture appeared on the big screen. Ida. But not like she had seen her on his mobile phone. This was from Ida's room. The video started, and Nina stood with her eyes locked on the screen over her, watching how Ida tried to escape from the camera at first. A man was holding her so she couldn't, and Nina recognized the Finn's gaunt face. He was the one holding her. And touching her. It took a hard grip to hold her in the picture, with his forearms pushed against Ida's breasts, while he whispered something to her. In the beginning she was screaming and kicking him. She continued to struggle as he pulled down her panties, but eventually she was just crying. Standing there naked, hunched over in front of the camera with her shoulders shaking. It seemed as if the guy holding the camera was starting to get bored, because the camera began to drift, pointing now at a couple of pale young men near Ida's desk. Nina had time to recognize Ulf's shocked face and shaved head. The young Roma guy from the car was standing next to Ulf with a strangely empty expression. As if he weren't really there. Someone mumbled something. Maybe it was Ulf. Eventually, the man with the camera gave up on aiming it at anything.

"Shut up now," he yelled. "Just shut up, you horny little bastard." Then the image on the screen froze.

Tommi turned around and looked calmly at Nina.

"You'd be surprised how popular this kind of shit is on the Internet . . . You can make a lot of money if you have the right material. Your daughter's cute, photogenic. We could make a new video. Just her and me."

The Finn stuck an almost comically pink, pointy tongue out between his tobacco-pale lips and slid it in and out suggestively. That was enough. Nina stared into his slightly bloodshot eyes and for a long, happy moment pictured herself digging her fingers into his eyes. Scratching, biting, kicking. Ferociously, over and over, until she was sure he would never move again. Would never again be able to hurt her and Ida. Ever.

But in reality she didn't do anything. Just stood there, frozen on the grease-stained gray carpet. Her whole body felt ice-cold, and it was hard to even turn her head. To breathe.

Nina thought about the radiation from Valby. About the rays that had penetrated everything, her and the children. And she knew that she ought to think it was important. But instead she closed her eyes and tried to picture the jacket. She had set it in the back seat along with the first aid kit and then . . .

She tried to remember everything from that evening. The nausea, the headache. The precarious drive to the Coal-House Camp. And then it hit her. There had been two jackets. When Magnus drove her to the hospital, he had scooped her stuff out of the Fiat and moved it over into his beloved Volvo. And there had been two jackets. Her's and that young Hungarian's.

"Magnus Nilsson," she said, swallowing. "My boss at

the clinic. It was all in his car when we left the Coal-House Camp." She let her head fall back, recalling the feeling of total weightlessness when Magnus had lifted her up and carried her into the hospital. Magnus, big, strong, and occasionally hot-tempered. She hoped to God he wouldn't be there when the Finn came looking.

AFTER THAT SHE was allowed to sit on the floor next to Ida. The Finn carefully secured her left arm to the heating pipe the same way, and after a fair amount of maneuvering they managed to get themselves into a more or less comfortable sitting position, with Nina's arm behind the back of Ida's head. Then the Finn disappeared out the door. Nina could hear the car on the gravel and guessed he was headed for the jacket in Magnus's Volvo. Mr. Suburbia was still sitting on the living room sofa, staring fixedly at the computer screen in front of him while Ida dozed, her head resting on Nina's shoulder.

Nina couldn't sleep.

Even though the fatigue sat in every muscle of her body with a paralyzing weight. Now she was worried about Magnus. Magnus and Ida. Because there was nothing to indicate that this was the end of it. It worried her that the Finn hadn't done anything to hide his identity or keep the location of this property a secret.

Nina looked down at Ida's tear-stained face as it rested heavily against her shoulder and again felt the same corrosive sense of impotence that had flooded through her when Tommi showed her the clip from the apartment. She should never have given them Magnus. She shouldn't have helped them find the fucking jacket. She may have postponed the unpleasantness for Ida by giving them Magnus, but that was all she had done. Postponed and delayed something, although she didn't quite know what.

The man on the other side of the radiator moved his uninjured hand a couple of centimeters up the pipe and moaned softly as he tried to push himself into a more upright position. Then he cleared his throat and out of the corner of her eye Nina saw that he was looking right at her.

"I'm sorry," he said.

Nina shifted slightly so she could see him. He looked terrible. His shirt was damp and filthy and covered with bloodstains presumably from both his face and his injured hand. His eyes were dull and washed-out.

"I was in your apartment. I should have stopped them," he continued. His English was easier to understand than the Finn's, possibly because he spoke more slowly. It took him a long time to find the right words. Nina couldn't be bothered to respond. She didn't have the energy to provide him with water, soap, and towel so he could wash his hands of the whole thing. She had seen the video. No one had been holding a gun to his head. No one had forced him to watch while someone ripped off her daughter's underwear. He was a free agent.

"She's fourteen years old," she said, noting much to her own irritation how the exhaustion and the seething rage made her voice tremble slightly.

The young man winced, and Nina knew that she should feel sorry for him. But she just didn't care.

"*I* would have stopped them," she snarled. "I would have stopped them no matter what."

Ida moved fitfully against Nina's chest, raising her obstinate head and looking over at the young man.

"Mom," she said, with a little of the old Ida's arrogant tone. "It wasn't Sándor. He couldn't help it. They had his brother. They killed his brother."

Nina sat there in total silence. She didn't react. Didn't make any doubting or shocked or sympathetic comments. She just felt the weight of her daughter's living body and tried not to think about the implication—that they had killed someone. That that was a line they had already crossed.

"**N**O MATTER HOW you look at it," Torben said stretching in his chair, "it is a secret organization in breech of some of this country's laws."

Søren felt almost as tired as before he had slept.

"They help deported refugees and other illegal aliens," he said. "They're sentimental do-gooders, for Christ's sake, not some gang of violent extremists."

They were surrounded by boxes of ring binders, confiscated from Peter Erhardsen's house in Vanløse. Names, dates, addresses, budgets. The man had a better grasp of who his "clients" were than most social service agencies. And absolutely no clue about how to run a covert operation. They could unravel his whole so-called Network based on his own meticulous lists.

"You of all people should know that idealistic, altruistic motives are no guarantee against terrorism. On the contrary. There is a risk that we're dealing with a group of people who might do something to promote their cause during the Summit."

"Yes, but not a dirty bomb, for God's sake." Søren studied Torben to see if he was playing devil's advocate or if he really believed this theory. He knew that privately Torben was less than thrilled with the current government's immigration policy, but that would only make him especially careful to keep his threat assessment objective and professional.

There was a knock on the door. It was Gitte.

"Our visitor from the NBH has arrived," she said.

"Good," Torben said. "Then let's try to get this business under control before it's too damn late."

Søren looked up abruptly and caught a glimpse of the revved-up tension underneath Torben's calm, professional demeanor. Torben noticed him noticing and subtly shrugged one shoulder.

"Central Station," he said. "Or the stadium on Wednesday during the international game. Don't you see? They don't even need to target any of the politicians at the Summit; they just need to hit Copenhagen. If we have a big, nasty radioactive bomb crater somewhere in the downtown area, the Summit won't happen, at least not right here, right now. And that might be enough of a victory."

Søren felt a chill down his spine. He was glad he wasn't running security right now. That he wasn't the one who had to decide how to divvy up the available equipment, where to position people with Geiger counters, and where not to. They couldn't cover all of Copenhagen—that was impossible. Someone would have to prioritize who and what should be protected, and for the rest, all they could do was hope.

"How big an area are we talking about?" he asked. "I mean, how big would the contamination zone be?"

Yet another understated shrug. "It depends entirely on how strong the explosives are and how much radioactive material there is," Torben said. "And maybe we'll know more about the latter after we've talked to our man from the NBH."

THE MAN FROM the NBH looked like a retired wrestler, Søren thought. Short, graying dark hair, strong shoulders, strong neck, low center of gravity, but definitely more muscle weight than fat. His name was Károly Gábor, and he radiated a calm professionalism that matched Torben's perfectly.

"We traced the radioactive material to this old, disused hospital," he said, pushing a button on his laptop so the projector showed a picture of the skeleton of a building and a little map indicating where it was located. "Apparently the Soviet troops abandoned some radiation-therapy equipment in the hospital's basement when they left in 1990. Unfortunately the radioactive substance was cesium chloride, which has both a very long half-life—about thirty years—and physical properties that allow it to bind very easily with its environment if the seal is broken."

A new picture—this time of people in yellow suits that resembled the ones currently decontaminating the soil in Valby. In this picture, however, there was a Latin American slum in the background.

"In terms of comparable events there's the Goiânia disaster in Brazil, in 1987, where careless handling of a similar unit resulted in the deaths of four people, and 249 others suffered serious radiation sickness. Like the device in Goiânia, the actual radioactive core in our unit was sealed in a ball-shaped lead capsule that rotated inside another lead ball, both with small openings so that when these two openings lined up, and only then, there would be a brief, controllable beam of radiation."

Cross sectional diagrams and animations helped him get his point across. The man had done his homework.

"In our case, however, the device was damaged

following an earthquake, and the outer casing had split, so the two young Roma who found it were able to open it and access the unit itself: a small cylinder packed full of cesium salt, which they put in a big paint bucket filled with sand. We questioned one of the two young men, an eighteen-year-old named László Erős, better known by his nickname, Pitkin. He is currently at a hospital in Miskolc being treated for radiation sickness but appears to be recovering. The second, sixteen-year-old Tamás Rézmüves, was identified from the photo you sent us. He's your corpse."

Gábor pushed a button again, and a photo appeared on the screen. Snow White, now alive, flashing a foolhardy smile at the cameraman. You could see a gap in his teeth, but it didn't diminish the effect of his charm.

"How did he end up buried in a gas tank in Valby?" Mikael asked.

"We think it's quite likely that he and his half-brother, Sándor Horváth, found a buyer in Denmark for the radio-active material and came up here to deliver the material. We believe their motive is exclusively financial, but we can't be sure. It appears that young Rézmüves was harboring a certain amount of anger at the Hungarian establishment. In terms of the buyer's identity, the only lead we can offer is the IP address we already gave you."

"We still haven't been able to find any connection between the IP address and the group of people in Valby," Søren said. "But we're working on it. What we do know, however, is that Sándor Horváth was in Valby."

"But you haven't found him?"

"No. His phone has been inactive since Saturday, he

hasn't used his credit card, and we don't have a single witness who has seen him since Saturday evening, when he apparently helped break into the apartment of one of the Danes who was helping the sick children in Valby, a nurse by the name of Nina Borg. She was the one who led us to Valby, after she was diagnosed with radiation sickness."

"And of course you've questioned her," Gábor said.

"Apparently she's just an overly idealistic nurse who was helping some people in need. But then . . ." Søren hesitated. How to word this? "Escaped" sounded so drastic. "She left the hospital with a youngish man we still haven't identified. We don't know where she is at the moment."

One of Gábor's eyebrows rose a couple millimeters, and Søren swore under his breath. No trace of Horváth, and then one of the case's lead witnesses just walks away without their having any kind of surveillance on her. The man must think they were amateurs. His phone vibrated in his pocket, but he ignored it. Whatever it was, it would have to wait until they finished the briefing.

He sensed Gitte fidgeting in the row of chairs behind him, and shortly afterward she leaned forward and handed him her phone.

"Boss," she whispered. "I think you need to hear this."

THEY HAD BROUGHT the boyfriend of Nina Borg's daughter into one of the interrogation rooms in Building C. He looked nervous and had a bruise on one cheek, presumably from Saturday night's attack.

He was alone—a five-foot-eleven teenager with a

shaved head in a black Iron Maiden T-shirt and a pair of camouflage hip-hop pants—because they hadn't been able to find his girlfriend Ida.

"We know each other from Greve," he explained. "I live across the street."

"I thought she lived in Østerbro?"

"Not anymore. Not since her mom went all glow-in-the-dark and contaminated their whole apartment. Now she lives with her dad's sister in Greve. But she still goes to Jagtvejen School, and we had agreed to meet there after school. But she didn't show up. And when I asked Anna, who's in her class, she said Ida hadn't been there for the last two periods."

Søren raised his index finger in Gitte's direction. She nodded and left the room. They hadn't found Ida at the address in Greve either. Of course Ida might just have gone to a friend's house, but too many of the people involved in this case were going missing. It wasn't too soon to push the panic button.

"Ulf, we'd like to hear a little more about the three men who attacked you."

He patiently led the boy through the statements, not pushing him, but providing opportunities. Was the first man taller than Ulf, or shorter? Was he a wearing a jacket, or a T-shirt, or a button-down? Did they speak English with the same accent, or did they have different accents?

"Different," Ulf said. "The one without the mask didn't really say anything. The two with tights over their faces . . . one of them was Danish, I think. The other one talked a little . . . kind of like those guys on *The Dudesons*."

The Dudesons? Søren thought.

"And what is that?" he asked.

"You know, the TV show. Those crazy guys from Finland who run around and do all kinds of weird stuff. Set themselves on fire or sit down on an anthill with no pants on, that kind of thing. Kind of like *Jackass*."

"Do you mean the guy might be Finnish?"

Ulf shrugged his T-shirt-clad shoulders. "I dunno. He just sort of sounded like them." Ulf looked down, apparently at the tabletop, but Søren could hear from his breathing that he was struggling with something. Tears? Disgraceful, unmanly tears? After all, the man who talked "kind of like those guys on *The Dudesons*" was also the man who had ripped the underwear off the boy's girlfriend while the other guy filmed it on his phone. That might raise strong emotions even in souls more phlegmatic than Ulf's.

"Why didn't she show up?" the boy asked, still without looking up. "Did something happen to her?"

"Let's not assume the worst," Søren said. But he thought to himself that if the *Dudesons* guy had taken the daughter, it was no longer a mystery why the mother had chosen to go off with him without protest.

"**T**HE POLICE ARE going to find us, right Mom? You can't be kidnapped in Denmark for that long. It's a small country. They can do all kinds of stuff with mobile phones and, and . . ."

Ida's voice was shrill, and she was searching feverishly for the right words in English as she looked dubiously from Sándor and back to Nina. Like the child of divorced parents, trying in vain to get a conversation going between mother and father.

Over on the sofa, Mr. Suburbia put an old James Bond movie into the DVD player and the sound of explosions rumbled out of the robust surround-sound system as Pierce Brosnan battled the villains. The flat screen's stand was bent so that everything tilted precariously to the right, but it didn't appear to detract from Mr. Suburbia's viewing pleasure.

"Of course they're going to find us," Nina said calmly, in Danish. "And even if they don't, I'll take care of you. We'll be all right."

Sándor seemed to guess what Nina was saying and nodded slightly as if to support her optimistic interpretation of their situation, but their eyes met briefly over Ida's head, and Nina saw the same conclusion in his eyes that she had reached. If they didn't do something . . . unless something happened soon, Tommi and Mr. Suburbia were going to kill them. All three of them, but probably Ida last.

IDA HAD FALLEN asleep again by the time Tommi came back.

The wind had picked up outside, and Nina could hear the rain rapping against the window over the radiator. Mr. Suburbia had made himself some instant soup using the electric kettle in the kitchen and conducted a long, quiet conversation on his phone that concluded with "kissy kissy, darling." Nina guessed he was talking to the source of the red ceramic mug on the coffee table. Frederik, that was his name, Sándor said. But she kept thinking of him as Mr. Suburbia.

A fresh James Bond movie was playing on the surround-sound system, this time one of the classics with Sean Connery, and Mr. Suburbia had put his feet up on the longer of the two sofas while he sipped his instant soup and supplemented the meal with a pack of chocolate cookies. Nina tried to figure out what time it was. They had taken her watch at the hospital, and her last accurate point of reference was when she was sitting in the car next to Tommi; the digital clock on the dashboard had said 2 P.M. when they arrived. Now a yellowish, rainy-day twilight filled the living room, and she estimated that it must be between 6 and 7 at night—she couldn't be any more precise than that.

They didn't hear Tommi coming until he was actually in the house, gliding through the living room door with slow, cat-like motions. He still had the broad-rimmed leather hat pulled squarely down over his forehead, and Nina could tell right away that his trip had been a success. He looked less tense and walked right over to Mr. Suburbia on the sofa, triumphantly waving a folded piece of paper.

"I got it."

The staccato Finnish accent caused Mr. Suburbia to turn and finally lower the cacophony of exploding cars and warehouses.

"Awesome," he said with emphasis, and for the first time since Nina had arrived at the property, he smiled enthusiastically. He stood up and tugged his shirt down over his modest potbelly. "Is that the name of the buyer?"

Tommi shook his head. "No, it's more some kind of code, but I already cracked it. Check this out." He unfolded the slip and pointed. "These could be dates, and these over here are phone numbers. It says text messages only."

He had already pulled out his phone and was starting to enter numbers. Mr. Suburbia was standing next to him, looking a little sheepish as he stared at the paper. He clearly hadn't understood the principle, which caused Tommi to switch over to a playful grin.

"Hey, dude, I'm not the accountant on this operation. Try and up your game, would you?"

He stopped his eager dialing and again let his finger run down over the paper on the table in front of them.

"Here are the different dates, and here . . . a new phone number for each day. This buyer is being super fucking cautious. Good for us. I'm texting him that we're ready to deliver the package."

Frederik nodded, and Nina could see that he was having a hard time containing an ecstatic grin that was almost identical to the Finn's. So. It was as trivial as that. This was about money. Probably quite a lot of money, but it was still just about the money.

Her nausea had returned and she was getting a little

dizzy from being tied in the same position for such a long time. She was still thirsty, but Sándor had already asked for water once and been told no.

"Then you'll just be needing to pee," as Mr. Suburbia had put it. He didn't want to have any trouble with them while Tommi was away, and now that the Finn was back, Nina didn't want to ask. She didn't want him to look at her, because if he did he would also notice Ida, and she wanted him to forget that Ida was here. She wanted to be invisible. For as long as possible.

The Finn went to the kitchen, came back with a beer can in his hand, and glanced briefly at James Bond, who was still playing on the crooked flat screen, without the sound now. Then he flopped down onto the love seat, most of which was taken up by the brown Lab. He slapped the dog on the nose. It raised its head and nipped playfully at the Finn's quick fingers, but then he hit it again, slapping the dog hard first on the nose and then on the forehead with the palm of his hand. The dog wagged its tail in confusion as yet another burst of hard slaps rained down on its head.

"Yeah, you want to play? Good dog!" The Finn landed a powerful punch on the forehead of the brown Lab, which finally appreciated the seriousness of the situation. Whining, it tumbled off the edge of the sofa and crawled under the coffee table to hide.

Mr. Suburbia leapt up from the end of the sofa.

"What the hell are you doing?"

"It shouldn't be up on the furniture," Tommi said.

"Keep your mitts off my dog," Mr. Suburbia shouted. "He has more right to be here than you do!"

Tommi pulled his chin in against his chest in feigned puzzlement.

"Well, well," he said. "That wasn't a very nice thing to say."

His tone sent a shiver down Nina's spine. Apparently it also had an effect on Mr. Suburbia.

"Just leave him alone," he said, but without the aggressive undertone he had used a moment earlier.

The lack of opposition almost seemed to frustrate the Finn. His restless eyes settled on the captives below the window. Nina tried to look away. To pretend they weren't there. But it was too late. The Finn was on his way across the living room floor, his steps quick and decisive.

"Hi, baby," he said to Ida, who had woken up in the middle of all the yelling. "You wanna be a movie star?"

He positioned himself in front of them with his legs spread, his crotch a few centimeters from Nina's face. She could smell some kind of cheap body shampoo mixed with nicotine and the cloying scent of fabric softener from those faded jeans. Nina looked up to meet his gaze, which caused him to pump his groin with a grin, so close that Nina reflexively pulled her head back, hitting it on the radiator behind her. This sent a little jolt through Ida. Nina prayed she was smart enough to sit still. Don't do anything, don't give him any excuse to touch you, she thought fervently. When driving on the roads between refugee camps around Dadaab, she had learned from the local women how to avoid trouble. Avoid drawing attention to yourself. Even the most hardened men liked to have an excuse when they committed rape. The girl with the defiant look and contempt in her voice was chosen first.

"Go away," Ida said. "Leave my mom alone."

Shut up, sweetheart, Nina thought. It's not your job to defend me!

Tommi smiled, a warm and disconcertingly normal smile.

"Man, are you cute," he said. "I think it's going to be a really good movie."

He squatted down in front of her and slid his hand down the front of her shirt.

"Leave her alone." Nina spoke quietly, with the same amount of emphasis on each syllable. No more than that. Not enough opposition to provoke him.

"Fucking let go of me," Ida hissed, trying to bite his hand.

No. No, Ida. Not like that!

The Finn's breathing had changed, and Nina could see his hand moving under the cotton fabric of Ida's T-shirt. Ida gasped, popped up onto her knees and awkwardly tried to wriggle away from him. Nina grabbed the only chance she could see. She slammed her fist upward, straight into his crotch, with everything she had.

She didn't hit him dead on, but still accurately enough that he staggered back a step moaning, with both hands over his crotch. As he stood like that, Sándor somehow managed to flip himself up on his hands, the bound healthy one and the wounded free one, and kick backward with both legs, bucking like a horse.

One of his heels hit the Finn in the face, right on his swollen black-and-blue nose. Tommi bellowed and kicked Sándor in the thigh, but Nina wasn't sure the Hungarian even noticed it. He was already doubled over, clutching his wounded hand, which had started bleeding again. A bruise on his thigh was probably the least of his concerns.

"Knock it off!" Mr. Suburbia shouted. Under the coffee table, the Labrador was barking furiously, although it showed no desire to get involved in the fight.

"I'll kill him," Tommi said. "This time I'll fucking kill him!" He grabbed for the fringed cowboy jacket he had tossed over the back of one sofa, but Mr. Suburbia beat him to it. He snatched the jacket and pulled something out of one of the pockets. A gun, of course. Nina was surprised only that it wasn't a gleaming silver six-shooter, but a dull black modern affair with a barrel that wasn't more than twelve or thirteen centimeters long.

"Give me that," Tommi hissed.

"Just knock it off, damnit." Mr. Suburbia said, looking irritated. Like a father interrupted in the middle of the evening news by a fight between his kids. "Are you coming totally unglued? First Tyson and now this? No more trouble now. You hear me?"

"But . . ." Tommi flung out his arms as if he were about to protest, and Nina was half expecting him to say that the others had started it.

Just then there was a *pling* from another pocket of the fringed jacket. Frederik awkwardly put down the pistol on the coffee table and pulled out the phone.

"It's from him," Frederik said. "It's going to be tonight. Nine-thirty. But he won't send the address until later." He looked up at Tommi again. "We're so close. Quit thinking with your cock. I want things low-key now. Smooth. That other stuff is going to have to wait."

The Finn shot Nina, Ida, and Sándor a collective angry look.

"Fine," Tommi said. "Then you can be the fucking babysitter."

The Finn flipped a defiant fuck-you finger at them all and vanished into the blue video room, presumably to relieve his frustration in the company of eighteen-year-old Sabrina.

Nina looked at Ida. There was barely suppressed panic in her dark eyes, and her bound arm was moving incessantly in an involuntary twitch.

"It's okay, sweetheart," Nina lied. "Nothing's going to happen. I'm here."

A **LITTLE AFTER SEVEN**, they finally hit the jackpot in the identification lottery. At that point Søren had had an unsatisfying conversation with Malee Rasmussen, who pretty much repeated the stock phrases he was familiar with from the recording with near surgical precision: "It's an investment. I didn't know there was anyone there. I haven't been there since February." He hadn't been able to find any holes in her shell, and finally he had had to admit defeat. Whatever she was afraid of, it made her completely immune to the pressure of more civilized interrogation methods.

Out of sheer desperation he had then spent almost twenty minutes watching a group of brain-dead young Finns subject themselves to various bizarre forms of bodily harm, all while laughing maniacally and yelling at themselves and each other. In English, with a strikingly pronounced Finnish accent. By the time his phone finally rang, he was profoundly grateful for the interruption.

It was his navy blue friend, Birgitte Johnsen.

"I just saw the description you sent out," she said. "Of the man in the video."

"Yes," Søren said. "Do you know him?"

"It could be Tommi Karvinen."

Søren sat up straight and slapped his pen down on the tabletop with a bang.

"A Finn?"

"Yup. One Nordic import we could certainly have done without. We suspect him of being heavily involved in trafficking, but the girls he's involved with don't talk. We haven't been able to nail him. Aside from an old narcotics conviction from the late 1990s, he just has one suspended conviction for aggravated assault from 2003."

"Suspended?"

"He beat up a john who had beat up a prostitute. His lawyer argued self-defense on the woman's behalf, and that won him some leniency."

"As in 'how chivalrous of him to defend her?'"

"Yes, but the most interesting thing . . ."

"Aha?" He could hear in Birgitte's voice that she was looking forward to telling him the next bit. But did she have to sound like a grandmother holding out a caramel and then pretending she wasn't going to let him have it?

"The prostitute, who of course was heard as a witness in the case, was Malee Rasmussen."

Yes!

"Give me everything you've got," he said. "Starting with the address."

All of a sudden his body was alive again. The feeling of defeat he'd been fighting all afternoon was gone. He leapt up and flung open the door to the hallway.

"Gitte!" he yelled. "Gitte, where are you?"

Christian came over to him with a printout in his hand.

"She just went downstairs for a power nap," he said. "But I have something for you."

Søren mechanically accepted the pages Christian was handing him.

"What is this?"

"The results from the Opel list."

"Give me just the highlights. Have we got something?"

"Not really. No IP addresses of particular interest. No one belonging to any known groups. No criminal records, apart from a guy who was apparently into alternative life-styles at some point back in the '70s and had a minor drug conviction. Solid pillars of society right down the list with an average age just over sixty, which I suppose isn't so surprising, considering the age of the car. These are people who bought German quality and kept it. The only thing is . . ." Christian paused.

Come on, Christian, not you too. Give me my caramel!

"Yes?"

"It's nothing too definite. The man is over eighty and retired. He worked for the city, in Buildings and Safety for damn near half a century. Not exactly obvious terrorist material."

"Christian, what the hell? What about him?"

"He just . . . well, more specifically, his wife, the house is in her name . . . they just took out a sizeable loan on the equity. And we can't see how they spent the money."

"How much?"

"Six hundred thousand kroner."

Okay. That wasn't exactly small potatoes.

"Well. I suppose we know he didn't spend it on a new car," Søren said.

"No. It could have been a holiday home or something like that, but if so it's not here in Denmark."

"Send Gitte over there when she wakes up."

"Will do. Where are you headed?"

Søren felt a famished predator's grin spreading across his face.

"Off to catch me a Finn," he said.

THE POLICE OFFICER was female. In a way, it was two shocks in one.

Of course Skou-Larsen was well aware that the police force employed countless women, but when there was a friendly young lady on one's doorstep, ringing one's doorbell, well, "Whoops, the police are here" wasn't exactly the first thing that popped into one's head.

"Has something happened to Helle?" he asked, as soon as he realized the meaning of the identification she was showing him.

"No, no," the policewoman said reassuringly. "We just need to follow up on all the leads in this case. Am I correct, sir, in my understanding that you own a 1984 Opel Rekord?"

"Yes." She could see it in the carport, he thought, if she turned her head a little. But he supposed they had to ask. "Model E," he said, to try to seem a little more accommodating. "An older car, of course, but very reliable. What is this in regard to?" She wasn't in uniform, so it couldn't be a traffic infraction. Or . . . did they not wear uniforms anymore?

"Would you mind if we came in for a moment, sir?"

We? It wasn't until then that he noticed the second police officer, who was still standing on the sidewalk talking into his phone. Skou-Larsen furrowed his brow, but it seemed rude to say no, and it would also look suspicious in their eyes.

"Not at all," he said. "My wife isn't home, but perhaps I could figure out how to make us some coffee."

The second police officer introduced himself as Mikael Nielsen, but didn't want to sit down.

"You guys mind if I take a look at the car while you talk?" Nielsen asked.

Skou-Larsen felt a wasp-sting of irritation at the officer's rude informality. You guys. As if he were talking to some street punk.

"Perhaps first you could just be so kind as to tell me what this case is about?" he suggested. "I can assure you that I haven't done anything illegal."

No one said, "No, of course not," or any other similarly placating phrases. Both Mikael Nielsen and that young lady—what was her name now? Nystrøm, Nyhus, Nymand—were just observing him with an expectant neutrality that he found disagreeable.

"Of course, sir, we could also wait for a warrant," Gitte Nymand said. Yes, that's what she said her name was.

He waved his hand in irritation.

"No," he said. "That's fine. Check whatever you damn well please, for Pete's sake."

"Thank you very much, sir," Gitte said, rewarding him with a warm smile. "The whole thing will go much quicker this way. For you as well."

He refused to let himself be mollified. She might be more polite than her colleague, but the signal was very clear: They were in charge, and they could invade his car and his home as it suited them. The affront stung, and he decided that he didn't feel like struggling with the coffee machine for their sake. Deeply ingrained manners made him wait until after she had sat down on the sofa before he allowed himself to settle into his favorite armchair.

Maybe it was good that Helle had that extra choir practice; with any luck, he could get this all over with and have the constabulary out of the house again before she came home.

"Let me just jump right in," Nymand said. "Several months ago, sir, you and your wife took out a loan for a little over half a million kroner. The loan was paid out in cash, which is rather unusual. Could you explain to me what the money was for?"

"Oh," Skou-Larsen said, suddenly feeling the light of understanding casting a reconciliatory glow over the invasion. "You're from the *fraud* squad."

"No, sir," Nymand said. "We're from the PET."

"But this obviously has something to do with that scam case in Spain," he said.

She didn't skip a beat. "Could you please tell me about it, sir," she said. "From your point of view, of course."

"I'm afraid my wife was taken in by a few brightly colored brochures and a salesman who was slightly too clever. And since the house is in her name, I didn't learn of her plans until it was too late. It was supposed to be a surprise, you understand. I'm almost eighty-five. And she thought it would be good for me to have someplace warmer to spend the winters."

Gitte nodded encouragingly, without interrupting.

"But it turned out the whole thing was a sham. The apartment my wife thought she bought doesn't exist. At least not outside the pictures in the brochure."

"Do you still have the brochure, sir?"

"Of course. Would you like to see it?"

He went to retrieve it from the drawer in Helle's

nightstand and then placed it on the rosewood coffee table in front of the police officer. PUEBLO PUERTO LAGUNAS it said in sunshine-yellow capital letters across the glossy front, and the pictures underneath were brimming with enough palm trees, pool umbrellas, and idyllic balconies to produce a stab of longing in any winter-weary Danish soul. Nor was Skou-Larsen completely immune to it. The idea of escaping the asthma-inducing fogs and winter bouts of arthritis was agreeable enough, but one didn't need to toss every scrap of judgment and healthy common sense out the window because of it.

"The problem is," Skou-Larsen said, "that the apartment my wife thinks she bought hasn't even been built yet. And in addition, it's already been sold to someone else. She keeps saying that there must have been some mistake, but I'm convinced the whole thing was a scam."

"I see. So the money was a down payment or a deposit?"

"Yes. A deposit."

"Mr. Skou-Larsen, we've no record of the money having been transferred to any other account, either here in Denmark or abroad. It was just cashed from the loan account the bank set up."

"I'm afraid my wife was so careless as to pay the sum in cash to a so-called agent in their sales office. I called them, but they claimed they had never heard of him. They said they don't even have agents in Denmark, just in Spain and one location in England. I think it was Brighton."

"So, sir, you believe your wife was the victim of a fraud?"

"I most certainly do. Wouldn't you call that a con job?"

"If it happened the way you describe, sir, I certainly would. We'll have to look into it more closely. In the meantime, perhaps you could tell me if you can remember what you were doing Saturday, May second, between 6 and 11 P.M.?"

Skou-Larsen was brought out of his rightful indignation with a jerk.

"What I was doing . . . ?" he said hesitantly. It sounded just like something one of those godawful mystery-novel detectives would ask the murder suspect. And he didn't see how it could be related to the fraud case. Unless the con man had met with some kind of accident? They had asked about the car, after all.

"I should think I was watching TV," he said hesitantly. "We usually do on Saturday. My wife likes those prime time dramas." Then he happened to think of something. "No, wait. I think that might be the Saturday I had to go to the clinic because I fainted. Doctors hardly ever make house calls anymore, you know, not even if you're practically dying. But once I got there, they changed their mind, and ended up admitting me to the hospital for the night."

"Which hospital?"

"Bispebjerg."

"And what was wrong with you, if you don't mind my asking?"

"Blood pressure. It was too low." At the hospital they claimed that he must have taken too many of his Fortzaar pills, but he was sure he hadn't. "They kept me in until Sunday, so I wasn't home that night."

The second policeman, Nielsen, returned from the

carport with a yellow device that reminded Skou-Larsen of the blood pressure monitor the doctor used, maybe because they had just been talking about that night at Bispebjerg Hospital. Instead of the blood pressure monitor's inflatable cuff, it had a stethoscope-like object connected to it by a spiral cord. Skou-Larsen noticed the two officers exchange a look and an infinitesimal shake of the head.

"We also need to check the house," the one named Nielsen said.

"Mr. Skou-Larsen was kind enough to give us permission to check anything we needed to," Gitte said quickly, and Skou-Larsen already regretted his rash words. Were they going to go rooting around in his closets and drawers and gape at his folded underwear now? But that wasn't what the young man was doing. Instead, he plugged a pair of headphones into his yellow box and started walking around waving the stethoscope-like instrument.

"I'm sorry, but what on earth is he doing?" Skou-Larsen asked. "What kind of device is that?"

At first he wasn't sure if Gitte was going to answer him. But after a brief pause, it came.

"It's a Geiger counter," she said. "Or more accurately, a Geiger-Müller counter. Mr. Skou-Larsen, does anyone besides you ever use your car? Your wife, perhaps?"

"Helle doesn't drive," he responded absentmindedly. A Geiger counter? In his house? "Does this have anything to do with that business in Valby? Why in the world would you think there's radioactivity in our home? Do we need to be evacuated?" His muddled brain reached all the way back to the safety drills from the '50s, and he started contemplating what he would need if he were going to spend the night in the air-raid shelter under Emdrup School. No, wait, it wasn't called that anymore. What was it now, Lundehus School? Did they even still have the bomb shelter? He could picture the old brochure clearly. IN THE EVENT OF WAR, it was called, with a foreword by former Prime Minister Viggo Kampmann, and gave information about "the destructive range of the new weapons" and the recommendation to keep enough emergency rations on hand for eight days. But this wasn't a nuclear war, this was . . . this was something else. You can't make an atomic bomb out of cesium, he told himself. But a Geiger counter—in his house?

"What is he looking for?" he managed to ask.

"Try to concentrate now, Mr. Skou-Larsen. Has anyone else used your car? Has it ever been stolen?"

"No," he said. "Never."

"Do you own a computer, sir?" Gitte asked.

"Uh, yes. Our son . . . he's good at sending e-mails and that kind of thing."

"We would like permission to copy the contents of your hard drive."

"Yes. But . . ." Suddenly he discovered that he had put his hand on her wrist, a move that took both of them by surprise. "Won't you tell me what's going on?" he asked, letting go of her again even though he actually wanted to keep holding on until she responded. It was unbearable, all of it. It was as if his home on Elmehøjvej were suddenly transformed into the setting for one of those absurdist 1960s dramas. They had been to see one, he recalled. With a title like *Happy Days*, he had expected it to be entertaining, but it was mostly sad, and Helle got angry and said it wasn't right to waste people's time with stuff like that. That was actually the last time they had been to the theater, apart from a musical or two.

Gitte gave him a look that was not entirely devoid of compassion, or so he thought.

"I'm sorry, Mr. Skou-Larsen. But as I said, we have to follow up on every lead. Even the more unlikely ones." She stood up. "Mikael?"

"Yes," came the muffled response from upstairs.

"Are you about done?"

"Just about."

A moment later, the policeman with the Geiger counter came back down to the living room.

"Clean," he said. "Just background radiation."

She nodded as if that was just what she had been expecting.

"There, you see now, Mr. Skou-Larsen. There's no reason to worry. We have to take your hard drive with us, or would you rather have us wait here until someone from IT can come out and make a copy?"

"Take it," he said hoarsely. The sooner he got them out of the house, the better. "We almost never use the computer. Not since Helle learned how to send text messages."

They left, after a polite goodbye—even from the rude young male officer. But Skou-Larsen was shaken and dazed, not sure that anything made sense anymore.

Thank God Helle hadn't been home . . .

RHODESIAVEJ. **THE STREET** name sounded so exotic, Søren thought, but ironically suburban neighborhoods in Denmark didn't come much more boring than this. Small boxy plots with slightly oversized boxy houses, most of them made of identical yellow brick.

The carport was empty. According to the motor vehicle registry, Tommi Karvinen was supposed to be the proud owner of a four-year-old BMW M6 Coupe, and that, at any rate, was nowhere to be seen.

Søren had managed to wangle two men from the evening shift's overworked staffing roster. Kim Jankowski had just turned forty but was still the less experienced of the two—he hadn't applied to the police academy until he was thirty-one, just before the age limit disqualified him, but had been extremely focused since then. Jesper Due Hansen was a couple of years younger and had just transferred to counterterrorism from the personal protection unit. He had inevitably been nicknamed "the Dove," not due to any particulary pacifist tendencies, but because of his avian middle name.

They drove past the address and parked farther away, where the car couldn't be seen from the house.

"The back garden abuts the Common," Jesper Due said. "It would be pretty easy to go in that way."

Søren nodded. "He may have hostages. So . . . nice and easy, right? Not too much noise. We don't want to escalate the situation."

He stationed Jankowski outside on Rhodesiavej, and then he and the Dove went down to the asphalt path that ran through the no man's land between the back gardens of the houses and the wide-open green spaces of the Common.

"We should have brought a dog," the Dove said. "Then we would have totally fit in."

They could see at least four people out walking their dogs on the Common; luckily three of them were quite far away, and the fourth was preoccupied with some form of training that involved an extraordinary number of toots on a dog whistle that unfortunately wasn't sufficiently high-pitched to be inaudible to human ears.

"It's that one," Søren pointed. "The brown wooden fence."

The Dove leapt over it first, in one quick, athletic bound. Søren followed a second later. Luckily Karvinen wasn't the type who went in for roses. His back garden was a big jungle of waist-high weeds, and the withered, yellow, knee-high grass from last year revealed that the lawn hadn't been mowed anytime recently. A thistle in the Eden of suburbia, Søren thought. How symbolic.

They both ran, bent double, up to the house and the patio. Yellow grass seeds stuck wetly to Søren's pants, and there was a strong stench of cat pee. The windows were bare and curtainless; the rooms inside had no lights on even though it was overcast and starting to get dark.

There was no one in the living room or the room next to it. Then Søren noticed some light coming from a basement window at the end wall of the house. He tapped his partner gently on the shoulder, and the Dove nodded and handed him the minicam—actually a miniature video camera on a stick, with a monitor so you could see what was going on in a room without having to stick your head up.

Søren lay down on his stomach in the dandelions and wormed his way along the foundation until he could put the minicam into position. Then he pulled back a little, sat up, and the Dove handed him the monitor. The Dove proceeded noiselessly around the house to check the windows in the other rooms.

The OLED monitor was about twice as big as a mobile phone. That was the most practical size for the field: You could operate it discreetly but still see the image clearly. What it provided Søren now was in razor-sharp high-definition; any sharper and he could have checked the girl's thighs for cellulite.

She was naked aside from a garter belt of the type that was never intended to hold anything other than a pair of kinky stockings. Very young, with long blonde hair that had been made even blonder with a little help from the cosmetics industry. Her eyes were pinpoint flashes of light in dark caves of mascara, and both of her nipples were pierced with wide gold rings. She was lying on a satiny black bed with her abdomen pushed up and forward as if she were writhing below an invisible lover. But there wasn't anyone else in the room as far as Søren and the minicam could tell.

"What the hell . . ." Søren mumbled to himself as the girl buried both hands in her crotch and rocked wildly back and forth. There was something unnatural about this . . . He fully appreciated that a young woman could have an intense erotic relationship with her own body, but this was more than a little teenage masturbation. Everything about the sight confronting him was purely for show. The girl's exaggerated facial expression of pleasure, her vigorous motions, that porn bed . . . The whole thing was designed to excite everyone but her.

She abruptly stopped her rocking and sat up. Waiting. Listening? He couldn't see whether there was a phone near her, but that would explain some of the superficiality of the performance. He could see her lips moving. She was saying something. Her face distorted for a brief instant into a grimace that had nothing to do with desire. Then she stuck her hand under one of the big, overstuffed silk pillows and brought out an object that had been stashed there.

It was, predictably enough, a dildo. A vinyl version of the male member in a size that bore no relation to reality. She pushed herself over to the edge of the bed, with her legs spread and her heels all the way up against her buttocks. She hesitated in a revealing moment of discomfort before opening her mouth in a parody of orgasm and slowly began pushing the behemoth between her legs.

Søren turned off the monitor. He knew that when they went in he would find a camera in the basement room with the porn bed. Probably a webcam. And somewhere out there, in Copenhagen or Amsterdam or Berlin, was a sleazebag who was paying for permission to give orders to the young girl. Orders she carried out, no matter how humiliating or uncomfortable.

The Dove was back.

"There's no one in the rest of the house," he said quietly. "How many down there?"

"One," said Søren, even though in a way he felt like he ought to count the sleazebag, too. "A young girl. And probably a webcam. I think she's providing paid sexual services over the Internet."

The Dove raised his eyebrows.

"Well, I guess that's one way to work from home," he said. "Shall we go in?"

Søren nodded. "Yes. She's here. She must know him. Maybe we can get her to tell us where he is."

THEY ENTERED QUIETLY. Jankowski dealt with the patio door without any major difficulties, and they crept down the stairs to the basement together. Now Søren could hear the sound, too.

"Show me your arrrse," the sleazebag commanded in strangely guttural English. "Yeah, that's right. Come to Daddy."

She was at it again with the vigorous thrusting motions, now down on all fours. The dildo was sticking out between the cheeks of her butt like some grotesquely docked tail. Her eyes were closed, and now that her face was turned away from the webcam, the act was over. Apart from a pained little wrinkle between her eyes, her face was completely devoid of expression.

The sleazebag on the Internet spotted them first.

"What the hell . . ." he swore.

The girl opened her eyes and screamed.

"Easy," Søren said in English, because he was pretty sure she wasn't Danish. "Police. We're not going to hurt you."

"Fuck," the male voice hissed, and there was a click and a brief bit of white noise from the speakers on the computer, which Søren hadn't been able to see with his minicam because it was hidden behind the bed.

Søren didn't care. If the girl was under eighteen, then Christian would deliver the sick sleazebag's IP address straight into Birgitte's eager hands. And if she was over eighteen, then there wasn't a damn thing they could do about it anyway. It wasn't illegal to buy sex online. And although he was pretty damn sure that the profit from the girl's efforts was going directly into Tommi Karvinen's till, it would no doubt be a thankless job to try and get her to admit it. Karvinen's girls don't blab, Birgitte had said.

Karvinen. *Dudesons.*

Oh, fuck.

He ran the mental tape one more time. *Show me your arrrse.* With the slurred S and the rolling guttural R sounds. Exactly like in the *Dudesons* episode when the insane Finn plunked himself down on an anthill with his backside bared.

It was him. The man on the other end of the Internet connection was Tommi Karvinen. And he had seen them.

NINA HAD BEEN feeling sick. She was pregnant with Ida, it was morning, and the morning sickness had overpowered her and made it hard for her to breathe. She was in bed next to Morten, trying to lie completely still in the sweat-dampened bedding as she listened to the traffic outside on the overpass. If she didn't move, she could sometimes postpone the inevitable. The sudden rush of saliva, the sharp burning feeling of vomit in her throat, and the hurried scramble to their tiny bathroom with its cold, black-specked terrazzo floor. Sometimes thinking about lemons and ginger and cool, fresh, green grass helped, too, and she tried thinking about the baby as a good thing. Something happy.

She rarely succeeded. She could see that her body had changed, her breasts were bigger, and just beneath the skin, there was a fine network of light-blue veins. Her flat stomach had also taken on a small, discreet bulge, and although she knew that there was a living being in there under her skin, she didn't really feel anything. It didn't have a face. It didn't exist, and as Nina lay on her knees on the cold terrazzo floor, the nausea finally over-taking her body, she sometimes wished the baby wasn't there, and that she and Morten didn't have to do this. Together. And with that thought came the anxiety of doing the whole thing wrong, because she didn't love the little unborn life enough. Because you were sup-posed to love your own baby. Weren't you? She didn't dare ask Morten if he loved the child, because he probably did. His feelings were always proper, healthy, and normal. Nina, on the other hand, felt panic and anxiety creeping in, from all the black crevices of her childhood. Mostly she was afraid of herself. The nausea washed over her again, and she was so terribly thirsty. But if she moved now, if she stood up now, there would be no going back.

Bang.

A door was yanked open in the outskirts of Nina's consciousness, and now there was someone yelling, too. She opened her eyes. The nausea was still there, but she wasn't lying in bed next to Morten, nor on the bathroom floor of their first apartment. Her left shoulder was painfully stretched, her arm still bent awkwardly behind Ida's neck and tied to the radiator. She must have dozed off, but not for very long, because there was still that same hazy, yellow half-light in the room.

"Fuck. We have to go. Now."

Tommi had stumbled into the living room, swearing and trying to zip up his jeans.

Mr. Suburbia got halfway up from the sofa and shot a questioning look at the Finn, who was now struggling to put on his worn white sneakers.

"What's going on? I thought we had to wait for the address."

"We're out of here *now*," Tommi hissed. "The police are at Rhodesiavej. They got Mini."

Something somewhere in the living room beeped, and the Finn looked around, searching, spotted his phone, and picked it up with a satisfied grunt. "I think we just got our address."

He browsed down through the menu.

"41 Lundedalsvej. This is it, Frederik."

Ida squirmed anxiously. She was wearing her favorite jeans, Nina noticed, a pair of skinny black jeans with ratty holes in the thighs and knees. She pulled her legs up against her chest so her bony white knees were visible. They were trembling faintly.

Mr. Suburbia stood there for a second staring mutely at Tommi.

"Rhodesiavej. How the hell did they find you?"

The Finn, who was now on his way over to Sándor in quick, decisive steps, sulkily shrugged. "No clue. It's not my fault. But Mini has got her passport and all that shit in the house, and if they look up her name, they'll find this place, too. So the new plan is . . ." He pulled a flimsy pocketknife out of his back pocket and was now standing in front of Ida, Nina, and Sándor. "The new plan is we get the money, I take a little trip to Thailand and enjoy some Asian cunt, and you slink off back to your house in the 'burbs and keep a low profile until the police find something else to waste their time on."

Mr. Suburbia looked like he had just woken up. He glanced around the living room, stuffed the laptop roughly into his computer bag and started randomly dumping DVDs, ring binders, loose change, and his red ceramic mug into a plastic bag. The Finn shot him an irritated look.

"Just leave all that shit, Freddie, and get over here and help me get this lot on their feet. I can't be doing every fucking thing by myself."

OUTSIDE, THE RAIN was coming down in a steady drizzle, and the moisture settled like a cool, wet film on Nina's face and hair, making her thirst burn worse than before. Ida and Sándor walked ahead of her across the wet, shiny gravel of the U-shaped drive in front of the house. Ida looked small and stooped, her backpack dangling absurdly from one hand as if she were just on her way home from a normal day at school. Sándor was holding himself straight in an almost-defiant way but kept his injured hand tucked against his belly, as if to protect it from the rest of the world. Tommi was behind them, with the gun aimed at their backs. He seemed a little less tense now that they were all out of the house but was hurrying them along the whole time. When they rounded the corner of the house, Nina felt a sharp shove, which almost sent her nose-first into the knee-high stinging nettles growing up along the wall.

"Faster!" Tommi yelled, loud enough that Ida and Sándor also got the message and obediently sped up. Nina got up slowly but then stumbled again without provocation and dropped to her knees in the wet, stinging stalks. The ground rolled dizzyingly beneath her, and for a brief panic-stricken second, she thought she wasn't going to be able to get back up again. What would he do then? Shoot her right there, in front of Ida? The thought flitted through her as she stared into the lush, dark-green jungle of nettles in front of her. She had broken the fall with her hands and felt her palms burn and sting as she struggled to regain her footing. Ida dropped back silently to pull her to her feet. Her daughter's face was unreadable, her eyes narrow, black cracks in a sheet-white mask.

"Stop right there."

Tommi barked the order in his heavy English, and Mr. Suburbia quickly skirted around Nina and Ida, his dog padding along at his heels. He stopped next to Sándor and cast an uncertain glance at Tommi. Mr. Suburbia looked like a man who was crumbling inside, Nina thought. If there had ever been any voice of authority inside that fancy polo shirt, it was gone now. This—whatever "this" was—was the Finn's territory.

"Where is the damn thing?"

Mr. Suburbia had pulled a long, thin metal hook out of his back pocket and was kicking around in the stinging nettles, searching, until his foot hit what he was looking for. A rusty metal lid. Maybe to a septic tank or an old oil tank of the illegal, buried variety?

"Here," he said.

In a way, Nina knew the instant she saw the lid. And yet she didn't believe it. Not until Mr. Suburbia hauled the lid of the tank back and called Ida over.

Ida didn't respond, just stood there, still with her back-pack in one hand.

"Come on. Get over here." Mr. Suburbia seemed annoyed and glanced hesitantly over at the Finn, as if he were waiting for some kind of instructions from him on how to get hostages to crawl down into black holes. But Ida kept close to Nina, her lips forming small, soundless prayers. Like when she was little and used to huddle in bed chanting whispered incantations against monsters.

"Get her down into the fucking tank," Tommi hissed. "I can't do it. I'm holding the gun. Come on already."

Mr. Suburbia took a step forward, grabbed Ida's arm

and started pulling her toward the yawning hole. He stepped over it clumsily and was now trying to lift Ida's feet off the ground so she would lose her footing, and he could stuff her into the hole. But his plan was doomed to fail. Ida finally let go of her schoolbag and stuck out her arms and legs in panic and started to make noises. Not screams, but sobbing pleas.

"Please don't. No. Please don't do this. Let me go."

And then, finally, Nina's feet left the ground, and she lunged at Mr. Suburbia, aiming for his eyes and nose and trying to dig her fingers into his face.

"Let. Her. Go."

Her words slipped out one by one in between each desperate attack on the man's mildly astonished face. Then he began to turn around, still with Ida struggling in his arms, so that Nina could only claw his shoulders and back.

A shot cracked with deafening loudness behind them, and out of the corner of her eye, she saw something brown and furry streak past her legs in a panic and continue through the stinging nettles into the field beyond. Mr. Suburbia swore loudly and called after the dog, and Nina gave it all she had and landed a proper blow for the first time, dead-on, somewhere just behind his ear. Then she was yanked back by the Finn's skinny, iron grip on the back of her neck.

"Knock it off, or I'll shoot you, your daughter, and your goat-fucking friend. Right now."

Nina slowly turned her head. The Finn was still holding the back of her neck with one hand and, with the other, aiming the gun at Sándor, who was standing beside him, still and pale. Sándor's injured left hand was clenched into a fist, but he had got no further than that.

Tommi loosened his grasp on her neck and instead pulled her all the way back, into an absurd embrace. She was standing with her back pressed against his chest while he pushed up her chin with the cold muzzle of the pistol. Nina tried to make eye contact with Ida, still dangling in Mr. Suburbia's grasp over the manhole, but Ida saw only the Finn and the gun under her mother's chin. Her eyes were crazed with fear.

"Psychology, Frederik," the Finn said. He was winded from the struggle and paused for a second to catch his breath. "You have to use a little psychology in situations like these."

Then he looked at Ida.

"There's nothing dangerous down there, baby. And it won't take that long. Your mom and the goat-fucker just have to help us with something. Then you can come up again. Nice and easy."

Ida shook her head faintly, and Nina could see her trying to bring her thoughts into some kind of order. Filter away the man's calm, almost friendly tone and hear what he was actually saying. She was confused.

"I could also put it another way," Tommi said then, without changing his intonation. "If you don't crawl down into that hole, right now, no fuss, I will blow your mom's jaw off."

This time the message hit home. Ida stared for a brief instant, looking from the Finn to Nina and back again. Her jaw muscles tensed, and Nina could see that she was trying to control her trembling. She didn't want to cry, probably for Nina's sake as much as her own. Nina herself wanted to scream, but didn't. Ida might not be aware how dangerous it was to be locked in a sealed tank. How quickly the oxygen got used up. And Nina wasn't going to explain that to her just now.

Without a word, Ida sat down on the edge of the hole, legs dangling. Then she slid down until only the very top of her shoulders stuck up amidst the stinging nettles. She slowly squatted, and Nina could hear a muffled scraping sound from Ida's knees as she crawled into the underground metal coffin.

"Chuck that down after her," the Finn said and pointed at her school bag with his pistol. "We can't leave it lying around, or someone might notice. And make sure you lock the inner lid."

Mr. Suburbia dropped the bag down into the tank and then hesitated a second. Glanced down at his polo shirt, up until now miraculously clean, and then knelt down with every sign of distaste. He stuck his head and upper body down into the darkness and, from the movement of his shoulders, seemed to be struggling with something big and heavy. There was the click of a well-lubricated padlock, and Mr. Suburbia popped back out of the hole, breathing hard.

Nina stood there as if she had been turned to stone.

"I have to go find Tyson," Mr. Suburbia said, looking around. "We can't leave without him."

The Finn snorted in irritation.

"Enough already. You can deal with the stupid mutt afterward. You might even ask the nice cops if they'll help you look." He turned Nina around to face him and looked at her with the seriousness of a doctor giving instructions to the parents of a dying child. "It's dangerous down there," he said. "In the tank. You can die from it, and right now the four of us are the only ones who know where your daughter is. But if you do as we say, I'm sure she'll make it out again just fine."

THE GIRL WAS sitting on the black bed, now dressed in a T-shirt, tight Levis, and a pair of red sneakers. Christian was on the floor whistling quietly and unconsciously as he connected his own custom-built box of computer tricks to the porn central with the webcam.

"Beatrice Pollini," Søren said, looking dubiously at the ID the girl had given him—a worn, dog-eared Italian passport. "Do we buy it?"

"No way she's nineteen," Jankowski said. "Seventeen at the very most."

"And I don't think she's Italian, either," Søren said. *"Come ti chiami?"* he asked. The girl smiled uncertainly.

"Good," she said. "Okay."

"That's not what you asked, is it?" Jankowski said.

"No. I asked her what her name is."

"Italian passports are some of the top scorers on the border police's list of forgeries," Jankowski said. "It's a whole industry."

Søren nodded. "It may well take some time. And that's exactly what we don't have. Christian, how's it going with that IP address?" He saw us, Søren thought, feeling the stress sizzling along his neural pathways. He has hostages, and he saw us. They could be looking at every kind of disaster right now.

Christian looked harassed. "Let me at least plug in the damn thing first, would you?" he said.

Søren raised his hands in a gesture of apology. "Just run her ID through the system," he told Jankowski. "I'll try and see if I can pry anything useful out of her." They had had to send Jesper Due back to the evening shift, which was screaming under the pressure.

"Beatrice is a difficult name," he said to the girl. "What do your friends call you?"

She stared at him with dark, deer-in-the-headlights eyes.

"Mini," she whispered. "Because I'm so small." And then she started crying, unnaturally quietly, as if she'd learned that making a noise just made things worse.

In my next life, Søren thought. In my next life, I want to do something else.

SURVIVE.

That was the single conscious plan in Nina's head. Survive, so she could tell someone where Ida was. Nothing else mattered.

And yet a twinge of . . . of horror ran through her when Sándor, on the Finn's orders, opened the door to the garage so, for the first time, she could see the source of Sándor's brother's death and her own illness. It was a completely normal paint can, the kind you keep wood preserver in—dented sheet metal, with a handle made out of strong steel wire. She wouldn't have given it a second glance if it had been sitting next to the jumble of rusty gardening tools leaning against the wall. But now that she knew what it was, her skin crawled, and it was hard not to think about the radiation penetrating her, invisible and unnoticed, seeking out her vulnerable internal organs and destroying them, cell by cell.

The stolen green van that the insane Finn had used

when he abducted her was parked in the driveway. He had placed a section of cement pipe inside the van on top of a couple of thick, cement paving slabs, and once they had eased the paint can with the cesium source into the concrete pipe section, two more pavers would go on top. In mechanical terms, the task was simple. Once the paint can was shielded on all sides by seventeen to eighteen centimeters of concrete, their forced proximity to it might actually be only minimally damaging.

At least it won't kill me before I can tell someone about Ida, she thought.

"You don't need to touch it," Sándor said. "If we take one of those and run the shaft through the handle on the can, we can carry it between us." He pointed to the gardening tools with his healthy hand.

Tommi and Mr. Suburbia were standing behind them, at a suitable distance, now clothed in protective masks, gloves, and white hooded outfits that said ENVIRO-CLEAN in big, black capital letters across the chest on the front and back. Nina and Sándor were not afforded the same luxury.

"Let's use the rake," Nina said. "It looks like it has the newest handle."

Sándor reached for it, but Nina beat him to it.

"It's better if I do it," she said. "I have two good hands."

He hesitated, but then nodded. If he messed up the maneuver and the paint can tipped, they would have radioactive sand everywhere, and that would just make a bad situation worse.

She coaxed the shaft of the rake under the wire handle and carefully dragged the paint can closer. Sándor grabbed the free end of the rake. They looked at each other. Nina nodded. Then they lifted, slowly and in unison. It was a matter of holding the handle perfectly level so the can didn't slide to one end or the other. Survive, Nina thought. Just survive.

SÁNDOR WAS STARING so hard at the can dangling between them that his eyes were starting to water. He kept his breathing slow and deliberate, focusing on holding the handle horizontal, completely horizontal, with no wobbling. Afterward he realized that the whole time it took to raise the can into the van and lower it down into the concrete pipe, he hadn't heard a single sound other than that of his own heartbeat. All his concentration, all his senses, were focused on that one, simple task.

"Nice," Tommi said waving the pistol. "Now the pavers."

They were perfectly standard garden pavers, sixty by sixty centimeters. Sándor couldn't grip the thick, rough edge of the square, concrete slabs with his injured hand, but he was forced to use it for support and balance. There was no way Nina would be able to lift the pavers alone. She looked like she was holding herself upright through sheer will power.

They moved the two slabs into place on top of the pipe section. Tommi inspected their work and apparently found it satisfactory. At any rate, he gave Sándor a pat of comaraderie on the shoulder with his gloved hand.

"Cool," he said. "Now you two hop in there, and keep it company. How do you say 'car' in Hungarian?"

The Finn's strange interest in Hungarian vocabulary no longer surprised Sándor. "*Autó*," he said in a monotone.

Tommi lit up behind the see-through plastic of his mask. "Hey," he said. "That's the same in Finnish. So it's true after all."

"What is?" Frederik said irritated. "What's true?"

"That Finnish and Hungarian are related. The Finno-Ugric language family and all that stuff."

Frederik glanced at the cement pipe in the back of the van." You don't think you could concentrate just a little on what's important here?"

"There's nothing wrong with expanding your horizons."

"For fuck's sake, Tommi. The word 'auto' doesn't have a goddamn thing to do with Finnish *or* Hungarian. It's from Latin. Get those two into the van so we can get going."

Tommi squinted. "You heard what the man said. Get in!"

The gun was pointed vaguely in their direction, but there was nothing vague about the look on the Finn's face. It radiated a clear-as-glass intensity even through the cheap plastic of the face mask. Nina clambered in without protest and shot Sándor a look that clearly said: No drama. Don't risk my daughter's life.

He wasn't so sure anymore that obedience and a low profile were their best survival strategy, but he didn't see any other options. The rear doors slammed shut with a hollow *claaaang*, and a moment later the van started moving.

"Where are we going?" Sándor asked Nina. "Do you know?"

She shook her head. He could only just see her. Not much light made it in through the small window between the back of the van and the driver's cabin.

"I heard the address," she said. "I just don't know where it is. Somewhere in Copenhagen, I think."

"To meet with some filthy rich sicko who wants to buy radioactive material," he said, not quite able to take his eyes off the makeshift cement container hiding the poisonous shit that had killed Tamás. "Nina, can we let them do it? How many people are going to end up dying the way Tamás did?"

She lowered her head so he could only see her dark hair.

"Ida" was all she said. "I can't think about anything else or anybody else."

The van rattled its way up over some small obstacle, turned sharply to the right, and continued more smoothly. They were heading toward the city.

SKOU-LARSEN'S HANDS WERE shaking. There was a stabbing sensation in his chest, and he decided that he probably ought to take one of his nitroglycerin pills. The sooner, the better, the doctor had said. It was better to ward off an attack than to try to treat one.

He still didn't understand. Didn't understand why a friendly, young police lady and a not-quite-as-friendly young policeman had spent more than an hour questioning him and checking out the car and the house with a Geiger counter. Or a Geiger-Müller counter, as they were now apparently called.

And it wasn't because he hadn't been paying attention. He'd been watching the experts on TV talking about the Summit and those dirty bombs—they always used the English words for "Summit" and "dirty bomb" even though Danish had perfectly adequate terms. He didn't understand why everything had to be English these days. He had listened to investigative radio reports about the problem of radioactive materials from Eastern Europe. He had plodded his way through that long article in *Berlingske Tidende* on "Why Denmark is a Target." He had also seen that documentary everyone was talking about—"The Making of a Terrorist" or something like that—about madrassas and training camps for suicide bombers. That video clip still stuck in his mind, the one of a young Muslim girl, no more than fourteen, talking about the greatness of Allah with a mixture of fear and pride in the dark gleam of her eyes a day before she blew herself and fourteen other people to smithereens on a street in eastern Bagdad.

He thought about the minarets in his backyard and of the dapper Mr. Hosseini and his mosque. It was hard to imagine Mr. Hosseini with an explosive belt full of TNT, but what did a terrorist actually look like?

They had asked about whether the Opel had been stolen, and he had said no. But now it suddenly occurred to him that there had been that day a few weeks ago when he'd had to adjust the seat. It was much farther forward than he cared for, which had puzzled him. Should he call the police lady and tell her that? What if someone had taken the car and put it back again without his having noticed?

Yet another stab in his chest. The pills. First he had to take one of those pills.

He trundled into the bathroom, careful not to hurry even though he was increasingly afraid that this was a heart attack coming on. Helle had put all his medications into a lunch-box-sized, white plastic crate in the cabinet over the sink. Centyl, aspirin, Fortzaar, Gaviscon, Nitromex. He shook a blister pack from the box, pressed the little tablet out of the foil, and put it under his tongue. There. Now it was just a matter of waiting. Breathing nice and easy, nice and easy. He sat down on the lid of the toilet and closed his eyes.

Then he opened them again. Because there was something missing, wasn't there?

Centyl, aspirin, Fortzaar, Gaviscon, Nitromex . . . but no box of Imovane. His sleeping pills were missing from the white crate.

He got up to see if they were elsewhere in the cabinet

and was overcome by a sudden wave of dizziness. He made a grab for the sink. The medicine crate flew off to one side and the Centyl bottle hit the toilet tank with a crack and shattered, scattering shards of glass and pale-green pills all over the floor tiles.

Skou-Larsen clung to the sink for a few minutes until his dizziness subsided. Pathetic old wreck, he snarled at himself. Hopeless, helpless, useless old man. What was that crude phrase of Claus's? Couldn't take a crap without busting the crapper.

Saying the word *crap* helped a little, even though it had just been quietly to himself. He tried again.

"Crap," he whispered to himself. "Everything is crap."

His respectable upbringing stirred uncomfortably in him. But where had it actually gotten him, being so impeccably *decent* his whole life? It hadn't protected him from having the police invade his home. And it certainly hadn't kept his marriage alive. His sense of propriety had settled like a membrane between him and Helle so they walked around playing their carefully rehearsed roles without ever talking about anything that really mattered.

Enough of that, he decided. When she comes home, I'm going to talk to her. *Really* talk to her.

He decided he had better clean up the broken glass first. And gather up the pills. There was no reason to let her see how close he had come to fainting. His physical frailty was only all too noticeable as it was.

It had been years since he had touched the vacuum cleaner, but he did know where it was—in the closet under the stairs. An older model Nilfisk, good Danish quality and very durable.

There was a padded envelope in the vacuum closet, on the shelf next to the vacuum bags and the neatly folded stack of dust cloths. A grayish- white envelope without an address.

What's that doing there? he thought. What a strange place to put it.

He opened it and peered into it.

It was full of five hundred kroner bills, and it didn't take him long to guess how much was in there.

About six hundred thousand kroner.

SØREN HAD BROUGHT the girl up from the basement and into the kitchen. His plan had been to suggest a cup of coffee to distract her and make the situation feel more normal, but the only visible coffee-making equipment was an espresso monstrosity the size of a small space station, and with the clock ticking in his head, the whole palaver of grinding beans and fumbling around with the settings and weird little filters was simply insurmountable.

The girl sensed his skepticism, and a tiny little pseudo-smile raised one corner of her mouth.

"We never use," she said. "Too hard."

She said "we," he noticed.

"Is Tommi your boyfriend?" Søren asked.

Her smile disappeared as if someone had erased it. She nodded, one time, a quick, abrupt motion.

"Where is he?" Søren asked, without much hope of receiving a helpful answer. Nor did he get one. She just shook her head.

"He not tell me."

Where was she from? Somewhere in Eastern Europe, probably, from the look of her. And if the Italian passport was bought in Italy, then it was likely to be one of the more southerly countries—former Yugoslavia, Bulgaria, maybe Albania. The false passport was probably as much to hide her age as her nationality, he guessed.

"How old are you, Mini?" he asked, to have some kind of baseline for what she looked like when she was lying.

"Nineteen." She looked him straight in the eye, but she couldn't keep her hands still. One hand flopped around restlessly in her lap, and as soon as she had delivered her lie, she looked away.

Good. One more time, just to test the theory.

"Where are you from? What country?"

"I am Italian girl." She looked at him, and this time both her hands and her feet were fidgety. Little Mini didn't like to lie.

He asked a couple of neutral questions and determined that she had been in Denmark for four months, that she had come to do some modeling work, that she was going to be in a movie soon. She actually believed all of this; Søren had to restrain a dark, bitter rage that wouldn't have done the interview the least bit of good. It was certainly possible, he thought, that they intended to film her. But the very idea of the kind of movie it would be made him want to smear Tommi Karvinen over a wide swath of Amager's asphalt.

Then he asked again if she knew where Karvinen was. And she fidgeted restlessly with one hand when she said no.

"Mini," he said in the plainest, clearest English he could think of. "He took a girl. A Danish girl. She's fourteen years old."

She didn't say anything, but the light in her eyes, which had sparked to life when she talked about her modeling career and her movie plans, died away again.

"Where did he take her?" Søren asked.

She pulled all her limbs in close to her body, like a spider when you blew on it. Self-preservation. Extreme self-preservation.

"Where is she?" he asked gently. "Don't you want to help her?"

She was hyperventilating. He could both see it and hear it. Slowly she keeled to one side on the chair. When he realized the chair was about to tip over, he reached out a hand to stop it, but he was a second too late. She slid onto the floor and lay there with her knees pulled up against her chest and her eyes closed. She actually *had* fainted, Søren confirmed. She wasn't pretending.

Suddenly Christian's broad silhouette appeared in the kitchen doorway. He looked down at the girl.

"What did you do to her?" Christian asked.

Søren maneuvered her gently onto her side, wadded up his dark windbreaker into a sort of pillow and pushed it in under her head. He shook his head.

"She was hyperventilating," he said. "Keeled right over. Do you have anything for me?"

"Yup. We got lucky. This little girl here officially owns a property a little farther out quite near the airport, just off Tømmerupvej. And get this—it's exactly where we traced the IP address back to."

"*Yes*. Jankowski and I will head out there." Pity the Dove had needed to take off, but there wasn't time to call him back. "Would you get an ambulance for this one?"

She was conscious again, he sensed. Lying there listening to their foreign voices in a language she didn't understand.

"An ambulance? But if she just hyperventilated . . . ?"

"Christian. Get her out of this house. Get her admitted to a nice, clean hospital with friendly people who will take care of her. We'll take it from there tomorrow.

Right? Just say she's unconscious, and you can't wake her up."

The penny finally dropped, Søren observed, and Christian merely nodded.

Without his jacket and with Jankowski on his heels, Søren trotted down the suburban street to where they had parked the car.

"What was wrong with the girl?" Jankowski asked as he slid in behind the wheel. "Did she just faint?"

Søren yanked his seatbelt into place with barely restrained fury.

"Drive," he said. "I don't know what the hell he does to terrorize these women. But it is going to stop right now!"

SÁNDOR AND NINA didn't talk. They just sat there next to each other as the throb of the diesel engine resonated inside the cold metal box of the van, drowning out most of the street sounds. The first time they stopped, Sándor started kicking the back doors with both legs, but Nina grabbed his arm.

"Ida," she said, and there was a feral imperative in her eyes that could not be ignored. "You risk getting my daughter killed."

The car started moving again, presumably they had just stopped for a red light.

His injured hand throbbed and pulsed in time with the diesel engine. His head hurt so much that he was wondering if it wouldn't be a relief to just let that Finnish psychopath shoot it off. His weary heart still had room for empathy for Nina and a shiver at the thought of that dark, subterranean oil tank and the girl down there, struggling not to gasp up the oxygen too fast and shorten the time she had left. But someone was going to have to try to think beyond that. He certainly understood that Nina couldn't do it. It was her child. But someone *had* to think about everyone else, about unsuspecting people sitting on the metro or going to sleep in a hotel bed or jumping up and down in the stands at a concert somewhere, not knowing that their world was about to be blown into a thousand pieces, into a thousand radioactive particles, in a week or a day or an hour.

Someone had to think about them.

Tamás hadn't. He had thought only about the money, about immediate injustices, about his family's survival and dreams. The metro passengers, the hotel guests, and the Copenhagen music fans weren't really people to him. The Roma in Valby had called him a *mulo*, an evil spirit. An impure death brought curses with it, and you couldn't die much more impurely than Tamás had.

When Sándor closed his eyes, it was Tamás he saw. Not a living memory of him, but a dead Tamás, who stared at him with burning eyes like the ghosts in Grandma Éva's stories, blazing eyes that cried blood. He wondered if he would ever be able to sleep again without seeing *Mulo*-Tamás in his dreams. He wondered if he would ever get the chance to go to sleep again at all or if it would all be over in an instant, with a bang he wouldn't even hear before the projectile smashed its way into his brain and snuffed everything out.

The van stopped. For longer this time, too long for it just to be a traffic light. Then it slowly drove forward again, now over a somewhat more uneven, bumpy surface.

Nina's eyes shone in the reflected lights from the driver's cabin, and she moved uneasily. Then the doors were flung open, and the Finnish psychopath ordered them out.

They were at a construction site, Sándor noted. Muddy tire tracks, pallets of drywall wrapped in plastic flapping gently in the breeze. Spotlights on high posts and sharply delineated black shadows in the May night darkness. Tommi had parked the van between two portable office trailers so it wasn't immediately visible from the street.

"He wants it inside," Tommi said. His face mask made his heavy accent even heavier, or maybe it was just because he was excited. "Come on. We're not going to get any money until he gets it where he wants it."

Sándor measured the distance with his eyes, but Tommi was too far away. He was rocking back and forth on his feet like an athlete getting ready to make his approach to the high jump, with a phone in one hand and the gun blatantly on display in the other. Either he figured no one could see them or he just didn't care. Frederik was nowhere to be seen. Maybe he was already inside the half-finished building a little further away, behind Tommi's agitated, rocking form.

Nina started to push the top slab off.

"Help the lady, now," Tommi said. "It isn't fair to let her do all the work, now, is it?"

Sándor helped her. Yet again they managed to work the rake under the paint can's wire handle. Yet again they balanced the can between them, and the need to maintain its equilibrium absorbed all his attention for a while. Right up until his heel struck something both soft and unyielding. He looked down, forgetting about the horizontal line of the rake handle, and then had to abruptly adjust his end before the can slid all the way down to him and spilled its sand on the ground.

It was a dog. A German Shepherd.

At first he thought Tommi had simply shot it, but there wasn't enough blood, and now he saw its rib cage rise in a brief gasp and the tongue hanging out of the dog's half-open mouth quivered, wet and pink. It wasn't dead, or at least not yet. He couldn't tell if someone had hit the dog and knocked it out or if it had been drugged in some way.

"Come on," Tommi said, with an actual hop of happiness. "Aren't you excited at all? The party is just beginning!"

TICK. **T**ICK. **T**ICK. Skou-Larsen could hear the antique French table clock on the linen cabinet tick loudly in the silence. He was sitting on the third step of the hallway stairs and couldn't make himself move any further.

She would be home soon. They rarely sang for more than two hours. Supposing she was actually singing.

I could call Ellen Jørgensen and ask, he thought. Mrs. Jørgensen lived a few streets away and was in the choir, too. Sometimes he drove her home after practice if he was picking Helle up anyway.

He didn't get up. The nitroglycerin had helped a little, even though he still wasn't feeling quite right. But the reason that he kept sitting there was . . . the real reason was that he just wasn't up to it. What was he going to do if Ellen told him he had made a mistake, that they didn't have an extra choir practice tonight?

Then he heard the garden gate click, and though he couldn't see out into the front yard from where he was sitting, he could hear the crunchy *click-click-click* sound of the gears on Helle's bicycle. His hearing was the only thing that still worked more or less as well as when he was younger. He struggled to his feet. His legs were all pins and needles; the hard staircase had taken its toll on the already poor blood supply to his lower extremities.

She realized immediately that something was wrong. Her eyes flitted from his face to the open vacuum closet, to the envelope sitting behind him on the steps.

"Give it to me," she said.

"Helle, we have to talk about this. What were you going to do with the money?"

"I hate it when you snoop in my things," she hissed, trying to push her way past him.

He propped his hand against the wall so she couldn't walk past him. Her face looked like it usually did when she had been out of the house—tastefully made up with a touch of light eye shadow and a bit of pale pink lipstick, just a hint, nothing vulgar. She had pulled her hair back into a loose bun, and she was wearing her Benetton shirt, the one he had bought based on the careful instructions from her wish list last year. He remembered how Claus had complained—"Mom, this isn't a wish list, this is an order form. Can't you just let us surprise you?"—but Skou-Larsen thought it was nice and reassuring to have such neat directions to follow. That way you wouldn't get it wrong.

She looked the way she always did. Completely the way she always did.

"This wouldn't have been necessary if you had done something," she said. "But you never actually get anything done, do you?"

"I'm going to put that money back in the bank tomorrow," he said patiently. "And then we need to have a power of attorney drawn up so Claus or I will also have to sign something before you can withdraw it again."

She wasn't listening to him anymore. He could tell from the distant but focused look that made him feel like just a random object standing in her way.

Suddenly she shoved him hard to one side, not with

her hands, but with her shoulder. He staggered and tripped on the bottom step, landing badly on his hip and heard the dry, little crack as he felt his thighbone snap and slide.

"Aaarhhh," he moaned and then again when the pain came, "Aaaaaaaarhh." The air wheezed out of him in an undignified, barely human sound.

She grabbed the envelope with the money.

"Call," he said through clenched teeth. "Call the ambulance."

She looked down at him with that sharp, concerned wrinkle between her brows.

"I don't have time now," she said. "You'll have to wait until I get back."

And then she left, with the envelope clasped to her chest.

Skou-Larsen heard the door slam but was no longer able to see it or her. It wasn't the pain from his broken femur now; it was a bigger, more all-encompassing pain radiating outward from the back of his head, obliterating the contours of his body and shutting down all his other senses.

I won't be here, he managed to think. When you come back, I won't be here anymore.

A black tide was swelling irresistibly within him. He couldn't hold on any longer and had to let it bear him away.

"**N**OT A SOUL," Jankowski said.

Grudgingly, Søren had to agree with him. The house was deserted.

"We were too slow," he said. He had alerted "the uniforms," as Torben referred to them, and had them send a squad car to block off the dirt road leading to the dilapidated farm, but it had been too late. Karvinen was gone and so were his hostages. The knowledge ate away at his gut, and he regretted that last cup of coffee.

"Get the techs out here, and let's see what we can find," Søren said, but he knew the likelihood of their finding anything they could use in time was depressingly small.

He took a deep, deliberate breath and tried to clear his thoughts. His feelings of rage and failure weren't going to do him any good, and they weren't going to do Karvinen's hostages any good either.

Tommi Karvinen wasn't some ingenious supercriminal. According to Birgitte, he had started out as an ordinary street pusher before moving into pimping, where he had channeled his talent for explosive, brutal violence into terrorizing both the girls and the customers as necessary. He obviously possessed sufficient intelligence to know who he could beat the crap out of without the police getting involved, and it was exactly this type of calculating instinct for self-preservation that made it hard for Søren to picture him as a fanatical bomber. His form of terror was more individual. He chose his victims with care and had an intense and intimate personal relationship with them; it was hard to see how he would get the same satisfaction from blowing random people to kingdom come.

So what did he want with the nurse and her daughter?

For one absurd, shaky moment, Søren imagined that the two things had absolutely nothing to do with each other. That Karvinen's motives had nothing to do with Valby or cesium or dirty bombs.

"Søren?"

"Yes. What now?"

"Just listen to the Geiger counter."

Søren stuck one of the two earphones into his ear. The dry, sonar-like beeping was significantly stronger as they approached the garage.

"Get Radiation Hygiene out here," he said. "Immediately."

He thought back to that flashy PowerPoint presentation. The cesium source didn't take up much room—the cylinder itself was smaller than an ordinary soup can. Could it be hidden somewhere in this garage?

He didn't want this hope to jinx it, but at the very least he knew they had been here. Karvinen fell back into place, inextricably tied to Valby and the dirty bomb scenario. It was all connected. It didn't make any sense yet, but it was all connected.

The wind was coming in across the flat fields, carrying the scent of seaweed and brine and jet fuel with it. With a sharp pang of longing, Søren thought of Susse and her white house and the hour's peace he had snatched for himself earlier in the day. Why had he set up his life so that most of his time was spent trying to get inside the heads of parasites like Karvinen?

Pull yourself together, he snarled to himself. Think. Do something. You can feel sorry for yourself later.

Suddenly he noticed a movement in the sea of stinging nettles at the corner of the farmhouse. He glided sideways, closer to the wall, and drew his sidearm. Waiting. Listening.

The nettles rustled again, and now he could hear something. Scraping, and whining. He slipped along the wall of the house in a couple of stealthy, sideways paces and peeked around the corner.

A slightly overweight, brown Labrador retriever looked up at him with golden brown eyes and wagged faintly. Then it went back to digging again, dirt and pebbles flying out between its hind legs.

Søren stuck his gun back in its holster. He was glad he hadn't had a chance to yell "Police!" or some other inappropriate action line. Instead he made a couple of encouraging clicks with his tongue so the dog looked up from his digging again.

"What are you up to, boy?" he asked.

The dog wasn't just trying to dig up a mouse hole. It had scratched and clawed the entire way around a rusty metal lid like one that might cover a well or sewer access.

Snow White. Suddenly Søren had a flashback to the cold morning hours outside the garage in Valby, digging up the underground gas tank and the body they had found in that dark, diesel-stinking sarcophagus.

Fuck.

No.

Not again.

His heart skipped a beat before it hammered on. Not the girl. Please God, not that poor fourteen-year-old girl.

Then he heard a sound that wasn't the dog's whining and scraping. A faint, metallic knocking. *Thunk-thunk-thunk. Thunk. Thunk. Thunk. Thunk-thunk-thunk.*

SOS.

"Jankowski!" he bellowed. "Get over here! Now!"

He dropped down onto his knees in the trampled nettles and tried to lift the lid with his fingers, but he couldn't get a proper grip. A screwdriver, a hook of some kind . . . something that could fit into those two holes in the lid. He tried with a ballpoint pen, but it snapped. Then he took his pistol and banged out a response rhythm with the butt so that she—in his head it was still the girl, he couldn't get his mind off her—so that at least she knew someone had heard her and that help was on the way.

"We're coming," he shouted. "We're going to get you out!"

IT WAS THE girl. Once they managed to wrench the outer lid away from the opening of the oil tank and cut the padlock off the specially mounted inner lid, what peered up at him was the chilled, pale face of a teenager. Her hands were bloody and her nails broken and chipped, and her fingers were convulsively clutching the bunch of keys she had been using to bang out her faint, scarcely audible SOS. Tears were streaming down her filthy cheeks and kept flowing even after they got her out and wrapped her in silver-colored heat blankets, given her water and sugar and more water.

"They have my mom," she said. "And Sándor. He's OK,

he isn't one of them, please don't hurt him. And they have that thing."

"The cesium unit?" Søren said.

"Yes. That. They want to sell it to some crazy old guy who's going to give them half a million kroner for it."

"Do you know where?" Søren asked, holding his breath. "Do you know where they're going to meet?"

The girl was still breathing in a strangely arrhythmic, jerky way. Søren was amazed she was holding it together as much as she was under the circumstances. That she could talk, think, and respond at all.

"Lundedalsvej," she said. "I wrote it down so I would remember it." She showed him her forearms and the big, black, smeared letters written zigzagged across her skin. "I used my mascara."

Søren wanted to give her a hug, but she wasn't the kind of girl who would have appreciated that. She was so clearly clinging to her self-control with an iron will that reminded him of her mother.

"Respect," he said instead, quietly and heartfelt. And was rewarded with a crooked, wobbly teenage smile.

Jankowski looked pensive.

"Lundedalsvej . . ." he said slowly. "Isn't that where . . . ?"

"Yes," said Søren. "That's where they're building that new mosque."

FREDERIK CAME RUNNING, skipping between the puddles so as not to muddy his boat shoes. Idiot, Sándor thought to himself, he has covered his whole body in protective gear but is still walking around in unprotected shoes.

"I parked the Touareg a few blocks away," Frederik said, winded. "So we can dump the van here. I'm assuming you stole it?"

"Yeah, yeah," Tommi said. "Come on. It's almost nine-thirty. And put on your mask, otherwise the rest of the hazmat suit isn't going to do any good."

Frederik pulled the hood up over his head and positioned the filter mask and protective goggles over his eyes, nose, and mouth.

The door to the single-story hall in front of the domed building was locked, but that didn't slow Tommi down.

"Take this," he said passing Frederik the pistol. Frederik took it but held it away from his body, awkwardly, very obviously uncomfortable with the weapon. Somehow that didn't make Sándor feel any better; he just got the sense that he could now be shot by accident as well as on purpose.

Tommi had fetched a screwdriver from the van and quickly and efficiently broke open the green double doors to the mosque.

"Wait here," he said.

He took the gun from Frederik and disappeared into the

building, but it didn't take long before he was back in the doorway again.

"All clear," he said. "He's not here yet."

With the paint can balanced between them, Sándor and Nina stepped into the dark reception hall. It smelled of turpentine and new wood, and plastic sheeting rustled under their feet with every step they took. The sharp light from the spotlights outside shone in through the arched windows, but otherwise it was dark, and it was harder to hold the rake handle level when you couldn't see it.

"Set it down," Frederik said. "And stay where you are. Now we wait."

He and Tommi stepped out of the light, and that made Sándor feel exposed and vulnerable standing here in the middle of the room, plainly visible as soon as anyone stepped through the door. Next to him, Nina had sat down on the floor with her head between her knees.

"Are you okay?" he asked.

"No," she said. "But what are you going to do about it?"

In the silence they heard the *pling* of a text message arriving. Tommi tossed the phone to Frederik. "Here," he said. "See what he wants."

There was a pause while Frederik fumbled around with the keys and read the message. "He wants it down in the gents'," he said. "Over to the left."

"Can he see us?" Tommi asked. "Where is old Moneybags?"

"Just do what he says," Frederik said. "The sooner we get out of here, the better." His voice was higher than usual, tense and nervous.

"Yeah, but not without the money."

Frederik crinkled his way across the plastic sheeting in his out-of-place boat shoes, and Sándor heard him open a door. Then there was a click, and the door became a shining rectangle in the darkness.

"The lights work over here," Frederik announced unnecessarily.

"Hello," Tommi suddenly yelled so loudly that the sound reverberated and startled them all. "Come out, come out, wherever you are! Show me the money!"

The only response was a new text message arriving with a *pling*.

"What?" Frederik mumbled. "Why the hell should we do that?"

"What did he say?"

Frederik showed Tommi the text message. Then he waved to Sándor.

"Come here. No, damn it. *With* the thing."

Sándor looked at Nina. She had collapsed on the floor, with an arm and a leg flung out to the side in a sloppy way that revealed that she wasn't just resting.

"Nina," he said.

She didn't respond.

"I think she's fainted," he said.

Tommi had his own simple test for that. He sauntered over to Nina's ragdoll body and kicked her so hard in the side that Sándor grabbed his own rib in automatic empathy.

There was absolutely no response.

If he was going to carry the can alone, he would have to touch it. He couldn't hold the rake handle in his injured hand, so he had to grab the paint can's wire handle in his healthy one.

"At least give me a pair of gloves!" he pleaded.

Frederik hesitated. Then he removed one of his own pale-yellow work gloves and tossed it onto the floor in front of Sándor.

"Here."

Sándor pulled it on. It was the wrong one, but it was still a whole lot better than touching the thing with his bare hand. He pulled the rake free and set it on the floor. Then he picked up the paint can. He held it as far away from his body as he could. It was heavy, and his arm quivered with the effort.

The lavatories were tiled in green and blue from floor to ceiling and had gleaming brass taps. There were no doors on the stalls yet, and down at the end, a water heater, some pipes, the main water shut-off valves, and an expansion tank were still exposed, not having been sealed away behind drywall or paneling yet.

"He wants it inside that," Tommi said, pointing to the hot water storage tank with the gun. "Just the whatsit, not the whole can."

That meant he was going to have to touch the actual source of the radioactivity. Sándor hesitated, on the verge of rebellion. Tommi didn't. He moved the pistol ever so slightly, so it would just miss Sándor, and fired.

The shot rang out between the tiled walls and a shower of small, sharp tile fragments sprayed Sándor's cheek, neck, and shoulder. And they heard a muffled scream from the ceiling over them.

Sándor and Tommi both looked up. The ceiling wasn't

totally finished. White panels were being mounted on a wood frame, and in the space above that, between bristling unconnected wires and exposed insulation, they could now both see that there was someone up there.

"You're coming down," Tommi hissed. "With or without holes. It's up to you."

At first it didn't seem like the person intended to obey, but when Tommi raised the gun again, the figure began moving with difficulty. With difficulty, because he or she was impeded by an astronaut-like protective suit of the type used for asbestos removal. The legs came first, and then the rest followed, with a wriggle and a twist, and the ceiling voyeur dropped down onto the floor between Sándor and Tommi.

The suit made it impossible to tell much other than that it was a human being. But Tommi was far more interested in the padded envelope the figure had taped to its chest.

"Payday . . ." he whispered, tearing the envelope free. "Money, money, money . . ."

He was actually singing it. Hoarsely and off-key, but it was unmistakably Abba.

Now, Sándor thought. Now, while he's not paying attention to anything else.

All he had was the sand-filled paint can. He swung it at the Finn's head with all his might, at this moment utterly indifferent to where the sand and cesium ended up.

He missed. Tommi jumped back, dropped the envelope, and fired the gun all in one motion.

SOMEONE HAD SET her on fire, and Nina knew she had to wake up. Now. The strange darkness enveloping her kept dragging her back; even when she succeeded in forcing her eyes open, it was as if her brain refused to come back online. The floor felt hard and cold against her hipbone and her shoulder. Then she realized that she wasn't actually on fire. The burning, throbbing pain was coming from the lower rib on her right side. A broken rib can perforate the lung, she thought woozily. Avoid sharp movements. But everything was moving. The room was a big teetering, swirling darkness that for a brief, absurd moment made her think of a gigantic hall of mirrors, the kind where everything is crooked and distorted. She was still desperately thirsty, and the floor she was lying on was terribly cold and dusty. There was dust in her mouth and on her hands.

Ida.

She pictured Ida in Mr. Suburbia's arms in the darkness in front of her. And Ida on her way down into her dark, subterranean tomb. Nina could hear voices and turned her head toward the sound. A narrow strip of light shone in from a half-open door a little further into the hall, and she recognized Mr. Suburbia's family-man silhouette next to the door. Nina swore to herself and lay still. Maybe he would think she was still unconscious. Tommi had probably stationed him there to keep an eye on her. Her eyes had adjusted to the darkness now so that she could see the wide double doors that led out to reality. It wouldn't take more than a few seconds of running, and once she was out . . . The pain in her side gave a brutal jab as she inhaled. Perforated lungs. She couldn't run if she had a punctured lung. If she ran, she could puncture a lung. Her thoughts chased each other around in circles, like white mice in a laboratory maze. It felt as if someone had plunged a chisel under her rib and wrenched at it. She didn't remember how it happened, but when she carefully ran her fingers over the lower edge of her ribcage, she felt a clear angle that shouldn't be there. A fracture, it was definitely broken. She wasn't running anywhere.

And Ida was still alone in the dark.

Bang.

The sound of the shot echoed through the empty, tiled hall and made Mr. Suburbia's silhouette cower.

"What the hell is going on?" he muttered.

He walked over to the doorway but appeared to change his mind and stayed put with his back against the doorframe, peering furtively into the next room. Apparently no one answered him, but they could still hear the Finn in there. It almost sounded as if he were singing.

Singing?

Mr. Suburbia glanced over at her, perplexed, then he turned around and disappeared into where Tommi and Sándor were.

Now, Nina thought. You can't die here. You have to do it now.

She tried to take shallow breaths as she pushed herself up off the floor with both arms. The pain in her side made everything go black before her eyes, and twice she was forced to stop altogether and wait for the world to slowly come into view again. Then she continued hobbling across the floor toward the exit.

Which was when the second shot rang out. She was so startled it almost knocked her over. But she still didn't look back.

She reached the door. Splinters from the damaged wood around the lock jutted out like barbs, and her fingers were too clumsy to open it silently. The wind from outside grabbed it and blew it all the way open with a distinctive bang. Then she was standing outside in the chilly May evening. The construction site's puddles glittered yellow-brown in the light from the overhead spotlights. She could see the paved road just a hundred meters away, and on the other side of it, a row of peaceful looking suburban homes with dark beech hedges and birch trees, their black branches swaying in the cool breeze. There were lights on and people at home in one of the closest ones.

Help, she thought. Get help for Ida.

She started walking toward the light, staggering but obstinate, and didn't stop despite hearing another three shots ring out from inside the mosque behind her.

THE SHOT RIPPED a hole in his side, right under his ribs. He felt it first as an impact, then as a burning, wet sensation. He was still standing, hadn't been dramatically hurled backward like in the action movies. He had, however, dropped the paint can.

"What the fuck are you doing?!"

The voice was Frederik's, but it was almost unrecognizable from the shock. Tommi was just laughing, a completely normal laugh, as if someone had said something really funny.

"Boom!" he said. "You're dead." And then the pistol clicked as he let yet another bullet slide forward into the chamber.

Sándor didn't want to fall. That would most definitely hurt, and he had already experienced enough pain. But his legs didn't ask for permission. They just crumpled beneath him, so he fell to his knees, and after that forward, and then onto his side. And, yes, it hurt.

There was yet another shot, but Sándor didn't feel anything. While the bang was still ringing in his ears, he saw the asbestos-suited figure spin halfway round and topple over onto the floor. Ah, he got shot this time, not you, Sándor thought with a strange sensation of remoteness, as if it were some sort of public statement that didn't pertain to him.

"Stop it," Frederik yelled.

"Why? Dude, it's a Muslim terrorist and a Gypsy. I'm doing the world a fucking service here."

Someone hoisted up Sándor's aching body. It was Frederik. The man put his arms around Sándor and supported him, almost affectionately, it felt like, but Sándor wished he would leave him alone. Then the man pushed something cold and metallic into Sándor's good hand and closed his fingers around it.

The grip of a pistol.

He forced his eyelids open. Yes, it *was* a pistol. A flat, little black one. Smaller than Tommi's.

"Shoot him," Frederik whispered. "He's insane! Shoot him before he kills us all . . ."

Why don't *you* shoot him? But his irritable question didn't make it any further than his mind. Frederik raised his hand, placed his index finger over Sándor's index finger on the trigger, and squeezed.

The back of the Finn's head exploded. Sándor just had time to see the singed black hole in the face mask, approximately where the man's mouth was. Then Tommi fell over and hit the tile floor with a jellyfish-like slap.

Frederik let go of Sándor and stood up. He stepped over the crumpled asbestos-suit-clad figure and leaned over Tommi.

Why is he holding Tommi's hand? Sándor wondered.

But that wasn't what Frederik was doing. He tore the gloves off Tommi's hands. Then he picked up Tommi's pistol and positioned it in Tommi's dead, floppy hand, wrapping the Finn's fingers around the grip, pretty much the way he had done with Sándor's uncooperative fingers.

He's going to shoot me, Sándor thought. And then he'll shoot Nina. And make sure the asbestos man is dead, too. And then he'll walk out of here, safe in the knowledge that no one can point their finger at Mr. Clean and say: He did it.

The flat, little pistol was still in his hand. He only had to lift it. Lift it and aim.

He couldn't.

Come on, phrala.

He heard the voice so clearly that for a crazy instant he was sure Tamás wasn't dead after all. It sent a jolt through him, and his finger curled around the trigger. And he fired.

Bang. Howl.

Frederik was standing in front of him with his hands folded as if he were in church, blood gushing out between his fingers. His little finger was missing.

"Fuck. Fuck. Fuck," he moaned, the pitch of his voice growing higher and higher with each repetition. He staggered out the door and disappeared.

Sándor contemplated whether he had the energy to drag himself out of the building. He wasn't sure. The asbestos-suited figure was lying still, a red stain on his chest, and Sándor couldn't tell if there was any life behind the mask. The paint can was a few meters from him, on its side, and the sand was slowly trickling out around the edges of the lid where it wasn't completely sealed. And the envelope with the money was also lying on the floor, so close that he could reach it if he stuck out his arm.

He stuck out his arm.

FIRST NINA KNOCKED on the door, which had a little knocker with a black cast-iron lion's head. But nothing happened. She was fairly sure she heard footsteps behind the solid front door, but it didn't open, and she regretted choosing the closest house. She should have moved farther away from the building behind her. If Tommi or Frederik came after her now, she would be totally exposed, standing there in front of this closed door. A wide-open target, a barely moving target. The pain in her side rose and fell with her much-too-rapid breathing, and each time she inhaled, new black dots danced in front of her eyes. They could shoot her right here, and no one would ever find out where Ida was.

She stepped over to the tall, narrow window next to the door and knocked on the glass, alternating between her knuckles and her palm.

"Hello!"

Her voice made almost no sound. The shout was there, in her throat, but her tongue and dry lips refused to cooperate. Anyway, now she could see a face on the other side of the glass. An older man dismissively waving a hand lightly covered with liver spots. Nina looked down at herself. She looked terrible. The dark-blue tracksuit was covered with construction dust, and her right arm jutted out awkwardly to the side to keep her from touching her rib. She tried to smile, but the face inside the window had already started backing away. Farther and farther away. She knocked again, but this time without much conviction.

"Hello? I need help!"

There was no response.

Nina turned around and stared back at the mosque behind her. Its front door was still open, but she didn't see any sign of Tommi or Frederik. The reflection of a light in the window of one of the portable office trailers at the construction site across the street made her jump, but it was just the streetlights swaying in the heavy wind.

Did she have the strength to try the neighbor's? Nina looked over at the house next door. Yet another red-brick fort with a single lit window and an impervious front door. She had the utterly stupid desire to cry. Like when she was little, standing alone on the playground with a scraped knee and hundreds of happy, laughing children around her. But it hadn't done any good then, and it wouldn't do any good now. She rubbed a hand over her eyes and looked around. There was a birdbath on the little lawn in front of the house, attractively surrounded by fist-sized red, granite rocks.

Nina hobbled down the steps with a firm grasp on the wrought iron railing. One step, two steps . . . she tried to ignore the pain when she bent down, but as she straightened up with a rock in her hand, she emitted a wheezing groan anyway.

She went back up the stairs and peered in the window. The man had withdrawn so far that she could see only his feet, nervously padding away. She raised the rock and slammed it into the window with all her might. The old man's double-glazing didn't surrender until she hit it for the third time, making a hole big enough to pass a fist through. Her reluctant helper had by this time retreated so far back into his hallway that all she could see was his feet, but that didn't matter.

"Call the police," she bellowed. "Now!"

SHE SAW THE patrol car long before the pensioner could have even picked up the phone. It drove past her without flashing lights or a siren, pulled up outside the construction site, and turned off its headlights.

Nina grabbed the stair railing and took the three steps down to the front walkway so fast that she crashed to her knees on the flagstones. She got up again and staggered, shuffling and shouting, as fast and as loud as her rib would permit.

"Help."

She didn't know how long it had been since Ida had crawled into that oil tank. One hour? Two hours? At any rate it had gotten dark out, and it had been way too long.

"Help." Nina picked up her pace. "Help. I need help."

This time she screamed for real.

BLOOD OR MONEY. This wasn't some vague hypothetical choice; it was a practical problem. The blood was flowing out of him with every single heartbeat, and his ability to move, think, and act was flowing away with it. Sándor didn't know if he was dying or not. Maybe there was no point in speculating about the future.

And the money. The money that Tamás had given his life for. It was all here in his hand, in a gray, blood-smeared envelope that was almost as thick as *Blackstone's International Law*.

He didn't have much time or many options. He clumsily got up onto all fours and couldn't get any farther than that. Walking and standing were not in his current repertoire. A stab of pain shot through his hole-riddled palm when he put his left hand on the floor, but if he was going to take that envelope, he would have to ignore the pain. It turned out you could reach a point when the pain became irrelevant. What mattered were the mechanics. What you could and what you couldn't do. He couldn't stand up without falling down. And if he fell, he would stay down. He could probably crawl on all fours if he used his left hand, too, so that's what he did.

He crawled past the person in the white suit. At the moment he didn't care who was lying there inside the suit, nor did he care if the man were alive or dead. He didn't have any spare energy to waste on anger or curiosity. Hand-knee, hand-knee, that was all that mattered. Past the Finn with only half a head. Out of the door. Out.

Halfway across the threshold he was hit by a wave of weakness. His arm buckled, he rolled halfway onto his side, but the doorframe stopped him and kept him from collapsing completely.

"You're not going to make it, *phrala*."

He looked up. There was Tamás, *Mulo*-Tamás with the red, bleeding eyes.

"Shut up," Sándor mumbled. "Out of my way! You know this whole thing is your fault, right?"

Mulo-Tamás didn't move. "Not just my fault," he said.

Sándor didn't have the strength to argue with an evil spirit that might not even be there. He tried to crawl farther, but his body wouldn't obey.

"I did it because I had to," *Mulo*-Tamás said. "So the family would survive. So we could get by. Who knows? If you hadn't turned your back on us, maybe I wouldn't have fucking needed to."

"Move," Sándor repeated feebly.

"You turned your back on us." *Mulo*-Tamás's bloody eyes burned. "You turned your back on your own people, your brother and your sisters, your own mother. Just so you could get by in the *gadjo* world. And where did it get you? Nowhere. Soon you'll be as dead as me. And what will happen to the family then? Your death is hardly any purer than mine."

Sándor's head sank.

"The money," Sándor mumbled. "Feliszia's school. The new roof. An apartment for Vanda. Tamás, I'm not turning my back on them."

"You just don't want anyone to know we exist."

"Yes. Yes, I do. Lujza is going to meet you all. If . . .

well, if she wants to." *I don't think I have the strength to love someone who isn't brave enough to be himself*, she'd said. But . . . what if he was brave enough now? What if he could stop being just half a person? Somewhere deep down, he knew perfectly well that that was why he backed down so easily, why he never stood up to confrontation, why he was afraid of the authorities and walked away from most fights—even the most important ones. A half person has a harder time keeping his balance than a whole one. Maybe it was about time he quit being a half-brother, too.

"*Phrala*," Sándor said. "Enough now, okay? *Te merav.* You're killing me."

But *Mulo*-Tamás wasn't there anymore. There was nothing there.

Sándor clung to the doorframe and managed to pull himself up onto his knees. The front hall was empty. Nina wasn't lying in the middle of the floor anymore, and he really hoped that was because she had managed to get away, and not because Frederik had dragged her off somewhere.

He wasn't going to be able to get away. He heard car doors closing and footsteps outside. He had minutes or maybe only seconds left until they were here.

His heart hammered in an attempt to force the blood around his body faster. He clung to the doorframe with both hands and managed to struggle to his feet. The hole in the ceiling was still there, but there was no chance he would be able to reach it and not much chance that he would avoid detection even if he could. But the money. Maybe he could get the money up there.

One try. He didn't think he had it in him to do any more.

Come on now, phrala. Do it!

He wasn't sure if the voice came from someone else or if it was from inside him. Wasn't sure if it was Tamás's or his own. Maybe it didn't matter, either. Maybe it was one and the same thing now.

He threw. Flung the envelope up, toward that dark opening up there. It was pretty much going to take a miracle, he thought. And that was exactly what he got—a perfect arc, with more strength than he actually had, and a precision that even on a good day would have been remarkable. The envelope disappeared through the opening into the jumbled chaos of wires and insulation material and darkness.

Sándor staggered a few more steps before his legs gave out. The fall almost killed him, but he managed to crawl another few meters. Then he could go no farther.

He lowered his head on to his one aching arm and lay down to wait for help or judgment. For whatever was going to come next.

Okay, *phrala*. You did what you could.

1

IDA'S ALIVE. IDA'S alive.

Nina hadn't noticed she was shaking until the officer had put his jacket across her shoulders. And then he had told her that someone had found Ida. And that she wasn't dead. She didn't hear much else of what he said, but it was as if she became aware of herself again in a different way. The pain in her ribs became real. The nausea and the throbbing in her head and her shaking hands, clutching the water bottle the policeman had handed her. They all felt like her, like parts of her. It hurt, but that meant she was alive again. And Ida was alive.

Nina sank back in the seat, watching the scene outside as pain throbbed rhythmically in her right side. There were three police cars parked along the curb now, but none of the officers were in sight. The door they had entered through gaped blackly at the parking lot, and the door to the office trailer was also open now and swinging in the wind. She hoped Sándor was alive. She hoped those shots that had been fired hadn't been meant for him, but she was consumed by relief over the news about Ida. It was as if there wasn't room for anything else right now.

A man was walking down the sidewalk. She wouldn't even have noticed him if he hadn't sped up as he went past the police cars. It was just a man in a pale raincoat, a man who was out taking a walk in the suburban neighborhood where he surely belonged. It was the low, white silhouettes of the police cruisers that were out of place. But instead of stopping out of curiosity to look at them, he hurried on. And that was why she recognized him.

It was Frederik. And it wasn't until she looked more closely that she saw there were quite a few things wrong with the picture Mr. Suburbia presented. The raincoat was too big to be his. And the one pocket, the one he was hiding his right hand in, sported a growing bloodstain.

The open door of the office trailer, swinging in the wind . . . the light she thought she had seen in the window of the hut. Had that been something more than a reflection from the spotlights bobbing on the swaying posts? Had Frederik been hiding there while he got his camouflage worked out?

Nina flung herself across the steering wheel in the front seat and hit the horn. The prolonged honk made the man cower like a gun-shy dog, but then he sped up to a run. And nothing else happened. The officers in the hall either hadn't heard her, or they were busy, preoccupied with something they thought was more important. Nina pushed the horn down again and held it. This time with the result that the curtains moved very slightly in the anxious old man's house. Well, that's not much help, Nina thought dryly.

I parked the Touareg a few blocks away. She suddenly remembered what Frederik had said as he came jogging back, skipping between the puddles in the parking lot, before they went into the mosque. If he made it to the car, he might actually escape. Frederik slowed back down to a just-out-for-an-evening stroll again as he rounded the corner. He was getting away.

Mr. Suburbia. Who had sat there drinking instant soup

out of his ugly red ceramic mug while Ida was strapped to that radiator.

Nina had ridden in the ambulance a few times while she was in training, and she had quickly picked up some of the more experienced EMTs' tricks. One of them was to leave a set of extra keys under one of the sun visors so any driver would be able to start the ambulance when the call came in. She leaned over the driver's seat in the police car and tilted the visor down. A key landed on the seat with a soft thump, and Nina gingerly shimmied her way into the driver's seat, pushed the clutch pedal down, and stuck the key in the ignition. She steered the car out onto Lundedalsvej and accelerated toward the corner, without being completely sure what her plan was. She just couldn't let him get away like that. Not after what he'd done to Ida. And Sándor. And his brother.

She caught sight of him a little farther down the road. He appeared calmer now. Once again looking more and more like a homeowner out for a neighborhood stroll. He didn't even glance over his shoulder when he turned down yet another side street and briefly disappeared from her view. Turning the corner herself, she was suddenly right on his tail, and this time he couldn't help but hear her. He turned around on the sidewalk and saw her. Looked into her eyes for the first time.

His hands came up out of his pockets. One was wrapped in blood-soaked toilet paper. The other was holding a gun. She didn't have time to see any more than that before he aimed the gun at her. He held it in his left hand with his arm out straight in front of him, in a way that wasn't totally convincing. Nina turned the wheel, slowed the patrol car down, and ducked to the right as the shot hit, causing white chunks of glass to rain down on her like a shower of ice. The right front tire bumped onto the curb, and the engine cut out.

She shook the glass fragments out of her hair. He was still there. He was standing right in front of the car's white hood, clumsily cocking the gun with his injured hand.

He was crying. Tears of pain, presumably, which was fair enough. And yet she couldn't shake the thought that it was the cry of a spoiled child. A child who had never before been in real pain.

She turned the key in the ignition and brought the engine back to life just as he raised his gun again. She let out the clutch a little too abruptly, and the car jumped forward in a kangaroo hop before stalling again. But that was enough. The thud on the bumper was firm and satisfying, and Mr. Suburbia disappeared under the front of the car with an indignant howl.

JUNE

A PLEASANT, GOLDEN LIGHT fell through the Venetian blinds, and the background noise of clattering trays and serving carts, voices and footsteps, and the distinctive suction-cup *shwoop* of the automated doors closing were pleasantly muffled. The month of June was in full bloom outside, and the chestnut trees were dropping their sticky yellow-white flowers left and right. Søren had cycled over to Bispebjerg Hospital in drizzle and rain showers, but now it had cleared up. They had let him hang his dripping rain pants and anorak in Ward K's staff locker room while he questioned Helle Skou-Larsen.

She lay with her face turned toward the light and her bed raised so that it was easier for her to look out. She didn't turn her head when he entered her room. If he wanted to see her facial expression, he would have to sit between her and the window, so he nodded quickly to the lawyer and pulled one of the mismatched visitor's chairs around to the other side of the bed.

"Hello, Mrs. Skou-Larsen," he said pleasantly. "How are you doing?"

She focused on him slowly. Her eyes were porcelain blue against her bloodless skin, and the subtle makeup couldn't completely cover her pallor and the dark, heavy bags under her eyes. There was a certain absurdity to the oxygen tube as an accessory to her pink lipstick, but her lung capacity was still far from optimal.

"Fine, thank you." Her voice sounded astonishingly

normal. Stronger than he would have expected, given her general frailty.

He showed her his identification.

"Søren Kirkegård, PET."

"Yes" was all she said.

"I'm sorry about your husband."

She showed no reaction.

Her lawyer got up off the only upholstered chair in the room.

"Mads Ahlegaard," he said, holding out his hand. "Let me just remind you that the doctors say this conversation will have to be limited to fifteen minutes."

"I'm aware of that," Søren said, sitting down on the flimsy, wooden chair. "Mrs. Skou-Larsen, I'm here to talk to you about your attempt to buy an illegal radioactive substance."

The words felt so inappropriate, as if they didn't really belong in the same universe as this middle-aged suburban housewife who went to choir practice once a week and played bridge every other Friday. And yet, that was exactly what she had done. They were now aware of most of her activities; they had found the Acer laptop she had used for the online searches that had ultimately put her in touch with Tamás Rézmüves, ten different pay-as-you-go phones she had bought at various locations around town, the remnants of her husband's supply of Imovane pills that she had used to sedate the guard dogs at the mosque— and possibly also her husband . . . They had found her fingerprints on the Opel Rekord's steering wheel and gear shift, despite the fact that she apparently hadn't driven a car since the '70s. They were pretty clear on *what* she'd done. What remained a mystery was *why*. The first theory was that she must have been subjected to some form of extortion or coercion, maybe from a radical right-wing extremist group, but there just weren't any indications that that was the case. It appeared the whole thing had been her own bright idea.

Now the doctors had finally given the green light for her to be questioned. And this was not a task Søren planned to assign to anyone else.

"Mrs. Skou-Larsen, what was the cesium chloride for?"

She looked past him, at the window. It was irritating that she wouldn't allow him to establish eye contact, but he wasn't going to let that show.

"Someone had to do something," she said. "You can't just let things slide."

"Yes, but what were you going to do?"

"It was getting so that you saw them everywhere," she said. "You couldn't go anywhere without . . . without them being there. Without them *looking* at you."

"Who?" he asked, even though he thought he knew the answer.

"Them. Those foreigners. It wouldn't bother me so much if it were just a few here and there, but there are just more and more of them." She looked right at him for the first time, a chilly glimpse of blue and white. "Did you know that they have almost twice as many children as do Danes?"

Where do people hear this nonsense? The question was on the tip of his tongue, but he restrained himself, smiling pleasantly instead.

"Yes, I can certainly understand how that might seem alarming."

"And then that new mosque. So close! At first I was so angry I almost couldn't sleep at night. But then . . ." She cut herself short, her eyes left him again and drifted sideways, toward the sunlight and the blinds. He had to prompt her to get her talking again.

"Then what, Mrs. Skou-Larsen?"

"Then I started thinking that maybe there was a reason for it. That it was *supposed* to be right here, so close that I could walk there. Because, of course, that made it easier."

"Yes, I can certainly see that."

"I'm *not* at all fond of driving," she said suddenly flashing him an apologetic, feminine smile. "My husband is always the one who drives. Or . . . well, he was."

But where there's a will, there's a way, thought Søren, picturing this seemingly helpless woman, slightly out of touch with reality, throwing herself into Copenhagen traffic in a twenty-five-year-old Opel Rekord, probably with her hands clutching the steering wheel so hard that her knuckles gleamed. They probably ought to be glad the Opel was an automatic, at least from a purely traffic-safety-related point of view. Had she intentionally chosen to access the Internet from a school where more than 70 percent of the students were not ethnically Danish? It was quite possible that Khalid's difficulties were due to an intentional if impersonal act of revenge on the part of this woman. No, helpless wasn't the right word for her.

"So you would prefer it if this mosque were . . .

removed?" Important not to use words like "destroyed," "blown to pieces," or "contaminated." Language mattered. He had to try to describe the act in such a way that she wouldn't distance herself from it.

She shook her head all the same.

"Removed? No, where did you get that idea from? That would ruin everything."

Søren was too professional to let her see how astonished he was. But it took an act of iron will.

"How would it ruin the whole thing?" he asked neutrally.

"Well, it just wouldn't have worked then."

"So you didn't intend to . . ." Oh, now there was no avoiding it. "It was not your intention to blow up the mosque?" That would explain why they hadn't found any trace of explosives, either at the house on Elmehøjvej or around the cultural center.

She looked indignant.

"Blow it up? Of course not. Why in God's name would I want to do that? What do you take me for? A criminal?"

And then she told him what she had actually planned to do.

As Søren cycled back from Bispebjerg Hospital, he had an almost irresistible desire to lie in a woman's arms. Not necessarily to have sex, although that might be nice, too. But to lie next to a warm, receptive body, to talk to a person who was lying so close to him that he could smell her breath, her sweat, her hair and skin. To rest his face in the hollow between her shoulder and her breast and feel her softness and warmth.

There just wasn't anyone.

Susse was the closest he came, right now. But she was with Ben at some concert in Randers, and besides he couldn't tell her anything of significance about the case, though much would surely come out later during the trial.

He cycled back to his office in Søborg, even though the Skou-Larsen interview was supposed to have been his last stop for the day. Going home to Hvidovre, to an empty house, a beer, and a microwave dinner from the freezer . . . no. Not now. Not today.

Torben was heading out to his Audi when Søren turned into the parking lot. He kicked his feet out of the toe clips and dismounted, hot and sweaty because he had ridden as fast as traffic had permitted, but not winded. Maybe he ought to just head down to the fitness room and run his brains out on the treadmill so he could quit thinking about women and emptiness and sources of radioactivity at least for as long as he could keep his pulse up around 190 BPM.

"Well?" Torben asked, turning his back on the Audi for a bit. "How did it go?"

"She was willing to cooperate up to a point. And it looks like she was acting completely on her own. Obviously we should run her through it a few more times once she is up to slightly longer sessions, but I didn't get the impression that she was hiding anything."

"No ties to extremists, no accomplices, no conspiracies?"

"Doesn't look that way. And I think we should be letting young Mr. Horváth go home soon. Her story supports his. She was actually dealing only with Tamás

Rézmüves, his half-brother. Sándor was just in the wrong place at the wrong time."

"Well, *we* can certainly release him," Torben said. "The question is whether the NBH will."

"Gábor seemed like a pretty reasonable man. Couldn't you put in a good word?"

Torben raised his eyebrows. "How did Sándor Horváth manage to win you over into his corner?"

"I just don't think there's any reason to ruin his life further."

Torben studied him for a moment. Then he said, "Okay. I'll talk to Gábor. That is if you're sure Mrs. Skou-Larsen's explanation is credible."

"As I said, I'd really like to talk to her again. But I'm fairly certain it'll bear up. She decided to procure some radioactive material over the Internet and install it in the hot water tank in the men's lavatory in that mosque."

"Did she say anything about why?"

"Yes." Søren opened the neck of his anorak, to alleviate some of the sweating. "It wasn't because she wanted to blow up anyone or anything. She was actually quite indignant when I suggested that. No, she just wanted to ensure that there wouldn't be so many of 'them.' And the reproductive organs are among the first to be affected when someone is exposed to radiation."

"Damn," said Torben, his hand moving halfway down to his testicles in a protective gesture before he caught himself.

"Yup. She just wanted to quietly and calmly sterilize the entire population of Muslim men in the area."

Torben shook his head. "People are crazy," he said helplessly. "How on earth are we supposed to predict what all the nutcases of this world are going to come up with? Sometimes I wish my job were just solving crimes *after* they've been committed. Nice, clean, and simple. Weren't you headed home?"

"Yes. I'm just going to go work out for a bit first."

Torben gave him a quick, manly slap on the back. "You want to see if you can outrow me one of these days when the weather's nice? Bring it on."

Søren forced a smile. He definitely had a competitive streak, but sometimes he found it tiring that everything had to be an incessant pissing contest.

AFTER HIS SIXTH interval running on the treadmill's 12 percent incline, he gave up. No matter how high he drove his pulse, he couldn't stop thinking. Frustrated, he took off his sweaty clothes and stood under the faintly chlorine-scented jet of water in the shower room. He lathered up his armpits and crotch. Curled his fingers around his cock and scrotum, wondering at everything this one organ signified. It defined him as a man; it made him a lover; it could have made him a father if he had wanted that and hadn't just backed away, forcing Susse to have her kids with another man.

It was completely unnecessary to sterilize him, he thought. He had managed that all on his own, with the choices he had made in his life.

In his mind's eye, he once again saw Helle Skou-Larsen's indignation when he had asked whether she were planning on blowing up the mosque. She did not believe in violence, she had said. She hadn't been planning on killing anyone. What did she look like, a murderer?

Søren didn't know what a murderer looked like anymore. And he supposed what she had wanted to commit wasn't homicide, not in the standard sense. Just a quiet, invisible murder of the future.

NINA WAS WAITING for the night.

It was still light outside, even though it was almost 10 P.M., and she had been lying on the guest bed in the clinic for more than an hour. Since she got out of the taxi, actually, dragging her scant possessions with her. She had bought a sleeping bag. Underwear. Two pairs of jeans. Socks, shorts, and T-shirts. And a toothbrush, of course. It was important to bring a toothbrush to your new home. Magnus had said she could stay at the clinic until she found a place to live, and somehow Nina was thinking that wouldn't happen right away. A new place to live meant something like an apartment. Maybe somewhere in Østerbro. Two bedrooms would suffice, surely. Then the kids could each have their own, and she could sleep in the living room when they were there. If they ever were. Anton would show up at regular intervals. Ida was less likely to. Nina had been granted permission to hug her one single time since their ordeal. Ida had wrapped both arms around Nina and cried into her neck, but she had also given her a look afterward that was completely different from her normal glare. For the first time in more than a year, it didn't feel like Ida was mad at her, but more . . . sick of it all. Disappointed, maybe.

You promised her that as long as you were with her, nothing bad would happen to her, Nina thought. Now she knows that isn't true. That her mother and father aren't strong enough to protect her from everything in this world.

Apparently the war between them had been called off and replaced with something else. Nina just didn't know what. But Ida hadn't come to see her since.

Morten came to the hospital a few times with Anton and had dutifully asked about her broken rib and her radiation sickness and the long-term effects, and he had also smiled, probably for Anton's sake, and talked a little about Anton's school and how the parent-teacher meeting had gone. He had traded shifts so he didn't need to go back to the North Sea until the summer vacation. He was thinking about looking for a new job, he had said. One where he wouldn't be away from home for two weeks out of four. But for the time being, his sister was helping with the logistics, and they were lucky that his brother-in-law worked in Copenhagen, not far from Ida and Anton's school.

They hadn't discussed difficult issues like custody. Not yet. "That can wait until you're well again," he had said.

And now she was well. Or recovered, anyway.

Her body was symptom-free, but the doctors said she should still count on having more infections than normal. She should go to the doctor for regular checkups. And remember to take her pills.

The springs in the guest bed sagged noisily every time she rolled over. The sleeping bag she had just taken out of its plastic wrap was way too warm. North Field Arctic, rated for extreme, subzero temperatures. But the sun had been beating on the clinic's south-facing windows all day, and the evening was muggy and still. She could hear young men yelling outside, drunk and aggressive.

Nina got up, pulled a shirt on over her underwear and

stuck her feet into the loose shorts she'd bought at Kvickly. She left her sleeping bag where it was and walked down the long walkway to the children's unit. In the security room, the night guard was sitting on the sofa sipping a cup of coffee and watching the ten o'clock news, with its endless scenes of violence and prophecies of doom. They were talking about terrorist threats and the melting polar icecaps and the global financial crisis. Nina snuck past without saying hello.

She found Rina in her room, all the way down at the end of the hall, wrapped up too warmly in the corner of her bed with her eyes closed, her breathing hot and fast. Sometimes she mumbled something or other and lashed out at something in the air. She was on medication now, Nina knew. She was sleeping better now. Nina opened the window facing the lawn and stood there for a moment looking out into the twilight before she lay down next to Rina.

Nighttime was the worst time at the Coal-House Camp, because at night they were all alone in the dark.

ACKNOWLEDGMENTS

An enormous thank you to the many people and organizations that generously gave their time and knowledge so that this book could be written:

Iringó Nemes
Orsolya Pánczél
Csilla Báder Lakatosné
Lajos Bangó
Magyarországi Roma Parlament, Budapest
Kata E. Fris
János Tódor
Szandra Váraljai
Amaro Drom and the residents of Csenyéte, Hungary
The Institute of Danish Culture in Kecskemét, Hungary
Laokoon Films, Budapest
Hans Jørgen Bonnichsen
Biljana Muncan
Knirke Egede
Hildegunn Brattvåg
Mary Lisa Jayaseelan and the Danish Refugee Council
Anne Karen Ursø and the Danish Red Cross
Christian Riewe
Kim Nielsen
Anita Frank
Lone-emilie Rasmussen

822   LENE KAABERBØL AND AGNETE FRIIS

Hans Peter Hansen
Henrik Laier
Gustav Friis
Kirstine Friis
Anna Grue
Alex Uth
Mette Finderup
Lotte Krarup
Lars Ringhof
Bibs Carlsen
Erling Kaaberbøl
Eva Kaaberbøl
Berit Weeler

In addition, the two authors would both like to assert that any errors or oversights are exclusively the fault of the other.

ABOUT THE AUTHORS

It wasn't exactly love at first sight when Lene Kaaberbøl and Agnete Friis met, but it was pretty damn close.

It was the year 2007 and Lene was at that time already a widely published bestselling author of children's books, while Agnete was still making a living as a journalist, writing only in what was left of her spare time as a mother of two young children, with her third child on the way.

The meeting was quite coincidental, in the way important meetings often are. Agnete was looking for a publisher for her second children's book, and Lene was looking for young talented writers for the small publishing house she was part-proprietor of at the time.

They met and had coffee. Or rather, they met and had coffee and tea. As with a lot of other issues, Lene and Agnete do not agree on choice of beverage. But they did agree to meet again, this time to kick-start the children's book together. Lene would be the coach and Agnete the talent. A couple of weeks later, Agnete rode her bike through the city of Copenhagen to meet up with Lene in her private home on the Copenhagen waterfront.

And that was when they fell in love—professionally, that is. In spite of their countless differences, they had one very important thing in common. They thought about writing in the exact same way, and they enjoyed talking about it.

In 2008, shortly after Agnete's book was published, Lene was first haunted by the image of a small naked boy in a suitcase. She knew that this was in no way something that belonged in one of her usual books for children. But the picture distracted her in her work and would not go away, so she finally came to the conclusion that she would have to do something about it—if possible with Agnete as copilot on her mission.

"She called me and read me the first page of *The Boy in the Suitcase*," Agnete says. "And I wanted so badly to say yes right away, but at that point my third child was only one month old, and I wasn't entirely sure that I could live up to the challenge. But after thinking hard about it for a couple of days, I finally said yes, and it was one of the best decisions I have made in my life. Not just because of the books we write together, but because having a writing partner and friend like that is absolutely wonderful."

"Finding someone you can work with in that very intimate fashion is a rare gift," says Lene. "I'm really, really glad I had the sense to recognize it at the time. It's been extremely rewarding to have someone there every bit of the way, laughing, sparring, critiquing, gossiping, killing darlings, and inventing people, places and stories that I could not have come up with on my own in a million years." Tongue in cheek, she adds: "Getting a ring-side seat to Agnete's busy and often highly entertaining family life is, of course, an added bonus."

The two authors have worked closely together since 2008, having published four books, the last one of which, *The Considerate Killer*, was published in the US in 2016.

Lene Kaaberbøl, 55, has an M.A. in English and Drama. A former high school teacher, she is now a full-time writer, with more than 40 books under her belt, most of them published all over the world. She started writing very early and had her first two novels published when she was only 15 years old. After living in Copenhagen for several years, she has moved to the tiny island of Sark with her three dogs, a laptop, a varying number of chickens, and a satisfyingly productive vegetable garden.

Things to know about Lene:
- She absolutely hates coffee but loves tea
- She likes to work in the morning
- She is a self-declared perfectionist and control freak when it comes to her books, but not her garden
- She likes living far away from anything that can distract her from what she feels is her most important task in life: to write

Agnete Friis, 41, is a journalist and now full-time writer. Beside crime fiction she has written children's books and biographies. She grew up in the countryside, but now lives in Copenhagen with her husband and three children. Although she enjoyed being a journalist, she enjoys being a fiction writer even more, because she sometimes finds it easier to write a true story when it's not really true.

Things to know about Agnete:

- She only drinks coffee when she is working
- She works whenever her children are not around, whatever time of day it is
- She is very far from being a perfectionist, although not as bad a slob as Lene might suggest
- She loves Copenhagen and will never leave the city again

Continue reading for a preview of
the next Nina Borg thriller

Death of a Nightingale

AUDIO FILE **#83:** Nightingale

"Go on," says a man's voice.

"I'm tired," an older woman answers, clearly uncomfortable and dismissive.

"But it's so exciting."

"Exciting?" There's a lash of bitterness in her reaction. "A bit of Saturday entertainment? Is that what this is for you?"

"No, I didn't mean it like that."

They are both speaking Ukrainian, he quickly and informally, she more hesitantly. In the background, occasional beeps from an electronic game can be heard.

"It's important for posterity."

The old woman laughs now, a hard and unhappy laughter. "Posterity," she says. "Do you mean the child? Isn't she better off not knowing?"

"If that's how you see it. We should be getting home anyway."

"No." The word is abrupt. "Not yet. Surely you can stay a little longer."

"You said you were tired," says the man.

"No. Not . . . that tired."

"I don't mean to press you."

"No, I know that. You just thought it was exciting."

"Forget I said that. It was stupid."

"No, no. Children like exciting stories. Fairy tales."

"I was thinking more along the lines of something real. Something you experienced yourself."

Another short pause. Then, "No, let me tell you a story," the old woman says suddenly. "A fairy tale. A little fairy tale from Stalin Land. A suitable bedtime story for the little one. Are you listening, my sweet?"

Beep, beep, beep-beep. Unclear mumbling from the child. Obviously, her attention is mostly on the game, but that doesn't stop the old woman.

"Once upon a time, there were two sisters," she begins clearly, as if reciting. "Two sisters who both sang so beautifully that the nightingale had to stop singing when it heard them. First one sister sang for the emperor himself, and thus was the undoing of a great many people. Then the other sister, in her resentment, began to sing too."

"Who are you talking about?" the man asks. "Is it you? Is it someone we know?"

The old woman ignores him. There's a harshness to her voice, as if she's using the story to punish him.

"When the emperor heard the other sister, his heart grew inflamed, and he had to own her," she continued. "'Come to me,' he begged. Oh, you can be sure he begged. 'Come to me, and be my nightingale. I'll give you gold and beautiful clothes and servants at your beck and call.'"

Here the old woman stops. It's as if she doesn't really

feel like going on, and the man no longer pressures her. But the story has its own relentless logic, and she has to finish it.

"At first she refused. She rejected the emperor. But he persisted. 'What should I give you, then?' he asked, because he had learned that everything has a price. 'I will not come to you,' said the other sister, 'before you give me my evil sister's head on a platter.'"

In the background, the beeping sounds from the child's game have ceased. Now there is only an attentive silence.

"When the emperor saw that a heart as black as sin hid behind the beautiful song," the old woman continues, still using her fairy-tale voice, "he not only killed the first sister, but also the nightingale's father and mother and grandfather and grandmother and whole family. 'That's what you get for your jealousy,' he said and threw the other sister out."

The child utters a sound, a frightened squeak. The old woman doesn't seem to notice.

"Tell me," she whispers. "Which of them is me?"

"You're both alive," says the man. "So something in the story must be a lie."

"In Stalin Land, Stalin decides what is true and what is a lie," says the old woman. "And I said that it was a Stalin fairy tale."

"Daddy," says the child, "I want to go home now."

"**G**UM?"

Natasha started; she had been sitting silently, looking out the window of the patrol car as Copenhagen glided by in frozen shades of winter grey. Dirty house fronts, dirty snow and a low and dirty sky in which the sun had barely managed to rise above the rooftops in the course of the day. The car's tires hissed in the soap-like mixture of snow, ice and salt that covered the asphalt. None of it had anything to do with her, and she noted it all without really seeing it.

"You do speak Danish, don't you?"

The policeman in the passenger seat had turned toward her and offered her a little blue-white pack. She nodded and took a piece. Said thank you. He smiled at her and turned back into his seat.

This wasn't the "bus," as they called it—the usual transport from Vestre Prison to the court—that Natasha had been on before. It was an ordinary black-and-white; the police were ordinary Danish policemen. The youngest one, the one who had given her the gum, was thirty at the most. The other was old and fat and seemed nice enough too. Danish policemen had kind eyes. Even that time with Michael and the knife, they had spoken calmly and kindly to her as if she hadn't been a criminal they were arresting but rather a patient going to the hospital.

One day, before too long, two of these kind men would put Katerina and her on a flight back to Ukraine, but that was not what was happening today. Not yet. It couldn't be. Her asylum case had not yet been decided, and Katerina was not with her. Besides, you didn't need to go through Copenhagen to get to the airport, that much she knew. This was the way to Central Police Headquarters.

Natasha placed her hands on her light blue jeans, rubbed them hard back and forth across the rough fabric, opened and closed them quickly. Finally, she made an effort to let her fists rest on her knees while she looked out at Copenhagen and tried to figure out if the trip into the city brought her closer to or farther from Katerina. During the last months, the walls and the physical distance that separated them had become an obsession. She was closer to her daughter when she ate in the cafeteria than when she was in her cell. The trip to the yard was also several meters in the wrong direction, but it still felt soothing because it was as if she were breathing the same air as Katerina. On the library computer Natasha had found Google Street View and dragged the flat little man to the parking lot in front of the prison, farther along Copenhagen's streets and up the entrance ramp to the highway leading through the woods that sprawled north of the city's outer reaches. It was as if she could walk next to him the whole way and see houses and storefronts and trees and cars, but when he reached the Coal-House Camp, he couldn't go any farther. Here she had to make do with the grubby satellite image of the camp's flat barrack roofs. She had stared at the pictures until she went nearly insane. She had imagined that one of the tiny dots was Katerina. Had dreamed of getting closer. From the prison, it was twenty-three kilometers to the Coal-House Camp. From the center of Copenhagen it was probably a few kilometers more, but on the other hand, there were neither walls nor barbed wire between the camp and her right now. There was only the thin steel shell of the police car, air and wind, kilometers of asphalt. And later, the fields and the wet forest floor.

She knew it wouldn't do any good, but she reached out to touch the young policeman's shoulder all the same. "You still don't know anything?" she asked in English.

His eyes met hers in the rearview mirror. His gaze was apologetic but basically indifferent. He shook his head. "We're just the chauffeurs," he said. "We aren't usually told stuff like that."

She leaned back in her seat and again began to rub her palms against her jeans. Opened and closed her hands. Neither of the two policemen knew why she was going to police headquarters. They had nothing for her except chewing gum.

The court case over the thing with Michael was long finished, so that probably wasn't what it was about, and her plea for asylum had never required interviews or interrogations anywhere but the Coal-House Camp.

Fear made her stomach contract, and she felt the urge to shit and pee at the same time. If only she could have had Katerina with her. If only they could have been together. At night in the prison, she had the most terrible nightmares about Katerina alone in the children's barrack, surrounded by flames.

Or Katerina making her way alone into the swamp behind the camp.

It was unnatural for a mother not to be able to reach out and touch her child. Natasha knew she was behaving exactly like cows after their calves were taken from them in the fall, when they stood, their shrill bellowing lasting for hours, without knowing which way to direct their sorrow. She had tried to relieve her restlessness with cold logic. They were not separated forever, she told herself. Katerina came to visit once in a while with Nina, the lady from the Coal-House Camp, who reassured Natasha every time that she would personally take care of Katerina. Rina, the Danes called her. They thought that was her name because that was what the papers said. But Rina wasn't even a name. It was what was left when an overpaid little forger in Lublin had done what he could to disguise the original text.

Maybe that was why she was here? Had they discovered what the man in Lublin had done?

Her dread of the future rose like the tide. Her jaw muscles tightened painfully, and when she crushed the compact piece of gum between her teeth, everything in her mouth felt sticky and metallic.

The policeman at the wheel slowed down, gave a low, triumphant whistle and slid the car in between two other cars in a perfect parking maneuver. Through the front window, Natasha could see the grey, fortress-like headquarters of the Danish police. Why were there thick bars in front of some of the windows? As far as she knew, it wasn't here by the entrance that they locked up thieves and murderers. It seemed as if the bars were just there as a signal—a warning about what awaited when the interrogations with the nice Danish policemen were over.

The fat cop opened the door for her. "This is as far as we go, young lady."

She climbed out of the car and buried her hands in the pockets of her down jacket. The cold hit her, biting at her nose and cheeks, and she realized that she had brought neither hat nor gloves. When you were in prison, the weather wasn't something that really mattered. She had barely registered the snow the day before.

The older policeman pulled a smoke out of his uniform jacket and lit it, gave an expectant cough. The young cop, who already had a hand on Natasha's arm, sighed impatiently.

"Just two minutes," said the heavyset one and leaned against the car. "We've got plenty of time."

The young one shrugged. "You really should stop that, pal. It's going to kill both you and me. I'm freezing my ass off here."

The old one laughed good-naturedly and drew smoke deep into his lungs. Natasha wasn't freezing, but her legs felt weak, and she noticed again that she needed to pee. Soon. But she didn't want to say anything, didn't want the policemen to rush. She looked up at the massive, squat building as if it could tell her why she was here. Relaxed uniformed and non-uniformed employees wandered in and out among the pillars in the wide entrance area. If they were planning to seal the fate of a young Ukrainian woman today, you couldn't tell, and for a moment, Natasha felt calmer.

This was Copenhagen, not Kiev.

Both she and Katerina were safe. She was still in Copenhagen. Still Copenhagen. Across the rooftops a bit farther away, she could see the frozen and silent amusement rides in Tivoli, closed for the season. The tower ride from which she and Michael and Katerina had let themselves fall, secure in their little seats, on a warm summer night almost two years ago.

The big guy stubbed out his cigarette against a stone island in the parking lot and nodded at Natasha. "Well, shall we?"

She began to move but then remained standing as if frozen in place. The sounds of the city reached her with a sudden violence. The rising and falling song of car motors and tires on the road, the weak vibration in the asphalt under her when a truck rumbled by, the voices and slamming car doors. She was searching for something definite in the babble. She focused her consciousness to its utmost and found it. Again.

"Ni. Sohodni. Rozumiyete?"

Natasha locked her gaze on two men who had parked their car some distance away—one of them wearing an impeccable black suit and overcoat, the other more casual in dark jeans and a light brown suede jacket.

"Did someone nail your feet to the pavement?" the young cop said, in a friendly enough fashion. "Let's keep moving." His hand pressed harder around her elbow, pushing her forward a little.

"I'm sorry," she said. She took one more step and another. Looked down at the slushy black asphalt and felt the fear rise in her in its purest and darkest form.

They worked their way sideways around a small row of dug-up parking spaces cordoned off with red-and-white construction tape. Long orange plastic tubes snaked their way up from the bottom of the deserted pit. Next to it was a small, neat pile of cobbles half covered by snow.

Natasha slowed down. Gently. Avoided any sudden movements.

The old guy looked back just as she bent down to pick up the top cobble. She smiled at him. Or tried to, at least.

"I'm just . . ."

He was two steps away, but the younger one was closer, and she hit *him*, hard and fast and without thinking. She felt the impact shoot up through the stone and into her hand and closed her eyes for an instant. She knew that the young cop fell in front of the old one, blocking his way, because she could hear them both curse and scrabble in the soap-like slush. But she didn't see it.

She just ran.

TRAVEL THE WORLD FOR $9.99

The first books in our most popular series in a new low price paperback edition

DENMARK

THE BOY IN THE SUITCASE
Lene Kaaberbol & Agnete Friis
ISBN: 978-1-61695-491-8

HOLLYWOOD

CRASHED
Timothy Hallinan
ISBN: 978-1-61695-276-1

LONDON

SLOW HORSES
Mick Herron
ISBN: 978-1-61695-416-1

WWII BERLIN

ZOO STATION
David Downing
ISBN: 978-1-61695-348-5

ENGLAND
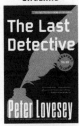
THE LAST DETECTIVE
Peter Lovesey
ISBN: 978-1-61695-530-4

WWII EUROPE

BILLY BOYLE
James R. Benn
ISBN: 978-1-61695-355-3

SWEDEN

DETECTIVE INSPECTOR HUSS
Helene Tursten
ISBN: 978-1-61695-111-5

AUSTRALIA

THE DRAGON MAN
Garry Disher
ISBN: 978-1-61695-448-2

LAOS

THE CORONER'S LUNCH
Colin Cotterill
ISBN: 978-1-61695-649-3

CHINA

ROCK PAPER TIGER
Lisa Brackmann
ISBN: 978-1-61695-258-7

ENGLAND
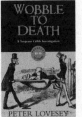
WOBBLE TO DEATH
Peter Lovesey
ISBN: 978-1-61695-659-2

ITALY

CONVERGING PARALLELS
Timothy Williams
ISBN: 978-1-61695-460-4

Other Titles in the Soho Crime Series

Stephanie Barron
(Jane Austen's England)
*Jane and the Twelve Days
of Christmas*
Jane and the Waterloo Map

F.H. Batacan
(Philippines)
Smaller and Smaller Circles

Quentin Bates
(Iceland)
Frozen Assets
Cold Comfort
Chilled to the Bone

James R. Benn
(World War II Europe)
Billy Boyle
The First Wave
Blood Alone
Evil for Evil
Rag & Bone
A Mortal Terror
Death's Door
A Blind Goddess
The Rest Is Silence
The White Ghost

Cara Black
(Paris, France)
Murder in the Marais
Murder in Belleville
Murder in the Sentier
Murder in the Bastille
Murder in Clichy
Murder in Montmartre
Murder on the Ile Saint-Louis
Murder in the Rue de Paradis
Murder in the Latin Quarter
Murder in the Palais Royal
Murder in Passy
Murder at the Lanterne Rouge
Murder Below Montparnasse
Murder in Pigalle
Murder on the Champ de Mars
Murder on the Quai

Lisa Brackmann
(China)
Rock Paper Tiger
Hour of the Rat
Dragon Day

(Mexico)
Getaway

Go-Between

Henry Chang
(Chinatown)
Chinatown Beat
Year of the Dog
Red Jade
Death Money

Barbara Cleverly
(England)
The Last Kashmiri Rose
Strange Images of Death
The Blood Royal
Not My Blood
A Spider in the Cup
Enter Pale Death
Diana's Altar

Gary Corby
(Ancient Greece)
The Pericles Commission
The Ionia Sanction
Sacred Games
The Marathon Conspiracy
Death Ex Machina
The Singer from Memphis

Colin Cotterill
(Laos)
The Coroner's Lunch
Thirty-Three Teeth
Disco for the Departed
Anarchy and Old Dogs
Curse of the Pogo Stick
The Merry Misogynist
Love Songs from a Shallow Grave
Slash and Burn
The Woman Who Wouldn't Die
The Six and a Half Deadly Sins
I Shot the Buddha

Garry Disher
(Australia)
The Dragon Man
Kittyhawk Down
Snapshot
Chain of Evidence
Blood Moon
Wyatt
Whispering Death
Port Vila Blues
Fallout
Hell to Pay

David Downing
(World War II Germany)
Zoo Station
Silesian Station
Stettin Station
Potsdam Station
Lehrter Station
Masaryk Station

David Downing cont.
(World War I)
Jack of Spies
One Man's Flag

Leighton Gage
(Brazil)
Blood of the Wicked
Buried Strangers
Dying Gasp
Every Bitter Thing
A Vine in the Blood
Perfect Hatred
The Ways of Evil Men

Timothy Hallinan
(Thailand)
The Fear Artist
For the Dead
The Hot Countries

(Los Angeles)
Crashed
Little Elvises
The Fame Thief
Herbie's Game
King Maybe

Mette Ivie Harrison
(Mormon Utah)
The Bishop's Wife
His Right Hand

Mick Herron
(England)
Down Cemetery Road
The Last Voice You Hear
Reconstruction
Smoke and Whispers
Why We Die
Slow Horses
Dead Lions
Nobody Walks
Real Tigers

**Lene Kaaberbøl &
Agnete Friis**
(Denmark)
The Boy in the Suitcase
Invisible Murder
Death of a Nightingale
The Considerate Killer

Heda Margolius Kovály
(1950s Prague)
Innocence

Martin Limón
(South Korea)
Jade Lady Burning
Slicky Boys